THE THREE
MUSKETEERS

ALEXANDRE DUMAS

THE THREE
MUSKETEERS

Introduction by Alan Furst

TRANSLATED BY
JACQUES LE CLERCQ

THE MODERN LIBRARY

NEW YORK

LIBRARY OF CONGRESS CATALOGING-IN-PUBLICATION DATA
Dumas, Alexandre, 1802–1870.
[Trois mousquetaires. English]
The three musketeers/Alexandre Dumas; introduction by Alan Furst;
translated by Jacques Le Clercq.
p. cm.
ISBN 0-375-75674-4
1. France—History—Louis XIII, 1610–1643—Fiction. 2. Swordplay—Fiction.
I. Title: 3 musketeers. II. Le Clercq, Jacques Georges Clemenceau, 1898–1972.
III. Title.
PQ2228.A34813   2001
843′.7—dc21   00-50096

ALEXANDRE DUMAS

Alexandre Dumas, who lived a life as dramatic as any depicted in his more than three hundred volumes of plays, novels, travel books, and memoirs, was born on July 24, 1802, in the town of Villers-Cotterêts, some fifty miles from Paris. He was the third child of Thomas-Alexandre Davy de la Pailleterie (who took the name of Dumas), a nobleman who distinguished himself as one of Napoleon's most brilliant generals, and Marie-Louise-Elisabeth Labouret. Following General Dumas's death in 1806 the family faced precarious financial circumstances, yet Mme. Dumas scrimped to pay for her son's private schooling. Unfortunately he proved an indifferent student who excelled in but one subject: penmanship. In 1816, at the age of fourteen, Dumas found employment as a clerk with a local notary to help support the family. A growing interest in theater brought him to Paris in 1822, where he met François-Joseph Talma, the great French tragedian, and resolved to become a playwright. Meanwhile the passionate Dumas fell in love with Catherine Labay, a seamstress by whom he had a son. (Though he had numerous mistresses in his lifetime Dumas married only once, but the union did not last.) While working as a scribe for the duc d'Orléans (later King Louis-Philippe) Dumas collaborated on a one-act vaudeville, *La Chasse et l'amour* (*The Chase and Love*, 1825). But it was not until 1827, after attending a British performance of *Hamlet,* that Dumas discovered a direction for his dramas. "For the first time in the theater I was seeing true passions motivating men and women of flesh and blood," he recalled. "From this time on, but only then, did I have an idea of what the theater could be."

Dumas achieved instant fame on February 11, 1829, with the triumphant opening of *Henri III et sa cour (Henry III and His Court)*. An innovative and influential play generally regarded as the first French drama of the Romantic movement, it broke with the staid precepts of Neoclassicism that had been imposed on the Paris stage for more than a century. Briefly involved as a republican partisan in the July Revolution of 1830, Dumas soon resumed playwriting and over the next decade turned out a number of historical melodramas that electrified audiences. Two of these works—*Antony* (1831) and *La Tour de Nesle* (*The Tower of Nesle,* 1832)— stand out as milestones in the history of nineteenth-century French theater. In disfavor with the new monarch, Louis-Philippe, because of his republican sympathies, Dumas left France for a time. In 1832 he set out on a tour of Switzerland, chronicling his adventures in *Impressions de voyage: En Suisse* (*Travels in Switzerland,* 1834–1837); over the years he produced many travelogues about subsequent journeys through France, Italy, Russia, and other countries.

Around 1840 Dumas embarked upon a series of historical romances inspired by both his love of French history and the novels of Sir Walter Scott. In collaboration with Auguste Maquet, he serialized *Le Chevalier d'Harmental* in the newspaper *Le Siècle* in 1842. Part history, intrigue, adventure, and romance, it is widely regarded as the first of Dumas's great novels. The two subsequently worked together on a steady stream of books, most of which were published serially in Parisian tabloids and eagerly read by the public. He is best known for the celebrated d'Artagnan trilogy—*Les trois mousquetaires* (*The Three Musketeers,* 1844), *Vingt ans après* (*Twenty Years After,* 1845) and *Dix ans plus tarde ou le Vicomte de Bragelonne* (*Ten Years Later; or The Viscount of Bragelonne,* 1848–1850)—and the so-called Valois romances—*La Reine Margot* (*Queen Margot,* 1845), *La Dame de Monsoreau* (*The Lady of Monsoreau,* 1846), and *Les Quarante-cinc* (*The Forty-Five Guardsmen,* 1848). Yet perhaps his greatest success was *Le Comte de Monte Cristo* (*The Count of Monte Cristo*), which appeared in installments in *Le Journal des débats* from 1844 to 1845. A final tetralogy marked the end of their partnership: *Mémoires d'un médecin: Joseph Balsamo* (*Memoirs of a Physician,* 1846–1848), *Le Collier de la reine* (*The Queen's Necklace,* 1849–1850), *Ange Pitou* (*Taking the Bastille,* 1853), and *La Comtesse de Charny* (*The Countess de Charny,* 1852–1855).

In 1847, at the height of his fame, Dumas assumed the role of impresario. Hoping to reap huge profits, he inaugurated the new Théâtre Historique as a vehicle for staging dramatizations of his historical novels. The same year he completed construction of a lavish residence in the quiet hamlet of Marly-le-Roi. Called Le Château de Monte Cristo, it was home to a menagerie of exotic pets and a parade of freeloaders until 1850, when Dumas's theater failed and he faced bankruptcy. Fleeing temporarily to Belgium in order to avoid creditors, Dumas returned to Paris in 1853, shortly after the appearance of the initial volumes of *Mes Mémoires* (*My Memoirs*, 1852). Over the next years he founded the newspaper *Le Mousquetaire*, for which he wrote much of the copy, as well as the literary weekly *Le Monte Cristo*, but his finances never recovered. In 1858 he traveled to Russia, eventually publishing two new episodes of *Impressions de voyage: Le Caucase* (*Adventures in the Caucasus*, 1859) and *En Russie* (*Travels in Russia*, 1865).

The final decade of Dumas's life began with customary high adventure. In 1860 he met Garibaldi and was swept up into the cause of Italian independence. After four years in Naples publishing the bilingual paper *L'Indépendant/L'Indipendente*, Dumas returned to Paris in 1864. In 1867 he began a flamboyant liaison with Ada Menken, a young American actress who dubbed him "the king of romance." The same year marked the appearance of a last novel, *La Terreur Prussiene* (*The Prussian Terror*). Dumas's final play, *Les Blancs et les Bleus* (*The Whites and the Blues*), opened in Paris in 1869.

Alexandre Dumas died penniless but cheerful on December 5, 1870, saying of death: "I shall tell her a story, and she will be kind to me." One hundred years later his biographer André Maurois paid him this tribute: "Dumas was a hero out of Dumas. As strong as Porthos, as adroit as d'Artagnan, as generous as Edmond Dantès, this superb giant strode across the nineteenth century breaking down doors with his shoulder, sweeping women away in his arms, and earning fortunes only to squander them promptly in dissipation. For forty years he filled the newspapers with his prose, the stage with his dramas, the world with his clamor. Never did he know a moment of doubt or an instant of despair. He turned his own existence into the finest of his novels."

Contents

Introduction

Alan Furst

From Alexandre Dumas, a precise and candid description of his particular view of history:

> I start by devising a story. I try to make it romantic, moving, dramatic, and when scope has been found for the emotions and the imagination, I search through the annals of the past to find a frame in which to set it; and it has never happened that history has failed to provide this frame, so exactly adjusted to the subject that it seemed it was not a case of the frame being made for the picture, but that the picture had been made to fit the frame.

This is the point of view of the historical novelist, who approaches the past as theater—the unending melodrama of saints and sinners, and who knows that history, eternally surprising, inspiring, disheartening, sometimes described as "one damn thing after another," will never fail him. It is all there. And it is all there to be used.

Dumas was in his early forties when he wrote *The Three Musketeers*, an age when novelists are believed to be entering their best creative years. He is traditionally described as "a man of vast republican sympathies," which, in contemporary terms, made him a believer in democracy, equality, and the rights of man. He had fought in the streets of Paris during the July revolution of 1830; would man the barricades in 1848; would aid

Garibaldi, with guns and journalism, in the struggle for Italian independence in 1860.

Such politics came to him by inclination, and by birth. His father, Thomas-Alexandre Davy de La Pailleterie, had taken the name of his African slave mother, Marie Dumas, and spent the early years of his life on the island of Santo Domingo. When the French Revolution made it possible for men without wealth or social connections to rise to power, the soldier Alexandre Dumas became General Alexandre Dumas, commanding the Army of the Alps in 1794, serving under Napoleon Bonaparte in Italy, and later in Egypt. But his relationship with Bonaparte deteriorated; his health was destroyed by two years in an Italian prison; and he died, a broken man, in 1806. His son, in time the novelist Dumas, was then four years old, but he would be told of his father's life, and he knew what it meant.

By 1844, France was ruled by Louis-Philippe, duc d'Orleans, a constitutional monarch known as "the bourgeois king," who presided over the golden age of the French bourgeoisie, a propertied class animated by the slogan *"Enrichissez-vous!"* (Enrich yourselves!) This was a period of transition, when corrupt capitalism was opposed by passionate idealism—the age of monarchy was dying, the age of democracy was just being born. The best insight into the period is to be found in the novels of Honoré de Balzac—Dumas's fierce literary rival. Balzac was virtually the same age as Dumas, and, like Dumas, rose from social obscurity and penury by producing a huge volume of work at an extraordinary pace. But Balzac wrote about contemporary life—the vanity, corruption and sexual politics of Paris in the 1840s—and was, throughout his fiction, essentially a novelist of vice. Dumas, on the other hand, was a novelist of virtue, though he had to go back two hundred years to find it.

Setting *The Three Musketeers* in the year 1625—at that distance, a contemporary American novelist might use the revolution of 1776—Dumas was summoning up a remote and heroic era. Yes, it was all *different* back then. Better. Still, it may be worth remembering that Dumas's musketeers are proud, courageous men, men without inherited money or the support of prominent family, who must fight their way through a world of political intrigue dominated by predatory, immoral people who scheme and connive, who will do virtually anything, to keep their wealth and position. So, if it is about anything, *The Three Musketeers* is about betrayal, fidelity, and, like almost all genre fiction, it is about honor. Honor lost, honor gained, honor maintained at the cost of life itself. By 1894, the sale of Dumas's works totaled three million books and eight million serials.

The Three Musketeers, the first book of the d'Artagnan trilogy, with *Twenty Years After* and *The Vicomte de Bragelonne* to follow, appeared in installments in the journal *Le Siècle* from March to July in 1844. It was written with help of a collaborator, Auguste Maquet, who also participated in the writing of *The Count of Monte Cristo.* Maquet would later claim significant authorship, and haul Dumas into court.

Dumas was accused, as well, of plagiarism, having used *The Memoirs of Monsieur d'Artagnan,* by one Courtilz de Sandras, published in Cologne in 1701, as source material. There he found not only d'Artagnan but Athos, Porthos, and Aramis; Tréville and his musketeers; Milady and her maid; and the Cardinalist Guards. From the annals of French history, he took the machinations, real or reputed, involving Louis XIII, Anne of Austria, Cardinal Richelieu, and the duke of Buckingham. Then he threw out whatever reality he found inconvenient and wrote what he liked.

In the real world of Europe in 1625, the continent was being torn apart by the Thirty Years War—a rather pallid name that obscures the cruel and brutal nature of its reality. Fighting on behalf of royal houses in conflict over religious issues and rights of succession, mercenary armies were paid by the right of pillage and ravaged the countryside, a strategy described as "war supports the war." In France, French Catholics suppressed a French Protestant minority, the Huguenots, who were supported by English Protestant money and arms. Serving as virtual regent for a weak king Louis XIII, Cardinal Richelieu was perhaps the greatest political figure of his time. Famously eloquent, determined and brilliant, Richelieu was a deeply ambitious man, but a devoted and faithful servant of king and country.

A popular novelist, however, must produce an archvillain, and Dumas gave the job to Richelieu. As the servant of Dumas's fictional requirements, Richelieu is merely political on the surface, as he undertakes a series of intrigues in a struggle for power with the king or with his English Protestant enemy, Buckingham. In *The Three Musketeers,* Richelieu is discovered to have deeper motives, a lust for revenge inspired by a romantic slight—a spurned advance—and, in general, by sexual jealousy. The cardinal, according to Dumas, was in love with the queen, Anne of Austria. The reader of 1844, hurrying off to buy this week's chapter in *Le Siècle,* likely suspected as much.

Serialized fiction read as a novel can, at times, be a slightly bumpy ride. The twists and turns of the story are intended not only to keep the reader reading, but to keep the reader *buying*. Thus the plot tends toward precipitous dives and breathtaking ascents, as peril and escape follow each other at narrow intervals, characters disappear and are brought back to life, and what seemed like the central crisis of the narrative is suddenly resolved, to be replaced by a second crisis.

The perfidious Cardinal Richelieu is a good example of this principle at work. He's a useful éminence grise at the beginning of the novel, as Cardinalist guards fight the king's faithful musketeers. But, when it's time for the story to end, he's too historical a figure to be vanquished with all the force that the conclusion of a romantic adventure demands. Thus the role of villain is shifted to Milady; the story can then take its chilling and violent turn; and justice, when it is at last achieved, can be, to say the least, severe.

Since writers of serials wrote for a weekly deadline, there was no such thing as regret or revision, and the reader may see rather more of the novel's scaffolding than the author would like. Dumas, characteristically, solved this problem with talent, and produced the best writing in *The Three Musketeers* in the latter third of the novel, for example the combination of battle and picnic at the Bastion Saint Gervais, during the attack on the Protestant stronghold at La Rochelle. This is easily one of the most insouciant scenes in all of literature, as the musketeers, intent on winning a tavern bet, occupy the bastion; sip wine; discuss matters of love and strategy; push a wall over on a raiding party; use the dead as mock defenders; and, finally, after four-hundred pages of action and intrigue, actually fire muskets!

This is but one pleasure among many. There is, throughout *The Three Musketeers,* a vast and magnanimous intelligence at work. The critic Jules Michelet described Alexandre Dumas as "an inextinguishable volcano," and "one of the forces of nature." He was certainly that. Born to write, and born to write about mythic times and mythic deeds, Dumas loved his characters and the elaborate story he fashioned for them. This is a telling trait in a novelist, the reader instinctively feels it, so gives himself to the story, lives in the time and place of its setting, and escapes, as surely as d'Artagnan ever escaped, from the drone of daily existence. That's the job of romantic fiction and it's done in *The Three Musketeers* on virtually every page. "All for one, and one for all!" And all for us.

AUTHOR'S PREFACE

Wherein It Is Proved
That Despite Their Names Ending in -os and -is,
the Heroes of the History We Are About to
Have the Honor to Relate
Have Nothing Mythological About Them

About a year ago, while I was engaged in research in the Royal Library for my *History of Louis XIV,* I chanced upon a volume called *The Memoirs of Monsieur d'Artagnan.* Like most works in a period in which authors could not tell the truth without risking a more or less lengthy sojourn in the Bastille, it was printed at Amsterdam. The publisher was one Pierre Rouge. The title fascinated me; I took the book home (with the permission of the Librarian of course) and I devoured its pages.

I do not intend to give a minute account of this curious work here; I merely indicate it to those of my readers who enjoy pictures of a given period. In it they will find a gallery of portraits penciled by a master; and, though most of these sketches may be traced on barracks doors or on the walls of taverns, yet they present the figures of Louis XIII, of Ann of Austria, of Richelieu, of Mazarin and of most of the courtiers of the period quite as vividly and faithfully as Monsieur Anquetil does in his *History of France.*

Now as everybody knows, what strikes the capricious mind of the poet does not always impress the mass of readers. So while I admired, as others doubtless will admire, the details I have just cited, my main preoccupation concerned a matter to which no one had paid the slightest attention previously.

In his *Memoirs,* Monsieur d'Artagnan relates that, on his first visit to Monsieur de Tréville, Captain of His Majesty's Musketeers, he met in the antechamber three young men belonging to the illustrious corps in which he was soliciting the honor of enrolling. Their names were Athos, Porthos and Aramis.

I must confess these three foreign names struck me. I immediately decided that they were pseudonyms under which D'Artagnan disguised names that were perhaps illustrious. Or else, perhaps, the bearers of these names had themselves chosen them on the day when, thanks to a whim, or discontent, or exiguity of fortune, they donned the uniform of a ranker in the Musketeers.

From then on I knew no rest until I could find some trace in contemporaneous works of these three names which had aroused my passionate curiosity.

The mere catalogue of the books I read with this object in view would fill a whole chapter, which might prove highly instructive to my readers but would certainly not amuse them. Suffice to say that, just as, discouraged at so much fruitless investigation, I was about to abandon my quest, I at last found what I was after. Guided by the counsels of my illustrious and erudite friend Paulin Paris, I consulted a manuscript in folio— Number 4772 or 4773, I forget which, in the catalogue of the Royal Library—entitled *Memoirs of Monsieur le Comte de la Fère, Concerning Some Events in France towards the End of the Reign of Louis XIII and the Beginning of the Reign of Louis XIV.*

The reader may imagine my immense joy when in this manuscript, my last hope, I came upon the name of Athos on Page 20, of Porthos on Page 27, and of Aramis on Page 31.

The discovery of a completely unknown manuscript, at a period in which the science of history has progressed to such an extraordinary degree, seemed to me to be almost miraculous. I therefore hastened to ask for permission to print it in order to present my candidacy to the Académie des Inscriptions et Belles Lettres on the strength of another's work in case I could not enter the Académie Française on the strength of my own—which is exceedingly probable! I must add that this permission was graciously granted. I do so in order publicly to refute the slanderers who maintain that we live under a government scarcely favorable to men of letters.

It is the first part of this precious manuscript which I now offer to my readers, restoring the fitting title that belongs to it.

Should this first part meet with the success it deserves (of which I have no doubt) I hereby undertake to publish the second part immediately.

In the meantime, since godfathers are second fathers, as it were, I beg the reader to hold myself and not the Comte de la Fère responsible for such pleasure or boredom as he may experience.

This being understood, let us proceed with our story.

THE THREE
MUSKETEERS

THE THREE GIFTS OF
MONSIEUR D'ARTAGNAN THE ELDER

Meung, a pretty market town on the Loire and the birthplace of Jean de Meung, author of the *Romance of the Rose*, was more or less used to disturbances of one sort or another because of the troublous times. But on the first Monday in April, 1625, it appeared as though all the armed hosts of the Huguenots had descended upon the place in order to make of it a second La Rochelle. The citizens, seeing the women fleeing over by the main street and hearing the abandoned children crying from the doorsteps, hurriedly donned their breastplates. Then, bolstering up their somewhat uncertain courage by seizing musket, axe or pike, they sped toward the hostelry *At the Sign of the Jolly Miller*. There they found a compact, everswelling group, all agog, milling about, full of curiosity and clamor.

Panics were frequent in France at that period; few days passed without some city or another recording an event of this sort in its archives. There were the nobles fighting among themselves, the King making war upon the Cardinal, and Spain battling against the King. Besides these conflicts, concealed or public, secret or patent, other riots were occasioned by brigands, beggars, Huguenots, wolves and knaves who attacked all comers. The citizenry always took up arms against brigands and wolves and knaves, often against the nobles and Huguenots, sometimes against the King, but never against the Cardinal or Spain.

Accordingly, custom being what it was, on the first Monday in April 1625, the burghers of Meung, hearing the tumult and seeing neither the red-and-yellow standard of Spain nor the livery of the Cardinal Duc de Richelieu, rushed toward *The Sign of the Jolly Miller*. One glance was enough to make clear to everybody what was causing all this hullabaloo.

A young man—but let us sketch his portrait with one bold stroke of the pen! Imagine, then, a Don Quixote aged eighteen ... a Don Quixote lacking breastplate, coat-of-mail or thighguards ... a Don Quixote clad in a woolen doublet, its blue faded into an indefinable color that combined a multitude of tints as dissimilar as the red of deepest Burgundy and the most celestial azure. . . . His face was long, thin and tanned, the cheekbones high (a sign of astuteness) and the jaw wide (the infallible mark of a Gascon, whether he wears a beret or no). As a matter of fact, the youth wore a beret, adorned with a feather of sorts. His glance was frank and intelligent, his nose hooked but finely chiseled. Too tall for an adolescent, too short for an adult, he looked like nothing so much as a farmer's son on a journey, were it not for the sword dangling from a belt of shagreen, which kept hitting against the calves of its owner when he walked, and against the bristling flank of his steed when he rode.

Our youth boasted a steed so noteworthy that no man could fail to take note of it. A Béarn nag, it was, twelve or fourteen years old, with a yellow coat and hairless tail, but not without swellings on its legs. As this nag walked with its head well below its knees, no martingale was necessary. Nevertheless, it managed to cover eight leagues a day regularly. Unfortunately the virtues of this horse were so well concealed under its weird coat and incongruous gait that, at a period when everybody was a connoisseur in horseflesh, its apparition at Meung (it had entered a quarter of an hour before by the Gate of Beaugency) created a sensation. And the discredit inspired by the beast naturally extended to its master.

This fact proved all the more painful to young D'Artagnan—to name the Don Quixote of this second Rosinante—because he was himself forced to acknowledge how ridiculous such a steed made him, excellent horseman though he was. Indeed, he had heaved a deep sigh as he accepted this gift from his father. He was aware, of course, that such a beast was worth at least twenty livres. But the words accompanying the gift were beyond all price.

"My son," said the old Gascon gentleman in that pure Béarn patois which Henry IV had never succeeded in shedding, "my son, this horse was born in your father's house some thirteen years ago, and here it has remained ever since. This ought to make you love the beast! Never sell it; let it die quietly and honorably of old age. If you should go to the wars with it, then care for it as faithfully as you would care for an old servant. At Court, should you ever have the honor to go there," Monsieur d'Artagnan the elder continued, adding parenthetically that it was an honor to which his son's ancient nobility entitled him, "be sure worthily to uphold the name of 'gentleman' which has been dutifully borne by your ancestors for more than five hundred years. Do this both for your own sake and for the sake of your own people—I mean your relatives and friends. Endure nothing from anyone save the Cardinal and the King. Nowadays a gentleman makes his way by his courage—do you understand?—by his courage alone! Whoever trembles for but a second has perhaps lost the bait which fortune held out to him in precisely that second. You are young. You ought to be brave for two reasons: first because you are a Gascon and second because you are my son! Never avoid a quarrel: seek out the hazards of high adventure. I have taught you how to wield a sword; you have muscles of iron and a wrist of steel. Fight at every opportunity, the more blithely because duels are forbidden and therefore it will be doubly brave of you to fight."

After a pause, D'Artagnan's father went on:

"I have nothing to give you, my son, except fifteen crowns, my horse and the advice you have just heard. To these, your mother will add a recipe for a certain balsam which she acquired from a gipsy woman. It possesses the miraculous virtue of curing all wounds which do not reach the heart. Take advantage of everything that comes your way; live happily and long!"

Then:

"One word more," the old man added. "I would wish to propose an example for you. Not mine, to be sure, for I have never appeared at Court; besides, I took part in the Religious Wars as a volunteer. No, I mean Monsieur de Tréville. He was formerly my neighbor; as a child, he had the honor of being a playmate of our King, Louis XIII, whom God preserve! Their games sometimes degenerated into battles in which the King did not always have the upper hand. The thumps and thwacks he received from Monsieur de Tréville inspired His Majesty with much esteem and friendship for his former playmate. Later, Monsieur de Tréville fought against others: on his first journey to Paris, five times ... from the death of the late King to the majority of the young King, seven times, excluding all the wars and the sieges he has been through ... from that date until now, I do not know how many times, possibly one hundred ... thus despite all edicts, ordinances Musketeers—in other words, leader of a legion of Caesars highly esteemed by His Majesty and dreaded by the Cardinal, who is known to dread nothing! Better still, Monsieur de Tréville earns ten thousand crowns per annum, which makes him a very great noble indeed. And he started from scratch, just like you!

"Go to him with this letter. And model your behavior upon his, in order to accomplish what he has accomplished."

Whereupon the old man buckled his own sword to his son's belt, kissed him tenderly on both cheeks, and gave him his blessing.

Leaving his father, the young man went to his mother's apartment where she awaited him with that sovereign remedy which, thanks to the advice we have reported, was subsequently to be employed so often. In this interview, the adieux were longer and more tender than in the other. It was not because Monsieur d'Artagnan failed to cherish his only son, but he was a man and he would have deemed it unworthy for a man to give way to his feelings; whereas Madame d'Artagnan was a woman, and more, a mother. So she wept copiously and, to the honor of Monsieur d'Artagnan the younger, notwithstanding the efforts he made to remain as firm as a future musketeer should be, nature prevailed, and he too shed many tears, half of which he managed at great pains to conceal.

That same day the youth set out on his journey equipped with his father's three gifts, namely, the fifteen crowns, the horse and the letter to Monsieur de Tréville. As may well be imagined, the advice had been thrown into the bargain.

With such a *vade mecum*, D'Artagnan was, morally and physically, an exact replica of Cervantes' hero, to whom we so aptly compared him when our duties as historian placed us under the necessity of sketching his portrait. The Spanish don took windmills for giants and sheep for armies; his Gascon counterpart took every smile for an insult and every glance for a challenge. Accordingly from Tardes in the Pyrénées all the way to Meung on the Loire, he kept his fist clenched or pressed his hand against the hilt of his sword ten times a day. Yet his fist did not crash down on any jaw nor did his sword issue from its scabbard. To be sure, the sight of the wretched nag excited many a smile as D'Artagnan rode by, but against the nag's flank rattled a sword of respectable length and over the sword gleamed an eye more ferocious than proud. Passersby therefore repressed their hilarity or, if hilarity prevailed over prudence, they attempted to laugh on one side of their faces only, as do the masks of the ancients. Thus D'Artagnan remained majestic and virgin in his susceptibility until he reached the inauspicious town of Meung.

There, as he was alighting from his horse at the gate of *The Jolly Miller*, without anyone—host, waiter or ostler—coming to hold his stirrup, D'Artagnan spied, through an open window on the ground floor, a gentleman of fine figure and proud, though somewhat sullen mien. This person was talking to two others who appeared to be listening to him with great deference. D'Artagnan, fancying quite naturally, according to habit, that he was the object of their conversation, listened attentively. This time

D'Artagnan was only in part mistaken; he himself was not being discussed, his nag was. Apparently the gentleman was treating his audience to an enumeration of all the nag's qualities; and the audience being highly respectful of the narrator, there were bursts of raucous laughter at every moment. If the suggestion of a smile sufficed to stir the ire of our Gascon we may readily imagine how this vociferous jollity affected him.

However, D'Artagnan first wished to examine the insolent fellow who dared make mock of him. His haughty glance fell upon the stranger, a man of forty or forty-five years of age, pale of complexion, with piercing black eyes, a nose boldly fashioned and a black, impeccably trimmed mustache. He wore a doublet and hose of violet, with trimming of like color and no other ornament save the customary slashes through which the shirt appeared. Though new, his doublet and hose looked rumpled, like traveling clothes long packed in a portmanteau. D'Artagnan took in all these details with the speed of the most meticulous observer and also, doubtless, with an instinctive presentiment that this stranger was to exercise a powerful influence upon his future life.

As D'Artagnan stared at the gentleman in violet, the latter was uttering the most sagacious and profound commentary on the nag of Béarn. His two auditors roared with laughter, at which the narrator actually smiled. This time, there could be no doubt whatsoever; D'Artagnan had been truly insulted. Convinced of it, he pulled his beret down over his eyes, and, attempting to copy certain courtly gestures he had picked up from noblemen traveling through Gascony, he stepped forward, his right hand on the hilt of his sword, his left against his hip. Unfortunately fast as he moved, waxing angrier at every step, he seemed to become more confused. Instead of the polite, lofty speech he had prepared as a challenge, his tongue could produce nothing better than a vulgar exclamation which he topped off with a furious gesture.

"Look here, Monsieur," he cried. "Look here, you, there, skulking behind that shutter . . . yes, I mean *you* . . . Look here! tell me what you are laughing at, will you, and we can laugh together!"

The gentleman's gaze moved slowly away from the nag and slowly toward its master, as though a certain lapse of time were requisite before he could understand how such extraordinary reproaches could be leveled at him. Then, when he could entertain no doubt on the matter, he frowned slightly. A moment later, in a tone of irony indescribable in its insolence, he replied:

"I am not aware that I was addressing you, Monsieur."

"Never mind," countered D'Artagnan, exasperated by this medley of insolence and good manners, of convention and disdain, "*I was* addressing *you!*"

The stranger eyed him again, smiled fleetingly as before, and, withdrawing from the window, walked slowly out of the inn. He took his stand two paces from D'Artagnan and stood there, rooted to the spot, staring at the horse. His tranquil manner and bantering air increased the hilarity of his auditors, who were still gathered around the window, watching the scene.

Seeing him approach, D'Artagnan drew his sword a full foot out of its scabbard.

"Upon my word, this horse is certainly a buttercup!" observed the stranger, pursuing his investigations. His remarks were addressed to his audience at the window; apparently, he was quite unconscious of D'Artagnan's exasperation although the youth stood between him and his audience. "This color is quite common in botany but until now it has been very rare among horses."

"Laugh all you will at my horse," said D'Artagnan angrily. He recalled how his hero, Monsieur de Tréville, had ridden a bob-tailed nag from the Midi to Fortune. "I dare you to smile at his master."

"As you may judge from my cast of features, Monsieur, I do not laugh frequently," the stranger replied. "But I intend to preserve the privilege of laughing whenever I please."

"As for me," cried D'Artagnan, "I will brook no man's laughter when it irks me."

"Well, well, Monsieur I dare say you are right," said the stranger edging away. But D'Artagnan was not the type of youth to suffer anyone to escape him, least of all a man who had ridiculed him so impudently. Drawing his sword at long last and for cause, he ran after the stranger, crying:

"Turn about, turn about, Master Jester!" he challenged. "Must I strike you in the back?"

"You strike *me?*" The stranger surveyed the young man with astonishment and scorn. "Come, lad, you must be crazy!"

Then, in subdued tones, as though talking to himself:

"What a bore!" he sighed. "What a find this buck would be for His

Majesty. The Royal Musketeers are combing the country to recruit just such hotheads."

He had barely finished speaking when D'Artagnan lunged at him so impetuously that this jest might have been his last. The stranger drew his sword, saluted D'Artagnan and took up his guard. But suddenly at a sign his two onlookers, backed up by the innkeeper, fell upon D'Artagnan with sticks, shovels and tongs. While this sudden onslaught held D'Artagnan, the stranger sheathed his sword as readily as he had drawn it.

"A plague upon these Gascons!" he muttered. "Put him back on his orange nag and away with him!"

"Not before I kill you!"

"Another Gascon boast! Really, these Gascons are incorrigible! Keep up the dance since that is what he wants! When he is tired, we will cry quits."

But the stranger did not suspect of what stubborn stuff his late adversary was made; D'Artagnan was never one to knuckle under. So the fight went on for a few seconds more, until D'Artagnan, exhausted, dropped his broken sword. Simultaneously, a cudgel struck him squarely on the forehead, bringing him to the ground, bloody and almost unconscious.

It was at this moment that the citizenry of Meung came flocking from all sides to the scene of action. The host, fearing a scandal, carried the wounded man into the kitchen where some trifling attentions were administered.

As for the stranger, he had resumed his stand at the window whence he stared somewhat impatiently upon the mob. Obviously put out by all this pother, he seemed to resent the fact that the crowd would not disperse.

"Well, how is this madman doing?" he inquired as the host poked his head through the door.

"Your Excellency is safe and sound, I trust?"

"Safe as a house and sound as a bell, my good host! But *I* am asking *you* what has happened to our young firebrand?"

"He is better now. He fainted quite away and before he fainted, he gathered all his strength to challenge and defy you!"

"Why, this fellow must be the devil in person!"

"Oh no, Your Excellency, he is no devil." The host shrugged his shoulders disparagingly. "We searched him and rummaged through his kit. All we found was one clean shirt and twelve crowns in his purse, which didn't stop him from cursing you roundly. He said that if this had happened in Paris instead of in Meung, you would have paid dearly for it."

"A prince of the blood, no less, incognito and full of threats."

"I have told Your Excellency all this so that you might be on your guard."

"Did he name any names!"

"He slapped his pocket and said—"

"What?"

"He said: 'We shall see what Monsieur de Tréville thinks of this insult.' "

"Monsieur de Tréville?" The stranger started. "He struck his pocket and mentioned Monsieur de Tréville? Come, come, my dear host, while your young man was unconscious, I'm sure you did not fail to look into this pocket. What did you find?"

"A letter addressed to Monsieur de Tréville, Captain of the Musketeers."

"Indeed!"

"Exactly as I have the honor to tell Your Excellency."

The innkeeper, who was not gifted with great perspicacity, failed to observe the other's expression as he received this news. The stranger moved away from the window, and frowning:

"The devil!" he muttered. "Can Tréville have set this Gascon on my trail? He is very young. Still, a sword thrust is a sword thrust, whatever the fencer's age. Besides, a youth arouses less suspicion than an older man."

Then he fell into a deep silence. After several minutes:

"Come, come, my good host, do please rid me of this crazy lad. I can't kill him and yet—" his expression was cold and threatening, "yet he is a great nuisance! Where is the fellow?"

"Upstairs in my wife's room. They are dressing his wounds."

"Did you take his rags and kit up? Did he remove his doublet?"

"All his stuff is downstairs in the kitchen. But if this young fool annoys you—"

"He annoys me very much. He has caused an uproar in your hostelry, a thing which respectable people cannot abide. Go upstairs, man, make out my bill, and summon my lackey."

"What! Is Monsieur leaving us already?"

"Of course. I told you to have my horse saddled. Have you done so?"

"Yes, indeed, Your Excellency. Your horse is ready—saddled for you to ride off."

"Good! Now do as I told you."

"Lord save us!" the host said. Examining the stranger: "Can he be afraid of this stripling?" he wondered.

An imperious look from the stranger sent him about his business and, bowing humbly, he withdrew.

"Milady must on no account be seen," the stranger mused. "She will be passing through here soon, in fact she's late already. I daresay I had better ride out to meet her. If only I knew what was in this letter to Tréville." Mumbling to himself, he made off for the kitchen.

Meanwhile the host, certain that the youth's presence had driven the stranger from his hostelry, ran upstairs to his wife's room. There he found D'Artagnan who had at last come to. Suggesting that the police would handle the youth pretty roughly for having picked a quarrel with a great lord—for he had no doubt that the stranger could be nothing less—the host persuaded D'Artagnan, weak though he was, to get up and to be off.

D'Artagnan rose. He was still only half-conscious, he had lost his doublet, and his head was swathed in a linen cloth. Propelled by the innkeeper, he worked his way downstairs. But as he reached the kitchen, the first thing he saw was the stranger, standing at the step of a heavy carriage with two large Norman horses in harness.

He was chatting urbanely with a lady who leaned out of the window of the coach to listen. She must have been about twenty years of age. D'Artagnan was no fool; at a glance, he perceived that this woman was young and beautiful, her beauty the more striking because it differed so radically from that of the Midi, where he had always lived. She was pale and fair, with long curls falling in profusion over her shoulders; she had large blue, languishing eyes, rosy lips and hands of alabaster. She was talking vivaciously to the stranger.

"So His Eminence orders me——?"

"To return to England at once. Should the Duke leave London you are to report directly to His Eminence."

"Any other instructions?" the fair traveler asked.

"They are in this box here. You are not to open it until you have crossed the Channel."

"Very well! And you? What will you do?"

"I go back to Paris."

"Without chastising this insolent youth?" the lady objected.

The stranger was about to reply. But before he could open his mouth, D'Artagnan, who had heard all, bounded across the doorsill.

"This insolent youth does his own chastising," he cried, "and this time, I trust, chastisement will not escape him!"

"Will not escape him?" the stranger echoed, frowning.

"With a woman present, I dare hope you will not run away again."

The stranger grasped the hilt of his sword. Milady, seeing this, cautioned:

"Remember that the least delay may ruin everything."

"You are right, Milady. Let us go our several ways!"

Bowing to the lady, he sprang into his saddle. The coachman whipped up his horses and galloped off in one direction; the stranger was ready to gallop off in the other when suddenly the host appeared. Seeing his great lord about to disappear without settling his score, mine host's affection yielded to the most profound contempt.

"What about my bill?" he shouted.

"Pay him, dolt!" said the stranger to his lackey, tossing a purse to him as they cantered off. The lackey checked his mount, flung three or four silver coins at the host's feet, and sped after his master.

"Oh, you coward! you wretch! you bogus gentleman!" cried D'Artagnan, springing forward in turn after the lackey. But his wounds had left him too weak to bear the strain of such exertion. He had not taken ten steps before he felt his ears ringing. A giddiness swept over him, a cloud of blood rolled over his eyes, and he fell in the middle of the street, crying:

"Coward! Coward! Coward!"

"A coward he is!" mine host agreed as he went to D'Artagnan's aid, flattering him as the hero of the fable flattered the snail he had scorned the evening before.

"Ay, he's a coward, a base coward!" D'Artagnan murmured. "But the lady! How beautiful she was!"

"Who?"

"Milady!" D'Artagnan faltered, as he fainted once again.

"Well!" thought the host. "I've lost two clients but I still have this one. I'm certain to keep *him* for a few days. That means eleven crowns to the good!"

(Eleven crowns represented the exact sum that remained in D'Artagnan's purse.)

The innkeeper had reckoned D'Artagnan's convalescence at one crown per day for eleven days, but mine host had reckoned without his guest. D'Artagnan rose next day at five o'clock, went down to the kitchen unaided and requested several things. First, he asked for certain ingredients, the nature of which have not been transmitted to us. Then he asked for wine, oil and rosemary, and, his mother's recipe in hand, he concocted a balsam with which he anointed his numerous wounds. He himself laid compress after compress upon them, steadfastly refusing the assistance of any physician. Doubtless, thanks to the efficacy of the gipsy salve—and perhaps to the absence of any medico—D'Artagnan felt much restored that evening and practically cured on the morrow.

D'Artagnan prepared to settle his score. His only extras were for the rosemary, oil and wine. The master had fasted while the yellow nag according to the innkeeper had eaten three times as much as a nag of such proportions could possibly assimilate. In his pocket D'Artagnan found only his worn velvet purse and the eleven livres which it contained. As for the letter to Monsieur de Tréville, it had vanished.

He began to search for it with utmost patience . . . to turn his pockets and gussets inside out over and over . . . to rummage time after time in his bag . . . to ransack his purse, opening it, closing it, and opening it again and again. . . . Then, convinced at last that the letter was not to be found, he flew for the third time into such a fit of fury that he might easily have required a fresh supply of wine and aromatic oils. Mine host saw this young firebrand on the rampage and heard him vow to tear down the establishment if his letter were not forthcoming. Immediately he seized a spit, his wife a broom, and his servants the very cudgels they had used two days before.

"Give me my letter!" D'Artagnan kept shouting. "Give me my letter or by the Holy Blood, I'll spit you through like ortolans!"

Unfortunately there was one circumstance which prevented him from carrying out his threat. His sword had been broken in two during his first conflict, a fact which we have chronicled but which he had completely forgotten. Accordingly when D'Artagnan sought to draw his blade, he found himself armed with no more than a stump eight or ten inches long, which the innkeeper carefully replaced in his scabbard. As for the rest of the blade, the host had pawkily set it aside in order to make of it a larding-pin.

Great as his disappointment was, it would probably not have deterred our young hothead if the innkeeper had not realized that the objection was perfectly justified.

"Yes, that's true!" said mine host, lowering his spit. "Where is that letter?"

"Ay, where *is* that letter?" D'Artagnan repeated. "Let me tell you that letter was addressed to Monsieur de Tréville. It *must* be found and if it isn't, Monsieur de Tréville will know the reason why!"

This threat completed the intimidation of the innkeeper. After the King and the Cardinal, Monsieur de Tréville was probably the most important figure in the realm, a constant subject of discussion among soldiers and even citizens. To be sure there was also the famous Father Joseph, but his name was never breathed above a whisper, so great was the terror inspired by the Gray Eminence, to give the Cardinal's familiar his popular nickname.

Throwing down his spit and ordering his wife and servants to cast away their respective weapons, the innkeeper himself inaugurated the search for the missing document.

"Was there anything valuable in your letter?" he asked after a few moments of futile endeavor.

"God's blood I should say so!" cried the Gascon. Had he not been counting on this letter to speed his advancement at court? "It contained my whole fortune!"

"Drafts on the Spanish Treasury?" mine host asked with a worried air.

"No," D'Artagnan answered. "Drafts on the Privy Treasury of His Majesty of France." Having expected to enter the King's service on the strength of this recommendation, he believed himself justified in hazarding this somewhat misleading reply without incurring the stigma of lying.

"God help us all!" wailed the host.

"It is of no moment!" D'Artagnan said with true Gascon phlegm. "It is of no moment! Money means nothing to me!" He paused. "But that letter meant *everything*! I would rather have lost one thousand pistoles than that letter!"

He might as readily have risked twenty thousand but a certain youthful modesty restrained him.

Just as the innkeeper, finding no trace of the letter, was about to commit himself to the Devil, a ray of light pierced his skull.

"That letter is not lost!" he said.

"What!"

"That letter is *not* lost! It was stolen from you!"

"Stolen? Who stole it?"

"The gentleman who was here yesterday. He came down here to the kitchen where you left your doublet. He was alone here for quite a while. I'll wager he stole your letter."

"You think so?" D'Artagnan asked. He was somewhat skeptical for he knew the letter better than anybody else. It was purely personal; how then could it have become valuable enough to steal? No servant, no traveler could have gained anything by possessing it.

"You say you suspect that impertinent gentleman?"

"Sure as I stand here! I told him you, Monsieur, were the protégé of Monsieur de Tréville; I said you even had a letter for this illustrious gentleman. Well, the stranger looked very much disturbed. He asked me where the letter was and went straightway down to the kitchen. He knew your doublet was there."

"He's the thief, then!" D'Artagnan scowled. "I shall complain to Monsieur de Tréville, and Monsieur de Tréville will complain to the King."

Majestically, he drew two crowns from his purse, handed them to the innkeeper, and made for the gate, mine host close on his heels, hat in hand. The yellow nag awaited him; he leaped into the saddle and rode off. His steed bore him without further misadventure to the Porte Saint-Antoine, the northern gate of Paris, where its owner sold it for three crowns—an excellent price, considering that D'Artagnan had pressed it hard during the last stage of his journey. The dealer to whom D'Artagnan sold it for the aforesaid nine livres did not fail to make it clear that he was disbursing this exorbitant sum solely because of the originality of the beast's color.

So D'Artagnan entered Paris on foot, carrying his kit under his arm, roaming the city until he found a room suited to his scanty means. It was a sort of garret situated in the Rue des Fossoyeurs—Gravediggers' Row— near the Luxembourg Palace.

Having paid a deposit, D'Artagnan took possession of his lodging and spent the rest of the day sewing. His specific task was to stitch on to his doublet and hose some ornamental braiding which his mother had ripped off an almost new doublet of her husband's and given to her son secretly. Next he repaired to the Quai de la Ferraille to have a new blade put to his sword. Then he walked back toward the Louvre, to ask the first musketeer he met where Monsieur de Tréville's mansion was. It proved to be in the Rue du Vieux Colombier, quite close to where D'Artagnan had taken a room. The circumstance appeared to him to augur well for the success of his journey.

After this, gratified with the way in which he had behaved at Meung, clear of all remorse for the past, confident in the present and full of hope for the future, he retired to bed and slept the sleep of the valiant.

This sleep, the sleep of one who was still a provincial, occupied him till morning. At nine o'clock he rose, dressed and set out for the mansion of the illustrious Monsieur de Tréville, the third personage in the kingdom, according to Monsieur d'Artagnan the elder.

II
THE ANTECHAMBER OF MONSIEUR DE TRÉVILLE

Monsieur de Troisville, as his family was still called in Gascony, or Monsieur de Tréville, as he had ended by styling himself in Paris, had begun life exactly as D'Artagnan. He had marched on the capital without a sou to his name; but he possessed that wealth of audacity, shrewdness and intelligence whereby the poorest and humblest Gascon gentleman often derives brighter hopes from his paternal heritage than the richest and loftiest nobleman from Périgord or Berry realizes materially from his. His insolent bravery, his still more insolent success at a time when blows were thick as hops, sped him to the top of that difficult ladder called Court favor. He had scaled it four steps at a time.

Monsieur de Tréville was a friend of the reigning King, Louis XIII, who, as is well known, venerated the memory of his father, Henry IV. Now Monsieur de Tréville's father had served Henry IV with unfailing loyalty during the Wars of Religion. The monarch could not reward him in coin of the realm, for he was short of that commodity all his life long and he used to pay his debts with the only staple he never had cause to borrow—a ready wit! So Henry of Navarre, having captured Paris and become King of France, being short of money, as we have said, authorized the late Monsieur de Tréville to assume for arms a lion or passant upon gules—in non-heraldic terms a golden lion walking and looking towards the right, with right forepaw raised, with the motto of *Fidelis et fortis,* loyal and brave.

This was of course a very great honor but it scarcely made for creature comfort, so that when the illustrious comrade of Henry IV died, he left his son his sword and his motto for only inheritance. Thanks to this double gift and the spotless name that accompanied it, Monsieur de Tréville was admitted into the household of the young prince. There he made such good use of his sword and proved so faithful to his motto that King Louis XIII, one of the good swordsmen of his kingdom, was wont to exclaim:

"Had I a friend about to fight, I would advise him to choose me in the first place to support him, then Tréville—or no, perhaps Tréville in the first place, then myself!"

Thus Louis XIII had a genuine liking for Tréville—a royal and selfish liking, true, but a liking nevertheless. At that unhappy period, it was important for the great to be surrounded by men made of such stuff as Tréville. Many might take for a motto the epithet of *brave,* which formed the second part of Tréville's motto, but few gentlemen could boast that of *loyal,* which constituted the first. Tréville was of this small group, and high among them for the rare combination of virtues that were his. He was intelligent, obedient and tenacious as a bulldog and blindly passionate in his valor. Quick of eye and prompt of hand, he seemed to have been endowed with sight only to discern who displeased the King and with an arm only to strike down the culprit, whether a Besme, a Maurevers, a Poltrot, a Méré or a Vitry. In short, until now, Tréville had lacked nothing save the golden opportunity; but he had lain in wait for it and vowed to seize it by its three hairs if ever it came within reach. It did, and the sovereign appointed Tréville Captain of his Musketeers, who in devotion or rather in fanaticism were to Louis XIII what his Ordinaries had been to Henry III and his Scots Guards to Louis XI.

Monseigneur Cardinal, Duc de Richelieu, did not lag behind the King in this respect. Seeing the impressive élite Louis XIII had recruited, this second—or shall we say this first?—the Cardinal, as actual ruler of France, determined to have his own private guard too. Thus there were two corps of guards, the King's and the Cardinal's, and these two powerful rivals vied with each other in attracting the most celebrated swordsmen, not only from all the provinces in France but from all the foreign states. Over their evening game of chess, Cardinal and King argued the merits of their respective soldiery, each vaunting the elegance and valor of his own. Officially, they condemned all duels and brawling but pri-

vately they incited their henchmen to quarrel, deriving immoderate pleasure in victory or acute chagrin in defeat. For this statement, we have the
authority of a gentleman whose *Memoirs* attest that he was involved in
some few of these defeats but in many more of these victories.

Tréville knew how to appeal to and profit by his master's foibles. His
skill in appraising these explains how he enjoyed the long and steadfast
favor of a monarch whom history does not record as particularly faithful
in his friendships. He paraded his musketeers before Armand Duplessis,
Cardinal and Duke, with a defiant air that made His Eminence's gray
mustaches bristle with impotent anger. Tréville had an admirable grasp of
the war methods of his period; he realized that when soldiers could not
live at the enemy's expense they must live off their fellow-countrymen.
His men formed a legion of devil-may-care fellows, quite undisciplined
except in regard to their Commanding Officer.

Loose in their ways, great drinkers, battle-scarred, His Majesty's
Musketeers—or rather Monsieur de Tréville's—roamed the city. They
were to be seen lounging in the taverns, strolling in the public walks and
attending all civic sports and entertainments, shouting, twirling their
mustachios and rattling their swords. They took immense pleasure in
jostling the Guards of Monseigneur Cardinal when they met; then they
would draw their swords in the open street, amid a thousand jests, as
though it were all the greatest sport in the world. Sometimes they were
killed, but they died certain of being mourned and avenged; often they
did the killing, but they were certain of not languishing in jail, for Monsieur de Tréville was there to claim them. Obviously then they praised
their Commanding Officer to the skies, they adored him, and, ruffians
though they were, they trembled before him like schoolboys before the
magister. Submissive to his least word, they were prepared to suffer death
in order to wash out the slightest affront.

Monsieur de Tréville employed this powerful weapon on behalf of the
King and the King's friends in the first place, then, in the second place on
behalf of himself and his own friends. For the rest, no line in the memoirs
of a period so fertile in memoirs, even those left by his enemies, accuses
this worthy gentleman of acquiring personal profit from the cooperation
of his minions—and heaven knows! he had enemies aplenty among both
writers and soldiers! Gifted with a genius for intrigue which made him a
match for the ablest intriguers, he remained a model of probity and
honor. More, despite grueling training and murderous duels, Monsieur

de Tréville had become one of the most gallant frequenters of boudoirs, the most subtle squire of dames and the most exquisite turner of pretty compliments of his day. Monsieur de Tréville's triumphs in the lists of Venus were as widely bruited as those of Bassompierre twenty years before—and that was saying a good deal! The Captain of the Musketeers was therefore admired, feared and loved, a state which constitutes the zenith of human fortune.

Louis XIV absorbed all the smaller stars of his Court in his own vast radiance, but his father, *pluribus impar,* more accommodating, suffered each of his favorites to retain his personal splendor, and each of his courtiers his individual value. Besides the levees of the King and the Cardinal, Paris at that time boasted more than two hundred others, minor ones but much frequented. Among these, Monsieur de Tréville's levee was one of the most avidly sought after.

In summer from six o'clock in the morning, in winter from eight, the courtyard of his mansion in the Rue du Vieux Colombier resembled an armed camp. Groups of fifty or sixty musketeers appeared to replace one another in relays so as always to present an imposing number; they paraded ceaselessly, armed to the teeth and prepared for any eventuality. In quest of favors, the office-seekers of Paris sped up and down one of those colossal staircases within whose space our modern civilisation could build an entire house. There were gentlemen from the provinces eager to enroll in the Musketeers and flunkeys in brilliant, multicolored liveries bringing and bearing back messages between their masters and Monsieur de Tréville. In the antechamber on long circular benches sat the elect, that is to say those fortunate enough to have been summoned. A perpetual buzzing reigned in this room from morning till night while Monsieur de Tréville, in an adjoining office, received visits, listened to complaints and gave his orders. To review both his men and his arms, he had but to step to his window, much as at the Louvre the King had but to step out on his balcony.

The day D'Artagnan appeared at the Hôtel de Tréville the assemblage was most imposing, particularly for a provincial newly arrived from his distant province. True, this provincial was a Gascon and at that period Gascons were reputed to be difficult to impress. Entering through the massive door with its long, square studs, he walked into the midst of a troop of swordsmen crossing one another as they passed, calling out, quarreling and playing tricks on one another. Only an officer, a great lord or a pretty woman could have moved through these turbulent, clashing waves of humanity.

Young D'Artagnan advanced with beating heart through this tumult and confusion, holding his long rapier tight against his lanky leg and keeping one hand on the brim of his felt hat with the half-smile of your provincial who wishes to cut a figure. Having got past one group, he breathed more easily but he realized that people were turning round to stare at him, and, for the first time in his life, D'Artagnan, who had hitherto entertained a very good opinion of himself, felt ridiculous.

Things were still worse when he reached the staircase to be confronted with the following scene. Four musketeers were amusing themselves fencing. Three were on the bottom steps, a fourth some steps above them; he, naked sword in hand, prevented or attempted to prevent the three from ascending, as they plied their agile swords against him. Ten or twelve comrades waited on the landing to take their turn at this sport. At first D'Artagnan mistook these weapons for foils and believed them to be buttoned, but he soon recognized by the scratches inflicted that every weapon was pointed as a needle and razor-sharp. Incidentally, at each scratch one of the fencers dealt an adversary, both spectators and the actors themselves roared with laughter.

The soldier temporarily defending the upper step kept his adversaries marvelously in check. The circle about the fencers grew denser as fresh candidates swelled the audience. The rules of the game were that when a man was hit, he must yield his turn to another candidate, and the man who hit him received an extra turn. In five minutes, the defender of the stairway pinked three men very slightly, one on the wrist, another on the chin, and the third on the ear, while he himself remained intact. This feat, according to the rules, won him three extra turns.

However difficult it might be—or rather, however difficult D'Artagnan pretended it might be—for them to impress him, this pastime left him gaping. In his home province, a land where every man is a hothead, he had seen somewhat more elaborate preliminaries before dueling; the *gasconnade*—that is, the impetuosity, courage, calm and swagger of these four fencers—eclipsed anything he had ever witnessed even in Gascony. It was as though he had been transported into that famous realm of giants which Gulliver was later to visit and where he was to be so frightened. But D'Artagnan had not yet reached his goal; he had still to cross the landing and the antechamber.

At the head of the stairs, the musketeers were not fighting, they were exchanging stories about women; in the antechamber they were exchanging stories about the Court. On the landing, D'Artagnan blushed; in the antechamber he shuddered. In Gascony his lively and vagrant imagination had rendered him formidable to young chambermaids and even sometimes to their young mistresses; but even in his most delirious moments, he had never dreamed of half the amorous wonders or a quarter of the feats of dalliance which he heard exposed here, with no detail omitted or attenuated, in connection with the loftiest names of the realm. But if his love of decency was shocked on the landing, his respect for the Cardinal was scandalized in the antechamber. There, to D'Artagnan's amazement, they were loudly and boldly criticizing the policy which made all Europe tremble; worse, they blamed the private life of the Cardinal, blithely indifferent to the fact that so many powerful nobles had been punished mercilessly for merely attempting to learn something about it. What! Was it possible that the great man whom Monsieur d'Artagnan the elder revered so deeply served as an object of ridicule to Monsieur de Tréville's musketeers? D'Artagnan could scarcely believe his ears as he heard these soldiers cracking jokes about His Eminence's bandy legs and His Eminence's crooked back. Some sang scurrilous lampoons about Madame d'Aiguillon, his mistress, and Madame de Combalet, his niece; others formed parties and laid plans to annoy the pages and guards of Monseigneur Duke and Cardinal.

However when by chance the King's name was thoughtlessly uttered amid all these cardinalist jests, it was as though a gag had suddenly been clamped down over all these jeering mouths. The speakers glanced hesitantly about them, apparently doubting the thickness of the partition separating them from Monsieur de Tréville's office. But a fresh allusion soon brought the conversation back to His Eminence and then laughter waxed boisterous as ever and a bright, cruel light was shed upon the least of his actions.

"Upon my word, these fellows will all be imprisoned and hanged!" D'Artagnan thought. He was terrified. "And that will be my fate, too. I have been listening to them and I have heard them; I shall undoubtedly be held as an accomplice. What would my good father say—father who so earnestly counseled respect for My Lord Cardinal—what would my good father say if he knew I was in the society of such heathens?"

Needless to say, then, D'Artagnan dared not join in the conversation.

But he was all eyes and all ears, jealous lest he miss the merest detail. Despite his faith in the paternal injunction, his tastes and instincts led him to praise rather than to blame the unheard-of things he was witnessing.

Although a stranger in the throng of Monsieur de Tréville's courtiers and making his first appearance in this antechamber, D'Artagnan was finally noticed. A flunkey went up to him and asked what he wanted. D'Artagnan gave his name very modestly, emphasized the fact that he was a fellow-countryman of Monsieur de Tréville and requested a moment's audience. The servant with a somewhat patronizing air promised to transmit his request in due season.

D'Artagnan, recovering from his first surprise, now had leisure to examine the persons and costumes of those about him.

The center of the most lively group was a very tall, haughty-looking musketeer dressed in so peculiar a costume as to attract general attention. He was not wearing the uniform cloak (it was not compulsory in those days of less liberty and more independence) but, instead, a sky-blue doublet, somewhat faded and worn, and over it, a long cloak of crimson velvet that fell in graceful folds from his shoulders. Across his chest, from over his right shoulder to his left hip, blazed a magnificent baldric, worked in gold and twinkling like rippling waters in the sun. From it hung a gigantic rapier.

This musketeer had just come off guard, coughed affectedly from time to time and complained of having caught a cold. That was why he was wearing his cloak, he explained to those around him, speaking with a lofty air and twirling his mustaches disdainfully. Everyone admired his gold-braided baldric, D'Artagnan more than anyone.

"After all, baldrics are coming in to fashion," said the musketeer. "It was wildly extravagant of me, but still they're the fashion! Besides, a man must spend his inheritance somehow."

"Come, Porthos, don't try to tell us your baldric comes from the paternal coffers!" another musketeer piped up. "I know better."

"What?"

"It came from the heavily-veiled lady I met you with two Sundays ago over by the Porte Saint-Honoré."

"No, by my honor, I bought it myself!" the man designated as Porthos protested. "On my faith as a gentleman, I paid for it out of my own purse."

"Yes," said a bystander. "Just as I bought this new purse with the money my mistress put in my old one!"

"It's true, though," Porthos insisted. "The proof of it is that I paid twelve pistoles for it." The general wonderment grew but the general doubt subsisted. "Didn't I, Aramis?" he concluded, turning to still another musketeer.

The companion whose corroboration he invited offered a perfect contrast to Porthos. Aramis was a young man twenty-three years old at most with a delicate and ingenuous countenance ... black gentle eyes ... cheeks rosy and downy as an autumn peach . . . and tenuous mustaches that marked a perfectly straight line over his upper lip.... He seemed mortally afraid to lower his hands lest their veins swell up; he would pinch his ear-lobes from time to time to preserve their smooth, roseate transparency. Usually he spoke little and always slowly; he bowed frequently and laughed noiselessly, baring beautiful white teeth which he seemed to care for as attentively as he cared for the rest of his person. At his friend's appeal, he nodded affirmatively.

Another musketeer changed the subject, addressing no one in particular.

"What do you think of the Chalais incident?" he inquired. "His esquire is telling the strangest tale!"

"And what does the esquire say?" Porthos asked pompously.

"He says he was in Brussels and there he met Rochefort, the *âme damnée* of the Cardinal. And guess in what circumstances?"

"Well?"

"Rochefort was disguised as a Capuchin friar, damn his soul! Thanks to his costume he was able to trick Monsieur de Laigues, fool that he is!"

"De Laigues is a fool, certainly," Porthos conceded. "But is this news reliable?"

"I had it from Aramis."

"You did?"

"Why yes, Porthos, I told you all about it yesterday. Let's drop the subject!"

"Drop the subject?" Porthos thundered. "That's *your* opinion!" He drew a deep breath. "Drop the subject, indeed! A plague on you, you draw your conclusions too quickly! What! The Cardinal sets a spy upon a gentleman? The Cardinal has this gentleman's letters stolen from him by a traitor, a brigand, a gallows bird? With the help of this scoundrel and thanks to this correspondence, the Cardinal has the head of Monsieur de Chalais severed skilfully from his shoulders? And you say 'Drop the subject!'

"And under what pretext does the Cardinal execute Chalais? Under the stupid pretext that Chalais plotted to kill the King and marry off Monsieur, the King's brother, to our Queen. No one knew a word about this intrigue. Yesterday you unraveled it to our general satisfaction. And now, while we are still gaping at the news, *you* say: 'Let's drop the subject!' "

"Very well, then," Aramis agreed. "Since you wish it, let us discuss the matter."

"Were I the esquire of poor Monsieur de Chalais," Porthos blustered, "I would give that criminal Rochefort a pretty hard time of it for a minute or two."

"Yes, I know!" Aramis countered suavely. "And you would get a pretty hard time of it yourself from the Red Duke!"

"The Red Duke! Bravo, bravo! The Red Duke!" Porthos cried, clapping his hands and nodding approval. "The Red Duke! What a capital coiner of *mots* you are, my dear Aramis. I shall make it my business to put that epithet in circulation all over the city, you may be sure! What a wit this lad Aramis is! What a pity you did not follow your early vocation! What a delightful abbé you would have made!"

"A temporary postponement!" Aramis answered, picking imaginary dust off his sleeve. "Some day I shall be a priest! Why do you suppose I am going on with my theological studies?"

"Ay, a priest he'll be, sooner or later!"

"Sooner!"

Another musketeer intervened:

"Aramis is waiting for one thing before he dons the cassock hanging behind his uniform."

"What is that?"

"For the Queen to produce an heir to the throne of France!"

"That is no subject for jesting!" Porthos objected. "Thank God the Queen is still of an age to bear a child!"

"My Lord Buckingham is said to be in France . . ."

The fleeting, sharp smile that accompanied this apparently simple statement left it open to a somewhat scandalous interpretation.

"Aramis, my friend, this time you are wrong. Your wit is forever leading you astray. If Monsieur de Tréville heard you, you would rue it."

"Are you presuming to lecture me, Porthos?"

"No, I—"

A flash of lightning blazed in the eyes of Aramis, eyes habitually so placid and kindly.

"Well?"

"My dear Aramis, make up your mind. Are you to be an abbé or a musketeer? Be one or the other, not both." Porthos paused. "You know what Athos told you the other day. He said you were all things to all men."

Aramis raised his arm violently.

"Come, let us not get angry," Porthos continued. "You know what Athos, you and I have agreed upon. Well, you visit Madame d'Aiguillon to pay court to her, you visit Madame de Bois-Tracy and you pay court to her, too. May I remind you that she is a cousin of Madame de Chevreuse? Rumor has it that you are quite far advanced in the good graces of Madame de Bois-Tracy."

Again, Aramis made an impatient gesture.

"Good Lord, don't bother to tell us about your luck with the ladies. No one wants to discover your secret; everybody knows you for a model of discretion. But since you possess that virtue, why the devil not apply it when you speak of Her Majesty the Queen? I don't care who plays fast and loose with King or Cardinal. But the Queen is sacred. If a man speaks of her, let it be with respect."

Aramis looked at his friend. He sighed.

"Porthos," he declared, "You are vain as Narcissus. I have told you this before, I tell you again. You know how I loathe moralizing, unless Athos does it. As for yourself, my fine friend, your baldric is far too magnificent to chime with your philosophy. If I care to become an abbé, I shall do so. Meanwhile I am a musketeer and as such I shall say what I please. At this moment, I am pleased to say that I find you very boring."

"Aramis!"

"Porthos!"

Their comrades hastily interfered:

"Come, come, gentlemen . . . Stop, Porthos . . . Look, Aramis . . . After all, he didn't mean it . . . Now, now. . . ."

The door of Monsieur de Tréville's study flew open. A lackey stood on the doorsill.

"Monsieur de Tréville will receive Monsieur d'Artagnan," he announced.

The door being open, those in the antechamber suddenly stopped talking. Amid the general silence, D'Artagnan walked across the room and entered the office, congratulating himself with all his heart at having so narrowly escaped the end of the extraordinary altercation.

III

THE AUDIENCE

Though Monsieur de Tréville was in a very bad humor at the moment, he greeted his young caller politely. D'Artagnan bowed to the ground and in his sonorous Béarn accent paid his profound respects. His southern intonation and diction reminded Monsieur de Tréville of both his youth and his country, a twofold remembrance which brings a smile to the lips of any man, old or young. But before bidding D'Artagnan to be seated, Monsieur de Tréville stepped toward the antechamber, waving his hand toward D'Artagnan as though to ask his permission to finish with other business before he began with him.

Standing by the open door, Monsieur de Tréville called three names. At each name, his voice gained in volume so that he ran the gamut between command and anger.

"Athos! Porthos! Aramis!"

At his summons, only two soldiers appeared, the musketeer of the golden baldric and the musketeer who would be an abbé. No sooner had they entered than the door closed behind them. Though they were not quite at ease, D'Artagnan admired their bearing; they were at once carefree, dignified and submissive. In his eyes they were as demigods and their leader an Olympian Jove, armed with all his thunderbolts.

D'Artagnan took stock of the situation. The two musketeers were here now, the door closed behind them, and the hum of conversation in the antechamber rose again, doubtless revived by speculation about why Porthos and Aramis were on the carpet. Monsieur de Tréville was pacing up and down in silence, his brows knit; he covered the entire length of his office, back and forth, three or four times, passing directly in front of the musketeers, who stood smartly at attention, as if on parade. Suddenly he stopped squarely in front of them, wheeled round to face them, and, surveying them angrily from top to toe:

"Do you gentlemen know what the King said to me no later than yesterday evening?" he demanded. "Do you know, gentlemen?"

There was a moment's silence. Then one of them replied:

"No ... No, Monsieur, we do not."

"I hope that Monsieur will do us the honor to tell us," Aramis suggested in his most honeyed tone as he made a deep bow.

"He told me that from now on he would recruit his musketeers from among the Cardinal's Guards."

"The Cardinal's Guards!" Aramis asked indignantly. "But why, Monsieur?"

"Because His Majesty realizes that his inferior wine needs improving by blending it with a better vintage."

The two musketeers blushed to the roots of their hair. D'Artagnan, completely in the dark about what was happening and considerably embarrassed, wished himself a hundred feet underground.

"Ay," Monsieur de Tréville went on, growing angrier apace, "His Majesty was perfectly right, for upon my word, the musketeers certainly cut a sorry figure at Court. Do you know what happened yesterday evening when His Eminence was playing chess with the King? Well, I'll tell you. . . .

"His Eminence looked at me with a commiserating air which frankly vexed me. Then he told me that my daredevil musketeers —those *daredevils,* he repeated with an irony that vexed me even more—had required disciplining. Then, his tiger-cat eye cocked at me, he informed me that my swashbucklers had made a night of it in a tavern in the Rue Férou and that a patrol of his Guards (I thought he was going to laugh in my face!) had been forced to arrest the rioters."

Monsieur de Tréville paused for breath.

"*Morbleu!* God's death, you must know something about it," he resumed. "My musketeers—arrested! And you were among them, don't deny it; you were identified and the Cardinal named you! But it's all my own fault, ay, it's my own fault because it is I who choose my men. Come, Aramis, tell me why the devil you asked me for a musketeer's uniform when a cassock would have suited you so much better? And you, Porthos? Of what use is that fine golden baldric of yours if all it holds up is a sword of straw? And Athos? ... By the way, where *is* Athos?"

"Monsieur," Aramis explained mournfully, "Athos is ill, very ill."

"Ill, you say? What's the matter with him?"

"We're afraid it's chicken-pox, Monsieur," Porthos improvised, deter-

mined at all costs to take part in the conversation. "But we hope not, because it would certainly disfigure him."

"The pox. There's a cock-and-bull story, Porthos! Chicken-pox at his
age! No, I know better. He was probably wounded or killed, I dare say. Oh,
if only I knew what has happened to him!"

Monsieur de Tréville began pacing his office again, then turned
fiercely on the culprits:

"*Sangdieu*, gentlemen! God's blood, I will not have my men haunting
disreputable places, I will not have them brawling in the streets, and I will
not have them fighting at every street corner. Above all, I will not have
them make themselves the laughingstocks of Monseigneur Cardinal's
Guards. These Guards are decent fellows, they are law-abiding and tact-
ful, they do not put themselves in a position to be arrested. And if they
did—I swear it!—they wouldn't *allow* themselves to *be* arrested. They
would prefer dying in their tracks to yielding an inch. Whereas self-
preservation, flight and surrender," he sneered, "seem to be the watch-
words of His Majesty's Musketeers."

During his long censure, Porthos and Aramis were shaking with rage;
they would cheerfully have strangled Monsieur de Tréville had they not
felt that it was the great love he bore them made him speak thus. Occasionally, one or the other would stamp on the carpet or bite his lips to the
quick or grasp the hilt of his sword so firmly that his hand paled. Their ordeal was the worse because they knew that Monsieur de Tréville's voice
carried over into the antechamber. There, of course, the assembled musketeers had heard Monsieur de Tréville call for Athos, Porthos and
Aramis, and they judged from his tone of voice that he was exceeding
wroth. Dozens of eavesdroppers glued their ears to the tapestry covering
the partition, shuddering at what they heard. Several glued their ears as
near the keyhole as they could, and, by a relay system, repeated their
leader's insults word for word for the benefit of the entire audience. In a
trice, from the door of the Captain's office to the gate on the street, the
whole mansion was seething.

"So His Majesty's Musketeers are arrested by the Cardinal's Guards,
eh?" At heart Monsieur de Tréville was as furious as any of his soldiers.
Yet he clipped his words, whetting and sharpening them until they were
so many stilettos plunged into the breasts of the culprits.

"Yes, six of the Cardinal's Guards arrest six Royal Musketeers! God's
death, I know what to do now. I shall go straight to the Louvre, submit my

resignation as Captain of the Royal Musketeers and apply for a Lieutenant's commission in the Cardinal's Guards. And *morbleu!* if he refuses, I will turn abbé!"

At these last words, the murmur outside, which had been steadily rising, crescendo, burst into a veritable explosion. Jeers, oaths, curses and blasphemy rent the air; it was *morbleu* here, *sangdieu* there, *morts de tous les diables,* upstairs and down, all over the mansion, with God and Satan serving with their bodily parts as pegs upon which to hang the most violent imprecations. D'Artagnan looked vainly about him for some curtain behind which to hide; failing to find any, he was seized with a wild desire to crawl under the table.

"I beg your pardon, Captain," said Porthos, flaring up, "but the truth is that we were evenly matched, six to six. They set upon us treacherously and unawares; before we could even draw our swords, two of our men were dead and Athos was grievously wounded. You know Athos, Monsieur! Well, Athos tried to get up on his feet twice and twice he fell down again. Meanwhile, we did not surrender, we were dragged forcibly away. Anyhow, before they got us in jail, we escaped."

"And Athos?"

"Well, Monsieur, they thought Athos dead and left him lying comfortably on the field of battle. What point was there in carrying off a corpse? There's the whole story for you. Devil take it, Captain, nobody ever won all the battles he fought in. Pompey the Great lost the Battle of Pharsala, I think, and King Francis the first, who so far as I have heard, was as good as the next man, suffered ignominious defeat at the Battle of Pavia."

"I have the honor to assure you, Monsieur, that I killed one guardsman with his own sword," Aramis put in. "Mine was broken at the first parry. I killed him or stabbed him, Monsieur; it is for you to choose which terminology you prefer."

Monsieur de Tréville appeared to be somewhat mollified:

"I did not know all this," he admitted. "From what I now hear, I suppose His Eminence was exaggerating."

Profiting by the fact that his Commanding Officer seemed to have calmed down, Aramis hazarded:

"I beg you Monsieur not to say that Athos is wounded. He would be desperately unhappy if the King should hear of it. The wound is a very serious one; the blade passed through his shoulder and penetrated into his chest. So it is to be feared that—"

Suddenly the door opened, the tapestry curtain was raised and a man stood on the threshold. He stood at attention, his noble head erect, his shoulders squared. His features were drawn, his face white.

"Athos!"

"Athos!" Monsieur de Tréville echoed in amazement.

"My comrades told me you had sent for me, Captain," the newcomer said in a feeble yet perfectly even voice, "so I came here to report to you. What is your pleasure, Monsieur?"

He was in regulation uniform, buttons ashine, boots glittering, belted as usual for duty, every inch a soldier. With a tolerably firm step, he advanced into the room. Monsieur de Tréville, deeply moved by this proof of courage, sprang to meet him.

"I was telling these gentlemen that I forbid my musketeers to expose their lives needlessly," he explained. "Brave men are very dear to the King and His Majesty knows that his musketeers are the bravest men on earth. Your hand, Athos!"

And without waiting for the other's reaction, Monsieur de Tréville seized his right hand and pressed it with all his might. In his enthusiasm he failed to notice that Athos, mastering himself as he did, could not check a twitch of pain. Athos turned even whiter than before.

The arrival of Athos had created a sensation in the Hôtel de Tréville. Despite the precautions his comrades had taken to keep his wounds a secret, news of his condition was common gossip. The door to Monsieur de Tréville's had remained open; his last words met with a burst of satisfaction in the antechamber. Jubilant, two or three musketeers poked their heads through the openings of the tapestry. Monsieur de Tréville was about to reprimand this breach of discipline when he felt the hand of Athos stiffen and, looking up, realized that Athos was about to faint. At that moment, Athos rallied all his energy to struggle against pain, but he was at length overcome and fell to the floor like a dead man.

"A surgeon!" Monsieur de Tréville ordered. "My surgeon or the King's. Anyhow, the best surgeon you can find. God's blood, unless you fetch a surgeon, my brave Athos will die."

At this, many of the musketeers outside rushed into Monsieur de Tréville's office (for he was too occupied with Athos to close the door upon them) and crowded around the wounded man. All this attention might have proved useless had not the physician so urgently summoned chanced to be in the mansion. Elbowing his way through the throng, he approached Athos. The musketeer was still unconscious, and, as all this noise and commotion was inconvenient, the first and most urgent thing the doctor asked was that Athos be removed to an adjoining room. Monsieur de Tréville immediately opened the door and pointed the way to Porthos and Aramis who carried off their comrade in their arms. Behind them walked the surgeon, and behind the surgeon, the door closed. Then, momentarily, Monsieur de Tréville's office, usually a place held sacred, became an annex to the antechamber as everybody commented, harangued, vociferated, swore, cursed and consigned the Cardinal and his guardsmen to all the devils.

An instant after, Porthos and Aramis reappeared, leaving only the surgeon and Monsieur de Tréville at their friend's side. Presently Monsieur de Tréville himself returned. Athos, he said, had regained consciousness and, according to the surgeon, his condition need not worry his friends; his weakness was due wholly to loss of blood.

Then the Captain of Musketeers dismissed the company with a wave of the hand and all withdrew save D'Artagnan, who did not forget that he had an audience and who, with Gascon tenacity, sat tight.

"Pardon me, my dear compatriot," Monsieur de Tréville said with a smile, "pardon me but I had completely forgotten you. You can understand that. A captain is nothing but a father charged with an even greater responsibility than the father of an ordinary family. Soldiers are just big children. But as I insist on the orders of the King, and more particularly the orders of the Cardinal, being carried out—"

D'Artagnan could not help smiling. Observing this Monsieur de Tréville judged that he was not dealing with a fool, and, changing the conversation, came straight to the point:

"I loved your father dearly," he said. "What can I do for his son? Tell me quickly, for as you see my time is not my own."

"Monsieur," D'Artagnan explained, "on leaving Tarbes and coming here, I intended to request you, in remembrance of the friendship you have cited, to enroll me in the musketeers. But after what I have seen here during the last two hours, I understand what a tremendous favor this would be. I am afraid I do not deserve it."

"It is indeed a favor, young man, but perhaps not so far beyond your hopes as you believe or affect to believe. At all events, His Majesty's Regulations are explicit on that point. I am sorry to have to tell you that no one is admitted to the musketeers unless he has fought in several campaigns or performed certain brilliant feats or served at least two years in some other regiment less favored than ours."

D'Artagnan bowed without replying. Disappointed as he was, the difficulties to be surmounted before becoming a musketeer made him all the more eager to achieve this. Monsieur de Tréville fixed a sharp, piercing glance upon his compatriot as though to read his inmost thoughts and continued:

"However, on account of my old comrade, your father, I want to do something for you, as I said. Our youths from Béarn are usually none too well off nor have I any reason to suspect that things have changed much since I myself left the province. I dare say you haven't brought any too much money up with you?"

D'Artagnan drew himself up proudly; his expression indicated clearly that he accepted alms of no man.

"Very well, young man, I understand," Monsieur de Tréville observed. "I know those airs; I myself descended upon Paris with four crowns in my purse and I would have fought with anybody who suggested that I could not buy up the Louvre!"

D'Artagnan drew himself up even more proudly as he realized that thanks to the sale of his nag, he was beginning his career with four crowns more than Monsieur de Tréville had possessed in similar circumstances.

"You ought, I say, to husband your resources however great they may be, but you ought also to perfect yourself in exercises befitting a gentleman. I shall write a letter today to the Director of the Royal Military Academy and he will admit you tomorrow at no expense to yourself. Do not refuse this small favor; our best-born and wealthiest gentlemen sometimes solicit it in vain. You will learn horsemanship, swordsmanship of all sorts, and dancing. You will make desirable acquaintances there and you can call on me from time to time to tell me how you are getting along and whether I can be of further service to you."

D'Artagnan, though a stranger to the manners of the Court, could not help feeling a certain coldness in this reception.

"Alas, Monsieur!" he mourned. "My father gave me a letter of introduction to present to you. Now I realize how much it would help me."

"I am indeed surprised that you should undertake so long a journey without that viaticum, that indispensable passport, which is the sole resource we poor Béarnais possess."

"I had one, Monsieur, and by God! the finest I could wish for. But it was treacherously stolen from me."

And he proceeded to relate the adventure of Meung, describing the unknown gentleman with the minutest detail and with a warmth and truthfulness that delighted Monsieur de Tréville.

"This is all very curious," Monsieur de Tréville declared after a moment's reflection. "You mentioned my name aloud then?"

"Yes, Monsieur, I confess I committed that imprudence. But why not? A name like yours must needs serve me as a shield on my journey. You will judge whether I often availed myself of its protection."

Flattery was very current in those days and Monsieur de Tréville loved incense as well as any king or cardinal. He could not restrain a smile of obvious satisfaction, but this smile soon disappeared. Returning to the adventure of Meung:

"Tell me," he asked, "did this gentleman have a slight scar on his cheek?"

"Yes, the kind of scar he might have if a bullet had grazed him. . . ."

"Wasn't he a fine-looking man?"

"Yes, splendid."

"Tall?"

"Ay."

"Fair complexion? Brown hair?"

"Yes, Monsieur, that's right, that's the man! How do you know him so well? If ever I find him again—and I will find him, I swear, even in hell—"

"He was waiting for a lady?"

"Yes, and he left after talking to her for a few moments."

"Do you happen to know what they talked about?"

"He gave her a box, told her it contained her instructions, and admonished her not to open it until she reached London."

"Was this woman English?"

"He called her Milady."

"It is *he*, it *is* he!" Tréville murmured. "I thought he was still at Brussels."

"Oh, Monsieur, if you know who this man is, pray tell me who he is and where he comes from. This would be the greatest favor you could possibly do me. If you will, then I shall release you from all your promises, even that of helping me eventually to join the musketeers. The only thing I ask of life is to avenge myself!"

"Beware of trying any such thing, young man," Tréville cautioned. "On the contrary, if you ever see him on one side of the street, make sure to cross to the other. Do not throw yourself against such a rock; it would smash you like glass."

"That will not prevent me, if ever I meet him, from—"

Suddenly Tréville eyed D'Artagnan suspiciously. Treachery might well lurk behind the fierce hatred the young traveler professed for the man who had stolen his father's letter—or so he said! Besides, this theft seemed an improbable thing at best. Might not His Eminence have sent this youth to set a trap for Tréville? Wasn't this pretended D'Artagnan an emissary whom the Cardinal sought to introduce into Tréville's household so that he might be close to him, win his confidence and then ruin him? The Cardinal had played this trick in a thousand other instances. Looking at D'Artagnan even more searchingly than before, Monsieur de Tréville was but moderately reassured by his expression, alive with astute intelligence and affected humility.

"I know he's a Gascon," he mused. "But he may be as much of a Gascon for Monseigneur Cardinal as he is for me. I shall test him."

His eyes fixed upon D'Artagnan's, he spoke slowly: "My boy, your father was my old friend and comrade. I believe this story of the lost letter to be perfectly true and I should like to dispel the impression of coldness you may have remarked in my welcome. Perhaps the best way to do so would be to discover to you, a novice as I once was myself, the secrets of our policy today."

He then went on to explain to D'Artagnan how the King and the Cardinal were the best of friends; their apparent bickering was only a stratagem intended to deceive fools. Monsieur de Tréville was unwilling that a compatriot, a dashing cavalier and a youth of high mettle, should be duped by such artifices and fall into the snare, as so many others had done before him to their ruin. He assured D'Artagnan of his devotion to both these all-powerful masters; he insisted that his most earnest endeavor was to serve both the King and the Cardinal. His Eminence, he added, was one of the most illustrious geniuses France had ever produced.

"Now, young man, rule your conduct accordingly. If for family reasons or through your friends or through your own instincts, even, you entertain such enmity for the Cardinal as we are constantly discovering, then let us bid each other adieu. I will help you as much as I can but without attaching you to my person."

There was a long pause.

"I hope my frankness will at least make you my friend," Monsieur de Tréville said at last, "because you are the only young man to whom I have ever spoken like this."

(Tréville was thinking: "The Cardinal knows how bitterly I loathe him. If he has set this young fox upon me, then he cannot have failed to indicate the best means of winning my favor. This spy, therefore, has been primed to rail at Richelieu for my benefit. If my suspicions are well-founded, my hypocritical protestations of loyalty to Richelieu should move this crafty youth to loose a torrent of abuse against His Eminence." But Monsieur de Tréville's calculations proved to be wrong.)

"I came to Paris with just the intentions you advise me to harbor, Monsieur," he replied candidly. "My father warned me to follow nobody but His Majesty, Monseigneur Cardinal, and yourself—whom he considered the three leading personages in the realm of France."

(Monsieur d'Artagnan the elder had indicated only Louis XIII and Richelieu, but his son thought the addition of Monsieur de Tréville would do no harm.)

"I have the greatest reverence for the Cardinal and the most profound respect for his actions," he continued. "So much the better for me, Monsieur, if as you say, you are speaking to me frankly, because, by so doing, you pay me the honor of sharing my opinion. So much the worse for me if you mistrust me, as well you may, because then I am damning myself in your eyes for speaking the truth. Still, I trust you will not esteem me any the less for my frankness since your esteem is the thing I hold dearest in life."

Monsieur de Tréville was overwhelmed with surprise. Such penetration and sincerity won his admiration but did not wholly dissipate his suspicions; the more this youth excelled others, the more dangerous he was if Tréville misjudged him. Nevertheless, he pressed D'Artagnan's hand, saying:

"You are an honest lad. But at present I can do for you no more than what I just offered. The Hôtel de Tréville will always be open to you. In time, you will have a chance to ask for me at all hours. Consequently you will be able to take advantage of all available opportunities and you will probably achieve what you desire."

"You mean, Monsieur, when I have proved myself worthy?" said

D'Artagnan. And, with all the familiarity of Gascon to Gascon: "Well, you may rest assured, you will not have to wait long!"

Whereupon he bowed, to take his leave, as if he considered the future so much putty in his hands to shape as he willed.

"Wait, wait!" Monsieur de Tréville laid a hand on his arm. "I promised you a letter to the Director of the Royal Academy. Are you too proud to accept it, my lad?"

"No, Monsieur, and I guarantee this letter will not fare like my father's; I will guard it so carefully that I swear it will be delivered. If anyone attempts to take it from me, may God have mercy on his soul!"

Smiling at this extravagance, Monsieur de Tréville left D'Artagnan in the embrasure of the window, where they had been chatting, and moved to his desk to write the promised letter. While he was doing this, D'Artagnan, with nothing to occupy him, drummed a tattoo on the window pane, and amused himself by watching the musketeers as they left the building, one by one, until turning the corner, they vanished.

The letter finished, Monsieur de Tréville sealed it, rose and advanced toward D'Artagnan, who stretched out his hand to receive it. Suddenly, to Monsieur de Tréville's amazement, his protégé turned crimson with fury.

"God's blood. . . ."

"What's the matter?"

D'Artagnan leaped across the room, crying:

"God's blood, he'll not slip through my fingers this time!"

"Who?"

"My thief!" D'Artagnan shouted as he rushed from the room. "Ah, coward! traitor! at last!"

"Devil take that madman!" Monsieur de Tréville grumbled. "Unless, failing in his mission, he is making a highly strategic escape."

IV

OF ATHOS AND HIS SHOULDER, OF PORTHOS AND HIS
BALDRIC, AND OF ARAMIS AND HIS HANDKERCHIEF

Mad with anger, D'Artagnan crossed the office in the three leaps and was darting toward the stairs, expecting to clear them four at a time, when, in his furious rush, he collided head foremost with a musketeer who was coming out of one of Monsieur de Tréville's private rooms. As D'Artagnan butted the man's shoulder violently, the other uttered a cry or rather a howl.

"Excuse me," said D'Artagnan, trying to start off again. "Excuse me but I am in a hurry."

He had scarcely gone down the first step when a hand of iron seized him by the belt.

"Oh! you're in a hurry, eh?" said the musketeer, blanching. "You're in a hurry so you run right into me and you say 'Excuse me' and you expect me to take it? Not at all, my lad. You heard Monsieur de Tréville speak somewhat cavalierly to us today and you think we can take that sort of thing from anybody. Let me set you right, comrade, you are not Monsieur de Tréville."

D'Artagnan recognized Athos who, having had his wounds dressed by the doctor, was on his way home.

"I assure you I did not do it on purpose," D'Artagnan apologized. "As it was an accident, I said 'Excuse me'. I should think that was sufficient apology. Once more, I say I am in a very great hurry—on my honor!—and I'll not say it again. Let me go, please, let me go about my business."

"Monsieur, you are far from courteous," Athos replied, loosing his hold of him. "It is obvious that you are newly come from some remote province."

D'Artagnan had already gone down several steps but at this remark he stopped short:

"*Morbleu*, Monsieur," he growled, "I may come from a distance but I warn you, you are not the man to give me lessons in deportment."

"Perhaps."

"If I were not in such a hurry and if I were not chasing somebody—"

"Monsieur-the-gentleman-in-a-great-hurry, you can find me again without running after me, if you see what I mean."

"And where, if you please?"

"Near the Carmes-Deschaux, you know, the Carmelite convent."

"At what time?"

"About noon."

"About noon. Very well. I shall be there."

"Try to be punctual because if you make me wait till a quarter past, I shall cut your ears off as you run."

"Good, I shall be there at ten to twelve."

And D'Artagnan set off as though borne by the Devil, confident that he would overtake the man of Meung whom he had seen sauntering down the street. But at the main gate, he saw Porthos talking to the soldier on guard. Between the two of them, there was just room for a man to pass; D'Artagnan, thinking he could whisk through, shot forward like an arrow between them. Unfortunately he had not reckoned with the wind. As he was about to pass, a gust blew out the portly musketeer's long cloak and D'Artagnan landed right in the middle of it. Porthos doubtless had his own reasons for not wishing to abandon this essential part of his costume, for instead of releasing the flap he held in his hand, he pulled it toward him. D'Artagnan was thus rolled up inside the velvet by a rotatory movement attributable to the persistency of Porthos.

Hearing the musketeer swear, he tried to emerge from under the cloak which was blinding him and sought to find his way from under its folds. Above all he must avoid marring the virgin freshness of the baldric Porthos set such store by. Opening his eyes timidly, he found his nose glued between the musketeer's shoulders flat against the baldric.

Alas, like most things in this world which have but appearance in their favor, the baldric was aglitter with gold in front, but behind it was of ordinary buff. Vainglorious as he was, if Porthos could not afford a baldric wholly of gold, he would have at least one-half of it. This explained the necessity of the cold he had complained of and the urgency of the cloak he sported.

"*Vertubleu,* you must be crazy to crash into people this way," Porthos grumbled as D'Artagnan kept wriggling behind him.

"Excuse me," said D'Artagnan, reappearing from under the giant's shoulder, "but I am in a great hurry. I was running after somebody and—"

"And you always go blind when you run, I suppose."

"No," D'Artagnan answered, somewhat nettled. "In fact, thanks to my eyes I can see a good many things other people don't."

He did not care whether Porthos understood the allusion or not. At all events, the musketeer gave free rein to his anger:

"Monsieur, I warn you, you stand an excellent chance of being disemboweled if you try pushing a musketeer about."

"Disemboweled? That's strong language, Monsieur."

"It befits a man accustomed to looking his enemies in the face!"

"Ha, that's no lie!" D'Artagnan laughed. "Certainly you wouldn't show them your back."

And enchanted with his wit, he went off, still chuckling over the semi-golden baldric. Porthos, foaming with rage, was about to fall upon him.

"Later, later!" D'Artagnan admonished. "When you haven't your cloak on."

"At one o'clock, then, behind the Luxembourg."

"Very well, then, at one o'clock."

D'Artagnan turned the corner of the street, looking carefully ahead and up and down the cross street. Slowly though the stranger had walked, he must still have outdistanced D'Artagnan while the Gascon was being detained by Athos and Porthos or he must have entered some house nearby. D'Artagnan inquired of passers-by if they had seen a person answering his enemy's description. He walked down as far as the ferry, came up again along the Rue de Seine and across the Croix-Rouse, but he found nothing, absolutely nothing. Yet this wild-goose chase helped him in a sense, for, fast as the beads of sweat ran down his forehead, his heart began to cool.

He retraced all the events that had occurred; they were numerous and ill-omened. It was scarcely eleven o'clock in the morning and yet in two short hours he had made three capital blunders. In the first place, he had disgraced himself in the eyes of Monsieur de Tréville, who could not but consider his withdrawal somewhat cavalier; in the second and third, he had invited dangerous duels with two men, each capable of slaying three D'Artagnans—with two musketeers, in short, with two of those heroes he admired so passionately that they throned it in his mind and heart over all others.

A sad plight! Certain of being killed by Athos, he was naturally unperturbed about Porthos. But as hope is the last thing a man will relinquish, D'Artagnan hoped against hope that he might survive both these duels, even though grievously wounded. Should this happen, he would profit by the following homily delivered by himself to himself.

"What a lunatic I was and what a clod I am! Poor brave Athos was wounded in the shoulder and I was fated to butt against it! Why he did not kill me then and there, God knows! He had ample cause to, I must have caused him fearful pain. As for Porthos—dear old Porthos!—my run-in with him was the drollest thing that ever happened to me!"

At the thought, the youth could not help roaring with laughter, but he looked very carefully about him to make sure lest his solitary laughter, unaccountable to any passer-by, be considered offensive.

"Funny it was, surely, but that doesn't make me any less of a driveling idiot. People simply don't go charging into others without warning and they don't dive under their cloaks to search for what isn't there. Porthos would certainly have excused me if I hadn't alluded to his cursed baldric. To be sure I didn't refer to it specifically; I employed subtle insinuation and hilarious innuendo. Ah, cursed Gascon that I am, I would crack a joke as I fried on the griddles of hell!"

His mirth spent, he continued to talk to himself with all the amenity he believed to be his due:

"Look here, D'Artagnan my friend, if you escape (which seems to me highly improbable) you must learn to be perfectly polite in the future. You must henceforth be admired and cited as a model of urbanity. To be mannerly and obliging does not make a man a coward. Look at Aramis, he is amiability and grace personified. Well, has anyone ever dreamed of calling him a coward? Certainly not, and I vow that from now on I shall take him as a model in everything. Ah, here he is!"

Walking forward and soliloquizing, D'Artagnan had arrived a few steps from the Hôtel d'Aiguillon and found Aramis by the main gate chatting gaily with three gentlemen of the Royal Guards. Aramis, for his part, perceived D'Artagnan too. But remembering that the youth had witnessed the angry scene with Monsieur de Tréville that morning, he felt loath to welcome one who had observed the Captain rebuking his musketeers. So he pretended not to see him. D'Artagnan, on the contrary, was still full of his plans of conciliation and courtesy, so with a deep bow and a most gracious smile, he approached the quartet. Aramis bowed his head slightly but did not smile. The four soldiers immediately broke off their conversation.

D'Artagnan at once perceived that he was intruding upon them, but he was not familiar enough with the manners of the fashionable world to know how to extricate himself gallantly from a false position. Here he was, mingling with people he scarcely knew and interrupting a conversation that did not concern him. He was racking his brains to find the least awkward means of retreat when he noticed that Aramis had dropped his handkerchief and, doubtless by mistake, had placed his foot over it. Here, thought D'Artagnan, was a favorable opportunity to make up for his tactlessness. With the most polished air he could summon, he stooped and drew the handkerchief from under the musketeer's foot, despite the efforts Aramis made to keep it hidden. Holding it out to Aramis, he said:

"Here, Monsieur, is a handkerchief I believe you should be sorry to lose."

Indeed, the handkerchief was richly embroidered and one of the corners bore a coronet and crest. Aramis, blushing excessively, snatched it from the Gascon's hand.

"Ah, ah, my most discreet friend," one of the guards said to Aramis, "will you persist in saying that you are not on good terms with Madame de Bois-Tracy when that charming lady is kind enough to lend you one of her handkerchiefs?"

The glance Aramis shot at D'Artagnan was a declaration of mortal enmity. Then, resuming his usual suave air:

"You are in error, gentlemen," he answered. "This handkerchief does not belong to me. I cannot imagine what maggot inspired Monsieur to hand it to me rather than to one of you. As proof of what I say, here is mine in my pocket."

Whereupon he produced his own handkerchief which was very elegant too and of fine cambric though that material was expensive at the period. But it lacked both embroidery and a crest. As he held it up, they could all see it was ornamented with a single cipher, its owner's.

This time D'Artagnan was not so hasty. He perceived his mistake. But the others refused to be convinced by the musketeer's denial. One of them addressed the musketeer with affected seriousness:

"If matters were as you pretend, my dear Aramis, I should be forced to ask you to hand over that handkerchief. Bois-Tracy is an intimate friend of mine and I will not allow his wife's property to be sported as a trophy."

"Your demand is ill-couched," Aramis retorted. "While I recognize the justice of your claim, I refuse it on account of the form."

"The fact is," D'Artagnan hazarded timidly, "I did not see the handkerchief fall from the pocket of Monsieur Aramis. He had his foot on it, that is all. Seeing his foot on it, I thought it was his."

"And you were completely mistaken, Monsieur," Aramis replied coldly, indifferent to D'Artagnan's efforts at reparation. Then, turning to the gentleman who had declared himself the friend of Bois-Tracy:

"As for you, Monsieur-the-Friend-of-Bois-Tracy, it occurs to me that I am on quite as intimate terms with him as you are. Thus this handkerchief might have fallen just as easily out of your pocket as out of mine."

"No, no! On my honor as a gentleman—"

"You are about to swear on your honor and I on my word, which will make it evident that one of us is lying. Look here, Montaran, we can do better than that. Let us each take one half."

"One half of the handkerchief?"

"Certainly!"

The other two guardsmen were enchanted:

"Quite right . . . perfectly fair . . . the judgment of Solomon . . . Aramis, you are certainly exceeding wise! . . ."

As they all burst out laughing, the affair, as may be supposed, had no untoward sequel. After a moment or two, the conversation ceased, the three guardsmen and the musketeer shook hands cordially and went off in opposite directions. D'Artagnan, meanwhile, stood sheepishly to one side.

"Now is my chance to make my peace with this gallant gentleman," D'Artagnan thought, and, agog with good intent, he hurried after Aramis, who had moved off without paying any attention to him.

"Monsieur, you will excuse me, I hope."

"Monsieur, allow me to observe that your behavior in this circumstance was not that of a gentleman."

"What, Monsieur! Do you suppose—?"

"I suppose you are not a fool, Monsieur. I also suppose that, though you come from Gascony, you must know that people do not step upon handkerchiefs without a reason. What the devil! The streets of Paris are not paved with cambric."

"Monsieur, you are wrong in trying to humiliate me," D'Artagnan replied, his natural aggressive spirit gaining the upper hand over his pacific resolutions. "I am from Gascony it is true; since you know this, I need not tell you that Gascons are anything but patient. When a Gascon has begged to be excused once, even for a foolish act, he is convinced that he has already done once again as much as he should have."

"Monsieur, what I said was not said in order to pick a quarrel with you. I am no bravo, thank God! I am but a temporary musketeer; as much, I fight only when I am forced to and always with the greatest repugnance. But this time the affair is serious because you have compromised a lady."

"Because *we* have compromised a lady, you mean."

"Why were you so tactless as to give me back the handkerchief?"

"Why were you so clumsy as to drop it?"

"I said and I repeat, Monsieur, that the handkerchief was never in my pocket."

"Well, Monsieur, you have lied twice, for I saw it fall."

"Ha! so that's the tone you assume, Monsieur the Gascon. Well, I shall have to teach you how to behave yourself."

"And I shall send you back to Mass, Monsieur l'Abbé, to a Mass said over your corpse. Draw, if you please, and instantly—"

"No, no, if you please, my fair friend, at least not here. Can't you see that we are opposite the Hôtel d'Aiguillon which is filled with a rabble of Monseigneur Cardinal's servants? How do I know that His Eminence has not deputed you to procure him my head? To tell you the truth, I am ridiculously attached to this head of mine; it seems to fit so symmetrically upon my shoulders. Of course I intend to kill you, don't worry on that score. But in a cosy, remote place where we will not be interrupted lest you be inclined to boast about your death in public."

"I agree, Monsieur, but do not be too confident. And bring along your handkerchief; whether it belongs to you or to somebody else, you will probably need it."

"Monsieur is a Gascon?"

"Yes, this monsieur is a Gascon and he never postpones a duel through prudence."

"Prudence, Monsieur, is a somewhat useless virtue for musketeers, I know. But it is indispensable to churchmen. Therefore as I am only a musketeer pro. tem., I intend to remain prudent. At two o'clock I shall have the honor of waiting for you at the Hôtel de Tréville. There, I shall apprise you of the best place and time we can meet."

The two young men bowed and parted. Aramis went up the street which led to the Luxembourg. D'Artagnan, having suddenly noticed the time, set out toward the Carmes-Deschaux.

"Decidedly, I shall not return," he mused. "But at least if I am killed, I shall be killed by a musketeer."

V

HIS MAJESTY'S MUSKETEERS AND THE CARDINAL'S GUARDS

D'Artagnan did not know a soul in Paris. He therefore went to his appointment with Athos without a second to support him, let alone two, content with those whom his adversary would have chosen for himself. Besides, he fully intended to offer the brave musketeer all suitable apologies—without weakness or servility of course—for he feared the usual outcome of an affair of this sort, when a young, vigorous man fights against one who is weak from his wounds. If conquered, he doubles the value of his adversary's triumph; if victorious, he is accused of having taken an unfair advantage of a handicap.

Now unless we have painted the character of our seeker after adventures unsatisfactorily our readers must already have noted that D'Artagnan was no ordinary man. Therefore while he kept repeating to himself that his death was inevitable, he was not going tamely and submissively to death as a man less courageous might have done in his place. Thinking over the different characters of the men he was about to fight against, he gained a clearer view of the situation. By offering sincere apology, he hoped to make a friend of Athos, whose lordly air and austere bearing he admired immensely. Unless he were killed outright, he flattered himself that he could frighten Porthos with the adventure of the baldric, an anecdote which, cleverly presented, could be told to everybody with the certainty of covering its master with ridicule. As for the astute Aramis, D'Artagnan was not seriously afraid of him:

"If I manage to last until I get to him, I shall dispatch him blithely," he murmured. "At any rate, I shall aim at his face, which was Caesar's advice to his soldiers before they joined battle with Pompey's. At worst, I shall at least have damaged that handsome mien he is so proud of."

Further, D'Artagnan was armed with that invincible stock of determination his father had communicated to him. He remembered the old hero's exact words: "Endure nothing from anyone save Monseigneur Cardinal and the King." Sped by this counsel, he flew rather than walked toward the monastery of the Carmes Déchaussés or Barefoot Carmelite Friars, which, in those days, was known as the Carmes Deschaux. It was a building innocent of windows and surrounded by barren fields, less frequented than the Pré-aux-Clercs as a dueling ground and usually chosen by men who had no time to lose.

When D'Artagnan arrived in sight of the bare space extending along the foot of the monastery wall, Athos had been waiting only five minutes. Twelve o'clock was striking. D'Artagnan was therefore as punctual as the Woman of Samaria and as the most rigorously casuistic of duelists might wish.

Though Monsieur de Tréville's physician had dressed the musketeer's wounds afresh, he was still suffering. D'Artagnan found him seated on a stone, waiting with that placidity and dignity which never forsook him. Seeing D'Artagnan draw near, Athos rose and came courteously to meet him; D'Artagnan, for his part, took off his hat and bowed so deeply that its feathers swept the ground.

"Monsieur, I have engaged two of my friends as seconds, but they have not arrived yet. I am surprised at the delay; it is not at all their custom."

"Monsieur," D'Artagnan answered, "I have no seconds. I arrived in Paris just yesterday. The only person I know in the city is Monsieur de Tréville. I was recommended to him by my father who has the honor of being a tolerably close friend of his."

After a moment's reflection, Athos asked:

"Monsieur de Tréville is the only person you know?"

"Yes, Monsieur."

"Look here, look here!" Athos grumbled. He was addressing D'Artagnan yet half of what he said was for his own benefit. "If I kill you, I shall be taken for a child-slaying ogre. Everybody will swear that I robbed the cradle!"

"No one will say our fight was too one-sided," D'Artagnan protested with a bow not devoid of dignity. "After all, you are doing me the honor of crossing swords with me although your wounds must be giving you considerable trouble."

"Ay, it is all very troublesome, I must confess. And you hurt me devilishly when you charged into me. But I shall fence with my left hand; I usually do so in such circumstances. Please do not think I am doing you a favor, I am either-handed. In fact, you will be at a disadvantage; left-handers can be pretty irksome for those who are not used to them."

"Monsieur," said D'Artagnan bowing again, "I assure you I am immensely grateful to you for your perfect courtesy."

"You are too kind," Athos replied, ever the gentleman. "Let us speak of something else, if you please." Then, as a twinge of pain seized him: *"Sangbleu!"* he cried. "You certainly hurt me. My shoulder is on fire!"

"If you would permit me—" D'Artagnan ventured timidly.

"What, Monsieur?"

"I have a miraculous balm for wounds. My mother gave it to me. I have had occasion to try it on myself."

"Well?"

"Well, I am certain that in less than three days this balm would cure you, Monsieur. After three days, when you are cured, I would still deem it a great honor to cross swords with you."

D'Artagnan spoke with a simplicity that did honor to his courtesy without casting the least doubt upon his courage.

"God's truth, Monsieur, there's a proposition I cannot but admire. Not that I accept it, but none save a gentleman born could have made it. That is how the paladins spoke in the days of Charlemagne, and were they not the very paradigm of chivalry? Unfortunately we do not live in the days of the great Emperor; we live under the rule of a Cardinal. However carefully we might try to guard our secret, people would learn we were about to fight and we would be prevented from doing so." He frowned as he looked at the horizon. "Confound it, will these fellows never come?"

"If you are in a hurry, Monsieur," D'Artagnan suggested in the same polite tone he had used before, "we might set to without your seconds. Do not stand upon ceremony; you may dispatch me as soon as you care to."

"I like you for those words," said Athos, nodding graciously. "They came from an intelligent mind and a generous heart. Monsieur, I prize men of your mettle. I see plainly that if we do not kill each other, I shall hereafter have much pleasure conversing with you. But let us wait for my friends, if you please; I have plenty of time and it would be more seemly." He had barely finished speaking when, looking up: "Here comes one of them!" he cried, as, to his surprise, D'Artagnan discerned the gigantic bulk of Porthos at the far end of the Rue de Vaugirard.

"What! Is Monsieur Porthos one of your seconds?"

"Certainly. Does that disturb you?"

"No, by no means."

"And here comes the second one!"

As D'Artagnan turned to follow the direction in which Athos was pointing, he perceived Aramis.

"What?" he cried, even more astonished than before, "Monsieur Aramis is your other second?"

"Of course. Don't you know that none of us is ever seen without the others? Musketeers and Guards, the Court and the city know us as the Three Inseparables. Of course, as you come from Dax or Pau—"

"From Tarbes—"

"From Tarbes, then, you are probably unaware of this fact."

"By my troth, you are well-named, gentlemen, and my adventure, should it make a stir, will certainly prove that your union is not founded upon contrasts."

Meanwhile Porthos came up, waved his hand to Athos, then, noticing D'Artagnan, stopped short, gaping with surprise. Incidentally he had changed his baldric and left off his cloak.

"Well, bless me! what does this mean?" he asked.

"This is the gentleman I am to fight with," Athos explained, pointing to D'Artagnan, then opening his palm in a gesture of salutation.

"But I am going to fight with him too!"

"Not before one o'clock, Monsieur," D'Artagnan reminded him.

"And *I* too am to fight with this gentleman," Aramis announced, joining the group.

"Not until two o'clock," D'Artagnan replied as casually as before.

Aramis turned to Athos:

"By the way, Athos, what are you fighting about?"

"By my faith, I'm none too sure. As a matter of fact, he hurt my shoulder. What about you, Porthos?"

"I'm fighting—" Porthos blushed a deep crimson. "I'm fighting because I'm fighting!"

Athos, whose keen eye lost no detail of the scene, observed a faint sly smile steal over the young Gascon's lips as he specified:

"We had a slight disagreement about dress."

"And you, Aramis?"

"Oh, ours is a theological quarrel." Aramis made a sign to D'Artagnan begging him to keep the cause of their difference a secret. Athos saw a second smile flit across D'Artagnan's lips.

"Indeed?"

"Yes," D'Artagnan agreed. "A passage in Saint Augustine upon which we could not concur."

"A clever fellow, this Gascon, no doubt about it," Athos murmured under his breath.

"And now that we are all here, gentlemen," D'Artagnan announced. "Allow me to offer you my apologies."

At the word "apologies," a cloud passed over the brow of Athos, a haughty smile curled the lips of Porthos, and a nod of refusal from Aramis proved more expressive than any words he might have said.

"One moment, gentlemen, you do not understand me." D'Artagnan objected. As he tossed back his head, the sunlight fell upon it, emphasizing its bold, sharp lines. "I am apologizing only in case I cannot settle my score with all three of you. Monsieur Athos has the first right to kill me, a fact which lessens the value of your claim, Monsieur Porthos, and makes yours, Monsieur Aramis, practically worthless. So I repeat, gentlemen, pray excuse me—but on that score alone! Come, on guard!"

With these words, accompanied by the most gallant gesture, D'Artagnan drew his sword. The blood had rushed to his head; at that moment he would have tackled all the musketeers in the kingdom as cheerfully as he was about to try conclusions with Athos, Porthos and Aramis. It was high noon; the sun in its zenith beat mercilessly down upon the dueling ground.

"It is very hot," Athos remarked, drawing his sword in his turn, "but I cannot take off my doublet. My wound has begun to bleed again and I would not wish to embarrass Monsieur by the sight of blood which he has not drawn from me himself."

"True, Monsieur, and, whether drawn by myself or anyone else, I vow I will always view with regret the blood of so gallant a gentleman. I will therefore fight in my doublet, like yourself."

"Come, come, enough of such compliments," Porthos growled. "Remember we are awaiting our turn."

"Speak for yourself, Porthos, when you utter such absurdities," Aramis broke in. "I, for one, hold that everything they said was well spoken and worthy of gallant gentlemen."

"When you please, Monsieur," said Athos, putting himself on guard.

"I was awaiting your orders, Monsieur," D'Artagnan replied, crossing swords. But the sound of the two blades clashing had barely died down when a company of the Cardinal's guards, commanded by Monsieur de Jussac, turned the corner of the convent.

"The Cardinal's Guards!" Porthos and Aramis cried. "Sheathe your swords, gentlemen . . . sheathe your swords. . . ."

But it was too late; the combatants had been seen in a position which left no doubt of their intentions.

"Ho, there!" Jussac called, advancing toward them and making a sign to his men to follow him. "Hallo, there, Musketeers! So you're fighting here, are you? And the edicts against dueling, what about *them?*"

"You are very generous, gentlemen of the guards," said Athos, full of rancor, for Jussac was one of those who had attacked him the day before.

"If we saw you fighting, I can promise you we would not try to interfere. Leave us alone, then, and you can enjoy a little fun without any trouble to yourselves."

"Gentlemen," said Jussac, "I much regret to have to tell you that this is impossible. We have our duty to accomplish. Sheathe, then, if you please, and follow us."

"Monsieur," said Aramis, parodying Jussac, "we would be delighted to obey your kindly invitation if it depended only upon ourselves. But unfortunately this is impossible. Monsieur de Tréville has forbidden it. Be off on your way, then; it is the best thing to do."

The raillery exasperated Jussac:

"If you disobey," he warned, "we shall charge you."

"There are five of them," Athos said in a low voice, "and only three of us. We shall be beaten again and we shall die here and now, for I swear I will never again face our Captain a beaten man."

Athos, Porthos and Aramis huddled together as Jussac marshaled his men. This short interval was enough to convince D'Artagnan. Here was one of those events that decide a man's entire existence; D'Artagnan must choose between King and Cardinal and forever abide by his choice. To fight meant to disobey the law, to risk his head, to attract in one instant the enmity of a minister more powerful than the King himself. He perceived all this quite clearly, and, to his credit, did not hesitate a second. Turning to the musketeers:

"Gentlemen," he said, "allow me to correct you, if you please. You said you were but three; it seems to me that there are four of us."

"But you are not one of us," Porthos demurred.

"True, I wear no musketeer's uniform but I have the spirit of a musketeer. My heart is a musketeer's; I feel it, Monsieur, and so I shall fight!"

"You may withdraw, young man," Jussac shouted, guessing D'Artagnan's intentions. "We will allow you to retire. Save your skin, lad; begone quickly."

D'Artagnan did not budge.

"Upon my word, you're a plucky fellow," said Athos, pressing the young man's hand.

"Come, come, make up your minds," Jussac urged.

"Look here," Porthos said to Aramis, "we must do something."

"This is very magnanimous of you, Monsieur," Athos told D'Artagnan, but the three musketeers, realizing how young he was, dreaded his inexperience. Athos summed up the situation: "We should still be but three, one of whom is wounded, plus a mere boy, yet everybody will say that there were four men fighting the guards."

"Yes, but shall we surrender?" Porthos asked indignantly.

"That *is* difficult!" Aramis agreed.

D'Artagnan, understanding their irresolution, pressed his point:

"Try me, gentlemen, and I swear on my honor that I will not leave this field if we are vanquished."

"What is your name, my brave fellow?" Athos inquired.

"D'Artagnan, Monsieur."

"Well then," cried Athos, "Athos, Porthos, Aramis and D'Artagnan, forward!"

"Come, along now, gentlemen, have you made up your minds to make up your minds?" Jussac asked for the third time.

"We have," Athos replied.

"And what is your choice?"

"We are about to have the honor of charging you," Aramis answered, raising his hat with one hand and drawing his sword with the other.

"So you're offering resistance, are you?"

"God's blood, are you surprised?"

At once the nine combatants rushed up to join battle furiously but not without method. Athos singled out a certain Cahusac, a favorite of the Cardinal's, Porthos paired off with Bicarat, and Aramis was faced with two adversaries. As for D'Artagnan, he was pitted against Jussac himself.

The young Gascon's heart beat as though it would burst, not with fear, thank God! for he welcomed danger, but with emulation. He fought like a furious tiger, turning dozens of times around his opponent and continuously changing his ground and his guard. Jussac, to quote a phrase then in fashion, was an epicure of the blade and he had had much practice, yet it required all his skill to defend himself; for D'Artagnan was energetic and nimble, departing every instant from the accepted rules of technique, attacking him on all sides at once yet parrying like a man with the greatest respect for his own epidermis.

At length these tactics exhausted Jussac's patience. Enraged at being held in check by an adversary he had dismissed as a mere boy, he lost his temper and began to make mistakes. D'Artagnan, though lacking in experience, was schooled in the soundest theory; the more wildly Jussac lunged, the more agile the Gascon became. Jussac, determined to have done with him, sprang forward and lunged to the full extent of his reach, aiming a terrible thrust at D'Artagnan; the latter whipped his blade under Jussac's, parrying in *prime*, and while Jussac was trying to get on guard again, D'Artagnan's blade darted like a serpent below Jussac's and passed through his body. Jussac fell like a log.

D'Artagnan then cast a swift, anxious glance over the field of battle. Aramis had killed one of his opponents but the other was pressing him warmly; nevertheless, Aramis was in good posture and able to look after himself. Bicarat and Porthos had just made counter-hits, Porthos receiving a thrust through his arm, Bicarat one through his thigh; but neither of these wounds was serious and they fought on ever more doggedly. Athos, wounded anew by Cahusac, grew increasingly pale but had not yielded an inch of ground; he had only changed his sword from one hand to the other and was now fighting with his left.

According to the dueling laws then in force, D'Artagnan was at liberty to assist whom he pleased. While endeavoring to ascertain which of his comrades stood in greatest need, he caught a glance from Athos. Its expression was of sublime eloquence. Athos would have rather died than appealed for help, but he could look and, in that look, ask for assistance. D'Artagnan, divining what Athos meant, sprang to Cahusac's side with a terrible bound, crying:

"My turn, Monsieur le Garde; I am going to slay you!"

Cathusac wheeled about. D'Artagnan had intervened in the nick of time, for Athos, who had been fighting on sheer nerve, sank on one knee.

"God's blood," he cried to D'Artagnan, "don't kill him, lad! I have an old bone to pick with him when I am fit again. Just disarm him, make sure of his sword. That's it! Oh, well done, well done!"

Athos gave vent to the last exclamation as he saw Cahusac's sword fly through the air and land twenty paces away. Both Cahusac and D'Artagnan leapt forward at the same time, the former to recover his weapon, the latter to capture it, but D'Artagnan, being more active, reached it first and placed his foot upon it.

Cahusac ran over to the guardsman whom Aramis had killed, seized his rapier and returned toward D'Artagnan. But on the way he met Athos, who had recovered his breath during the short respite D'Artagnan had afforded him and who wished to resume the fight lest D'Artagnan kill

Cahusac. D'Artagnan realized that he would be disobliging Athos not to leave him alone, and, a few minutes later, Cahusac fell, pinked in the throat.

At the same instant Aramis placed his sword-point on the breast of his fallen adversary and forced him to beg for mercy. This left only Porthos and Bicarat to be accounted for. Porthos was indulging in all manner of braggadocio and swagger, asking Bicarat what time of day it might be and congratulating him on the fact that his brother had just obtained a company in the Regiment of Navarre. But, jest as he might, he was making no headway for Bicarat was one of those men of iron who never cry quits until they fall dead.

Meanwhile it was imperative to finish the fighting soon. There was danger of the watch coming by and picking up all the duelists, wounded or not, royalists or cardinalists. Athos, Aramis and D'Artagnan, surrounding Bicarat, called on him to surrender. Though one against four and wounded in the thigh, Bicarat was determined to hold out. Jussac, rising on his elbow, cried out to him to yield. But Bicarat, like D'Artagnan, was a Gascon; he turned a deaf ear and laughed as though it was all a huge joke. Between two parries he even found time to point with his sword at a patch of earth and, parodying a verse from the Bible, declare mock-heroically:

"Here shall Bicarat perish, alone of them which are beside him!"

"But they are four to one," Jussac remonstrated. "Leave off, I command you."

"Oh, if you command me, that's another thing," Bicarat agreed. "You are my superior officer, it is my duty to obey you."

And, springing backward, he broke his sword across his knee to avoid having to surrender it, threw the two pieces over the convent wall, and crossed his arms, whistling a cardinalist air.

Bravery is always honored even in an enemy. The musketeers and D'Artagnan saluted Bicarat with their swords and returned them to their sheaths. Next, D'Artagnan, with the help of Bicarat, the only adversary still on his feet, carried Jussac, Cahusac and the guardsman Aramis had wounded, under the porch of the convent, leaving the dead man where he lay. Finally they rang the convent bell and, taking along four cardinalist swords as trophies of victory, they set out, wild with joy, for Monsieur de Tréville's mansion.

Arm in arm, they strode, occupying the whole width of the street and, as every musketeer they met swelled their ranks, in the end their progress was a triumphal march. D'Artagnan was delirious with happiness as he marched between Athos and Porthos, squeezing their arms affectionately.

"If I'm not a musketeer yet," he told his new-found friends as they swung through the gateway of the Hôtel de Tréville, "at least I've begun my apprenticeship, don't you think?"

VI

His Majesty King Louis the Thirteenth

The affair caused a sensation. In public Monsieur de Tréville scolded them roundly but he congratulated them in private. Then, as no time must be lost in reaching the King and winning him over, he hastened to the Louvre. It was too late; His Majesty was already closeted with My Lord Cardinal and too busy, he was told, to receive him. That evening he went to the King's gaming-table. His Majesty was winning, and, being very miserly, was in an excellent humor. Seeing Monsieur de Tréville at a distance, the King cried:

"Come, Monsieur le Capitaine, come here so I may chide you. Do you know that His Eminence has been complaining again about your musketeers, ay, Captain, and with such passion that he is out of sorts this evening? These musketeers of yours are devils incarnate and gallowsbirds all!"

Seeing at first glance how things would turn, Monsieur de Tréville hastened to deny the accusation. On the contrary, he insisted, his soldiers were kindly creatures and meek as lambs. He would personally warrant that they had but one desire, namely to draw their swords only in His Majesty's service. But what were they to do? The Cardinal's Guards were forever picking quarrels with them and they were obliged to defend themselves, if only for the honor of the corps.

"Hark at Monsieur de Tréville," the King commented. "Hark at the man! Anybody would imagine he was speaking about the members of a religious order. In fact, my dear Captain, I've a good mind to take away your commission and give it to Mademoiselle de Chemerault, to whom I promised an abbey. But I do not think I will take you at your word. I am called Louis le Juste and justice shall prevail, Monsieur. By and by we shall see...."

"It is because of my faith in that justice, Sire, that I shall calmly and patiently await the good pleasure of Your Majesty."

"Wait then, Monsieur, wait; I shall not keep you long."

Luck was turning against the King. As his winnings began to shrink, he was not sorry to find an excuse whereby to *faire Charlemagne*, to use a gambling term whose origin I do not know but which means to leave the table when one is in pocket. His Majesty rose and pocketing his winnings, turned to a courtier:

"La Vieuville," he said, "take my place, for I must speak to Monsieur de Tréville about an urgent matter. Ah, I had eighty louis before me! Put down the same sum so that those who have lost money will have no cause for complaint. Justice comes first!"

Then, turning to Monsieur de Tréville, he walked toward the window.

"Well, Monsieur, you say that His Most Illustrious Eminence's Guards sought a quarrel with Royal Musketeers?"

"Yes, Sire, just as they always do."

"How did it happen? Tell me all about it. A judge must hear both sides of any question."

"Well, Sire, it was like this. Three of my best soldiers, Athos, Porthos and Aramis, decided to go on a jaunt with a young fellow from Gascony to whom I had introduced them that morning. The party was to take place at Saint-Germain, I believe, so they decided to meet at the Carmelite convent. Here they were molested by De Jussac, Cahusac, Bicarat and two other guardsmen who certainly did not repair to such a place in such numbers without intending to flout the laws against dueling.

"I do not accuse them, Sire. But I leave Your Majesty to judge what five armed men could possibly want in so deserted a place as the convent pasture.

"Seeing my musketeers, the cardinalists changed their minds; their private grievances gave way to party hatred."

"Ay, Tréville, how sad to see two parties in France, two heads to one kingdom. But this can't go on forever!"

"Your Majesty's servants devoutly hope so."

"So the Cardinal's Guards picked a quarrel with the King's Musketeers?"

"That probably happened but I cannot swear to it, Sire. Your Majesty knows how difficult it is to arrive at the truth, unless a man be gifted with that admirable instinct which has caused Louis XIII to be named Louis the Just. . . ."

"Right again, Tréville. But your three musketeers were not alone. They had a youth with them."

"True, Sire, but one of the three was wounded. Thus the Royal Musketeers were represented by three soldiers, one of whom was wounded, plus a mere stripling. They stood up to five of the Cardinal's stoutest guardsmen and laid four of them low."

"What a victory for us!" The King beamed. "A complete victory!"

"As complete a victory, Sire, as Caesar won over Vercingetorix at the Bridge of Cé."

"Four men, you say . . . one of them wounded . . . and a mere lad. . . ."

"A lad ridiculously young, Sire. But he behaved so proudly on this occasion that I take the liberty of recommending him to Your Majesty."

"His name?"

"D'Artagnan, Sire . . . the son of one of my oldest friends . . . the son of a man who served throughout the Civil War under His Majesty, your father, of glorious memory."

"He acquitted himself well, eh?" The King placed one hand on his hip and twirled his mustache with the other. "Tell me more, Tréville. You know how much I enjoy tales of fighting and warfare."

"As I told you, Sire, D'Artagnan is little more than a boy. As he has not the honor of being a musketeer, he was in civilian dress. The Cardinal's guardsmen, realizing at once that he was very young indeed and that he did not belong to the corps of musketeers, invited him to withdraw before they attacked."

"Aha! you see, Tréville, it was they who attacked, eh? That is quite clear, eh?"

"It is, Sire. Well, when they called on him to withdraw, he told them that he was a musketeer at heart, that he was wholly devoted to the King, and that he chose to remain with His Majesty's servants."

"A brave lad!"

"He was as good as his word, Sire. Your Majesty can be proud of him. He pinked De Jussac, to the Cardinal's vast annoyance."

"He wounded De Jussac? *He*, a mere boy? De Jussac, one of the top swordsmen in the kingdom."

"Well, Sire, this youth felled De Jussac."

"I want to see him, Tréville, I want to see him. If anything can be done, we shall make it our business. . . ."

"When will Your Majesty deign to receive him?"

"Tomorrow at noon, Tréville."

"Shall I bring him alone?"

"No, bring all four of them, I wish to thank them at once. Loyal servants are rare; they deserve to be rewarded."

"We shall report at noon tomorrow, Sire!"

"Good!" the King said. Then fidgeting nervously: "Er—the back staircase, Tréville, come up the back staircase. There's no point in letting His Eminence know—"

"Of course, Sire."

"You understand, Tréville, an edict is an edict and, after all, dueling has been banned."

"But this was no duel, Sire, it was a brawl. The proof is that five of the Cardinal's Guards set upon my three musketeers and Monsieur d'Artagnan."

"Quite so," the King agreed. "All the same, Tréville, make sure to take the back staircase."

Tréville smiled at the monarch's weakness but there was satisfaction in his smile, too, for he felt he had accomplished something by prevailing upon this child to rebel against his master.

That evening the four stalwarts were informed of the honor bestowed upon them. Having been long acquainted with the King, the musketeers were not particularly impressed, but D'Artagnan, his Gascon imagination aflame, saw in this summons the making of his future fortune. All night long, he dreamed golden dreams.

By eight o'clock next morning he was calling for Athos; he found him fully dressed and ready to go out. As their audience with the King was not till noon, Athos had arranged to play tennis with Porthos and Aramis at a court near the Luxembourg stables. He invited D'Artagnan to join them. The Gascon, ignorant of a game he had never played, nevertheless accepted. What else was he to do during the next four hours?

Porthos and Aramis were already on the court, playing together; Athos, who was an excellent athlete, passed over to the other side and, with D'Artagnan as a partner, challenged them. But though Athos played with his left hand, his first shot convinced him that his wound was still too recent to permit of such exertion. D'Artagnan therefore remained alone and, as he declared his complete ignorance of the game, they simply tried rallying, without scoring their points. A smashing ball from Porthos just missed hitting D'Artagnan in the face; had it done so, D'Artagnan would have been compelled to forego his audience with the King. As in his Gascon imagination his whole future life depended upon this meeting, he bowed politely to Porthos and Aramis, declaring that he would not resume the game until he knew enough about it to play with them on equal terms. Then he returned to a seat in the gallery close to the court.

Unfortunately for D'Artagnan, one of His Eminence's Guards was among the spectators. Still chafing at the defeat his comrades had suffered just the day before, he had promised himself to seize the earliest opportunity to obtain revenge. He now saw his chance, and, turning to his neighbor:

"I am not surprised this youth is afraid of a tennis ball," he drawled. "He must surely be a 'prentice musketeer."

D'Artagnan started as though a serpent had stung him. Then he turned and stared at the guardsman.

"La!" the cardinalist continued, twirling his mustache insolently, "you may stare at me as long as you like, my little gentleman, I have said what I have said."

"Your words are too clear to require a commentary," D'Artagnan replied. "I beg you to follow me out of here."

"And when, pray?" the guardsman asked banteringly.

"At once, if you please."

"By the way, do you know who I am?"

"I haven't the faintest idea and I don't care."

"You're wrong, there. If you knew my name, perhaps you would be more careful."

"What *is* your name?"

"Bernajoux, at your service."

"Well, Monsieur Bernajoux, I shall wait for you at the door."

"Proceed, Monsieur, I shall join you in a minute."

"Do not hurry, Monsieur. We must not be seen going out together. Any witnesses at our interview might cramp our style."

"True, true," the guardsman agreed.

He was surprised that his name had made no impression on the Gascon, for he was known to everybody, everywhere, with perhaps the solitary exception of D'Artagnan. His Eminence the Cardinal might heap up edicts against dueling to his heart's content, Bernajoux continued to figure as instigator or liquidator of daily brawls.

Porthos and Aramis were so intent on their game and Athos so busy observing them that they did not notice D'Artagnan's exit. True to his word, D'Artagnan stood by the door, waiting; a moment later, Bernajoux joined him. With no time to lose because of his audience with the King, D'Artagnan looked up and down the street, found it empty, and decided to fight then and there.

"Upon my word, though you may be called Bernajoux," he said, "it is lucky you have only a 'prentice musketeer to deal with. But never mind, I shall do my best. On guard, please!"

"This is no place to fight," the other objected. "We would be better off behind the Abbey of Saint-Germain or in the Pré-aux-Clercs."

"What you say makes excellent sense," D'Artagnan agreed. "Unfortunately, I have very little time to spare; I have an appointment at twelve sharp. On guard, then, Monsieur, I beg you."

Bernajoux was not the man to entertain two requests to draw; an instant later, his sword glittered in the sunlight and he swooped down on D'Artagnan, thinking to intimidate him. But D'Artagnan had served his apprenticeship the day before. Fresh from a spectacular victory and fired by hopes of favors soon forthcoming, he was determined not to budge an inch. So the two swords were hilt to hilt and, as D'Artagnan stood his ground, it was Bernajoux who had to retreat. In doing so, Bernajoux's sword deviated from the line of guard; D'Artagnan at once freed his blade by passing it under his adversary's, and lunged, pinking Bernajoux on the shoulder. Then D'Artagnan stepped back and, according to the rites of dueling, raised his sword to salute his defeated foe.

But Bernajoux would have none of it. Assuring D'Artagnan that he was unscathed, he rushed blindly at him, actually spitting himself upon the Gascon's sword. As he did not fall, he refused to declare himself conquered. Instead, he kept retreating towards the mansion of the Duc de La Trémouille, in whose service he had a relative. D'Artagnan, unaware of how serious Bernajoux's wounds were, kept pressing him and would no doubt have struck him a third deadly blow. But the noise from the street had reached the tennis court. Two fellow-cardinalists, who had seen Bernajoux leave after an exchange of words with D'Artagnan, rushed out, sword in hand, and swept down upon him. Close on their heels came Athos, Porthos and Aramis and, just as the cardinalists attacked D'Artagnan, the three musketeers intervened to drive them back. Bernajoux suddenly fell, exhausted. Since there were now four royalists against two cardinalists, the latter cried for help.

"*A nous, l'Hôtel de La Trémouille!* To the rescue! To the rescue!"

Immediately, all those in Monsieur de la Trémouille's mansion, coming to the aid of the cardinalists, fell upon the victors. Our four friends set up an antiphonal cry: "*A nous, mousquetaires!*" summoning their comrades to the fight.

This appeal was widely and briskly heeded, for the musketeers, notorious foes of His Eminence, were correspondingly popular. Usually men from the Royal Companies of Guards cast their lot in with the musketeers against the henchmen of the man Aramis had dubbed the Red Duke. Three guardsmen from the company of Monsieur des Essarts happened to be passing; two of them immediately joined in the fray while the third ran off to the Hôtel de Tréville to seek reenforcements. As usual there were plenty of musketeers on the premises; they ran to their comrades' help and the mêlée became general. Very soon, the musketeers and their allies prevailed; the Cardinal's guardsmen and Monsieur de La Trémouille's servants beat a hasty retreat into the Hôtel de La Trémouille, slamming the gates just in time to prevent their pursuers from entering after them. As for Bernajoux, he had been picked up and conveyed to safety early in the battle; his condition was critical.

Excitement was at its height among the musketeers and their supporters. Somebody suggested that they set fire to the Trémouille mansion to punish Monsieur de La Trémouille's servants for their insolence in daring to make a sally against the Royal Musketeers. The motion, duly seconded, was received enthusiastically; ways and means were being blithely debated, when, as luck would have it, the clock struck eleven. D'Artagnan and his friends recalled their audience with the King and because they could not fight it out then and there, they prevailed on their friends to retire. The royalists decided to hurl some paving stones against the gates but the gates were too solid and they soon tired of the sport. Besides, the leaders of the enterprise had left the group and were on their way to the Hôtel de Tréville. Arriving there, they found the Captain of Musketeers awaiting them; he was already informed of their latest escapade.

"Quick, to the Louvre," he said, "we must get there before the King has been influenced by His Eminence. We will describe this business as a consequence of yesterday's trouble and pass the two off together."

Accordingly the four young men and their Commanding Officer set off for the Royal Palace. To Monsieur de Tréville's amazement, he was told that the King had gone stag-hunting in the forest of Saint-Germain. Monsieur de Tréville asked to have this information repeated to him no less than twice; each time, his companions noticed that his face darkened.

"Did His Majesty plan yesterday to go hunting?"

"No, Your Excellency, it was all quite sudden," the valet replied. "The Master of Hounds called this morning to say that he had marked down a stag last night for His Majesty's benefit. At first the King said he would not go, but he could not resist a day's hunting, so he left shortly after dinner."

"Did His Majesty see the Cardinal?"

"Most probably, Your Excellency," the valet answered. "I saw His Eminence's horses being harnessed. I asked where he was going and they told me to Saint-Germain."

"The Cardinal has stolen a march on us," Monsieur de Tréville told his protégés. "I shall see His Majesty this evening, gentlemen, but I advise you not to venture to do so."

This advice from a man who knew the King only too well was unassailable. They agreed to return home to await further developments.

For his part, Monsieur de Tréville determined that he had best register an immediate complaint. He therefore dispatched a servant with a letter to Monsieur de La Trémouille, begging him to expel the Cardinal's guards from his house and to rebuke his servants for their audacity in making a sortie against the Royal Musketeers. But Monsieur de La Trémouille, already prejudiced by his esquire, Bernajoux's kinsman, replied that neither Monsieur de Tréville nor his soldiers had reason for complaint. On the contrary, he, De La Trémouille was the offended party because the musketeers had assailed his servitors and planned to burn his mansion. The debate between these two nobles might have been endlessly protracted as each, quite naturally, persisted in his opinion. Happily Monsieur de Tréville imagined an expedient likely to end it quickly. He would go personally to call upon Monsieur de La Trémouille.

The two nobles exchanged polite greetings, for, though they were not friends, they respected each other. Both were men of courage and honor and as Monsieur de La Trémouille was a Protestant, saw the King seldom, and belonged to no party, he generally allowed no bias to affect his social relations. On this occasion, however, his manner though courteous was cooler than usual.

"Monsieur," said the Captain of Musketeers, "each of us believes that he has cause for complaint against the other. I have come here to attempt to clear up our misunderstanding."

"I am perfectly willing, Monsieur, but I warn you that I have made inquiries and that the fault lies wholly with your musketeers."

"You are too fair-minded and reasonable a man, Monsieur, not to entertain a proposition I should like to make."

"Make it, Monsieur, I am at your service."

"How is Monsieur Bernajoux, your esquire's kinsman?"

"Very ill indeed. His wound in the arm is not dangerous but he was run through the lungs too, and the doctor is much alarmed."

"Is he still conscious?"

"Certainly."

"Can he talk?"

"Yes, but with difficulty."

"Well, Monsieur, let us go to his bedside and call upon him to tell us the truth in the name of that God Whom he may have to face all too soon. I am perfectly willing to let him judge his own cause and to abide by whatever he says."

Monsieur de La Trémouille thought the matter over for a moment, found the suggestion eminently reasonable, and agreed. Together he and Tréville repaired to the sickroom. As they entered, the patient tried desperately to rise in his bed, but his strength failed him; exhausted, he fell back on the pillows. Monsieur de La Trémouille picked up a vial of salts and pressed it against Bernajoux's nostrils; in a few moments the guardsman came to. Unwilling to appear to be exerting pressure, the Captain of Musketeers suggested that Monsieur de La Trémouille himself question Bernajoux.

The upshot of it all was exactly as Tréville had foreseen. Hovering between life and death, Bernajoux made a clean breast of everything that had occurred. This was all that Monsieur de Tréville desired. Wishing Bernajoux a speedy convalescence, he took leave of Monsieur de La Trémouille, returned to his mansion, and immediately sent word to the four friends, inviting them to dinner.

The Captain of Musketeers entertained the most distinguished company in Paris, short of cardinalists. Quite naturally, therefore, the conversation throughout dinner dealt with the two setbacks His Eminence's Guards had suffered. D'Artagnan, as the hero of both fights, was showered with congratulations, to the delight of Athos, Porthos and Aramis. It was not out of good fellowship alone that they envied him no whit of his success; they had themselves so often had their turn in similar circumstances that they could well afford to leave him his turn.

Toward six o'clock, Monsieur de Tréville announced that it was time to go to the Louvre. The hour of the audience granted by His Majesty was long since past, so instead of claiming entrance up the back staircase, he led the four young men into the antechamber. The King had not returned from hunting. The courtiers and others waited for about a half-hour. Suddenly all the doors were thrown open and an usher announced His Majesty the King. D'Artagnan trembled with anticipation; he was thrilled to the core for he felt that the next few minutes would probably decide the rest of his life. Anxiously, he stared at the doorway through which the monarch was to enter.

Louis XIII appeared, his henchmen in his wake. He was clad in dusty hunting dress; his high boots reached over his knees and he held a riding-crop in his right hand. At first glance D'Artagnan realized that His Majesty was very much out of sorts.

The royal displeasure, obvious though it was, did not prevent the courtiers from lining up, right and left, to form a human avenue down which His Majesty might proceed. At court, it is better to be noticed even with an angry eye than not to be seen at all. The three musketeers, therefore, did not hesitate to step forward. As for D'Artagnan, he stood behind them. Though the King knew Athos, Porthos and Aramis, he swept by without a word or glance of recognition; but as he passed Monsieur de Tréville and looked at him a moment, Tréville outstared his master. Grumbling, His Majesty entered his apartment.

"Things are going badly," Athos commented, smiling. "We shall not be appointed Chevaliers of the Royal Order this time."

"Wait here for about ten minutes," Monsieur de Tréville told his protégés. "If I do not return by then, it will be useless to stay on; go back to the Hôtel de Tréville."

Obediently they waited ten minutes, fifteen, twenty; finally, apprehensive of what might be happening, they withdrew.

Monsieur de Tréville marched boldly into the King's rooms to find a very glum Majesty, ensconced in an armchair, beating his boots with the handle of his riding-crop. This did not prevent the Captain of Musketeers from inquiring phlegmatically after the royal health.

"Bad, Monsieur, bad as can be," the King answered. "I am bored, I am bored stiff!"

Indeed, Louis XIII suffered chronically from ennui. Often he would lead a courtier to the window, invite him to gaze out upon the scene below, and say: "Monsieur, let us suffer boredom together!"

"What? Bored? I thought Your Majesty had been enjoying the pleasures of hunting."

"Pleasures, Monsieur? Fine pleasures indeed! I don't know whether it's because the game leaves no scent or because the dogs have no noses, but everything is arseyturvy! We started a stag of ten branches and chased him for six hours; we were just about to take him, Saint-Simon was raising his horn to blow the mort, when before we could catch our breath, the whole pack took to the wrong scent and dashed off after a two-year-old. I shall be forced to give up hunting just as I had to give up falconry. Ah, I am a very unhappy monarch, Monsieur, I had only one gerfalcon and he died the day before yesterday."

"Indeed, Sire, I understand your discomfort. It was a great misfortune. But you still have a number of falcons, sparrowhawks and tiercets."

"And not a man to train them. Falconers are disappearing; I alone know the noble art of venery. Let me die and all will be over; people will hunt with gins, snares and traps. If I only had time to train a few pupils! But no! The Cardinal will not give me a moment's respite, what with his talk about Austria, his talk about England, his talk about Spain. Ah, speaking of His Eminence, I am much annoyed at you, Monsieur de Tréville."

Here was the chance Monsieur de Tréville had been waiting for. Knowing the King of old, he realized that all these complaints were but a prelude and a means whereby his master roused himself to the proper pitch of anger.

"Have I been so unfortunate as to incur Your Majesty's displeasure?" asked the Captain of Musketeers, feigning the greatest astonishment.

Without replying directly to the question:

"Is this how you perform your duties, Monsieur?" the King continued. "Did I appoint you Captain of Musketeers so that your men should assassinate a soldier, disturb a whole quarter and try to set fire to Paris, while you stand by without opening your mouth?" The King paused a moment, then added judiciously: "But perhaps I am too hasty in rebuking you. Doubtless the rioters are in prison and you have come to tell me that justice has been done."

"Sire," Monsieur de Tréville answered calmly. "On the contrary, I have come to ask *you* for justice."

"Against whom?"

"Against slanderers."

"Well, well, here is something new! I suppose you are going to tell me that your three damned musketeers, Athos, Porthos and Aramis, plus your lad from Béarn, did not fall upon poor Bernajoux like so many maniacs? I suppose they didn't treat him so roughly that by this time he is probably dead? I suppose they didn't lay siege to the mansion of the Duc de La Trémouille and even attempt to burn it? This would be no great misfortune in time of war, for the place is a nest of Huguenots. But in times of peace, what a frightful example! Come now, can you deny this?"

"Who told you this fine story, Sire?"

"Who told me this fine story? Who but one who watches while I sleep, who labors while I amuse myself, and who governs everything at home and abroad, in France and in all Europe."

"Your Majesty is doubtless referring to God, for I know of no one save God who stands so high above Your Majesty."

"No, Monsieur, I mean the prop of the State, my only servant, my only friend, the Cardinal!"

"His Eminence is not His Holiness, Sire."

"What do you mean by that, Monsieur?"

"I mean that only the Pope is infallible and that his infallibility does not extend to cardinals."

"Do you propose to tell me that the Cardinal is misleading me? You are accusing him, eh? Come, speak up; tell me frankly, are you accusing him?"

"No, Sire, but I say that the Cardinal has been misled. I say that he is ill-informed. I say that he was over-hasty in accusing His Majesty's Musketeers, that he is unjust to them, and—I repeat—that he has not gone to the proper sources for his information."

"The accusation comes from Monsieur de La Trémouille himself. What do you say to that?"

"I might answer, Sire, that he is personally too much involved in the matter to be a very impartial witness. But I shall do nothing of the kind, for I know Trémouille to be a loyal gentleman. I therefore refer the whole thing to him—but on one condition, Sire!"

"Which is—?"

"That Your Majesty will summon him here, that you will question him in private, and that I may see Your Majesty as soon as you have seen him."

"What? You will subscribe to anything Monsieur de La Trémouille may say?"

"Yes, Sire."

"You will abide by his advice?"

"Absolutely."

"And you will agree to any conditions he sets?"

"Certainly."

"La Chesnaye!" the King called. "La Chesnaye!" The monarch's confidential valet, who never left the door, entered the room. "La Chesnaye," said the King, "send somebody immediately to find Monsieur de La Trémouille. I wish to speak to him this evening."

As the valet withdrew, the Captain of Musketeers turned to the King:

"Your Majesty promises not to see anyone else in the meantime."

"I promise."

"Tomorrow, then, Sire?"

"Until tomorrow, Monsieur."

"At what time, if it please Your Majesty?"

"At any hour you will."

"But if I came too early, I would be afraid of awakening Your Majesty."

"Afraid of awakening me? Do I ever sleep? No, Monsieur, it is a long time since I had a good night's rest. I sometimes doze, that is all. Come as early as you like, say at seven. But heaven help you if your musketeers are guilty."

"If my musketeers are guilty, Sire, the culprits shall be delivered into Your Majesty's hands for you to dispose of them at your pleasure. Does Your Majesty require anything further? You have but to speak, Sire, I am ready to obey."

"No, Monsieur, no. I am not called Louis the Just without reason. Tomorrow, then, Monsieur, until tomorrow."

"Till then, and God preserve Your Majesty."

Poorly though the King might sleep, Monsieur de Tréville slept still worse. At half-past six next morning, the three musketeers and D'Artagnan were awaiting him; he took them with him but gave no encouragement and made no promises nor did he hide the fact that their luck, and even his own, depended on a throw of the dice. At the foot of the rear stairway, he asked them to wait. If the King was still angry at them, they could depart unseen; if His Majesty consented to receive them, they had only to be called.

In the King's private antechamber, Monsieur de Tréville learned from La Chesnaye that they had not been able to reach Monsieur de La Trémouille at his mansion the night before, that he had returned too late to obey the summons, that he had only just arrived, and was even now closeted with His Majesty. The Captain of Musketeers was highly pleased at this news, for he could be certain that no foreign suggestion could insinuate itself between Monsieur de La Trémouille's testimony and himself. In fact after some ten minutes, the door of the King's closet opened and the Duc de La Trémouille came out.

"Monsieur de Tréville," said the duke, "His Majesty has just sent for me to inquire into the circumstances of what happened yesterday morning at my mansion. I told the King the truth, namely that the fault lay with my people and that I was ready to apologize. Since I have the good fortune to meet you here, I beg you to forgive me and to consider me always your friend."

"Monsieur le Duc," Tréville replied, "I was so confident of your loyalty that I asked for no other defender before His Majesty. I see that I was not mistaken; I thank you. There is still one man in France who measures up to what I said of you."

"Well spoken!" cried the King. "Since he claims to be a friend of yours, Tréville, tell him I should like to be a friend of his. But he neglects me. Why, it is nearly three years since I saw him last."

"My thanks, Sire, my warmest thanks. Of course I do not refer to Monsieur de Tréville, but I beg Your Majesty to believe that those whom you see at all hours of the day are not your most devoted servants."

"So, you heard what I said, Monsieur le Duc. So much the better, so much the better!" the King declared. "Well Tréville, where are your musketeers? I told you the day before yesterday to bring them along; why haven't you done so, pray?"

"They are downstairs, Sire, and with your permission La Chesnaye will bid them come up."

"Yes, let them come up immediately. It is almost eight o'clock and I expect another visitor at nine. Go, Monsieur le Duc, and please come back to see me occasionally. Come in, Tréville."

The duke saluted and retired; as he opened the door, the three musketeers and D'Artagnan, escorted by La Chesnaye, appeared at the top of the staircase.

"Come in, my brave lads," the King called. "Come in, I am going to scold you."

The musketeers advanced bowing, D'Artagnan close behind them.

"What the devil!" the King exclaimed. "Seven of His Eminence's Guards crushed by you four in two days! That's too many, gentlemen, too many! If you go on at that rate, the Cardinal will have to recruit a new corps and I to apply the dueling edicts with utmost severity. One man, now and then, I don't mind much; but seven in two days, I repeat, is too many, much too many."

"As Your Majesty sees, my men have come, contrite and repentant, to make their apologies."

"A fig for their contrition and repentance," the King said. "I place no confidence in their hypocritical faces, particularly that Gascon face over there! Come here, Monsieur."

D'Artagnan, aware that the compliment was addressed to him and assuming a most shamefaced air, came forward.

"Why, you told me he was a young man! This is a boy, Tréville, a mere boy! Do you mean to say it was he who dealt Jussac that master-stroke?"

"Yes, and he accounted for Bernajoux as well."

"Indeed?"

"And besides this," Athos put in, "had he not rescued me from Bicarat, I would certainly not have the honor of making my very humble obeisance to Your Majesty at this moment."

"La, this lad from Béarn is a very devil! *Ventre-Saint-Gris,* as the King my father used to say! . . . I suppose this sort of work involves the slashing of many doublets and the breaking of many swords. And Gascons are always poor, are they not?"

"Sire, I can guarantee that they have not yet discovered any gold mines in their mountains. Yet God owes them this miracle as a reward for the way they championed the King, your father."

"Which amounts to saying that the Gascons made a King of *me* too, for I am my father's son, eh, Tréville? Well, that's all true and I shall not deny it. La Chesnaye, go rummage through all my pockets and see if you can find forty pistoles; if you do, bring me the money. And now, let us see, young man: your hand upon your conscience, tell me exactly how all this came about."

D'Artagnan related the adventure of the day before in full detail: how he had been unable to sleep for joy at his approaching audience with His Majesty . . . how he had called at his friends' three hours before the appointment . . . how they had gone to the tennis court together . . . how, afraid of being struck in the face by a ball, he had been ridiculed by Bernajoux . . . how Bernajoux had very nearly paid for his jeers with his life . . . and finally how Monsieur de La Trémouille, who had had nothing to do with the matter, almost lost his mansion because of it. . . .

"That is what I fancied," the King murmured. "Your account agrees in every particular with Trémouille's. Poor Cardinal! Seven men in two days, and his very best men, too! But, that will do, gentlemen, you hear, that will do. You have taken your revenge for the affair of the Rue Férou and even exceeded it; you ought to be satisfied."

"If Your Majesty is, then so are we," said Monsieur de Tréville.

"Yes, I am quite satisfied." Taking a handful of gold from La Chesnaye and putting it into D'Artagnan's hand: "Here you are!" the King said. "Here is a proof of my satisfaction."

The notions of pride which are universally observed today did not prevail in the seventeenth century. Gentlemen received gifts of money from the King's hand without feeling in any way humiliated. D'Artagnan pocketed his forty pistoles without scruple; on the contrary, he thanked His Majesty heartily.

"There," said the King looking at the clock, "there, now that it's half-past eight, you may withdraw. (I told you I was expecting a caller at nine.) Thank you for your devotedness, gentlemen; I can continue to rely upon it, can I not?"

The four assured His Majesty that nothing was too much to do in his service, that their loyalty was boundless and that, for his sake, they would allow themselves to be cut to pieces.

"Good, good, but keep whole; that will be better and you will be more useful to me." As they retired, he turned to Tréville, and added, in a low voice: "I know you have no room in the musketeers, and besides we decided that a trial period elsewhere is necessary before entering that corps. So I beg you to place this young man in the company of guards commanded by Monsieur des Essarts, your brother-in-law."

The Captain of Musketeers nodded affirmatively.

"Ah, Tréville, I rejoice at the face His Eminence will make when he finds this out. He will be furious; but I don't care, I am doing what is right."

The King waved good-bye to Tréville who, joining the four companions, found D'Artagnan dividing his forty pistoles among them.

As His Majesty had foreseen, the Cardinal was really furious, so furious, indeed, that for a week he kept away from the King's gaming-table. This did not prevent the King from being as affable to him as possible whenever they met or from asking him in the most kindly tone:

"Well, Monsieur le Cardinal, how fares it with that poor Bernajoux and that poor Jussac of yours?"

VII
HOME LIFE OF THE MUSKETEERS

When the four young men were outside the Louvre, D'Artagnan consulted his friends on what use he might best make of his share of the forty pistoles. Athos suggested he order a good meal at *The Sign of the Fir Cone,* an excellent tavern. Porthos urged him to engage a lackey. Aramis proposed that D'Artagnan provide himself with a suitable mistress.

The banquet took place that very day, with the lackey serving them at table, for Athos had ordered the meal and Porthos had furnished the lackey. D'Artagnan's domestic was called Planchet; he hailed from Picardy. Porthos had picked him up by the bridge at the Quai de la Tournelle, having found him leaning over the parapet and watching the rings that formed as he spat into the water.

Porthos vowed that this occupation gave proof of reflective and contemplative disposition; he therefore engaged him without further recommendation. The musketeer's noble bearing had won Planchet over immediately and he congratulated himself on serving so elegant a gentleman, but Porthos soon disabused him by explaining that he already had a valet called Mousqueton, that his mode of life though considerable would not support two servants, and that Planchet must enter D'Artagnan's service. However, when Planchet waited at the dinner given by his master and saw him take out a handful of gold to pay for it, he believed his fortune made and he gave thanks to Heaven for his luck in meeting such a Croesus. He persevered in this illusion even after the feast, for with its remnants he repaired his long abstinence. But when he made his master's bed that evening, his chimeras vanished like so much smoke. D'Artagnan's was the only bed in the apartment, which consisted of an antechamber and a bedroom; Planchet had to sleep in the antechamber on a coverlet which D'Artagnan stripped from the bed and had thenceforth to do without.

Athos, for his part, had a valet named Grimaud (the word means ignoramus and, by extension, a scribbler) whom he had trained to serve him in a singularly original manner. He was an extraordinarily taciturn man, this Athos! He had been living in the strictest intimacy with his comrades Porthos and Aramis for five or six years; during all that time they could remember having often seen him smile but they had never once heard him laugh. His words were brief and expressive, conveying all that was meant and no more, with never any embellishments, embroideries or arabesques. His conversation dealt with hard facts, with never an episode or interlude of fantasy.

Although Athos was barely thirty years old, strikingly handsome and remarkably intelligent, he was never known to have had a mistress. He never spoke of women. To be sure he never prevented others from doing so in his presence but this sort of talk, to which he contributed only bitter comment and misanthropic observations, was obviously disagreeable to him. His reserve, his severity and his silence made almost an old man of him. In order not to depart from his habits, he had accustomed Grimaud to obey his slightest gesture or a mere movement of his lips. He spoke to him only under the most exceptional circumstances.

Though Grimaud entertained a strong attachment to his master's person and a great veneration for his character, he feared him as he feared fire. Sometimes, believing he understood what Athos desired, he would hasten to execute the order received and do precisely the contrary. Athos would then shrug his shoulders and, without losing his temper, give Grimaud a sound thrashing. On these occasions, Athos would speak a little.

Porthos, as we have already seen, was by character quite the opposite of Athos. Porthos not only talked much but he talked loudly and, to do him justice, without caring whether anybody was listening to him or not. He talked for the pleasure of talking and for the pleasure of hearing himself talk on all subjects except the sciences, explaining this omission by the inveterate hatred he had borne scholars since childhood. Less distinguished in bearing and manner than Athos, he was conscious of his inferiority; in the early days of their intimacy, this had often caused him to be unjust toward his friend, whom he sought to outshine by the brilliance of his sartorial effects. But in his simple musketeer's uniform, with only his way of tossing back his head or of advancing his foot, Athos at once regained the place that was his due, relegating the ostentatious Porthos to a subordinate position. Porthos consoled himself by filling Monsieur de Tréville's antechamber and the guardroom at the Louvre with his amatory triumphs, which Athos never mentioned. At the present moment, having passed from the judiciary to the military, from the legist's lady to the warrior's wife, Porthos was concerned with nothing less than a foreign princess who was enormously fond of him.

The old proverb says: "*Tel maître, tel valet;* like master, like man." Having considered Grimaud, valet to Athos, let us now consider Mousqueton, who served Porthos in like capacity.

He was a Norman rejoicing under the pacific name of Boniface (a term applied to artless or witless persons) until Porthos made him change it to the infinitely more sonorous name of Mousqueton. He agreed to serve Porthos on condition he be merely clothed and lodged, but on a handsome scale; in return, he worked elsewhere two hours a day at a job which provided for his other wants. Porthos accepted the bargain for it suited him perfectly. He would have doublets fashioned out of his old clothes and spare cloaks for Mousqueton; thus, thanks to a very skilful tailor who made the clothes look as good as new by turning them (his wife was suspected of wishing to lure Porthos away from his aristocratic habits) Mousqueton cut a very dashing figure when he waited upon his master.

As for Aramis, we believe we have presented his character clearly enough; besides, we shall be able to follow it and those of his companions in their development. His lackey was named Bazin and he came from the province of Berry. Because his master hoped to take Holy Orders, the servant was always clad in black, as becomes the domestic of a churchman. He was a man of about thirty-five or forty, mild, peaceable and chubby. In his spare time, he would read pious words; when required, he could whip up a dinner for the two of them that boasted few dishes but excellently prepared. In conclusion, he was dumb, blind, deaf and of unimpeachable loyalty.

Now that we are at least superficially familiar with the masters and lackeys, let us summarily observe the quarters they occupied.

Athos lived in the Rue Férou, within two steps of the Luxembourg. His apartment consisted of two small rooms, agreeably furnished, in a lodging house maintained by a woman, still young and really handsome, who cast warm, tender glances at him in vain. Here and there the walls of his

humble abode shone with vestiges of past splendors. There was, for instance, a richly embossed sword which obviously belonged to the age of
François I; its hilt, studded with precious stones, was alone worth two
hundred pistoles. Yet in his moments of direst need, Athos had never
sought to pawn or sell it. This sword had long been an object of immense
envy to Porthos who would have given ten years of his life to possess it.

One day, having an appointment with a duchess, he tried to borrow it.
Athos, without saying a word, emptied his pockets, gathered all his jewels,
purses, aglets and gold chains, and offered the lot to Porthos. As for the
sword, he told him, it was sealed to the wall and would not come down
until its master moved out of these lodgings.

In addition to this sword, there was a portrait of a nobleman of the time
of Henry III, dressed with the greatest elegance and wearing the blue ribbon of the Order of the Holy Ghost. Certain features common to the subject of the portrait and Athos indicated that this great lord, a Knight of the
Order of the King, was his ancestor.

Besides these, a casket of magnificent goldwork, bearing the same crest
as sword and portrait and forming a middle ornament to the mantelpiece,
displayed a massive elegance utterly out of keeping with the rest of the
furniture. Athos always carried the key to this casket on his person. But
one day he chanced to open it in the presence of Porthos who was convinced that it contained nothing but letters and papers—love-letters,
doubtless, and family papers. . . .

Porthos lived in an apartment of vast dimensions and very sumptuous
appearance in the Rue du Vieux-Colombier. Whenever he chanced to
stroll by with a friend, he would point to his windows, at one of which
Mousqueton was certain to be standing, dressed in full livery, and, raising
head and hand, exclaim sententiously:

"That is where I live!"

Yet as he was never to be found at home and never invited anybody in,
the true riches of this palatial residence remained a mystery. . . .

As for Aramis, his modest abode consisted of a boudoir, a dining room
and a bedroom, all on the ground floor, overlooking a tiny garden, green,
fresh, shady and safe from the eyes of prying neighbors.

D'Artagnan, intellectually curious like most enterprising people, did
his best to try to discover the key to the pseudonyms under which Athos,
Porthos and Aramis cloaked their identities. He was particularly interested in Athos, whose high nobility could be detected in his merest ges-

ture. But Monsieur de Tréville alone possessed this secret. Vainly D'Artagnan sought to pump Porthos for information about Athos and to draw out Aramis on the subject of Porthos. All he could find out about Athos was the following.

Porthos knew no more about his taciturn comrade than was self-apparent. Rumor had it that Athos had suffered desperate crosses in love and that a tragic betrayal had poisoned his existence. What this treachery was and who were the principals in this drama, nobody knew.

The life of Porthos, except for his real name, was an open book; his vanity and indiscretion made him as transparent as crystal. One factor alone—the excellent opinion Porthos entertained of himself—might conceivably have led an investigator astray.

Aramis, while appearing anything but secretive was a very repository of arcana; he replied meagrely to the questions asked him about others and he eluded those concerning himself. One day D'Artagnan, questioning Aramis at length about Porthos, learned the current rumor about the latter's success with a princess. His curiosity whetted, he sought to find out something of his interlocutor's amours.

"And you, my friend, you who are constantly speaking about the baronesses, countesses and princesses of others?"

"I beg your pardon, I speak of them because Porthos himself did. As you have noticed, he is not averse to parading his good fortune. Believe me, my dear D'Artagnan, if I had them from any other source or if they had been given me in confidence, I can think of no confessor more discreet than I."

"I am sure of that, my dear Aramis. Yet it seems to me that you are quite familiar with armorial bearings. I seem to remember a certain embroidered handkerchief to which I owe the honor of your acquaintance."

This time Aramis, far from being angry, assumed his most modest air and replied in a friendly tone:

"Don't forget, my dear friend, that I intend to become a churchman; I therefore eschew all mundane and fashionable pleasures. The handkerchief you saw was not mine; it had been mislaid at my house by a friend. I had perforce to pick it up in order not to compromise him and the lady he loves. As for myself, I have no mistress and do not desire one. In this, I follow the judicious example of Athos, who is as celibate as I."

"Devil take it, you are not an abbé, you are a musketeer!"

"A musketeer provisionally—ad interim, as the Cardinal says—a musketeer in spite of himself. At heart I am a churchman, believe me. Athos and Porthos dragged me into this rôle to occupy my mind, because, at the moment I was being ordained, I had a little difficulty with . . . Oh well, never mind! This must be boring you and I am wasting your valuable time."

"Not at all, I am much interested and I have nothing to do for the moment."

"That may be. But I have my breviary to read, then I must compose some verses which Madame d'Aiguillon begged of me, then I must go to the Rue Saint-Honoré to buy some rouge for Madame de Chevreuse. So you see, my dear friend, that if you are not in a hurry, I most certainly am."

With which he held out his hand most cordially and took his leave of his companion.

Since despite repeated efforts, this was all D'Artagnan could learn about his new friends, he determined to believe for the present all that was said of their past and to look to the future for more extensive and authoritative revelations. Meanwhile, the life of the four young men was pleasant enough. Athos gambled and as a rule, unluckily; yet he never borrowed a sou from his companions though his own purse was ever at their service, and when he played on credit, he invariably awakened his creditor by six o'clock next morning to pay his debts.

Porthos was erratic. When he won, he was insolent and splendiferous; when he lost, he disappeared completely for several days to reappear subsequently with pallid face and drawn features but money in his purse.

As for Aramis, he never placed a wager; he was the unconventional musketeer and the most unconvivial comrade imaginable. Sometimes at dinner when, amid the flush of wine and geniality of conversation, everybody expected to stay on for two or three hours, Aramis would glance at his watch, rise, and, with a gracious smile, take leave of the company. He was off, he said, to consult some casuist with whom he had an appointment, or he must go home to write a treatise and therefore begged his friends not to disturb him. At which Athos would smile in that charming, melancholy way that illumined his noble countenance, and Porthos, draining his glass, vowed that Aramis would never be anything but a village priest.

Planchet, D'Artagnan's lackey, endured his master's prosperity with noble zeal, and, his daily wage of thirty sous in his pocket, returned to his lodgings blithe as a chaffinch and a model of affability. But when the winds of adversity began to sweep across the dwelling in the Rue des Fossoyeurs—in other words when the forty pistoles of Louis XIII were more or less gone—he launched into a series of complaints which Athos considered nauseous, Porthos unbecoming, and Aramis ridiculous. Athos advised him to dismiss the fellow; Porthos agreed but insisted that Planchet be roundly thrashed before being dismissed; Aramis contended that a good master should heed only the compliments paid him.

"Easy enough to say," D'Artagnan objected. "You, Athos, live with Grimaud, you forbid him to talk, your life is a complete silence, and so you never have words with him . . . you, Porthos, live like a magnifico and therefore are a god to your valet Mousqueton . . . and you, Aramis, forever intent upon your theological studies, inspire your valet Bazin, a mild religious sort of man, with the most profound respect. . . . But what about *me?* I have no settled means and no resources, I am neither a musketeer nor even a guardsman. How on earth can I inspire Planchet with affection, terror or respect?"

His three friends acknowledged that the matter was serious. It was, they added, a family affair. Valets were like wives, they must be placed at outset upon the footing they were subsequently to remain. They advised D'Artagnan to think it all over with great care.

D'Artagnan did exactly that. First, he gave Planchet a cautionary but healthy drubbing; then, Planchet drubbed, he forbade him ever to leave his service, and, for good measure, he told him:

"The future cannot fail to prosper me, I am but waiting for the better times that must inevitably come. If you stay with me, your fortune is made. I am much too good a master to allow you to forfeit it by granting you the dismissal you request."

D'Artagnan's firmness won the approval of his three friends, and, equally important, that of Planchet, who said no more about quitting his service. And so their comradely, happy-go-lucky life went on. D'Artagnan, fresh from his province in a world that was bafflingly novel, fell in easily with their habits.

In winter they would rise at eight o'clock, in summer at six, and report immediately at Monsieur de Tréville's to receive orders and to see how the land lay. Though not a musketeer, D'Artagnan performed this duty with touching punctuality; he mounted guard whenever one or another of his friends was on duty. People at the Hôtel de Tréville knew him and considered him a good comrade. Monsieur de Tréville, who had liked him from the first and who bore him a real affection, never ceased to commend him to the King.

The three musketeers thought the world of him. They would all meet, three or four times daily, whether for dueling, business or pleasure. Each was the other's shadow and from the Luxembourg to the Place Saint-Sulpice or from the Rue du Vieux-Colombier to the Luxembourg they were soon known as The Inseparables.

Meanwhile Monsieur de Tréville was working on D'Artagnan's behalf as keenly as he had promised. One fine morning the King ordered Monsieur le Chevalier des Essarts to admit D'Artagnan as a cadet in his company of guards. As he donned the guardsman's uniform, D'Artagnan sighed, for he would have given ten years of his life to exchange it for that of a musketeer. But Monsieur de Tréville assured him he could do so only after his trial period of two years in another regiment, unless, in the meantime, he found an opportunity to render His Majesty some signal service or to distinguish himself by some brilliant action.

D'Artagnan a guardsman, what could Athos, Porthos and Aramis do but reciprocally mount guard with him when he was on duty? Thus Monsieur le Chevalier des Essart's company, by admitting one D'Artagnan, found itself four men the stronger.

VIII

Concerning a Court Intrigue

Like all good things in this world, the forty pistoles of Louis XIII, having had a beginning, came to their appointed end, which placed the four comrades in an awkward situation. At first, Athos supported the group for a while out of his own pocket . . . next Porthos succeeded him, and, thanks to one of his customary disappearances, kept them going a fortnight . . . next Aramis came to the rescue with good grace and a few pistoles he had obtained, so he said, by selling some theological books . . . next as they had done so often, they appealed to Monsieur de Tréville who advanced them some money on their pay, but these advances did not go very far with three musketeers who were heavily in arrears and a guardsman who as yet had had no pay at all. . . .

Finally, realizing they were about to fall into dire want, they managed by a last desperate effort to raise eight or ten pistoles with which Porthos was despatched to the gaming-table. Unfortunately he was not in luck; he lost every sou plus twenty-five pistoles for which he pledged his word. Then their want became actual distress as the four hungry friends, followed by their four hungry lackeys, haunted the quays and guardrooms of the city to prove that Aramis was right in saying:

"It is wise to sow meals right and left in prosperity in order to reap a few in time of need."

Athos was invited four times and each time brought his friends and their lackeys along; Porthos was invited six times which provided them all with six more meals; Aramis was invited eight times (as we have seen he was a very quiet man but much sought after) and eight times his friends shared his good fortune. D'Artagnan, who as yet knew no one in the capital, unearthed a priest from his own province who supplied a light breakfast with chocolate, and a cornet of the guards who furnished a dinner at his home. The Gascon took his troop to the priest's, where they devoured a stock of food that would have lasted the cleric two months, and to the home of the cornet, who did wonders. But as Planchet remarked:

"People do not eat once for all time even when they eat a great deal."

D'Artagnan felt humiliated at having procured only one meal and a half for his companions—breakfast at the priest's could only be counted as a half-meal—in return for the banquets Athos, Porthos and Aramis had procured him. He fancied himself a burden to the group, forgetting in his wholly youthful good faith that he had entertained them for a whole month. His plight gave him considerable food—for thought! He came to the conclusion that this coalition of four young, brave, enterprising and active men ought to have some other object than swaggering about the city, taking fencing lessons and playing practical jokes that were more or less witty.

In fact, four men devoted to one another whether their purses or lives were involved . . . four men always supporting one another, never yielding, and executing singly or together the resolutions they had made in common . . . four arms threatening the four cardinal points or concentrated upon a single point . . . in brief, four such men as they, must inevitably, by open or underground means, by minework or in a trench, by cunning or by force, open up a way toward their goal, however fiercely defended or distant it might seem. . . . The only thing that surprised D'Artagnan was that his friends had not thought of this.

He, for his part, was thinking seriously of it, racking his brain to find a direction for this single force four times multiplied. And the longer he meditated, the surer he became that, as with the lever Archimedes sought, Athos, Porthos, Aramis and D'Artagnan would succeed in moving the world. Suddenly there was a light knock at the door; D'Artagnan awakened Planchet and ordered him to open it.

(The phrase "D'Artagnan awakened Planchet" must not lead the reader to believe that it was night or that day had not yet broken. No, it was afternoon; it had just struck four. Two hours before, Planchet had asked his master for some dinner, to which D'Artagnan replied by quoting the proverb "*Qui dort, dîne;* he who sleeps, dines." And Planchet dined by sleeping.)

A stranger entered, a man of unassuming appearance, obviously a simple bourgeois. Planchet would have relished, by way of dessert, to overhear the conversation, but the man told D'Artagnan that what he had to say was both important and confidential, and solicited a private interview. D'Artagnan therefore dismissed his valet and requested his visitor to be seated. During the short silence that ensued, the two men looked at each other appraisingly. Then D'Artagnan bowed, to signify that he was ready to listen. The stranger began:

"I have heard Monsieur spoken of as a very courageous young man. This well-deserved reputation emboldens me to confide a secret to him."

"Speak, Monsieur, speak," D'Artagnan replied, instinctively sensing that the matter might prove profitable.

The stranger paused again, then went on:

"I have a wife who is seamstress to Her Majesty the Queen. My wife is not lacking in either virtue or beauty. Though she brought but a small dowry, I was induced to marry her about three years ago because Monsieur de La Porte, the Queen's cloakbearer, is her godfather and befriends her."

"Well, Monsieur?"

"Well, Monsieur," the stranger repeated, "well, Monsieur, my wife was abducted yesterday morning as she was leaving her workroom."

"By whom was your wife abducted?"

"I know nothing for certain, Monsieur, but I have my suspicions."

"And whom do you suspect?"

"A man who has been pursuing her for a long time."

"The devil you say—"

"Let me add this, Monsieur: I am convinced that there is more politics than love in this business."

"More politics than love?" D'Artagnan murmured with a thoughtful air. "And what do you suspect?"

"I hardly know whether I should tell you what I suspect—"

"I beg you to observe, Monsieur, that I am asking absolutely nothing of you; it was you who came to me to tell me that you had a secret to confide in me. Do just as you please; it is not too late to withdraw."

"No, Monsieur, you seem to be an honest young man and I have confidence in you. Frankly, I do not believe my wife has been arrested because of any love affair of her own but rather because of the conduct of a lady far mightier than herself."

"Ah ha! I see!" D'Artagnan commented knowingly and, pretending to be familiar with Court affairs, he added:

"Can it be on account of the amours of Madame de Bois-Tracy?"

"Higher, Monsieur, higher."

"Of Madame d'Aiguillon?"

"Higher still, Monsieur."

"Of Madame de Chevreuse?"

"Higher, much higher."

"Of the—" D'Artagnan checked himself.

"Yes, Monsieur," his terrified visitor replied so low as to be almost inaudible.

"And with whom?"

"With whom else could it be save with the Duke of—?"

"The Duke of—?" D'Artagnan repeated, hiding his ignorance and bewilderment.

"Yes, Monsieur," the stranger interrupted, even more faintly than before.

"But how do you know all this?"

"How do I know it?"

"Exactly: how do you know it? No half-confidences now, or—you understand?"

"I know it through my wife, Monsieur, I heard it from her own lips!"

"And your wife? Where did she learn this?"

"From Monsieur de La Porte. Didn't I tell you my wife is his goddaughter? And isn't he Her Majesty's most confidential retainer? Well, Monsieur de La Porte placed my wife near Her Majesty in order that our poor Queen might at least have someone she could trust, abandoned as she is by the King, spied upon by the Cardinal, and betrayed by everybody."

"Ah, your story is taking shape!"

"Now, my wife came home four days ago, Monsieur. (I must explain that one of the conditions she made on accepting the position was that she should visit me twice a week, for, as I had the honor to tell you a moment ago, she loves me dearly.) Well, she came home and she told me that at that very moment Her Majesty was frightened."

"Indeed?"

"Ay, His Eminence, it would seem, pursues and persecutes her more than ever. He cannot forgive her the incident of the Saraband. You know the story of the Saraband, Monsieur?"

"Of course I know it!" D'Artagnan answered. Though he had never even heard of it, he must appear to know everything that was going on.

"So the Cardinal's feelings are stronger than hatred now; he is moved by the lust of vengeance."

"Is that so?"

"And the Queen believes—"

"Well, what does Her Majesty believe?"

"She believes that someone has written to the Duke of Buckingham in her name."

"In the Queen's name?"

"Ay, in order to persuade him to come to Paris and, once here, to draw him into some trap."

"Devil take it, what a tale! But what has your wife to do with all this, Monsieur?"

"Her devotion to the Queen is well known. Somebody therefore wishes either to remove her from her mistress or, by intimidating her, to learn Her Majesty's secrets, or to win her over and use her as a spy."

"That seems plausible," D'Artagnan agreed. "But what about the man who abducted her? Do you know him?"

"As I said, I think I know him."

"His name?"

"That, I do not know. But I do know he is a creature of the Cardinal's, the tool of His Eminence's will."

"You have seen him?"

"Ay, my wife pointed him out to me one day."

"Is there anything particularly noticeable about him, any distinctive feature?"

"Ay, certainly. He is a nobleman of lofty bearing . . . black hair . . . a swarthy complexion . . . eyes piercing as drills . . . very white teeth . . . and a scar on his temple. . . ."

"A scar on his temple!" D'Artagnan murmured. "Very white teeth . . . eyes piercing as drills . . . a swarthy complexion . . . black hair . . . a lofty bearing. . . . Why, that's my man of Meung!"

"Your man, you say."

"Yes, yes! but that has nothing to do with it. No, I am wrong; on the contrary that simplifies matters considerably. If your man is mine, I shall avenge two wrongs at one blow, that's all! But where can I find this man?"

"I'm sure I don't know."

"Would you happen to know where he lives?"

"No. One day I was accompanying my wife back to the Louvre and he came out as she went in. That was when she pointed him out to me."

"Devil take it, blast and confound it! all this is very vague!" D'Artagnan cursed. Then: "Look here, how did you hear your wife had been abducted?"

"Monsieur de La Porte told me."

"Did he give you any details?"

"He knew none himself."

"Did you obtain any other information?"

"Ay, Monsieur, I received—"

"What?"

"Er—I am afraid I am committing a serious indiscretion."

"There you are, back on the same tack. This time I must point out that you have gone too far to retreat now."

"*Mordieu,* I'm not retreating," the other swore, hoping the blasphemy might bolster his courage. "Besides, as sure as I am Bonacieux—"

"So your name is Bonacieux?"

"Ay."

"You were saying: 'As sure as I am Bonacieux—' Forgive me for interrupting, but I think your name is not unfamiliar."

"Possibly, Monsieur; I am your landlord."

"Ah, you are my landlord!" said D'Artagnan, half-rising and bowing to his visitor.

"Ay," said the visitor pertinently. "You have been here three months,

have you not, Monsieur? Of course I realize how with your important oc-
cupations, you have forgotten to pay me my rent. But since I have not
bothered you about this, I thought you would appreciate my tact."

"Believe me, my dear Monsieur Bonacieux, I am truly grateful to you
for your consideration. As I told you, if I can be of any service to you—"

"I take you at your word, Monsieur, and, as I was about to tell you, as
sure as I am Bonacieux, I believe in you implicitly."

"Go ahead, then; go on with what you were about to say."

Bonacieux took a sheet of paper from his pocket and presented it to
D'Artagnan.

"A letter?"

"Ay, Monsieur, I received it this morning."

It was dusk; the room was swathed in shadows. D'Artagnan moved
toward the window to read it, Bonacieux at his heels. Unfolding the paper,
D'Artagnan read:

> Do not look for your wife. She will be sent back to you when her services
> will have ceased to be of use. Do you but take one step to attempt to find
> her, you are irremediably lost.

"That is positive enough," D'Artagnan remarked. "But after all it is
merely a threat."

"Ay, but a threat that terrifies me, Monsieur. I am no soldier or duelist,
and I dread the Bastille."

"Hm! I'm no keener on the Bastille than you are. Were it but a question
of dueling—"

"Ah, Monsieur, you cannot imagine how much I have been counting on
you in this connection."

"Really."

"I have seen you constantly surrounded by musketeers, men of the
proudest and most resolute bearing. I recognized them immediately as
belonging to Monsieur de Tréville and therefore enemies of the Cardinal. Naturally, I supposed that you and your friends would be delighted at
once to do the Queen Justice and the Cardinal an ill turn."

"Undoubtedly, we—"

"I also bethought me that in view of the three months' rental about
which I have said nothing—"

"Yes, yes, yes, you have already used that argument. I find it excellent."

"I also thought that so long as you remain under my roof, if I were never to mention the rent again—"

"Very good! What else?"

"Well . . . to go further . . . I thought I would make bold to offer you, say, about fifty pistoles . . . if it proved necessary . . . I mean if you should happen to be short of cash at the moment, which I am certain is not the case. . . ."

"Admirable! So you are a rich man, my dear Monsieur Bonacieux."

"I am comfortably off, Monsieur, that's all. I have scraped together an income of something like two or three hundred thousand crowns: first in the haberdashery business—I started in small wares—but particularly in an investment I made. I ventured some funds in the most recent voyage of Jean Mocquet, the celebrated navigator. You can judge for yourself, then, Monsieur, how I—But look, look!"

"What?"

"Over there!"

"Where?"

"In the street, facing your house, on the doorsill opposite: a man wrapped in a cloak."

Suddenly both recognized their man:

"It's the man I told you about!" said Bonacieux.

"It's the man I'm after!" cried D'Artagnan, springing across the room for his sword. "This time he will not escape me."

Drawing his sword from its scabbard, he rushed out of the apartment. On the staircase he met Athos and Porthos; they separated as D'Artagnan sped between them like a dart.

"What's up? Where are you off to? What's the matter?"

"The man of Meung!" D'Artagnan cried as he disappeared.

He had more than once told his friends about his adventure with the sinister stranger and the apparition of the beautiful English traveler to whom his enemy had confided some important missive. The musketeers had long since formed their own opinions about the incident.

According to Athos, D'Artagnan must have lost his letter in the skirmish. From D'Artagnan's description, the stranger must have been a gentleman; no gentleman could possibly debase himself to pilfer a letter.

According to Porthos, the imbroglio was due to love. A lady had given her cavalier a rendezvous or vice versa and D'Artagnan, yellow nag and all, had interrupted them.

According to Aramis, affairs of this kind were buried in mysteries it was better not to fathom.

Athos and Porthos understood, from D'Artagnan's cry, what the young Gascon was about. He would either meet his man of Meung and dispatch him promptly or he would lose sight of him; in either case, he would return home. Accordingly, they continued to walk upstairs.

When they entered D'Artagnan's room, it was empty. Bonacieux, fearing the consequences that must inevitably attend the encounter between D'Artagnan and his arch-enemy, had judged it prudent to decamp.

Which was quite in keeping with the description he himself had given of his character.

IX

D'ARTAGNAN TO THE FORE

As Athos and Porthos had foreseen, D'Artagnan returned within a half-hour. Once again he had missed his man. Sword in hand, D'Artagnan had run up and down all the neighboring streets to no avail. He found nobody who looked like the prey he had hoped to stalk. The man of Meung had vanished, as by magic, into thin air. Baffled, he presently decided to do what he should perhaps have done in the first place, namely knock at the door against which his enemy had been leaning. But this proved useless; though he slammed down the knocker ten or twelve times, no one answered. Presently some of the neighbors, alerted by the noise he was making, appeared on their doorsteps or poked their heads out of the window, and D'Artagnan was variously assured that the house had been uninhabited for six months. He himself could see that doors and windows were tightly locked.

While D'Artagnan was running through the streets and knocking at doors, Aramis had joined his companions. When D'Artagnan returned home he found his friends waiting in full force.

"Well?" asked Athos with pessimistic calm as D'Artagnan burst in, his brow bathed in perspiration, his face black with anger.

"Well?" said Porthos jauntily.

"Well?" said Aramis in a tone of discreet encouragement.

"Well—" D'Artagnan threw his sword on the bed, "well, that man must be the devil in person. He vanished like a phantom, a shadow, a spectre."

"Do you believe in apparitions, Porthos?" Athos inquired.

"I believe only in what I have seen. I have never seen an apparition, therefore I do not believe in apparitions."

"The Bible orders us by law to believe in them," Aramis remarked. "Did not the ghost of Samuel appear to Saul? Belief in apparitions constitutes an article of faith; I would deplore it if any doubts were cast on this matter, Porthos."

"At all events, man or devil, body or shadow, illusion or reality that man was born for my damnation," said D'Artagnan. "His flight, gentlemen, has caused us to lose a wonderful piece of business by which we might have gained a hundred pistoles if not more."

"How so?" Porthos asked.

"What!" Aramis exclaimed.

Athos, true to his philosophy of reticence, merely cast D'Artagnan a questioning glance. Just then Planchet craned his neck through the doorway to try to catch some fragments of the conversation.

"Planchet," D'Artagnan ordered, "go down to my landlord, Monsieur Bonacieux, and tell him to send up half-a-dozen bottles of Beaugency wine. It is my favorite tipple."

"So you have credit with your landlord, eh?"

"Yes, I established credit today. If his wine is bad, never mind; we will send him to find something more palatable."

"We must use and not abuse," said Aramis sententiously.

"I have always maintained that D'Artagnan was the most brainy of the four of us," said Athos. D'Artagnan bowed at the compliment and Athos relapsed into his wonted silence.

"Look here, why don't you explain all this to us?" Porthos suggested.

"Yes, tell us everything, my dear friend," Aramis agreed. "Unless the honor of some lady is involved, in which case you would do better to keep your story to yourself."

"You may set your mind at rest, Aramis, my story will not harm anybody's reputation."

Then word for word he related all that had passed between his landlord and himself, concluding with the startling information that Madame Bonacieux's abductor and D'Artagnan's enemy at the *Sign of the Jolly Miller* in Meung were one and the same man.

Having sampled the wine like a connoisseur and nodded to indicate that he found it good, Athos declared:

"You are in luck, D'Artagnan, your worthy landlord seems good for fifty or sixty pistoles. The only question to debate is whether these fifty or sixty pistoles are worth the risk of four heads."

"You forget there is a woman in the case," D'Artagnan protested, "a woman who was carried off, a woman who is probably being threatened, and perhaps even being tortured, and all because she is faithful to her mistress."

"Careful, D'Artagnan, go easy! In my opinion, you are overzealous about Madame Bonacieux's fate," Aramis cautioned. "Woman was created for our destruction; it is from woman that we inherit all our afflictions."

As Aramis uttered this maxim, Athos frowned and bit his lips.

"I'm not worried about Madame Bonacieux," D'Artagnan answered, "but about the Queen. The King neglects her, the Cardinal persecutes her, and her friends are being killed one after the other."

"Why does she love what we hate most in the world, the Spaniards and the English?"

"Spain is her native land," D'Artagnan explained. "It is quite natural that she should love the Spaniards; are they not children of the same soil as herself? As for your second reproach, I have heard say that she does not love the English, but rather one Englishman."

"Upon my faith," said Athos, "that Englishman deserves to be loved. I never saw a man of nobler aspect in all my life."

"And he dresses better than anyone in the world," Porthos added. "I was at the Louvre the day he scattered his pearls. I picked up two that I sold for ten pistoles apiece. Do you know him, Aramis?"

"Quite as well as you do, gentlemen. I was with those who arrested him in the gardens at Amiens. (Monsieur de Putange, the Queen's equerry, had let me in.) I was at the seminary at the time. The whole adventure seemed to me to be a cruel blow for the King."

"If I knew where the Duke of Buckingham was," said D'Artagnan, "nothing could prevent me from taking him by the hand and leading him to the Queen's side, if only to enrage the Cardinal. After all, gentlemen, our true, sole and eternal enemy is His Eminence. If we could find some way to play him a cruel trick, I confess I would gladly risk my head."

"Please set me right about what your haberdasher-landlord told you," said Athos slowly. "Did he say the Queen believed that Buckingham came to Paris on the strength of a forged letter?"

"That is what the Queen fears."

"Wait, wait a minute!" Aramis commanded.

"What for?" asked Porthos.

"Go on talking; I shall try to recall the exact circumstances," Aramis answered, falling into a brown study.

"I am convinced," D'Artagnan said, "that the abduction of the Queen's seamstress is connected with what we have been discussing and perhaps even with the presence of Buckingham in Paris."

"That Gascon is full of ideas!" Porthos said admiringly.

"I like to hear him speak," said Athos, "his patois delights me."

"Gentlemen, please listen to what I am about to tell you," Aramis broke in.

"Go ahead!"

"We are listening!"

"We are all ears."

"Yesterday," said Aramis, "I happened to be at the house of a learned doctor of theology whom I sometimes consult about my studies."

Athos smiled.

"He lives in a quiet, unfrequented quarter; his tastes and profession require it," Aramis continued. "Now, just as I was leaving his house. . . ."

Aramis paused.

"Well, just as you were leaving his house?"

Aramis appeared to be making a great effort to master himself. He was like a man who, having launched full-sail into a lie, suddenly runs afoul of some unforeseen obstacle. But his three friends were staring at him, their ears were wide open, and he had no means of retreat.

"This doctor has a niece," Aramis went on.

"Ah, he has a niece!" said Porthos meaningfully

"A very respectable lady," Aramis insisted, as the others burst into peals of laughter. "If you laugh or if you doubt my word," Aramis warned, "you shall hear nothing further."

"We believe like Mahometans and we are mute as tombstones," said Athos.

"Very well then, I shall go on. This niece I mentioned often calls on her uncle; she happened to come yesterday while I was there and I had to offer to see her into her carriage."

"So your theologian's niece sports a carriage, eh?" Porthos interrupted, talkative as usual. "Congratulations on your distinguished acquaintances."

"I have had occasion to observe to you more than once, Porthos, that you are most indiscreet," Aramis answered. "That sort of thing does you much harm in the eyes of the ladies."

"Gentlemen, gentlemen," cried D'Artagnan, who began to glimpse what the outcome of the story might be. "This matter is serious. Let us not jest. Go ahead, Aramis, carry on."

"All right, D'Artagnan. Suddenly I saw a gentleman, a tall dark man very much like your man of Meung—"

"Perhaps it was my man!"

"It may well have been," Aramis agreed. "Anyhow, he advanced towards me, followed at an interval of ten paces by five or six men. 'Monsieur . . .' he said courteously to me, and 'Madame . . .' to the lady on my arm . . ."

"The doctor's niece!"

"Porthos, hold your tongue, you're unbearable!"

" '. . . Monsieur, Madame, will you be good enough to step into this carriage without offering the slightest resistance or making the least noise?' "

"He took you for Buckingham!" D'Artagnan exploded.

"I rather believe so."

"But the lady?" Porthos persisted.

"He took her for the Queen," D'Artagnan said.

"Exactly," Aramis assented.

"That Gascon is the Devil!" cried Athos. "Nothing escapes him."

"As a matter of fact," Porthos opined, "Aramis is about as tall as the dashing Duke and has something of the same build. Still, I should imagine the uniform of a musketeer—"

"I wore an enormous cloak."

"In July!" Porthos gasped. "Devil take it! Is your doctor of theology afraid somebody might recognize you?"

"I can understand how the spy might have mistaken your person, Aramis, but your face—"

"I wore a large, wide-brimmed hat."

"Heavens!" Porthos laughed. "What elaborate precautions you take to go to study theology!"

"Gentlemen, gentlemen," D'Artagnan urged, "let us waste no more time in jesting. Let us rather separate and look for the haberdasher's wife. She holds the key to the riddle."

"Do you really think so, D'Artagnan?" Porthos curled his lip contemptuously. "A woman of such humble standing."

"She is the goddaughter of La Porte, confidential valet to the Queen.

Didn't I tell you that? Besides, on this occasion Her Majesty may deliberately have sought the support of a person of modest station. The heads of those high in rank are very conspicuous and the Cardinal's eyesight is of the best."

"The first thing to do," Porthos counseled, "is to drive a bargain, and a good one, with your haberdasher."

"That's useless," D'Artagnan replied. "I have an idea that if Bonacieux fails to pay us, we shall be paid handsomely by another party."

Suddenly footsteps resounded on the stairs, the door flew open and the luckless haberdasher rushed in.

"Save me, gentlemen, for the love of Heaven, save me!" he wailed. "There are four men downstairs who came to arrest me. Save me, save me!"

Porthos and Aramis sprang to their feet; D'Artagnan intervened hastily:

"Not so fast, gentlemen!" He motioned to them to sheathe their half-drawn swords. "It is not courage we need now, but prudence—"

"Are we to stand here," Porthos stormed, "and allow—"

"You will allow D'Artagnan to do as he thinks best," Athos declared. "He is, as I said before, the brainiest one of our lot. For my part, I am prepared to obey him. Do whatever you wish, D'Artagnan."

At that moment, the four bailiffs appeared at the door of the antechamber but seeing four musketeers standing there, fully armed, they seemed somewhat hesitant about entering.

"Come in, gentlemen, come in," D'Artagnan called to them. "This is my apartment and we are all faithful servants of the King and of the Cardinal."

"So you have no objection to our carrying out our orders, gentlemen?"

"On the contrary, we would assist you if that were necessary."

"What on earth is D'Artagnan saying?" Porthos muttered.

"You're a simpleton!" Porthos whispered. "Silence!"

The wretched haberdasher protested in a whisper:

"But you promised me—"

"We can save you only by remaining free ourselves," D'Artagnan whispered. "If we appeared eager to defend you, we would be arrested too."

"All the same, it seems to me—"

"Come, gentlemen, come," said D'Artagnan, aloud. "I have no reason to defend Monsieur here. I saw him today for the first time in my life. He can tell you in what circumstances we met; he came to collect the rent for my lodgings. Is this true or no, Monsieur Bonacieux? Answer!"

"That is quite true," the landlord answered. "But Monsieur has not told you—"

"Not a word about me, not a word about my friends, and above all, not a word about the Queen, or you will ruin everybody without saving yourself!" D'Artagnan cautioned Bonacieux. Then aloud to the bailiffs: "Come, gentlemen, take this fellow away!" With which he pushed the stunned haberdasher into the arms of the bailiffs. "You are a fine rascal, my man," he told Bonacieux. "Imagine coming to dun me for money— me, a musketeer! Away with him, take him to prison! Gentlemen, once again I beg you, take him into custody and keep him behind bars as long as ever you can. That will give me time to pay him."

The myrmidons of the law, mouthing their thanks, took away their prey. But just as they were about to go downstairs, D'Artagnan clapped their leader on the shoulder:

"Come, I must drink to your health and you to mine!" he said jovially, filling two glasses with the Beaugency he owed to Monsieur Bonacieux's liberality.

"You do me too much honor," said the leader of the posse, "I accept, and thanks for your kindness, I'm sure."

"Well then, here's to you, Monsieur—Monsieur—? What *is* your name?"

"Boisrenard."

"Your health, then, Monsieur Boisrenard."

"To yours, honored gentleman! And what is your name, if I may make so bold—?"

"D'Artagnan."

"Here's to your health, Monsieur."

"But first and foremost, above all healths," cried D'Artagnan, as if carried away by his enthusiasm, "I drink to the King and the Cardinal!"

Had the wine been bad, the bailiff might have questioned D'Artagnan's sincerity; but the wine was good, and he was convinced.

"What devilish villainy have you been up to?" Porthos inquired after the bailiff had joined his companions. "Shame on us, shame! Four musketeers have just stood by without moving a finger and allowed an unfortunate fellow who called for help to be arrested under their very noses! And the gentleman responsible for all this has to hobnob with a bailiff. For shame!"

"Look here, Porthos," Aramis said. "Athos has already told you that you are a simpleton. May I add that I completely share his opinion? As for you, D'Artagnan, you are a great man. When you step into Monsieur de Tréville's shoes—as undoubtedly you will—I shall ask you to use your influence to secure me an abbey."

"Well, I *am* in a maze," Porthos exclaimed. "Do you mean to say you approve of what D'Artagnan did?"

"Why of course I do!" Athos told him. "I not only approve of it but I offer him my heartiest congratulations."

"And now, gentlemen," said D'Artagnan without troubling to explain his conduct to Porthos, "*All for One and One for All*—that is our motto, is it not?"

"But still, look here, I—" Porthos demurred.

"Hold up your hand and swear!" Athos commanded.

"Swear, man!" Aramis insisted.

Overcome by the example of his comrades yet grumbling nevertheless, Porthos raised his hand and, with one voice, the four friends repeated the slogan dictated by D'Artagnan:

"All for One and One for All!"

"Excellent!" D'Artagnan approved. And as though he had done nothing all his life save issue orders: "Let us each go his own way now. And remember! From this moment on, we are at war with His Eminence the Cardinal!"

X

CONCERNING A MOUSETRAP IN THE
SEVENTEENTH CENTURY

The invention of the mousetrap is not a modern one. When, long ago, human societies, in the process of formation, invented the police, the police invented the mousetrap.

As most of our readers are still unfamiliar with the slang of the Rue de Jérusalem and as fifteen years have elapsed since we applied the word mousetrap to the thing in question, it is perhaps pertinent to explain exactly what a mousetrap is.

When in a house of any kind a person suspected of a crime has been arrested, the arrest is kept secret. Four or five men are posted in ambush in the front room of the prisoner's apartment. The door is opened to all who knock but, as it closes, the visitor becomes a prisoner. Thus within two or three days almost all the habitués of the house are in the hands of the police. Such then is the mousetrap.

Monsieur Bonacieux's residence then became a mousetrap; whoever appeared was seized and investigated by the Cardinal's men. However, as a special passage led to the second floor, where D'Artagnan lodged, his callers were exempt from molestation.

Besides no one save the three musketeers ever came there. They reported that they had all made careful independent investigations but to no avail; Athos had even gone so far as to question Monsieur de Tréville, a step which, in view of this worthy musketeer's usual reticence, had much surprised his Captain. But Monsieur de Tréville knew nothing save that the last time he had seen the Cardinal, the King and the Queen, the Cardinal looked very anxious, the King seemed worried and the Queen's bloodshot eyes betrayed either a sleepless night or much weeping. This last circumstance was not particularly striking, for since her marriage the Queen had known vigils and tears aplenty.

Monsieur de Tréville urged Athos scrupulously to observe his duty to the King and particularly to the Queen, and to convey the same orders to his companions.

As for D'Artagnan, nowadays he never stirred from his quarters. He turned his room into a sort of observatory. From the watchtower of his windows, he saw all who, entering the house, walked into the trap. He also removed a plank of the flooring and cleared enough of the foundation so that there was but a mere ceiling between him and the inquisition room below. Thus he could hear everything that passed between the Cardinal's spies and their victims.

Those arrested were first submitted to a minute search of their persons. Then, almost invariably, they were asked:

"Has Madame Bonacieux given you anything to deliver to her husband or to another party? Has Monsieur Bonacieux given you anything to deliver to his wife or to another party? Has either of them confided anything to you by word of mouth?"

"If they knew anything they would not question people in this manner," D'Artagnan mused. "Now what do they want to find out? Exactly this: whether the Duke of Buckingham is in Paris and whether he has had or is due to have an interview with the Queen."

This idea was constantly uppermost in D'Artagnan's mind especially since everything he had heard seemed to confirm its probability. Meanwhile the mousetrap—and D'Artagnan's vigilance—never relaxed for a moment.

On the morrow of Monsieur Bonacieux's arrest, late in the evening, on the stroke of nine, Athos left D'Artagnan's to call at Monsieur de Tréville's. Planchet, who had not yet made the bed, was setting to work when there was a knock at the street door. The door immediately opened and closed; someone was caught in the mousetrap!

D'Artagnan leapt to his listening-post and lay flat on his belly, his ear to the ground. Soon he heard cries, then moans which someone was apparently trying to stifle. Assuredly this was no mere exchange of questions and answers.

"Devil take it," D'Artagnan thought. "It sounds like a woman. Probably they're searching her and she's resisting. They're using force, the swine. . . ."

In spite of his prudence it was all D'Artagnan could do not to interrupt the scene.

"But I tell you I am the mistress of this house, gentlemen," cried the unhappy woman. "I tell you I am Madame Bonacieux; I tell you I belong to the Queen."

"Madame Bonacieux!" D'Artagnan murmured. "Have I found the person everyone is looking for?"

"You are exactly the lady we were awaiting."

The voice grew more and more indistinct, then a series of bumps shook the wainscoting; no doubt the victim was struggling as fiercely as a lone woman could struggle against four men.

"Pardon, gentlemen, pard—" murmured the voice. Then it lapsed into inarticulate sounds.

"They have gagged her, they are going to drag her away." D'Artagnan rose to his feet as though mechanically propelled by a spring. "My sword? Good, here it is! Planchet!"

"Monsieur?"

"Go fetch Athos, Porthos and Aramis. One of the three will surely be at home. Tell them to come here at once, fully armed. Tell them to run. Oh, I remember, Athos is at the Hôtel de Tréville."

"But where are *you* going, Monsieur?"

"I'm going down through the window, it's quicker. You put back the boards, sweep the floor, go out by the front door and off to where I told you."

"Oh, Monsieur, Monsieur, you are going to get killed."

"Hush, idiot!" said D'Artagnan. Vaulting over the windowsill, he clung to it for a moment, then dropped without mishap to the ground which fortunately was no very great distance. A second later, he was knocking at the street door, murmuring as he did so:

"It's my turn to get caught in the mousetrap, but God help the cats that pounce on a mouse like me."

The sound of his knock brought the tumult within to an abrupt halt; steps were heard approaching, the door opened and D'Artagnan, sword drawn, rushed into Monsieur Bonacieux's apartment. This door clicked shut upon him.

Immediately the whole neighborhood heard loud cries, a stamping of many feet, a clash of swords, and a prolonged smashing of furniture. Those who, surprised at this bedlam, went to their windows to ascertain its cause, were rewarded by seeing the street door flung open again and four black-clad men emerging. These did not walk or run, they actually flew out like so many frightened crows, strewing furniture and ground with feathers from their wings or, in other words, patches of their clothes and tatters from their cloaks.

D'Artagnan emerged the victor without much effort, for only one of the officers was armed and he defended himself only for form's sake. True, the three others attempted to fell the young man with chairs, stools and crockery, but two or three scratches from the Gascon's blade terrified them. A scant ten minutes sufficed to put them to rout, leaving D'Artagnan undisputed master of the field of battle.

Such neighbors as had opened their windows with the habitual phlegm of Parisians in these times of riot and perpetual brawls, now closed them quite as phlegmatically. Seeing the four men in black disappear, they knew instinctively that for the moment at least the fun was over. Besides it was growing late and in those days, as today, early to bed was the watchword in the Luxembourg quarter.

Left alone with Madame Bonacieux, D'Artagnan turned toward where the poor woman lay back, deep in an armchair, half-conscious. One swift glance revealed a charming woman of twenty-five or twenty-six, with dark hair, blue eyes and a slightly retroussé nose, admirable teeth and a complexion marbled with rose and opal. There however ended whatever resemblance she bore to a lady of rank: her hands were white but without delicacy, her feet did not bespeak your lady of quality. Happily D'Artagnan was not yet acquainted with such niceties of social distinction.

While he was surveying Madame Bonacieux and had, as we have said, reached her feet, he noticed a fine cambric handkerchief lying on the floor. True to habit, he picked it up. In one corner he recognized the same crest he had seen on the handkerchief which had almost caused Aramis to cut his throat.

Ever since that occasion D'Artagnan looked askance at handkerchiefs with crests on them, so without a word he put this one back into Madame Bonacieux's pocket.

At that moment, Madame Bonacieux recovered her senses. Opening her eyes, she cast a glance of terror about her, then realized that the apartment was empty and that she was alone with her liberator. Smiling, she stretched out her hands to him—and Madame Bonacieux had the sweetest smile in all the world!

"Ah, Monsieur, you saved me! Pray let me thank you—"

"Madame, you owe me no thanks. I did what any gentleman would have done in my place."

"Oh, but I do owe you thanks, Monsieur, and I hope to prove to you that you have not befriended an ingrate. But tell me . . . those men . . . I took them for robbers at first . . . What did they want with me? . . . And why isn't Monsieur Bonacieux here?"

"Madame, these men were far more dangerous than any robbers could be, they were agents of the Cardinal. As for your husband, he isn't here because he was picked up yesterday and taken to the Bastille."

"My husband in the Bastille! Oh, my God! What has he done? Poor dear man, he is innocence personified."

And something like a smile fluttered over her face.

"What has he done?" D'Artagnan echoed. "I think his only crime consists in having at once the good fortune and misfortune to be your husband."

"But Monsieur, then you know—?"

"I know that you were abducted, Madame."

"Who did it, Monsieur? Do you know? If you *do* know, then please, please tell me who it was!"

"You were abducted by a man forty or forty-five years old, with black hair, a swarthy complexion, and a scar on his left temple."

"That's right, that is the man. But his name, what is his name?"

"Alas, Madame, I do not know."

"Was my husband aware that I had been abducted?"

"He received a letter telling him about it from the abductor himself."

"Does he suspect the reason for my abduction?" Madame Bonacieux asked with some embarrassment.

"I believe he attributed it to political motives."

"I myself did not think so at first but now I believe just as he does," said the young woman. "Then my dear husband did not for a moment suspect me?"

"Never for a moment, Madame; he was too sure of your virtue and proud of the love you bear him."

Again, an almost imperceptible smile stole over the roseate lips of the comely young woman.

"How did you escape?" D'Artagnan asked.

"I took advantage of a few minutes when they left me alone. As I had known since morning why I was abducted, I was determined to escape. I knotted my bedsheets together and let myself down through the window. Then, thinking my husband would be at home, I rushed here."

"To put yourself under his protection?"

"No, no, poor dear man! I knew quite well that he was incapable of defending me. But he could serve us in another way, so I wished to talk to him."

"About what?"

"I cannot tell you that because it is not my secret."

"In any case, Madame (though I am a guardsman, let me recall you to prudence), in any case, this is scarcely a place for an exchange of confidences. The men I put to flight will soon return with reinforcements; if they find us here, we are ruined. To be sure, I sent word to three of my friends, but who knows whether they can be reached?"

"Yes, you are right! Let us fly, let us escape!" Considerably frightened, she slipped her arm through D'Artagnan's and urged him forward.

"But where to?" D'Artagnan asked. "Where shall we fly to?"

"First let us get away from this house; afterwards we shall see."

Without bothering to close the door behind them, the young couple walked quickly down the Rue des Fossoyeurs, turned into the Rue des Fossés Monsieur-le-Prince, and did not stop until they reached the Place Saint-Sulpice.

"Now what shall we do?" D'Artagnan asked. "To what address may I have the honor of accompanying you?"

"I must own I am at a loss how to answer," she told him. "I intended to have my husband go to Monsieur de La Porte to ascertain what has been happening at the Louvre for the last three days and whether I could safely go back there."

"Surely I can go to Monsieur de La Porte."

"Perhaps so. Still there is one drawback. They know Monsieur Bonacieux at the Louvre so they would let him pass. They do not know you."

"But surely there must be a concierge or doorman at some wicket of the Louvre who is devoted to you and thanks to a password—"

Madame Bonacieux looked earnestly at the young man:

"Suppose I give you this password, will you promise to forget it as soon as you have used it?"

"I promise on my word of honor and on my faith as a gentleman," said D'Artagnan in accents too fervent to leave room for any doubt as to his sincerity.

"I believe you. You appear to be an honorable man. Besides, your services might well make your fortune."

"Without thought of reward, I shall do all I can to serve the King and to be useful to the Queen. Pray believe me your friend."

"But I—where shall I go meanwhile?"

"Is there nobody who can put you in touch with Monsieur de La Porte?"

"I dare not trust anyone."

"Ah, I have it! . . . . we are but a few steps from where Athos lives . . . yes, that's it! . . . ."

"Who is Athos?"

"One of my friends."

"But what if he is at home? What if he should see me?"

"He is not at home. I shall lock you in and take the key away with me."

"Suppose he returns?"

"He will not return. Even if he did, he would be told that I brought a lady there and that she was in his apartment."

"Of course you realize how compromising that will be."

"What matter? Nobody knows you. In a desperate situation like ours, we can afford to overlook a few social conventions."

"Let us go to your friend's house. Where does he live?"

"Rue Férou, just around the corner."

As D'Artagnan had foreseen, Athos was out. D'Artagnan picked up the key, which was always given him, and introduced Madame Bonacieux into the little apartment.

"Make yourself at home," he said. "Stay here, bolt the door and let no one in unless you hear three raps, so: two fairly hard raps, close together, and after an interval, a third rap, much lighter."

"Good. Now may I give you your instructions."

"I am all attention."

"When you reach the Louvre, go in at the wicket by the Rue de l'Echelle and ask for Germain."

"Yes?"

"When Germain asks you what you want, say two words: 'Tours' and 'Brussels'. Immediately he will place himself at your orders."

"What shall I tell him to do?"

"Tell him to fetch Monsieur de La Porte, valet to Her Majesty."

"And when he has fetched him?"

"You will ask Monsieur de La Porte to come here to me."

"That offers no difficulty. But—"

"But what?"

"But where and how shall I see you again?"

"Do you wish very much to see me again?"

"Certainly."

"Then you may count on me. Meanwhile, do not fret."

"I depend on your word."

"You may do so unreservedly."

D'Artagnan bowed to Madame Bonacieux, darting the most loving glance he could possibly concentrate upon her petite, slight person. As he was starting down the stairs he heard the door being closed, double-locked and bolted. In two bounds he reached the Louvre; as he entered the wicket at the Rue de l'Echelle, the clock struck ten. The whole drama we have described took place within just one half-hour.

Everything happened just as Madame Bonacieux had indicated. At the given password, Germain bowed; ten minutes later, Monsieur de La Porte was at the porter's lodge; in two words D'Artagnan informed him of everything including the whereabouts of Madame Bonacieux. La Porte made sure of the address where his godchild waited. Then he left at a run, but he had not taken ten steps before he hastened back.

"Young man, let me give you a piece of advice!"

"What?"

"You may get into trouble because of what has just happened."

"Really?"

"Yes. Have you by any chance some friend whose clock runs too slow?"

"Monsieur, I—"

"Go call on him. Let him testify that you were at his house at nine-thirty. In a court of justice that is what we call an alibi."

D'Artagnan, finding this counsel prudent, hurried off to Monsieur de Tréville's. But instead of going into the reception room with the rest of the crowd, he asked to be shown into the Captain's study. As he frequented the Hôtel so assiduously, his request was granted; Monsieur de Tréville was informed that his young compatriot, having something important to communicate, solicited a private audience. Five minutes later, Monsieur de Tréville was asking D'Artagnan what he could do to be of service and what occasioned a visit at so late an hour.

"I beg your pardon, Monsieur, I did not think twenty-five minutes past nine was too late to wait upon you."

(Left alone to wait for the Captain, he had of course turned back Monsieur de Tréville's clock three quarters of an hour.)

"Twenty-five past nine!" cried Monsieur de Tréville, looking at his clock. "But that's impossible."

"Clocks don't lie, Monsieur."

"That's true. But I would have thought it was much later. Well, tell me what I can do for you?"

D'Artagnan proceeded to spin Monsieur de Tréville a long yarn about the Queen. He voiced the fears he entertained with respect to Her Majesty; he repeated what he had heard about the Cardinal's plans with regard to Buckingham, carrying the whole thing off with such calm and such candor that Monsieur de Tréville was duped the more easily because he had himself noticed some fresh trouble brewing between Cardinal, King and Queen.

As Monsieur de Tréville's clock struck ten D'Artagnan took his leave. Thanking him for the information he had brought, the Captain of Musketeers urged him always to keep the service of King and Queen at heart. At the foot of the staircase, D'Artagnan suddenly remembered that he had forgotten his cane. He therefore ran upstairs again, returned to Monsieur de Tréville's office, and, with a turn of the finger, set the clock right again so that on the morrow no one would know it had been tampered with. Then, certain that he had secured a witness to prove his alibi, he sauntered downstairs and found himself in the street.

XI
IN WHICH THE PLOT THICKENS

Having paid his visit to Monsieur de Tréville, D'Artagnan, deep in thought, took the longest possible way homeward. And of what was he meditating as he strayed from his path, gazed at the stars, and found himself now sighing, now smiling?

He was thinking of Madame Bonacieux. To an apprentice musketeer, she represented virtually the ideal of love. Pretty, mysterious, privy to almost all the secrets of the Court, her delicate features reflecting such charming gravity, she might be supposed not entirely indifferent to him. So fond a hope acts like an irresistible magnet to novices in love. Moreover D'Artagnan had delivered her out of the hands of the demons who had sought to violate her privacy and do her bodily harm. Did not this important service establish a bond of gratitude which might well assume a more tender character?

How swiftly our dreams soar on the wings of imagination! Already D'Artagnan saw himself being accosted by a messenger from the young woman and receiving from his hands a note appointing a meeting or a gold chain or a diamond even. As we have seen, young cavaliers accepted presents from their King without shame; and in that period of easy morals, they were no more delicate with regard to their mistresses. Invariably the ladies left them some valuable and lasting token of their affection, as though they were attempting to conquer the fragility of masculine sentiments by the solidity of feminine gifts.

Men unblushingly made their way in the world thanks to the largesse of women. Those women whose sole assets consisted in their beauty made a glad gift of that, whence doubtless the proverb: "*La plus belle fille du monde ne peut donner que ce qu'elle a,* The fairest maid in the world can give no more than what she has!" But those who were rich gave a part of their money as well, and many a hero of that gallant period would neither have won his spurs in the first place nor his battles afterward were it not for the purse his mistress fastened to his saddle-bow.

D'Artagnan possessed nothing. The bashfulness of your provincial—that slight patina, that ephemeral blossom, that down on a peach—soon evaporated before the blasts of scarcely orthodox advice the three musketeers offered their friend. D'Artagnan, following the strange customs of the times, considered himself fighting the campaign of Paris, just as though he were on active service on the battlefield. On the Flanders front, the Spaniard; on the Paris front, woman—in either place an enemy to contend with and contributions to be levied!

In all justice to D'Artagnan it must be added that at this moment he was moved by nobler and more generous sentiments. When the haberdasher confessed to being a wealthy man, D'Artagnan concluded that, Bonacieux being the ninny he was, Madame probably held the pursestrings. But this in no wise influenced the feelings that swept over him the moment he saw her. Mercenary calculations entered almost not at all into his awakening love. We say "almost not at all" because the idea of a youthful, comely, graceful and intelligent woman being rich into the bargain, far from detracting from incipient love, serves on the contrary to intensify it.

Affluence provides a host of little amenities and frills which prove most becoming to a beauty. Shapely slippers on her feet, white stockings of sheer material, a silk dress, a lace guimpe and a dainty ribbon in her hair do not make an ugly woman pretty, but they do make a pretty woman beautiful. And a woman's hands especially! What wonders money can do for women by sparing them from working! Truly, to be beautiful, a woman's hands must be idle.

As we have not concealed the state of D'Artagnan's fortune, the reader well knows that he was no millionaire. To be sure he hoped to become one some day but the date set in his own mind for this happy change was still far distant. Meanwhile, how painful to see the woman one loves longing for those myriad trifles that constitute feminine happiness and to be unable to satisfy her wants. When a woman is rich and her lover is not, she can at least buy what her lover cannot afford to give her; she usually gratifies these indulgences with her husband's money and without thanks to him.

D'Artagnan, eager to become the most passionate of lovers, was al-

ready her devoted friend. Amid his amorous designs upon the haberdasher's wife, he did not forget his comrades. The comely Madame Bonacieux was just the woman to stroll on his arm in the Plaine Saint-Denis or
through the fair of Saint-Germain with Athos, Porthos and Aramis for
company. How proud D'Artagnan would be to display such a conquest!

Now when people have walked any length of time, they get quite hungry, as D'Artagnan had himself noticed. So D'Artagnan, his inamorata and
his comrades, their stroll done, would enjoy charming little dinners at
which he visualized himself pressing the hand of a loyal friend on one
side, and, on the other, the foot of an adoring mistress. And, were his
friends out of funds, he saw himself as their financial savior.

What about Monsieur Bonacieux whom D'Artagnan had delivered
into the hands of the officers, betraying him publicly after his private
promises to save him? It must be confessed that D'Artagnan did not
vouchsafe him a thought or, if he did, he decided that the haberdasher was
in the proper place, wherever it was. Is not love the most selfish of all passions?

(Let our readers reassure themselves. If D'Artagnan forgot or feigned
to forget his landlord, pretending not to know whither the wretched man
had been carried away, *we* have not forgotten him and *we* know where he
is. But for the moment let us do as the amorous Gascon did. Presently our
worthy haberdasher will reappear.)

Dreaming of his future amours, apostrophizing the night and gazing at
the stars, D'Artagnan was returning up the Rue du Cherche-Midi, or
rather Chasse-Midi as it was then called. As Aramis lived in this quarter,
he suddenly thought he would pay Aramis a visit to explain why he had
dispatched Planchet to him with immediate orders to rush to the mousetrap.

"If Aramis was at home when Planchet arrived," D'Artagnan said, "he
must have gone straight to the Rue des Fossoyeurs. There he would have
found no one or at best Athos and Porthos. So all three are in complete ignorance of what has happened. I owe them at least an explanation for having disturbed them."

Thus he spoke aloud. But silently, to himself, he thought that a visit to
Aramis offered him a chance of talking about pretty little Madame Bonacieux, who at this point filled his head if not his heart. To look for discretion in a first love is irrelevant. First loves are accompanied by a joy so
excessive that it must be allowed to overflow or it will stifle a man.

For the past two hours Paris had been swathed in darkness and the streets were practically deserted. Eleven o'clock struck from all the clocks of the Faubourg Saint-Germain. The night was mild. D'Artagnan passed down a lane which is now the Rue d'Assas. From the Rue de Vaugirard came the cool fragrance of the Luxembourg gardens, freshened by the dews of evening and the breeze of night. Gratefully D'Artagnan breathed in the redolence of flower and grass and tree. Afar, muffled by stout shutters, echoes of drinking songs floated out from taverns scattered across the plain. At the foot of the lane, D'Artagnan turned to the left, for Aramis lived between the Rue Cassette and the Rue Servandoni.

D'Artagnan had just passed the Rue Cassette and could see the door of his friend's house, nestling under a clump of sycamores and clematis that formed a vast leafy arch above. Suddenly a shadowlike form issued from the Rue Servandoni. That form was wrapped up in a cloak, and D'Artagnan first thought it was a man but the slenderness of the figure, the hesitancy of the gait and the insecurity of the steps convinced him that it was a woman. As if uncertain of the house she sought, she kept looking up to get her bearings, stopped, retraced her steps, and once again approached. D'Artagnan was seized with curiosity.

"Shall I go offer my services?" he wondered. "Judging by her step, I would say she was young; perhaps she is pretty! Yes, but a woman scarcely ventures on the streets at this hour unless she is going to meet her lover. A pox on it! To disturb a lovers' rendezvous is no way to begin an acquaintance!"

Meanwhile the young woman kept coming forward counting the houses and the windows. This was neither long nor difficult, for there were but three houses in that part of the street and only two windows looking out upon it: one in a pavilion parallel to that of Aramis, the other in the pavilion Aramis occupied.

"*Pardieu!*" said D'Artagnan to himself as he recalled the theologian's niece, "*Pardieu,* how droll if this belated dove were bound for my friend's house! Upon my soul, it looks very much like it. Ah, my dear Aramis, this time my curiosity shall be satisfied!"

And he drew back, making himself as thin as possible, as he took his stand on the darkest side of the street near a stone bench set in a niche. The young woman continued to advance, betraying herself not only by her light step but also by a soft cough—a signal, thought D'Artagnan—which suggested a sweet voice. Either a corresponding signal settled the doubts of the nocturnal adventuress or she needed no aid to recognize that she had reached the end of her journey; at all events, she stepped resolutely forward and, with finger crooked, rapped three times, at equal intervals, on the musketeer's shutter.

"It *is* Aramis!" D'Artagnan murmured. "Ha, Monsieur Hypocrite, this time I've caught you studying theology."

Scarcely was the rapping done when the window opened and a light appeared through the slats of the shutter.

"Ah ha!" said our quidnunc, "the pretty caller was expected! There, the shutters will open in a minute and the lady will climb over the window sill, entering by escalade, to use a technical term. Very neat, very neat indeed."

To his vast astonishment, however, the shutter remained closed, the light that had shown for a moment disappeared, and once again darkness reigned.

D'Artagnan, sensing that this could not last long, kept his eyes peeled and his ears pricked up for the next move. He was right. After a few seconds two sharp raps were heard inside; the young woman in the street replied by a single rap and the shutter opened ever so slightly.

The reader may judge with what avidity D'Artagnan looked and listened. Unfortunately the light had been moved into another room. But his eyes were accustomed to the night; and besides, according to report, the eyes of the Gascons, like those of cats, possess the faculty of seeing through the dark.

The young woman drew a white object from her pocket and unfolded it quickly into the shape of a handkerchief, then drew her interlocutor's attention to one corner of it. D'Artagnan suddenly recalled the handkerchief he had found at Madame Bonacieux's feet, which in turn reminded him of the one he had pulled out from under the feet of Aramis.

What in the Devil's name could this handkerchief mean to these people?

From his point of vantage, D'Artagnan could not distinguish Aramis, but he felt certain it was his friend within conversing with the lady without. Curiosity prevailed over prudence. Making the most of the couple's preoccupation over the handkerchief, he emerged from his hiding-place and swift as lightning but stepping with the utmost caution, flattened himself against an angle of the wall, whence he could see into the room Aramis occupied.

Looking in, he almost cried out, so great was his surprise. It was not with Aramis the midnight visitor was conversing but with another woman! He perceived her clearly enough to recognize the clothes she wore but he could not make out her features.

The woman inside now drew a handkerchief from her pocket and exchanged it for the one the visitor had shown her. The two women spoke a few words more and presently the shutter was closed. The visitor turned back and passed within four steps of D'Artagnan, lowering the hood of her mantle. But her precaution was too late; D'Artagnan had recognized Madame Bonacieux.

Madame Bonacieux! Already when he had seen her draw the handkerchief from her pocket a suspicion had flashed through his mind, but he dismissed it. After all, was it likely that Madame Bonacieux, having sent for Monsieur de La Porte to conduct her back to the Louvre, would be running about the streets of Paris alone at half-past eleven at night at the risk of being abducted a second time?

Her errand must be one of immense importance. And what is the most important errand for a woman of twenty-five? Love.

Was she exposing herself to such hazards on her own account or for the sake of somebody else? There, thought D'Artagnan, lay the whole problem as the demon of jealousy gnawed at his heart as bitterly as though he were already her accepted lover. Well, there was a very simple means of finding out where Madame Bonacieux was going; he need but follow her.

Seeing the young man as he detached himself from the wall like a statue walking out of its niche and hearing his footsteps resound so near her, Madame Bonacieux uttered a little cry and fled.

D'Artagnan, running after her, had no difficulty in overtaking a woman burdened by a long, heavy cloak; he came abreast of her before she was one-third of the way down the street. The unfortunate woman was exhausted not by fatigue but by terror, and when D'Artagnan laid his hand on her shoulder, she fell to one knee and cried in a choking voice:

"Kill me if you like, I shall not tell you anything."

D'Artagnan slipped his arm around her waist and drew her to her feet; as he felt that she was about to faint, he hastily comforted her by protestations of devotion. Such protestations meant nothing to Madame Bonacieux for a person might make them while harboring the most evil intentions in the world; but the voice that uttered them meant everything to her. Despite her confusion, she thought she recognized that voice; she opened her eyes, cast a glance at the man who had terrified her, and recognizing D'Artagnan, gave a cry of joy.

"Oh, it is you! Thank God! Thank God!"

"Yes, it is I, whom God has sent to watch over you."

"Was that why you followed me?"

The moment she recognized her supposed enemy to be a friend, all her fears vanished. She flashed him a coquettish smile.

"No," D'Artagnan told her, "I must confess it was chance threw me in your way. I saw a woman tapping at the window of one of my friends."

"Of one of your friends?"

"Certainly, Aramis is one of my best friends."

"Aramis? Who is he?"

"Come, come, you're not telling me you don't know Aramis?"

"This is the first time I have ever heard his name."

"And I suppose it is the first time you ever went to his house?"

"Assuredly."

"And you did not know that a young man lived there?"

"No."

"A musketeer?"

"No, indeed."

"So you weren't looking for Aramis?"

"Absolutely not. Besides, as you saw, I was talking to a woman."

"That is quite true. But the woman is probably a friend of Aramis—"

"I don't know anything about that."

"She must be if she lives in his apartment."

"That is none of my business."

"But who is she?"

"Oh, that is not my secret."

"My dear Madame Bonacieux, you are the most attractive and the most mysterious of women."

"Is what you call my mystery a handicap?"

"No. On the contrary, you are adorable."

"Give me your arm, then."

"Gladly. And now?"

"Now escort me; I have a call to make."

"Where?"

"Where I am going."

"But where *are* you going?"

"You will see because I shall ask you to leave me at the door."

"Shall I wait for you?"

"That will be unnecessary."

"Will you come back from there unaccompanied?"

"Maybe yes, maybe no."

"Will the person accompanying you be a man or a woman?"

"I don't know yet."

"I shall find out!"

"How?"

"I shall wait until you come out."

"In that case, good-bye."

"Why so?"

"I do not need you."

"But you asked me to—"

"I asked a gentleman to aid me, not a spy to shadow me."

"The word 'spy' is a harsh one."

"What do *you* call a man who trails people against their will?"

"I call him indiscreet."

"The word 'indiscreet' is too mild."

"Well, Madame, I see I must do as you wish."

"Why did you forgo the merit of doing so at once?"

"Is there no merit in repentance?"

"Are you really repentant?"

"Frankly I scarce know if I am or not. But this I do know: I promise to do whatever you wish if you will allow me to accompany you where you are going."

"And you will leave me afterward?"

"Yes."

"Without waiting for me to come out again?"

"Yes."

"On your word of honor?"

"By my faith as a gentleman. Take my arm and let us go."

Half-laughing, half-trembling, she slipped her arm through his and together they strolled up the Rue de La Harpe. Reaching the end of the street, the young woman appeared to hesitate, just as she had done in the Rue de Vaugirard. Yet she seemed by certain signs to recognize a particular door and, going toward it:

"Now, Monsieur," she said, "this is where I have business to do. A thousand thanks for your honorable company; it has saved me from all the dangers I would have faced had I come alone. But now I have reached my destination, the time has come for you to keep your word."

"And you will have nothing to fear on your way home?"

"I shall have nothing to fear but robbers."

"And are robbers nothing?"

"What could they take? I haven't a sou on me."

"You forget that beautiful embroidered handkerchief with the crest in the corner?"

"What handkerchief?"

"The one I found at your feet and put back into your pocket."

"Hush, hold your tongue, man! You must be mad to be so foolhardy! Do you wish to destroy me?"

"You see, you are still in danger since a single word makes you tremble and you admit you would be ruined if anyone heard me saying it. Oh, come, Madame, please," he cried, seizing her hands and gazing ardently into her eyes, "please be more generous. Confide in me. Can you not see by my eyes that my heart is filled with sympathy and devotion?"

"Truly, I can. Ask me my own secrets and I shall hold nothing back. But you are asking me to divulge the secrets of others—which is a very different matter."

"No matter, I shall discover them. Since these secrets may have an influence over your life, they must become my secrets too."

"Beware of doing anything of the sort!" the young woman replied so earnestly that D'Artagnan gave an involuntary start. "Please, please do not meddle in anything that concerns me; please do not seek to aid me in what I am accomplishing. I ask you this in the name of the interest I have inspired in you and in the name of the service you rendered me, which I shall never forget. Rather, believe everything that I have told you. Do not bother about me; I no longer exist for you, it is as though you had never laid eyes on me!"

"Must Aramis do so likewise?" D'Artagnan asked in an access of pique.

"You mentioned that name two or three times and I told you I did not know him, Monsieur."

"You don't know the man at whose shutter you knocked? Now, now, Madame, you take me to be too credulous."

"Be honest, Monsieur. You manufactured this story and invented this character in order to make me talk."

"I am manufacturing and inventing nothing. I am speaking the naked truth."

"You say that a friend of yours lives in that house?"

"I say and repeat for the third time: a friend of mine lives in that house and his name is Aramis."

"This misunderstanding will be cleared up later," the young woman murmured, "but for the present, Monsieur, please be silent."

"If you could see plainly into my heart, you would discover so much curiosity that you would have pity on me and so much love that you would satisfy my curiosity at once. A woman has nothing to fear from the man who loves her."

"You speak very suddenly of love," she objected, shaking her head.

"That is because love has come upon me very suddenly, because I was never in love before and because I am only nineteen."

The young woman eyed him shyly.

"Listen to me, Madame, I am already on the scent," D'Artagnan continued. "Three months ago I almost fought a duel with Aramis over a handkerchief like the one you showed the woman in his house, a handkerchief bearing the same crest, I am sure."

"Monsieur, I assure you that you are wearying me with all this questioning."

"But you, Madame, prudent as you are, just think: if you were to be arrested and that handkerchief seized, wouldn't you be compromised?"

"In what way? The initials are mine, C. B. for Constance Bonacieux."

"Or for Camille de Bois-Tracy."

"Silence, Monsieur! Once again, silence! If the dangers I myself face cannot stop you, think of those *you* are facing."

"I?"

"Yes, you. By knowing me you are in danger of imprisonment or even of death."

"Then I refuse to leave you."

"Monsieur," the young woman implored, her hands clasped, "Monsieur, in the name of Heaven, on the honor of a soldier and the courtesy of a gentleman, please, please be off. Hark! midnight is striking, the hour of my appointment."

"Madame," said D'Artagnan bowing, "I cannot refuse a request couched in such terms. Be content, I will go my way."

"You won't follow me, you won't watch me?"

"I shall go straight home."

"Ah, I was sure of it, I knew you were a gentleman," said Madame Bonacieux.

Seizing her outstretched hand, D'Artagnan kissed it ardently. Then, with that naïve brutality which women often prefer to the affectations of politeness (because it betrays the depths of a man's thoughts and establishes the triumph of feeling over reason) he murmured:

"Ah, would to God I had never seen you!"

"Well, well, I will not say the same about you!" Her voice was almost caressing and she squeezed the hand that still clung to hers. "What is lost today is not lost forever. Who knows, some day I may be free to satisfy your curiosity."

"Will you promise the same to my love?" D'Artagnan asked, overcome with joy.

"Oh, as to that, I will not commit myself. It depends on the feelings you may stir in me."

"So that today, Madame—"

"Today, Monsieur, my feelings do not go beyond gratitude."

"You are too beautiful," D'Artagnan sighed, "and you take advantage of my love."

"No, of your generosity! Pray believe me, Monsieur, with certain people, everything works out well."

"Oh, you have made me the happiest of mortals! Do not forget this evening, do not forget your promise."

"Rest assured, in good time and at the proper place, I shall remember everything. And now go, go in Heaven's name! I was expected promptly at midnight and I am late."

"Five minutes late."

"Yes, but in certain circumstances, five minutes are five centuries!"

"To a person in love."

"Who told you I was not meeting a lover this evening?"

"A lover is waiting for you!" D'Artagnan cried indignantly. "A lover!"

"Oh dear! so the argument is to begin all over again?" she sighed, half-smiling, half-impatient.

"No, no, I'm off, I'm leaving; I believe in you and I wish to enjoy my devotion even were that devotion stupid. Farewell, Madame, farewell."

As if it required the most violent effort to make him release the hand he held in his, he sprang away from her and started running down the street while she rapped three times at regular intervals. When he reached the street corner, he turned around; the door had opened and shut again, the haberdasher's pretty wife had disappeared.

D'Artagnan pursued his way. He had given his word not to watch Madame Bonacieux. Had his very life depended upon this visit of hers or upon the person who was to accompany her, D'Artagnan would nevertheless have returned home, because he had so promised. Five minutes later he was in the Rue des Fossoyeurs.

"Poor Athos!" he muttered. "How can he possibly have guessed what all this is about? He probably fell asleep waiting for me or else he went home to be informed that a woman had called there. A woman under his roof! Well, why not? Aramis certainly had a woman in his place. All this is very strange and I am most curious to know how it will end."

"It will end badly, Monsieur," said a voice which he recognized as Planchet's. Soliloquizing as people so often will when they are preoccupied, D'Artagnan had turned into the alley that led to his staircase.

"What do you mean, badly? Explain yourself, idiot! What has happened?"

"All sorts of misfortunes."

"What?"

"To begin with, Monsieur Athos was arrested."

"Arrested? Athos arrested? What for?"

"He was found in your room. They mistook him for you."

"Who arrested him?"

"Guards brought by those men in black that you drove off."

"Why didn't he give them his name? Why didn't he tell them he knew nothing about the whole business?"

Planchet explained to his master that Athos had been careful to do no such thing. On the contrary, drawing Planchet aside, he had said: "Your master knows all about this, I know nothing; he needs his liberty, I don't need mine. The police will think they have arrested him; that should give him time. In three days, I shall tell them who I am and they will have to let me go."

"Bravo, Athos! noble heart! how typical of him! . . . But tell me, Planchet, what did the officers do?"

"Four of them took him away I don't know where, either to the Bastille or to Fort L'Evêque. Two stayed with the men in black, rummaging through everything and seizing all your papers. There were two more; while all this was going on, they were mounting guard at the door. When it was all over, they went away, leaving the house empty and wide open."

"And Porthos and Aramis?"

"I could not reach them. They did not come."

"But they may still come at any moment. You left word that I was expecting them, eh?"

"Yes, Monsieur."

"Well, you sit tight here, Planchet, and don't budge. If they come, tell them what happened. The house may be watched, it's too dangerous to meet here; tell them to wait for me at the *Sign of the Fir Cone*. I am off to Monsieur de Tréville's to inform him of all this, then I will go to the tavern."

"Very good, Monsieur."

"Mind you stay, Planchet. You're not afraid?"

"Don't worry, Monsieur," the lackey replied. "You see, you don't really know me yet. I can be brave when I put my mind to it. That's the whole point: to put one's mind to it. Besides, I come from Picardy."

"You would rather be killed than quit your post?"

"Yes, Monsieur. There is nothing I would not do to prove my attachment to my master."

"Capital!" D'Artagnan mused. "Apparently I adopted the best possible method with this lad. I shall use it again on occasion."

Then, fast as his legs could carry him—they were by now somewhat weary from their labors that day—D'Artagnan sped away toward the Rue du Vieux-Colombier. Monsieur de Tréville was not at his mansion; his company was on guard at the Louvre and he was with his company.

D'Artagnan knew he must see the Captain of Musketeers in order to inform him of developments; he must somehow try to enter the Louvre. Surely his uniform, identifying him as a guardsman in Monsieur des Essart's company would serve him as passport?

Following the Rue des Petits-Augustins, he reached the quay and turned to the right in order to cross the Seine over the Pont Neuf. For a moment he had thought of taking the ferry but, as he put his hand mechanically into his pocket, he noticed that he had not the wherewithal to pay his fare.

As he reached the corner of the Rue Guénegand, he saw two persons coming out of the Rue Dauphine, a man and a woman. Their appearance struck him and, as he looked carefully at them, he realized that the woman looked very much like Madame Bonacieux and her cavalier like Aramis. The woman still wore that black mantle which D'Artagnan could visualize outlined on the shutter of the Rue de Vaugirard and on the door of the Rue de La Harpe. The man wore the uniform of a musketeer. The woman's hood was pulled down over her ears and the man held a handkerchief up to his face.

They took the bridge, which was also D'Artagnan's road since he was bound for the Louvre, he several paces behind them. D'Artagnan had not gone thirty feet before he was convinced that the woman was Madame Bonacieux and the man Aramis. And, as his suspicions increased, a wave of jealousy swept across his heart. So he was betrayed both by his friend and by the woman whom he already cherished as a mistress! Madame Bonacieux had sworn to him by all the gods that she did not know Aramis, and a quarter of an hour later he found her arm in arm with the musketeer!

D'Artagnan did not reflect that he had known the haberdasher's pretty wife for just three hours, that she owed him nothing more than a modicum of gratitude for saving her from the men in black, and that she had promised him nothing. He considered himself an outraged, betrayed and ridiculed lover; the blood rushed to his face, anger possessed him and he determined to unravel the mystery.

The couple, noticing they were being followed, redoubled their speed. D'Artagnan sped forward, passed them and then turned round so as to meet them squarely in front of the Samaritaine in the lamplight. D'Artagnan stopped dead and they too halted before him. Then the musketeer stepped back and:

"What do you want, Monsieur?" he asked in a voice and with a foreign accent which immediately proved that D'Artagnan had been mistaken in one part of his conjectures.

"It is not Aramis!" he blurted.

"No, Monsieur, it is not Aramis. By your exclamation, I see you have mistaken me for someone else, and so I excuse you."

"You excuse me?"

"Yes," replied the stranger. "And since you have no business with me, kindly step aside and let me pass."

"You are right, Monsieur, my business is not with you but with Madame."

"With Madame? But you do not know her."

"I beg your pardon, Monsieur, I know her very well."

"Ah," Madame Bonacieux sighed reproachfully. "I had your promise as a soldier and your word as a gentleman. I hoped I could rely on that!"

"And I, Madame," said D'Artagnan somewhat embarrassed, "you had promised me—"

"Please take my arm, Madame," said the stranger, "and let us go on."

Meanwhile D'Artagnan, dazed, downcast and shocked, stood his ground. The musketeer advanced two steps and pushed D'Artagnan aside. D'Artagnan sprang backward and drew his sword. At the same time, swift as lightning, the stranger drew his.

"In the name of Heaven, Milord!" cried Madame Bonacieux throwing herself between the combatants and seizing their swords.

"Milord!" cried D'Artagnan, suddenly enlightened. "Milord! I beg your pardon, Monsieur, but can you possibly be—?"

"My Lord Duke of Buckingham," said Madame Bonacieux in an undertone. "And now you may ruin us all."

"Milord, Madame, I ask a hundred pardons. But I love her, Milord, and I was jealous. You know what it is to love, Milord. Pray forgive me and tell me how I may risk my life to serve Your Grace?"

"You are a worthy young man," said Buckingham extending a hand which D'Artagnan pressed respectfully. "You offer me your services and I accept them gladly. Follow us at a distance of twenty paces. If any one shadows us, kill him."

D'Artagnan allowed the Duke and Madame Bonacieux to take twenty steps ahead; then he followed, fully prepared to execute the orders given him by Charles the First's minister. Happily, he found no opportunity to offer the Duke this proof of his devotion, for the young woman and the handsome musketeer entered the Louvre by the wicket near the Rue de l'Echelle without any interference.

D'Artagnan immediately repaired to the *Sign of the Fir Cone* where he found Porthos and Aramis waiting for him. As for the evening's adventures, he gave his friends no explanation other than that he had himself managed the affair for which he had summoned them.

And now, carried away as we are by our narrative, we must leave our three friends to themselves and follow the Duke of Buckingham and his guide through the labyrinths of the Louvre.

XII
GEORGE VILLIERS, DUKE OF BUCKINGHAM

Madame Bonacieux and the Duke entered the Louvre without difficulty, for she was known to be a servant of the Queen's household and he wore the uniform of Monsieur de Tréville's Musketeers, who were on guard that evening. Moreover Germain, the porter, was devoted to Her Majesty's interests. Were anything to go wrong, Madame Bonacieux would have to take the blame for introducing her lover into the Louvre. That was all: she assumed every risk, her reputation would be ruined of course, but what does the reputation of a haberdasher's wife amount to in a world inhabited by great personages?

Once inside the courtyard, they followed the wall for about twenty-five paces until they came to a small door in the servants' quarters, open by day but usually closed at night. It yielded to Madame Bonacieux's pressure and they passed into utter darkness; fortunately the Ariadne of the moment knew all the turnings and windings of this part of the Louvre, assigned to servants of Her Majesty's Household. Her hand in the Duke's hand, she tiptoed down passages, closed door after door behind her, groped her way through the dark, grasped a banister, felt with her foot for the bottom step and began to walk up a staircase. The Duke counted two stories, then Madame Bonacieux turned to the right, followed a long corridor, descended a flight of stairs, went a few steps farther, introduced a key into a lock, opened a door, and pushed His Grace into an apartment lighted only by a nightlight.

"You must wait here, My Lord Duke," she whispered.

Then she went out by the same door which she locked from the outside, leaving her companion literally a prisoner.

Alone as he was, Buckingham did not experience an instant of fear; indeed one of his most salient characteristics was his search for adventure, his love of romance. A brave, rash, enterprising man, he was not risking his life in this sort of affair for the first time. He had learned that the message from Anne of Austria, on the strength of which he had come to Paris, was a snare; but instead of returning to England, he had, abusing his present plight, warned the Queen that he refused to depart without seeing her. At first the Queen would have none of it; presently, fearing that the Duke, exasperated, might commit some folly, she had consented reluctantly. In fact she had planned to meet him and to urge his immediate departure on the evening of Madame Bonacieux's abduction; but since Madame Bonacieux was to fetch the Duke and lead him into the royal presence, the interview had perforce to be postponed.

For two days, as nobody knew what had become of the haberdasher's wife, everything remained in suspense; but once free again and in touch with La Porte, Madame Bonacieux was available to serve her royal mistress.

Left alone in the small boudoir, Buckingham walked toward a mirror; his musketeer's uniform, fitting him perfectly, was most becoming to him. Now thirty-five years old, he passed rightfully for the handsomest gentleman and most gallant cavalier in France or England. The favorite of two kings, immensely rich, all-powerful in a realm with which he played merry havoc to gratify a whim and then pacified to indulge a fancy, George Villiers, Duke of Buckingham, led one of those fabulous existences which have remained through the centuries to astound posterity.

Self-confident, convinced of his own power, certain that the laws which bound other men could not possibly hamper him, he made straight for whatever goal he had set himself, even were it so lofty and splendent that another man must be insane even to contemplate it. Thus, having succeeded in approaching the beautiful and haughty Anne of Austria several times, he had won her love by dazzling her.

George Villiers stood before the glass, running his fingers through his long fair hair to restore the curls which his hat had disordered. Then he twirled his mustache and, his heart swelling with joy and happiness and pride at being so close to the moment he had yearned for so long, he smiled with hope and confidence.

Suddenly a door concealed in the tapestry opened and a woman appeared. Seeing this apparition in the mirror, Buckingham uttered a cry. It was the Queen.

Anne of Austria, then twenty-six or twenty-seven years of age, was at the height of her beauty. Her bearing was that of a queen or a goddess; her eyes, sparkling like emeralds, were of matchless splendor yet filled with sweetness and majesty. Her mouth was small and rosy, and though her under-lip, like that of all the princes of the House of Austria, protruded slightly, it was eminently gracious in her smile and profoundly haughty in her scorn. Her skin was much admired for its velvety softness; her hands and arms, surprisingly white and delicate of texture, were celebrated by all the poets of the age. And her hair, very blond in her youth, had turned to a warm chestnut; curled very simply and amply powdered, it framed her face so admirably that the most rigid critic could only have desired a little more rouge and the most exacting sculptor a nose somewhat more delicately chiseled.

Buckingham stood before her, lost in awe of her beauty. Never had the Queen appeared to him so lovely at Court balls, fêtes and entertainments as she did in this moment clad in a simple gown of white satin and accompanied by Dona Estefana, the only one of her Spanish duennas whom the King's jealousy or the Cardinal's persecution had not banished from her side.

The Queen took two steps forward, Buckingham threw himself at her feet; before she could prevent him, he had kissed the hem of her gown.

"My Lord Duke," said the Queen, "you must already know that *I* did not write to you."

"I do. Alas! a madman I, to dream that snow might melt and marble thaw. But what will you, Madame, a lover believes in love. My journey has not been in vain; at least I have seen you."

"You know very well, My Lord, how and why I am here now. Indifferent to my anguish, you insisted on staying here at the risk of your life and the peril of my honor. I am here now to tell you that everything parts us: the depths of the seas, the enmity of kingdoms, the sanctity of oaths sworn. To struggle against such obstacles is sacrilege, My Lord. I tell you we must never meet again."

"Speak on, Madame, speak on: the warmth of Your Majesty's voice defeats the harshness of your words. You spoke of sacrilege, but surely such sacrilege lies solely in the separation of two hearts that were made for each other."

"My Lord Duke, you forget I never told you I loved you."

"But Your Majesty never told me that you did *not* love me. To tell me this now would be an ingratitude too great on Your Majesty's part. Oh, tell me, Madame, where shall you, queen as you are, ever find a love like mine . . . a love which neither time nor absence nor despair can quench . . .

a love content to thrive upon a lost ribbon, a stray glance, a random word. . . .

"I first set eyes upon you, Madame, three years ago, and ever since I have loved you nobly and ardently as I did that day. Shall I describe the gown you wore, shall I cite each article of apparel that I remember? I see Your Majesty as clearly now as I did then. You were seated, Spanish-fashion, upon square cushions . . . you wore a green satin dress stitched with silver and gold . . . your sleeves hung down caught by diamond clasps, over your arms—your beautiful arms! . . . You wore a close ruff, a cap of the same color as your dress, and athwart your cap, a heron's feather. . . .

"Ah, Madame, I have but to close my eyes in order to see you just as you were then, and to open them again in order to find you as you are now, one hundred times more beautiful."

"Foolish man!" the Queen murmured, too weak to find fault with a lover who had cherished her image so faithfully in his heart. "Do not feed the flame of a vain passion with such memories."

"By what else shall I live, Madame? What else have I but memories, which are my happiness, my treasure and my hope. Each time I have beheld Your Majesty, it was as a new diamond which I enclosed in the casket of my heart. Here is the fourth jewel Your Majesty has let fall from the heights where you dwell and how avidly I gather it! Only four times, Madame: the first which I have described . . . the second at the Hôtel de Chevreuse . . . the third in the gardens at Amiens—"

"I beg you, My Lord Duke, never to speak of that evening," said the Queen, blushing.

"No, Madame, on the contrary, let us speak of it always, for it was the most fortunate and radiant evening of my life. How soft the night, Madame, do you remember? How mild, how balmy the air and how blue the sky, studded with silver stars! That night, Madame, I contrived to be alone with you for one instant . . . that night you were ready to tell me all the loneliness of your life and the sorrows of your heart . . . you leaned upon my arm, Madame, ay, upon this very arm . . . as I bowed my head I could feel your hair grazing my cheek, and each time it touched me, I trembled like a coward . . . You were a queen, my queen, ah! you cannot know what divine felicity and what paradisical joy fill one such moment! Take my riches, my fortune, take my glory, take all the days I have yet to live, I would gladly exchange them for a moment like that moment, a night like that night. That night, Madame, I dare swear it! that night Your Majesty loved me!"

"My Lord, the beauty of the gardens . . . the spell of the evening . . . the fascination of your glance—oh! the thousand and one circumstances that sometimes unite to destroy a woman!—all these were heavy upon me that fatal evening. . . . But you saw it, My Lord: the Queen come to the aid of the faltering woman. At the first word you dared speak, with the first word I mustered to answer your temerity, I called for help."

"True, Madame, and any love but mine would have perished at this ordeal, but mine emerged more ardent, more eternal! You thought to escape me by returning to Paris; you believed I would not dare quit the treasure over which my master had appointed me to watch. But what did all the treasures of the world mean to me, and all the kings of the universe? A week later I was back again, Madame. That time you had nothing to say to me; I had risked my favor and my life to see you for a fleeting second. I did not even touch your hand, and you forgave me, seeing me so submissive and repentant."

"Yes, but as you well know, My Lord, calumny pounced upon all these follies in which I took no part. The King, excited by the Cardinal, made a terrible scene; Madame de Vernet was dismissed, Putange was exiled and Madame de Chevreuse fell into disgrace. And remember, My Lord, when you sought to return as Ambassador to France, His Majesty himself opposed it."

"That is why France is now about to pay for her King's refusal with a war. Now that I may no longer see you, Madame, I can at least arrange to have news of me reach you day by day. What do you suppose lies behind my plans for the occupation of the Isle of Ré and for our league with the Protestants of La Rochelle? This, no more and no less: the pleasure of my seeing you.

"I cannot hope to fight my way to Paris, sword in hand; I know this all too well. But a war, Madame, ends in a peace, a peace requires a negotiator, that negotiator might well be myself, Madame. No one would then dare to refuse me. So I shall return to Paris, I shall see you again, I shall savor a moment of ecstasy! Thousands of men, it is true, will lose their lives for my joy, but what matter so but I see Your Majesty again? Is this folly, Madame, is it insanity? I dare not say. But tell me, Madame, when did ever woman find a lover more deeply in love, when did ever queen find a servant more ardent?"

"My Lord, you call to your defense arguments that accuse you the more strongly. These proofs of love that you invoke are almost crimes."

"That is because you do not love me, Madame. If you loved me, how differently you would feel! If you loved me, oh! if but you loved me, I would be too happy, I would perish for very delight."

The Queen sighed.

"Your Majesty mentioned Madame de Chevreuse; alas, she was less cruel than you, for Lord Holland loved her and she responded to his love."

"Madame de Chevreuse was not a queen," Anne of Austria replied, overcome, in spite of herself, by the depths of Buckingham's love.

"So you would love me, Madame, were you not queen; ah, tell me that you would love me! Let me believe that only the dignity of your rank makes you so cruel to me . . . let me believe that were you Madame de Chevreuse, poor Buckingham might have hoped . . . I thank you Madame, I thank my beauteous sovereign one hundredfold for her most gracious words."

"No, My Lord, you misunderstand . . . you misconstrue my meaning. . . ."

"Madame, I find my happiness in illusion and error; I pray you mercifully to leave them me. You have told me I was drawn to Paris as into a trap, which may cost me my life—"

"God forbid!" The Queen's terror revealed her interest in Buckingham more clearly than words could do. "My Lord—"

"Madame, I must tell you that for some time I have felt a strange presentiment . . ." he smiled, at once melancholy and charming, "Who shall say? I may die sooner than I imagine. . . ."

"But, My Lord—"

"I do not mention this, Madame, to frighten you. Forget what I said . . . it was ridiculous . . . I take no heed of such dreams . . . But your words and the hope you have suggested would prove to be a royal wage for even my life—"

"I too feel strange portents; I too dream dreams; I too, queen though I be, saw a vision. It was you, My Lord, lying wounded on a couch, your blood flowing from your veins."

"In my left side . . . a knife wound. . . ."

"Yes, My Lord, but who can have told you of it? It was but a dream which I confessed to God alone and in my prayers—"

"I ask no more so but you tell me that you love me, Madame."

"I ... I ... ?"

"If you do not love me, then why does God send the same dreams to us? Could we feel the same presentiments in common if our existences were not one? You love me, Madam, and you will weep my death."

"Ah, God, be merciful to give me strength. I beg Your Grace to go. Whether I love you or not is another question, but I implore you, My Lord, to depart. I shall not make myself privy to perjury; take pity on me and go. If you were struck down here in France and I were held responsible for your death, I myself would die of grief. Pray go, Monsieur, by your love, pray leave me."

"How beautiful Your Majesty is in this supreme moment! How fervently your servant Buckingham worships you!"

"Go, I beg you. You will come back later, as ambassador, as minister, surrounded by guards who will defend you and watch over you. Then at least I shall have no cause to fear for your days, then I shall delight in seeing you."

"Shall I believe this?"

"You must, My Lord—"

"Madame, let me beg as a token of your indulgence some object which comes from you ... something to prove to me that I am not dreaming ... something that you have worn on your person ... something I may wear in turn ... a ring, a necklace, a chain. ..."

"Will you leave if I give what you ask?"

"Assuredly."

"At this very instant?"

"Ay."

"You will quit France? You will return to England?"

"I swear it."

"Wait then, wait, My Lord—"

The Queen went back to her apartment, returning almost at once with a small rosewood coffer, the Royal and Imperial coat-of-arms stamped upon it in gold:

"My Lord, here is a gift by which to remember me."

Buckingham took up the casket, fell to one knee ...

"You promised me to leave," the Queen reminded him.

"I shall be true to my word, Madame; your hand and I go."

Her eyes closed, the Queen offered him one hand, resting heavily with the other upon Dona Estefana, for she felt about to faint. Passionately Buckingham pressed his lips to the Queen's fingertips, then rose.

"If I am still alive within six months," he vowed, "I shall see Your Majesty again though I upset the universe to do so." Then faithful to his promise, he stumbled from the room.

Madame Bonacieux was awaiting him; with the same caution and the same luck they made their way successfully out of the Louvre.

XIII

OF MONSIEUR BONACIEUX

By now the perspicacious reader will have perceived that the author seems to have paid but scant attention to one of his characters, despite the latter's precarious plight. What of Monsieur Bonacieux, that worthy martyr to the political and amorous intrigues of an age when political and amorous intrigues went cheek by jowl?

The officers who had arrested him led him straight to the Bastille . . . shuddering with fright, he was marched past a platoon of soldiers who were loading their muskets . . . then he was taken down a subterranean gallery where he met with the bawdiest insults and the harshest of physical treatment. . . . No one could have supposed him to be a gentleman; he was therefore handled as the veriest clodhopper.

After a half-hour or so, a clerk arrived to put an end to his tortures if not to his disquiet with orders to lead Monsieur Bonacieux to the Bureau of Investigation. Usually prisoners were questioned in their cells, but Monsieur Bonacieux's presence in jail did not warrant such niceties. Two guards seized him, trundled him across a court, propelled him down a corridor flanked by sentinels, thrust open a door and pushed him into a small room to face a table, a chair and a Commissioner. The Commissioner was seated on the chair and busy writing at a table. The guards led the prisoner to the table, and at a wave of the Commissioner's hand moved out of earshot. The Commissioner continued sedulously to examine the papers before him, then suddenly looked up, and Bonacieux glimpsed a surly mouth . . . a pointed nose . . . a pair of yellow protruding cheeks . . . a pair of tiny eyes, bright and piercing . . . a man half-ferret, half-fox . . . a head emerging atop an exaggerated neck much as a turtle's head emerges from its shell. . . .

The Commissioner asked Monsieur Bonacieux his family name, his Christian name, his age, his profession and his domicile, to which the accused replied:

"Joseph-Michel Bonacieux; fifty years old; haberdasher (retired); residence, Number 11 Rue des Fossoyeurs." This settled, there was no more questioning; instead, the Commissioner read a long lecture on the dangers an obscure bourgeois might incur by interfering with public affairs, topping this exordium with a lengthier exposition celebrating the deeds and power of His Eminence the Cardinal:

"An incomparable minister, hum! The conqueror of previous ministries, hum! An exemplar of ministers to come, hum! A statesman whose acts no sane man, hum! would oppose."

Part Two of his speech done, Monsieur le Commissaire fixed his hawk eyes on poor Bonacieux, inviting him to ponder upon the extreme gravity of his plight. Our haberdasher needed no such invitation, his mind was already made up; he swiftly consigned Monsieur de La Porte to the Devil for marrying him off to Constance, especially since Constance was a servant in the Queen's Household. At bottom Bonacieux's character was a mixture of profound egoism and sordid avarice, flavored with a dash of extreme cowardice; any love he might bear his young wife was secondary to selfishness, greed and fear. Carefully he thought over what his questioner had said, then replied coolly:

"Monsieur le Commissaire, I beg you to believe I yield to none in admiration for the personality and merit of His Incomparable Eminence whom we have the honor to serve."

"If that is so, why are you in the Bastille?"

"Why am I here? How am I here? I simply cannot tell you, Monsieur, because I do not know myself. But certainly I never caused My Lord Cardinal the slightest displeasure—not consciously, at least!"

"Why do you suppose you stand here accused of high treason?"

"High treason! High treason! Why do *you* suppose a wretched haberdasher who loathes the Huguenots and abhors the Spaniards stands here accused of high treason? Come, Monsieur, think it over. How could I possibly be suspected of anything?"

The Commissioner stared, cleared his throat, and:

"You have a wife, Monsieur Bonacieux, have you not?"

"Ay, Monsieur," the haberdasher acknowledged. (Here's where my troubles begin, he thought to himself.) "I mean I *had* a wife."

"You *had* a wife? What *do* you mean? Where is she?"

"They took her away, Monsieur."

"So: 'they took her away!' Humph!" (To Bonacieux the 'Humph' complicated matters all the more.)

"So they took her away. Who, Monsieur? Do you know who abducted her?"

"I think so."

"Who?"

"By your leave, Monsieur le Commissaire, I would not dare accuse anyone . . . I only have suspicions. . . ."

"Whom do you suspect? Come on, speak out, man!"

This question put Monsieur Bonacieux in a very tight corner. Should he deny or should he confess? Denial would imply that he knew too much, confession that he was eager to co-operate; he therefore determined to tell everything. Eagerly he said:

"I suspect a tall dark man . . . a distinguished-looking gentleman . . . a great lord, I dare say . . . if I am not in error, it seems to me that he followed us . . . my wife and me . . . several times . . . when I waited for her at the Louvre to take her home. . . ."

At this point, Monsieur le Commissaire gave evidence of a certain anxiety:

"His name?"

"I wouldn't know his name, Monsieur. But if ever I saw him, I could spot him out of a thousand."

"Out of a thousand, eh?" The Commissioner frowned. "Out of a thousand, you say?"

Bonacieux, with a sense of past blunder and impending ruin, mumbled:

"What I mean is . . . I mean, Monsieur. . . ."

"You mean that you would recognize him out of a thousand. Very well, so much for today. Meanwhile, I shall report that you know who abducted your wife."

"I didn't say I knew him. On the contrary. . . ."

"Prisoner dismissed! Take him away."

"Where, Monsieur le Commissaire?"

"Clap him into a cell!"

"What sort of cell?"

"Clap him into the handiest cell you find so but it be secure!"

The Commissioner's indifference filled Bonacieux with horror:

"Alas, alas," he mused, "misfortune has fallen upon my gray hairs. Undoubtedly my wife committed some horrible crime . . . I am suspected of being her accomplice . . . I shall pay for it, all on her account . . . she has probably confessed I know what all this is about . . . I shall suffer because woman is a weak vessel . . . the Commissioner said 'the handiest cell you can find' . . . I know: one night, twelve short hours, and then the wheel, the gallows . . . Ah God, have mercy on my soul! . . ."

The guards, hardened by use to the lamentations of prisoners, whisked Monsieur Bonacieux off while the Commissioner wrote a summary report of the proceedings.

Though his cell was not too disagreeable, Bonacieux could not sleep a wink. All night long he sat rooted to his stool, trembling at the slightest rumor; and, when the first rays of daylight crept into his cell, the dawn seemed to him dismal and funereal. Suddenly the bolts of his door shot back and he gave a terrible start. Yes, now surely they had come to take him to the scaffold. When, to his surprise, he saw no executioner but instead the Commissioner and the clerk of yesterday's interview, he was ready to embrace them both.

"This trouble you are in has become ever so much more complicated overnight," the Commissioner informed Bonacieux. "I advise you to tell the whole truth. Only full repentance will appease the Cardinal's anger."

"But I am ready to say everything, at least everything that I know. Won't you please question me, Monsieur?"

"Well, in the first place: where is your wife?"

"She was abducted."

"But at five-thirty yesterday afternoon, thanks to your efforts, she escaped."

"My wife? Escaped? Poor, poor woman! If she escaped, I swear it is no fault of mine!"

"You visited your neighbor Monsieur d'Artagnan yesterday. You had a long conversation with him. What was your business?"

"Yes, yes, Monsieur le Commissaire, yes, it is true, I confess I acted foolishly in visiting Monsieur d'Artagnan."

"The purpose of your visit?"

"I called to beg him to help me find my wife again. I thought I was right in looking for her. But apparently I was wrong and I beg your pardon most humbly."

"How did Monsieur d'Artagnan react to your proposal?"

"Monsieur d'Artagnan promised to help me. Alas, I soon realized that he was betraying me."

"You are attempting to obstruct justice, my good man. Do you deny that Monsieur d'Artagnan agreed to drive away the police officers? Do you deny that he kept your wife in hiding?"

"Monsieur d'Artagnan abducted my wife! Monsieur le Commissaire, what on earth do you mean?"

"Fortunately Monsieur d'Artagnan is in our hands. We shall at once confront you with him."

"By my faith, I ask for nothing better," cried Bonacieux. "I shall not be sorry to see the face of somebody I know."

"Show Monsieur d'Artagnan in," the Commissioner ordered. The guards admitted Athos.

"Monsieur d'Artagnan," said the Commissioner, "will you please state what happened between you and Monsieur here?"

"But Monsieur," Bonacieux objected, "this is not Monsieur d'Artagnan."

"What? This is not Monsieur d'Artagnan?"

"No, not by any manner of means."

"Then what is Monsieur's name?"

"I cannot tell you, Monsieur le Commissaire. I do not know this gentleman."

"You do not know him?"

"No, Monsieur."

"You have never seen him?"

"Yes, I have seen him, but I do not know his name."

"Your name, Monsieur," snapped the Commissioner.

"Athos," the musketeer replied.

"That is not a man's name," the wretched interrogator protested, losing his head. "Athos is the name of a mountain."

"Athos is nevertheless my name."

"But you said your name was D'Artagnan?"

"*I* said that?"

"Certainly you did."

"No, Monsieur le Commissaire. Somebody asked me was I Monsieur d'Artagnan; I said: 'Do you really think so.' The guards declared they were positive I *was* D'Artagnan. Who was *I* to contradict them? After all, I might have been wrong about my own identity."

"Monsieur, you are insulting the majesty of the law."

"In no wise, Monsieur."

"You are Monsieur d'Artagnan."

"There, you see, once again I hear I am Monsieur d'Artagnan."

"Monsieur le Commissaire," Bonacieux interrupted, "*I* can tell you there is not the least doubt about the matter. Monsieur d'Artagnan is my lodger and, though he does not pay his rent, or rather because he does not pay his rent, I most certainly know him. Monsieur d'Artagnan is a youth barely nineteen or twenty years old; this gentleman here must be at least thirty. Monsieur d'Artagnan serves in the Guards under Monsieur des Essarts; this gentleman belongs to Monsieur de Tréville's Musketeers. Just look at his uniform, Monsieur le Commissaire, look at his uniform."

"By God, that's true!" the Commissioner gasped. But before he could take action, the door swung open and one of the gatekeepers of the Bastille introduced a messenger who handed the Commissioner a letter.

"Oh, poor woman, poor woman!" sighed the Commissioner, as he finished reading the message.

"What's that? What did you say? Whom are you talking about? Not my wife, I hope."

"Precisely: your wife. You're in plenty of trouble now, believe me!"

"But look here, Monsieur le Commissaire," cried the haberdasher, overcome, "will you be good enough to tell me how I can get into worse trouble because of what my wife may be doing while I languish in prison?"

"It is quite simple. Your wife is carrying out the diabolical plans which the pair of you previously agreed upon."

"I swear to you, Monsieur le Commissaire, that you are making a most tragic mistake. I know nothing about what my wife was supposed to be doing, I am completely foreign to what she may have done, and if she has made a fool of herself, I renounce her, I abjure her, I curse her."

"Come, Monsieur le Commissaire," said Athos disdainfully, "if I am no longer needed here, pray send me somewhere else. I find your Monsieur Bonacieux a very tiresome person."

"Take the prisoners back to their cells." The Commissioner included Athos and Bonacieux in the same gesture of dismissal. "See that they are guarded more closely than ever."

"I must observe," Athos declared with his usual phlegm, "that you are interested in Monsieur d'Artagnan, I scarcely see how I can replace him."

"Do as I said," the Commissioner told his guards. "Watch these men carefully!"

Athos shrugged his shoulders and followed the guards silently, but Monsieur Bonacieux set up howls of lamentation. Led back to the same cell he had occupied the night before, he sat there all day, weeping like a real haberdasher. As he himself had said, he was no soldier. In the evening, at about nine, just as he was preparing to retire, he heard steps echoing ever louder and closer in the corridor. The door of his cell was flung open and the guards appeared. Then an officer, close behind the guards, commanded:

"Follow me!"

"Follow you?" cried Bonacieux. "Follow you at this hour? Where to? O Lord, where to?"

"Where we are commanded to lead you."

"But that is no answer, Monsieur."

"It is the only answer we can give you."

"O God, O God," cried the wretched haberdasher, "now indeed I am lost."

Moving like an automaton, he followed the familiar corridor, crossed a courtyard, then another large building in front of which stood a carriage, flanked by four guards on horseback.

"Get in," said the officer, hoisting him on the seat and settling himself on Bonacieux's right. A guard locked the door, and the rolling prison moved off, slow as a hearse. Through the padlocked windows, the prisoner could see a house here, a pavement there, but, a true Parisian, he recognized each street by its stones, signboards and lamp-posts. As the carriage approached Saint-Paul, where prisoners from the Bastille were usually executed, he all but fainted. Twice he made the sign of the Cross, then realized he was spared. The carriage rolled on.

Further on, a new wave of terror swept over him as the carriage passed by the Cimetière Saint-Jean, the burial place of State criminals. But he found consolation in recalling that their heads were usually severed from their bodies before interment, whereas his head was still on his shoulders.

Next the carriage moved towards the Place de Grève; he identified their itinerary by the pointed roofwork of the Hôtel de Ville. Suddenly the carriage whisked under an arcade and Bonacieux knew all was over.

"Monsieur l'Officier," he cried, "let me confess my sins."

The officer refusing, Bonacieux screamed so shrilly that the other threatened:

"Shut up, idiot, or I'll clap a gag on you!"

Bonacieux considered these words minatory yet reassuring. Were he destined for execution on the Place de Grève, no gagging was necessary, for the carriage was arriving . . . was crossing . . . and now had left the fatal spot far behind. . . .

One more station to his Calvary remained: the Croix-du-Trahoir. This time, no doubt remained, for all minor criminals were put to death there. What vanity for the haberdasher to flatter himself that he was worthy of Saint-Paul or the Place de Grève! Alas, no: journey's end was surely the Place de la Croix-du-Trahoir! He could not yet distinguish that dreadful cross but he could almost feel it advancing to meet him. Twenty paces from it, he heard a tumult of voices. The carriage stopped.

This was more than poor Bonacieux could stand. Crushed by the emotions he had undergone, our haberdasher uttered so feeble a moan that you would have sworn it was the last sigh of a dying man.

This time he really fainted.

XIV

THE MAN OF MEUNG

The crowd near the Croix-du-Trahoir was not awaiting a victim; it was contemplating a man who had just been hanged. The carriage stopped for a moment, then pursued its way along the Rue Saint-Honoré, to turn down the Rue des Bons-Enfants, and finally pull up before a low square door. Two guards hundled Bonacieux, supported by the officer, down a corridor, up a stairway, and suddenly by a wholly mechanical process, Bonacieux found himself in an antechamber.

He walked as a somnambulist, dimly perceiving objects as through a mist, apprehending sounds that he could not identify. Had his life depended upon it, he could have summoned no gesture of apology, no cry for mercy. He occupied a hard wooden bench, a dazed man, his back glued to the wall, his arms hanging limply at his sides, in exactly the place where the guards had deposited him.

Presently he looked about him. There seemed to be no sign of danger ... he saw no object threatening his life ... he realized that he sat on a comfortably upholstered bench ... the walls were lined with handsome Cordovan leather ... great red damask curtains, fastened by gold clasps, fluttered at the window. ...

Gradually, convinced that his fears were exaggerated, he proceeded to wag his head up and down, right and left. As nobody seemed to object to this, he gathered sufficient courage to pull back first his right leg, then his left; finally, with the help of both hands, he lifted himself from the bench and rose to his feet.

Just then an officer—a man of pleasant mien—opened a door, said a few words to somebody within, and turning to the haberdasher:

"Are you Bonacieux?"

"Yes, Monsieur l'Officier," Bonacieux stammered, more dead than alive. "At your service, Monsieur."

"Step in here, please," said the officer, effacing himself to allow a startled, silent Bonacieux to enter a room where he sensed that he was being expected. It was a large room, set aside from the rest of the mansion and richly tapestried; weapons of all kinds adorned the walls; a fire burned in the grate though it was but late September. A square table stood conspicuously in the middle of the room, covered with books and papers, and over them a huge map of the city of La Rochelle.

A man stood with his back to the fireplace. Of medium size, of proud and haughty mien, he had a noble brow, piercing eyes, and a thin face, its thinness emphasized by a slight mustache and a short tapering beard. Though he was scarcely thirty-six or at most thirty-seven, his hair, mustache and beard were turning gray. He wore no sword but otherwise he looked every inch a soldier. A patina of dust on his buff boots indicated that he had been riding on horseback that day.

It was Armand-Jean Duplessis, Cardinal de Richelieu. But nothing in his appearance suggested the man as he is represented today. Here was no broken-down old man, suffering like a martyr, his body bent, his voice failing, his frame buried in an armchair as in a tomb, a being still alive only by virtue of his genius and standing up to all Europe only by virtue of his inflexible will. No, here was the Cardinal as he really looked at this period, a gallant and gifted cavalier, already frail, physically, but sustained by that moral power which made him one of the most extraordinary men who ever lived. Here was the statesman who had upheld the Duc de Nevers in his Duchy of Mantua, who had captured Nîmes, Castres and Uzès, and who, even now, was preparing to drive the British from the Isle de Ré and to besiege La Rochelle.

At first glance nothing in his appearance denoted a prince of the Church; only those who knew him could have guessed who he was.

The unhappy haberdasher stood by the door; the man by the fireplace gazed at him piercingly as though to read every circumstance of his past. After a moment of silence, he asked:

"Is this the man Bonacieux?"

"Yes, Monseigneur."

"Good. Give me those papers, please. Thank you; you may withdraw."

The officer picked up a sheaf of papers from the table, handed them to the gentleman, bowed low and retired. Bonacieux recognized these papers as the record of his examination at the Bastille. From time to time, the gentleman by the fireside raised his eyes from the script and plunged them, daggerlike, through Bonacieux's heart. After ten minutes of reading and ten seconds of scrutiny the Cardinal must have decided that no man with a face like Bonacieux's could have plotted against the State. Still, it might be useful to question him further.

"You are accused of high treason," he said slowly.

"So I have been told, Monseigneur." Bonacieux was careful to address his questioner by the title he had heard the officer use. "But I swear I know nothing of all this."

"You have plotted with your wife," the Cardinal repressed a smile, "with Madame de Chevreuse and with My Lord Duke of Buckingham."

"No, Monseigneur, but I have heard my wife mention those names."

"Under what circumstances?"

"I heard my wife say that the Cardinal de Richelieu lured the Duke of Buckingham to Paris in order to ruin both him and the Queen."

"Your wife said that?" the Cardinal demanded.

"Yes, Monseigneur. But I told her she was wrong to talk about such things. I said that His Eminence was incapable—"

"Hold your tongue, fool!"

"That is exactly what my wife said, Monseigneur."

"Do you know who abducted your wife?"

"No, Monseigneur."

"Yet you have suspicions."

"Ay, Monseigneur, I *had* suspicions. But I dismissed them after talking with Monsieur le Commissaire."

"Your wife escaped. Did you know that?"

"I learned it in prison, Monseigneur. I was told of it by Monsieur le Commissaire, a most kindly and understanding gentleman."

Again the Cardinal repressed a smile:

"Then you are ignorant of what has happened to your wife since her flight?"

"Ay, Monseigneur. Doubtless she returned to the Louvre."

"She had not returned by one o'clock this morning."

"Ah God! What can have happened to her?"

"We shall find out, you may be sure. No one can conceal anything from the Cardinal. The Cardinal knows everything."

"In that case, Monseigneur, do you think the Cardinal would kindly tell me what has happened to my wife?"

"He may and he may not. First, you must confess all you know of your wife's relations with Madame de Chevreuse."

"Monseigneur, I know nothing at all. I have never seen Madame de Chev—"

"When you went to call for your wife at the Louvre, did you always take her straight home?"

"Almost never. She always had to do some shopping. I usually left her at the draper's."

"What draper's?"

"There were two, Monseigneur."

"Where did they live?"

"One in the Rue de Vaugirard, the other in the Rue de La Harpe."

"Did you accompany your wife into these houses?"

"Never, Monseigneur. I used to wait at the door."

"What excuse did she give you for going in alone?"

"She gave me no excuse. She told me to wait and I waited."

"What an accommodating husband you are, Monsieur Bonacieux!"

The haberdasher thrilled as he heard himself addressed by name. Things seemed to be going better; perhaps his trouble was clearing up.

"Would you recognize the doors of these houses?"

"Certainly."

"Where exactly are these drapers' establishments?"

"Number 25 Rue de Vaugirard, Number 75 Rue de La Harpe."

"Excellent!" the Cardinal commented. Then he took up a silver bell, rang it and, addressing an officer who appeared immediately:

"Find out if Rochefort is here," he whispered. "If so, send him in at once."

"The Comte de Rochefort is here and craves immediate audience with Your Eminence."

("Your Eminence," Bonacieux thought, his eyes agoggle.)

Five seconds later, the door opened, a person entered—

"That's the man," Bonacieux cried.

"The man?"

"That's the man who abducted my wife."

His Eminence again shook the silver bell. The officer reappeared:

"Hand this fellow over to the guards. I shall want him presently."

"No, no, Monseigneur, it is *not* the man ... I made a mistake ... I was thinking of another man who does not look like this gentleman at all ... This gentleman here is a respectable man...."

"Take away this idiot," the Cardinal said curtly. Once again Bonacieux found an officer picking him up bodily and conveying him forcibly to a pair of guards.

The gentleman whose entrance caused Bonacieux's dismissal watched his exit impatiently. As soon as the door closed, he turned to the Cardinal:

"They saw each other," he whispered.

"You mean—?"

"The Queen ... the Duke...."

"Where?" asked the Cardinal.

"At the Louvre."

"Are you sure?"

"Certain, Monsieur le Cardinal."

"How do you know this?"

"I heard it from Madame de Lannoy. Your Eminence knows how devoted she is to your interests."

"Why did she not inform me earlier?"

"By chance or by intention, Her Majesty made Madame de Surgis sleep in her chamber; she kept her at her side all day. Madame de Lannoy was denied access—"

"Well, we have been roundly beaten. The point now is to take vengeance."

"Your Eminence may count upon my wholehearted efforts...."

In answer to the Cardinal's further questions, Rochefort explained what had happened. The Queen was with her ladies-in-waiting in her bedroom when a servant presented Her Majesty with a handkerchief from her laundress, where-upon Her Majesty displayed much concern. In spite of the rouge on her cheeks, she turned very pale and asked her ladies to await her for ten minutes. She left through the door of her alcove.

"Why didn't Madame de Lannoy inform you of this at once?" the Cardinal interrupted.

"Madame de Lannoy could not make out what was going on. The Queen had told her ladies to wait for her; Madame de Lannoy dared not disobey Her Majesty."

The Queen, Rochefort reported, was away from her bedchamber for three-quarters of an hour; Dona Estefana alone accompanied her. She returned, picked up a small rosewood casket stamped with her coat-of-arms, and went away again. This time she was not gone long, but she returned without the casket.

"Does Madame de Lannoy know what was in this casket?"

"The diamond studs His Majesty gave the Queen."

"And Her Majesty returned without the casket?"

"Yes, Your Eminence."

"Madame de Lannoy thinks Her Majesty gave it to Buckingham."

"She is certain of it."

"How can she be certain?"

"During the course of the day, Madame de Lannoy, as Lady of the Queen's Wardrobe, looked for this casket, seemed worried not to find it and finally asked the Queen about it—"

"And the Queen—?"

"The Queen blushed. She explained embarrassedly that, having broken one of the studs the day before, she had sent it to her goldsmith to be repaired."

"We must immediately find out from the goldsmith if this is true or not."

"Send to the jeweler's at once to find out if the repairs were made."

"I have already done so, Your Eminence."

"And the goldsmith—?"

". . . knows absolutely nothing about the matter."

"Good, good, Rochefort, all is not lost! Perhaps, indeed, everything is for the best."

"Indeed I have no doubt that Your Eminence's genius—"

". . . will yet repair the blunders of his agent! Is that what you mean?"

"That is precisely what I would have said had Your Eminence let me finish my sentence."

"Meanwhile, do you know where the Duchesse de Chevreuse and the Duke of Buckingham are hiding?"

"No, Monseigneur. My agents could discover nothing positive on that score."

"*I* happen to *know*."

"*You*, Monseigneur?"

"Yes. Or at least I have shrewd suspicions. One stayed at 25 Rue de Vaugirard, the other at 75 Rue de La Harpe."

"Does Your Eminence wish me to have them arrested?"

"Too late. Both will have fled by now."

"We should at least make sure of this."

"Well, take ten of my guardsmen and search both houses thoroughly."

"I shall go instantly, Monseigneur."

Left alone, the Cardinal reflected for an instant, then rang the bell a third time. The same officer reappeared.

"Bring the prisoner in again," the Cardinal ordered.

Monsieur Bonacieux was introduced afresh and, at a sign from the Cardinal, the officer withdrew.

"You have deceived me," the Cardinal said sternly.

"I? I deceive Your Eminence!"

"When your wife went to the Rue de Vaugirard and the Rue de La Harpe, she was not calling on drapers."

"What was she up to then, dear God?"

"She was visiting the Duchesse de Chevreuse and the Duke of Buckingham."

"Yes," cried Bonacieux, recalling what he could of these errands. "Your Eminence is right. Several times I told my wife it was surprising to find drapers living in such houses, without signs at the door. But she always laughed at me. Ah, Monseigneur," the haberdasher threw himself at the statesman's feet, "how truly you are the great Cardinal, the man of genius whom all the world reveres."

Petty as was his triumph over so base a creature as Bonacieux, His Eminence nevertheless savored it gratefully for a moment. Then, almost immediately, inspired anew, he smiled ever so fleetingly and offered the haberdasher his hand.

"Come, rise, friend, you are a worthy man."

"The Cardinal has touched my hand! I have touched the hand of the great man! The great man has called me his friend."

"Yes, my friend, yes," said the Cardinal with that paternal tone which he could assume on occasion, but which did not deceive those who knew him, "as you have been unjustly suspected, you shall be rewarded. Here, take this purse; it has one hundred pistoles in it. And pardon me for misjudging you."

"*I* pardon *you*, Monseigneur!" Bonacieux hesitated to take the purse, fearing that the Cardinal was jesting. "But Your Eminence is free to arrest me, to have me tortured, even to have me hanged; you are the master and I can have nothing to say. *I* pardon *you*, Monseigneur. You cannot mean that!"

"My dear Monsieur Bonacieux, you are acting most generously and I thank you. Take this purse and let there be no hard feelings between us."

"Hard feelings? No, Monseigneur, I am delighted—"

"Adieu, then. Or rather au revoir, for I hope that we shall meet again."

"Whenever Monseigneur wishes. I am always at Your Eminence's orders."

"We shall meet again often, you may be sure. I have enjoyed our conversation very much."

"Oh, Monseigneur!"

"Au revoir, Monsieur Bonacieux." The Cardinal motioned him out. "Au revoir."

Bonacieux bowed to the very ground and retreated, bowing. When he reached the antechamber, the Cardinal heard him shouting at the top of his lungs:

"Vive Monseigneur! Long live His Eminence! Hurrah for the Cardinal!"

This vociferous manifestation of the haberdasher's enthusiasm brought another fleeting smile to the Cardinal's lips. As the cheers faded into the distance:

"Good!" said His Eminence. "There goes a man who would give his life for me."

Then he returned to the map of La Rochelle on his table and, having examined it minutely, picked up a pencil and traced the line along which, eighteen months later, the famous dyke was to block the port of the beleaguered city. Rochefort entered. Though lost in the most vital and detailed planning, the Cardinal nevertheless looked up and rose eagerly.

"Well?"

"Well, Your Eminence, a young woman of some twenty-six years of age stayed in the Rue de Vaugirard; a man of about forty in the Rue de La Harpe. The lady spent four days here, the gentleman five; she left last night, he this morning."

"It was our friends, of course!" The Cardinal glanced at the clock. "Too late now to catch them: Madame de Chevreuse is at Tours, Buckingham at Boulogne. We shall have to settle all this in London."

"What are Your Eminence's orders?"

"The strictest silence about what has happened . . . let the Queen believe herself perfectly secure, she must not dream we know her secret . . . she must be made to believe we are following up some other plot. . . . send for the Keeper of the Seals."

"What has Your Eminence done with that fellow—"

"What fellow?"

"The haberdasher Bonacieux."

"All that could be done with such a man. From now on he will spy on his wife night and day."

The Comte de Rochefort bowed deeply. Here was a master of intrigue making of a conventional salutation a tribute to genius.

Richelieu sat down, penned a letter, stamped it with his private seal, and rang the bell. The orderly officer entered for the fourth time.

"Send for Vitray," the Cardinal ordered. "Tell him he is to go on a journey."

An instant later, Vitray, booted and spurred, stood before the Cardinal.

"Vitray," said His Eminence, "you are to leave immediately for London. You must not stop a moment on the way. You will deliver this letter to Milady. Here is an order for two hundred pistoles; call on my treasurer and get the money. You shall have as much again if you return within six days, your mission accomplished."

The messenger bowed, took the letter and the order, and retired without a word.

The letter read:

Milady

You are instructed to go to the first ball or public ceremony that His Grace the Duke of Buckingham may attend. He will wear on his doublet twelve diamond studs; you will approach him and cut off two of them.

You are to inform me as soon as you have these studs in your possession.

XV
MEN OF LAW AND MEN OF THE SWORD

Next day Athos being still absent, D'Artagnan and Porthos reported his disappearance to Monsieur de Tréville. As for Aramis, he had obtained a leave of absence for four days; it was believed he had gone to Rouen on family affairs.

Now Monsieur de Tréville was father and friend to his soldiers, the humblest and most obscure of them, in musketeer uniform, was as certain of his help and support as he could be of a brother's.

Accordingly Monsieur de Tréville repaired instantly to the bureau of the Lieutenant Provost, the highest police magistrate; the officer in command of the Croix Rouge district was summoned and some time later reported that Athos was in custody at the Fort L'Evêque prison. He had gone through the same questionings and investigations as Bonacieux had gone through and had been brought face to face with the haberdasher. He had refused to speak up because he wished to allow D'Artagnan the time necessary to carry out his plans. This interval assured, Athos boldly declared his own name, expressing some surprise that his identity had been confounded with that of D'Artagnan. He added that he knew neither Monsieur nor Madame Bonacieux ... that he had never spoken to either ... that he was involved in these idle proceedings only because he had called on his friend Monsieur d'Artagnan at ten o'clock ... that he had previously dined at Monsieur de Tréville's until shortly before ten ... and that several gentlemen of rank, including the Duc de La Trémouille, could testify to that effect. ...

Now men of the long robe are at all times eager to be revenged upon men of the long sword; but the firm and direct statement Athos presented took the magistrate somewhat aback and the names of Monsieur de Tréville and the Duc de La Trémouille were indeed impressive.

Athos was then sent to the Cardinal but unfortunately the Cardinal was closeted with the King at the Louvre. At precisely that time, Monsieur de Tréville, having left first the Lieutenant Provost, then the Governor of the Fort l'Evêque prison, arrived to call upon the King. As

Captain of Musketeers, Monsieur de Tréville had privileges of access to the royal presence at all times.

It was common gossip that the King was violently prejudiced against the Queen. The Cardinal, who in matters of intrigue, was infinitely more wary of women than of men, made a point of encouraging his master's prejudices. Among these, one of the chief irritants was the friendship Anne of Austria entertained for Madame de Chevreuse. Between them these two women occasioned His Majesty more anxiety than the wars with Spain, the quarrel with England and the troublous state of his country's finances. He was firmly convinced that Madame de Chevreuse served the Queen not only in her political activity but—more torturous still!—in her amorous intrigues.

The mere mention of Madame de Chevreuse's name infuriated the King. Had she not been exiled to Tours, was she not supposed to be in that city? How then dared she come to Paris and stay there five days as if there were no police in the capital? And here was the Cardinal reporting these facts quite blandly. The King flew into a towering rage.

Capricious and unfaithful as he was, His Majesty nevertheless prided himself on the epithets of Louis the Just and Louis the Chaste, a crochet which history will find it difficult to explain to posterity save by deeds and facts that fly in the face of logic.

For the King it was offensive enough to learn that Madame de Chevreuse had come to Paris. But he was angry beyond belief when he heard that the Queen had renewed relations with her by correspondence . . . that the two women had formed what was then mysteriously called a cabal . . . that he, the Cardinal himself, on the point of unraveling the most mysterious details of this intrigue, was suddenly foiled   that the Cardinal, in possession of all necessary proof, was about to arrest, *in flagrante delicto,* the Queen's emissary to the banished Madame de Chevreuse . . . that at this moment a musketeer had dared interrupt the course of justice in the most violent fashion . . . and that this same musketeer had fallen, sword in hand, upon honest men of the law who were investigating the affair in the line of duty. . . .

Losing all self-control, Louis XIII started toward the Queen's apartment, his features set in that mute, pale indignation which when it broke out drove this monarch to commit the most pitiless cruelties. And yet, so far, the Cardinal had not breathed a word about My Lord Duke of Buckingham.

At exactly this point Monsieur de Tréville entered, cool, polite and impeccably clad. Realizing from the Cardinal's presence and the King's sullen rage what had occurred, Monsieur de Tréville felt very much as Samson must have felt among the Philistines. Louis XIII had his hand on the doorknob when Monsieur de Tréville entered. The King swung round:

"Your arrival is timely, Monsieur," he said testily, for when he lost his temper he was incapable of dissembling. "I have just learned some pretty things about your musketeers."

"Sire," Tréville countered phlegmatically, "*I* have some pretty things to tell Your Majesty about his men of law."

"Pray explain," the King commanded haughtily.

"I have the honor to inform your Majesty," Monsieur de Tréville continued coolly as ever, "that a party of commissioners, investigators and policemen—excellent folk, I have no doubt, but apparently rabid enemies of all who wear the King's uniform—took it upon themselves to enter the house of one of my musketeers. They dared arrest him without warrant, led him away through the streets and tossed him into the prison of Fort L'Evêque. I say without warrant, Sire, because they refused to show me any order; and when I say one of *my* musketeers, I should more properly say one of *your* musketeers. I hasten to add that the soldier in question is a man of irreproachable conduct and of almost illustrious repute. Undoubtedly Your Majesty recalls him favorably; his name is Athos."

"Athos?" the King mechanically repeated. "Yes, as a matter of fact I do know that name."

"If Your Majesty recalls," Monsieur de Tréville insisted, "Monsieur Athos is the musketeer who, in the untoward duel you know of, had the misfortune to wound Monsieur de Cahusac so grievously." Tréville paused a moment to make his point, then, turning to the Cardinal: "By the way, Monsieur le Cardinal, I trust Monsieur de Cahusac has recovered."

"Quite, thank you," the Cardinal replied, biting his lips.

"May it please Your Majesty, here are the facts. Monsieur Athos had gone to call upon one of his friends who was out. The friend is a young man from Béarn, a cadet in Your Majesty's Guards; Monsieur des Essarts is his commanding officer. Athos had barely made himself comfortable at his friend's and taken up a book while awaiting his friend's return when a motley crew of bailiffs and soldiers laid siege to the house, broke down several doors—"

(The Cardinal made a sign to the King, as if to say: "That was on account of the matter I just mentioned.")

"We know all about *that!*" the King retorted. "It was all done in our service."

"Then it was also in Your Majesty's service that one of my musketeers, an innocent man, was seized, hemmed in between two guards like a malefactor and, gallant gentleman though he is, was paraded through the streets to serve as the laughing stock of an insolent rabble? This gentleman, I may add," Monsieur de Tréville's voice rose ever so slightly, "this gentleman," he emphasized, "has shed his blood at least a dozen times on behalf of Your Majesty and he is ready to do so again."

"Indeed?" The King seemed somewhat shaken. "Is that what actually happened?"

"Monsieur de Tréville has failed to mention an important fact, Sire," the Cardinal commented drily. "One hour previously this innocent musketeer and paragon of gallantry, his sword in hand, struck down four commissioners who had been sent personally by myself to inquire into a matter of the highest importance."

"I defy Your Eminence to prove that!" cried Monsieur de Tréville with typically Gascon frankness and soldierly bluntness. "Exactly one hour previously, Monsieur Athos—who, I may say confidentially, is a man of lofty rank—had just finished doing me the honor of dining at my board and was conversing in my drawing room with the Duc de La Trémouille, the Comte de Châlus and myself."

The King glanced quizzically at the Cardinal.

"Official reports do not lie," the Cardinal said meaningfully in reply to the King's mute query. "The officers of the law who were molested drew up this official record which I have the honor to bring to Your Majesty's attention."

Tréville broke in: "Is the written testimony of a man of law to be compared to the word of honor of a soldier?"

"Come, come, Tréville, hush!"

But Tréville persisted:

"If His Eminence entertains the slightest suspicion against one of my musketeers, the justice of Monsieur le Cardinal is famed enough for me to demand an inquiry of my own."

"If I am not mistaken," the Cardinal observed impassively, "a Béarnais, a friend of this musketeer's, lives in the house which my police raided."

"Your Eminence means Monsieur d'Artagnan?"

"I mean a young man you have taken under your wing, Monsieur."

"Yes, D'Artagnan, Your Eminence, precisely."

"Do you not suspect this young man of giving bad counsel to—"

"To Monsieur Athos, a man double his age?" Monsieur de Tréville asked wonderingly; and, before the Cardinal could reply, "No, Monseigneur, I do not suspect anything of the kind. Besides, Monsieur d'Artagnan also spent the evening with me."

"Well, well!" the Cardinal exclaimed. "Everybody seems to have spent the evening with you."

"Does His Eminence venture to doubt my word?" Tréville asked hotly.

"Heaven forbid!" the Cardinal said piously. "But tell me, at what time was he at your house?"

"I can tell Your Eminence *that* quite positively. Just as he arrived I happened to notice that it was half-past eight by the clock though I had thought it was later."

"And at what time did he leave your house?"

"At ten-thirty—an hour after the event."

The Cardinal, who did not for a moment question Tréville's integrity, felt victory slipping through his fingers. Here was a mystery he must solve. "After all, Monsieur," he went on, "Athos was certainly picked up at the house in the Rue des Fossoyeurs."

"Is one friend forbidden to visit another? Is a musketeer in my company forbidden to fraternize with a guardsman in Monsieur des Essart's?"

"Yes, when they meet in a house that is suspect."

"Quite so, Tréville," the King remarked. "The house is under suspicion. Perhaps you did not know it?"

"Indeed, Sire, I did not. Of course some part of the house may bear investigation but not Monsieur d'Artagnan's apartment. That, I can swear to! If I can believe what the young man says, Sire—and I do—Your Majesty has no more devoted servant and the Cardinal no more profound admirer."

The King turned toward His Eminence and, with a suggestion of malice:

"Surely this must be the youth who wounded De Jussac in that unfortunate encounter near the convent of the Carmelites?"

The Cardinal blushed.

"Yes, Sire," Tréville put in quickly. "And he wounded Bernajoux the day after. Your Majesty has an excellent memory!"

"Come, what shall we decide?" the King asked His Eminence.

"That concerns Your Majesty more than myself," the Cardinal replied. "I maintain that he is guilty."

"And I deny it!" Tréville retorted. "But His Majesty has judges and those judges will decide."

"Agreed!" said the King. "Let us refer the matter to the judges. It is their business to judge and judge they shall!"

"And yet," Tréville commented. "In these sorry times, it seems a pity that the noblest of men must be subjected to obloquy and persecution.

"The Army will resent it, I am sure; are your soldiers varlets that the police may molest them for alleged misdemeanors?"

These words were deliberately insolent; Tréville hoped for an explosion. Does not a mine sprung burst afire and does not fire shed considerable light?

"Misdemeanors!" The King scowled. "Misdemeanors indeed! And what do *you* know about them, Monsieur? Stick to your musketeers and do not annoy us with such statements. To hear you speak, if by ill luck some musketeer should happen to be arrested, all France is in danger. Good heavens! What a pother about one musketeer! By God, I shall arrest ten of them, fifty, a hundred, the whole company without tolerating a whisper of comment."

"So long as the musketeers are victims of your suspicion, Sire, the musketeers are guilty. Therefore, as Your Majesty sees, I am prepared to surrender my sword. Having accused my musketeers, the Cardinal will, I am sure, proceed to accuse me. Accordingly I prefer to constitute myself a prisoner with Monsieur Athos, who is already under arrest and with Monsieur d'Artagnan who doubtless soon will be."

"You Gascon firebrand, will you have done?" said the King.

"Sire," Tréville replied evenly, "pray order my musketeer to be returned to me or else to be tried by process of law."

"He shall be tried," said the Cardinal.

"So much the better then. I shall request His Majesty to allow me to plead in his behalf."

The King, fearing a public scandal, suggested:

"If His Eminence had not certain personal motives . . . ?"

"Excuse me, Sire," the Cardinal interrupted, forestalling what he knew the King was about to say. "The moment Your Majesty considers me prejudiced, I beg to withdraw."

"Come now, Tréville," the King urged, "will you swear by my father that Monsieur Athos was at your house during the event and that he had no hand in it?"

"By your glorious father and by yourself whom I love and revere above all else in the world, I swear it!"

"Pray reflect, Sire," the Cardinal coaxed, "if we release the prisoner, we shall never discover the truth."

"Monsieur Athos will be at hand," Tréville retorted, "ready to testify whenever the gownsmen care to question him. He will not desert, Monsieur le Cardinal, rest assured of that. I will be personally answerable for him."

"Of course he will not desert," the King agreed, "and he can always be found, just as Monsieur de Tréville has said. Moreover—" here the King lowered his voice and glanced beseechingly at His Eminence, "let us give them apparent security. It is good policy to do so."

This policy of Louis XIII made Richelieu smile.

"Order it as you will, Sire; you possess the right of pardon."

"The right of pardon is applicable only to the guilty," Tréville demurred, eager to have the last word, "and my musketeer is innocent. It is not an act of mercy you are about to perform, Sire, but an act of justice."

"He is now at Fort L'Evêque?"

"Yes, Sire, held incommunicado, in solitary confinement, like the lowest of criminals."

"The devil, the devil!" murmured the King. "What must we do?"

"Sign the order for his release, Sire. That will be the end of it," the Cardinal proposed. "I believe with Your Majesty that Monsieur de Tréville's guarantee is more than sufficient."

Tréville bowed respectfully, with a joy not unmixed with fear; he would have preferred stubborn resistance on the part of the Cardinal to this sudden compliance. The King signed the order for release; Tréville accepted it with alacrity. Just as he was leaving, the Cardinal gave him a friendly smile and said to the King:

"A perfect harmony reigns between the Commanding Officer of Your Musketeers, Sire, and his soldiers. That is really very profitable for the service and reflects honor upon all concerned."

Monsieur de Tréville was not fooled by these honeyed words. The

Cardinal would play him some nasty trick or other, and in short order. Who had ever outwitted the Cardinal with impunity? The Captain of Musketeers realized he must make haste, too, for the King might change his mind at any moment. After all it was harder to send a man back to the Bastille or to Fort L'Evêque once he had been released than to detain a man already behind bars.

When, after a triumphant entry into Fort L'Evêque, he liberated Athos he found that the musketeer's quiet indifference had not forsaken him.

Later as soon as Athos met D'Artagnan: "You have had a narrow escape," he told him. "You bested De Jussac; I have just paid the price for your gallantry. But your account with Bernajoux remains to be settled and I advise you to be careful."

Indeed, Monsieur de Tréville had good reason to mistrust the Cardinal and to sense that all was not finished yet. Scarcely had the Captain of Musketeers closed the door behind him than His Eminence said to the King:

"Now that we are alone again, Sire, let us converse seriously, if it please Your Majesty." He paused a moment, then added significantly: "Sire, Buckingham has been in Paris five days; he left Paris this morning."

XVI

Wherein Monsieur Pierre Séguier, Chancellor of France and Keeper of the Seals, Looks More Than Once for a Bell to Ring as Lustily as He Was Wont to Do of Yore

To describe the impression these few words made upon Louis XIII is impossible. The King flushed, then paled; the Cardinal knew at once that his cause had recovered all the ground it had lost.

"My Lord Buckingham in Paris! What brought him here?"

"Doubtless he came to plot with Your Majesty's Huguenots and Spanish enemies."

"No, *pardieu*, no! He came to plot against my honor with Madame de Chevreuse, Madame de Longueville and the Condés."

"Surely not, Sire. Her Majesty is far too discreet to risk such a scandal. And she loves Your Majesty too dearly."

"Woman is a weak vessel, Monsieur le Cardinal. As for her loving me much, I have my own opinion on that score."

"Nevertheless, Sire, I still maintain that the Duke of Buckingham came to Paris on a political errand."

"And *I*, Monsieur le Cardinal, insist that he came for other reasons. If the Queen is guilty, she shall rue it."

"As a matter of fact," the Cardinal continued, "much as I hate to dwell upon such a betrayal, Your Majesty does remind me of an important point. In accordance with Your Majesty's orders, I have questioned Madame de Lannoy several times. This morning she told me that two nights ago the Queen had sat up till a very late hour, that the following morning she had wept a great deal, and that she had spent most of that day writing."

"Ah, she has been writing to him," the King said angrily. "Monsieur le Cardinal," he added, "I *must* have the papers of the Queen!"

"But how can we seize them, Sire? Obviously neither Your Majesty nor I can undertake to do so."

"How did we go about it in the case of the wife of the Maréchal d'Ancre?" cried the King, now in a towering rage. "Eight years ago, I recall, she plotted against the State. Well, we searched her apartment first, then we searched her person, and we found enough to send her to the stake as a witch."

"Madame la Maréchale d'Ancre was but a florentine adventuress, Sire, that is all; whereas the august spouse of Your Majesty is Anne of Austria, Queen of France, one of the mightiest princesses on earth."

"She is all the more guilty for that very reason, Monseigneur; the more she has forgotten the exalted position she occupies, the lower she has fallen. Besides I have long since decided to put an end to all these petty political and amorous intrigues. There is a certain La Porte in her household, is there not?"

"Ay, Your Majesty, I confess I believe him to be the mainspring of all this business."

"Then you agree with me that the Queen is betraying me?"

"I repeat, Sire, I believe that the Queen is plotting against the power of her King, but I do not say she is plotting against his honor."

"And I tell you she is guilty on both counts. Her Majesty does not love me, she loves another, she loves the infamous Buckingham! Why did you not have him arrested while he was in Paris?"

"Arrest the Duke of Buckingham? Arrest the Prime Minister of King Charles the first? How can you think of it, Sire? What a scandal! Then, suppose Your Majesty's suspicions proved justified—and I continue to doubt it—what a terrible mess, what a desperate scandal!"

"But since he behaved like a vagabond and a thief, you should have—"

Louis XIII stopped, frightened at what he was about to say; Richelieu, craning his neck, waited in vain for the word which had died on the monarch's lips.

"I should have—?"

"Nothing, nothing!" said the King. "But all the while he was in Paris, you kept your eye on him?"

"Yes, Sire."

"Where did he lodge?"

"Number 75 Rue de La Harpe."

"Where is that?"

"Near the Luxembourg Palace."

"You are sure he did not meet the Queen?"

"I believe the Queen too loyal to you to have done so."

"But they corresponded. It was to *him* the Queen wrote all day yesterday. Monsieur le Cardinal, I must have those letters."

"But Sire—"

"Monsieur le Cardinal, I must have them at all costs."

"I beg Your Majesty to observe—"

"Are you too betraying me, Monseigneur? Why do you constantly oppose my will? Are you too in league with the Spaniards and the English, with Madame de Chevreuse and with the Queen?"

"Sire," the Cardinal sighed, "I believed I had proved myself above suspicion."

"Monsieur le Cardinal, you heard me: I will have those letters."

"There is but one way—."

"What is that?"

"Monsieur Séguier, Keeper of the Seals, might be entrusted with this task; it rests entirely within the competence of his post."

"Let him be sent for instantly."

"He is probably waiting for me now. We had an engagement this evening, when Your Majesty summoned me, I left word for him to await my return."

"Let him be sent for instantly."

"Your Majesty's orders shall be executed, but—"

"But what?"

"But the Queen may perhaps refuse to obey."

"To obey my orders?"

"Yes, if she does not know these orders come from the King."

"Well then, to dispel any doubts she might have on that matter, I shall go tell her myself."

"I beg you to remember, Sire, that I have done everything in my power to prevent a misunderstanding between Her Majesty and yourself."

"Yes, Monseigneur, I know you are very indulgent—perhaps too indulgent—where the Queen is concerned. In fact, I warn you, we shall have cause to take up that matter presently."

"Whenever it shall please Your Majesty. Meanwhile I shall always remain happy, nay proud, Sire, to assure perfect harmony between my royal masters."

"Good, Monsieur le Cardinal, good. Now, pray send for the Keeper of the Seals; I go to call upon the Queen."

With which the King departed.

The Queen was surrounded by her ladies-in-waiting, Madame de Guitaut, Madame de Sablé, Madame de Montbazon and Madame de Guéménée. In one corner sat the Spanish Lady of the Bedchamber, Dona Estefana, who had followed the Queen from Madrid. Madame de Guéménée was reading aloud and everyone was listening attentively save the Queen, who, on the contrary, had suggested this reading. While pretending to listen, Her Majesty pursued the thread of her own thoughts.

These thoughts, though intent upon love, were tinged with melancholy. The Queen was recalling how she was deprived of her husband's confidence ... how relentlessly the Cardinal's hatred dogged her footsteps ... how Richelieu had never forgiven her for repulsing a more tender sentiment on his part ... how the Queen Mother, Marie de Medici, had once granted Richelieu the favors Anne now refused ... how Richelieu's rancor had pursued the Queen Mother for years after the liaison was over ... how Anne herself had seen her most devoted followers, her most intimate confidants and her most cherished favorites struck down on every side. ... Truly, she was like those unfortunates who are damned with a fatal gift ... she brought ruin to everything she touched ... her very friendship was a fated signal for the persecution of those she befriended ... Madame de Chevreuse and Madame de Vernet in exile ... and now La Porte himself did not conceal from her that he expected to be arrested at any moment. . . .

The Queen was plunged in the darkest of these reflections when the door suddenly opened and the King loomed before her.

Madame de Guéménée stopped dead in the middle of a sentence and dropped the book on her lap. The ladies all rose. A deep silence ensued.

As for the King, he strode rudely past the ladies and stopped squarely in front of the Queen.

"Madame," he said hoarsely, "you are about to receive a visit from the Chancellor who will communicate to you certain matters with which I have charged him."

The unhappy Queen, ceaselessly threatened with divorce, exile and even trial at law, paled under her rouge and automatically inquired:

"But why this visit, Sire? What can the Chancellor tell me that Your Majesty cannot himself tell me?"

For all answer, the King turned on his heel just as the Captain of the Guards, Monsieur de Guitant, announced the Chancellor. By the time Monsieur Séguier, Chancellor and Keeper of the Seals, appeared, the King had vanished through another door. Séguier entered, half smiling, half blushing.

Séguier was by nature the drollest of men. He owed his success to the fact that Des Roches Le Masle, a canon of Notre Dame, who had once served the Cardinal, had referred him to Richelieu as a completely reliable man. The Cardinal trusted him and found no cause to regret it.

Séguier was the subject of numerous anecdotes not the least of which is the following.

After a stormy youth, he retired to a monastery to expiate, for a while at least, the follies of his adolescence. But on entering this holy place, the penitent could not shut the door behind him fast enough to prevent his besetting temptations from following him in. Relentlessly they obsessed him. When he confessed this to the Superior, the latter, seeking to protect him as much as possible, recommended that to exorcise the demon of temptation, Séguier resort to the bell-rope, pulling it with all his might. At the tell-tale clangor, his fellow-monks would know that one of their brothers was being beleaguered by Satan; and the entire community would forthwith take to their prayers.

To the future Chancellor and Keeper of the Seals, this advice seemed eminently sound. He fell heartily to work exorcising the Evil Spirit by dint of the long, frequent and effortful prayers of his fellows. But Satan was not to be so readily dislodged from a bastion so comfortable, familiar and stalwart. Accordingly, fast as the monks increased their supplications, Satan redoubled his temptations so that the bell clanged full-peal day and night.

So extreme was the penitent's desire for mortification that presently the monks no longer had a moment's respite. Day and night they did nothing but walk upstairs and down to chapel. Their ordinary duties called for *matins* at midnight, for *lauds* at sunrise, for *prime* at six, *terce* at nine, *sext* at noon, *none* at three, *vespers* at sunset and *compline* at nine. Now over and above these prayers they were forced to leap up from their bedside, or forsake their work, or forfeit their recreation at any moment and prostrate themselves, night and day, in cell, shop or garden.

Whether Satan abandoned the struggle or the monks grew weary of it remains unknown. But within three arduous months Séguier reappeared in the world with the reputation of having been possessed of the Devil more thoroughly than any man on record.

Forsaking monastic life, Séguier took to the law ... was promoted President of the High Court in his uncle's stead ... embraced the Cardinalist Party, which showed no little wisdom on his part ... became Chancellor ... served His Eminence with zeal in the latter's successive hatred of Marie de Medici and Anne of Austria ... prompted the judges in the Chalais affair ... encouraged the activities of Monsieur de Laffemas ... and finally invested with the Cardinal's complete confidence—so richly earned—he attained the singular commission he was now about to execute. ...

As Séguier entered the Queen was still standing as etiquette demanded until the King had left. The moment he entered she sat down and motioned to her ladies to be seated again on cushions and taborets. In a tone of extreme hauteur she demanded:

"Monsieur, what do you wish? Pray what brings you here?"

"Madame, I am here in the name of the King. My purpose, in all honor and with all respect due to Your Majesty, is to make a thorough examination of Your Majesty's papers."

"What, Monsieur? A search? A search of *my* papers? This is an outrage!"

"I most humbly implore Your Majesty's pardon. In this instance I am but the instrument of the King. His Majesty has just left you, having himself prepared you for my visit."

"So, Monsieur, I am a criminal, it seems? Very well, then; pray search my effects. Estefana, give Monsieur the keys to my drawers and my desk."

For form's sake the Chancellor inspected these, but the Queen would not have entrusted so important a letter to drawer or desk. Having opened, closed and re-opened a variety of drawers and rummaged through a congeries of pigeonholes, he must now perforce bring matters to a head. For all his hesitation, it was his duty now to search the person of the Queen herself. He therefore stepped forward and with the most embarrassed and perplexed air imaginable, ventured:

"Now, Madame, I have come to the principal and most delicate point of my investigation."

Either the Queen did not understand or preferred not to. She looked at Monsieur Séguier, Chancellor and Keeper of the Seals:

"Which is—?"

"Madame, His Majesty is convinced that Your Majesty has written a certain letter which has not been dispatched as yet. This letter is neither in your desk nor in your cabinets. But it must be somewhere."

The Queen drew herself up to her full height and eyed Séguier almost threateningly:

"Do you dare lay hands upon your Queen?" she demanded.

"Madame, I am a faithful subject of the King. Whatever His Majesty commands, I am in duty bound to accomplish."

"I see!" The Queen looked down scornfully at the Chancellor. "It is true I wrote a letter which has not been sent off. The letter in question is—here!" And she pressed a beautiful, tapering hand against her bosom.

"I must beg Your Majesty to give me that letter."

"I shall give it to none but the King, Monsieur."

"Madame, had His Majesty desired to receive the letter in person, he would himself have asked you for it. But, I repeat, it is *I* who am charged with requesting it of you and if you do not give it up—"

"Well?"

"Well, Madame, it is *I*, again, who am charged to take it from you."

"What! I do not understand. What do you mean?"

"I mean, Madame, that my orders are far-reaching. In fact I am authorized to search for the suspicious paper even on Your Majesty's person."

"How shameful!"

"I therefore beg Your Majesty to comply with the King's order."

"Such conduct is infamous. Do you realize that, Monsieur?"

"His Majesty commands, Madame; I can but obey and beg you to excuse me."

"I will not suffer it!" The Queen shuddered, at this offense to her dignity. Was she, a daughter of imperial blood, to submit to such humiliation? Angrily she cried: "I would rather die!"

Séguier made a deep bow. It was quite evident that he did not intend to draw back a single step; he had his mission to accomplish and accomplish it he would. Indeed, he stepped forward to do so, much as an attendant steps forward in a torture chamber to prepare the victim for the executioner. Tears of rage welled up in the Queen's eyes.

The Queen was of course a woman of great beauty. The task might well be considered a delicate one; but the King was too desperately jealous of Buckingham to consider being jealous of anyone else.

At the moment, no doubt, Monsieur Séguier, Chancellor and Keeper of the Seals, looked all about him for the famous bellrope that might save him from temptation. Failing to find it, he determined to obey the King's instructions and stretched out his hand toward the place where the Queen had admitted the paper lay. The Queen took a step backwards; she turned white as a sheet. Her left hand clutching the edge of a table for support, with her right she drew a paper from her breast and handed it to the Chancellor.

"Here is the letter, Monsieur," she said in a tremulous, choking voice. "Pray take it and deliver me of your odious presence."

The Chancellor, who was trembling with a totally different emotion, took the letter, bowed to the ground, and withdrew. The door had scarcely closed upon him when the Queen fell half-fainting in the arms of her ladies-in-waiting.

Without pausing to examine the letter, Séguier bore it forthwith to the King who took it with anxious hand, looked for the address which was missing, turned very pale and opened it slowly. Then, seeing by the first words that it was addressed to the King of Spain, he read it rapidly.

The letter contained a complete plan of attack against the Cardinal. The Queen invited her brother and the Emperor of Austria (offended as they were by Richelieu's eternal policy of attempting to humble the House of Austria) to threaten war against France unless the Cardinal was dismissed. Of Love, there was not a single word from beginning to end.

Highly elated, the King inquired whether the Cardinal were still in the

Louvre, and, learning that His Eminence awaited His Majesty's orders in the royal sanctum, rejoined him immediately.

"You were right, Monsieur le Cardinal, and I was wrong," he admitted. "The intrigue is wholly political; there is no question whatever of love in this letter. On the other hand, there is a great deal about you."

The Cardinal took the letter, read it attentively once, then reread it: "This should convince Your Majesty to what lengths my enemies will go," he opined. "They threaten you with two wars, Sire, unless you dismiss me. Frankly, were I in Your Majesty's place, I should yield to such powerful pressure. For my own part I admit I would be genuinely pleased to retire from public affairs."

"What, Monseigneur? What?"

"I mean, Sire, that my health is sinking under this burden of unceasing labor and endless strife. I doubt very much whether I can possibly undergo the fatigues of the Siege of La Rochelle. I honestly think Your Majesty would do well to appoint either Monsieur de Condé or Monsieur de Bassompierre or some other professional soldier to conduct the campaign rather than myself who am a Churchman, constantly diverted from my vocation to undertake matters for which I have scant aptitude. Undoubtedly you will be the better off for it, Sire, both at home and abroad."

"Monsieur le Cardinal, I understand you perfectly. You have my promise that I shall punish all those mentioned in this letter, including the Queen herself."

"Ah, Sire, God forbid! Her Majesty must not suffer the slightest annoyance, nay inconvenience, on my account! Her Majesty has always imagined me to be her worst enemy; but you, Sire, can readily attest that I have always warmly espoused her cause even against yourself."

"True."

"Were the Queen to betray Your Majesty's honor, it would be quite another matter and I would be the first to urge you to vouchsafe the guilty no mercy. Here, happily, that is not the question, for Your Majesty has just acquired fresh proof of the Queen's innocence."

"True again, Monseigneur, you were right on that score as usual. Nevertheless the Queen has incurred my displeasure and more."

"It is you, Sire, who have now incurred hers. In all honesty were the Queen to be seriously offended I could well understand it. I must say Your Majesty treated her with considerable severity...."

"So shall I always treat my enemies and yours, Monseigneur, however exalted their positions and whatever perils befall me in so doing."

"I am the victim of the Queen's enmity, not you, Sire. To Your Majesty, she is a devoted, submissive and irreproachable wife. Pray allow me then, Sire, to intercede with Your Majesty on her behalf."

"Let her humble herself then and come to me first."

"On the contrary, Sire, deign to set the example. Were you not wrong in the first place to suspect Her Majesty?"

"What? *I* am to make advances? Impossible."

"Not wholly impossible, Sire, if you condescend. I beg you—"

"But how? How am I to—?"

"Your Majesty might do well to find some means of giving the Queen pleasure."

"For instance?"

"For instance, a ball; Your Majesty knows how fond the Queen is of dancing. I am certain the Queen's resentment will melt before an attention of the sort."

"Monseigneur, you know I dislike certain worldly pleasures."

"Her Majesty will be the more grateful to you for overcoming that aversion, Sire. Besides it will give the Queen an opportunity to display the beautiful diamond studs you gave her for her birthday. Her Majesty has not yet worn them."

"We shall see, Cardinal, we shall see," the King answered, overjoyed that the Queen was at once guilty of a crime which caused him no worry and innocent of a betrayal he had dreaded. Perhaps the Cardinal was right; perhaps a reconciliation was in order. "We shall see, yes, but upon my word, you are too indulgent, Monsieur le Cardinal."

"Sire, leave severity to your Ministers, clemency is the royal virtue. Exercise it and you will find yourself the happier for it."

The clock struck eleven, the Cardinal rose, bowed low and begged leave to retire, not without imploring his master to compose his royal and marital difficulties.

On the morrow the Queen, after the seizure of her letter, expected serious trouble or leastways sullen and acrimonious reproach. To her amazement the King called upon her and seemed to be making overtures for a reconciliation. Her first instinct was to repel them; she was too cruelly hurt in her womanly pride and queenly dignity to relent so suddenly. But presently, after consultation with her ladies-in-waiting, she was persuaded to forget the indignities she had suffered. At least she appeared to have forgotten them. Taking advantage of this favorable moment, His Majesty announced his intention of giving a fête in the near future.

A fête was so rare a thing in the Queen's life that, as the Cardinal had divined, the mere mention of such gaiety scattered the last traces of resentment from her features, if not from her heart. When she inquired eagerly what day the fête was to take place the King replied that he would have to consult the Cardinal. Indeed, day after day the King consulted His Eminence and day after day His Eminence found some pretext or other to temporize. Time passed and Her Majesty was left in suspense for ten days....

But Monsieur le Cardinal's period of suspense was two days shorter. Forty-eight hours before he had communicated with the King, who in turn immediately communicated with the Queen, His Eminence received a missive from London which read:

> I have them but I cannot leave London for want of money. Pray send me five hundred pistoles and within four or five days of receipt I shall be in Paris.

The day the Cardinal received this note, His Majesty asked the usual question; His Eminence, counting on his fingers, mused:

"She says she will arrive within four or five days of receipt . . . it will take four or five days to get the money to her . . . it will take her four or five days to return . . . eight days minimum, ten days average, twelve at the outside, allowing for contrary winds, accidents and the frailty of woman. . . ."

"Come, Monsieur le Cardinal, have you decided upon the date?"

"Yes, Sire. Today is the twentieth of September. The Aldermen of the City are giving their fête on October third. A most auspicious date, it suits our purpose perfectly, for Your Majesty will not appear to have gone out of your way to be favoring the Queen. And," the Cardinal added in a casual, urbane tone, "pray remember to tell Her Majesty the day before the fête—that is, October second—that you should be pleased to see how beautifully her diamond studs become her."

XVII

MONSIEUR BONACIEUX AND HIS LADY

The King was somewhat surprised at the Cardinal's insistence; here for
the second time His Eminence was referring to the diamond studs. What
mystery lay under that insistence?

In those days, of course, the police had not yet attained the perfection
of ours, but it was nevertheless excellent. King Louis had been humiliated
more than once by the Cardinal who seemed better informed than he
concerning the royal household. He therefore hoped that a conversation
with Anne of Austria might shed some light on current problems. Then
he could in turn surprise the Cardinal with some secret, which Richelieu
either knew or did not know, but which would anyhow greatly enhance
him in the eyes of his minister.

His Majesty proceeded to the Queen's apartment and as usual uttered
fresh threats against her henchmen and henchwomen. Anne of Austria
bowed her head in silence and allowed the torrent to flow on, hoping the
spate would eventually spend itself. But this was not what Louis XIII had
in mind; His Majesty wanted a discussion from which he might glean
some information. For he was convinced that the Cardinal was brooding
over some one of those terrible surprises he knew only too well how to
spring. His Majesty gained his end by dint of persistent accusation.

Exhausted by these vague attacks, the Queen protested: "Why do you
not tell me what is on your mind? What have I done? What sort of crime
am I supposed to have committed? Surely Your Majesty cannot make all
this to-do over a letter I wrote my brother?"

The King, at a loss for an answer, decided to divulge the news he had
intended to spring upon her at the last moment.

"Madame," the King said with dignity, "there will soon be a ball at the
Hôtel de Ville. In order to do honor to our worthy aldermen, I propose
that you appear in ceremonial costume; I am particularly eager that you
wear the diamond studs which I gave you on your birthday. That is my answer."

The answer was terrible indeed. Anne of Austria imagined that Louis
XIII knew all and that the Cardinal had prevailed upon him to employ
this protracted eight-day pretense, which in any case was quite in keeping with his nature. She blanched, leaned on the console for support and

looked up in silent terror. His Majesty kept his eyes riveted on that slender, admirable hand, now bloodless and as though of wax.

"You understand, Madame?" he said, enjoying her embarrassment to the full, but without guessing what had caused it. "You understand?"

"Yes, Sire. I understand."

"You will appear at this ball?"

"Yes."

"With those studs, Madame?"

"Yes."

The Queen grew paler still. The King, noticing it, gloated with that cold cruelty which was one of his worst traits.

"Then we agree," he said abruptly. "That was all I had to say, Madame."

"But what day will the ball take place?"

The Queen's question was so faint and so pathetic that instinctively Louis XIII realized that he must ward it off.

"Oh, very shortly Madame," he replied. "As a matter of fact, I have forgotten the exact date. I shall ask the Cardinal."

"So it was the Cardinal who told you of this fête?"

"Certainly. Why do you ask?"

"So the Cardinal suggested you invite me to wear my studs?"

"Well, Madame, he—"

"It was he who suggested it?"

"He or I, what matter? Is the suggestion so outlandish?"

"No, Sire, certainly not—"

"Then you will appear?"

"Yes, Sire."

"Good," said the King, retiring. "Good! I shall count upon it."

The Queen curtsied less out of etiquette than because her knees were giving way under her. The King went away delighted.

"I am lost, lost," the Queen murmured. "The Cardinal knows everything; the King is but his tool. But the King will learn the truth soon enough. Oh, my God, my God, my God . . ."

She knelt upon a cushion and prayed, her head bowed, her arms trembling. Her plight was desperate, for Buckingham had returned to London and Madame de Chevreuse was in exile at Tours. More closely watched than ever, the Queen understood that one of her ladies-in-waiting or maidservants had betrayed her. But who was the culprit? As La Porte could not possibly leave the Louvre, there was not one soul in all the world in whom she could place her trust. Contemplating the impending catastrophe and her helplessness, she burst into sobs.

"Can I be of use to Your Majesty?" A voice filled with gentleness and pity intruded upon the Queen's misery. "Can I be of help?"

The Queen turned sharply round; there was no mistaking the expression of sympathy in that voice. Here was a friend in time of need. As she looked up, Madame Bonacieux stepped into the Queen's apartment. She had been busy sorting gowns and linen in one of the closets when the King entered; now, timidly, she ventured forth.

The Queen gasped at this intrusion; in her dismay she did not immediately recognize La Porte's protégée.

"You have nothing to fear, Madame," said the young servant. "I am Your Majesty's, body and soul. Remote as I am from Your Majesty and lowly though my station be, I think I can find a way to help you."

"*You*? Great Heavens, *you*! I am betrayed on all sides. Can I trust in *you*?"

Madame Bonacieux fell to her knees:

"Madame," she vowed, "I swear upon my soul that I am ready to die for Your Majesty." That cry of loyalty sprang from her innermost heart; its fervor and sincerity were unmistakable. "Ay, Madame," the young woman continued, "there are traitors here in the Louvre! But by the Holy Name of the Virgin, I swear that no one is more devoted to Your Majesty than I am. These studs the King requests of you—you gave them to the Duke of Buckingham, did you not? They were in a little rosewood box which he took away with him. Am I mistaken?"

"Ah, God, ah, God!" the Queen moaned.

"We must get those studs back, Madame."

"Of course, my child! But how? What to do? How to go about it?"

"Someone must be sent to the Duke."

"But who? Who? Whom can I trust?"

"Have faith in me, Madame; do me this honor, my Queen, and I shall find the messenger, I promise you."

"But I shall have to write a message!"

"Yes, of course, Madame. Two words in Your Majesty's writing and your own seal will suffice."

"But two words might bring about my arrest, divorce and exile!"

"Perhaps, if your message were to fall into the hands of an enemy. But I promise I can have it delivered safely to the Duke."

"So I must place my life, my honor and my reputation in your hands?"

"Ay, Madame, you must. I know I can save you."

"But how?"

"Madame, my husband was freed only two or three days ago; I have not yet had time to see him. He is a good, honest man; he has never loved or hated anyone on earth. He will do anything I wish. One word from me and he will go to London without even knowing what tidings he bears. And he will deliver Your Majesty's letter to the address she desires, without even knowing it is from Your Majesty!"

Fervidly the Queen grasped the young woman's hands and looked deep into her eyes. Convinced of her servant's sincerity, the Queen embraced Madame Bonacieux.

"Do it," she vowed, "and you will save the life and honor of your Queen."

"But, Madame, these are not at stake. The service I beg to render is slight indeed. Alas, are you not the victim of treacherous plots?"

"True, all too true, my child!"

"Then give me that letter at once, Madame. Time presses."

The Queen went to her desk, wrote two short lines, sealed her message with her private seal, and handed it to Madame Bonacieux.

"We are forgetting one very important thing," she said.

"What is that, Madame?"

"Money."

"Ay!" Madame Bonacieux blushed. "I must confess to Your Majesty that my husband—"

"Your husband has none. Is that what you mean?"

"Oh, yes, he has plenty, but he is very stingy. No one is perfect and avarice is his besetting sin. But Your Majesty must not worry about all this. We shall find some way—"

"The truth is that I have no money either," the Queen confessed. "But wait!" She picked up her jewel-case: "Here," she said breathlessly, "here is a ring of great value, I am told. It is a gift from my brother, the King of Spain; it belongs to me, I can dispose of it as I wish. Take this ring, sell it and let your husband leave for London at once."

"You shall be obeyed within an hour, Madame."

"You see the address," the Queen added, almost inaudibly. "This message goes to His Grace the Duke of Buckingham, London."

"The letter will be delivered to him in person."

The Queen grasped Madame Bonacieux's hands and sighed: "You generous child!"

Madame Bonacieux kissed the Queen's hands, concealed the paper in her bodice and hastened away.

Ten minutes later she was at home. As she told the Queen, she had not seen her husband since his liberation. She was therefore unaware of his change of feeling toward the Cardinal; nor did she know that this change had been intensified by two or more visits from the Comte de Rochefort. The latter had become Bonacieux's best friend; he had easily persuaded the haberdasher that his wife's abduction was no criminal act but merely a political measure.

Madame Bonacieux found her husband alone. The poor fellow was with utmost difficulty restoring some order in his house. The furniture was completely destroyed and the closets were empty, for justice is not one of the three things which King Solomon named as leaving no traces of their passage. As for the servant, she had fled when her master was arrested; the wretched girl was so panic stricken that after leaving Paris she did not stop until she reached Burgundy, her native province.

Immediately upon his return, the worthy haberdasher had notified his wife that he was safe at home. She had replied by congratulating him and promising that the earliest moment she could steal from her duties would be devoted to paying him a visit.

This earliest moment had been delayed five whole days, which under any other circumstances might have seemed a long time to friend Bonacieux. But the visit he had paid to the Cardinal and the succeeding visits the Comte de Rochefort had paid him, provided ample food for thought, and, as everybody knows, such food makes time pass swiftly. This was all the more true in Bonacieux's case because all his thoughts were rosy indeed. Rochefort called him his friend, his dear Bonacieux, and never ceased telling him how highly the Cardinal prized him. Already the haberdasher fancied himself on the high road to honors and fortune.

Madame Bonacieux for her part had been thoughtful too, but truth to tell, on a subject alien to ambition. In spite of herself, her thoughts constantly reverted to the handsome and brave youth who seemed so much in love with her. She had married Monsieur Bonacieux at the age of eighteen; she had always lived among her husband's friends, people hardly capable of inspiring a young woman whose heart and soul were above her social position. She had remained virtuous and decent. But a title exerted a great influence over the bourgeoisie at this period. D'Artagnan was of gentle birth; furthermore, he wore the uniform of the guards, which, next to that of the musketeers, was most admired by the ladies. He was handsome, young and adventurous; he spoke of love as a man who loved and was eager to be loved in return. In all this there was certainly enough to turn a head only twenty-three years old, and Madame Bonacieux had just reached that happy age.

Husband and wife had not seen each other for over a week during which the most serious events had occurred to both. But when at length they met, it was with a feeling of preoccupation on both sides. However, Monsieur Bonacieux manifested genuine delight as he advanced toward his wife with open arms.

Madame Bonacieux raised her head, presenting her brow to his kiss.

"Let us talk a little," she suggested.

"What?" Bonacieux exclaimed in astonishment.

"Yes, let us talk. I have something of the greatest importance to tell you."

"As a matter of fact, I too would like to discuss several serious matters with you. First, will you please explain the circumstances of your abduction?"

"That is not important just now."

"Well then, what is important? Do you want to discuss my stay in prison?"

"I heard of it the day you were arrested," Madame Bonacieux explained. "But I knew you were guilty of no crime or intrigue; I knew you possessed no knowledge that could compromise you or anyone else. So I attached no more importance to your arrest than it warranted."

"You speak very lightly of it, Madame," Bonacieux retorted, hurt at his wife's lack of interest. "Do you realize that I spent a day and a night in a dungeon in the Bastille?"

"Oh, a day and a night pass very quickly. Let us forget your captivity and return to the matter that brings me here."

"What? The matter that brings you here!" The haberdasher was wounded to the quick. "Are you not here to see a husband from whom you have been separated for a week?"

"Yes, that first! But there is also something else."

"Speak out."

"Something of the greatest interest . . . something on which our future fortunes depend. . . ."

"Our fortunes have changed considerably since I last saw you, Madame Bonacieux. In fact I should not be surprised if, sooner or later, our fortunes were to excite the envy of a great many people."

"Indeed, yes! Especially if you follow the instructions I am about to give you."

"Instructions? *You*—about to give *me*—"

"Yes, *you*. There is a good and holy deed to be done, Monsieur, and a great deal of money to be made into the bargain."

Madame Bonacieux knew that by talking of money she was attacking his weakest spot. But a man (even a haberdasher) who has once spoken to Cardinal Richelieu (if only for ten minutes) is no longer the same man.

"A great deal of money to be made?" said Bonacieux, pursing his lips.

"Yes, a great deal."

"How much, roughly?"

"About a thousand pistoles."

"I see! Obviously what you are about to ask of me is very serious?"

"Ay!"

"What is to be done?"

"You must set out immediately. I shall give you a paper which you must not part with on any account whatever. You are to deliver that paper into the proper hands."

"And where am I to go?"

"To London."

"I go to London! Look here, you are joking! I have no business in London."

"Others require that you go then."

"Others? Who are those others? I warn you I will never again act without knowing what is what. I wish to know not only what risks I run but for whose sake."

"An illustrious personage is sending you, an illustrious person awaits you. The reward will exceed your expectations, that I can promise you."

"More intrigues, always intrigues!" Bonacieux grumbled. "Thank you,

I have had my fill of them. His Eminence the Cardinal has enlightened me on that score!"

"The Cardinal? You saw the Cardinal?"

"He sent for me," the haberdasher answered proudly.

"And you went? What rashness!"

"I must confess I had no choice one way or the other; I was marched off between two guards. I must also confess I did not know His Eminence—at that time."

"So he ill-treated you? He threatened you?"

"He gave me his hand and called me his friend—his friend, do you understand, Madame? I am a friend of the great Cardinal."

"Of the great Cardinal!"

"Do you perchance deny him that title, Madame?"

"I deny him nothing. But I tell you that the favor of a minister is ephemeral. A man must be mad to attach himself to a minister! There are powers superior to his which do not depend on the whim of an individual or the outcome of an event. It is around these powers that we should rally."

"I am sorry, Madame, but I recognize no power other than that of the great man I serve."

"You serve the Cardinal?"

"Ay, Madame, and as his servant, I will not permit you to participate in plots against the security of the State or to assist in the intrigues of an alien woman whose heart is devoted to Spain. Fortunately we have the great Cardinal: his watchful eye observes and penetrates to the bottom of the human heart."

Bonacieux was repeating word for word a phrase which he had heard Comte de Rochefort utter. His poor wife, who had counted on her husband and vouched for him to the Queen, shuddered at the danger which she had so narrowly avoided and at her present helplessness. There was one consolation: she knew her husband's weakness and more particularly his cupidity; therefore she did not despair of bringing him round to her purpose.

"So you are a cardinalist, Monsieur?" she exclaimed. "You serve the party who mistreat your wife and insult your Queen."

"Private interests are of no import against the interest of all," Bonacieux observed sententiously. "I am for those who support the State."

This was another quotation from the Comte de Rochefort; he had committed it avidly to memory against such time as he could trot it out.

"The State? Do you know what this State you speak of actually is?" Madame Bonacieux shrugged her shoulders. "Be satisfied with living as a plain, straightforward bourgeois; turn to that side which holds out the greatest advantages."

"Well, well!" Bonacieux slapped a plump round bag which jingled at his touch, "what do you say of this, Madame Preacher?"

"Where does that money come from?"

"Can't you guess?"

"From the Cardinal?"

"From him and from my friend the Comte de Rochefort."

"The Comte de Rochefort! Why, it was he who carried me off!"

"That is quite possible, Madame."

"And you accept money from that man?"

"Why not? You yourself seem scarcely worried about your abduction. I suppose you were carried off for political reasons."

"Yes, I was. They carried me off in order to make me betray my sovereign; they hoped by torturing me to wring from me confessions that might compromise the honor and perhaps the very life of my august mistress."

"Madame, your august mistress is a perfidious Spaniard. What the Cardinal has done, was well done."

"Monsieur, I knew you for a coward, a miser and an idiot. But I never supposed you were infamous."

Bonácieux, who had never seen his wife angry, retreated before this outburst of conjugal wrath:

"Madame, what are you saying?" he asked, incredulous.

"I am saying that you are a wretched creature!" she insisted, as she noted that she was regaining some influence over her husband. "You meddle with politics, do you? *You?* And with Cardinalist politics at that? Why, you are selling yourself body and soul to the Devil—for money!"

"No, it's the Cardinal."

"It is all one and the same thing! Who says Richelieu, says Satan."

"Hold your tongue, Madame, hold your tongue, we may be overheard."

"Yes, you are right. I should be ashamed to have anyone know of your cowardice."

"But what on earth do you want me to do? Tell me!"

"I have told you already. I want you to leave instantly, Monsieur, and faithfully to carry out the mission with which I have deigned to charge you. If you do this, I shall forgive and forget everything, and—" she held out her hand to him,—"I will give you my love again."

Bonacieux was a coward and a miser but he loved his wife. He was touched. A man of fifty cannot long bear a grudge against a wife of twenty-three. Madame Bonacieux saw he was hesitating.

"Well, have you made up your mind?" she asked.

"But, my love, think of what you require of me! London is far away, very far away! And the mission you suggest may well offer considerable danger."

"What matter, if you avoid it?"

"No, Madame Bonacieux," the haberdasher decided, "No, no, no, I positively refuse. Intrigues terrify me. I have seen the Bastille, yes, Madame, that I have! Ugh, it's a ghastly place; the very thought of it gives me gooseflesh. I was threatened with torture; do you know what torture is? Wooden blocks wedged in between your legs till the bones burst! No, I shan't go; decidedly not! By Heaven, why don't you go yourself? Upon my word, I think I have been mistaken about you; you sound like a man and a madman at that!"

"And you—you're a woman, a miserable, stupid and besotted woman! So you are scared, are you? Well, if you do not leave immediately, I shall have you arrested by order of the Queen and clapped into that Bastille you dread so much."

Bonacieux carefully weighed the respective angers of Queen and Cardinal; the latter easily won the day.

"You have me arrested by order of the Queen," he threatened, "and I shall appeal to His Eminence."

Madame Bonacieux saw she had gone too far; she was terrified at her boldness. For a moment, lost in dread, she contemplated his stupid countenance and read in it all the invincible resolution of a fool overcome by fear.

"Well, so be it," she said, "perhaps you are right after all. A man knows more about politics than a woman, especially a man like you, Monsieur Bonacieux, who have met the Cardinal. And yet it is very hard," she added, "that my husband, upon whose affection I thought I could rely, treats me so ungraciously and will not gratify a whim of mine."

"The trouble is that your whims may carry one too far," Bonacieux replied triumphantly. "I mistrust them."

"Very well, I give up the idea! Let us say no more about it."

Bonacieux now recalled somewhat belatedly that Rochefort had admonished him to discover his wife's secrets.

"You might at least tell me what you expected me to do in London?" he suggested.

"There is no point in your knowing," she answered, with instinctive mistrust. "It was a trifling matter . . . one of those purchases that interest women . . . and we might have made a good profit on the transaction. . . ."

But the more she excused herself, the more important he believed her secret to be. He therefore decided to hasten to the Comte de Rochefort to tell him that the Queen was seeking a messenger to send to London.

"Pray forgive me if I must leave you now, dear Madame Bonacieux," he said unctuously. "I did not know you were coming to see me, so I made an appointment to meet a friend. I shall be back soon, and, if you wait, I will escort you to the Louvre."

"Thank you, Monsieur, you can be of no service to me. I shall return to the Louvre alone."

"As you please, Madame Bonacieux. Shall I see you soon again?"

"Probably. Next week, I hope, my duties will afford me a little liberty; I shall take advantage of it to come here and tidy up. This place is a shambles."

"Very well, I shall expect you. You are not angry with me?"

"Who, I? Not in the least."

"We shall meet shortly then?"

"Yes, in a few days."

Bonacieux kissed his wife's hand and set off hurriedly.

"Well, well!" Madame Bonacieux mused as soon as her husband had shut the street door and she was alone. "Poor idiot, all he required to crown his baseness was to become a Cardinalist! And I vouched for him to the Queen; I promised my poor mistress—Ah, dear God! the Queen will take me for one of those wretches in the Louvre who spy upon her night and day. Alas, Monsieur Bonacieux, I never did love you much; now, things are worse than ever. I hate you and I vow you shall pay for it."

Suddenly, hearing a rap at the ceiling, she raised her head. Through the plaster, she heard a voice from the floor above. A man was saying:

"Dear Madame Bonacieux, please open the side door; I shall come downstairs at once."

XVIII
LOVER AND HUSBAND

Passing through the side door, D'Artagnan announced:

"Forgive me, Madame, if I say so, but your husband is a sorry specimen."

"You heard our conversation?" Madame Bonacieux asked anxiously.

"Every word."

"How could you overhear us?"

"I have a system, Madame, known only to myself. By this system, I also overheard the somewhat more lively conversation you had with the Cardinal's police."

"What did you learn from all this?"

"I learned a great deal. First, I discovered that your husband is a simpleton and a fool, which is fortunate for me ... Secondly, I gathered that you are in distress, which pleases me beyond words because it affords me a chance to serve you ... Third, I realized that to do so I was willing to risk all the fires of Hell ... Fourth and last, I ascertained that the Queen needs a brave, intelligent, devoted man to go to London on her behalf. ... Personally, I possess three of these four requisite qualities. That is why I am here."

Madame Bonacieux dared not speak; but her heart leaped for joy and her eyes shone with all the brightness of her secret hope.

"What pledge can you offer?" she asked timidly. "This mission is a weighty one."

"My pledge will be the love I bear you. You have but to command; I am at your orders."

The young woman paused, wondering whether she dared confide in so young a man. "You are but a boy!" she whispered. D'Artagnan protested that there were plenty of older men who could vouch for him.

"I admit I would be more comfortable if you —"

"Do you know Athos?"

"No."

"Porthos?"

"No."

"Aramis?"

"No, I do not," Madame Bonacieux said helplessly. "Who are these gentlemen?"

"They belong to His Majesty's musketeers. Have you heard of Monsieur de Tréville, their Captain?"

Madame Bonacieux admitted that she knew him—not personally of course, but she had often heard people cite him to the Queen as a brave and loyal gentleman. When D'Artagnan suggested that Tréville might betray her to the Cardinal, she dismissed it as impossible. D'Artagnan then proposed that she reveal her secret to Tréville:

"Ask Tréville," he insisted, "whether I can be trusted with so urgent, precious and terrible a secret?"

"But my secret does not belong to me. I am not at liberty to divulge it."

"You were about to divulge it to Monsieur Bonacieux," the Gascon objected.

"Ay, Monsieur, just as a woman leaves a letter in the hollow of a tree or pins a note on a pigeon's wing or fastens a message under the collar of a dog."

"Yet you must know I love you."

"So you say."

"I am an honorable man."

"I believe it."

"I have pluck . . . I have initiative . . . I can shift for myself and for others, too. . . ."

"Oh, I am sure of that!"

"Then use me . . . let me help you . . . put me to the test . . . !"

As Madame Bonacieux looked at him, her last doubt vanished. There was such ardor in his eyes and such conviction in his voice that she could not but trust him. For her, it was a case of risk all, lose all; the Queen's cause could be ruined as easily by too excessive caution as by excessive confidence. In all sincerity, her private feelings toward her young champion were what compelled her to speak frankly.

"I yield to your protestations and I accept your assurances," she said. "But, God be my witness, I swear upon His Presence here and now that if you betray me I shall kill myself and you will be held responsible."

"Madame, for my part, I can only swear by God that, if I die before carrying out your orders, your secret will go with me to the grave."

Madame Bonacieux told him all that worried her now and all that had worried her when they met near the Louvre the night he had challenged her mysterious escort.

This explanation amounted to a mutual declaration of love.

D'Artagnan was radiant with joy and pride; the woman he loved had confided her deepest, purest secret! Confidence and passion made of him a very Titan.

"I go," he vowed, "I go at once!"

"How can you go? What of your Captain and your regiment?"

"Upon my soul, you had made me forget such things. Dear Constance, you are right; I must get a furlough immediately."

"One more obstacle!" Madame Bonacieux sighed.

"Not a serious one!" D'Artagnan assured her after a moment's reflection, "I shall hurdle it, I promise you."

"But how?"

"I shall call on Monsieur de Tréville this very evening and request him to obtain leave for me from his brother-in-law, Monsieur des Essarts."

"But there is something else," she said hesitantly.

"Namely—"

"Perhaps you have no money?"

"*Perhaps* is an exaggeration!"

Madame Bonacieux opened a wardrobe; out of it she drew the bag which her husband had been fondling so lovingly half an hour earlier:

"In that case, here! Take this!"

"The Cardinal's money!" D'Artagnan roared with laughter.

"How do you know?"

"You forget I saw everything."

"Ah, yes! Well, the Cardinal's money is a tidy sum."

"By God! How entertaining to save the Queen with His Eminence's money!"

"You are a most charming and witty young man; believe me, Her Majesty will not prove ungrateful."

"I need no reward," D'Artagnan protested. "I love you and you allow me to tell you so; that in itself is more happiness than ever I dared hope."

"Hush!"

"What is the matter?"

"Voices . . . in the street. . . ."

"Voices?"

"My husband's voice . . . I recognize it. . . ."

D'Artagnan rushed to the door, bolted it:

"He shall not come in before I leave. Give me time to get away. Then you can let him in."

"But what of me? How can I account for Bonacieux's money if he finds me here?"

"You are right, we must both leave!"

"But he will see us."

"Then you must come upstairs with me."

"You say that in a tone which frightens me." There were tears in her eyes. D'Artagnan, deeply touched, fell to his knees.

"In my rooms," he assured her, "you will be as safe as in a church, I pledge my word as a gentleman."

"Let us go! I trust you, my friend."

D'Artagnan cautiously unbolted the door and, light as shadows, the pair slipped out into the alley and mounted the stairway to D'Artagnan's apartment.

Once there, for greater safety, the young man barricaded the door. They moved to the window and through a slit in the shutter espied Monsieur Bonacieux talking to a cloaked figure. At the sight of this man, D'Artagnan leaped up and, half-drawing his sword, sprang toward the door.

It was the man of Meung!

"What are you doing! You will ruin us both."

"But I have sworn to kill that man!"

"Your life is now devoted to a nobler cause; from this moment on, it is not yours to risk. In the Queen's name, I forbid you to face any danger other than that of your journey."

"And in your own name, you order nothing?"

"In my own name," she replied with great emotion, "I beg you to listen. I think they are talking about me."

D'Artagnan returned to the window and listened carefully. Meanwhile Monsieur Bonacieux had opened the front door and, seeing his apartment empty, had rejoined the cloaked man.

"She's gone," he announced. "Probably back to the Louvre."

"You're sure she had no suspicions?"

"No," Bonacieux replied self-sufficiently. "She is too superficial a woman for that."

"Is the young guardsman at home?"

"I don't think so. His shutters are closed; I see no light."

"We must make sure."

"How?"

"By knocking at his door."

"I shall ask his manservant."

"Go ahead!"

Bonacieux took the same stairway the fugitives had taken, stopped at D'Artagnan's landing, and knocked at the outer door. The lovers, within, held their breath, startled. There was no answer from the front room because Porthos had borrowed Planchet that evening in order to make a show. D'Artagnan, of course, was careful to give no sign of life.

"There's no one there," Bonacieux reported.

"Never mind, let us go to your rooms. We shall be safer there than in the doorway."

"Oh, Lord," said Madame Bonacieux, "now we can't hear them!"

"Nonsense, we shall hear all the better." Removing four of the floorboards, D'Artagnan spread a rug over the aperture he had made, went down on his knees, and motioned to Madame Bonacieux to stoop too. Shoulder to shoulder, they crouched listening.

"You're sure there is no one?" the stranger was asking.

"I will answer for it."

"And you think your wife—"

"She has gone back to the Louvre!"

"She spoke to no one but yourself?"

"I am sure of it."

"That point is important, you understand?"

"Then the news I brought you has some value?"

"Great value, my dear Bonacieux, great value!"

"The Cardinal will be pleased with my efforts?"

"I have no doubt he will be jubilant."

"Our great Cardinal!"

"You are quite sure your wife mentioned no one by name?"

"I think not."

"She mentioned neither Madame de Chevreuse nor Lord Buckingham nor Madame de Vernet?"

"No. She only said she wished me to go to London to serve the interests of some illustrious person."

("The traitor," Madame Bonacieux murmured.

"Silence!" D'Artagnan warned, taking a hand which she abandoned to him.)

"Never mind," the stranger went on. "You were a ninny not to pretend to accept the commission . . . you would now be in possession of the letter . . . the State which is being threatened would have been saved . . . and you. . . ."

"And I?"

"Well, the Cardinal would probably have given you letters of nobility."

"Did he tell you so?"

"Yes, I know he meant to surprise you in some such way."

"All is not lost, Monsieur, my wife adores me and there is still time."

("The dolt," murmured Madame Bonacieux.

"Silence!" D'Artagnan warned again, pressing her hand still more firmly.)

"What do you mean: there is still time?" the stranger challenged Bonacieux.

"I shall go to the Louvre and ask for Madame Bonacieux . . . I shall tell her that I have thought things over and that I accept . . . I shall get the letter . . . and I shall speed to the Cardinal. . . ."

"Well, be off then, quickly. I will return soon to learn the result of your errand."

Whereupon the stranger left the room.

("The swine!" said Madame Bonacieux, overcome by her husband's infamy.

"Silence!" D'Artagnan repeated, crushing her hand as in a vise!)

A sudden terrible howling interrupted the lovers. Downstairs, Monsieur Bonacieux had just discovered the disappearance of his money bag and was crying: "Help! Thieves! I've been robbed!"

("Oh my God," Madame Bonacieux wailed, "he will rouse the whole neighborhood!")

Bonacieux kept howling for a long time, but as such cries were frequent in the Rue des Fossoyeurs, they attracted no attention, especially since the haberdasher's house had lately fallen into disrepute. Seeing that no one came, Bonacieux emerged, still howling, his voice trailing off into the distance as he disappeared down the Rue du Bac.

"Now that he's gone, it is your turn to go!" Madame Bonacieux told D'Artagnan. "Courage, my friend, but, above all, caution! Remember you owe yourself to the Queen."

"To her and to you, darling Constance," D'Artagnan said passionately. "Rest easy, my love, I shall return worthy of Her Majesty's gratitude. And shall I return worthy of your love?"

For only answer, the young woman blushed deeply. A few moments later, D'Artagnan left the house, hidden under a greatcoat, its skirt raised cavalierly by his rapier.

Madame Bonacieux followed him with her eyes with that long fond look a woman lavishes upon the man she loves. When he had turned the corner she fell to her knees and, clasping her hands:

"Dear God!" she prayed. "Protect the Queen! And protect me! Amen!"

XIX

PLAN OF CAMPAIGN

D'Artagnan went straight to the Hotel de Tréville. Within a few minutes he knew the Cardinal would learn everything from that infernal stranger, obviously his agent. D'Artagnan realized he had not a moment to lose.

His heart overflowed with joy. Here was an opportunity both to win glory and to make money, and, for primary encouragement, one which had just brought him close to the woman he adored. From the very beginning then, chance offered him more than he had dared to ask of Providence.

Monsieur de Tréville was in his drawing-room with his usual company. D'Artagnan was shown directly to his study whence he sent word that he awaited the Captain on a matter of extreme urgency. He had not long to wait; five minutes later Monsieur de Tréville joined him. One glance at the young Gascon's radiant expression told the Captain that something new was afoot.

On his way to the mansion, D'Artagnan had wondered whether he should unbosom himself to Monsieur de Tréville or merely ask for a free hand in conducting an affair of utmost secrecy. But Monsieur de Tréville had always been so wonderfully kind to him, he was so completely devoted to the King and Queen, and he hated the Cardinal so cordially, that the young man decided to tell him everything.

"You asked for me, young man?"

"Yes, Monsieur, I did. You will forgive me for disturbing you when you learn the importance of my errand."

"Well?"

"Monsieur, the Queen's honor, perhaps her very life, are at stake."

"What!" Monsieur de Tréville looked about him to make sure they were quite alone. "What do you mean?"

"I mean that chance has put me in possession of a secret—"

"—which I hope, young man, you will guard with your very life—"

"—but which I must confide to you, Monsieur. You alone can help me accomplish the mission I have just received from Her Majesty."

"Is this secret yours?"

"No, Monsieur, it is the Queen's secret."

"Did the Queen permit you to divulge it?"

"No, Monsieur, I have been pledged to the deepest secrecy."

"Then why were you about to—?"

"Because, I repeat, without you I can do nothing, Monsieur."

"Keep your secret, young man, and tell me what you wish."

"I beg you to ask Monsieur des Essarts to grant me a two-week furlough."

"When?"

"This very night."

"You mean to leave Paris?"

"On a mission."

"Can you tell me where?"

"To London."

"Is anyone seeking to prevent you from reaching your destination?"

"The Cardinal would, I believe, give the world to stop me."

"You are going alone?"

"Quite alone."

"In that case you will never get beyond Bondy, I swear it on the faith of a Tréville."

"How so, Monsieur?"

"You will be murdered en route."

"Then I shall die in the attempt!"

"But your mission will not be accomplished."

"True!"

"Believe me," Monsieur de Tréville said earnestly, "in undertakings of this kind the chances are about four to one against. There should be four of you!"

"Well, Monsieur, three of your musketeers are dear friends of mine: Athos, P—"

"Yes, I know. Can you use them and pledge them to secrecy? You were on the point—"

"We four are as blood brothers, Monsieur. You need but tell them you trust me, they will take me at my word."

"I can give each of them a two-week furlough, no more. Athos is bothered by his wound, let him go to the waters at Forges; Porthos and Aramis may well accompany the invalid. Their orders will serve to prove that I authorize the journey."

"Monsieur is a hundred times too generous!"

"See them at once and arrange everything tonight. Oh, yes, I was forgetting about Monsieur des Essarts! Go file your request with him at once. If some Cardinalist spy is already at your heels, His Eminence knows you have visited me. You can justify this visit by reporting officially to Monsieur des Essarts."

D'Artagnan made out his application; Monsieur de Tréville, receiving it, assured him that his furlough and those of his friends would be in their hands by two o'clock in the morning.

"May I ask you, Monsieur, to send mine in care of Athos?" D'Artagnan requested. "I think it highly unwise to go home."

"Very good. Farewell and bon voyage!" Monsier de Tréville paused. "By the by, have you any money?"

D'Artagnan turned, tapping the Bonacieux bag which was in his pocket.

"Enough?"

"Three hundred pistoles."

"Plenty! Enough to take you to the end of the world! Proceed, young man!"

As D'Artagnan bowed, Monsieur de Tréville offered his hand which D'Artagnan shook gratefully. Since his arrival in Paris, he had always found this great soldier a kindly, sincere and helpful friend.

His first visit was to Aramis, whom he had not called on since that evening on the bridge when he mistook him for Buckingham. The few times they had met in the interval, Aramis had seemed profoundly depressed.

Finding Aramis awake but gloomy and pensive, he inquired perfunctorily about this gloom and pensiveness. Aramis replied that his feeling rose from a commentary on Chapter XVIII of Saint Augustine's *Confessions*.

"I have to translate it into Latin by next week," Aramis said, "and it's a thorny job!"

They continued their discussion of Saint Augustine of whom Aramis spoke at length. They discussed other matters of current interest. Suddenly there was a knock at the door; a lackey wearing the livery of Monsieur de Tréville loomed in the doorway.

"What is this?" Aramis asked.

"The leave of absence Monsieur requested."

"I requested no leave of absence, my good man. There must be some mistake!"

"Hush, Aramis, and be thankful for small mercies," D'Artagnan said royally. Then turning to the lackey: "As for you my friend, here is half a pistole for your pains. Pray convey to Monsieur de Tréville the sincere thanks of Monsieur Aramis. And so, away with you!"

"Do you mind telling me what all this means?" Aramis asked meekly after the lackey had bowed himself out.

"It means a fortnight's leave," D'Artagnan explained. "Fall in and follow me."

"How can I leave Paris now without know—?"

"—without knowing what has become of *her*, eh?"

"Who?"

"The lady who was here . . . the lady of the embroidered handkerchief. . . ."

Aramis turned deathly pale:

"Who told you there was a lady here?"

"I saw her."

"You know who she is?"

"I might venture a shrewd guess."

"Look here, D'Artagnan, as long as you know so much, can you tell me what has happened to her?"

"I dare say she went back to Tours."

"To Tours? Yes, that's right. I realize you know her. But why did she leave town without telling me?"

"She was afraid of being arrested."

"Why has she not written?"

"For fear of compromising you."

"My dear D'Artagnan, here I was a dead man and lo! you revive me! I thought myself despised and betrayed . . . I wondered why I had not heard from her . . . Ah, you cannot imagine how happy I was to see her again . . . I could not dream she would risk her life for my sake. . . . Yet why else would she have returned to Paris?"

"For the same reason that is sending us to England tonight."

"I don't understand—"

"You will later. Meanwhile, my dear Aramis, allow me to model my discretion on that of the niece of your theologian."

Aramis smiled as he remembered the evasive yarn he had told his inquisitive friends one evening.

"So long as you are sure she has left Paris," he said, "nothing keeps me here. I am ready to follow you. Where are we off to?"

"First we must see Athos. If you want to come along, do make haste; time is short. If you are with me, tell Bazin."

"Bazin is going with us?"

"Perhaps. Anyhow, he had better follow us now."

Aramis summoned Bazin and gave him the necessary instructions, and:

"Off we go," he said, picking up his cloak, his sword and his three pistols. He opened several drawers in search of cash. Convinced this was useless, he followed D'Artagnan. How, Aramis wondered, could this young cadet in the guards know about the lady he had sheltered? How again could he know what had become of her? Aramis placed his hand on D'Artagnan's arm and asked earnestly:

"You have spoken of this lady to no one?"

"To no one on earth."

"Not even to Porthos and Athos?"

"I have not breathed the slightest word to either."

"Thank heavens!"

And, his mind at rest on this important point, Aramis breathed more easily.

They found Athos with his orders in one hand and Monsieur de Tréville's letter in the other.

"Can you explain the meaning of this leave and this letter?" Athos asked in astonishment, then proceeded to read:

My dear Athos,

As I know your health absolutely requires it, I am perfectly willing for you to take a fortnight's rest.

Go to the spa at Forges, then, or to any other spa that you prefer, profit by the waters, and come back thoroughly fit.

Cordially yours,
De Treville

"That letter and that leave," D'Artagnan explained, "mean that you must follow me, Athos."

"To the waters at Forges?"

"There or elsewhere."

"On the King's Service?"

"The King's or the Queen's. Are we not servants of both Their Majesties?"

Just then Porthos came in:

"Look here, friends," he said, "here is a queer thing for you! Since when are furloughs granted to musketeers without their being requested?"

"Since the day musketeers have friends to ask for leaves on their behalf."

"Aha! then something is brewing, eh?"

"Yes we are going—" Aramis informed him.

"To what country?" Porthos interrupted.

"Upon my soul, I know less than nothing about it," Athos confessed. "Ask D'Artagnan."

"We are leaving for London, gentlemen," D'Artagnan announced.

"For London? What the devil are we going to do in London?"

"That is something I am not at liberty to tell you, gentlemen. You will have to trust me blindly."

"But to go to London we must have money," Porthos objected, "and I haven't a sou."

"Nor I," said Aramis.

"Nor I," said Athos.

"I have," D'Artagnan said triumphantly as he drew his treasure from his pocket and placed it on the table. "This bag contains three hundred pistoles. Let us each take seventy-five; that is enough to take us to London and back. Besides, don't worry, all of us will not reach London."

"Why, pray?"

"Because in all probability some one or other of us will be held up on the way!"

"Is this a campaign we are undertaking?"

"A most dangerous one, I warn you."

"Well, if we're risking our lives," Porthos complained, "I would like to know in what cause."

"What on earth for?" Athos asked.

"I agree with Porthos," said Aramis.

"Does the King usually give you his reasons in matters of this sort? No. He tells you gaily: 'Gentlemen, there is fighting in Flanders, or in Gascony. Go fight there!' And off you go! Why do you go? You do not even bother to think why?"

"D'Artagnan is right," Athos declared. "Here are our three furloughs from Monsieur de Tréville and here are three hundred pistoles from God knows where. So let us go get ourselves killed wherever we are told to. Is life worth the trouble of asking so many questions? D'Artagnan, I am ready to follow you."

"I too," Porthos assured the Gascon. "You may count on me," Aramis chimed in. "Anyhow I am not sorry to be leaving Paris; I need some distraction."

"You will have distraction aplenty, gentlemen, you may be sure of that," D'Artagnan promised.

"When are we to leave?" Athos inquired.

"Immediately; we have not a minute to lose."

Pandemonium broke loose as the young men summoned their lackeys.

"Ho, Grimaud, my boots, properly polished and set out for me!" Athos cried.

"Planchet, home at once to furbish my equipment!" D'Artagnan commanded.

"Mousqueton, I will give you five minutes to get my gear in shape!" Porthos said in lordly fashion.

"Bazin, you know what to do," Aramis counseled.

"Fetch up our horses from the stables," D'Artagnan ordered.

When the lackeys were gone, Porthos asked:

"What is our plan of campaign? Point one: where are we bound for?"

"Calais," said D'Artagnan. "That is the shortest route to London."

"No one has asked me for my advice," Porthos said, "but I will volunteer it. A party of four, setting out together, would attract too much attention. I therefore suggest that D'Artagnan give each of us his instructions. I am willing to go by the Boulogne road to blaze the trail; Athos can leave two hours later on the Amiens road, Aramis can follow us along the Noyon road, and D'Artagnan can do as he sees fit. I think it would be wise for D'Artagnan to join us eventually by whatever route he sees fit. And I do advise him to wear Planchet's livery while Planchet, disguised as a guardsman, impersonates D'Artagnan."

"To my way of thinking," Athos observed, "this matter is not one for lackeys. A gentleman may betray a secret by chance, a lackey invariably sells it!"

"The plan suggested by Porthos seems to me unfeasible," D'Artagnan commented, "if only because I am myself at a loss to tell you what to do. All I can tell you is this: I have a letter to deliver but I cannot make three copies of it, because it is sealed. Therefore in my opinion we should all travel together. The letter is here, in this pocket. . . ."

And he tapped his breast.

"If I am killed," he went on, "one of you must take it and ride on; if *he* is killed, a third will take his place, and so on. One thing alone matters: the letter must reach its destination."

"Bravo D'Artagnan, I agree!" said Athos. "We must be logical about all this. I am supposed to go to the spa of Forges; instead, I shall go to the seaside, for I can choose my place of convalescence. If anyone tries to stop us, I have but to show Monsieur de Tréville's letter, and you, my friends, your furlough orders; if we are attacked, we fight back; if we are sent up for trial, we will swear we were bound for a holiday at the seaside. Four men, each on his own, are too easily destroyed; four men, shoulder to shoulder, form a troop. We will arm our lackeys with pistols and light muskets; if an army is sent out against us, we shall give battle; and as D'Artagnan said, the survivor will deliver the message. . . ."

"Well spoken, Athos!" Aramis congratulated his friend. "You do not speak often, but when you do, you speak like Saint John of the Golden Mouth. I see eye to eye with Athos and I suggest we adopt his plan. What about it, Porthos?"

"I am with you. Since D'Artagnan bears the letter, he should be in charge of operations. Let him order, we will obey."

"Very well, I vote for the plan Athos outlined," D'Artagnan decided. "Let us leave within a half-hour!"

Whereupon four right hands moved toward the money bag, four palms seized seventy-five pistoles each, and four men separated in order to prepare for the forthcoming campaign.

XX
The Journey

At two in the morning our four adventurers left Paris by the Gate of Saint-Denis. So long as it was night, they exchanged no word, awed as they were by the darkness, and imagining ambushes on every side. But with the first light of dawn their tongues were loosened and with the sun their gaiety revived. It was like on the eve of battle; their hearts throbbed, their eyes danced, and they felt that the life they were perhaps to lose was, after all, a good thing.

The appearance of the caravan was most impressive; their black horses, their martial air, and that squadron training which makes a musketeer's mount keep in perfect step with his fellows would have betrayed the strictest incognito. The lackeys followed, armed to the teeth.

All went well as far as Chantilly which they reached at eight in the morning. Eager for breakfast, they alighted at an inn under a sign displaying Saint Martin giving half his cloak to a beggar. The lackeys were told to keep the horses saddled and to be ready to set off again immediately.

Our friends entered the common room and sat down. A gentleman who had just arrived by the Dammartin road was breakfasting at the same table. He started talking about the weather, the travelers answered, he drank their healths, and they returned the politeness.

But just as Mousqueton came to announce that their horses were ready and our friends rose, the stranger proposed to Porthos that they drink to the Cardinal. Porthos replied that he would like nothing better if the stranger would, in turn, drink to the King. The stranger countered that he recognized no other King but His Eminence. Porthos called him a drunkard; the stranger drew his sword.

"You were foolish," said Athos, "but, never mind, you can't draw back now. Kill the man and join us as soon as you can."

All three remounted their horses and left at a gallop while Porthos was promising his opponent to puncture him with every thrust known to fencing.

"There goes victim Number One," said Athos after they had advanced some five hundred paces.

"But why did the fellow choose Porthos?" Aramis asked.

"Porthos spoke louder than the rest of us," D'Artagnan explained. "The fellow took him for our leader."

"Ah, this lad from Gascony is a well of wisdom," Athos murmured.

And the travelers continued on their way.

At Beauvais they stopped to give their horses a breathing spell and to wait for Porthos. After two hours, Porthos having failed to arrive or to forward news, they resumed their journey.

A league from Beauvais, at a place where the road narrowed between two high banks, they came upon a dozen men who, taking advantage of the fact that the road was unpaved at that spot, seemed to be busy digging holes to deepen the muddy ruts.

Aramis, fearing to soil his boots in this artificial trench, cursed them roundly. Athos sought to restrain him but it was too late. The workmen started to jeer at the travelers; at their insolence even the phlegmatic Athos lost his head and urged his horse against one of them.

At this the workmen retreated as far as the ditch from which each produced a hidden musket. The result was that our seven travelers were literally riddled with bullets. Aramis received one which pierced his shoulder; Mousqueton another which embedded itself in the fleshy parts which prolong the small of the back. Only Mousqueton fell from his horse—not that he was badly hurt, but as he could not see his wound he fancied himself more seriously hurt than he was.

"This is an ambush," said D'Artagnan. "Don't waste a shot! Let us be off!"

Aramis, wounded though he was, seized his horse's mane and was borne off headlong with the rest. Mousqueton's horse, rejoining the group, galloped on in formation, riderless.

"That will give us a remount," said Athos.

"I would prefer a hat," D'Artagnan remarked. "Mine was carried away by a bullet. How very fortunate that I did not carry my letter in it."

"Look here," Aramis said anxiously, "do you realize they'll kill poor Porthos when he comes up?"

"If Porthos were on his legs he would have joined us long ago. I fancy that on the dueling ground that so-called drunkard sobered up miraculously!"

They galloped on for another two hours at top speed though their horses began to give signs of failing.

Hoping to avoid trouble, the cavalcade had chosen side roads but at Crèvecoeur Aramis declared he could go no further. In truth, it had required all the courage hidden beneath his polished manners and his suave grace to bring him that far; he kept growing paler and paler and he had to be held up on his horse. So they left him at an inn with Bazin who, to be frank, was more of a nuisance than a help in a skirmish, and they started off again, hoping to sleep at Amiens.

"*Morbleu!*" Athos cried to D'Artagnan, as they raced off, the cavalcade reduced to themselves and Grimaud and Planchet, "I vow I won't play into their hands again; no one will make me open my mouth or draw my sword till we reach Calais!"

"Let us make no vows; let us gallop if our horses can manage it!"

And the travelers dug their spurs in their horses' flanks, thanks to which vigorous stimulation the steeds regained their strength. The quartet reached Amiens at midnight and alighted at the *Sign of the Golden Lily.*

The host looked like the most honest man on earth; he received them with a candlestick in one hand and his cotton nightcap in the other. He begged to lodge the masters each in a comfortable room, but unfortunately these charming rooms were at opposite ends of the inn. D'Artagnan and Athos refused. The host protested that he had no other rooms worthy of Their Excellencies, to which Their Excellencies replied that they would sleep on mattresses in the public chamber. The host was insistent but the travelers held their ground and he had perforce to do their bidding.

They had just arranged their bedding and barricaded the door from within when there was a knock at the courtyard shutter. They asked who was there and recognized the voices of Planchet and Grimaud.

"Grimaud can take care of the horses," Planchet volunteered, "and if you gentlemen are willing, I shall sleep across the doorway. Thus you will be certain that no one can reach you."

"On what will you sleep, Planchet?" D'Artagnan asked. The valet produced a bundle of straw. "Very well!" D'Artagnan acquiesced. "Mine host's face inspires me with scant confidence; it is altogether too affable."

"I quite agree," said Athos.

Planchet climbed in through the window and settled himself across the door; Grimaud went off to lock himself in the stable, promising that he and the four horses would be ready by five o'clock in the morning.

The night passed off quietly enough though at about two o'clock someone tried the door. Planchet awoke with a start, crying, "Who goes there?"

"A mistake," came the answer. "Your pardon!"

And the intruder withdrew.

At four o'clock in the morning they heard a terrible riot in the stables. Grimaud had sought to awaken the stable boys; they had turned upon him and beaten him severely.

Opening the window of the stable, Athos and D'Artagnan saw the poor lad lying senseless on the ground, his head split. Some ostler had struck him from behind with the handle of a pitchfork.

Planchet ran to the yard to saddle the horses. They were utterly foundered; only Mousqueton's, which had run riderless for about six hours, was fit to proceed. However, it appeared that, by some inconceivable error, a veterinary, who had been sent for to bleed the host's horse, had bled Mousqueton's instead.

All this was becoming most annoying. Perhaps these successive accidents were the result of chance; but they might quite as probably be the result of a plot. Athos and D'Artagnan returned to the inn while Planchet set out to find out whether there were not three horses for sale in the neighborhood. At the gate of the inn, Planchet saw two horses, fresh, strong and fully equipped; they would have suited his masters perfectly. Inquiring to whom the nags belonged, he was told their owners had spent the night at the inn and were now settling their accounts with the landlord.

Athos went downstairs to pay the bill while D'Artagnan and Planchet waited for him at the street door. The host's office was in a low-ceilinged back room to which Athos was requested to go. Entering without the least mistrust, he found the host alone, seated at his desk, one of the drawers of which was half-open. Athos took two pistoles from his pocket to pay the bill; the host accepted the coin and then, having turned it over in his hands several times, suddenly shouted that it was counterfeit: "I shall have you and your confederate arrested as coiners," he cried.

"You blackguard!" Athos advanced toward him. "I'll cut your ears off."

At the same instant four men, armed to the teeth, entered by side doors and fell upon Athos.

"I'm trapped," Athos yelled at the top of his lungs, "Run, D'Artagnan! Spur, Spur!" And he fired two pistols.

D'Artagnan and Planchet needed no further invitation. Unfastening their horses from the gatepost they leaped upon them, buried their spurs in their flanks, and set off at full gallop.

"Do you know how Athos fared?" D'Artagnan asked of Planchet as they raced on.

"Monsieur, I saw a man fall at each of his shots. As I glanced through the glass door, I caught sight of him using his sword to advantage."

"Athos is a brave man. What a shame we must leave him behind. Ah, well! perhaps the same fate awaits us two steps hence! Forward Planchet, forward; you're a plucky fellow!"

"I told Monsieur I was a Picard. We of Picardy come up to scratch! Besides, Monsieur, I am in my homeland, here, and that puts me on my mettle."

Spurring on, master and lackey reached Saint-Omer without drawing bit. There they gave their horses a breather, holding their bridles under their arms for fear of some mishap, and had a bite of food, standing on the road. A few minutes later they started off again.

At a hundred paces from the gates of Calais D'Artagnan's horse sank under him; the blood flowed from his nose and eyes and nothing could be done to get him up again. Planchet's horse was still available but, having stopped at long last, now refused to budge. Congratulating themselves on being so close to the city, D'Artagnan and Planchet abandoned their mounts and ran toward the port. On the way Planchet drew his master's attention to a gentleman and his lackey who were some fifty paces ahead. Catching up with the pair at the port, D'Artagnan noted that their boots were covered with dust. The gentleman was bustling about authoritatively, asking here and there whether he could find passage for England immediately.

"Nothing easier," said the skipper of a vessel about to sail, "but we had orders this morning to allow no one to sail without express permission from Monsieur le Cardinal."

"I have that permission," the gentleman said, drawing a paper from his pocket, "here it is!"

"Monsieur must have it certified by the Governor of the Port," said the skipper. "When that is done, please give me first choice. I've a fine vessel and a crack crew."

"Where shall I find the Governor?"

"At his country house."

"Where is that?"

"About three-quarters of a mile out of town. Look Monsieur, you can see it from here—over there, at the foot of that little hill—that slate roof ..."

"Thank you," said the gentleman and, with his lackey, he made for the Governor's country house, D'Artagnan and Planchet following at an interval of five hundred paces. No sooner outside the city than D'Artagnan quickened his pace, overtaking the gentleman just as he was entering a little wood.

"Monsieur," he said, "You appear to be in a vast hurry."

"I could not be more pressed for time, Monsieur."

"I am distressed to hear that, Monsieur, for I too am pressed for time and I was about to ask a favor of you."

"What favor, pray?"

"To allow me to precede you."

"Impossible! I have covered sixty leagues in forty-four hours and I must be in London tomorrow at noon."

"*I* have covered the same distance in forty hours and *I* must be in London tomorrow at *ten* o'clock in the morning."

"Truly, Monsieur, I am extremely sorry but I arrived here first and will not pass second."

"Truly, Monsieur, I am quite as sorry, but I arrived here second and shall pass first."

"*Service du Roi,* I am on His Majesty's Service," the gentleman declared.

"*Service de Moi,* I on my own service!" D'Artagnan countered.

"Come, Monsieur, I think you are picking a needless quarrel."

"*Parbleu,* what else, my friend?"

"What do you want?"

"Would you like to know?"

"Certainly."

"Well then, I want your movement orders. I have none and need some."

"You are jesting, I presume."

"I never jest."

"Let me pass!"

"You shall not pass!"

"My dear young man, I shall blow your brains out. Ho, Lubin! my pistols!"

"Planchet, *you* handle the lackey, *I* shall manage the master."

Emboldened by his first exploit, Planchet sprang upon Lubin and, being young and lusty, soon had Lubin flattened out, Planchet's bony knee pinning Lubin's narrow chest to the ground.

"Carry on, Monsieur," Planchet called. "My man is accounted for."

The gentleman drew his sword and sprang upon D'Artagnan but he met more than he had bargained for. Within three seconds D'Artagnan pinked him thrice, dedicating each thrust as he dealt it: "One for Athos!" he cried. "One for Porthos!" and at the last, "one for Aramis!"

At the third thrust the gentleman fell like a log. D'Artagnan, believing him dead or at least in a faint, advanced to seize the order but, just as he stretched out his hand to search for it, the wounded man, who had not relinquished his sword, pinked D'Artagnan in the chest, crying:

"And one for you!"

"And one for me," D'Artagnan cried in a fury, nailing him to the earth with a fourth thrust.

This time the gentleman closed his eyes and fainted. D'Artagnan plucked the order from the pocket into which he had seen the gentleman stuff it. It was in the name of the Comte de Vardes.

Then, casting a last glance at the handsome youth he was leaving there, lying senseless and perhaps dead, D'Artagnan heaved a sigh over that inexplicable fate which drives men to destroy one another in the interests of people who are strangers to them and who often do not suspect their very existence. But he was soon roused from these reflections by Lubin who was howling for help with all his might. Planchet grasped Lubin by the throat and pressed on his gullet as hard as he could.

"He won't even whimper while I have him like this," he announced. "But so soon as I let go of him, Monsieur, he squeals like a stuck pig. You see, he's a Norman and Normans are a pig-headed lot."

Indeed, all but choked, Lubin still attempted to shout for help.

"This will settle him," D'Artagnan said, taking his handkerchief and gagging the lackey.

"Now Monsieur, let us string him up to a tree."

This accomplished they drew the body of the Comte de Vardes close to the lackey. Night was falling. As the stranger and his lackey were both immobilized a few feet within the wood they would probably remain there until the morrow.

"Now to the Governor's!" said D'Artagnan briskly.

"But you are wounded, Monsieur?"

"Oh, that's nothing. Come, let us attend to our most urgent business, we can attend to my wound later. It is a mere scratch."

They soon reached the worthy official's country house; the Comte de Vardes was announced; D'Artagnan entered.

"You have an order signed by the Cardinal?" the Governor asked.

D'Artagnan produced the order.

"Hm! quite regular and explicit."

"Of course, Monsieur. I am one of the Cardinal's most faithful servants."

"Apparently His Eminence is anxious to prevent someone from crossing to England."

"Yes, Monsieur, one D'Artagnan, a gentleman from Béarn, who set out for London with three of his friends."

"Do you know him personally?"

"Do I know—"

"D'Artagnan?"

"Intimately, Monsieur."

"Pray describe him to me, then."

"Nothing could be simpler," D'Artagnan assured him. And he proceeded to furnish the most minute description of the Comte de Vardes.

"Is he accompanied by anyone?"

"Yes, by a valet named Lubin."

"We will keep a sharp lookout for them," the Governor promised, "and if ever we lay hands on them, His Eminence may be sure they will be returned to Paris under heavy guard."

"By doing so, my dear Governor, you will have deserved well of the Cardinal," D'Artagnan said unctuously.

"Will you be seeing His Eminence on your return, Monsieur le Comte?"

"Why, of course."

"Tell him, I beg you, that I remain his humble servant."

"I shall not fail to do so."

Delighted with this assurance, the Governor countersigned the passport and handed it to D'Artagnan. Unwilling to lose a moment of his precious time in idle compliments, the Gascon bowed to the Governor, thanked him and took his leave. Once out of doors, master and lackey set off at top speed; taking a long détour, they skirted the wood, entering the town by another gate. As they reached the harbor, they found the vessel still ready to sail and the skipper awaiting them alongside.

"Well?" he asked as D'Artagnan appeared.

"Here is my pass, signed and countersigned."

"And the other gentleman?"

"He will not leave today," D'Artagnan explained. "But never mind: I will pay for both of us."

"In that case we shall set sail at once."

"The sooner the better," D'Artagnan agreed, leaping into the rowboat, Planchet behind him. Five minutes later they were aboard the vessel. It was high time, too, for they were barely half-a-league at sea when D'Artagnan saw a flash and heard a detonation as the cannon announced the closing of the harbor.

At last he had an opportunity to examine his injury. Happily, as he had thought, it was not serious: the point of the sword, striking a rib, had glanced along the bone, and his shirt, matted over the wound, had staunched the blood. But he was exhausted and when they laid out a mattress on deck for him, he sank gratefully upon it and promptly fell into a deep sleep.

At daybreak, the vessel was a few leagues off the English coast; the breeze had been slight all night and the sailing slow. By ten o'clock the craft dropped anchor in Dover harbor. Half an hour later D'Artagnan set foot on English soil, crying:

"Here I am at last!"

But that was not all, they must get to London. In England the post was well organized and post-horses readily available; D'Artagnan and Planchet took advantage of this and, preceded by a postilion, they reached the capital within four hours.

D'Artagnan did not know London and he could not speak one word of English, but he wrote the name of Buckingham on a piece of paper and everyone to whom he showed it, pointed out the way to the Duke's mansion.

The Duke was at Windsor, hunting with the King. D'Artagnan inquired for the Duke's confidential valet, who had accompanied him in all his travels and spoke perfect French. He explained that he had come from Paris on a matter of life and death and that he must speak to his master immediately.

The assurance with which D'Artagnan spoke convinced Patrick on the spot. The minister's minister therefore ordered two horses to be saddled forthwith and himself accompanied the young guardsman. As for Planchet, he had been lifted from his horse stiff as a ramrod; the poor lad's strength was well-nigh spent. D'Artagnan, on the contrary, seemed fresh as a daisy.

At Windsor Castle they inquired for the Duke and were told that the King and Buckingham were in the marshes two or three leagues distant. As they reached the place twenty minutes later, Patrick recognized his master's voice, calling his falcon back to him.

"Whom am I to announce to His Grace?" Patrick asked.

"The young man who one evening challenged him on the Pont-Neuf, opposite the Samaritaine."

"A somewhat peculiar introduction, Monsieur, if I may say so."

"You will find it as good as any other."

Patrick rode off, located the Duke, and announced that a messenger awaited him, identifying the messenger as directed.

Buckingham recalled the incident at once. Suspecting that something vital was going on in France, he hastened to ask where the messenger was. Recognizing the uniform of the guards, he rode straight up to D'Artagnan. Patrick kept discreetly in the background. At once, Buckingham, reining in his horse, cast all discretion to the winds. Voicing all his fear and love:

"Has any harm befallen Her Majesty?" he asked.

"I think not, Milord. Nevertheless, I believe Her Majesty to be in great danger from which Your Grace alone can save her."

"I? God help me, I would be only too happy to be of service to the Queen. Speak, man, speak up!"

"Pray read this letter, Milord."

"A letter from whom?"

"From Her Majesty, I think."

"From Her Majesty!" Buckingham repeated, turning so pale that D'Artagnan feared he was about to faint. His hands trembling, he broke the seal.

"Why is this letter ripped here?" Buckingham asked, his finger on a portion of the letter where the paper was pierced through.

"I had not noticed that, Milord," D'Artagnan said. "The Comte de Vardes made that hole when his sword pinked my chest."

"Are you wounded?" Buckingham asked, unfolding the letter.

"Nothing serious, Milord, a mere scratch."

"Great Heavens, what have I read?" Buckingham cried aghast. Then, imperiously: "Stay here, Patrick, or rather find the King wherever he is and tell His Majesty that I beseech him to excuse me but that a matter of the utmost importance calls me to London." Turning to D'Artagnan: "Come, Monsieur, come!" he ordered.

And both set off toward the capital at full gallop.

XXI

LADY CLARK

Along the way the Duke drew from D'Artagnan not all that happened but what D'Artagnan himself knew. By adding what he recalled to what information the young Gascon gave him, Buckingham was able to form a pretty exact idea of the state of affairs. The Queen's letter was short and scarcely informative but it afforded ample confirmation of how serious the situation must be. What surprised him most was that the Cardinal, so vitally interested in preventing the youth from reaching England, had been powerless to intercept him. In the face of this astonishment, D'Artagnan told him how carefully the voyage had been planned and what precautions had been taken . . . how devoted his three friends had been . . . how he had left them scattered along the road, bathed in their blood . . . how he had come off successfully save for the sword thrust which had pierced the Queen's letter . . . and in what terrible coin he had repaid Monsieur de Vardes. . . . Listening to D'Artagnan's plain matter-of-fact account, the Duke looked at the Gascon from time to time in wonder as if he could not understand how so much prudence, courage and devotion could belong to a man who looked barely twenty.

The horses went like the wind and in no time at all they reached the gates of London. D'Artagnan imagined that on arriving in the city the Duke would slacken his pace, but no! Buckingham rode on at top speed, heedless of any pedestrians so unfortunate as to stand in his path. As they crossed the city he ran down at least three people without even turning to see what had become of his victims. D'Artagnan followed amidst cries which sounded very much like curses.

Entering the courtyard of his mansion, Buckingham dismounted and without bothering about his steed, tossed the reins over its neck and rushed to the front steps. D'Artagnan followed suit except that he did show a little more concern for the noble animals whose worth he had been able to appreciate. He was pleased to see four grooms rushing from kitchen and stables to attend to the horses.

The Duke walked so fast that D'Artagnan had some trouble in keeping up with him. They passed through several apartments furnished with an elegance which even the greatest noblemen of France could not imagine; presently they reached a bedroom which was at once a miracle of taste and splendor. In the alcove of this room was a door cut through a tapestry; the Duke opened it with a small gold key which he wore on a chain of the same metal around his neck. Out of discretion, D'Artagnan lingered back, but as Buckingham passed through the door he turned around and noting the young man's hesitation:

"Come in, my friend, come in," he invited, "and if you are so fortunate as to be admitted to Her Majesty's presence, pray tell her what you have seen."

Encouraged by this invitation, D'Artagnan followed the Duke who closed the door behind them. They were in a small chapel tapestried with Persian silk and gold brocade and brilliantly lighted by a great number of wax tapers. Above a kind of altar and beneath a blue velvet dais, surmounted by red and white plumes, was a life-size portrait of Anne of Austria, so strikingly faithful that D'Artagnan uttered an exclamation of surprise. It was as though the Queen stood there before them about to speak.

Above the altar and beneath the portrait, was the casket which held the diamond studs. The Duke approached the altar, kneeled as a priest might have knelt before a crucifix, and then opened the casket. From it he drew a large bow of blue ribbon sparkling with diamonds:

"Here," he said, "here are these precious diamonds with which I had vowed to be buried. The Queen gave them to me, the Queen requires their return. So be it. Her will be done, like that of God, in all things."

Slowly, one after the other, he kissed the beloved studs with which he must reluctantly part. Suddenly he uttered a terrible cry.

"What is it, Milord?" D'Artagnan exclaimed anxiously. "What is the matter?"

"The matter?" Buckingham winced; he was shaking like a leaf.

"Milord, what——?"

"All is lost!"

"But—?"

"Two of the studs are missing. There are only ten here!"

"Can you have lost them, Milord? Do you think they have been stolen?"

"They have been stolen and the Cardinal is responsible. Look, the ribbons which held them have been cut with scissors."

"If they were stolen—if Milord suspects anyone—perhaps that person still has them—"

"Wait, wait!" cried the Duke. "The only time I wore these studs was at a ball given by the King at Windsor a week ago. Lady Winter, with whom I once had a falling out, stood beside me quite long as we made up our differences. Yes, that's it! That reconciliation was nothing but a jealous woman's revenge. I have not laid eyes on her since. That woman is an agent of the Cardinal's."

"Then he has agents all over the world?"

"Yes, yes, everywhere." Buckingham gnashed his teeth with rage. "He is a terrible enemy." There was a long silence. Then, passionately: "Tell me, when is this ball in Paris to take place?"

"Next Monday."

"Next Monday. Five days from now. Ah, we have time and time aplenty!" Flinging open the door: "Patrick!" he called, "Patrick!"

Imperturbable, as though he had not left the spot, Patrick stood at attention by the doorway.

"Patrick, send for my jeweler and my secretary!"

The promptness with which the servant withdrew bore eloquent testimony to his discretion and obedience. Buckingham had mentioned the jeweler first but the secretary was the first to appear because he lived in the ducal mansion. He found Buckingham seated at a table in his bedroom, writing orders in his own hand.

"Jackson," said the Duke, "you will call upon the Lord Chancellor immediately and inform him that I commit these orders to him for execution. I wish them to be issued forthwith."

"But Your Grace, if the Lord Chancellor asks me what reasons prompted you to adopt such an extraordinary measure, what shall I answer?"

"Tell him that such is my good pleasure and that I account for my pleasure to no man."

The secretary smiled:

"Is My Lord Chancellor to forward this reply to the King if His Majesty should happen to inquire why no vessel of his is to leave any British port?"

"Very well, Jackson!" Buckingham drew a deep breath. "Should His Majesty so inquire, the Lord Chancellor is to reply that I am determined on war and that this measure is my first act of hostility against France."

The secretary bowed and retired.

"Well, we are safe on that score," Buckingham said jauntily. "If the studs have not yet left for France they will not arrive before you."

"How so, Milord?"

"I have just clapped an embargo on all vessels at present in His Majesty's ports. Without express permission not one of them can weigh anchor!"

D'Artagnan stared with stupefaction at this man who, invested with unlimited power by his sovereign, was thus abusing the royal confidence to serve his amours. D'Artagnan's expression was so candid that Buckingham could not fail to read his thoughts. He smiled.

"Yes, yes!" he said impetuously, "Anne of Austria is my true Queen. At one word from her, I would betray my country, my sovereign and my God. She asked me not to send the Protestants of La Rochelle the aid I had promised them; I have not done so. I broke my word, but what of that? Did I not bow to Her Majesty's wishes? Have I not been richly rewarded? Have I not my obedience to thank for the portrait you just saw?"

D'Artagnan mused on the mysterious and tenuous threads upon which the destinies of great nations and the lives of mere men are sometimes hung. He was lost in these thoughts when the goldsmith entered.

O'Reilly, master of his guild, was an Irishman; among the most skilled workmen of Europe, he earned, as he himself admitted, one hundred thousand livres a year from Buckingham's custom alone.

"Come in here, O'Reilly, come in!" Buckingham led the goldsmith into his chapel. "Look at these studs and tell me what they are worth apiece."

O'Reilly cast a single glance at the elegant mounting of the jewels . . . estimated the worth of each stud . . . looked at the whole display rapidly to make sure he was accurate in his appraisal . . . and without hesitation:

"Fifteen hundred pistoles apiece, and beauties they be, M'Lud," he said pontifically.

"How soon can you make two studs to match these ten, O'Reilly?"

"A week, Your Grace."

"O'Reilly, I will give you three thousand pistoles for each of the two studs if I can have them by the day after tomorrow."

"M'Lud, have them you shall!"

"You are worth your weight in gold, Master Goldsmith, but that is not all. These studs must not be entrusted to anybody; the work must be done here, under this roof."

"Impossible, M'Lud. No one else can make new studs to look like the others, Your Grace, even if I say so as shouldn't."

"That is why you are now a prisoner here, my dear O'Reilly. Even if you wanted to leave this hospitable dwelling at this moment, you could not do so. Come, my friend, make the best of it. Name any of your workmen you need and tell me what tools they must bring along."

O'Reilly knew the Duke; he realized that any objection would be futile and he made up his mind then and there.

"May I let my wife know, please, M'Lud?"

"Certainly. You may even see her, my dear O'Reilly. Your captivity will be a mild one, rest assured. And because every inconvenience calls for compensation, here—over and above the price of the studs—here are a thousand pistoles to console you for the trouble I am giving you."

D'Artagnan could not recover from his surprise as he saw how this statesman played ducks and drakes with men and millions. As for the jeweler, he wrote to his wife, enclosing the draft for a thousand pistoles and asking her to send his most skilful apprentice . . . an assortment of diamonds (he specified names and weights) . . . the required tools which he carefully listed . . . his nightshirt and a change of clothes. . . . Buckingham led him to the apartment allotted to him. within a half-hour it was transformed into a workshop. A sentry was stationed at each door with orders to allow only Patrick to go in and no one to go out.

Having settled this matter, Buckingham turned his attention to D'Artagnan.

"Now, my young friend," he said affably, "all England is yours. What can I do for you? Say what you want and it shall be done."

"Thank you, Milord, the one thing I crave is a bed to lie down on."

Buckingham assigned D'Artagnan a room adjoining his own. He wished to keep the lad close at hand, not because he mistrusted him but because he wished to have someone to whom he could constantly talk about the Queen.

An hour later an ordinance was published in London forbidding the departure from all British ports of vessels bound for France; even the mail packet was to be held up. Public opinion viewed this act as a declaration of war between the two kingdoms. Two days later, at eleven o'clock, the new studs were finished, their lustre and workmanship so perfect that neither Buckingham nor even an expert dealer could have distinguished them from the others. The Duke summoned D'Artagnan immediately.

"Here are the studs you came to fetch," he said, "I trust you will report that I have done all that was humanly possible."

"Milord need have no qualms on that score," D'Artagnan assured him. "I shall tell what I have seen." Buckingham nodded. "But Your Grace has not given me the casket," D'Artagnan said in surprise.

"The casket would only be an encumbrance, my friend." Buckingham sighed. "Besides, I treasure it, for it is all I have left of the Queen's. You will tell Her Majesty that I am keeping it."

"I shall deliver your message word for word, Milord."

"And now," Buckingham resumed looking earnestly at the young man, "how can I ever repay my debt to you?"

D'Artagnan blushed; obviously the Duke was trying to get him to accept some gift. But the idea that the blood of his comrades and his own were to be paid for with English gold was strangely repugnant.

"Let us understand each other, Milord," he said courteously. "Let us see things clearly at outset in order to avoid misapprehension. I am in the service of the King and Queen of France. I am a Royal Guardsman; my Commanding Officer, Monsieur des Essarts, like his brother-in-law, Monsieur de Tréville, is particularly attached to their Majesties. Your Grace sees therefore under what auspices I have come here. What is more, I might perhaps never have undertaken all this had I not wished to please someone who is my lady, just as the Queen is yours."

The Duke smiled: "Yes, I see! Indeed, I dare say I know the lady you refer to. It is—"

"I have not mentioned her name, Milord—"

"True, Monsieur. My debt of gratitude for your devotion therefore belongs to that lady—who shall remain nameless."

"Exactly, Milord. At this moment, with war looming between our countries, I confess I can see nothing in Your Grace but an Englishman, hence an enemy. I need not add that I would therefore have greater pleasure in meeting you on the field of battle than in Windsor Park or in the halls of the Louvre. Nevertheless, nothing will prevent me from carrying out my mission in every detail or from laying down my life, if necessary, in so doing. But I repeat: I will accomplish this without Your Grace having cause to thank me at this time any more than at our first meeting."

"We Englishmen say: 'Proud as a Scot,' " Buckingham murmured.

"We Frenchmen say: 'Proud as a Gascon,' " D'Artagnan replied, bowing. "The Gascons are the Scots of France."

"Come now, you cannot leave like this. Where are you off to? How will you get away?"

"That's true."

"Upon my soul! you Frenchmen are cocksure!"

"I had forgotten that England was an island and you were its king."

"Go to the port, ask for the brig *Sund,* and give the Captain this letter. He will convey you to a little harbor where you are surely not expected; it is used by fishermen only."

"The harbor of—?"

"Saint-Valéry! But listen: when you land there, go to a mean-looking little inn on the front. It has no name or sign, it is a mere fishermen's hovel; you can't mistake it, it is the only such place."

"And then?"

"You will ask for the host and say: *Forward!*"

"Which means?"

"*En avant*—that is the password. He will give you a fully saddled horse and tell you what road you are to take. In this way you will find four relays on your route. If you will give your Paris address at each relay, the four horses will follow you there. You know two of them already and, as a lover of horseflesh, you seem to have appreciated them; you saw how they brought us from Windsor. You may take my word for it that the two others are just as good. These horses are equipped for campaigning. Proud though you are, you will not refuse to accept one for yourself and one for each of your companions. Remember that they will serve you to make war against us. The end justifies the means, as you Frenchmen put it, does it not?"

"Yes, Milord, I accept with pleasure!" D'Artagnan bowed low. "Please God, we shall make good use of your gift."

"Now your hand, young man. Perhaps we shall meet soon on the field of battle. Meanwhile, we part good friends, I trust."

"Ay, Milord, but with the hope of soon becoming enemies."

"Have no fear on that score, I promise you that."

"I count on your word, Milord!"

D'Artagnan bowed again and hastened to the port.

Opposite the Tower of London, he found the *Sund* and gave the Captain his letter; the Captain had it certified by the Governor of the Port and they set sail at once.

Fifty vessels were waiting to set out as soon as the prohibition was lifted. As the *Sund* passed close alongside one of them, D'Artagnan fancied he saw a familiar figure—the woman of Meung, the woman whom the stranger had called Milady and whom our Gascon had thought so beautiful. But thanks to the swift tide and to the brisk wind the *Sund* passed so quickly that he caught little more than a glimpse of her.

Next day at about nine o'clock he landed at Saint-Valéry and immediately looked for the inn Buckingham had mentioned. He easily identified it by the riotous noise within; already there was excited talk of speedy and certain war between England and France, and the happy sailors were carousing to celebrate it.

D'Artagnan made his way through the crowd, found the host and whispered: *Forward!* The host immediately motioned to him to follow, went out by a door leading to the yard, advanced to the stable where a horse, ready-saddled, awaited, and asked D'Artagnan if he needed anything else.

"I want to know the route I am to take."

"Go from here to Blangy and from Blangy to Neufchâtel. At Neufchâtel, at the *Sign of the Golden Harrow,* give the innkeeper the password and you will find a horse, ready-saddled, just as you did here."

"What do I owe you?"

"Everything is paid for, Monsieur, and handsomely, too," the host said importantly. "Be off then and God speed you!"

"Amen," breathed D'Artagnan, setting off at full gallop.

Four hours later he was at Neufchâtel. Faithfully he followed the instructions he had received; at Neufchâtel, as at Saint-Valéry, he found a fully saddled mount waiting for him. He was about to transfer the pistols from one saddle to another when he noticed that his new mount was already furnished with similar ones.

"Your address in Paris?"

"Hôtel des Gardes, Monsieur des Essarts, Commanding Officer."

"Good."

"What route am I to take?"

"The Rouen road, but do not go through the city; skirt it on your right. At the hamlet of Ecouis, you will find an inn—the only one—*The Sign of the French Arms*. Don't judge it by appearances; you will find a horse as good as this one in the stables."

"Same password?"

"Exactly."

"Good-bye, host."

"Farewell, Monsieur. Do you need anything?"

D'Artagnan shook his head, waved his hand and made off at full speed. At Ecouis the same scene was repeated: a host equally obliging . . . a fresh fully equipped horse . . . a request for his Paris address . . . a statement of the same . . . a wave of the hand and a cloud of dust as he galloped off toward Pontoise. . . .

Here he changed horses for the last time and at nine o'clock galloped into the courtyard of the Hôtel de Tréville. He had covered nearly sixty leagues—in twelve hours.

Monsieur de Tréville received him as if he had seen him that very morning. But, on shaking his hand a little more warmly than usual, he told him that Monsieur des Essart's company was on guard duty at the Louvre that night and that he might repair at once to his post.

XXII

In Which Their Majesties Dance La Merlaison, a Favorite Ballet of the King's

On the morrow all Paris was agog with talk of the ball which the City Aldermen were to give in honor of the King and Queen. Their Majesties were to dance the famous La Merlaison, the King's favorite ballet.

For the past week feverish preparations for this important occasion had made the Hôtel de Ville hum with activity. The city carpenters erected scaffolds to seat the ladies invited . . . the city grocer had furnished the reception rooms with two hundred white waxen torches, a piece of luxury unheard of at that period . . . no fewer than twenty violinists were to play, at double their usual wage on condition, rumor said, that they played the night through. . . .

At ten o'clock in the morning the Sieur de La Coste, Ensign in the King's Guards, followed by two officers and several archers of the Corps of Guards, called upon the City Registrar, Clément, to demand the keys of all doors, rooms and offices in the building. These keys were handed over to him instantly; each bore a label to identify it. From that moment Monsieur de La Coste, as supreme Security Officer, was charged with guarding every inch of the premises.

At eleven o'clock Captain du Hallier, of the guards, appeared with fifty archers who immediately took up their stations at the posts assigned them in the Hôtel de Ville.

At three o'clock, two companies of guards reported, one French, the other Swiss. The French company was composed half of Monsieur du Hallier's men, half of men under Monsieur des Essarts.

At six in the evening the guests began to arrive. Fast as they entered, they were ushered to their seats on the scaffolding in the great hall.

At nine o'clock Madame la Première Présidente, wife of the Chief Magistrate, swept into the City Hall. Next to the Queen she was the most important personage of the fête. She was received by the notables of the city and shown to a loge immediately opposite the one the Queen was to occupy.

At ten o'clock, the King's collation, consisting of preserves, confitures and other sweetmeats, was prepared in the little chamber facing the church of Saint-Jean and placed in front of the silver service of the City, which was guarded by four archers.

At midnight loud cries and vociferous cheers rose from the street, marking the King's progress as he passed through the city from the Louvre to the Hôtel de Ville along thoroughfares illumined with colored lanterns.

Aldermen and City Councilors, wearing their broadcloth robes and preceded by six sergeants, each of whom bore a torch, advanced to attend upon the King. Meeting His Majesty on the steps, they stopped while the Provost of the Merchants made the official compliment of welcome. His Majesty replied by excusing himself for his late arrival, blaming it on Monsieur le Cardinal who had detained him until eleven o'clock to discuss matters of State.

His Majesty, in full dress, was accompanied by His Royal Highness, Monsieur Duc d'Orléans and brother to the King, by the Comte de Soissons, who was later to attempt to assassinate Richelieu, by the Grand Prior, in all the splendor of his ecclesiastical robes, by the Duc de Longueville, a third-rate politician, governor of Normandy, by the Duc d'Elboeuf, the husband of a legitimized daughter of Henry IV, by the Comte d'Harcourt, d'Elboeuf's son, by the Comte de La Roche-Guyon, descendant of a heroine of the Hundred Years' War, by Monsieur de Liancourt, a profligate redeemed by his young wife, by the Comte de Cramail, author and wit who was to be imprisoned by Richelieu for twelve years, by Monsieur de Baradas and by the Chevalier de Souveray.

No one in the crowd failed to notice that the King looked glum and preoccupied.

A dressing-room had been prepared for the King and another for Monsieur, with masquerade dress in each; the same had been done for the Queen and Madame la Première Présidente. The nobles and ladies of Their Majesties' suites were to dress two by two in chambers prepared for the purpose. Before entering his dressing-room, the King left orders to be notified as soon as the Cardinal arrived.

Half an hour later loud cheers were heard, proclaiming the Queen's arrival; aldermen and councilors, as before, followed the sergeants to the steps of the City Hall where they repeated the ceremony of welcome.

The Queen entered the great hall. To the public she too, like the King, looked sad and, above all, fatigued. Just as she arrived the curtains of a small gallery, which had until then remained closed, were suddenly parted to reveal, for an instant, the pale face of the Cardinal. His eyes, piercing bright, were fastened upon those of the Queen; and as he noted that she was not wearing the diamond studs, a smile of fierce, cruel joy passed over his lips. The Queen lingered a while to receive the compliments of the city gentlemen and to reply to the salutations of their ladies.

Suddenly the King appeared at one of the doors of the hall with the Cardinal. His Majesty wore no masquerade and the ribbons of his doublet were scarcely tied; His Eminence was dressed as a Spanish Cavalier. The Cardinal was speaking in a low voice and the King, listening, was pale as wax. His Majesty made his way through the crowd, bowed to the Queen and, in a broken voice, said:

"Well, Madame, pray why are you not wearing your diamond studs? Did I not tell you how pleased I should be to see how they become you?"

The Queen, looking around her, descried the Cardinal in the background, smiling diabolically.

"Sire," she replied, in faltering tones, "I feared something might happen to them in such a throng."

"There you were wrong, Madame! If I presented them to you it was because I wished you to wear them. I repeat, you were quite wrong, Madame."

The King's voice trembled with anger, the bystanders wide-eyed and completely bewildered, stood aside, wondering what could be the matter.

"I can easily send for them, Sire," the Queen offered. "They are at the Louvre; within a few minutes Your Majesty's wishes will be fulfilled."

"Pray do so, Madame, pray do so as quickly as possible. The ballet is to begin within an hour."

Curtseying, the Queen followed the ladies who were to conduct her to her dressing-room. The King returned to his.

There was a buzz of chatter. Surprise and confusion filled the hall; everyone had noticed that something was awry between King and Queen, but both had spoken so low that the bystanders had discreetly stepped aside. Thus no one had overheard anything. The violins began to play at their loudest but nobody listened.

The King was the first to emerge from his dressing-room, clad in a hunting costume of great elegance; this type of dress became him best and now he really looked like the first gentleman of his kingdom. He was followed by Monsieur and the other nobles, similarly apparelled.

The Cardinal drew near the King and handed him a tiny casket; opening it, the King found two diamond studs.

"What does this mean?" he asked in astonishment.

"Nothing, Sire! But if the Queen wears her studs—which I very much doubt—I beg you to count them. Should you find that the Queen wears but ten, Sire, pray ask Her Majesty who could have stolen the two that are here?"

The King looked blankly at the Cardinal and was about to ask him something when suddenly a cry of admiration rose up on all sides. It was the Queen, making her entrance. If His Majesty appeared to be the first gentleman of the realm, the Queen was undoubtedly the most beautiful woman in all France. The habit of a huntress suited her marvelously well, setting off her figure to excellent advantage. She wore a beaver hat with blue feathers, a tight-waisted jacket of pearl-gray velvet fastened with diamond clasps, and a skirt of blue satin embroidered with silver. On her left shoulder sparkled the diamond studs, on a bow of the same color as her plumes and her skirt.

The King trembled with joy, the Cardinal with anger, but they were still too far from the Queen to count the studs. Her Majesty was wearing them, to be sure, but were there ten or twelve?

At that moment the violins gave the signal for the ball to open. The King advanced toward Madame la Première Présidente, who was to be his partner; His Royal Highness Monsieur advanced toward the Queen. They took their places and the ballet began. His Majesty figured opposite the Queen and every time he passed her he devoured those studs with his eyes but could never pause long enough to count them. A cold sweat glistened on the Cardinal's brow as he watched. The ballet, which had sixteen figures, lasted a full hour.

When it was finished, amid enthusiastic applause, each gentleman led his lady back to her place; but the King, availing himself of his privilege to leave his lady where she stood, advanced eagerly toward the Queen.

"I thank you, Madame, for deferring to my wishes," he said graciously, "but I believe two of your studs are missing, I am bringing them back to you."

Whereupon he handed the Queen the two studs the Cardinal had given to him.

"What, Sire!" cried the Queen, feigning surprise, "you are giving me two more! Then I shall have fourteen in all!"

The King, at last in a position to count, could scarcely believe his eyes. Turning aside sulkily, he summoned the Cardinal and, sternly:

"Well, Monsieur le Cardinal," he asked, "what does this mean?"

"It means, Sire, that I wished to present Her Majesty with those two studs but, not venturing to present them myself, I adopted this means of doing so."

The Queen flashed him a smile which for all its brilliant graciousness yet proved that she was not duped by this ingenious piece of gallantry.

"I am the more grateful to Your Eminence," she said blandly, "because I am sure these two studs have cost you as much as the other twelve cost the King."

Then, having bowed to the King and the Cardinal, the Queen went back to her dressing-room.

And so these events took place among the most illustrious—King, Queen and Cardinal—while other important or frivolous activities occupied the flower of French nobility, the cream of the magistracy, and the choicest Parisian citizenry. Meanwhile, anonymous and unseen, a young Gascon, a guardsman, the man to whom Anne of Austria owed her extraordinary triumph over the Cardinal, was lost in a throng gathered at one of the doors. With pardonable satisfaction, he had surveyed a scene comprehensible to four people alone: the King, the Queen—the Cardinal and—himself!

The Queen made her exit and D'Artagnan was about to go home when he felt a light touch on his shoulder. Turning around he saw a young woman who beckoned him to follow her. This young woman wore a black velvet mask, but despite this precaution, taken against others rather than against him, he recognized his quondam guide, the alert, sprightly and shapely Madame Bonacieux.

The evening before, they had barely exchanged a few words in the quarters of Germain, at the gatekeeper's lodge. So eager was the lover, with the objects and message he brought, and so eager was his lady to communicate both to the Queen, that love was neglected and Madame Bonacieux tarried but a few moments. This evening, however, D'Artagnan hoped for better, moved as he was by both love and curiosity. As he followed her on and on through corridors that became more and more deserted, he sought to stop the young woman, grasp her and look into her eyes if only for an instant. But, quick and elusive as a bird, she always slipped through his hands. Whenever he sought to speak, her finger placed over her lips, in a little imperious gesture full of charm, enjoined silence, reminding him that he must obey blindly and in every particular. Finally, after winding to left and right down various passageways, through vestibules and across landings, Madame Bonacieux opened a door and ushered him into a small antechamber that was completely dark. There again she bade him be silent, placing her finger upon *his* lips *this* time. Then she opened an inner door concealed by a tapestry, a brilliant light spread through the room, she disappeared, and all was silence and darkness again.

D'Artagnan stood motionless for a moment, wondering where he was and what was about to happen. Presently a ray of light penetrated into the chamber ... he felt a current of warm perfumed air ... he heard the voices of two, then three ladies conversing ... he could not distinguish what they said but he noted the refinement and ceremony of their tones ... the word *Majesty* occurred several times ... so he could but conclude that he was in a chamber adjoining the Queen's dressing-room. . . .

He stood there waiting in the shadows. Now the sounds from the next room came more clearly. The Queen sounded cheerful and happy, at which her ladies seemed to be somewhat astonished, for, as everyone knew, Her Majesty was usually worried and anxious. D'Artagnan actually caught a few words of the conversation. As a lady with a high, slight voice congratulated the Queen on her new-found gaiety, he heard Her Majesty reply that she was stimulated by the beauty of the fête and the pleasure the ballet had given her. Since it is never permissible to contradict a Queen, whether she smile or weep, the ladies vied with one another in hymning the praises of the Aldermen and Councilors of the good City of Paris.

Although D'Artagnan did not know the Queen, he soon distinguished her voice from the others, first by a slight foreign accent, then by that tone of domination natural to sovereigns. He heard the voice approach then withdraw from the door; then, almost imperceptibly, the knob turned and the door opened stealthily and ever so slightly. D'Artagnan even saw the shadow of a person who, walking up and down, occasionally intercepted the light.

At length a hand and arm of wondrous form and whiteness appeared through the tapestry. D'Artagnan, understanding that this was his recompense, fell to his knees, grasped the outstretched hand and respectfully pressed it to his lips. Before he realized what had happened, the hand was withdrawn and, as he looked down, blinking, at his own hand, he saw and felt an object in his palm, a hard, bright object which he recognized as a ring. Then, the door was promptly closed and D'Artagnan once again found himself in complete darkness.

Our Gascon placed the ring on his finger and again waited; obviously all was not yet over. After the reward of his devotion surely he would receive that of his love. Besides, though the ballet was done, the festivities had scarcely begun: supper was to be served at three o'clock and the clock of Saint-Jean had just struck a quarter to three.

The sound of voices in the next room gradually diminished, the echo of departing footsteps reached him, and the door to the corridor suddenly opened. Madame Bonacieux entered briskly.

"You, at last!" cried D'Artagnan.

"Hush!" she commanded, pressing her hand on his lips. "Not a sound! You must go away at once just as you came."

"But when shall I see you again? When? And where?"

"You will find a note from me waiting at your home. Begone now, I implore you; begone and God bless you!"

Quickly she pushed D'Artagnan out of the room. He obeyed like a child, without venturing objection or resistance—which proves conclusively that he was genuinely in love with her.

XXIII
THE RENDEZVOUS

D'Artagnan ran home immediately. Though it was past three in the morning and he had to go through some of the most ill-famed and dangerous quarters of Paris, he met with no misadventure. As everybody knows, drunkards and lovers are protected by a special deity.

He found the door to his passage ajar, climbed the staircase and knocked gently, two short raps followed by three, as agreed upon between him and his lackey. He had sent Planchet home from the Hôtel de Ville two hours before and, according to instructions, Planchet was sitting up awaiting his arrival.

"Did anyone bring me a letter?" D'Artagnan asked eagerly.

"No, Monsieur."

D'Artagnan's face fell.

"No, Monsieur, nobody *brought* you a letter," Planchet went on, "but there is a letter here which seems to have come of itself."

"What on earth do you mean, ass?"

"I mean to say that when I came home, I had the key to your apartment in my pocket . . . I had that key, Monsieur, and I never let it out of my hands . . . and yet I found a letter for you sitting up on the green tablecover in your bedroom like a white tulip in a bunch of ferns. . . ."

"Where is the letter?"

"I left it where it lay, Monsieur." Planchet drew a deep breath. "Begging your pardon, Monsieur, it is not natural for letters to come into people's houses like that. Had the window been open or even half open, I should think nothing of it; but no, Monsieur, everything was tight shut. I beg Monsieur to beware; I vow there's witchcraft in all this."

While Planchet was expatiating, D'Artagnan ran to his bedroom and tore open the letter. It was from Madame Bonacieux and ran as follows:

Great thanks are due you and await your presence so that they may be given you.

Pray come this evening at about ten o'clock to Saint-Cloud and wait opposite the lodge that stands at right angles to the mansion of Monsieur d'Estrées.

C. B.

Reading this note, D'Artagnan felt his heart dilate and contract with the delicious spasms that torture and caress the hearts of all true lovers. Here was the first note he had received from a woman, the first meeting ever granted him; his heart swelled with the intoxication of joy and he felt about to faint at the very portals of that terrestial Paradise known as Love.

Planchet, worried at his master's impetuous exit and at the long silence that ensued, stood between sitting-room and bedroom, scratching his ear. Why was his master so excited and why did he successively flush and grow pale?

"Well, Monsieur," he opined, "was I right? Is this some dirty work or did I guess wrong?"

"You are quite wrong, Planchet and to prove it here is a crown for you to drink to my health."

"I am much obliged to Monsieur for the money; and I promise to follow your instructions exactly. All the same, letters which suddenly materialize in houses that are bolted and locked—"

"—fall from Heaven, obviously."

"Then Monsieur is happy?"

"Happy as a king, Planchet, happy as the day is long, happy as a clam at high water...."

"Begging Monsieur's pardon, may I take advantage of his happiness by going to bed?"

"Certainly, my lad. Off with you!"

"May all the blessings of Heaven fall upon you, Monsieur. All the same, that letter...."

Planchet withdrew, shaking his head; even D'Artagnan's liberality had not quelled his doubts. Left alone, D'Artagnan read the note over and over; then he kissed it over and over and held it up before him, gazing avidly at the lines traced by the febrile hand of his beautiful mistress.

After much ado he went to bed and fell into a deep sleep crowned with golden dreams.

Rising at seven o'clock in the morning, he summoned Planchet who at his second call opened the door, his countenance still dark with anxiety.

"Planchet, I shall probably be gone all day," D'Artagnan announced. "Your time is your own until seven o'clock this evening. At seven be ready, with two horses."

"So we are in for it again, Monsieur? Where will their bullets pepper us—in the head, in the back or in the bowels?"

"You will take along your musketoon and a pair of pistols."

"I knew it . . . I was certain . . . that accursed letter. . . ."

"Cheer up, lad, don't be afraid! We are off on a little jaunt!"

"Ay, Monsieur, like the jaunt we took the other day, when it rained bullets and ambushes grew underfoot."

"Well, if you are really frightened, Monsieur Planchet, I shall go alone. Better a man by himself than with a whimpering acolyte."

"Monsieur does me wrong; after all, Monsieur has seen me at work, I think."

"Certainly, you were brave on one occasion. But I thought you had used all your courage up."

"In a tight spot, Monsieur will see that I can still hold my own. I am only begging you not to squander my efforts if you care to use them for long."

"Have you pluck enough to come along with me tonight?"

"I trust so, Monsieur."

"Then I can count upon you."

"I shall be ready, Monsieur, at seven sharp. But I thought Monsieur had only one horse in the stables at the Hôtel des Gardes."

"There may be only one now; by this evening there will be four."

"So Monsieur's journey was by relays?"

"Precisely," D'Artagnan said, taking his leave.

At the front door he found Monsieur Bonacieux; he intended to pass without exchanging any words but the good haberdasher greeted him with such cordial politeness that his lodger felt compelled not only to return his salutation but to pass the time of day with him. Besides, how could our Gascon fail to entertain a certain condescension for a husband whose wife he was to meet that very evening at the place appointed?

D'Artagnan approached Bonacieux with the most amiable air he could assume.

The conversation quite naturally revolved upon the unhappy man's imprisonment. Monsieur Bonacieux, unaware that D'Artagnan had overheard his conversation with the man of Meung, described all the tortures he had undergone at the hands of that monster, Monsieur de Laffémas, whom he repeatedly qualified as the Cardinal's hangman. He lingered at great length, almost lovingly, upon the Bastille and its amenities (bolts, cranks, screws, racks, scourges, thumbscrews, and wheels) and its wickets, dungeons, loopholes and gratings. . . .

D'Artagnan listened with exemplary politeness and when Bonacieux was done inquired:

"What about Madame Bonacieux? Did you find out who abducted her? I recall I owe the pleasure of your acquaintance to that unhappy circumstance!"

"Ah, Monsieur, they took good care not to tell me that and my wife has sworn to me by all that's sacred that she does not know. But you yourself, Monsieur?" he continued in the most genial tone, "What have *you* been up to these last few days? I haven't laid eyes on you and your friends for over a week . . . and it happens I saw Planchet cleaning your boots, Monsieur . . . and I vow you could not have picked up all that mud and dust on the pavements of Paris. . . ."

"Right you are, my dear Monsieur Bonacieux. My friends and I took a little trip."

"Did you go far from Paris?"

"Heavens, no, only forty leagues or so; we took Monsieur Athos to Forges for a cure. My friends stayed on there."

"But *you* came back, eh?" the haberdasher asked in the most roguish and jocular tone. "A handsome, smart young fellow like yourself doesn't relish furloughs away from his mistress. I dare say some pretty lady has been awaiting you here with the utmost impatience."

D'Artagnan roared with laughter:

"Upon my faith," he declared, "I must confess you are right and the more readily because I see there is no concealing anything from you. Yes, of course I was expected here, and yes again, I was most eagerly awaited, I assure you!"

A slight shadow passed across the nondescript brow of the haberdasher, too slight by far for D'Artagnan to notice.

"Undoubtedly Monsieur will be rewarded for his diligence," Bonacieux hazarded with a slight change of voice which D'Artagnan noticed no more than he had noticed the change in Bonacieux's facial expression. D'Artagnan laughed again.

"Come, my dear landlord, what are you driving at with your apparently artless questions?"

"Monsieur misjudges me. I only wondered whether you would be coming home late?"

"Why such interest in my movements, my dear host? Do you intend to sit up waiting for me?"

"No, no, Monsieur, you do not understand. But since my arrest and the robbery committed in my house, I am frightened every time I hear a door open, especially at night. Heavens, why not? After all I am no swordsman!"

"Well, do not be alarmed if I return at one or two or even three in the morning. Indeed, do not be alarmed if I do not return at all."

This time Bonacieux turned so pale that D'Artagnan, perceiving his discomfiture, asked him what was the matter.

"Nothing, nothing!" Bonacieux said hastily. "But ever since my misfortunes I am subject to dizzy spells which come upon me suddenly; I just felt a cold shiver. Pay no attention to it; you have but one thing to occupy your mind, and that is your own happiness!"

"Then I shall be very busy for I am ecstatically happy."

"Already? Aren't you somewhat previous? I thought you said it was this evening—"

"Well, this evening will come, thank God! Probably you are looking forward to it as impatiently as I am. Are you expecting Madame Bonacieux to visit the conjugal domicile tonight?"

"Madame Bonacieux is not at liberty this evening," the haberdasher said gravely. "Her duties detain her at the Louvre."

"So much the worse for you, my dear host, so much the worse for you. As for me, when I am happy, I wish the whole world to be so. But apparently that is impossible!"

And D'Artagnan strode off, roaring with laughter over a joke he thought he alone could appreciate.

"Have a good time!" Bonacieux growled in a sepulchral tone. But D'Artagnan was out of earshot and anyhow, in his present mood, would have noted nothing amiss even if he had heard. He was bound for Monsieur de Tréville's in order to substantiate the vague report he had submitted on his fleeting visit the night before.

D'Artagnan found the Captain of Musketeers highly elated. The King and Queen had been charming to him at the ball. It is true the Cardinal was particularly sullen and at one o'clock, pleading illness, left the Hôtel de Ville. But their Majesties stayed on making merry until six o'clock in the morning.

"And now, my young friend," Monsieur de Tréville lowered his voice and glanced carefully around, making sure they were quite alone, "now let us talk about you. Obviously your happy return has something to do with the King's joy, the Queen's triumph and the Cardinal's confusion. You will have to be very cautious indeed."

"What have I to fear, Monsieur, so long as I enjoy the favor of Their Majesties?"

"You have everything to fear, believe me! The Cardinal is not the man to have a joke played on him without settling accounts with the jokester. And I venture to think that the jokester in question is a certain young Gascon of my acquaintance."

"Do you think the Cardinal knows as much as you, Monsieur? Do you think he suspects I have been to London?"

"My God, were you in London? Was that where you found that beautiful diamond I see on your finger? Take care my dear D'Artagnan, a gift from an enemy is not particularly profitable. There is some Latin verse to this effect . . . let me think . . . ?"

D'Artagnan had never succeeded in cramming the barest rudiments of Latin into his head; his ignorance had been the despair of his tutor. And so he hemmed and hawed, mumbling: "Yes, Monsieur, I seem to recall some such line . . . it goes. . . ."

"Of course there is," Monsieur de Tréville broke in, for he had at least a smattering of letters, "in fact Monsieur de Benserade, the poet, was quoting that very line just the other day. Wait! Here it is:

Timeo Danaos et dona ferentes.

"Ah, yes, Monsieur," D'Artagnan agreed, quite nonplussed.

"It means," Tréville went on:

"Beware the foe bringing gifts."

"This diamond does not come from an enemy, Monsieur," D'Artagnan explained. "It comes from the Queen."

"From the Queen, eh? It is indeed a truly royal jewel; it must be worth a thousand pistoles if it's worth a sou. And through whom did the Queen send you this gift?"

"Her Majesty gave it to me personally."

"Where?"

"In the small room adjoining her dressing-room at the Hôtel de Ville."

"How did this happen?"

"It happened whilst I was kissing Her Majesty's hand—"

"You kissed the Queen's hand!" Monsieur de Tréville looked at D'Artagnan more closely.

"Her Majesty did me the honor to grant me this signal favor."

"In the presence of witnesses? How rash of her, how terribly rash!"

"No, Monsieur, do not worry, no one saw the Queen!"

And D'Artagnan related every circumstance of the night before.

"Oh, woman, woman!" the old soldier philosophized. "Who can fail to recognize her by her romantic imagination! Everything that smacks of mystery charms her! You saw an arm, no more! Should you meet the Queen you would not recognize her; should she meet you, she would not know who you are."

"I daresay not, Monsieur, but thanks to this diamond . . ."

"Look here, young man, let me give you a piece of advice, sound advice, the advice of a friend—"

"I would be much honored, Monsieur."

"Well, go to the nearest jeweler and sell him that diamond for whatever he will give you. However much of a bargainer he may be, you will get at least eight hundred pistoles for it. Pistoles are an anonymous commodity and your ring is terribly personal. Remember it may betray whoever wears it."

"I, sell this ring—? I sell a ring which comes to me from my Queen! Never!"

"Then at least turn the diamond inwards, silly lad! Do you think anyone believes a cadet of Gascony finds such jewels in his mother's jewel-case?"

"I still do not see what I have to fear," D'Artagnan argued.

"Oh, nothing at all," Monsieur de Tréville said airily. "You are as safe as a man resting on a mine whose fuse is burning."

Monsieur de Tréville's solemn and positive tone gave the young Gascon some pause; he felt somewhat worried.

"The devil, Monsieur, what am I to do?"

"Be constantly and steadfastly on your guard. The Cardinal has a long memory and a long reach. Take my word for it, he will play you some sorry trick."

"But what can he do, Monsieur?"

"Good Heavens, how can I tell? His Eminence has all the devil's calendar of tricks at his command. The best you can possibly hope for is to be arrested."

"Even His Eminence would not dare to arrest a soldier in His Majesty's service?"

"Did they hesitate about arresting Athos!" Monsieur de Tréville sighed. "Advice is cheap, but I beg you to take that of a man who has been at Court for thirty years. Do not lull yourself in security or you are done for. On the contrary, I insist, look out for enemies on every hand. If anyone picks a quarrel with you, even a child of ten, avoid it... if you are attacked, day or night, take to your heels shamelessly . . . if you cross a bridge, test every board of it for fear that one might give way underfoot... when you pass a house being built or repaired, look up lest a stone fall on your head . . . if you stay out late, be sure your lackey follows you and be sure he is armed, if, incidentally, you are sure you can trust your lackey. . . . Suspect everyone: your friend, your brother, your mistress—especially your mistress!"

D'Artagnan blushed, and mechanically:

"My mistress? Why should I suspect her more than anyone else, Monsieur?"

"Because the Cardinal uses mistresses to the best advantage; they are his most efficient agents. Women have been known to sell their lovers down the river for ten pistoles. Witness Delilah, or do you remember the Bible?"

D'Artagnan thought of his appointment with Madame Bonacieux that very evening. But, to his credit, Monsieur de Tréville's misogyny could not prejudice him against his pretty landlady.

"By the way," Monsieur de Tréville inquired, "what of your three comrades?"

"I was about to ask you, Monsieur, if you had news of them?"

"No. None."

"Well, Monsieur, I lost them by the wayside: Porthos at Chantilly with a duel on his hands ... Aramis at Crèvecoeur with a bullet in his shoulder ... and Athos at Amiens accused of counterfeiting...."

Monsieur de Tréville pointed out that these three instances were proof of the Cardinal's long reach:

"How in the devil's name did *you* get away?" he concluded.

"By a miracle, Monsieur, I must confess. The Comte de Vardes pinked me in the chest but I nailed him down to a Calais byroad like a butterfly on a tapestry."

"De Vardes, eh? A cardinalist, a cousin of Rochefort's, I know them! But stop, my friend, I have an idea."

"Ay, Monsieur."

"Were I you, I would—"

"What, Monsieur?"

"I would get away while His Eminence was looking for me in the city ... I would very quietly take the road to Picardy ... I would enjoy myself riding over a pleasant countryside ... and I would make inquiries about the fate of my comrades who, I dare say, richly deserve that courtesy on your part...."

"Monsieur, your advice is excellent and I promise to set out tomorrow."

"Tomorrow? Why not tonight?"

"Tonight, Sir, I am unavoidably detained in town."

"Come, lad, I know: some bird of amorous passage, eh? Heigh-ho, youth will be served! Still, I repeat, please take care of yourself: it was woman by whom we fell when Adam fell, frail as we are, and woman will ruin us one and all, so long as we draw breath!" (Monsieur de Tréville was of Gascon and Protestant stock but a good soldier withal.) "Take my word for it, lad," he concluded. "Away with you this evening."

"Impossible, Monsieur."

"You have pledged your word to spend the night in town?"

"Yes, Monsieur."

"Well, that puts a different complexion upon present matters." Monsieur de Tréville stroked his beard. Then suddenly: "If you're not killed tonight—and well you may be—will you set out tomorrow?"

"Absolutely, Monsieur, on my word of honor."

"Do you need any money?"

"I still have fifty pistoles. That should certainly serve my needs."

"And your friends?"

"I doubt whether they need money, Monsieur. Each of us had seventy-five pistoles when we left town."

"Shall I see you before you leave?"

"I doubt it, Monsieur, unless something new turns up."

"Well, good luck to you, lad."

"Thank you, Monsieur."

D'Artagnan left Tréville, more than ever touched by his paternal solicitude for the men under him, his musketeers, the crack soldiers of the Army. He had a busy evening before him. He must visit Athos, Porthos and Aramis in turn. He did so, to discover that none of them had reported home; their lackeys, too, were absent, and there was no news of masters or servants. D'Artagnan, by now desperate, would have sought news of them from their mistresses—Porthos was cherished by an attorney's wife . . . Aramis had a highly-placed lady in the offing . . . Athos stood alone . . . But he did not know who their mistresses were. Passing by the Hôtel des Gardes, he looked into the stable. Three of the four horses Lord Buckingham had given him were already in their stalls; Planchet, much impressed, had groomed down two of them.

"Monsieur, how glad I am to see you!"

"Why, Planchet?"

"Do you trust Bonacieux, Monsieur?"

"As I would the plague."

"How right you are, Monsieur."

"But why do you ask me?"

Planchet scratched his brow.

"Well, Monsieur, this is what happened," he explained. "While you were talking to Monsieur Bonacieux, I watched him. I didn't hear a word you said but I saw him fidgeting about and I swear he turned pale and blushed and looked very uncomfortable. . . ."

"Nonsense, Planchet!"

"Monsieur did not notice all this, for Monsieur was too much preoccupied by the letter he had just received. But Planchet was on guard, Planchet was suspicious of a letter that appeared in our house supernaturally, and Planchet watched every change of expression on our landlord's face."

"So you—"

"So I found his every expression full of guile—"

"Indeed?"

"Pray listen, Monsieur. So soon as you turned the corner of the street, Bonacieux picked up his hat, closed the door and ran down the street."

"Right, Planchet, the man is a suspicious character. Never mind though; we will pay no rent until we thrash all this out."

"Monsieur jests, but we shall see—"

"Cheer up, Planchet, what is written is written."

"Does Monsieur insist on our evening's outing?"

"Of course I do. The more I suspect Bonacieux, the more firmly I intend to keep my appointment."

"Then Monsieur is determined—?"

"My mind is made up, Planchet, I shall go through with this. Be here at nine, I shall come by for you."

The lackey concluded that all hope of persuading his master to abandon his rash intent was irremediably lost. Fetching a deep sigh, he set to currying the third horse. As for D'Artagnan—at bottom a cautious fellow—instead of going home he called to dine with the Gascon priest who had once before befriended him and the musketeers, when, out of pocket, they had breakfasted with him, chocolate included.

XXIV

THE LODGE

At nine o'clock D'Artagnan, true to his word, stopped at the barracks of the Royal Guards. Planchet awaited him, fully armed. The fourth horse had arrived. D'Artagnan made sure that Planchet had his musketoon and one pistol, both primed; he himself slipped two pistols in his holsters and they rode off. It was very dark. Under cover of the darkness, they made off unseen, Planchet some ten paces in his master's wake.

D'Artagnan crossed the quais, left town by the Porte de La Conférence and followed the road to Saint-Cloud, a pleasanter and more beautiful road than it is now.

So long as they were in the city, Planchet kept at a respectful distance; but as the road loomed up before them, ever darker and more deserted, he kept inching up closer so that as they reached the Bois de Boulogne he rode abreast of his master. Truth to tell the huge branches of the trees as they waved in the wind and the reflection of the moon in the black thickets afforded Planchet a certain anxiety. D'Artagnan could not but notice that his lackey was uneasy.

"Well, well, Planchet, what is the matter?"

"This may sound funny, Monsieur . . . I mean . . . I mean: Don't you find that woods are very much like churches."

"How so, Planchet?"

"Well, Monsieur, we daren't speak aloud in either."

"Why not, Planchet? Are you afraid?"

"Yes, Monsieur, that I am."

"Afraid of what?"

"Afraid of being overheard, Monsieur."

"Of being overheard?" D'Artagnan laughed. "Is there anything immoral in our conversation? Who could possibly object to it?"

Planchet, sighing, returned to his besetting idea.

"Monsieur," he said, "There is something about Bonacieux . . . something evil in his eyebrows and something downright vicious in the play of his lips. . . ."

"Why mention Bonacieux now?"

"Monsieur, a man thinks as he can, not as he will."

"That is because you are a coward."

"Monsieur, cowardice and caution are horses of a different color; I am cautious, not cowardly. Prudence is a virtue."

"And you are very virtuous, eh?"

"Look Monsieur, there to the left. Don't you see a musket gleaming? Let us duck quickly—"

"God help us," D'Artagnan mused, "this wretch of a lackey will end by terrifying me." He recalled Monsieur de Tréville's advice in all its particulars. ("Be sure your lackey follows you," Tréville had said, "if incidentally, you are sure you can trust your lackey.") And D'Artagnan roused his horse to a trot, Planchet clinging to him like his shadow.

"Are we to ride on and on all night, Monsieur?" Planchet inquired.

"No, Planchet, you have gone far enough."

"I, Monsieur? And what of you?"

"I am going on a little."

"And you are leaving me here alone, Monsieur?"

"Are you frightened?"

"Not in the least, Monsieur. But I beg leave to observe that it is turning very cold and likely to turn colder . . . that cold brings on chills . . . that chills cause rheumatism . . . and that a lackey with rheumatism is worse than useless, particularly to as active a master as you, Monsieur. . . ."

"Very well, Planchet, if you feel cold, you can go into one of those huts there. Turn in, keep warm, and wait at the door for me at six sharp tomorrow morning."

"Begging your pardon, Monsieur, I respectfully ate and drank up the crown Monsieur gave me this morning. I have not a sou and if I should happen to need the wherewithal to warm up—"

"Here's half a pistole, Planchet. Remember: tomorrow at six."

D'Artagnan dismounted, tossed his steed's bridle to Planchet, and muffling himself snugly in his coat, vanished into the darkness. He was not out of sight before Planchet, shivering with cold and eager to thaw out, made for the hovel, which looked like a typical suburban tavern, and knocked loudly at the door.

Meanwhile D'Artagnan took a side path and presently reached Saint-Cloud. There, instead of following the main street of the village, he turned behind the château, found a tiny lane, and in a few minutes reached the lodge which, the note had said, stood "at right angles to the mansion of Monsieur d'Estrées."

It was very bleak and stood in a very lonely spot. On one side the outer wall of the mansion loomed high above the lane; on the other a tall hedge screened off a small garden at the end of which stood a shabby hut. D'Artagnan, having reached the place appointed, waited; having received no instructions about announcing his presence, he took up his stand between hedge and wall. All was silence, an eerie silence that made him feel a hundred leagues from the capital. He glanced carefully about him, then leaned against the hedge, staring across the garden and beyond the lodge at the dense fog that swathed the mysterious immensity of Paris. Faintly, out of the shadowy void, he could distinguish a few lights, so many stars twinkling faintly over Sodom and Gomorrah. . . .

Dismal though the prospect was, D'Artagnan found everything to his taste; dark though the night, his ideas were roseate and opaque, they glimmered diaphanous through the shadows. Presently the chimes of the church of Saint-Cloud boomed the hour of ten. As D'Artagnan counted the strokes, happy and expectant as he was, he could not help feeling how lugubriously this sonorous bronze voice echoed across the unfriendly night. At the last stroke, his heart racing within him, he stared up at the lodge, all the windows of which were shuttered save one on the first floor. A dim light shone through this window, silvering the foliage of a clump of linden trees that rose, thick and powdery, beyond the garden. His eyes fixed on this light, D'Artagnan thrilled at the thought that within this cheerful room Madame Bonacieux awaited him.

Lost in charmed anticipation, D'Artagnan waited blithely for a half-hour, staring up at one part of the ceiling, which was clearly visible, admiring its gilded mouldings, and speculating how lavish the apartment might be. The belfry of Saint-Cloud sounded the half-hour.

This time quite unconsciously D'Artagnan shuddered. Perhaps he was beginning to feel the cold and mistook a wholly physical sensation for a mental impression. Suddenly he decided that he had made a mistake. Doubtless in his eagerness he had misread his instructions and his appointment was for eleven o'clock. Stealthily he drew close to the window and, thanks to a faint ray of light, managed to read his letter again. He had not been mistaken, the appointment was for ten o'clock.

By now somewhat uneasy at the silence and loneliness, he returned to his post. Eleven o'clock struck.

Now he thought fearfully that something might have happened to Madame Bonacieux. Nervously he clapped his hands three times, the usual signal of lovers, but there was no answer, not even an echo. Somewhat annoyed, he decided that his inamorata had perhaps fallen asleep while waiting for him. He approached the wall and attempted to scale it but it had been recently plastered; he could obtain no hold on it and he broke several fingernails in the effort. Looking about at a loss, he saw the trees again, shimmering in the light from the room above; perhaps by climbing the tallest of them he could look into the room. The tree offered no difficulty; after all, D'Artagnan was only twenty and his schoolboy habits were still fresh. Swift as a squirrel, he scurried from branch to branch; in a few moments his keen gaze enjoyed an unobstructed view into the lodge. The sight that greeted him sent a cold shiver through his body: he had to hug the branch on which he perched to keep himself from falling.

Straining his eyes to gaze through a perfectly transparent window, D'Artagnan was horrified at the scene he beheld. The mild, subdued light of the lamp, shining steadfastly, revealed a scene of frightful disorder. One window was broken ... the door to the room had been forced and, smashed in, hung limply on its swollen hinges ... a table, obviously set for supper, lay overturned, its four legs gaping ... the floor was strewn with fragments of glass and crushed fruits. . . . There could be no doubt of it, the room had witnessed a violent, desperate struggle; D'Artagnan even thought he detected shreds of clothing amid this grotesque disorder and traces of blood on tablecloth and curtains.

Aghast, D'Artagnan climbed down from his point of vantage, his heart thumping against his ribs. He must find further clues, he must discover what had happened by examining everything about him, coolly and scrupulously as a judge. The soft light still glimmered across the cold dark shadows. Looking about him, D'Artagnan noticed that the ground underfoot seemed to have been trampled upon. There were marks of carriage wheels, of horses' hoofs and of men's footsteps. Obviously the carriage had driven in from the direction of Paris and, describing a circle, driven off again toward the city. Or vice-versa. At all events its wheels had left no trace in the damp earth beyond the lodge.

Pursuing his investigations, D'Artagnan suddenly came upon a glove. It lay close to the wall ... a woman's glove undoubtedly ... and torn ... its palm muddy, the top immaculate ... the type of perfumed glove an eager lover longs to snatch from a shapely hand ... but a glove which had been wrenched off that hand in a violent tussle. . . .

As the impact of his discoveries made itself felt, an icier and more abundant sweat broke in large beads over D'Artagnan's forehead. A terrible anguish gripped him, his heart was oppressed, his breath came short and fast. Striving for self-control, he told himself that this lodge had nothing to do with Madame Bonacieux ... that his Constance had specified he was to stand opposite the lodge, not to enter it ... that her duties might conceivably have kept her in Paris ... that a jealous husband had prevented her coming. . . . And yet he realized this was but wishful thinking. An inevitable instinct, filled with foreboding, convinced him beyond peradventure of reasoning, that misfortune was upon him.

A savage rage swept over him as, losing all sense of reality, he ran ahead down the lane as though the Devil himself were at his heels. Time passed and he ran on, this way and that, until eventually he found himself at the riverside in front of the ferry. The boatman was at hand; D'Artagnan questioned him feverishly.

At seven o'clock that evening, the boatman said, he had rowed a lady across the river. The lady wore a heavy black cloak and wrapped it closely about her as though wishing to go unrecognized and for that very reason he had looked at her attentively. She was, he added, both young and pretty. Of course young and pretty women had come to Saint-Cloud in the past, came to Saint-Cloud daily, and would continue to come to Saint-Cloud in the future, all of them chary of recognition. Nevertheless D'Artagnan felt certain that the boatman's client was Constance Bonacieux.

By the light in the boatman's shed, he read his inamorata's note once again to make sure of its contents. No, there could be no doubt: the appointment was for Saint-Cloud and nowhere else, for ten o'clock and at no other time, and in front of Monsieur d'Estrées' lodge. D'Artagnan's worst fears were confirmed; something terrible had occurred.

He ran back to the château, hoping against hope that in his absence some new development might shed light on the mystery.

The lane was still deserted; the same calm, soft light still shone from the window. In despair he looked about him and once again saw the dark silent hut at the end of the garden. Someone must surely live there, he thought, someone who might have heard or seen what had happened and who might be persuaded to talk.

The gate of the enclosure was shut but he vaulted over the hedge and despite the angry barking of a dog—he noticed it was chained— approached the hut.

To his first frantic knocking there was no reply. He stood quite still for a moment, his heart heavy as lead. A deathly silence reigned over the tumble-down dwelling, a silence as sinister as that he had found at the lodge. But fully aware that this was his last resort, he kept knocking with a sort of blind fury.

Presently he fancied he heard a slight noise within, a timid noise as though someone was fearful of being overheard amid the silence. D'Artagnan at once stopped knocking and pleaded to be admitted; his voice was so full of anxiety and promise, so appealing in its terror and persuasive in its cajolery that the most fearful of persons could not have apprehended any danger. At length an old worm-eaten shutter swung ajar on creaky hinges but was slammed shut as soon as the rays of a wretched lamp in one corner of the hovel had lighted up D'Artagnan's sword-belt, the pommel of his sword and the butts of the pistols in his holsters. Swift though the movement was, D'Artagnan nevertheless managed to catch a glimpse of an old man's head.

"In the name of Heaven, listen to me," he begged. "I have been waiting for someone who has not come; I am dying of anxiety. Has any mishap occurred here? Have you noticed anything untoward in the last few hours? Speak, I implore you!"

Slowly the window swung open again and the same face appeared again, looking even paler than before. D'Artagnan told his story simply and accurately without mentioning any names of course: how he had an appointment with a young woman . . . how he had been invited to wait near the lodge . . . how he had waited and, seeing no one, had climbed the tree . . . and what he had seen when he looked into the house. . . .

The old man listened to him attentively with an occasional nod of approval; when D'Artagnan had finished he shook his head with a rueful air that presaged nothing good.

"What is it?" D'Artagnan cried in alarm. "For God's sake, tell me everything."

"Ah, Monsieur, ask me no questions, I beg of you for if I told you what I had seen some evil would surely befall me."

"So you saw something, eh? If so, in the name of Heaven, tell me exactly what happened!" D'Artagnan tossed the old man a pistole. "Tell me what you saw and I give you my word as a gentleman that I shall not repeat one syllable of it."

The old man read such suffering and such sincerity in D'Artagnan's expression that he motioned to him to listen and said in a low voice:

"It was just about nine o'clock. I heard a noise in the land and wondered what it could be. As I went to my door I could see somebody at the gate in the hedge, trying to get in. I am a poor man, Monsieur, I own nothing worth stealing, so I opened. Three men stood by the gate. Over there in the shadows stood a carriage with two horses; a groom, a few paces away, held three saddle horses which doubtless belonged to my three visitors.

" 'Well, gentlemen,' I cried, 'what can I do for you?'

" 'Have you a ladder?' one of the gentlemen asked me. From his tone and air, I judged him to be the leader of the group.

" 'Ay, Monsieur, the ladder I use when I pick my fruit.'

" 'Lend it to us and then go back to your house again. Here is a crown for your trouble. Now remember this! However much we may threaten you, you will probably watch us and listen to us; but if you breathe one word of what you see or hear, you are a dead man.'

"With these words, he flung me a coin which I picked up and he took my ladder.

"I shut the hedge gate behind them and went back into the house but I went right out through the back door and stole through the shadows to that clump of elders yonder. From there I could see everything without being spotted.

"The three men drew the carriage up quietly and a little man got out, a fat, short elderly man with graying hair and dressed in mean black clothes. He climbed the ladder very carefully, glanced slily into the room, came down as quietly as he had gone up, and told the others:

" 'She's there, all right!'

"Then the man who had spoken to me went to the lodge, drew a key from his pocket and opened the door; then he went in, closed the door behind him and disappeared; then I saw the two others climbing the ladder. The little old man stayed by the door of the carriage; the coachman tended the carriage horses, the lackey held the saddle horses.

"All at once, Hell broke loose in the lodge, what with the screaming and howling of a thousand devils. A lady rushed to the window and opened it as if to jump out; but when she saw two men on the ladder, she ran back into the room. They immediately climbed in, more quickly than I can tell you, Monsieur.

"Then I saw no more, but I can tell you this: there was a hullabaloo and a smashing of furniture such as I hope never to hear again. The lady cried for help, but what could I do, old as I am, Monsieur, and against six men? The lady's cries grew fainter and fainter. Then two men came down the ladder with the lady in their arms. They carried her into the carriage, the little old man got in too and slammed the door shut. A minute later the one who had stayed in the lodge shut the window and came out through the front door. He went over to the coach and looked in to make sure the lady was there. His two companions were already mounted and waiting for him. The lackey jumped on the box beside the coachman and the carriage set off briskly with the three riders for escort.

"There you have the story, Monsieur. After that the only thing I heard was yourself knocking and the only thing I saw were your weapons shining in the dark."

Overcome by the horror of this story, D'Artagnan stood stock-still, gaping, whilst all the demons of jealousy and anger rioted in his heart. The old man, more deeply moved by the youth's mute despair than he could have been by cries and tears, said compassionately:

"Come, my good gentleman, do not take on so! There is still hope, Monsieur. They did not kill your lady, and that's a comfort."

"Can you tell me anything about the ringleader?"

"I never saw him before, Monsieur, I never knew any of them."

"But you spoke to him? You saw him?"

"Oh, you want me to tell you what he looked like?"

"Yes, exactly!"

"Well, Monsieur, he was a tall, dark, spare man with a swarthy complexion, black mustaches and eyes as black as the ace of spades. He looked like a nobleman."

"That's the man!" D'Artagnan gasped. "Once again and for ever, my demon, the man of Meung." He wrung his hands, then, more calmly: "What about the other man?" he asked.

"Which one do you mean?"

"The little oldish one."

"Oh, he was no nobleman, Monsieur, I can vouch for that. Besides he did not wear a sword and the others ordered him about every which way."

"Some lackey, I dare say," D'Artagnan murmured. And, as he thought of his mistress: "Poor woman, poor woman!" he sighed. "What have they done to you?"

"You swore to keep my secret, Monsieur?" the old man reminded him.

"I repeat my promise. I gave you my word as a gentleman; a gentleman has but one word, my friend, so you need worry about nothing."

With a heavy heart D'Artagnan retraced his steps toward the ferry, a prey to the most sanguine sentiments one moment and to the bitterest the next. Now he hoped that it could not have been Madame Bonacieux who was so brutally attacked and he looked forward to finding her at the Louvre on the morrow; now he feared she had had some intrigue with a jealous rival who had surprised her and carried her off. Doubt, grief and despair made their battleground of his heart.

"Ah, God! if only my friends were with me!" he exclaimed. "Athos, Porthos, Aramis, you would give me some hope of finding her. But who knows what on earth has become of you?"

It was past midnight. The next thing to do was to find Planchet. D'Artagnan called successively at five taverns where a light was burning but found Planchet in none. At the sixth, he decided that his search was vain. He had made arrangements to meet his lackey at six in the morning and the lackey's time was his own so that he appeared punctually. Further, he reflected, by remaining close to the spot where the tragedy had occurred, he might perhaps discover some fact to shed light on the appalling mystery. D'Artagnan therefore settled down in the sixth tavern, ordered a bottle of the best wine and, ensconced in the darkest corner of the room, determined to wait for daybreak. But here again his hopes were vain; though he strained his ears, he heard only oaths, coarse jokes and insults bandied about by the laborers, lackeys and carters who comprised the distinguished clientèle of the inn. There was not the merest hint of a scandal or abduction and no faintest clue to put him on the scent of his unhappy and beloved Constance. Having downed his bottle, for want of anything else to do, he decided to sit on in order to pass the time and to avoid suspicion. Sinking back comfortably into his corner, he composed himself for sleep. He had experienced a great ordeal, to be sure; but on a man of twenty, sleep exercises its imprescriptible rights though the sleeper's heart be utterly broken.

Toward six o'clock in the morning, D'Artagnan awakened with all the discomfort that usually follows a bad night. He was not long in tidying his rumpled clothes, making sure that his diamond was still on his finger, his purse in his pocket and his pistols in his belt. He rose, paid for his bottle and ventured out to try if he might have better luck in his search for his lackey than the night before. Through the damp gray mist the first object he discerned was honest Planchet, two horses in hand, waiting by the door of a disreputable looking tavern—a blind pig, so to speak—which D'Artagnan had passed the night before without even suspecting its existence.

XXV

OF WHAT HAPPENED TO PORTHOS

D'Artagnan did not go straight home. Instead he stopped off to call on Monsieur de Tréville. Taking the stairs three at a pace, he determined to tell the Captain of Musketeers about all that had befallen him. Monsieur de Tréville could give him excellent advice and since he saw the Queen daily could perhaps find out something about poor Constance, who was assuredly paying dearly for her devotion to her mistress.

The Captain of Musketeers listened patiently to his young protégé's story. His serious attention proved that he saw more in the matter than a mere love affair. When D'Artagnan had finished:

"This all reeks of the Cardinal," he commented.

"But what can be done, Monsieur?"

"Nothing, absolutely nothing, for the time being. You must leave Paris as soon as possible just as I told you last night. For my part I shall see the Queen and tell her about the disappearance of her maidservant. Probably Her Majesty knows nothing of it. At any rate I shall inform her and perhaps I shall have good news for you on your return."

D'Artagnan knew that, although a Gascon, Monsieur de Tréville was not a man to make promises that he did not intend to keep; usually indeed he went beyond his word. Very grateful for past favors and confident in the future, he bowed deeply as he took his leave of the old soldier. Monsieur de Tréville for his part felt a lively interest in his brave and resolute young compatriot. Shaking D'Artagnan's hand affably he wished him a pleasant journey.

Encouraged by Monsieur de Tréville's attitude, D'Artagnan resolved to follow his advice immediately and made for the Rue des Fossoyeurs. Planchet would be waiting but his packing required supervision. There was Monsieur Bonacieux too.

D'Artagnan found his landlord on the doorstep, clad in morning dress and staring up at the sky. All that the prudent Planchet had said about the Bonacieux's sinister personality the evening before now recurred to D'Artagnan's mind and as he drew near he looked at his landlord more closely than he had ever done. The fellow's complexion was yellow and sickly with that pallor which indicates an excess of bile in the blood. To be sure that might be accidental, yet D'Artagnan perceived something particularly crafty and perfidious in his wrinkled features. A rascal does not laugh in the same manner as an honest man nor does a hypocrite shed tears in the same way as a man of good faith. All falsehood is a mask which, however well fashioned, reveals its shams upon close inspection. To D'Artagnan it seemed that Monsieur Bonacieux wore a mask and a very ugly one to look upon at that.

Repelled by Bonacieux's unpleasing exterior, our Gascon intended to pass by without speaking but Monsieur Bonacieux accosted him as he had done the day before.

"Well young man!" he declared with mock joviality, "we seem to have made quite a night of it, eh? Home at seven in the morning, I see! You do turn things topsy-turvy, I declare; you come home to sleep just as other folk are setting out to work."

"No one can hold *that* against *you,* Monsieur Bonacieux; *you* are a model of conventional behavior. Of course I cannot blame you. When a man possesses as young and as pretty a wife as you do, he need not seek happiness elsewhere because happiness comes to meet him, does it not?"

Bonacieux turned pale and smiled wrily.

"What a gay blade you are, Monsieur; you *will* have your joke, won't you? But what the deuce were you up to last night?" He stared at D'Artagnan's boots. "Very muddy, eh? Dirty work at the crossroads?"

D'Artagnan, having surveyed his own boots, noticed that the haberdasher's shoes and stockings were muddy too. Suddenly D'Artagnan thought: a fat, short, elderly man with graying hair and dressed in mean black clothes ... a man who was no nobleman for he wore no sword ... a man whom the others ordered every which ways ... a lackey, no doubt ... Bonacieux himself! Yes, D'Artagnan was sure of it; the husband had actually presided at the brutality and outrage visited upon his wife.

A fury seized D'Artagnan; his fingers itched to grasp the haberdasher by the throat and throttle him. But for all his ardor our Gascon was prudent, too; effortfully he mastered himself. Bonacieux, frightened, stepped back but as the door behind him was closed, he had perforce to stand his ground.

"Come, my good man, you're joking! Did you mention dirty work at the crossroads? God help me, if my boots could do with a sponging, your shoes and stockings could do with a brush! Have you been gadding about too, my dear landlord? By God, that would be unpardonable for a man of your age with a wife as beautiful as Madame Bonacieux."

"No, no, no, Monsieur, I was not gadding about. I went out to Saint-Mandé to find out about a servant. I cannot do without one and you remember the last one left the night I was arrested. It was muddy going, I can tell you."

To D'Artagnan the fact that Bonacieux cited Saint-Mandé was eminently suspicious for Saint-Mandé was south west of Paris, Saint-Cloud north east. Bonacieux's guile offered D'Artagnan a glimmer of consolation, the first he had experienced. If the haberdasher knew where his wife was, somewhere and somehow he might be persuaded by forcible means to divulge his secret. The question was to change what D'Artagnan considered a probability into an absolute certainty.

"My dear landlord, do you mind if I do not stand on ceremony with you?" D'Artagnan inquired.

"Of course, go ahead, Monsieur."

"I'm parched with thirst; as you know nothing makes a man so thirsty as lack of sleep! May I go drink a glass of water in your kitchen? After all, as neighbor to neighbor—"

And without awaiting his landlord's permission, he went quickly into the house. As he passed through the apartment a rapid glance at the bed told him that no one had slept in it; therefore Bonacieux must have returned only an hour or two ago; therefore, again, he must have accompanied his wife to her place of confinement or, leastways, to the first relay.

"Many, many thanks, Monsieur Bonacieux," D'Artagnan said as he drained his glass. "I am much obliged. Now I shall go up to my place and have Planchet brush my boots. When he is done I will send him down to you to look after your shoes and stockings if you like. One good turn deserves another."

With which he left the haberdasher somewhat dazed by their singular parting and more than a little nervous that he had perhaps been hoisted by his own petard. At the top of the stairs D'Artagnan found Planchet plunged in abject confusion.

"Ah, Monsieur," the lackey wailed, "we are in for still more trouble. It never rains but it pours! I was wondering when you would come home."

"What is the matter?"

"I will give you a hundred guesses, Monsieur, a thousand, if necessary. Imagine who called on you while you were away?"

"When?"

"Half an hour ago, Monsieur, when you were with Monsieur de Tréville."

"Well, who? Speak up, man."

"Monsieur de Cavois!"

"Monsieur de Cavois?"

"In person!"

"The Captain of His Eminence's Guards?"

"Himself!"

"Did he come to arrest me?"

"I couldn't quite tell, Monsieur, but I suspect so, in spite of his wheedling manners."

"So he was pleasant, eh?"

"Sweet as a nut, Monsieur. He was honey dripping from the comb."

"You don't say so!"

"I do indeed, Monsieur. He told me he came at the express command

of His Eminence to offer you His Eminence's compliments and beg you
to proceed with him to wait upon His Eminence."

"What did you say, Planchet?"

"I answered that it was impossible because you were not at home, as he
could see for himself."

"What did he say then?"

"He said you should not fail to call on him in the course of the day. And
he whispered this, Monsieur, very polite and very mysterious, too!"

Planchet stopped, nursing his dramatic effect.

"Well, what, lad?"

"He whispered: 'Tell your master that His Eminence is very well disposed toward him and that his fortune may perhaps depend upon this interview.' "

D'Artagnan smiled:

"That kind of trap seems too clumsy to be of the Cardinal's making."

"You know I saw right through it myself, Monsieur. I said that you
would be desperately disappointed on your return."

Monsieur de Cavois had then asked Planchet where his master had
gone; the lackey had volunteered the information that D'Artagnan had set
off for Troyes in Champagne the evening before.

"Planchet, my friend, you are worth your weight in gold!" D'Artagnan
said, chuckling.

"Well, Monsieur, you see it's like this . . . I thought that if you really did
want to see Monsieur de Cavois, you could always put me in the wrong by
saying you had not left. . . . In that case, *I* would be the one caught in a lie
. . . but I'm no gentleman, Monsieur, so I can lie now and then and be
damned to the consequences. . . ."

"No, no, Planchet, don't worry: your reputation as a truthful man remains intact!" D'Artagnan smiled, then briskly: "We are leaving town in a
quarter of an hour," he announced.

"God bless me, I was on the point of giving Monsieur just that advice,"
the lackey said, slapping his hip. "But without seeming too curious, might
I ask Monsieur where we are off to?"

"You said I had gone to Champagne; we will therefore set off in the opposite direction. Remember, I should like to find out what has happened
to Athos, Porthos and Aramis; and I am sure you would like news of Grimaud, Mousqueton and Bazin."

"Of course, Monsieur, I am ready to leave at any moment. If I may say so, Monsieur, I think the air of the provinces will be a bit healthier for us in the next few days."

"Right you are, Planchet, pack up and off we go! I shall leave the house casually, my hands in my pockets, so that nobody suspects anything. Meet me at the barracks." D'Artagnan recalling Planchet's misgivings the night before, added generously: "By the by, Planchet, you were certainly right about the landlord. That haberdasher seems to me to be one of the vilest specimens of humanity I have ever encountered."

"Well, Monsieur, even if I say it who shouldn't, I can tell a man's nature by his face, ay, that I can. . . ."

D'Artagnan sauntered out, as arranged, and to make assurance doubly sure, visited the lodgings of his three friends. There were no tidings of them or messages anywhere, except that *chez* Aramis, D'Artagnan found a letter of signal calligraphy and balsam redolence. Arriving at the Hôtel des Grades before Planchet, D'Artagnan went to the stables and saddled his own horse. Ten minutes later his lackey arrived, bearing his portmanteau.

"Capital!" D'Artagnan exclaimed. "Now saddle the three other horses."

"Does Monsieur think we shall travel faster with three extra horses?" Planchet's expression was a picture of shrewdness.

"No, my witty friend," D'Artagnan replied, "but if we have five horses the three musketeers can ride home, provided we find them alive."

"I have my doubts, Monsieur, but God's mercy is boundless!"

"Amen," said D'Artagnan as he leaped into his saddle. And they parted at the gate of the Hôtel des Gardes, one to leave town by the Porte de La Villette, the other by the Porte de Montmartre, having arranged to meet beyond Saint-Denis, a piece of strategy which they punctually carried out with the most fortunate results. Together D'Artagnan and Planchet entered Pierrefitte.

Planchet was admittedly more daring in the daytime than after nightfall. But his native caution never forsook him an instant; having forgotten no incident of their first journey, he looked upon everyone they met on the road as an enemy. Accordingly he kept taking off his hat and holding it in his hand, at which D'Artagnan repeatedly reprimanded him with some asperity, for such excessive politeness might well cause Planchet to be taken as the lackey of a man of no consequence. At all events, whether the people they met were touched by Planchet's urbanity or whether this time no one lay in ambush for them, the two travelers arrived at Chantilly without mishap and repaired to the inn of the Grand Saint-Martin, where they had put up on their previous journey.

The host, impressed by a client with three remounts, advanced respectfully to greet them on the threshold. As they had already traveled eleven leagues, D'Artagnan considered it advisable to stop awhile at the inn even though Porthos were not there; he also deemed it prudent not to ask at once what had happened to the portly musketeer. Without asking any questions whatever D'Artagnan dismounted, left his lackey to attend to the horses and entered a small private room. Ordering the best wine and heartiest meal the house could afford, he confirmed the landlord's favorable impression, and was served with miraculous celerity.

The Regiment of Guards was known to be recruited from among the noblest gentlemen of the realm and, flanked by a lackey and three extra horses—magnificent nags they were, too—D'Artagnan cut a considerable swath. His uniform might be simple and anonymous but his air and his retinue compelled a certain respect. The landlord therefore served him in person and D'Artagnan, observing this attention, ordered him to bring two glasses.

"By my faith, my dear host," he paused a moment to fill both glasses, "By my faith, I ordered your best wine; if you have disappointed me, you shall suffer for it in the exact measure in which you have sinned. I hate to drink alone; you shall therefore join me; let us clink glasses and drink to each other's health. Further, to drink a toast that can hurt nobody's feelings, let us drink to the prosperity of your establishment."

"Monsieur does me much honor and I thank you most sincerely for your kind wishes."

"No, my dear host, make no mistake; there is probably more selfishness in my toast than you imagine. The only inns where guests are well received are the prosperous ones; other places, shabby and down at heels, make a gust the victim of his host's embarrassments. God preserve me from them!" The landlord bowed. "I travel a great deal, you know, especially on this road, and I should like to see all innkeepers coining money!"

"Indeed yes, Monsieur, if I am not mistaken I have had the honor of seeing you before."

"That is very likely: I have come through Chantilly at least ten times and stopped at your place at least four times or five. As a matter of fact I was last here some ten or twelve days ago, with some friends of mine, some musketeers."

"Really, Monsieur!"

"Yes. One of them, a somewhat stout gentleman, had a slight argument with a man totally unknown to any of us, who picked some kind of a quarrel with him."

"Why, yes, of course, Monsieur, I recall the incident. Monsieur is doubtless referring to Monsieur Porthos?"

"Exactly; he was traveling with us. Come, my dear host, tell me frankly: has anything untoward befallen Monsieur Porthos? He was a very cheerful traveling companion."

"Monsieur must have observed that Monsieur Porthos was prevented from continuing his journey."

"True: he promised to join us at Beauvais and we haven't seen him since."

"He did us the honor of remaining here, Monsieur."

"What? He is still here?"

"Ay, Monsieur, under this very roof. Indeed, I must confess to Monsieur that we are somewhat worried—"

"Worried about what—?"

"About certain expenses, Monsieur. Begging your pardon, Monsieur Porthos is a lavish gentleman."

"Well, if he has run up a bill, my dear landlord, he is certainly in a position to pay his score!"

"Monsieur's words are a solace to my soul!" The host sighed. "You see we advanced considerable cash to Monsieur Porthos and this very morning the surgeon swore that if Monsieur didn't pay him he would hold me responsible. Unfortunately it was I who sent for him!"

"Monsieur Porthos is wounded, then?"

"That I cannot tell!"

"What do you mean? Surely you of all people should know—?"

"Ay, Monsieur, men in my position cannot tell all they know. We must observe a landlordly discretion. And when the owner of an inn is told that his ears are answerable for what his tongue might say—"

"Tell me, may I see Monsieur Porthos?"

"Certainly, Monsieur; just take the stairs, walk up one flight and knock at the door of Number One. But be sure to say who you are."

"Why so?"

"Well, Monsieur, something terrible might happen to you."

"What, for instance?"

"Monsieur Porthos might easily mistake you for one of my staff. God help us, he might lose his temper and spit you like a fowl or blow your brains out."

"What on earth have you done to him?"

"We simply asked him for money, Monsieur."

"The devil you say! Now I understand everything. Don't you realize that when Monsieur Porthos is out of funds, any reference to money is apt to anger him?"

"We thought so too, Monsieur. But you see, we run this house on strictly businesslike lines, Monsieur; we make our bills out day by day and present them to our guests every Saturday. Maybe we chose the wrong moment to approach Monsieur Porthos. At any rate he flew into a towering rage and committed us to all the devils of hell. To be sure he had been gambling the night before."

"Gambling, eh? And with whom?"

"Good Lord, Monsieur, how can I tell? There was a gentleman in my inn, a very pretty gentleman indeed, but how should I know who he was? Anyhow, Monsieur, Porthos challenged him to a game of lansquenet."

"And I suppose poor Porthos lost all his money!"

"Not only his money, Monsieur, but even his horse. You see, when the nobleman was about to leave, I spied his lackey saddling the horse Monsieur Porthos had ridden. My wife and I told the lackey he was wrong but he said: 'Mind your own business, this horse belongs to us.' Imagine, Monsieur."

"Well, what happened next?"

The landlord proceeded to unfold his tale of woe. Having gone to inform Monsieur Porthos that his horse was being taken away, he was greeted with a volley of oaths for his pains. How dared a swine of a landlord doubt the word of a gentleman's lackey? How dared he venture to doubt an honorable guest? If the stranger had said that the horse was his, his it was and he could take it wherever he pleased. ("How typical of Porthos!" D'Artagnan murmured.) The landlord went on to explain that he soon realized no money was forthcoming; he had therefore hoped that Monsieur Porthos would at least condescend to honor a rival inn, *At the Sign of the Golden Eagle*, with his patronage. But no, Monsieur Porthos replied that the Grand Saint-Martin was very comfortable and that he intended to remain there. This statement was too flattering for the host to dispute it; he therefore merely suggested that Monsieur Porthos vacate

Room Number One, the handsomest in the hostelry, and move to a small but very comfortable room on the third floor. To this Monsieur Porthos replied that he was expecting his mistress to arrive at any moment and, since she was one of the greatest ladies at court, Monsieur Porthos intended to continue to occupy Room Number One because any other apartment would be unbefitting the lady and dishonoring to the hostelry of the Grand Saint-Martin, let alone to its landlord. While recognizing the truth and pith of the valid argument Monsieur Porthos advanced, mine host undertook to argue, whereupon Monsieur Porthos, brooking no discussion, seized a pistol which lay close at hand and delivered an ultimatum. He would, he swore, blow out the brains of anyone who rashly took it upon himself to meddle with affairs that concerned him, Monsieur Porthos, alone. Ever since, the landlord concluded, no one save the lackey, Mousqueton, dared enter Room Number One.

"So Mousqueton is here too?"

"Ay, Monsieur! five days after you left, the lackey returned, sullen and somewhat the worse for wear. It seems his journey did not agree with him. To tell you the truth, Monsieur, that lackey is considerably nimbler and spryer than his master. For the sake of Monsieur Porthos, he turns everything topsy-turvy; you see, Monsieur, God help us, he commandeers things right and left. Instead of waiting for us to refuse him something, he goes ahead and pinches it!"

"Ay, Mousqueton has always proved both enterprising and devoted to his master."

"Yes, Monsieur, I dare say; but if I found such enterprise and devotion four times a year, I would go bankrupt."

"Not at all; Porthos will pay you."

The landlord cleared his throat and heaved a sigh of doubt.

"My dear host, Monsieur Porthos is protected by an illustrious lady who would not permit him to languish here for the mere pittance of a week's rent."

"Well, Monsieur, if Monsieur will suffer me to speak freely—"

"Of course, my good man—"

"Well then, I will tell Monsieur not only what I surmise but what I know—"

"Go ahead, landlord—"

"Begging your pardon, Monsieur, this illustrious lady—"

"Yes—?"

"—this illustrious lady is no illustrious lady, Monsieur."

"What in the world do you mean?"

"I mean the illustrious lady—"

"Speak up, man!"

"The illustrious lady—hm!—may I count upon Monsieur's confidence—?"

"Of course; I give you my word as a gentleman—"

"Well, Monsieur, I know the lady in question—"

"You know her—?"

"Well, Monsieur, you see it was like this . . . Monsieur Porthos gave us a note addressed to his Duchess . . . we were meant to post the letter. . . . The valet had not arrived, Monsieur, so we had to do the needful because Monsieur Porthos was confined to his room—"

"Quite so. What then?"

"We did not post the letter, Monsieur, for the mails are not very safe. So I took the liberty of using one of my grooms who was going to Paris and I told him to deliver the letter himself. I was following the instructions of Monsieur Porthos, was I not? He was so insistent about the letter reaching its addressee!"

"I dare say; go on."

"Well, Monsieur, do you know who the illustrious lady is?"

"No, my friend, I have merely heard Monsieur Porthos mention her casually—"

"Monsieur, begging your pardon, she is no duchess; she is the wife of an aged attorney at the Châtelet. Her name is Coquenard and though at least fifty she plays the jealous coquette. When I first saw the letter, Monsieur, I thought it odd that a duchess lived in the Rue aux Ours!"

"How do you know all this?"

"Well, Monsieur, when the old lady received the letter, she flew into a great rage. She hinted that Monsieur Porthos was a trifler and had been wounded in a duel over a woman."

"So he *was* wounded, eh?"

"God help us, what have I said?"

"You said that Monsieur Porthos was wounded."

"Forgive me, Monsieur, I am all too indiscreet. Monsieur Porthos forbade me to mention it."

"Why?"

"Well, Monsieur, you see it happened like this. Monsieur Porthos boasted about riddling the stranger like a sieve but it was the stranger who pinked him, for all his boasting. Now you know what a proud gentleman Monsieur Porthos is, and how vainglorious he is, if I may say so, save in respect to his Duchess. Would you believe it, Monsieur, he wrote to Madame Coquenard all about his adventure and his gory wound but he forbids anyone else to mention it!"

"So he's in bed with a wound, eh, landlord?"

"A masterly wound it is, Monsieur; your friend is certainly hard to kill. God bless us."

"You saw the duel?"

"Ay, Monsieur, that I did. I was curious, that I was; and I saw the whole thing without the gentlemen knowing I was watching."

"Tell me what happened, landlord."

"Well, Monsieur, it was soon over, I warrant you. They fell into guard and before Monsieur Porthos could say knife, the stranger put three inches of steel in his chest . . . Monsieur Porthos fell back with a crash . . . the other gentleman pressed his swordpoint delicately to the throat of Monsieur Porthos and Monsieur Porthos gave in. . . . When the gentleman insisted on knowing whom he had bested and Monsieur Porthos told his name, he helped Monsieur Porthos back to the inn, apologized for having mistaken Monsieur Porthos for a certain Monsieur D'Artagnan, and rode away."

"So it was Monsieur D'Artagnan the gentleman sought to fight with?"

"So it would seem, Monsieur."

"Can you tell me what has become of this Monsieur D'Artagnan?"

"No, Monsieur, I never saw him before and I have not seen him since."

"Good, I know what I want. You told me Monsieur Porthos was—"

"—One flight up, Monsieur. Room Number One, the best in the house. I could have rented it ten times over."

"Pray don't worry, my dear host!" D'Artagnan laughed. "Monsieur Porthos will pay you with funds furnished by Madame la Duchesse de Coquenard."

"Duchess or lawyer's wife, Monsieur, let her but draw her purse-strings and I shall be delighted. But you see, Monsieur, between you and me, she seemed to be fed up with the demands Monsieur Porthos made upon her and with his infidelities. She swore she wouldn't send him a sou."

"Did you give your guest this message?"

"We were very careful to do nothing of the kind, Monsieur, because he would have found out how we delivered the letter."

"So he still expects the money?"

"Why, yes, Monsieur. Just yesterday he wrote again, but this time his lackey posted the letter."

"And the Duchess—I mean Madame la Procureuse—the lawyer's wife—is old and ugly?"

"At least fifty years old, Monsieur, and my man Pathaud reported that she was no pleasure to behold!"

"Never mind, landlord, the uglier she is, the more generous she will be. Besides, Monsieur Porthos can't owe you so very much."

"Well, no, Monsieur, not *very* much: just a matter of twenty pistoles so far, not counting the doctor. Oh no! Monsieur Porthos is a very generous man; he denies himself nothing. I can see he is used to lordly living."

"Well, my dear host, if his mistress forsakes him, I'm sure he will not lack friends. Cheer up, take things in your stride, and pray continue to treat him with all the courtesy his situation demands."

"Monsieur promised me not to breathe a word about the lawyerling duchess, eh? Monsieur will not betray my confidence in regard to the wound?"

"I have given you my word!"

"You see, Monsieur, if he knew I had told you, he would kill me!"

"Rest easy, my dear landlord; Monsieur Porthos is not so fierce or diabolic as he would have you believe."

With which D'Artagnan nodded to the host and climbed the stairs, leaving the good man somewhat more cheerful about two things he seemed to value very much—the money owed him and his life. At the top of the stairs, he saw a monstrously conspicuous door, with, over the panel, a gigantic sign, traced in black ink, reading Number One. D'Artagnan, knocking, was summoned to enter. He was greeted with a hilarious spectacle.

Porthos lay back in bed in sumptuous comfort; he was playing lansquenet with Mousqueton, just to keep his hand in. A spit loaded with partridges was turning gaily before the fire; at either side of the spacious chimney piece, on twin andirons, stood two chafing dishes over which two boiling stewpans exhaled the most fragrant odor of *gibelotte*—fricassee of hare—and *matelotte*—a fish stew with prevailing flavors of wine, onions and herbs. The top of a writing desk and the marble cover of a chest of drawers loomed aglitter with empty bottles.

Seeing his friend, Porthos cried out with joy:

"D'Artagnan? You? I can scarcely believe my eyes! By God, you are welcome, my dear fellow. Forgive me for not rising to greet you." Then with a certain degree of embarrassment, Porthos added: "Have you heard about me?"

"No!"

"You haven't talked to the landlord?"

"No, Porthos, he told me where to find you and up I came."

Porthos heaved a sigh of relief.

"Tell me all about yourself, Porthos?" D'Artagnan asked.

"Ah, it's a sorry story," Porthos sighed. "You left me here fighting against a stranger . . . I had dealt him three neat thrusts . . . I was about to settle him with a fourth . . . and, guess what happened?"

"What?"

"I tripped on a stone and sprained my knee."

"What dreadful luck!"

"Ay, my friend, it's God's truth! Happily for the cad I was fighting, I couldn't dispatch him. He had enough of it and took to his heels. . . . And you, D'Artagnan?"

"I am quite well, as you see. But tell me about your knee? It keeps you abed, I dare say."

"Yes, my friend, it's an infernal nuisance, but in a few days, I shall be up and about!"

"Why didn't you go back to Paris, Porthos? You must find it terribly boring here?"

"I wanted to go back to Paris. It *is* boring here, too, but I must confess—"

"What?"

"Well, as you may judge, I was terribly bored here. And I had the seventy-five pistoles you lent me. So I gambled with a gentleman who happened to be staying here overnight; I invited him up for a game of dice. He accepted and very swiftly transferred your seventy-five pistoles from my pocket to his, not to mention my horse, which I lost to him in a last, desperate effort to recoup. But enough of my woes, my dear D'Artagnan, tell me about yourself."

"Well my friend, you know the old proverb: *Unlucky at play, lucky in love.*

You are too happy in your amours not to suffer an occasional reverse in dicing. After all you're a very fortunate fellow! Surely your duchess will not fail but come to your rescue."

"To tell you the truth, my friend, I've had a spot of bad luck in that direction," Porthos confessed in the most careless and airy tone imaginable. "I did write to her to send me some fifty louis or so which I needed very much, because as you know I was in a tight spot—"

"And—?"

"—and I can only conclude that the Duchess must have been away in the country because I received no answer—"

"Well, well!"

"Having heard nothing from her, I sent her a second letter yesterday. I explained that matters were even more urgent than I had said in letter Number One. But *you* my friend, what about *you?* I must confess that, confined to my bed as I was, I felt very anxious about you."

"Oh, I've been very well. But your landlord, my dear Porthos," D'Artagnan pointed to the full saucepans and empty bottles, "your landlord seems to be doing his share, eh?"

"The host is doing an indifferent job, my friend, his treatment of us has been so-so. Four days ago he had the cheek to present his bill and I had to toss both him and the document out of the door of my apartment. This made me a victor of sorts and a conqueror, if you like; but as you see, I am in constant fear of being stormed out of my stronghold and I have perforce to remain armed to the teeth night and day."

D'Artagnan laughed jovially as he asked: "Don't you sally forth occasionally, my friend?" And once again he surveyed the empty bottles and the fragrant saucepans.

"Not I, alas," Porthos vouchsafed. "As you see, my wretched knee nails me to my bed. But Mousqueton does an occasional job of foraging and so we do not lack for provisions." Porthos turned to his lackey: "Mousqueton, as you see, we have reinforcements; you must produce rations for Monsieur D'Artagnan who is doubtless both hungry and thirsty."

"Mousqueton, a favor, I beg you?"

"Yes, Monsieur."

"Pray tell Planchet how you go about foraging; your recipe would be invaluable to him. I may be besieged and beleaguered at any time, just as Monsieur Porthos has been; and if this happened, I would welcome attentions from Planchet such as those you lavish on your master."

Mousqueton stared modestly at the ground.

"It's no trick, Monsieur," he said, "all you need is to be nimble and spry. I happen to have been brought up in the country and my father in his leisure moments used to do a bit of poaching now and again—"

"What did he do when he worked?"

"He toiled at a job I have always thought a very prosperous one."

"Namely?"

Mousqueton fetched up a deep sigh and told the heroic story of his father. It was at the time of the Wars of Religion; Catholics and Huguenots were vying with one another in violence. Monsieur Mousqueton père watched the Catholics exterminating the Huguenots and vice-versa all in the name of God. He evolved and compounded a mixed belief which permitted him now to be Catholic, now Protestant.

He was accustomed to strolling behind the hedges that border the roads, his blunderbuss over his shoulder. His activity was at once limited and unlimited by the choice between two positions. If he passed a Catholic, the Protestant religion immediately prevailed in his mind; he would lower his gun and, when he was within ten paces of the stranger, he would engage in a conversation which invariably resulted in the stranger's parting with his purse in order to save his life. If, on the other hand, he came upon a Protestant, in all fairness to Monsieur Mousqueton père, his son was compelled to admit that his sire was so overcome with a fervor of Catholic zeal that he found it difficult to conceive how he had attacked a follower of the Mother Church just a few moments before.

"My father was a stout believer in the superiority of our Holy Catholic faith," Mousqueton added sententiously. "And I myself am a devout practiser. But faithful to his all-embracing principles, he made my older brother a Huguenot."

"What happened to your worthy father?" D'Artagnan inquired. And volubly Mousqueton related that the fate of this worthy and eclectic citizen had been unfortunate indeed. One day he was caught in a sunken road between a Catholic and a Huguenot with whom he had had previous dealings; they both recognized him, joined forces and hung him to a tree. Mousqueton, the good Catholic, and his brother, the good Protestant, happened to be drinking in the village inn when the two assassins ordered a magnum of wine and boasted of their dastardly exploit.

"What did you do, my lad?" D'Artagnan asked.

"We let them talk, Monsieur, and they had their story out, talking a bellyful. Then my brother and I parted; he went north to wait for the Catholic, I south to wait for the Huguenot. Two hours later the situation was well in hand; we had settled both of them in wonder, gratitude and tribute at our father's foresight for bringing us up in different faiths."

"Your father must have been a most intelligent fellow, Mousqueton. Tell me something about the poaching he did in his leisure moments."

"Monsieur, he was marvelously skilled in poaching. It was he taught me first how to lay a snare and to ground a line. He was a past master, Monsieur, and I an apt pupil. So you can understand that when I found our shabby host serving us up lumps of meat fit for clodhoppers, I decided to do something about our delicate stomachs; Monsieur Porthos and I are not used to eating poorly! So I went back to poaching, Monsieur. As I strolled in the woods of Monsieur le Prince de Condé, I set a snare here and there in the runs; and as I reclined on the banks bordering His Royal Highness's waters, I slipped a line or two into his fishponds. Wherefore, praise God! we lack for no partridge or hare or carp or eel, as Monsieur will presently witness. These are light healthy foods, Monsieur, specially indicated for persons who are sick or recuperating from arduous duties."

"But the wine, Mousqueton? Does your host furnish it?"

"Well, Monsieur, yes he does and no he doesn't."

"What do you mean?"

"He furnishes our wine, yes; but no, he is not aware he has that honor."

"Come, come, Mousqueton, explain yourself. Your conversation opens up vistas that deserve elucidation."

"Well, here's the story, Monsieur. By chance in the course of my fairly wide travels, I once met a Spaniard, Monsieur, who had been in many a country and seen the New World too."

"What in Heaven's name has the New World to do with the empty bottles on that desk and on that chest of drawers?"

"Patience, Monsieur, I beg you; I will tell you all in good time."

"Right, Mousqueton, proceed; I am all ears."

Mousqueton thereupon related that the Spaniard in question had a lackey who had accompanied him on a voyage to Mexico. The lackey was a compatriot of Mousqueton and a lively intimacy grew up between them because they had much in common. They both loved hunting, particularly, and Mousqueton's friend used to tell him how in the plains of the pampas the natives hunt the tiger and wild bull with what they call lassos—just simple running nooses with which they down the fiercest animals. At first Mousqueton was skeptical because he could not imagine how even a heathen could toss the end of a rope a distance of thirty paces with such deadly accuracy. Nevertheless Mousqueton's colleague proved his point.

"And this is how, Monsieur: he placed a bottle thirty paces away and each time he cast his rope he caught the neck of the bottle in his running noose. He was as good a teacher as my father and I as ready a pupil and, since Nature has endowed me with certain aptitudes, today I can toss a lasso as accurately as any man in the world."

D'Artagnan shrugged his shoulders and urged Mousqueton to come to the point.

"Ah, the point, Monsieur? Well, you see our host has a very respectably stocked cellar but he insists on wearing the keys on his person. But fortunately the cellar boasts a loophole; I cast my lasso through this loophole and, as I know where the best wines stand, I direct my lasso in that quarter."

Mousqueton bowed modestly, adding:

"Now Monsieur understands the relation between the New World and the bottles which now grace our desk and our chest of drawers. Perhaps Monsieur would care to sample one of our bottles and tell us quite frankly what he thinks of our wares."

"Thank you, Mousqueton, unfortunately I have just breakfasted."

"Well, Mousqueton, lay the table and while you and I breakfast, Monsieur D'Artagnan can tell us what he has been doing these last ten days."

"Willingly," D'Artagnan said. And whilst Porthos and Mousqueton ate with the appetites of convalescents and with that brotherly cordiality which unties men in times of adversity, D'Artagnan told how Aramis, wounded, had remained at Crévecoeur . . . how Athos, accused of counterfeiting, had been left fighting off four men at Amiens . . . and how he, D'Artagnan, had been forced to run the Comte de Vardes through the body in order to reach England. . . . There D'Artagnan's confidences stopped; he merely added that on his return from England he brought back four magnificent horses, one for himself and one for each of his comrades, and that the one destined for Porthos was stabled in the inn. . . .

At that moment Planchet entered to inform his master that the horses were sufficiently refreshed and that they could all reach Clermont that night. Since D'Artagnan was tolerably reassured about Porthos and very anxious to obtain news of Aramis and Athos, he shook hands with the portly convalescent, telling him what he meant to do. Probably he would be returning through Chantilly; he therefore proposed to call for Porthos on the way if Porthos were still at the Hostelry of the Grand Saint-Martin.

Porthos replied that in all probability his knee would not permit him to leave yet a while; besides, he must stay at Chantilly to await the reply from his duchess.

"May the reply be prompt and favorable," our Gascon said and, recommending Porthos to Mousqueton, he settled the musketeer's debt to the inn. Then, with Planchet relieved of one horse, he rode off toward Crèvecoeur....

XXVI
Of Aramis and His Thesis

D'Artagnan had said nothing to Porthos about his wound or about his precious duchess. Our young man from Béarn was young, to be sure, but he was wise and prudent beyond his years. He had therefore pretended to believe all the vainglorious musketeer had told him, for he was convinced that no friendship can stand the strain of a secret discovered, particularly when that secret involves a man's pride. Again, a man always enjoys a certain feeling of mental superiority over those whose lives he knows better than they suspect. Further, D'Artagnan planned other intrigues for the future and was resolved that his three friends could be instrumental in making his fortune for him; he therefore was not at all sorry to grasp beforehand the invisible strings by which he hoped to move them.

Yet as he journeyed onward a profound melancholy weighed heavily upon his heart. He thought of the young and pretty Madame Bonacieux who was to have given him the reward of his devotion; but in all justice to him it must be confessed that his sorrow rose less from regret at the happiness he had missed than from his fear that some misfortune had befallen the poor woman. In his opinion there was no doubt she had become a victim of the Cardinal's vengeance, and as everyone knew, the Cardinal's vengeance was a terrible thing. How D'Artagnan himself could have found favor in the minister's eyes was a complete mystery to him; doubtless Monsieur de Cavois would have revealed this to him had D'Artagnan been at home when the Captain of the Cardinal's guards called upon him.

Now nothing makes time pass more quickly and shortens a journey more effectively than thoughts which absorb the thinker's every faculty. External existence seems to resemble a deep slumber of which this thought is the dream. Under its influence time becomes measureless and space loses all distance. We leave our place and arrive at another—that is all; of the interval between places nothing remains in the memory save a vague mist in which a myriad confused images of trees, mountains and landscapes are blurred beyond recognition. A prey to such an hallucination D'Artagnan covered the eight leagues between Chantilly and Crève-coeur at whatever gait his horse chose to adopt; of what he had seen on the road, he remembered nothing. It was not until he glimpsed the inn where he had left Aramis that he came to, and shaking his head, brought his horse up to the door at a trot.

This time it was no host but a hostess who greeted him. A canny physiognomist, he took in at one glance the plump, merry countenance of the mistress of the place, understanding at once that he need not dissemble and that he had nothing to fear from anyone with so cheerful an air.

"My dear Madame," he asked before dismounting, "could you tell me what has happened to a friend of mine, whom we were obliged to leave here about twelve days ago?"

"Does Monsieur mean a handsome young man? Twenty-three or twenty-four years old? A gentle, pleasant-spoken and very well-built young man?"

"Your description fits him like a glove. What's more, he was wounded in the shoulder."

"True, Monsieur."

"Well, what about him?"

"He's still here, Monsieur."

D'Artagnan leaped off his horse, tossed the reins to Planchet and:

"God help us, Madame," he cried, "you restore me to life. Where is my dear Aramis? I long to embrace him again; I vow I cannot wait to see him."

"Begging your pardon, Monsieur, I doubt whether he can see you just now."

"How so? Has he a lady with him?"

"God forbid, Monsieur; by Jesus, Mary and Joseph, what are you saying? No, he is with no woman."

"Well then, whom is he with?"

"With the curé of Montdidier and the Superior of the Jesuits of Amiens."

"Good Lord, can the poor fellow have taken a turn for the worse?"

"No, Monsieur, on the contrary. But after his troubles the grace of Heaven seems to have touched him and he has decided to take up Holy Orders."

"Ah, yes, I had forgotten he was but a musketeer *pro tem.*"

"Is Monsieur still eager to see him?"

"More than ever, I assure you."

"Well, Monsieur has only to take the right-hand staircase off the court-yard and knock at Number Five on the second floor."

Following her instructions D'Artagnan found one of those outside stairways that may still be seen today in the courtyard of old inns. But it was no easy task to penetrate into the presence of the future abbé; the passages to the chamber Aramis occupied were guarded as closely as ever the alleys of the gardens of Armida in Tasso's *Jerusalem Delivered*. Bazin, stationed in the corridor, barred all entrance the more intrepidly because after years of trial he now found himself within sight of the goal he had so steadfastly dreamed of.

Ever since he could remember, poor Bazin had longed to serve a churchman and, year after year, he had been longing for the day when Aramis would at last exchange the uniform for the cassock. It was only his master's frequent promises that the moment was almost at hand which kept Bazin in the service of a musketeer—a service in which, he was wont to add, his soul was in constant jeopardy.

Bazin was therefore overjoyed; this time in all probability his master would not retract. The combination of physical hurt and moral pain had surely produced the desired result! Suffering both in body and soul, Aramis had at last fixed his eyes and his thoughts upon religion, Bazin was sure. Ay, two horrible accidents had befallen him: the sudden disappearance of his mistress and the wound in his shoulder! Happily now he had come to regard these as warnings from an all-too indulgent Heaven!

In his present frame of mind then Bazin could not have imagined anything more unwelcome than D'Artagnan's arrival, which must needs cast his master back again into the vortex of mundane concerns that had swept him along for so many years. Bazin therefore resolved to defend the door bravely and since, betrayed by the hostess, he could not say that Aramis was absent, he attempted to prove to the visitor that it would be the height of indiscretion for him to disturb Monsieur Aramis in the midst of a pious conference which had begun that morning and which, Bazin was certain, would go on far into the night.

D'Artagnan, regardless of this eloquent discourse and in no mood to engage in polemic discussion with his friend's valet, simply moved him aside with one hand and with the other turned the handle of the door to Room Number Five.

He found Aramis clad in a black gown, his head surmounted by a sort of round, flat, black headdress not unlike a skull cap; the musketeer was seated at an oblong table covered with scrolls of paper and huge volumes in folio. At his right sat the Superior of the Jesuits; at his left the Curé of Montdidier. The curtains, half-drawn, permitted only the most discreet subdued daylight to enter the room, a penumbral glow calculated to encourage the most beatific contemplations. Any worldly object that might generally strike the eye on entering a young man's room—particularly when that young man is a musketeer—had disappeared as if by enchantment. Further, no doubt in fear lest the sight of his swords, pistols, plumed hat, embroideries and laces of all sorts might recall Aramis back to the follies of this world, Bazin had carefully put them away. Nothing of the normal equipment of a young man of fashion was visible; in the stead and place of such objects, D'Artagnan thought he perceived a whip for self-flagellation hanging from a nail on the wall.

Hearing the door open, Aramis looked up and recognized his friend. But to D'Artagnan's immense surprise his appearance seemed to make but a slight impression on an Aramis lost in supraterrestrial speculation.

"Good day to you, my dear D'Artagnan," Aramis said with utter calm, "believe me, I am happy to see you."

"And I too," D'Artagnan assured him, "although I am not yet quite certain that this is Aramis."

"And why not, my dear friend?"

"I feared I had mistaken your room and walked in upon some churchman. Then when I saw these two Fathers by your side I suddenly thought you were dangerously ill."

The two men in black, guessing at once what D'Artagnan meant, looked almost threateningly at him but this did not feaze him.

"Perhaps I am disturbing you, my dear Aramis," D'Artagnan suggested. "Unless my eyes mistake me, you were busy making confession to these gentlemen—?"

Aramis blushed ever so slightly and:

"You are not disturbing me," he assured D'Artagnan. "On the contrary, my dear friend, I vow I am delighted to note that you have come back from your travels safe and sound." (D'Artagnan congratulated himself silently on the fact that Aramis seemed to have returned to earth; indeed he was coming around at last and high time, too!) "This gentleman is a friend of mine," Aramis explained unctuously to the two clerics. "He has just escaped considerable danger."

"Praise God!" and "God be praised, Monsieur!" the ecclesiastics intoned, bowing in unison.

"I did not fail to praise Him, Your Reverences," D'Artagnan countered, returning their salutation.

"Your arrival is most timely, my dear D'Artagnan," Aramis continued smoothly. "By taking part in our discussion you can perhaps shed some light of your own upon the subject we were discussing. Monsieur le Principal, Superior of the Jesuits at Amiens, and Monsieur le Curé of Montdidier and I are arguing about certain theological problems which have long fascinated us. I am sure I would welcome any contribution you might care to make to our discussion."

"The opinion of a man of the sword can carry no weight," D'Artagnan protested, somewhat uneasy at the turn the conversation was taking. "Surely the learning of these gentlemen can settle all your doubts?"

Again the two men in black bowed in unison.

"Not at all, my dear D'Artagnan, I know your opinion will be much appreciated," Aramis pursued in honeyed tones. "Here is the point: Monsieur le Principal believes that my thesis ought to be very dogmatic and didactic."

"Your thesis? You are presenting a thesis?"

"Of course he is," the Jesuit replied. "For the examination preceding ordination, a thesis is always requisite."

"Ordination!" D'Artagnan echoed, flabbergasted, for he still could not bring himself to believe what both the hostess and Bazin had told him. "Ordination!" he repeated, looking in bewilderment at the trio before him.

Aramis sat back in his armchair with the same easy grace he would have assumed on a formal visit to the bedside of a lady of the Court. Nonchalantly he looked down at his hand, as white and as dimpled a hand as the fairest woman might boast; then he dropped his arm so that the blood might flow down to his fingertips. "Well, D'Artagnan, just as I told you, Monsieur le Principal would wish my thesis to be thoroughly dogmatic, whereas I would prefer it to be thoroughly idealistic. That is why Monsieur le Principal has proposed this subject: *Utraque manus in benedicendo clericis inferioribus necessaria est—*"

D'Artagnan, whose education was rudimentary, did not flinch at this learned quotation any more than he had flinched when Monsieur de Tréville had uttered certain incomprehensible words about gifts he believed D'Artagnan had received from the Duke of Buckingham.

Aramis however was not duped by the Gascon's imperturbability. With exquisite tact he added urbanely:

"I need scarcely translate the Latin for you as you know it means *That it is indispensable for priests of the inferior orders to employ both hands when they bestow the benediction.* Monsieur le Principal assures me the topic has not been treated and I myself see what magnificent possibilities it offers."

"An admirable subject!" the Jesuit confirmed and "Admirably dogmatic!" the Curé approved, for, about as well versed in Latin as D'Artagnan, he observed the Jesuit's every move in order to keep in step and echo him verbatim. As for D'Artagnan, he remained totally indifferent to the zeal and enthusiasm of the clerics. "*Prorsus admirabile,* admirable indeed," Aramis continued blandly, "but the subject requires a profound study of both the Scriptures and the Church Fathers. In all humility, D'Artagnan, I confessed to these ecclesiastical savants that my duties in mounting guard and serving the King have caused me to neglect my studies somewhat. Accordingly, *facilius natans,* swimming in my own waters, so to speak, I ventured that a subject of my own choosing might offer to these arduous theological problems something of the comfort moral science offers to the study of metaphysics in the realm of philosophy."

D'Artagnan felt bored to tears, so too the Curé.

"See what an exordium!" the Jesuit commented.

"*Exordium,*" the Curé repeated for want of something to say.

"*Quemadmodum inter coelorum immensitatem,*" Aramis said, "All ways are good so but we reach the vast world of heaven!" As he glanced at D'Artagnan to see what effect all this produced, he saw but a vast yawn, fit to break even a Gascon's jaw. "Let us speak French, Father," he urged the Jesuit, "Monsieur D'Artagnan will enjoy our conversation the more."

"Ay, gentlemen, I confess I am tired out after my journey and all this Latin confuses me."

Somewhat vexed, the Jesuit agreed; the Curé glanced gratefully at D'Artagnan and the Jesuit went on:

"Let us see, my friends, what sense is to be derived from this gloss . . ." He sighed cavernously, "Moses, the servant of God . . . he was but a servant, remember . . . Moses, I say, blessed with his hands, you understand . . . he had acolytes hold up his two arms while the Hebrews fell victoriously upon their enemies . . . in other words, he blessed with both hands. . . . Besides, what does the Gospel say? It says *imponite manus* not *imponite manum,* the hands, plural, not the hand."

"Imponite manus," the Curé echoed with an appropriate gesture, "lay on *both* hands!"

"Of course in the case of Saint Peter there was a slight difference," the Jesuit continued. "His successors, the Popes said: *Porrige digitos,* bless with the fingers." He coughed. "Do you follow me?" he asked hopefully.

"Certainly," Aramis exclaimed gleefully, "but the point is a subtle one."

"The fingers," the Jesuit insisted, "Saint Peter blessed with the fingers; the Pope therefore blesses with his fingers. And with how many fingers does he perform the benediction? With three, naturally: one for the Father, one for the Son, and one for the Holy Ghost."

Seeing the three disputants cross themselves, D'Artagnan did likewise. The Jesuit droned on:

"His Holiness the Pope is the direct successor of Saint Peter; he therefore represents the three divine powers, the Holy Trinity. All others, *ordines inferiores* or the lower orders of the ecclesiastical hierarchy, bless only in the name of the Archangels and Angels. The humblest clerics, our deacons, say, and our sacristans, bless with Holy Water sprinklers which represent an indefinite number of fingers extended in the act of Holy Benediction!" He sighed. "There," he continued sententiously, "you have the matter in a nutshell!" But he was not yet done. *"Argumentum omni denudatum ornamento, I have presented my argument in unadorned simplicity,"* he insisted and, carried away with excitement: "I fully expect to write two volumes meaty as these," he vowed, slapping an in-folio Saint Chrysostom of such weight and bulk that the table all but collapsed under it.

The impact of his palm and the tremulous table legs caused D'Artagnan to shudder. Aramis broke in.

"I must pay tribute to the beauty of this thesis, Father," he said humbly, "but it overwhelms me. For my part I had chosen another text and I beg you to tell me if it pleases you, my dear D'Artagnan. It is: *Non inutile est desiderium in oblatione,* or better, *a little regret is not unbecoming in an offering to the Lord."*

"Stop, stop!" the Jesuit warned. "That thesis borders on heresy; I find an almost identical proposition in the *Augustinus* of Jansenius, the heresiarch whose work will sooner or later be burned by the public executioner. Have a care, my young friend, you seem to incline toward false doctrines that may spell your ruin."

"Your ruin!" the Curé seconded, shaking his head sorrowfully.

"You are skirting that famous question of free will which is a deadly shoal. You are steering straight for the insinuations of the Pelagians and near-Pelagians."

"But Reverend Father—" Aramis ventured, somewhat taken aback by the shower of arguments falling about his head.

The Jesuit, giving him no time to make his point, challenged:

"How are you going to prove that we ought to regret the world when we offer ourselves to God? The dilemma is clear; listen! God is God, the World is the Devil, to regret the World is to regret the Devil. That is my conclusion."

"Mine too," said the Curé.

"But I beg of you . . ."

"*Desideras diabolum, you yearn for the Devil,* O unhappy man!" said the Jesuit pontifically.

"Ay, he yearns for the Devil!" the Curé groaned. "Poor young man, I implore you not to hanker after Satan!"

For D'Artagnan the whole scene was incomprehensible and the language so much Greek, let alone Latin. Was this a madhouse? Was he turning as mad as the people in it? Hampered by his lack of dialectic, he sank graciously into silence. Aramis, polite and suave as ever, but with unmistakable symptoms of impatience, was saying:

"Please hear me out, Father. I never said anything about regretting the world or hankering after Satan. You will at least grant that I could not utter a statement so unorthodox—"

As though rehearsed to do so, both Jesuit and Curé raised their arms to Heaven. This gave Aramis a brief inning.

"I appeal to you D'Artagnan, would it not be an act of ill grace to offer to the Lord a gift which filled one with disgust?"

"By God, yes!"

Jesuit and Curé rose simultaneously in their chairs, then sank back.

"I start from this simple syllogism," Aramis continued. "One: The World is not wanting in charm; Two, I quit the World and thus make a sacrifice; and Three, I obey the injunction of the Scriptures which command us to make a sacrifice unto the Lord."

"True," said the Jesuit, and "Yes, yes," said the Curé.

"What is more, I have written a rondeau about the whole problem." Aramis pinched his ears to redden them and twiddled his hands to make them white. "It is not a very good poem but I showed it to Monsieur Voiture last year and he was kind enough to say he liked it."

"A rondeau!" the Jesuit said contemptuously.

"A rondeau!" the Curé repeated mechanically.

"Do let us hear it, my dear Aramis!" D'Artagnan begged, welcoming an opportunity to take part in the discussion. "It will at least clear the air a bit!"

"I fear not, D'Artagnan, for it is a highly religious piece; it is theology expressed in verse."

"The devil you say, Aramis!"

"Well, anyhow, here it is, since you asked for it," Aramis said with a diffidence not exempt of a shade of hypocrisy. And he read:

> Vous qui pleurez un passé plein de charmes
> Et qui traînez des jours infortunés,
> Tous vos malheurs se verront terminés
> Quand à Dieu seul vous offrirez vos larmes—
>   Vous qui pleurez!

> All ye who weep for dulcet pleasures past,
> Your lives unfortunate and unbefriended,
> Soon shall your chronicle of woe be ended
> When that God greets your proferred tears at last,
>   All ye who weep!

D'Artagnan and the Curé evinced a certain satisfaction at the recitation but the Jesuit persisted in his opinion:

"Beware of a profane taste in theological style," he warned. "Remember Saint Augustine's dictum: *Severus sit clericorum sermo, let the preacher speak strictly to the point.*"

"Ay, let the sermon be clear!" the Curé approved.

"And," the Jesuit hastened on, aware that his acolyte misunderstood his Latin, "I am sure your thesis will please the ladies. I foresee the sort of success Maître Patru obtains when he pleads a cause in the law courts to the delight of an audience of sighing women."

"Please God you speak true," cried Aramis delighted.

"There, you see," the Jesuit scolded, "the world still speaks through you, *altissima voce, loud as it can.* You follow the world, my young friend, and I much fear Grace has not visited you."

"Rest easy, Father, I can answer for myself."

"With all the arrogance of worldly presumption!"

"I know what I am about, Father; I have made up my mind!"

"Yet you persist in supporting that thesis, my son?"

"I feel called upon to support that thesis and no other. I shall therefore continue to work on it tomorrow, Father, and I hope you will be satisfied with the corrections I shall bring to it, thanks to your advice."

"Work slowly and diligently," the Curé counseled. "I am sure we are leaving you in the best possible frame of mind to carry you successfully along the path you have chosen."

"Yes, the ground of the Lord is richly sown," said the Jesuit. "We need not fear lest one portion of the seed fall upon stone or another upon the highway nor lest the *birds of Heaven have eaten of the rest, aves coeli comederant illam!*"

D'Artagnan, at the end of his tether, muttered: "God choke, stifle and plague you with your Latin!"

"Farewell, my son," said the Curé. "I shall come back tomorrow."

"Farewell until tomorrow, my rash young friend," said the Jesuit. "You give promise of becoming a light of the Church; God grant that this light prove not to be a consuming fire."

For over an hour D'Artagnan had been gnawing furiously at his nails; now he was down to the quick. The two men in black rose stiffly, bowed ceremoniously to Aramis and D'Artagnan, and moved toward the door. Bazin, who had been standing by, overhearing the entire controversy with pious jubilation, sped forward toward them, picked up the breviary the Curé had left on a chair and the missal the Jesuit had forgotten, and ushered the clerics out with much respectful consideration. Aramis accompanied his guests to the foot of the stairs, then rejoined D'Artagnan who was still lost in thought.

Left alone at last the two friends were lost in an embarrassed silence;

one or the other must perforce break it and D'Artagnan appeared set upon leaving this honor to his comrade. Aramis therefore broke the ice.

"As you see," he volunteered, "I have reverted to my original ideas."

"So I perceive, Aramis; Grace has indeed visited you in all its power, if I may quote your clerical friend."

"My plans of retirement were formed long since, as you know. Indeed I mentioned them to you, did I not?"

"True, but I thought you were joking."

"Joking about anything as serious as that?"

"Well, we certainly joke about death."

"Yes, D'Artagnan, but we are wrong because death is the gateway to salvation or ruin."

"Granted, my dear Aramis, but pray spare me theologics; you must surely have had enough of them for one day. As for me I have just forgotten practically all the small Latin I ever learned. Also I happen to have had no food since ten o'clock this morning and I confess I am devilishly hungry."

"We will dine shortly, my friend. Only I must remind you that it is Friday, so I cannot eat meat or witness the eating of it. If you can put up with my humble dinner, you are indeed welcome. We are having tetragons—"

"Tetragons? What do you mean? I thought tetragons had something to do with geometry?"

"No, I mean simply spinach, to which we will add some eggs. Incidentally this is a serious infraction of the rules because eggs are actually meat, for out of them come your chickens."

"It scarcely sounds like succulent fare, my dear Aramis, but I will put up with it for the sake of your company."

"I appreciate your sacrifice, my dear fellow. It may not benefit your body but it will surely benefit your soul."

D'Artagnan then questioned Aramis about his intention to take up Holy Orders. What would their friends say about it, and how would Monsieur de Tréville take it? D'Artagnan suggested that many people might look upon Aramis as a deserter. His friend replied that he was not about to enter the Church but rather to re-enter it. He had forsaken the Church for the World; he had acted against his sincerest principles by donning the uniform of a musketeer. Surely D'Artagnan must know all this.

"I?" D'Artagnan asked in amazement. "I know nothing whatever about it, Aramis."

"Well, the Scriptures say 'Confess yourselves to one another'—James, V, 16—and so I will confess myself to you, my friend."

"And I, being a decent sort of fellow, will grant you absolution beforehand."

"Do not make light of holy things, my friend."

"No offense meant, my dear fellow. Fire away, I am listening!"

"Well, I had been at the seminary ever since the age of nine and I was within three days of my twentieth birthday. All was settled; I was certain of becoming an abbé and my life was marked out quite definitely. Then one evening as I was visiting a house which I frequented with much pleasure—one is young after all, and the flesh is weak!—an officer who was jealous of me because I used to read the *Lives of the Saints* to the mistress of the house, chanced to enter suddenly without being announced. That evening I had translated an episode concerning Judith; I had just read my verses to the lady, who was loud in her praise and, leaning on my shoulder, was reading them a second time. Her position, which I must admit was somewhat intimate, wounded the officer's feelings. He said nothing at the time, but when I left he followed me out and caught up with me.

" 'Monsieur l'Abbé,' he said, 'do you care for canings?'

" 'I cannot say, Monsieur,' I replied, 'no one has ever dared give me one.'

" 'Well, then, listen to me, Monsieur l'Abbé: if you ever return to the house where I met you this evening, I shall give you a sound drubbing.'

"I think I must have been frightened; at any rate I turned very pale, I felt my knees giving way, I sought for some reply, but, finding none, I kept silent. The officer was awaiting my reply but, seeing it so slow in coming, he burst into laughter, turned on his heel, and went back into the house.

"I returned to the seminary.

"Now I am a gentleman born and I am hot-blooded, as you may have noticed, my dear D'Artagnan; the insult was a terrible one, and though none but I knew of it, I felt it alive, stirring and festering in the depths of my heart. Accordingly I informed my superiors that I did not feel sufficiently prepared to be ordained and at my request the ceremony was postponed for a year.

"I promptly sought out the best fencing master in Paris, arranged to take lessons from him every day for a whole year and I never missed a single one. Then on the first anniversary of the day I was insulted, I hung my cassock on a peg, assumed the costume of a cavalier and attended a ball given by a lady of my acquaintance which I knew my man was to attend. It was in the Rue des Francs-Bourgeois, quite close to La Force.

"My officer was there as I had expected; I went up to him as he was singing a love song and ogling a lady. I interrupted him in the middle of the second verse.

" 'Monsieur,' I asked, 'do you still object to my returning to a certain house in the Rue Payenne? And do you still intend to cane me if I choose to disobey you?'

"He looked at me with considerable astonishment and said:

" 'Monsieur, what is your business with me? I am sure we have never met.'

" 'I am the little abbé who reads the *Lives of the Saints* and translates Judith into verse,' I informed him.

" 'Ah, yes, yes, yes, I remember now,' the officer replied in a jeering tone, 'well, what do you want of me?'

" 'I would like you to take a little turn with me outside.'

" 'Tomorrow morning, if you wish, and with the greatest pleasure.'

" 'No, not tomorrow morning but immediately, if you please!'

" 'If you absolutely insist—'

" 'I do.' "

" 'Come along then,' the officer said. 'As for you, ladies, pray do not disturb yourselves. Just allow me enough time to kill this gentleman and I will return to finish the last verse of our song.'

"We went out. I took him to the Rue Payenne, to exactly the same spot where a year before, hour for hour, he had paid me the compliment I mentioned. It was a magnificent moonlit night. We drew our swords and at the first pass I killed him outright."

"The devil!" D'Artagnan exclaimed.

"Now as the ladies did not see their singer return," Aramis continued, "and as he was found in the Rue Payenne with a great sword wound through his body, it was supposed that I had done him this favor. The matter obviously created some scandal and I had perforce to renounce the cassock, temporarily at least. Athos, whose acquaintance I made at that period, and Porthos, who had shown me several effective tricks of fencing beyond those my master taught me, both prevailed upon me to solicit the uniform of a musketeer. The King had been very fond of my father who fell at the siege of Arras; my request was granted and here I am now. But you can readily understand how the time has come for me to return to the bosom of the Holy Church."

"But why today rather than yesterday or tomorrow, Aramis? What has happened to you today to give you such sorry ideas?"

"This wound, my dear D'Artagnan, has come to me as a warning from Heaven."

"Your wound! Nonsense! Your wound is just about healed and I swear it is not your wound that gives you the greatest pain at this moment!"

"What should it be then?" asked Aramis, blushing.

"Another wound, Aramis, the wound in your heart, a deeper and bloodier wound inflicted by a woman."

In spite of himself a flame sparkled in the eyes of Aramis.

"Come, do not speak of such things," he declared, masking his emotion under a feigned indifference. "What? I, Aramis, to think of such things and suffer the pangs of love! *Vanitas vanitatum, O Vanity of Vanities!* So you think I have lost my head—let alone my heart—eh? And for whom? For some gay chambermaid or inviting doxy I may have met in a garrison town? Faugh, you disgust me!"

"Forgive me, Aramis, but I thought you aspired to something nobler than chambermaids and doxies?"

"I, aspire to something higher? I, a poor musketeer, a beggar, a mere anonymous cipher who abominates slavery and finds himself very much of a misfit in a sorry makeshift world?"

D'Artagnan wagged his head dubiously.

"Dust am I and to dust I return," Aramis went on with increasing melancholy. "Life is replete with humiliations and sorrows; all the threads that bind it to happiness break one by one in the hollow of a man's hand. And that is truest of the golden threads!" Aramis passed from dejection to a certain bitterness: "My dear D'Artagnan," he begged, "believe me, if you have any wounds, then make sure to conceal them. Silence is the last of the joys vouchsafed the unhappy. Beware of ever giving anyone an inkling of what you suffer, for the curious suck our tears as flies suck the blood of a wounded heart."

It was D'Artagnan's turn to heave a deep sigh.

"Alas, dear Aramis, it is my own story you are relating."

"How do you mean?"

"Well, a woman I loved—a woman I adored—has just been taken away from me by force. I do not know where she is; I cannot guess where her abductors have lodged her. Is she in prison? Is she dead? I know nothing of it."

"At least you have the consolation of knowing that she did not leave you of her own free will," Aramis pointed out. "At least you can be sure that if you have no news of her, it is because she is held incommunicado. While I—"

"While you—? What?"

"Nothing, my friend, nothing!"

"And so you are renouncing the world forever, eh? Your decision is irrevocable and the die is cast."

"Forever and ever. Today you are my friend D'Artagnan; tomorrow you will be no more to me than a shadow, or even less, for you will have ceased to exist for me. As for the world, it is but a sepulchre, no more, no less."

"Damn it, all that you say is really very sad."

"What would you have me say? My vocation commands, I can but obey." D'Artagnan smiled but made no answer. Aramis continued, "Yet, while I still am of this earth, I should wish to speak of you and of our friends."

"I too should wish to speak of *you*, Aramis. Unfortunately you are so utterly detached from everything. Love, you spurn as a snare and a delusion, your friends are shadows, and the world is a sepulchre."

"You will find this out for yourself some day," Aramis sighed.

"Well, then, let us drop the subject," D'Artagnan proposed. "I am perfectly willing to burn this letter I have here."

"A letter?"

"A letter which doubtless reports some new infidelity on the part of your chambermaid or doxy."

"What letter?" Aramis asked eagerly.

"A letter which was delivered at your lodgings in your absence and which I picked up there."

"A letter from whom?"

"Oh, from some heartbroken servant wench or some despondent light-of-love in a garrison town. It might even come from no less a personage than the chambermaid of the Duchesse de Chevreuse. I can easily imagine the soubrette having to return to Tours with the Duchess and, to appear smart, pilfering some of her mistress's scented note paper and sealing her letter with a duchess's coronet."

"What in the world—?"

"Confound it, I think I must have lost that letter," D'Artagnan said maliciously as he pretended to search for it. "But no matter! Happily the world is a sepulchre, men and consequently women are but shadows, and love is a lure which you spurn."

"D'Artagnan, D'Artagnan, please! You are killing me! Put me out of my misery!"

"Well, here is the letter at last!" D'Artagnan said blithely. "I don't know how I could have misplaced it."

Aramis sprang up, seized the letter and proceeded to read or rather to devour it, his face radiant.

"I dare say the gay chambermaid has a cheery style!" D'Artagnan observed nonchalantly.

"Oh, thank you, D'Artagnan, thank you!" Aramis cried in a delirium of joy. "She was forced to return to Tours . . . she is not unfaithful to me . . . she loves me still. . . . Come, my dear friend, let me embrace you. I am overwhelmed with sheer, rapturous happiness."

In their animal exuberance the pair began to dance around the venerable volume of Saint Chrysostom, which presently fell to the floor. The pages of the thesis were close to the toes of the dancers, so what should they do but trample them underfoot or kick them like so many footballs? At that moment Bazin entered with omelette and spinach.

"Away with you, wretch!" Aramis shouted, flinging his theological cap in the lackey's face. "Go back where you came from. And for God's sake, remove those ghastly greens and those putrid eggs instanter! Order a well-larded hare, a fat capon, a leg of mutton rich with garlic and at least four bottles of the best old Burgundy!"

Bazin, completely at a loss to explain his master's sudden change of mood, gaped helplessly at him; in his surprise, he allowed the omelette to slip into the spinach and the spinach to plop on to the floor.

"Now is the moment for you to consecrate your existence to the King of Kings," D'Artagnan exalted. "If you would honor him, I remember a phrase: *Non inutile desiderium oblatione!*"

"To the Devil with you and your Latin! Let us drink, my dear D'Artagnan, let us drink aplenty while the wine is fresh, let us drink mightily and, whilst we do, tell me about what is happening in the civilized world."

XXVII
Of Athos and of His Wife

Having told Aramis everything that had occurred since their departure from the capital, having downed a dinner which dispelled his fatigue, having seen all thought of a thesis vanish from the mind of Aramis, and having delighted in the musketeer's high spirits:

"Now all that remains for us to do is to find out what has happened to Athos," D'Artagnan said with pardonable satisfaction.

"Do you think he has come to grief?" Aramis asked. "Surely not Athos, who is so cool, so brave and such an expert swordsman?"

"True, Aramis, no one values his skill and his courage more than I. But I prefer to think of his blade clanging against the steel of gentlemen than against the staves of varlets. I am afraid he has been struck down by a rabble of churls; those fellows strike hard with their cudgels and they do not stop when they draw blood! That is why I confess I would like to set off as soon as possible."

"I will do my best to accompany you, D'Artagnan. But I must say I scarcely feel up to riding horseback very vigorously. Only yesterday I tried using that scourge you see hanging on the wall and I was in too much pain to continue that pious discipline of flagellation."

"Well, Aramis, who ever heard of anyone trying to cure a gunshot wound by whipping himself with a scourge, however consecrated? But of course you were ill and illness makes a man light-headed indeed, so I forgive you for your excesses."

"When do you mean to set out?"

"Tomorrow at daybreak. Rest as soundly as you can tonight; tomorrow if you are fit, we will ride off together."

"Good night then and until tomorrow!" Aramis said. "Your nerves may be of iron, but you could do with a bit of rest yourself, D'Artagnan."

Next morning when D'Artagnan called on Aramis he found his friend at the window.

"What on earth are you staring at?" he asked.

"Upon my word I was admiring those three magnificent horses which the stable boys are grooming. What a princely joy to ride on such steeds!"

"Well, my dear Aramis, that joy will be yours, for one of them belongs to you."

"Either stop joking this early in the morning, my friend, or tell me which horse is mine?"

"Whichever of the three you choose, Aramis; I myself have no preference."

"What about that sumptuous caparison?" Aramis inquired skeptically. "I suppose it is also mine."

"Of course!"

"Come, D'Artagnan, you are fooling . . ."

"No, I have ceased to fool ever since you decided to give up speaking Latin and reverted to French."

"Do you mean to say that those gilded holsters, that velvet horsecloth and that saddle studded with silver are mine too?"

"They are as much your own as that steed pawing the ground belongs to me and the one prancing belongs to Athos."

"The Devil you say! Magnificent beasts, they are!"

"I am very glad you like them."

"Only the King could have made you such a present."

"It could hardly have been the Cardinal. But never mind where they came from, Aramis; just remember that one of them is yours."

"I choose the one that ginger-headed stable boy over there is pacing."

"It is yours for the asking, Aramis."

"Praise God, this is enough to banish all my pain; I could ride that horse with thirty bullets inside me. Bless my soul, look at those handsome stirrups! Ho, Bazin, come here at once!" A dull and dispirited Bazin shuffled in. "Polish up my sword, prepare my hat, brush my cloak, and load my pistols instantly!"

"Your last order is unnecessary," D'Artagnan broke in. "There are loaded pistols in the holsters." Bazin sighed. "Come, Bazin, do not take things amiss. People may gain the Kingdom of Heaven under all sorts of conditions! Paradise is not reserved exclusively for clerics."

"Alas, Monsieur, my master was already such a skilled theologian," Bazin sighed, tears in his eyes. "He might have become a bishop or even a cardinal."

D'Artagnan suggested that the unhappy Bazin reflect for a moment. What did it profit a man to take up Holy Orders? It did not shelter him from war; His Eminence the Cardinal was himself about to campaign with a helmet on his head and a pike in his fist. There was also Monsieur de Nogaret de La Valette. What of him? He, too, was a cardinal and how often had his lackey had to prepare lint to dress His Eminence's wounds?

"True, all too true," Bazin groaned; "we live in a topsy-turvy world."

As they reached the stables Aramis became more alert. As his horse was led up:

"Hold my stirrups, Bazin," he commanded and sprang into the saddle with his usual agility and grace. But after a series of vaults and curvets, the noble animal had bested his noble master and Aramis, grown very pale, swayed in the saddle. D'Artagnan, foreseeing such a possibility, had kept his eye on him; at just the right moment he caught up with the horse, stood by and received a fainting Aramis in his arms. With Bazin's help he escorted Aramis to his chamber.

"You were too weak and it is better so," he told his friend. "Be sure to take good care of yourself. I will go alone in search of Athos."

"You are a man of iron and brass," Aramis whispered.

"No, I am lucky, that is all. But tell me what you expect to do while I am gone. What about glosses *in re* the fingers, *vide* Benediction? No nonsense, eh?"

Aramis smiled.

"I shall write poetry," he said.

"Good, my friend; verses fragrant with the perfume of the gay chambermaid who attends upon Madame de Chevreuse. Incidentally you might teach Bazin the laws of prosody; he would surely find them consoling. As for the horse, ride him from time to time every day; it will help restore you."

"Never you worry, D'Artagnan, I shall be ready to follow you the moment you return."

Whereupon they parted and D'Artagnan, having charged Bazin and the mistress of the inn to take the best possible care of Aramis, trotted off along the road to Amiens. Several problems assailed him. How was he to find Athos, if find him he could? And in what state? He had left his friend in a very critical condition; Athos might very easily have been killed. Here was a gloomy prospect but one he must face. As he rode on, the silent Planchet by his side, he felt lost in perplexity. Now he frowned angrily, now he sighed in desperation; but he was sure of one thing, he would exert vengeance if vengeance were called for.

Of all D'Artagnan's friends, Athos was the eldest and therefore the most remote from him, apparently, in tastes and interests. Yet of all his friends it was Athos he preferred.

D'Artagnan admired the man's noble bearing, his unmistakable distinction . . . he admired the occasional flashes of grandeur which burst from out the modest shadows in which he usually chose to remain . . . he admired the unfailing serenity and equanimity which made of Athos the best of companions . . . he admired his forced, somewhat mordant gaiety, which was always both gentle and wise . . . he admired his courage, which might have seemed rash, had it not sprung from the rarest self-control . . . and finally, he admired Athos most because he felt drawn toward him more through respect than through friendship. . . .

Monsieur de Tréville, for instance, was a great nobleman, a gallant man and a finished courtier, yet when in the mood for it Athos had nothing to suffer by comparison with the Captain of Musketeers. Pondering over the immense superiority Athos enjoyed, D'Artagnan recalled many facets of his friend's personality: Athos, of medium height but built in such flawless proportions . . . Athos who more than once, when wrestling with Porthos, a giant whose physical strength was proverbial, had felled him . . . Athos, with his finely chiseled features, his proud stance of head, his glittering eyes and his aristocratic nose . . . Athos, with his chin so like that of Brutus . . . Athos, alive with the high indefinable gifts of grandeur and grace . . . Athos, who never looked after his hands yet they were the envy of Aramis who cultivated his with the extensive aid of almond paste and perfumed oils . . . Athos, whose voice was at once incisive and mellow . . . Athos, who inevitably lurked modestly and obscurely in the background, yet who possessed a compendious knowledge of the world, an easy familiarity with the ways of the most brilliant society, and the air of a thoroughbred, did he but lift his little finger. . . .

Was a meal being enjoyed, then Athos presided better than any other, seating his or his host's guests scrupulously according to their rank, whether they were born to it or had achieved it themselves. There was no detail of heraldry or procedure which he did not have at his fingertips: he knew thoroughly all the noble families of the kingdom, their genealogy, their marriages, their arms, their mottoes and the origins of these. Etiquette possessed no smallest detail with which he was not conversant. He was familiar with all the rights the great landowners enjoyed, he was profoundly versed in the arts of venery and falconry and one day, during a discussion of the subject, he had amazed even King Louis XIII, who was a past master in such matters.

Like all the great nobles of that period, he rode, fenced and shot to perfection. What is more, his education had been so little neglected that even with regard to scholastic studies—which were so direly neglected by the gentlemen of his times—he could afford to smile at the scraps of Latin which Aramis served up and which Porthos pretended to understand. Several times indeed, to the vast astonishment of his friends, when Aramis had allowed some error to escape him, it was Athos who replaced a verb in its right tense and a noun in its appropriate case. Best of all in him was his unassailable probity in an age when soldiers compounded so easily with their religion and consciences, lovers with the rigorous delicacy of our own period, and the poor with God's Seventh Commandment. Truly, this Athos was a very extraordinary man.

And yet, despite his rare nature, his noble fibre and his unique essence, Athos could occasionally be seen sinking insensibly into the welter of material life much as old men sink into physical and moral imbecility. Athos in his hours of privation—and they were not infrequent—would lose all trace of his brilliance and it was as though a star had suddenly been snuffed out. On such occasions the demigod having vanished, Athos was scarcely a human being. His head lowered, his eyes glazed, his speech lumbering and thick, he would gaze dully for hours at a time at his bottle or glass, or at Grimaud, who, accustomed to obey him by signs, read his every wish and promptly fulfilled it. If the four friends happened to assemble at such a time, the sole contribution Athos made to the conversation was a laconic, effortful comment. To make up for his obstinate silence, Athos alone drank to the capacity of four heavy drinkers without betraying his bibacity save by a more accentuated frown and a deeper melancholy.

D'Artagnan, ever curious about any problem, had often sought to account for this phenomenon but to no avail; how and why Athos lapsed into such stagnation he had failed to ascertain, shrewdly though he observed his friend. Athos never received any letters nor indulged in any activity of which all his friends were not fully aware. Wine could not be held primarily responsible for his dejection; on the contrary, he drank only in order to combat it—alas! in vain. Gambling was not responsible for his atrabilious state, for, unlike Porthos who commented on the vagaries of Chance with songs or curses, Athos, gambling, remained impassive, winner or loser. One night at the Musketeers' Club he won six thousand pistoles, then promptly lost all his winnings, then mortgaged his gold-embroidered dress belt and then recouped all without turning a hair. Indeed he emerged from the ordeal one hundred louis to the good, without ever having raised or lowered his handsome dark eyebrows one whit, without his hands losing their pearly hue or betraying the slightest tremor, and without his conversation, which had been particularly agreeable that evening, ceasing one moment to be so. Finally his depression did not spring, as so often happens with our English neighbors, from the climate; Athos was gloomier than ever toward the finest season of the year, the months of June and July being particularly difficult for him.

For the present he seemed to have no worries; when anybody spoke of the future, he merely shrugged his shoulders. His secret, then, was concerned with the past, as D'Artagnan had vaguely heard from one musketeer or another.

The mystery which surrounded his entire person served to heighten people's interest in this man whose eyes and whose mouth, even in moments of abject drunkenness, had never revealed anything about himself, however insidiously he had been questioned.

"Alas!" D'Artagnan said. "Poor Athos may well be dead at this moment, and dead by my fault! It was I who dragged him into this business, of which he knew neither the origin nor the outcome, and from which he had nothing to gain."

"There's something else too," Planchet replied. "We must remember that we probably owe our lives to him, Monsieur. It was Monsieur Athos who warned us to get away and after he had emptied his two pistols, what a terrible clatter he made with his sword! You would have thought that twenty men, or rather twenty furious devils, were falling upon him."

The lackey's comment redoubled D'Artagnan's eagerness to ascertain what fate had befallen Athos. Our Gascon spurred on his horse though it needed no goading, for he was already galloping smartly and making excellent time. By about eleven o'clock in the morning, Amiens loomed up before them; a half-hour later they drew up before the accursed inn.

The perfidy of the landlord rankling in D'Artagnan's heart, he had more than once planned a dire vengeance which offered him some consolation in mere anticipation of it. His hat drawn low over his eyes, his left hand on the pommel of his sword, his right hand cracking his whip against his leg, he strode forward resolutely. The host advanced, bowing, to meet him.

"Do you recognize me?" D'Artagnan asked sharply.

"No, Monsieur, I have not that honor," the host replied very humbly, his eyes dazzled by the brilliant style in which D'Artagnan traveled.

"What? You mean to say you don't know me?"

"No, I do not, Monsieur."

"Well, let me refresh your memory. About a fortnight ago, more or less, you had the audacity to accuse a gentleman of passing counterfeit money. What has become of this gentleman?"

The host paled before D'Artagnan's threatening manner and Planchet's immediate adoption of the same.

"Ah, Monsieur, pray don't mention the matter," he cried in the most lachrymose tone, "ah, God! I have paid dearly for that mistake, unhappy wretch that I am!"

"But the gentleman, I say, the gentleman, what has become of him?"

"I implore you to deign to listen to me, Monsieur, and to be merciful. I beg you to do me the favor of being seated."

D'Artagnan, mute with anger and anxiety, took a seat, stern and comminatory as a veteran judge. Planchet stood proudly at attention close to his master's armchair.

"This is what happened, Monsieur," the landlord went on tremulously. "I will tell you all, for now I *do* recognize you. You are the gentleman who left when I had that unfortunate difference with the gentleman you mentioned."

"I am indeed. So you see you have little mercy to expect if you do not tell me the whole truth!"

"Be good enough to hear me, I beg you, and you shall hear it in every tragic detail."

"I am listening."

"I was warned by the authorities that a notorious counterfeiter would arrive at my inn with several companions disguised as guards of musketeers. I was supplied with an accurate description of your physical appearance, my noble gentlemen, of your horses, your lackeys and all the rest."

"Go on, go on!" D'Artagnan urged impatiently, knowing immediately from what source so exact an identification came.

"The authorities sent me a reinforcement of six men and, acting upon their strict orders, I took all measures necessary to secure the persons of the alleged coiners."

"Again!" D'Artagnan exclaimed, his blood boiling at the ugly word.

"Forgive me for mentioning such things, Monsieur, but they form my excuse. The authorities had terrified me and you know that an innkeeper must keep in with the authorities."

"But where is the gentleman? What has happened to him? Is he dead? Is he alive?"

"Patience, Monsieur, I am coming to that. You know what happened and—" here the host paused, adding with an astuteness which was not lost upon D'Artagnan, "and your precipitate departure seemed to authorize what occurred. The gentleman, your friend, defended himself desperately. Unfortunately for him, through some silly misunderstanding, his valet had quarreled with the six officers who were disguised as stable boys—"

"Ah, you scoundrel, all of you were in the plot. I don't know what stops me from exterminating the whole pack of you."

"Oh no, Monsieur, God bless me, there was no plot at all and we were not in agreement, as you shall see! Your friend—pray forgive me for not calling him by the noble name which he doubtless bears but I do not know it—your friend put two officers out of action with his two shots. Then he retreated, covering his retreat with his sword and thus accounted for one of my men and for myself. He did not wound us, he stunned us with a blow of the flat side of the blade."

"For God's sake, will you have done, you villain!" D'Artagnan shouted. "Tell me what happened to Athos?"

"Well, Monsieur, he retreated as I told you, sword in hand, fighting every inch of the way, till he backed up above the stairway leading to the cellar. The door happened to be open, your gentleman appropriated the key, stepped back, slammed the door behind him and by God! he locked himself in. As the authorities knew where to lay hands on him, they left him there, free to do as he willed."

"I see," D'Artagnan said wryly. "As you did not wish to slaughter him, you decided to make him your prisoner instead."

"Our prisoner, Monsieur! God help us, he imprisoned himself, I swear it! And he had done a pretty job of work: one man killed on the spot, two men badly wounded, and plenty of damage to the house. The casualties were carried away by their comrades and to this day I have heard nothing whatever about them. For my part, Monsieur, as soon as I came to my senses, I called upon Monsieur the Governor, told him all that had happened and asked him what to do with the prisoner. But the Governor was flabbergasted; he assured me he had no idea of what I was talking about: the orders I had mentioned did not come from him, he said, and if I had the stupidity or impertinence to mention his name in connection with this brawl, he would have me promptly hanged. It seems I had made a mistake, Monsieur: I had helped arrest an innocent gentleman while the coiners escaped."

"But Athos, you imbecile, what of Athos?" D'Artagnan stormed, his indignation fanned by the cynicism of the authorities. "What happened to *him?*"

"By your leave, as I was anxious to right the wrongs I had done the prisoner, I betook myself straightway to the cellar to set the gentleman free. But Heaven preserve us, Monsieur, that gentleman was no longer a man, he was a forty-power demon! When I suggested he was free, he insisted it was nothing but an ambush; he would leave the cellar, he said, only upon his own conditions. Of course I fully realized what a scrape I was in for having dared to lay hands on one of His Majesty's musketeers; so I told the gentleman very humbly that I would accept anything he proposed."

"Get on, man, get on!"

" 'First,' the gentleman said, 'I want my valet sent down here fully armed.' "

"We hastened to comply with this order, for as Monsieur can well understand we wished to do all your friend desired. Monsieur Grimaud— he told us his name though he is mum as the grave—Monsieur Grimaud was therefore carried down to the cellar, wounded though he was. Then his master, having admitted him, barricaded the door again, and ordered us to stay where we belonged."

"But where is he, where is Athos?"

"In the cellar, Monsieur."

"What, you wretch! You have been keeping him in the cellar all this time?"

"Merciful Heaven, no, Monsieur! *I keep him* in *my* cellar? Oh, you have no idea of what he is up to! If only you could persuade him to leave and come up for air, I would be grateful to you for the rest of my days, I would adore you as I adore my patron saint."

"So he is in your cellar? I shall find him there?"

"No doubt about it, Monsieur; he insisted on staying there. We pass him down some bread at the end of a pitchfork every day through a vent;

but, wellaway! it is not bread and meat that he absorbs most. Once I tried to go down with two of my servants but he flew into a towering rage; I heard the gentleman priming his pistols and the lackey cocking his musketoon. When I asked what they purposed, the gentleman replied that they had forty bullets to fire and would not hesitate to fire them to the last one if we so much as attempted to set foot in the cellar."

D'Artagnan smiled.

"Well, Monsieur, I went to see the Governor. He told me that I had got exactly what I deserved and that it would teach me not to insult noble and honorable gentlemen who sought lodging in my hostelry."

Again D'Artagnan laughed uncontrollably at the landlord's woebegone expression.

"What has happened since?" he asked.

"Since then, begging your pardon, we have been leading the most miserable existence imaginable. All our supplies are in that cellar: our choicest wines in bottles, other wines in casks, our beer, our spices, our bacon, our sausages! As we are not permitted to go down there, we are compelled to refuse food and drink to our clients. Our inn is losing customers and money every day. Another week with your friend in the cellar and I shall be a ruined man."

"Which you richly deserve, you scoundrel. Could you not tell by our looks that we were people of quality and not coiners?"

"Ay, Monsieur, all too true! But hark! there he goes, off into a rage again!"

"Somebody probably disturbed him," D'Artagnan suggested.

"But *I* can't help it, Monsieur. Two English gentlemen have just arrived."

"What of that?"

"Well, the English are fond of good wine, as you well know, and these two gentlemen ordered my best. My wife probably requested permission of your friend to enter the cellar and as usual it was probably refused. Ah, God, listen! What a hullabaloo! Has all Hell broken loose in my respectable inn?"

D'Artagnan heard an uproar rising from the cellar and, preceded by the host who wrung his hands and followed by Planchet who kept his musketoon ready for action, he headed toward the theatre of operations.

The two English gentlemen were exasperated; they had ridden hard and long and were dying of hunger and thirst.

"But this is an outrage!" one of them cried in excellent French, though with a foreign accent.

"How dare this lunatic prevent these good people from getting their own wine out of their own cellar!" the other demanded.

"Let us break in!"

"Yes, and if he gets too wild, we'll kill the fellow!"

"Just one moment, gentlemen," D'Artagnan cautioned, drawing his pistols from his belt. "Nobody is to be killed, if you please!"

"Come on, gentlemen, try to get in!" Athos challenged calmly from the other side of the door. "Let one of these sham ogres put his face in here and we shall see what we shall see!"

Brave as they appeared, the Englishmen looked at each other hesitatingly. It was as though the cellar housed some very real and ravenous ogre, a giant hero of popular legend into whose cavern no man ventured with impunity.

There was a moment of silence, after which the Englishmen determined not to give in. After all, their pride was at stake, and to withdraw would be humiliating. The angrier of the pair went down the six steps leading to the cellar door and kicked it furiously.

"Planchet," D'Artagnan ordered, cocking his pistols, "I will handle the one up here, you answer for the one kicking at the door."

The Englishmen turned. "Gentlemen, you asked for a fight, did you not? Well, I promise you a hot one."

"God in Heaven!" cried Athos cavernously from the lower darkness. "It is D'Artagnan I think. Yes, that voice is unmistakable."

"Right you are, Athos, here I am, friend!" the Gascon shouted.

"Good, D'Artagnan, we will give these trespassers a little exercise, eh?"

The Englishmen had drawn their swords but they found themselves caught between two fires. Again they hesitated. But, as before, their pride prevailed. A further kicking split the door from top to bottom.

"Take cover, D'Artagnan," Athos warned crisply. "I am about to fire!"

But D'Artagnan knew better. Here was a case for common sense and D'Artagnan's common sense never abandoned him.

"Gentlemen," he shouted, "pray think what you are about! As for you, Athos, patience! Gentlemen, you are courting trouble, and if you persist we will riddle you from crown to toe. My lackey and I have three shots apiece for you and the cellar can produce as many. Should you survive, we have our swords and I promise you we know something of swordplay.

Allow me to settle your problem, gentlemen, and my own. Presently you shall have all you want to drink, I assure you."

"If there's any wine left," Athos jeered.

A cold sweat broke over the landlord's face and, judging by his wriggling, doubtless trickled down his spine.

"If there's any wine left," he echoed dully.

"There must be plenty down there," D'Artagnan said. "Never you worry, landlord, two men cannot have drunk your cellar dry. Gentlemen, sheathe your swords if you will."

"Agreed, Monsieur, if you return your pistols to their holsters."

"Certainly, with the greatest of pleasure, gentlemen." Whereupon, setting the example, D'Artagnan obeyed the injunction and, turning to Planchet, motioned to him to uncock his musketoon.

Convinced by this gesture, the Englishmen, grumbling, returned their swords to their scabbards. D'Artagnan then told how Athos had come to be imprisoned in the cellar and the Englishmen, gentlemen both, agreed that the innkeeper was at fault.

"And now, Milords, go back to your apartment; I warrant you that within ten minutes you shall have all the wine you care to order."

The Englishmen bowed in appreciation and withdrew.

"We're alone now," D'Artagnan called. "Do please open the door, Athos."

"Certainly, right away!"

A great sound of shuffling, a creaking of logs and a groaning of beams ensued, as the beleaguered Athos in person dismantled his bastions and counterscarps. A few seconds later the broken door parted and Athos poked his pallid face between the split panels to survey the situation. They embraced heartily. Then as D'Artagnan sought to drag his friend from his damp quarters he realized that Athos was reeling and tottering.

"Were you wounded?" he asked anxiously.

"No, no, no, no, no, my dear fellow, I'm dead drunk, that's all, drunk as David's sow! Never a man made a better job of getting royally and imperially drunk as your friend Athos. Praise God and bless my landlord, I must have personally and individually downed at least one hundred and fifty bottles. I have enjoyed your hospitality, my dear host," he added, bowing to the innkeeper.

"God help us, Monsieur, if your lackey has drunk one half of that, then I am a ruined man and might as well close shop."

"Come, landlord," Athos protested, "Grimaud is a well-bred and seasoned lackey. He would not have taken upon himself to drink of the same vintages as I. No, my friend Grimaud drank only from the cask. Incidentally, I think he neglected to fasten the bung."

D'Artagnan burst into peals of laughter that changed the landlord's chills into a burning fever. Suddenly Grimaud appeared behind his master, his musketoon on his shoulder and his head vacillating like some tipsy satyr portrayed by Rubens. He was soaked front and back in a fatty liquid that the innkeeper recognized as his choicest olive oil.

In single file, Athos, D'Artagnan, Grimaud, the innkeeper and his wife proceeded across the public room and went upstairs to the best apartment in the inn, commandeered by D'Artagnan. Mine host and his wife hurried to the cellar, armed with lamps, to take a rapid inventory of their stock. Finding their own property accessible at long last, they faced a hideous spectacle.

Beyond the barricade which Athos had shattered in order to emerge—fagots, planks, kindling wood, logs, beams and empty barrels massed according to the most elaborate arts of obsidional strategy—there were great puddles of olive oil here and deep pools of wine there, over which swam a flotsam and jetsam which, on closer scrutiny, turned out to be the bones of hams consumed. The entire left corner of the cellar revealed a pyramid of empty bottles. A little further along, a barrel, minus its spigot, was spilling the last drops of its crimson blood. Here, as over a battlefield, to quote the bard of antiquity, were destruction and death. Out of fifty long saveloy sausages which once hung from the rafters, only ten remained.

Mine host groaned, mine hostess gasped, then host and hostess screamed to high heaven. So loud were their plaints that, piercing the cellar vault, they actually reached D'Artagnan's ears. He was much moved but Athos did not even turn his head to listen.

In the cellar a species of fury followed upon amazement and rage. The host, seizing a spit, rushed to the room our friends occupied.

"Wine ho, landlord!" Athos ordered as the innkeeper made his appearance.

"Wine!" the landlord bawled unable to believe his ears. "Why, you have already drunk more than one hundred pistoles' worth of it. God have mercy upon my soul, I am lost, ruined, destroyed, bankrupt and undone."

"What will you, we were thirsty!" said Athos.

"Ah, God, Monsieur, if only you had been content to drink! Why did you have to smash my bottles?"

"You yourself edged me into a heap of bottles which collapsed when I leaned against them. You have only yourself to blame."

"But I have lost all the oil in my cellar."

"Oil is a sovereign balm for wounds, landlord. My poor lackey Grimaud had to treat the wounds you inflicted upon him."

"My sausages are all eaten up."

"I dare say there are plenty of rats in your cellar."

"You shall pay for all this," the innkeeper cried in exasperation.

"Oh, you simple fool, you double ass and you triple knave—" Athos rose to his feet, swayed and then subsided, for he had taxed his strength to the utmost. D'Artagnan, riding crop in hand, came to his friend's rescue.

The host, drawing back, burst into tears.

"Perhaps this will teach you to act more courteously toward the guests God sends your way," D'Artagnan said sternly.

"God?" the innkeeper sighed. "You mean the Devil, Monsieur."

"Look here, landlord, if you persist in annoying us I vow the three of us will barricade ourselves in your cellar merely to see whether the damages are as great as you claim."

"Ay, gentlemen, begging your pardon, I am in the wrong, I admit. But every error finds its forgiveness in the bosom of God! You are noblemen and I but a poor innkeeper. Surely you will have pity on me."

"If you go on in that strain," Athos said, "you will break my heart. Already tears are about to flow from my eyes as the wine flowed from the casks in your cellar. We are not the devils we seem, my good man; come, stand up closer and let us talk all this over quietly."

The landlord approached gingerly.

"Come, my good host, you have nothing to fear."

"Thank you, Monsieur."

"Listen, my good man," Athos continued, "while I recall what happened. As I was about to settle my score, I laid down my purse on the table."

"Ay, Monsieur."

"There were sixty pistoles in that purse."

"Ay, Monsieur."

"Where is the money?"

"I deposited it at the City Registrar's; it was supposedly counterfeit money, was it not?"

"Very well, produce my purse and you can keep the money that was in it."

"Surely Monsieur knows that the authorities never relinquish anything they lay their hands on. Had your money been counterfeit, there might be a chance; but as luck would have it, your coins were sound."

"Well, my good friend, all that is *your* problem! It does not concern me personally, the more so since I have not a sou."

D'Artagnan came to the rescue:

"How much is that horse worth?" D'Artagnan asked.

"Monsieur's horse is in the stable," the landlord put in eagerly.

"How much is that horse worth?" D'Artagnan asked.

"Fifty pistoles at most," the landlord answered shrewdly.

"It is worth eighty," D'Artagnan insisted. "Keep it, host, and let us forget the whole matter."

"What!" Athos objected. "You are selling *my* horse? my trusty Bajazet? And pray how shall I manage in the forthcoming campaign? Do you expect me to ride pickaback on Grimaud?"

"No, Athos, I have brought you another horse to take the place of your Bajazet."

"And a magnificent animal it is, too, Monsieur!" the landlord commented.

"Very good," Athos drawled. "Now that I have a younger and handsomer mount, keep the old one, landlord, and fetch us up some wine."

"What wine do you desire?" the host smirked, his serenity and cheer once again in the ascendant.

"Some of that wine at the very back of your cellar, my good man, just next to the laths. There are twenty-five bottles of it left; all the rest were broken when I fell backwards. Bring up six of them, host."

"The man is a cask, a vat, a tun!" the innkeeper mused. "If he stays here another fortnight and pays for what he drinks, I shall catch up on my losses and even start making a profit again."

"Don't forget to take up four bottles of the same to the two English gentlemen," D'Artagnan ordered, as the host disappeared.

"Now that we are alone, my dear D'Artagnan," Athos said as soon as the door closed, "what about Porthos and Aramis? Tell me what has been going on; I am hungry for news."

274 · Alexandre Dumas

D'Artagnan told his friend how he had found Porthos in bed with a sprained knee and Aramis cheek by jowl over a doctoral table with a brace of theologians. Just as he finished the landlord reappeared with six bottles and a ham which, fortunately for him, had not been stored in the cellar.

"Your news is good," Athos said as he filled his glass and D'Artagnan's. "So much for Porthos and Aramis. But you, my friend, what of you, what happened to you personally? You look anything but happy."

"Ah, my dear Athos, I am the unhappiest of us all!"

"You unhappy, my good D'Artagnan. Come, how are *you* unhappy? Tell me."

"I shall tell you later."

"Later? Why later? Because you think I am drunk, D'Artagnan? Mark my words, D'Artagnan, and remember this: my ideas are never so clear as when I am in wine. Speak up, then, I am hanging on your every word."

D'Artagnan related his adventure with Madame Bonacieux as Athos listened in complete silence; then, when D'Artagnan was done:

"All these things are but trifles," he commented, "mere trifles!"

"I know that is your favorite expression, Athos; you dismiss the most harrowing events as mere trifles. That comes very ill from you who have never been in love."

Athos, who had been staring down at the table, suddenly drew himself up; his dull vacant glaze lighted up for an instant, then turned listless and glassy as before.

"True," he admitted quietly, "true! I have never been in love."

"Therefore my-dear-friend-with-the-heart-of-stone, I beg you to acknowledge that you are wrong to be so hard upon those of us who are tender-hearted."

"A tender heart means a broken heart; tenderness spells despair."

"What do you mean, Athos?"

"I mean that love is a lottery and the winning ticket brings but death. Believe me, you are very fortunate to be on the losing side, my dear D'Artagnan. And if I have any advice to give you it is this: always lose in the lottery of love!"

"She seemed to love me so dearly!"

"She *seemed* to, eh?"

"No, she *did* love me."

"What an infant you are! No man ever lived but believed his mistress loved him desperately and no man but discovered that he had been gulled and duped."

"No man save you, Athos, who never had a mistress."

"True, true!" Athos repeated after a moment's silence. "I never had a mistress." He cleared his throat. "Ah, well, let's drink!"

"Philosopher as you are, remote from our human sentimentalities, pray instruct and sustain me. I want to know why love's course never runs smoothly. And above all, I crave consolation."

"Consolation for what?"

"For my deep misfortune, Athos."

"Your unhappiness is laughable!" Athos shrugged his shoulders.

"Not to me, Athos!"

"I dare say not." Athos looked up at D'Artagnan. "I wonder what you would say if I were to tell you a real love story?"

"One which happened to you?"

"Or to a friend of mine, ay. What matter?"

"Tell me your story, Athos, please."

"Let us drink instead. Drinking is better than story-telling."

"They are not mutually exclusive. Drink up and talk away, Athos!"

"Right! Not a bad idea!" Athos drained his glass then refilled it. "The two pastimes go together very well."

"Fire away then, Athos, I am all attention."

Athos collected himself and as he did so D'Artagnan perceived that he grew pale apace. He was at that stage of intoxication where your vulgar topers fall asleep, but he, of course, remained upright and awake and seemed to be dreaming aloud. There was something frightening in this somnambulism of drunkenness.

"You insist on hearing my story?"

"I do indeed, Athos, pray go ahead!"

"Very well then, you shall have your wish. I shall tell you everything exactly as it happened. Here goes!" Drawing a deep breath, he launched into his narrative:

"One of my friends," he began, then with a melancholy smile he interrupted his story: "Please to observe this happened to one of my friends not to me—" and, resuming: "One of my friends, a count in my native province—Berry, that is—a man as nobly born as a Dandolo or a Montmorency, once fell in love. He was twenty-five, the girl sixteen and beautiful beyond description. There was an ardor and a spirit in her which, piercing through the ingenuousness of her age, stamped her more of a poet than a woman. She was not of the type that pleases and attracts, she intoxicated and enraptured any man who came within a mile of her. She lived in a small straggling township with her brother who was a curé. Nobody knew where they came from but seeing how beautiful she was and how pious her brother, nobody ever inquired. Rumor had it that they were well born. My friend, the hero of this tale, was the seigneur of the country. He might easily have seduced her or if he preferred taken her by force, for his power was unlimited. Who, indeed, would have come to the help of two strangers, two persons utterly unknown, come from God knows where? Unfortunately he was an honorable man; he married her, fool, idiot, imbecile that he was!"

"How so, if he loved her?"

"Patience, D'Artagnan and you shall see!" Athos gulped down the contents of half his glass. "My friend took her to his château and made her the first lady of the province and, to do her justice, she acquitted herself brilliantly of her rank."

"What happened then?" D'Artagnan asked.

"One day my friend was out hunting in the woods with his wife." Athos lowered his voice and spoke very rapidly. "She fell from her horse and fainted. The Count rushed to help her and, as she had difficulty in breathing, he slashed her bodice with his dagger, baring her throat and shoulders." Suddenly Athos burst into shrill, forced peals of laughter. "And guess what he found on her right shoulder?" he concluded.

"How could I know? Tell me, if you will."

"A fleur-de-lis," said Athos, "yes, a fleur-de-lis. She had been branded by the Royal Executioner." And Athos drained his glass at one gulp.

"How horrible!" cried D'Artagnan, "I can't believe it!"

"Gospel truth, I swear it. That angel my friend adored was a fiend; he discovered not only that she was a thief but that she had stolen the sacred vessels from a church."

"And what did your friend do?"

"He was a great nobleman, D'Artagnan; he enjoyed the right of petty and superior justice on his own domain. He tore her clothes to pieces, tied her hands behind her back, and hanged her to a tree."

"Good God, Athos, a murder!"

"Exactly: a murder, no less!" Athos turned pale as a corpse. "But I seem to have no wine," he added hastily, and, seizing the last remaining bottle by the neck, he drained it at a single draught as though it were an ordinary wineglass. Then he buried his head between his hands while D'Artagnan gazed at him, mute and horror-stricken. For a moment neither spoke. Presently Athos rose to his feet and forgetting to keep up the fiction of his friend the nobleman:

"That cured me of beautiful, poetical and loving women!" he wound up. "May God grant you the same enlightenment but less painfully! Come let us drink up."

"So the Comtesse is dead?" D'Artagnan stammered.

"Of course, dead as a doornail. But give me your glass, D'Artagnan. Oh, I see! no more wine! Well, have some ham then, fellow my lad, we really can't drink any more."

"What about her brother?" D'Artagnan asked timidly.

"Her brother?"

"Yes, the priest?"

"Oh, I made inquiries about him in order to have him hanged too. But he stole a march on me. He had left his curacy just the day before."

"Was it ever discovered who the wretch was?"

"Oh, he was probably the first lover and the accomplice of that angel of beauty, a worthy fellow who had pretended to be a priest in order to marry off his mistress and thus provide for her future. I trust he has been hanged, drawn and quartered since."

"My God, what a ghastly tale!" D'Artagnan exclaimed, dazed by the relation of this gruesome adventure.

"Come, try some of this ham, D'Artagnan; it is delicious," Athos said, cutting a slice which he placed on the young man's plate. "What a pity there were not four more such hams in the cellar; then I might have downed fifty bottles more!"

D'Artagnan could endure this conversation no longer; it would have driven him crazy. Allowing his head to sink between his hands and screening his eyes, he pretended to fall asleep.

"These young fellows don't know how to drink nowadays," Athos said, looking at him pityingly, "yet this lad is one of the stoutest and best!"

XXVIII
The Return

D'Artagnan was astounded by the recital of this terrible secret. More than one fact about this partial revelation seemed to him obscure. It had been made by a totally drunken man to one who was only half drunk, yet despite the vagueness which the fumes of two or three bottles of Burgundy impart to the brain, D'Artagnan, awaking the next morning, could recall word for word everything Athos had said. It was as though, while Athos spoke, sentence by sentence had been impressed upon D'Artagnan's memory. The doubts D'Artagnan entertained only increased his eagerness to arrive at a certainty. Accordingly he repaired to his friend's room, firmly resolved to renew the conversation of the evening before. But he found Athos fully himself again, in other words the shrewdest and most impenetrable of men. After they had exchanged a hearty handshake, the musketeer, anticipating D'Artagnan, broached the matter first.

"I was very drunk yesterday, my dear D'Artagnan," he confessed. "I could tell it this morning from the feel of my tongue which was still very thick and from the beat of my pulse which was still very fast. I wager I must have talked an awful lot of nonsense."

And he gazed at D'Artagnan with an earnestness that embarrassed our Gascon.

"No, Athos, I don't think so. As I remember you said nothing out of the ordinary."

"Well, you surprise me very much. I thought I had told you a most harrowing tale!"

And again Athos looked at the other as though to read his innermost thoughts.

"Upon my word, I must have been even drunker than you, Athos, for I remember nothing."

Athos was not taken in.

"You cannot have failed to notice how every man has his particular kind of drunkenness, sad or gay. In my own case, wine engenders melancholy and when I am in my cups I am possessed by a mania to tell all the lugubrious tales my foolish nurse ever crammed into my brain. That is a failing of mine, a serious one I admit; but apart from that, I drink pretty well."

Athos spoke so very naturally that D'Artagnan's conviction was shaken. Anxious to ascertain the truth D'Artagnan ventured:

"Oh, so that's it! Now I remember dimly as though it was a dream; we spoke of people being hanged, didn't we?"

"There, you see how it is!" Athos replied, growing still paler and forcing a laugh. "I was sure of it: the hanging of people is my particular nightmare, the obsession of Athos drunk."

"I think you told me something about—wait, my memory seems to be returning—yes, you told me about a woman—"

"Ay, that is it!" Athos answered, turning almost livid. "I must have spun my favorite yarn about the blonde woman. When I tell that one, I am indeed dead drunk."

"You told me the story of a tall blonde woman who was very beautiful, who had extraordinary blue eyes, and . . ."

"And who was hanged!"

"Precisely! She was hanged by her husband who was a nobleman of your acquaintance," D'Artagnan supplied, looking intently at Athos.

"Bah, now you see how a drunken man can compromise a friend when he does not know what he is saying," Athos remarked, shrugging his shoulders as though he considered himself an object of pity. "I certainly will never get drunk again, D'Artagnan; it is really a ghastly habit."

D'Artagnan made no comment. Then changing the subject suddenly Athos said: "By the way, I must thank you for the horse you brought me."

"You like it, eh?"

"Yes, but it is no horse for hard work."

"You're mistaken there, Athos, I rode him almost ten leagues in less than an hour and a half and he looked as though he had merely walked once around the Place Saint-Sulpice."

"Heavens, you begin to awaken my regrets."

"Regrets?"

"Yes, D'Artagnan. You see, I got rid of that horse."

"How?"

"Let me explain, my friend. Here are the simple facts. I got up this morning at six o'clock. You were sleeping like a log and I did not know what to do with myself. I was still stupefied by last night's debauch. As I went into the common room I heard a guest, an Englishman, haggling with a horse-dealer over a mount. (His own died yesterday from a stroke.)

I drew near and, finding that he was offering a hundred pistoles for a fine burned-chestnut nag:

" 'Look you, Monsieur,' I said, 'I too have a horse for sale.'

" 'And a very handsome horse at that, Monsieur,' he replied. 'I saw him yesterday; your friend's lackey was walking him.'

" 'Do you consider him worth a hundred pistoles?' I asked.

" 'Certainly. Will you sell him to me at that price?'

" 'Certainly not! But I will play with you for him.'

" 'Play at what?'

" 'At dice.' "

No sooner said than done, Athos told an increasingly apprehensive D'Artagnan. The Englishman, it seemed, had agreed at once.

"I lost the horse," Athos confessed, "but I did win back the saddle." And as D'Artagnan looked somewhat put out: "Are you annoyed?" he asked candidly.

"Yes, I admit I am, Athos. That horse was to have made us conspicuous on the battlefield; it was an identification, a pledge and a remembrance. Honestly, Athos, you were wrong to gamble it away."

"Well, my friend, put yourself in my place. I was bored to death, and anyhow, I swear I do not like English horses. Besides, if it is merely a question of being recognized by someone, the saddle will surely suffice; it is certainly conspicuous enough! As for the horse, we can find some excuse for explaining away its disappearance. What the devil, a horse is mortal; suppose mine had glanders or the farcy."

D'Artagnan looked as glum as ever.

"I am much vexed that you should set such store by horseflesh, my friend, because I am not yet at the end of my story."

"What else have you done, Athos?"

"After losing my horse with a throw of nine against a ten—rotten luck, eh?—I was inspired to stake yours. A capital idea, don't you think?"

"An idea perhaps, but surely you did not put it into execution?"

"Of course I did!"

"Confound it!" D'Artagnan said, greatly disturbed.

"What then?"

"I threw the dice and I lost."

"You lost my horse?"

"I lost your horse with a throw of seven against the Englishman's eight. Short of one point! You know the saying."

"Athos, I vow you have taken leave of your senses."

"That is what you should have told me yesterday, my dear fellow, when I was spinning all those foolish yarns. This morning it is too late for such strictures. So to be frank, D'Artagnan, I lost your horse with all his harness, accoutrement and equipment."

"But this is ghastly!"

"Wait, lad, you have not heard all. You know I would make a very competent gambler if I was not so stubborn; but I get stubborn, just as when I drink. So I got stubborn again . . ."

"But what could you wager? You had nothing left?"

"On the contrary, my friend, we still had that diamond sparkling on your finger. I noticed it yesterday and thought: what a valuable piece!"

Panic-stricken, D'Artagnan fumbled for his ring.

"My diamond!" he gasped.

"Precisely," Athos went on suavely. "And since I am a connoisseur, having owned quite a few myself, I estimated it at one thousand pistoles."

D'Artagnan, overcome with fright, said:

"Merciful Heavens! I *do* hope you did not mention my diamond!"

"On the contrary, my friend. You must understand that your diamond was now our only resource. With it I might win back our horses and our harnesses and even enough cash to get us home."

"Athos, I am appalled; I shudder!"

"Well, I mentioned your diamond to the English gentleman who, it appears, had noticed it too. What the devil, my lad, you simply cannot walk around with a star from Heaven on your finger and expect no one to notice it. That would be ludicrous."

"Get on, Athos, get on, my friend, I implore you. I swear your sangfroid and phlegm are driving me mad."

"This is what happened: we divided the diamond into ten parts, each worth one hundred pistoles."

"Bah!" D'Artagnan said, anger seizing him as violently as ever Minerva seized Achilles by the hair in the *Iliad,* "You are badgering me in jest. You want to make me lose my Gascon temper."

"*Mordieu,* I have never been less in a mood for jesting. I should have liked to see you in my place. What in God's name would *you* have done? Here I had been out of circulation for a whole fortnight; I had not seen a human face except Grimaud's which I know by heart; my sole consolation was our host's wine—excellent wine, I admit—for it provided me with the handsomest possible means of stultification and stupefaction."

"That was no reason for staking my diamond," D'Artagnan protested, clenching his fists in a nervous spasm.

"Do hear me out," Athos replied. "Remember: we had ten parts of the diamond to gamble for, each worth one hundred pistoles. We agreed that we would play these ten points and then there was to be an end to it. At the thirteenth throw, I had lost everything! Number thirteen has always been fatal; it was on July thirteenth that I—"

"God's body!" cried D'Artagnan, rising angrily from the table. Today's story erased from his memory all trace of the tragic story he had heard the night before. "I—"

"Patience, my friend," Athos counseled. "Mine was a sound plan. That Englishman was a crackpot or at least an eccentric like many of his race. I saw him conversing with Grimaud two mornings ago; and Grimaud immediately reported back to me that the Milord wished to attach him to his household. What could *I* do, knowing all this, but set up Grimaud, my silent Grimaud, as a stake divided into ten parts, each worth one hundred pistoles."

Vexed though he was, D'Artagnan could not help laughing at the comicality of the situation:

"You used Grimaud as a stake?" he asked incredulously, roaring with laughter.

"Yes," Athos pursued nonchalantly, "and with the ten parts of Grimaud, who is not worth a decatoon *in toto,* I won back your diamond. Now, tell me if persistence is not a lofty virtue?"

Somewhat relieved, D'Artagnan gave free run to his mirth:

"Very funny!" he said. "I haven't heard as amusing a story in years!"

"You may well imagine that finding my luck turning, I immediately staked the diamond again."

"The devil you did!" said D'Artagnan glowering once more.

"I won back your harness, I won back my own harness, I won back my horse, then I lost my horse again. To cut a long story short, I emerged with your harness and mine and that's where we stand now. I must say I had made a superb throw, so I let it go at that and left off."

D'Artagnan breathed as though the weight of the entire hostelry had been lifted off his chest.

"My diamond is still safe then?" he asked timidly.

"Safe as houses, my dear fellow. And we still have the harnesses of your Bucephalus and mine."

"But of what use can our harnesses be without horses?"

"D'Artagnan, I have an idea about that problem."

"Athos, you make me shudder."

"Look here, you haven't gambled for a long time, have you?"

"No, I have not, and I swear I have no desire to do so."

"Ah, D'Artagnan, no man must ever swear to anything lest he prove forsworn."

"What do you propose, Athos?"

"Luckily my Englishman and his companion are still here. I noticed that he seemed very regretful about the harnesses; you seem to set great store by your horse. If I were you, I would stake the harness you possess against the horse I lost for you."

"But surely your Englishman will not be interested in just one harness?"

"Well, then, lad, stake the pair of them! I am not as selfish as you!"

Despite his prudence, D'Artagnan felt the subtle influence of Athos prevailing insidiously upon him.

"Would you really do that, Athos?" he asked, in great perplexity.

"As I am an honest man, ay; I vow I would risk both harnesses at one throw."

"But having lost both horses, I am particularly anxious to save the equipment."

"Stake your diamond, then!"

"No, Athos, never; that is quite another thing. I could never do that!"

"Devil take it, I would propose staking Planchet," Athos said, "but that has been done already and probably the Englishman would object."

"Truth to tell, my dear Athos, I would prefer to stake nothing."

"What a pity!" Athos said coldly. "That Englishman's pockets are bulging with pistoles. Come along, lad, try one throw; one throw is soon cast."

"What if I lose?"

"You will win."

"But if I *lose?*"

"Then you will forfeit the harnesses."

"Done!" said D'Artagnan recklessly. "Here goes for one throw."

Athos went off in search of the Englishman whom he found in the stables, viewing the harnesses with a covetous eye. The moment was auspicious. Athos was able to impose his own conditions: both harnesses against either one horse or one hundred pistoles at the winner's choice. The Englishman, calculating rapidly, realized that the harnesses were worth a hundred and fifty pistoles apiece. He and Athos shook hands to seal the bargain.

After the usual courtesies had been exchanged, D'Artagnan took up the dice and, with trembling hand, rolled a trey! Athos, shocked as he noted how pale his friend turned, merely remarked:

"Ha, partner, that was a sorry throw!" and, nodding toward the Englishman: "Our adversary will have his horses fully equipped."

Triumphant, the Englishman did not even bother to shake the dice but threw them on the table without looking down, so certain was he of victory. D'Artagnan meanwhile turned aside to conceal his disappointment and vexation.

"Look at *that*!" Athos remarked in his usual calm tones. "There's an extraordinary throw for you. Upon my word, I've only seen it happen four times in my life. A pair of aces losing to a trey!"

The Englishman looked down at the table, incredulous, then surprise loomed large over his features; D'Artagnan, following his glance, was overcome with pleasure.

"Ay," Athos continued, "only four times in my life. Once when we were playing with Monsieur de Créquy; another time at my own place in the country when I had a château; a third at Monsieur de Tréville's, to our general amazement; and a fourth at an inn where I threw two aces, losing a hundred louis and a supper into the bargain."

"So, Monsieur, you have won back your horse!" the Englishman said ruefully.

"I have indeed!"

"And there is to be no revenge?"

"You recollect, Monsieur, that our conditions stipulated no chance for retrieval," Athos pointed out.

"True, Monsieur, that was agreed upon. Your horse will be restored to your valet."

"One moment, Milord," Athos broke in. "With your permission, I should very much like to have a word with my friend, here."

"Pray do, Monsieur."

Athos drew D'Artagnan aside.

"Well, tempter, what more do you want of me? To have me throw again, I suppose."

"No, D'Artagnan, I just want you to think things over carefully."

"Think what things over?"

"You want to take your horse back, don't you?"

"Of course I do."

"Well, you are wrong. Were I you, I would take the hundred pistoles. As you know you staked the harnesses against the horse or one hundred pistoles in cash, at your choice."

"I know that."

"Well, I would take the money."

"And I intend to take the horse."

"I repeat, you are wrong, D'Artagnan. What on earth can two of us do with but one horse? I cannot ride behind you; we would look like the two sons of Aymon in search of their brother. And surely you would not dream of humiliating me by prancing along beside me on that magnificent steed. For my part, D'Artagnan, I would not hesitate a moment; I would take the hundred pistoles. Remember we need money to get back to Paris."

"That horse means a great deal to me, Athos."

"There again you are wrong, my friend. A horse shies or slips and he suffers an injury; a horse bucks and he breaks a leg; a horse eats out of a manger in which an infected horse has eaten and he comes down with glanders. There is a horse—or rather one hundred pistoles—irremediably lost. Again, a master must feed his horse, whereas on the contrary one hundred pistoles feed their master!"

"But how shall we get back to Paris?"

"Quite easy! We will ride our lackeys' horses. People can always tell by our looks that we are persons of quality."

"So we are to cut a shabby figure on the wretched ponies of our lackeys while Aramis and Porthos caracole on their chargers beside us?"

"Aramis!" Athos laughed. "Porthos!" His laughter gained momentum.

"What is so hilarious about that?" D'Artagnan inquired, completely at a loss.

"Nothing, nothing, let us continue our argument."

"So your advice is—?"

"—to take the hundred pistoles, D'Artagnan! With such a sum we can live like kings till the end of the month. We have undergone a great deal of grueling fatigue, my friend; it will do us a lot of good to relax a little."

"To relax! I, relax? No, no, Athos! As soon as I reach Paris, I shall go search for the beautiful and unhappy woman I love."

"All right, which do you think will help you most in your quest; one hundred jingling golden coins or a horse? Take the money, my friend, I repeat; take the hundred pistoles."

D'Artagnan needed but one reason in order to surrender and this last reason seemed convincing. Besides, by refusing to do as Athos suggested, he feared lest he appear selfish and niggardly in the eyes of his friend. He therefore acquiesced and chose the hundred pistoles which the Englishman paid out on the spot.

Then they prepared eagerly to depart. To make their peace with the landlord, over and above the old horse Athos had given him, cost them six pistoles. D'Artagnan and his friend bestrode the nags of Planchet and Grimaud respectively, the lackeys following afoot in their wake, carrying the saddles on their heads. Ill-mounted though our friends were, they soon outpaced their lackeys, reaching Crèvecoeur long before them. From afar they sighted Aramis, seated at the window, leaning over the sill in deep melancholy and, like Sister Ann in Bluebeard, scanning the horizon.

"Ho, Aramis!" D'Artagnan shouted. "What the devil are you doing there?"

"So it's you, my friends! Greetings, D'Artagnan! Good day to you Athos!" Then when they had shaken hands: "I was meditating upon the celerity with which the goods of this world leave us," Aramis confessed. "My handsome English horse has just vanished amid a cloud of dust; he is a living image of the fragility of earthly things. All life may be summed up in three words: *erat, est, fuit;* ay, friends, it was, it is, and it has been!"

"Which means—?" D'Artagnan asked, vaguely suspecting what was to come.

"Which means that I have just made a fool's bargain. I was swindled. I got only sixty louis for a horse that, judging by his gait, can cover five leagues an hour at an easy trot."

D'Artagnan and Athos burst out laughing.

"My dear D'Artagnan," Aramis apologized, "pray do not be too angry with me, necessity knows no law. Besides, I am the person most severely punished because that rascally horsedealer has cheated me out of at least fifty louis. Ah, you two fellows are good managers; you ride your lackeys' horses and have your own magnificent mounts led by hand gently and by easy stages."

Just then a market-cart, which had turned into the Amiens road, drew up before the inn. Grimaud and Planchet emerged, the saddles on their heads. The cart was returning empty to Paris and the two lackeys, in return for their transportation, had agreed to slake the driver's thirst along the road.

"What's this? Aramis cried as he saw them arrive. "Saddles? Nothing but saddles?"

"Don't you understand?" Athos asked.

"Bless me, I did just the same, my friends. Some obscure instinct made me keep my harness too! Ho, Bazin, bring my new saddle and carry it along with those Planchet and Grimaud are wearing!"

"What about your clerics?" D'Artagnan asked. "What have you done with them?"

"I invited them to dinner the next day," Aramis replied, "and incidentally they have some capital wine in this inn, my friends. I did my very best to make my clerics tipsy to such effect that the Curé forbade me to doff my uniform and the Jesuit implored me to help him enlist in the musketeers."

"Without a thesis, eh Aramis!" D'Artagnan laughed. "I demand he be admitted without a thesis."

"Since then," Aramis continued, "I have been living most agreeably. I have begun a poem in lines of one syllable, a fairly difficult task but all merit consists in overcoming difficulties. The theme is worldly, gallant and erotic. I will read you the first canto; it consists of four hundred lines and can be read in just one minute."

"In other words, my dear Aramis—" D'Artagnan hated poetry almost as heartily as he did Latin, "add the merit of brevity to the merit of difficulty and your work will triumph on two counts."

"What is more," Aramis enthused, "my poem breathes the noblest and most irreproachable of passions. You shall hear for yourselves, my friends."

They chatted a few minutes about their plans.

"So we return to Paris, eh?" Aramis exclaimed joyfully. "Bravo! I am ready at a moment's notice. We shall join good old Porthos; that will be great fun. You can have no idea how much I have missed that great simpleton. You cannot imagine him selling his horse, no, not for a kingdom! I long to see him astride his magnificent beast, his buttocks firmly ensconced in his sumptuous saddle. I am certain he will look like the Great Mogul."

D'Artagnan and Athos stayed an hour to rest their horses; Aramis settled his bill and put Bazin in the cart with his colleagues. And so they set forth to join Porthos.

They found him up and about, much less pale than he had been on D'Artagnan's first visit. Porthos was seated at a table which, though he was alone, was set for four. The dinner consisted of meats succulently dressed, of choice wines and of superb fruits.

"Ha, by God!" he exclaimed, rising to greet them. "Your arrival is wonderfully timed, gentlemen. I was just beginning with soup; you must dine with me."

"Well, Porthos, Mousqueton certainly did not lasso such bottles as these!" D'Artagnan said admiringly. "And unless my eyes mistake me, I see a crisply larded fricandeau and a filet of beef—"

"I am recuperating, I have to build myself up," Porthos explained. "Nothing can weaken a man more than these damned sprains. Have you ever sprained your knee, Athos?"

"No, I have not. But I remember a sword-thrust I received in our skirmish in the Rue Férou. For a fortnight it had exactly the same effect on me as your sprain has on you."

"Surely this dinner was not intended for you alone, Porthos, was it?" Aramis inquired.

"No, Aramis, I was expecting several gentlemen of the neighborhood who have just sent word to me that they cannot come. You two shall take their places and I shall lose nothing by the exchange. Ho, Mousqueton, bring up some chairs and double the number of bottles."

After ten minutes of hearty eating, suddenly Athos asked: "Do you know what we are eating here?"

"I," said D'Artagnan, "am eating *veau piqué aux cardons et à la moelle* and I must confess I have always enjoyed veal stuffed with prawns and marrow."

"I," said Porthos, "am enjoying some *filets d'agneau*, the best lamb I have tasted in many moons."

"I," said Aramis, "am savoring *blanc de volaille;* a more succulent breast of chicken I never tasted."

"You're all mistaken, gentlemen," Athos announced gravely, "you are eating horseflesh."

"What?—We are eating what?" D'Artagnan asked in bewilderment.

"Horseflesh!" Aramis repeated in disgust.

Porthos alone made no reply.

"Ay, Porthos, horseflesh, that's what we're eating, isn't it?" Athos went on. "And the saddle as well, probably."

"No, gentlemen, I kept the harness," Porthos confessed.

"Upon my word," Aramis declared, "we are all alike. Any one might think we had tipped each other the wink to dispose of our horses!"

"Ah well!" Porthos sighed. "That horse made my visitors ashamed of theirs and I could not bear to humiliate them."

"And I suppose your duchess is still taking the waters, too, eh, Porthos?" D'Artagnan asked.

"Yes, unfortunately she is." Porthos looked around the table. "I had to get rid of the horse you gave me, D'Artagnan. As a matter of fact the Governor of the province—one of the guests I expected to dinner this evening—took a fancy to my horse so I gave it away."

"You gave it away?"

"God help us, yes, *gave* is the word. That animal was worth at least one hundred and fifty louis but the niggardly fellow would only pay me eighty."

"Without the saddle?" Aramis asked.

"Yes, without the saddle."

"You will observe, gentlemen," Athos declared, "that our friend Porthos still made the best bargain of any of us."

A roar of laughter rose vociferously to the rafters, leaving poor Porthos utterly at a loss; but when the reason for the general hilarity was made clear to him, he joined in noisily as usual.

"Well, thank Heaven we are all in funds!" D'Artagnan said.

"Not I," Athos replied. "I found the Spanish wine at the inn where Aramis was staying so excellent that I forwarded six hampers of it—sixty bottles in all—in the cart with our lackeys. This has considerably depleted my resources."

"Don't count on me!" Aramis warned. "You must realize that I have given practically my last sou to the church of Montdidier and to the Jesuits of Amiens. Remember too that I have assumed obligations which I must keep, namely, Masses to be said for myself and for you, too, gentlemen. I am confident these will prove to be of the greatest benefit to us."

"As for me," said Porthos, "don't you suppose my sprain cost me a considerable sum? Don't forget either that Mousqueton was wounded. I had to call in the surgeon twice a day and he charged me double because that idiot of a Mousqueton had managed to get himself shot in that portion of his anatomy which is usually shown only to apothecaries. I warned the lad roundly never to get himself wounded there again."

"Indeed, indeed!" said Athos, exchanging a smile with D'Artagnan and Aramis, "I see you behaved most generously toward the poor fellow. You are a good master, Porthos."

"In brief," Porthos replied, "after paying my bill, I shall have only thirty crowns left at most."

"I, roughly a dozen pistoles," Aramis volunteered.

"In other words we are as rich as Croesus!" said Athos. "By the way, D'Artagnan, how much have you still left of your hundred pistoles?"

"My hundred pistoles! Good Lord, I gave you fifty of them."

"You did?"

"Of course I did, on my word as a—"

"Oh, yes, now I remember."

"And I paid the innkeeper six pistoles."

"The scoundrel! Why on earth pay him six pistoles?"

"You told me to."

"True, true. I am really much too kind-hearted. Well, in brief, how much have you got?"

"Twenty-five pistoles."

"Making, all told?"

"Four hundred and seventy-five livres," D'Artagnan replied for, like Archimedes, he was a lightning calculator.

"When we get to Paris," Porthos said cheerfully, "we shall still have four hundred, plus our saddles."

"But what about our troop horses?" Aramis asked.

"Well, out of the four horses our lackeys own we can make two horses for the masters to ride and we can draw lots for who does so," Athos suggested. "With the four hundred livres we now have, we can conjure up a half a horse for one of the two dismountees. Then by scraping the linings of our pockets we can hand D'Artagnan a tidy sum. He has a steady hand; we can go stake the money in the first gaming-house we find. And that is that!"

"Let us get on with our dinner," Porthos urged. "The food is getting cold."

Relieved of anxiety as to the future, the quartet fell to, doing ample justice to the repast; the remains were consigned to Messrs. Mousqueton, Bazin, Planchet and Grimaud.

In Paris D'Artagnan found a letter from Monsieur de Tréville advising him that upon his request the King had just granted him the high favor of transfer from the guards to the Royal Musketeers in the not too distant future. As this transfer fulfilled D'Artagnan's most ambitious dream in life—except of course his desire to find Constance Bonacieux—he ran, filled with joy, to tell his friends the good news. He had left them but a half-hour before, cheerful as could be; he now found them dejected and apprehensive. They had repaired to the house of Athos, a fact which betrayed circumstances of considerable import.

Monsieur de Tréville had just notified them that His Majesty was definitely resolved to open the campaign on May the first and that they must immediately look to their equipment. The four philosophers gazed blankly at one another, stunned. Monsieur de Tréville never jested in matters of discipline.

"How much do you think your equipment will cost you?" D'Artagnan queried.

"There's no telling," Aramis answered ruefully. "We have just finished estimating the cost with the most strictly Spartan economy. So far each of us needs fifteen hundred livres."

"Four times fifteen equals sixty," said Athos. "Total: six thousand!"

"For my part," said D'Artagnan, "it seems to me that with a thousand livres apiece . . . to be sure I am not speaking as a Spartan but as a procurer. . . ."

The word *procurer* roused Porthos from his trance. A procurer was not only a man who furnished things required, he was also a *procureur,* a procurator, a lawyer!

"Ha!" he cried. "That gives me an idea!"

"Congratulations," Athos said breezily. "I confess I myself have not the shadow of the wraith of one." He sighed. "As for D'Artagnan, gentlemen, his delight at becoming a musketeer has driven him quite insane. A thousand livres, forsooth! I warn you I need two thousand just for myself."

"Four times two make eight," said Aramis. "We need eight thousand livres for our horses. Of course we have our saddles."

Athos waited until D'Artagnan, leaving to pay his visit of thanks to Monsieur de Tréville, had closed the door behind him.

Then confidentially:

"There is one thing you have forgotten, gentlemen," he said.

"What?"

"What's that, Athos?"

"Neither of you has mentioned the priceless diamond that sparkles whenever D'Artagnan raises his hand. Devil take it, D'Artagnan is too good a comrade to leave his brothers in want when he wears a king's ransom on his ring-finger."

XXIX

OF THE HUNT FOR CAMPAIGN OUTFITS

The most preoccupied of the four friends was certainly D'Artagnan, though as a guardsman he could be much more easily equipped than the musketeers who were all of high rank. But our Gascon cadet, as we have seen, was of a provident, almost avaricious nature and withal—who shall explain the paradox?—almost as vain as Porthos. For the moment beyond his vanity D'Artagnan was bestirred by a far more unselfish anxiety. Despite all his careful inquiries he had not obtained the slightest clue of Madame Bonacieux's fate. Monsieur de Tréville had broached the subject to the Queen who had no notion of the young woman's whereabouts but who promised to instigate a search for her. But Her Majesty's promise was all too vague and D'Artagnan continued to worry.

Athos steadfastly refused to leave his room; he was determined not to lift a finger to secure his campaign outfit.

"We have a whole fortnight before us," he told his friends, "and if I have found nothing—or rather if nothing has come to find me in the meantime—God will provide. I am too good a Catholic to blow my brains out. Instead I shall pick a juicy quarrel with four of His Eminence's Guards or with eight Englishmen, fighting until one of them kills me, which, given the odds, cannot fail to happen. It will thus be reported that I died for the King: and I shall have done my duty without the expense of an outfit."

Porthos continued to stroll and saunter about, here and there, his hands behind his back, tossing his head and proclaiming:

"I shall follow up an idea of mine!"

Aramis, apprehensive and for once neglectful of his personal appearance, maintained an obdurate silence.

From these disastrous details it may readily be seen what desolation reigned in the community.

Like the horses of Hippolytus who shared their master's fate when Neptune destroyed him, each lackey was as tragically situated as his master. Mousqueton collected a store of breadcrusts for future fare at the table of Porthos . . . Bazin, inveterately religious, forsook his master Aramis and haunted the churches of the city . . . Planchet, of no use to D'Artagnan, spent his time contemplating the flight of flies across the room . . . and Grimaud, whom even the general disaster could not move to break the silence Athos imposed upon him, heaved sigh upon sigh, deep and baleful enough to move stones. . . .

Athos never stirred from his apartment. The three others would venture forth early in the morning and return late at night. They spent the livelong hours in wandering through the streets, their eyes glued to the pavement in hopes of finding some purse a passer-by might carelessly have dropped. Indeed they looked like so many bloodhounds following up a trail. When they met they all wore the same desolate look which, being interpreted, meant:

"Haven't you found anything?"

At length Porthos, who had been the first to hit upon an idea, pursued it earnestly and was the first to act. One day D'Artagnan saw him strolling toward the Church of Saint Leu and followed him instinctively. Porthos stopped on the threshold of the holy place to twirl his mustache carefully and to smooth out his goatee, a gesture which invariably prefaced the most triumphant intentions. As D'Artagnan was careful to keep hidden, Porthos believed himself unobserved. Porthos went into the church and took his stand against a pillar; D'Artagnan, following him closely, leaned against the other side of it.

The church happened to be very crowded because a popular preacher was delivering a sermon. Porthos took advantage of this to ogle the ladies;

thanks to Mousqueton's kind offices, his outward and visible form gave no hint of his inward and stomachic distress. True his hat looked somewhat worn, his plume was somewhat faded, his galloons were somewhat tarnished and his laces somewhat frayed. But in the dim light of the church such trifles were not noticeable: Porthos was still the same handsome Porthos.

On the bench nearest the pillar Porthos adorned and D'Artagnan used for cover sat a lady, graced with a sort of ripe beauty; she was a whit yellowish, to be sure, and a jot dry, but erect and haughty withal under her black hood. Porthos kept casting furtive glances upon her, then his eyes roved, taking wing like butterflies at large over the nave.

For her part the lady, blushing from time to time, kept darting mercurial glances toward the inconstant Porthos, whereupon Porthos immediately looked everywhere save in her direction. Obviously his attitude piqued the hooded lady; D'Artagnan noted that she bit her lips fiercely, scratched the tip of her nose, and fidgeted nervously in her seat.

Porthos, aware of the lady's every move, answered each sigh of her vexation by twirling his mustache, stroking his goatee and making signs at a lady seated close to the choir—a pulchritudinous lady and doubtless of high station, for she was attended by a young Negro who bore the cushion upon which she knelt, and by a maidservant who held the emblazoned bag which contained her prayer book.

The lady in the black hood, who followed the glances of Porthos through all their meanderings, realized that they often rested quite fondly on the lady with the velvet cushion, the Negro and the maidservant. Porthos meanwhile was playing a shrewd game. It was with a slight almost imperceptible narrowing of his eyelids, with a finger placed upon his lips, and with trenchant little smiles that he was torturing the disdained beauty. Whereupon, while reciting her *mea culpa,* she beat her breast and cleared her throat so vigorously that everyone, including the lady with the red cushion, turned to stare at her. Porthos stood his ground, paying no need whatever; he understood well enough, but he turned a deaf ear to this desperate appeal.

The lady with the red cushion—she was indeed very beautiful—made a deep impression on the lady with the black hood, who saw in her a rival very much to be feared; she made a deep impression on Porthos who found her much prettier than the lady in the black hood; and she made a deep impression on D'Artagnan as he recognized in her the lady of Meung, of Calais and of Dover, whom his persecutor, the man with the scar, had addressed as Milady.

Without losing sight of the lady with the red cushion, D'Artagnan kept his eye on Porthos, deriving much amusement from the musketeer's manoeuvres. Obviously he thought the lady in the black hood must be the attorney's wife from the Rue aux Ours; the proximity of the Church of Saint-Leu to her residence corroborated D'Artagnan's conjecture. Further he deduced that Porthos was attempting to take his revenge for his defeat at Chantilly when Madame Attorney had shown herself so recalcitrant with her cash.

But amid all this D'Artagnan noticed that no lady responded to the gallantries Porthos was lavishing. These were but chimeras and delusions. And yet in true love and authentic jealousy, are not chimeras and delusions the great realities?

The sermon over, Madame Attorney advanced toward the holy font; Porthos, preceding her, dipped not one finger in the holy water but his entire hand. The lady in the black hood smiled, believing that Porthos was making this gesture for her sake. But she was speedily and cruelly disillusioned. When she stood just three paces behind him he turned his head and stared earnestly at the lady with the red cushion who, having risen from her knees, was now drawing near, followed by her little Negro and her maidservant. Just as the beauty came up to Porthos, he withdrew his dripping hand from the basin, the fair worshipper laid her delicate hand lightly upon his great paw, smiled, made the sign of the cross, and left the church.

This was all too much for the attorney's wife; she was now convinced that there must be some intrigue between this lady and Porthos. Had Madame Attorney been a great lady she would have fainted, but being only a lawyer's wife she was content to address the musketeer with a concentrated fury:

"So, Monsieur Porthos," she raged. "You offer no holy water to *me*!"

At the sound of her voice, Porthos started like a man who has been rudely awakened from a hundred years of slumber.

"M-m-ma-madame!" he cried, "is it really you? How is your husband, our dear Monsieur Coquenard? Still as stingy as ever? Where can my eyes have been not to have spied you during the two hours this sermon lasted?"

"I kneeled but two paces away from you, Monsieur, but you failed to see me because you had eyes for none but the lovely lady to whom you just gave holy water."

Porthos feigned embarrassment.

"Oh!" he mumbled. "You noticed—?"

"Anyone but a blind man could notice—"

"Ah yes," Porthos volunteered nonchalantly, "the lady is a duchess of my acquaintance and I have considerable difficulty in meeting her because of her husband's jealousy. But today she sent me word that she was coming to this sorry church, buried in this vile quarter, just for the sake of seeing me a moment."

"Monsieur Porthos, would you be so kind as to offer me your arm for five minutes? I would be happy to talk to you for a while."

"With the greatest of pleasure, Madame!" Porthos said affably, winking joyously to himself, much as a gambler does as he mocks the dupe he is about to pluck. D'Artagnan, passing by in pursuit of Milady, beheld the triumphant gleam in the musketeer's eye and hurried on.

"Well, well, well!" he mused, reasoning after the strangely facile morality of that gallant period, "there goes one musketeer who will probably raise his campaign equipment in short order!"

Yielding to the pressure of Madame Attorney's arm as a skiff yields to the rudder, Porthos and his lady reached the cloister of Saint-Magloire, a little-frequented spot with a turnstile at each end. By day beggars sat there devouring their crusts or a few children played their simple games.

"Oh, Monsieur Porthos!" the lawyer's wife gasped. Then she looked carefully about her to make certain that only the usual people were in the cloisters: "Oh, Monsieur Porthos, you certainly seem to be a great conqueror!"

"I, Madame?" Porthos swelled like a frog. "Why so?"

"What of the signs you made just now in church? What of the holy water? That lady must be a princess at least, what with her little Negro and her maidservant!"

"No, no, Madame, you exaggerate. She is merely a duchess."

"What about that footman waiting at the door and the carriage with that coachman in full livery?"

Porthos had seen neither footman nor carriage but his lady, with all the curiosity of a jealous woman, had missed nothing. Porthos regretted that he had not immediately made the lady of the red cushion a princess.

"Ah, you are the pet of the most beautiful ladies of fashion, Monsieur Porthos!" she sighed.

"To be sure, with the physique Nature has conferred upon me, you may well imagine that I have a certain success in society."

"Dear God, how quickly men forget!" Madame Attorney cried, raising her eyes to Heaven.

"No more quickly than women, I dare say," Porthos countered. "Take my case, Madame: was I not your victim? There I lay, wounded, dying . . . the surgeon had given me up . . . there I suffered, I the scion of an illustrious family . . . I who had trusted in your friendship . . . almost dead of my wounds—and of hunger! . . . I in a mean inn at Chantilly . . . while you did not once deign to reply to the burning letters I addressed to you. . . ."

"But Monsieur Porthos—" The lawyer's wife wrung her hands helplessly as she felt herself judged by the behavior of the greatest ladies of the period and irrevocably condemned. "But Monsieur Porthos—"

"For your sake I broke with the Baronne de—"

"I know—"

"For your sake I gave up the Comtesse de—"

"Monsieur Porthos, do not crush me."

"The Duchess de—"

"Monsieur Porthos, pray be generous!"

"You are right, Madame. I will not finish."

"You see, it is my husband who refuses to hear of my lending—"

"Madame Coquenard, kindly remember the first letter you wrote to me. For my part it remains graven upon my memory."

The attorney's wife groaned.

"Besides, the sum you wished to borrow was rather large—"

"Madame Coquenard, I gave *you* the preference! I need only have written to the Duchesse de—but no, I must not mention her name, for I am utterly incapable of compromising a woman! But this I *do* know: I had but to write one line to her and she would have sent me fifteen hundred."

The lawyer's wife began to weep softly.

"Monsieur Porthos, I assure you that you have punished me severely enough. I swear that if ever you are in such straits again, you have but to turn to me in all confidence."

"Fie, Madame, fie!" Porthos said, as if disgusted. "Let us not talk of money, if you please, it is humiliating."

"Then you no longer love me!" Madame Attorney asked in a slow, tragic voice.

Porthos maintained a majestic silence.

"And that is your only answer! Alas! I understand."

"Think of how deeply you have offended me, Madame!" Porthos spread his hand over his heart. "That hurt rankles here!" he added thumping his chest.

"I will make amends, my dear Porthos, honestly I will."

"Besides, what did I ask of you?" Porthos continued with a good-natured shrug of the shoulders. "A loan, nothing else. After all, I am not an unreasonable man. I know you are not rich, Madame Coquenard; I know your husband is forced to bleed his poor clients to squeeze a few paltry crowns from them. Oh, if you were a countess, a marchioness or a duchess, it would be something else again and you would be unpardonable."

Madame Attorney was plainly piqued.

"Let me tell you, my dear Monsieur Porthos, that my safe—though it be the safe of an attorney's lady—is probably better stocked than those of all your aristocratic minxes who are so long on affectation and so short on cash!"

"Then you have doubly offended me, Madame," Porthos answered, releasing her arm from his own, "for if you are wealthy, Madame Coquenard, there is no excuse for your refusal."

"When I implied I was wealthy," the lawyer's wife said cautiously, aware she had gone too far, "you must not take the word literally. I am not exactly wealthy, but I am comfortably well off."

"Come, Madame, let us say no more about it, I beg you. You have misunderstood me and all sympathy and fellow-feeling we entertained is forever dead."

"How ungrateful you are, Monsieur Porthos!"

"Those words come ill from *you*, Madame Coquenard."

"Begone then to your beautiful duchess, I shall not detain you."

"She is a comely woman as I recall."

"Come, Monsieur Porthos, once and for all: tell me, do you still love me?"

"Alas, Madame," Porthos sighed affecting the deepest melancholy, "we are about to go to the front in a campaign which I feel will cost me my life—"

"Oh, don't even *think* of such things!" said the lawyer's wife bursting into tears.

"Something tells me that in this lottery of life, my number is up," Porthos continued even more melancholy.

"Be honest and confess that you have found a new love."

"No, Madame, I am giving you the plain, unvarnished truth. No new-found lady stirs me; on the contrary, deep in my heart something speaks to me of you. But within a fortnight, whether you know it or not, this fatal campaign opens. I shall be frightfully busy acquiring my equipment; then I must visit my family in far away Brittany to obtain the sum necessary for my departure." Porthos, watching Madame Attorney's face, saw it as the final battleground upon which the forces of love and avarice struggled. "And," he concluded sumptuously, "since the duchess you just saw in church has estates near ours, we purpose to travel together. Journeys, as you know, pass more quickly and more merrily in company than alone."

"Have you no friends in Paris then, Monsieur Porthos?"

"I thought I had, but apparently I was mistaken."

"Oh, but you have friends here, Monsieur Porthos, I vow you have." She herself seemed considerably surprised at her vehemence. "Come to our house tomorrow. You will figure as the son of my aunt, therefore my cousin ... you hail from Noyon in Picardy ... you have several lawsuits to settle in Paris ... and you seek an attorney to press them. ... Can you remember all of that?"

"Perfectly, Madame."

"Pray come at dinner time."

"Very well."

"Be sure, too, dear Monsieur Porthos, to stand upon your guard. Be wary. My husband is seventy-six years old but a shrewd man—"

"Seventy-six, God help us, there's a noble age, Madame."

"You mean an *old* age, Monsieur Porthos! And so you understand," Madame Attorney cast a significant glance at Porthos, "fortunately my marriage contract makes me the inheritor of my husband's fortune."

"His whole fortune?"

"His whole fortune, Monsieur Porthos."

"My dear Madame Coquenard, I clearly perceive that you are an eminently provident woman." Porthos squeezed her hand.

"So we are reconciled, dear Monsieur Porthos?" she simpered.

"For life!" Porthos simpered in return.

"Farewell, sweet traitor!"

"Farewell, forgetful charmer."

"Tomorrow, angel!"

"Tomorrow, love of my life."

XXX

MILADY

D'Artagnan followed Milady out of the church, saw her step into her carriage and heard her order the coachman to drive to Saint-Germain. He knew it was useless to try to keep up with a vehicle drawn by two powerful horses. He therefore made his way to the Rue Férou to call upon Athos. In the Rue de Seine he met Planchet, who had paused to look into the show window of a pastrycook's and was lost in ecstasy as he surveyed a brioche of the most luscious and toothsome appearance.

"Well, Planchet, a fine sight, eh?"

"What does Monsieur wish me to do?"

"Take your eyes off that cake and go to the stables of Monsieur de Tréville! Saddle a horse for myself and you—" D'Artagnan blessed the moment when the Captain of Musketeers had given him carte blanche— "and take them to the Rue Férou where I shall be waiting with Monsieur Athos."

"Very good, Monsieur."

D'Artagnan found Athos at home, draining a bottle of the Spanish wine he had brought back from the expedition into Picardy. Athos signaled to Grimaud for a glass which Grimaud, wordless as usual, produced silently. Then the Gascon told Athos of what he had seen in the Church of Saint-Leu and how Porthos stood an excellent chance of outfitting himself in the very near future.

"For my part I am not worrying," Athos observed coolly. "No woman will pay for *my* equipment."

"Come now, Athos, what woman would be indifferent to you, handsome, well-bred and a nobleman to your fingertips? What queen or princess could be safe from your solicitations if but you deigned to solicit?"

"My poor D'Artagnan!" Athos shrugged his shoulders and motioned to

Grimaud to fetch up another bottle of wine. "I swear you are the veriest babe in arms!"

Suddenly Planchet poked his head meekly through the door to announce to his master that the horses were ready.

"What horses?" Athos demanded.

"Two horses that Monsieur de Tréville puts at my disposal," D'Artagnan explained suavely. "I am off for a jaunt to Saint-Germain."

"What on earth are you going to do at Saint-Germain?" Athos inquired.

D'Artagnan told him how he had seen the lady of Meung. It was not she, beautiful though she was, whom he sought to find again but his archenemy, the man in the black cloak, the man with the scar near his temple.

"I see," Athos observed contemptuously, his manner suggesting a vast pity for humanity in general. "You are in love with this lady as deeply as you were once in love with Madame Bonacieux."

"Nonsense, Athos! All I want is to clear up the mystery in which she plays a part. I cannot explain why, but I have a curious feeling that this woman, strangers though we are, exercises a powerful influence upon my life."

"Undoubtedly, D'Artagnan. Why bother to look for a woman once she is lost? Madame Bonacieux is lost, so much the worse for her. Let her shift for herself."

"No, Athos, you are mistaken. I love my poor Constance more than ever. Alas, if I knew where she was, I would cheerfully go to the ends of the earth to save her from her enemies. But I know nothing; all my investigations have proved useless. And after all a man must find amusement somewhere."

"Very well, amuse yourself with Milady, my dear fellow; I wish you the best of luck."

"Come, Athos, instead of shutting yourself up here as though you were under arrest, why not go for a ride with me through the forest of Saint-Germain?"

"My dear D'Artagnan, I ride when I own a horse. When I have none, I walk."

Such misanthropy would have offended D'Artagnan from any one but Athos. He smiled.

"That is where we differ," he said, "I am not so proud as you; I ride any nag I can get. Good-bye, Athos."

"Good-bye to you, lad!" the musketeer replied, motioning to Grimaud to uncork the bottle he had just brought in.

D'Artagnan and Planchet set off briskly toward Saint-Germain. All along the road the young Gascon reflected upon what Athos had said about Madame Bonacieux. Although not given to sentimentality, D'Artagnan had been deeply stirred by the beauty and charm and loyalty of the haberdasher's wife. As he said, he was ready to go to the ends of the earth in quest of her; but the earth being round has very many ends, so he knew not which way to turn. Meanwhile he proposed to investigate Milady. She had spoken to the man in the black cloak, therefore she must know him. And D'Artagnan was certain that the man in the black coat had carried off Madame Bonacieux the second time, just as he had carried her off the first. Thus when D'Artagnan told himself that by going in search of Milady he was going in search of Constance, he was lying only by half, which does not make a man much of a liar.

Lost in these thoughts and occasionally spurring on his horse in his impatience of a solution, D'Artagnan soon reached Saint-Germain. He passed the lodge where Louis XV was to be born ten years later. Then as he rode up a quiet, deserted street, looking to right and left in hope of finding some trace of the beautiful Englishwoman, suddenly he drew up his horse. On the ground floor of a pretty house which, as was then the fashion, had no window looking out onto the street, he fancied he recognized a familiar face. Immediately Planchet verified his suspicion by drawing D'Artagnan's attention to that face rising up from amid the flowers lining a small terrace.

"Look, Monsieur," Planchet said, "do you recall that gaping, blinking face?"

"I cannot say for sure, I thought I—"

"*I* know, Monsieur, it's poor old Lubin, the lackey of the Comte de Vardes whose score you settled so nicely a month ago at Calais on the road to the Governor's country house!"

"Of course, so it is. Now I recognize him. Do you suppose he will recognize you?"

"I doubt it, Monsieur. He was having much too hard a time of it to remember who it was drubbed him."

"Well, go talk to the fellow and try to find out if his master is dead."

Planchet dismounted and walked up to Lubin, who, as he had expected, failed to identify him. The two lackeys engaged in friendly conversation while D'Artagnan turned the two horses into a lane, circled the house, and returned to listen to the conference from behind a hedge of hazel bushes. Presently he heard the rumble of a carriage approaching and he saw Milady's coach draw up in front of him. He was absolutely certain it was she because he had an unobstructed view of her. D'Artagnan crouched down to avoid observation.

Milady leaned out of the window, her lovely blonde head clearly visible, to give orders to her maid, a most attractive girl in her early twenties, spry and alert, the typical soubrette of a lady of quality. The maid jumped from the step upon which, according to the custom of the times, she had been sitting, and made for the terrace where D'Artagnan had first caught sight of Lubin.

D'Artagnan followed the girl's progress with his eyes when suddenly an order from within the house summoned Lubin indoors; Planchet, left alone, stared about him to try to find out which way his master had gone. The maid then approached Planchet, whom she mistook for Lubin, and handed him a note.

"This is for your master," she said.

"For my master?" Planchet replied in astonishment.

"Yes. The message is urgent, too. Take it quickly."

Then she ran back to the carriage which had turned around and was headed homeward, jumped onto the step, and the carriage drove off.

Planchet twirled the note between his fingers. Then, accustomed as he was to passive obedience, he jumped down from the terrace, ran toward the lane and met D'Artagnan some sixty feet away.

"A note for you, Monsieur."

"For *me?* Are you sure?"

"Certainly, Monsieur. The soubrette said: 'For your master!' I have no other master but you, so . . . A fetching little baggage, that maid!"

D'Artagnan opened the letter and read:

A person who takes more interest in you than she is willing to confess, wishes to know on what day it would suit you to take a walk in the forest of Saint-Germain.

Tomorrow at the Hostelry of the field of the Cloth of Gold a lackey in black and red livery will await your reply.

"Ha, things are warming up considerably!" D'Artagnan exclaimed. "It seems that both Milady and I are anxious about the health of the same person. Tell me, Planchet, how is our good Monsieur de Vardes? Apparently very much alive."

"Indeed yes, Monsieur, that is as alive as can be expected, what with the wounds of four neat sword-thrusts. I fear the dear gentleman is still very weak thanks to your treatment, for he has lost buckets of blood. As I expected, Lubin did not recognize me. He told me our adventure from beginning to end."

"Bravo, Planchet, you are the monarch of lackeys. Now to horse again and let us overtake that carriage."

This did not take long; within a few minutes they sighted the carriage drawn up by the roadside, an elegantly dressed cavalier at the door. The conversation between Milady and the gentleman was so animated that D'Artagnan stopped on the far side of the carriage without being noticed by anyone but the pretty soubrette. Milady and the stranger were talking in English, a language D'Artagnan did not understand. But from the intonation and pitch of her voice, D'Artagnan easily perceived that the beautiful Englishwoman was very angry indeed. And she concluded her remarks with a gesture that left him in no uncertainty about the nature of her feelings, as she rapped her fan so forcefully on her knee that the delicate feminine weapon broke into a thousand pieces.

The cavalier laughed heartily which seemed still further to exasperate Milady. D'Artagnan, believing it was high time he intervene, drew up to the door on his side of the carriage and, doffing his hat respectfully, said:

"Madame, may I offer you my services? I notice this gentleman has incurred your displeasure. Speak but one word, Madame, and I will undertake to chastise him for his lack of courtesy."

Milady turned toward him in great astonishment.

"Monsieur," she replied in excellent French, "I should welcome your protection but for the fact that the person I am quarreling with is my brother."

"Pray excuse me, then, Madame; you must realize I was ignorant of that."

The stranger bent low over his horse's head to look through the carriage window.

"What is this simpleton talking about?" he asked. "Why doesn't he go about his business?"

D'Artagnan in turn leaned down to look through the carriage window from his side, and:

"Simpleton, yourself!" he declared. "I am staying here because such is my good pleasure."

The cavalier spoke a few words in English to his sister.

"I am addressing you in French," D'Artagnan remonstrated. "Pray do me the favor of replying in the same language. You may be Madame's brother but you are not mine, thank God!"

It might be thought that Milady, timid as women generally are, would interfere at this point in order to prevent the quarrel from going too far. On the contrary, she threw herself back in the carriage and called coolly to the coachman:

"Home, Basque, at once!"

As the carriage drew away, the pretty soubrette, clearly impressed by D'Artagnan's good looks, cast an anxious glance of farewell at him. The horses trotted off, leaving the two men face to face with no material obstacle between them.

The cavalier made a move as if to follow the carriage but D'Artagnan caught at his bridle and stopped him dead. For, angry as he was, he was further enraged on recognizing in the stranger the Englishman of Amiens who had won his horse outright from Athos and come perilously close to winning D'Artagnan's diamond.

"Monsieur," D'Artagnan cried, "you seem to be even more of a simpleton than I am: you have forgotten a previous quarrel that we have not yet settled."

"So it is you, my friend," the Englishman answered, recognizing our Gascon. "It looks as though you must always be playing at some game or other."

"Indeed, yes. You may recall it is time I had my inning. I am eager to find out, Monsieur, whether you handle a sword as adroitly as you handle a dice box?"

"You can see perfectly well that I carry no sword. Do you enjoy playing the braggart before a man unarmed?"

"I trust you have a sword at home, Monsieur. If not, I happen to have two and we can dice for who is to wield which."

"That is quite needless," the Englishman answered haughtily. "I have plenty of such playthings."

"Well then, Monsieur, pray pick out your longest toy and let me see the color of it this evening."

"Where, if you please?"

"Behind the Luxembourg, a delightful place indicated in every way for the game I suggest we play."

"Agreed: I shall be there."

"Your hour?"

"Six o'clock."

"By the by, Monsieur, you doubtless have one or two friends to second you?"

"I have three who will be honored to join in our amusement."

"Three? Splendid! The very thing! I too have three friends who will support me. I might add that three is my lucky number."

"May I ask who you are, Monsieur?"

"I am Monsieur D'Artagnan, a Gascon gentleman, serving in the Royal Guards; my Commanding Officer is Monsieur des Essarts."

"I am Lord Winter, Baron of Sheffield."

"Your servant, Monsieur le Baron, though your names are hard to remember."

Whereupon D'Artagnan bowed, set spurs to his horse and galloped off toward Paris. As usual when a crisis occurred he made straight for the Rue Férou where he found Athos reclining on a large sofa, waiting, as he said, for his campaign equipment to come to find him. D'Artagnan related all that had happened save the circumstance of Milady's letter to Monsieur de Vardes.

Athos was delighted to learn that he was to fight against an Englishman; it represented his sole ambition and delight in life. They lost no time in dispatching the lackeys for Porthos and Aramis who were speedily informed of the situation.

Porthos drew his sword from his scabbard and made passes at the wall, springing back from time to time to flex his knees like a dancer ... Aramis, who was still working on his poem, closeted himself in the room Athos used for a study, requesting to be left alone until the moment came to draw swords ... Athos motioned to Grimaud for a bottle ... and D'Artagnan, elaborating a promising and pleasurable little plan of his own, smiled now and again in anticipation of future joys. ...

XXXI

ENGLISHMEN AND FRENCHMEN

At the appointed hour our four friends and their lackeys repaired behind the Palais du Luxembourg to an inclosure used as grazing ground for goats. Athos gave the herder a coin to insure his withdrawal; the lackeys were posted as sentinels. Soon another party of four drew up in a coach, entered the enclosure and joined the musketeers. Then, according to English custom, introductions were in order.

The Englishmen, all men of high rank, were not only surprised but considerably disturbed by the odd names of their adversaries. When Athos, Porthos and Aramis announced their names Lord Winter objected.

"But, gentlemen, we do not know who you are. We refuse to fight against persons with such names; they are names of shepherds!"

"As you have guessed, Milord, these are but names we have assumed," Athos explained:

"That makes us the more eager to know your real names," the Englishman answered.

"You were perfectly willing to gamble with us, whatever our names," Athos objected. "In fact, you won our horses without being particularly formal about it."

"True, but we risked only our money; now we are risking our lives. A gentleman gambles with anybody, he fights only with his fellow-gentlemen."

"True enough!" Athos conceded, and, drawing his own adversary aside, he whispered his real name. Porthos and Aramis followed suit and three of the four Englishmen were convinced they were not dealing with shepherds.

"Are you satisfied?" Athos asked his adversary. "Do you consider me noble enough to condescend to cross swords with me?"

"Certainly, Monsieur," said the Englishman, bowing.

"Well then, may I tell you something?" Athos asked coldly.

"If you will."

"I say this: You would have done better not to ask me who I am."

"Pray why?"

"Because I am down on the records as a dead man and I propose to remain so. I shall therefore be compelled to kill you in order to keep my life a secret."

The Englishman smiled as at a joke but Athos spoke in deadly earnest.

"Are you ready, gentlemen?" Athos asked and, as friend and foe agreed, "On guard, then!" he cried.

At once eight swords flashed across the rays of the setting sun and the combat began with a fury natural between men who had double reason to be vindictive. Athos fenced calmly and methodically as at a practice bout in a fencing hall; Porthos, sobered by his mishap at Chantilly, sparred with careful strategy; Aramis, Canto III of his poem unfinished, hastened to get done with the fighting.

Athos was the first to dispatch his adversary. One thrust sufficed; as he had prophesied, the Englishman fell dead, pierced through the heart. Porthos was the second to settle his opponent, who fell to the grass with a wound in the thigh. The Englishman meekly surrendered his sword and Porthos, picking him up in his arms, carried him back to his coach. Aramis harried his opponent so forcefully that the Englishman, having retreated over fifty paces, took frankly to his heels amid the jeers of the lackeys.

As for D'Artagnan, he first stood purely and simply on the defensive; eventually, when he saw he had exhausted his opponent, he disarmed him with a *flanconade,* a turn of the wrist in *quarto.* The Englishman, swordless, took a few steps backward, but his foot slipped and he fell to the ground. One leap and D'Artagnan was on him, his sword point on the other's throat.

"I could kill you, Monsieur," cried the Gascon, "for you are at my mercy. But I prefer to grant you your life for the sake of your sister."

D'Artagnan smiled as widely in triumph of the fulfilment of his plans as he had smiled in hatching them.

Delighted with his opponent's courtesy, the Englishman rose, embraced D'Artagnan, shook hands all round and patted the three musketeers on the back. Then, since Porthos had already carried his adversary back to an alarmed English coachman and Aramis had put *his* Englishman to flight, they turned their attention to the dead man.

As Porthos and Aramis undressed him, hoping desperately that he was not mortally wounded, a heavy purse fell to the ground. D'Artagnan picked it up and handed it to Lord Winter.

"What the devil shall I do with *that?*" the Englishman asked.

"Will you be so kind as to return it to his family?"

"His family would not be interested," the Englishman answered. "His death brings them fifteen thousand louis a year. Give the purse to your lackeys for a tip."

D'Artagnan pocketed it.

"And now my friend, if I may call you so," Lord Winter said to D'Artagnan, "I shall present you to my sister, Lady Clark, this very evening. I should like her to feel as cordially toward you as I do. She is not out of favor at Court; indeed, she might well put in a word for you that might serve in the future."

D'Artagnan, blushing, made a bow. Suddenly Athos came up to him.

"What about the purse?" he whispered.

"I was planning to give it to you, my dear Athos."

"To me? Why, pray?"

"Because you killed him. The spoils of victory—"

"Can you imagine me stripping an enemy? What do you take me for?"

"You know the customs and fortunes of war," D'Artagnan explained. "Do not those customs apply to dueling?"

"I never did that even on the battlefield!"

Porthos shrugged his shoulders; Aramis, pursing his lips, showed approval.

"Very well," D'Artagnan agreed. "Let us give this money to the lackeys as Lord Winter suggested."

"To the lackeys, ay," cried Athos. "Not to ours, but to the Englishmen's lackeys."

Taking the purse from D'Artagnan, Athos tossed it to the English coachman.

"This is for you and your friends," he said.

Such generosity in a man utterly destitute struck even Porthos. The story of it, repeated throughout Paris by Lord Winter, made a vast impression on every one save Messrs. Grimaud, Bazin, Mousqueton and Planchet.

Taking leave of him, Lord Winter gave D'Artagnan Milady's address—6 Rue Royale, in the fashionable quarter of town—and offered to call for him. D'Artagnan suggested the Englishman stop by for him at eight o'clock; he would be visiting Athos then, and they could conveniently leave from there.

His forthcoming meeting with Milady filled our young Gascon's mind. Recalling the strange circumstances in which she had entered his life, he was convinced that she must be some creature of the Cardinal's, yet he felt invincibly drawn to her by some incomprehensible fascination. He had certain qualms, too. Would Milady recognize him as the man she had encountered at Meung and at Dover? Again, the fact that she must know him to be a friend of Monsieur de Tréville's and therefore devoted body and soul to the King, would necessarily deprive him of some part of his present advantages; known by Milady and knowing her as he did, he would be dealing with her on an equal footing. As for her incipient affair with the Comte de Vardes, our presumptuous Gascon gave it but scant thought, even though that dandy was young, handsome, rich and high in the Cardinal's favor. After all, a man of twenty and born in Tarbes does not worry over such trifles.

First, D'Artagnan went home to dress in the most flamboyant fashion his wardrobe permitted, then he called on Athos and as usual told his friend everything. Athos listened to his plans; then, shaking his head, advised him somewhat bitterly to be circumspect.

"What?" Athos protested. "You have just lost a woman whom you considered good, charming, perfect, and here you go running headlong after another."

D'Artagnan felt the truth in the reproach.

"I loved Madame Bonacieux with my heart," he explained. "I love Milady with my head. If I am so eager to be introduced to her, it is mainly because I want to ascertain what part she plays at Court."

"What part she plays at Court? Heaven help us, from all you have told me, that should be pretty obvious. She is some emissary of the Cardinal's, a woman who will surely draw you into some trap. Look out, my boy; all this might well cost you your head!"

"The devil! My dear Athos, apparently you always see the dark side of things!"

"My dear fellow, I mistrust women, especially blondes. Why not? I have learned that lesson to my cost. You did tell me Milady was a blonde, didn't you?"

"She has the most beautiful fair hair imaginable," D'Artagnan exclaimed lyrically.

"My poor D'Artagnan, God help you."

"No, no, Athos, I simply want to find out what's what. That done, I shall withdraw."

"Very well," Athos said phlegmatically. "Go ahead and find out what's what!"

Lord Winter arrived punctually and Athos, warned in good time, disappeared into the adjoining room. As it was close to eight o'clock, the two set off on their errand. A handsomely appointed carriage waited below and two mettlesome, spanking horses brought them to the Place Royale in a few minutes.

Lady Clark received D'Artagnan ceremoniously. Her mansion was remarkably sumptuous, and although most English residents had left or were about to leave France because of the war, she had quite recently expended considerable money on her house. Obviously then the general measure which drove the English home did not apply to her.

Presenting D'Artagnan, Lord Winter said:

"Sister, here is a young gentleman who held my life in his hands. I insulted him and I am an Englishman, which gave him two reasons for abominating me. Nevertheless, he refused to take advantage of his victory. Pray thank him, Madame, if you have any affection for me."

Milady frowned slightly, a faint shadow spun cloudlike over her radiant brow and a most peculiar smile appeared on her lips. Observing these three reactions, D'Artagnan felt something like a shudder pass through him. The brother saw nothing of this for he was busy playing with Milady's favorite monkey, which was tugging at his doublet.

"Pray let me welcome you, Monsieur," said Milady in a voice whose singular gentleness belied the symptoms of ill-humor D'Artagnan had just observed. "Today you have won an eternal claim to my gratitude."

The Englishman then turned toward them and related the duel in full detail; Milady listened with the greatest attention, but, despite the effort she made to dissimulate, it was clear that this recital vexed her. The blood rose to her head; her slender foot tapped a nervous tattoo under her gown. Still unaware of anything amiss, Lord Winter completed his story, then rose and crossed the room to a table bearing a bottle of Spanish wine and an assortment of glasses on a magnificent salver. Filling two glasses, he nodded to D'Artagnan to drink.

D'Artagnan realized that to refuse to toast an Englishman was considered most discourteous; he therefore went over to the table and took up the second glass. He did not, however, lose sight of Milady; in the mirror he noticed an extraordinary change in her expression. Now that she believed herself to be unobserved, a fierce malevolent spark kindled her eyes and she gnawed savagely at her handkerchief.

The comely maid that had admitted them now came in again and said something in English to Lord Winter. He immediately asked permission of D'Artagnan to retire, excusing himself on the grounds of urgent business and charging his sister to obtain his pardon.

D'Artagnan shook hands with Lord Winter and returned to Milady. With surprising mobility her features had regained their gracious composure; only a few little spots of red on her handkerchief betrayed the fact that she had bitten her lips so hard as to draw blood. What lovely lips they were, too, D'Artagnan thought, proudly chiseled, sensitive and coraline.

The conversation took a more cheerful, livelier turn. Milady appeared to have completely recovered. She explained that Lord Winter was not her brother but her brother-in-law; she had married the youngest of the family who left her a widow with one child. This child was Lord Winter's only heir, unless Lord Winter were to marry. From Milady's remarks, D'Artagnan sensed that a veil of mystery covered her, but he could not yet see under this veil.

A half-hour of conversation convinced D'Artagnan that Milady was a compatriot; she spoke French with a purity and elegance that left no doubt on that score.

D'Artagnan, profuse in gallant speeches and lavish in protestations of devotion, uttered a good deal of nonsense; Milady, accepting it, smiled benevolently upon the gushing Gascon. When it was time for him to retire, he took leave of her, the happiest of mortal men.

On the staircase he met the pretty soubrette who brushed gently against him as she passed and, blushing to the roots of her hair, apologized for having touched him. So sweet was her voice, so charming her manner, that D'Artagnan granted her his pardon instantly.

Next day he called on Milady again to be received even better than the evening before. Lord Winter was absent, so Milady did the honors of the house. She seemed to take a great interest in him. Where did he hail from, she asked, who were his friends, and had he ever thought of entering the Cardinal's service?

For a lad of twenty, D'Artagnan was, as we have seen, extremely prudent. Remembering his suspicions of Milady, he praised His Eminence to the skies, and assured her that he would certainly have joined the Cardinal's guards instead of the Royal Guards had he happened to know Monsieur de Cavois as he knew Monsieur de Tréville.

Milady, changing the subject not too pointedly, asked D'Artagnan quite casually if he had ever been in England. He replied that he had been sent there by Monsieur de Tréville to negotiate for a supply of horses and that he had brought four back. Twice or thrice in the course of the conversation Milady bit her lips; D'Artagnan gathered that she realized she was dealing with a Gascon who played a cautious game.

Leaving at the same hour as on the previous evening, D'Artagnan again met Kitty, the attractive soubrette, in the corridor. She looked at him with an unmistakable expression of fervor but D'Artagnan, absorbed by thoughts of the mistress, had no eyes for the servant's demonstration.

On the morrow, D'Artagnan returned to Milady's for a third time, and the next day for a fourth; each time Milady received him more graciously than the last, and each time, either in the corridor or on the staircase, he encountered the comely soubrette. But as we have said, D'Artagnan paid no attention to poor Kitty's persistent overtures.

XXXII

A Dinner at the House of an Attorney-at-Law

Brilliantly as Porthos had fought in the fray, he did not forget his engagement for dinner with Madame Coquenard. Next day toward one o'clock he had Mousqueton brush, dust, sponge and press his uniform. Then, trim and smart, he strolled off toward the Rue aux Ours, a man doubly favored by the fortunes of war and love.

His heart beat fast but not with a youthful, impetuous love like that of D'Artagnan. No, a more material and practical interest stirred his blood. At last he was about to cross the mysterious threshold which led to the unknown stairway, which led to the unexplored corridor, which led to the office, which led to the safe of Maître Coquenard, Attorney-at-Law. Coin by ancient coin, bill by assigned bill, the lawyer's fortune had progressed along the same path. Now Porthos was following triumphant in its wake.

Many a time in his dreams Porthos had visioned the lawyer's ample coffer. Surely it was a long, deep and capricious receptacle, padlocked, bolted, barred and fastened to the floor. How often and in what detail

Madame Attorney had described it! Today her somewhat wrinkled but not unshapely hands were to open it to his jubilant gaze.

And he, Porthos, a wanderer over the face of the earth, a man without family or fortune, a soldier accustomed to inns, taverns, cheap lodgings and pothouses, this epicure had been forced to content himself with what chance offered in the way of a friend treating him to a wretched meal. Now at least he was to enjoy the amenities of a comfortable home, to partake of good family meals and to revel in those little personal attentions which, the harder a man is, the sweeter they seem, as old soldiers say.

To be received in the capacity of a cousin ... to sit at a good table every day ... to unfurrow the yellow wrinkled brow of the aged attorney ... to teach the clerks the highest subtleties of such card games as bassette and lansquenet or such dice games as passe-dix ... to pluck them, too, taking as fee for an hour's lesson, their savings of a month ... what a delightful prospect! ...

Amid his rosy dreams, Porthos did not forget the uncomplimentary traits attributed to attorneys even at that period (and still prevalent!). They were ever reported to be a stingy crew given to cheeseparing and frequent fasts. Still, save for occasional acts of parsimony, which Porthos had always found highly inopportune, Madame Attorney had been tolerably liberal—for a lawyer's wife. Accordingly Porthos expected to find a household run on an ample and gracious scale.

But at the front door he was seized with misgivings. The approach was unprepossessing: a dingy, stinking passage ... a dank stairway barely lighted by a few rays that filtered through a barred window from an adjoining courtyard ... and, on the second floor, a squat door studded with enormous nails like the main gate of the Grand Châtelet prison....

Porthos rapped at the door. A tall gangling clerk, pallid under a forest of tousled hair, opened, bowing with the air of a man forced to respect a lofty stature (which indicated strength), a uniform (which indicated valor) and a ruddy countenance (which indicated a familiarity with good living).

Behind the tall clerk stood a medium-sized clerk, and behind the medium-sized clerk, a third rather tall clerk, and behind him a diminutive errand boy of some twelve summers. Three and a half clerks all told, which in those days represented a most prosperous practice.

Though the musketeer was not expected before one o'clock, Madame Attorney had been watching the clock since noon, counting upon her suitor's heart and perhaps his stomach to bring him earlier. Thus she entered the office from her private apartment just as her guest entered from the stairs and the worthy lady's appearance rescued him from considerable embarrassment. The clerks eyed him with curiosity and, not knowing quite what to say to this ascending and descending scale, Porthos stood tongue-tied.

"It is my cousin," Madame Coquenard said. "Come in, do come in, Monsieur Porthos."

The name of Porthos produced its effect on the clerks who began to laugh; but as Porthos turned around sharply, the faces of the lawyerlings quickly recovered their wonted gravity.

Madame Coquenard led her suitor through the antechamber, where the clerks were, and the office where they were supposed to be—a dark airless room littered with files of all sorts of papers. Emerging from the office they passed the kitchen on the right and entered the drawing room.

These various successively intercommunicating rooms scarcely filled Porthos with optimism. Through all these open doors, voices carried disagreeably, he thought, and the privacy of conversation suffered. Worse, while passing by, he had cast a swift investigating glance into the kitchen; to the shame of Madame Attorney and to his own deep regret, he admitted to himself that it possessed no roaring fire with great spits turning before it, and none of the bustle and animation which generally prevail in that sanctuary of delicious fare when a good meal is in the making.

The attorney must have been warned of a cousinly visit, for he showed no surprise at the sight of Porthos, who approached with an easy air and bowed courteously.

"It seems we are kinsmen, Monsieur Porthos," he remarked, rising yet supporting his weight on the arms of his cane chair. Swathed in a black doublet in which his slender body was all but lost, the old man was sharp, dry, sallow, and wizened. His little gray eyes, which glittered like carbuncles, and his grimacing mouth seemed to be the only features still alive in his face. Unfortunately for him his legs were beginning to refuse to serve the bony structure of his body; in the last six months of this weakness, he had become virtually a slave to his wife. Her cousin was accepted with resignation, no more. A nimble Maître Coquenard, firm on his legs, would have declined all relationship with Monsieur Porthos.

"Ay, Monsieur, we are cousins," Porthos confirmed, without losing countenance, for he had never expected an enthusiastic reception in this quarter.

"On the distaff side, I believe?" the attorney asked maliciously.

Porthos missed the point and, taking the query to be a proof of naïveté, chuckled softly under cover of his bushy mustache. Madame Coquenard, who knew that an ingenuous attorney was rare indeed among that species, smiled a whit and blushed a great deal.

From the moment Porthos appeared, Maître Coquenard had been casting anxious glances at a large chest that stood facing his oak desk. Porthos realized that this chest, though not similar in shape to the chest of his reveries, was nevertheless the blessed receptacle he had designs on. "Curious," he thought, congratulating himself, "curious that the reality stands several feet higher than the object of my dream."

Maître Coquenard delved no further into his genealogical research. Turning his worried glance from the solid chest to the solid countenance of Porthos, he merely asked:

"Surely our cousin will favor us by dining with us once before he goes off to the wars, eh, my dear?"

This time Porthos registered the thrust full in the pit of his stomach. Apparently Madame Coquenard felt it too, for she replied:

"My cousin will not return if he finds we have treated him poorly. If on the contrary he enjoys himself here, he still has only very little time to spend in Paris and even less time to devote to us. We should therefore beg him to grant us almost every free moment we can spare until he goes away."

This succour coming to Porthos at the very moment he had been attacked in his gastronomic hopes inspired the musketeer with lively feelings of gratitude toward Madame Coquenard.

"Oh, my legs, my poor legs, where are you?" the attorney groaned, attempting to smile.

Presently the dinner hour arrived and the trio adjourned to the dining room, a large dark room opposite the kitchen.

The clerks, who must have inhaled perfumes unusual to the house, were of military punctuality and stood waiting, their stools in their hands, to be invited to sit down. Their jaws moved in a preliminary activity that augured gargantuan disposal of what meats might fall under their teeth. Naturally the errand boy was not admitted to the honors of the master's table. Watching the starvelings, Porthos thought:

"By God, were I my cousin, I would not keep such a gluttonous crew!

Why, they look like shipwrecked sailors who have been without food for six long weeks!"

Madame Coquenard rolled her husband in on a chair equipped with casters; Porthos helped her to trundle him up to the table. The lawyer had scarcely entered when he began to twitch his nostrils and exercise his jaws as the clerks had done.

"Ha!" he exclaimed, "here is a most inviting soup!"

"What the devil can they smell that is so extraordinary in this soup?" Porthos grumbled to himself as he looked down upon a pale bouillon, abundant but innocent of any meat, with, on its surface, some crusts floating as scarce as the islands of an archipelago!

Madame Coquenard smiled and, upon a sign from her, they all sat down eagerly. First Maître Coquenard was served, next Porthos; next Madame Coquenard filled her own plate, exhausting the bouillon; then the dampened crusts went to the impatient clerks. At this moment the dining-room door opened of itself with a creak; through the half-open leaves, Porthos caught sight of the errand-boy. Not permitted to partake of the feast, the stripling was nibbling at his bread in the hall, stationed strategically there in order to flavor it with the twin aromas of dining room and kitchen.

After soup the maid brought a boiled fowl, at which splendor the eyes of the diners bulged dangerously from their sockets.

"It is easy to see you love your family dearly, Madame," the attorney observed with a smile almost tragic. "You are certainly treating your cousin to a rare feast."

The wretched fowl was thin and covered with the type of coarse bristly skin which, sharp and thin though the bones are, remains impenetrable. Obviously someone had searched for the fowl long and assiduously ere finding it lurking on the perch to which it had retired to die of old age.

"This is sad indeed," Porthos mused. "Heavens knows, I respect my elders, but I don't think much of them served up to me boiled or roasted."

Looking about him to see whether anyone shared his opinion, he was astounded to observe nothing but gleaming eyes devouring in anticipation that sublime fowl which was the object of his own contempt.

Madame Attorney drew the dish toward her . . . skilfully detached one black drumstick which she placed on her husband's plate . . . cut off the neck which with the head she put aside for herself . . . lopped off a wing for Porthos . . . and returned the bird to the maid who bore it away virtually intact. . . . Maid and bird vanished before the musketeer found time to examine the variations which disappointment can mark upon the human countenance, according to the character and temperament of those who experience it.

A dish of haricot beans was ushered in to replace the fowl—an enormous dish from which peeped a few rare mutton bones that might be supposed at first glance to have some meat on them. But the clerks were not duped by this fraud; their lugubrious glances froze into an expression of resignation. Madame Coquenard distributed this delicacy to the young men with all the moderation of a shrewd housewife.

It was now time for the wine to appear. From a diminutive stone crock, Maître Coquenard poured a third of a glass for each of the young men and about the same quantity for himself, then passed the vessel along to Porthos and to Madame Coquenard. The clerks filled their glasses, adding two parts of aqua pura to the one part vouchsafed them. Whenever they had drunk half a glassful, they kept adding water. By the end of the meal, what had been a beverage of deep crimson turned to the palest topaz.

Very timidly, Porthos toyed with his chicken wing and shuddered as he felt Madame Coquenard's knee seeking his under the table. He also drank half a glass of the sparingly served wine which he recognized as a horrible Montreuil, the horror of all practiced palates. Seeing him guzzle the wine undiluted, the attorney sighed.

"Wouldn't you care for some of these beans, Cousin Porthos?" Madame Coquenard inquired in a tone that implied: "Take my word for it, don't touch them!"

"Devil take me if I taste a single one!" Porthos muttered; then, aloud: "No, thank you, Cousin, I have eaten my fill."

A silence fell upon the company. Porthos was utterly at a loss. The attorney repeated several times:

"Ah, Madame, I congratulate you. Your dinner was a feast for the gods. Lord, how copiously I have eaten!"

In point of fact, the lawyer had sipped his bouillon, scraped the black foot of the unsavory fowl, and pared the only mutton bone which bore the semblance of any meat on it. Porthos, suddenly deciding he was the victim of a hoax, twirled his mustache and knit his eyebrows. But no! the knee of Madame pressed gently against his own, counseling patience.

This silence and the interruption in the service of the meal were unintelligible to Porthos, but it held a terrible meaning for the clerks. At a glance from the attorney, seconded by a smile from Madame Coquenard, they shuffled slowly to their feet, folded their napkins even more slowly, bowed and withdrew, as the attorney said solemnly:

"Go young men, go promote your digestion of this succulent food by working as hard as you can."

The clerks gone, Madame Coquenard rose and took up from the sideboard a piece of cheese, some quince jam, and a cake she herself had made with almonds and honey. Her husband frowned at what he considered her extravagance. Porthos pursed his lips at these starvation rations. He even looked around to see if the dish of beans were still available but it had vanished.

The attorney was squirming in his chair.

"A banquet to be remembered forever!" he said. "*Epulœ epulorum,* a real feast. Lucullus dines with Lucullus!"

Porthos glanced obliquely at the crock by his side; perhaps with wine, bread and cheese, he might be able to eke out what had not yet amounted to a snack. But the crock was empty, a fact which neither the lawyer nor his lady seemed aware of.

"Well, I know where *I* stand!" he thought resentfully.

He passed his tongue over a small spoonful of quince and found his teeth caught in the glutinous substance of Madame Attorney's cake.

"Now," he said to himself, "the sacrifice is consummated. Cheer up, Porthos, you still have hopes of peeping with Madame Coquenard into her husband's strong box."

After the luxuries of so luxurious a meal—excessive, he termed it—Maître Coquenard felt the need of a siesta. Porthos devoutly hoped the old fool would take his snooze then and there, but no! refusing to listen to reason, he insisted on being taken back to the drawing room, fussing and grumbling until he had been wheeled up to his chest over which, for greater safety, he hoisted his legs. He then relapsed into a sonorous slumber.

His wife led Porthos to an adjoining room and began to lay the groundwork for a reconciliation.

"You can come and dine three times a week," Madame Coquenard said archly.

"Thank you, Madame, but I should hate to take advantage of your kindness. I must look to my equipment."

"True," she admitted, groaning. "That unfortunate equipment."

"Ay, Madame."

"What does your equipment consist of, Monsieur Porthos?"

"Well, it is rather elaborate, Madame. As you know the musketeers are a crack corps. We require many things which would be useless to the Royal Guards or to the Swiss Guards."

"Tell me more, Monsieur, give me details."

"Well—" Porthos hedged. He much preferred naming a lump sum to offering a bill of particulars.

She looked at him encouragingly.

"Well," Porthos said, "all this may amount to—"

She waited, tremulous.

"To how much?" she asked. "I hope not more than—," she stopped, at a loss for words.

"Well, it will certainly not exceed twenty-five hundred livres. As a matter of fact, if I am careful I can probably manage with two thousand livres."

"Two thousand livres! Why, that's a fortune!"

Porthos made a significantly deprecatory grimace which Madame Coquenard understood perfectly.

"I asked you to tell me some of the items," she explained, "because I have many relatives and connections in business. I am sure I could obtain things for you at one hundred percent less than you could get them for yourself."

"Ah well, if that is what you meant—"

"Yes, dear Monsieur Porthos, that is all I meant. For example, to begin with, you do need a horse, don't you."

"Yes, I do indeed."

"Well, I have just the thing for you."

"Ah, so much for the horse!" Porthos beamed. "Of course I need a complete equipment for him too. It consists of a variety of things that only a musketeer can buy. That shouldn't amount to more than three hundred livres."

"Three hundred livres!" Madame Attorney sighed. "Very well then, three hundred livres!"

(Porthos smiled angelically. On one hand there was the saddle, a gift from My Lord of Buckingham; on the other, three hundred livres which he could quickly pocket!)

"Then there is a horse for my lackey. And my valise. And—no! as for my weapons, I need not trouble you, I already have them."

"A horse for your lackey?" Madame Coquenard faltered. "Surely you are doing things on a very lordly scale, my friend."

"Do you take me for a beggar, Madame?"

"No, I only meant to say that a pretty mule often looks quite as well as a horse. It seems to me that if you get Mousqueton a pretty mule—"

"So be it, Madame, a pretty mule for Mousqueton. I have seen the greatest Spanish grandees whose whole suites were mounted on mules. But of course you understand, Madame, a mule with plumes and bells—"

"That is quite easy."

"There remains my valise, Madame—"

"Do not fret, dear Monsieur Porthos, my husband has five or six valises. You shall choose the best. There is one in particular which he always preferred to travel with; it is huge; it could hold all the world."

"So your valise is empty, Madame?" Porthos inquired, naïvely.

"Certainly," Madame Attorney replied, matching his candor.

"But the valise I need is a well-fitted one, my dear."

Again Madame sighed profusely.

(At the time, Molière had not written his play *L'Avare;* the avarice of the attorney's lady was not yet outdone by the celebrated Harpagon.)

Item by item, the rest of the equipment was successively broached, taken under advisement, discussed and settled. In the end, Madame Attorney pledged herself to give eight hundred livres in money and to furnish the horse and the mule which were to have the honor of carrying Porthos and Mousqueton to glory. There terms agreed upon, Porthos took his leave of his inamorata. Madame sought to detain him by gazing tenderly at him from under lowered lashes. But Porthos pleaded the exigencies of duty and the lawyer's wife had perforce to yield in prerogative to His Majesty the King.

The musketeer returned home hungry as a hunter and angry as a bear.

XXXIII

THE SOUBRETTE AND HER MISTRESS

Meanwhile as we have said, despite the cries of his conscience and the wise counsels of Athos, D'Artagnan became more infatuated with Milady hour by hour. Convinced that she must inevitably respond sooner or later, our adventurous Gascon never once failed to pay her his daily court.

One evening when he arrived, his head in the air and as light of heart as a man who awaits a shower of gold, he found Milady's chambermaid under the gateway of the mansion. This time pretty Kitty was not content merely to touch him as he passed, she took him gently by the hand.

"Good!" thought D'Artagnan, "her mistress has charged her with some message for me; the soubrette is about to appoint some rendezvous which Milady dared not make orally."

And he looked at the pretty girl with the most triumphant air imaginable.

"May I have two words with you, Monsieur le Chevalier?" the maid stammered.

"Speak, my child, speak, I am listening."

"Here? Impossible. What I have to say is too complicated and above all too secret."

"Well, what shall we do?"

"If Monsieur le Chevalier will follow me?" Kitty suggested shyly.

"Where you please, my dear child!"

"Then come!"

So Kitty, who had not released his hand, led him up a little dark winding staircase and, after ascending about fifteen steps, opened a door.

"Come in here, Monsieur le Chevalier; we shall be alone here and we can talk at our ease."

"And whose room is this, my dear child?"

"This is my room, Monsieur le Chevalier; it communicates with my mistress's by that door. But you need not fear. She will not hear what we are saying; she never goes to bed before midnight."

D'Artagnan gazed around him. The little room was charming in its neatness and taste; but in spite of himself he stared at the door which Kitty said led to Milady's chamber. Reading his secret thoughts, Kitty heaved a deep sigh.

"So you do love my mistress very dearly, Monsieur le Chevalier?" she asked.

"Ay, more than I can say, Kitty. I am mad about her!"

Kitty breathed another sigh.

"Alas, Monsieur," she said, "that is a great pity!"

"Why in the devil's name is that a pity?"

"Because my mistress does not love Monsieur at all."

"What!" D'Artagnan gasped. Then "Did she charge you to tell me so?" he asked.

"Oh, no, Monsieur! Out of my regard for you, I resolved to tell you myself."

"I am much obliged to you, my dear Kitty—for your intention only, because you must confess that your information is scarcely agreeable."

"In other words you think I am wrong?"

"It is always difficult to believe such things, my dear child, if only because of pride."

"Then you don't believe me?"

"I confess that until you deign to give me some proof of what you advance, I—"

"What do you think of this?" Kitty demanded, drawing a little note from her bosom.

"Is it for me?" D'Artagnan asked, snatching the letter.

"No, it is for someone else."

"For someone else?"

"Yes."

"His name, tell me his name!" cried D'Artagnan.

"Read the address."

D'Artagnan, obeying, read: *For Monsieur le Comte de Vardes.*

The memory of the scene at Saint-Germain flashed across the mind of the presumptuous Gascon. In a move as quick as thought he tore open the letter, in spite of Kitty's warning cry as she realized too late what he had done.

"Good Lord, Monsieur le Chevalier, what are you doing?"

"What am I doing?" said D'Artagnan. "Why, nothing, nothing at all." And he read:

You have not answered my first note. Are you indisposed or have you forgotten the glances you favored me with at the ball of Madame de Guise? Monsieur le Comte, I offer you an opportunity now; do not let it slip through your fingers.

D'Artagnan turned pale, as he felt all the pangs of what he believed to be his wounded love but what of course was merely self-love.

"Poor dear Monsieur D'Artagnan!" Kitty whispered in a voice full of compassion, pressing the young man's hand anew.

"Do you pity me, little one?"

"Ay, truly, with all my heart, for I know what it is to be in love."

"You know what it is to be in love?" D'Artagnan echoed, looking at her attentively for the first time.

"Alas, yes!"

"Well then, instead of pitying me, you would do much better to help me to avenge myself on your mistress."

"And what sort of vengeance would you take?"

"I want to triumph over her and supplant my rival."

"I shall never help you to do that, Monsieur le Chevalier."

"Why not?"

"For two reasons."

"What reasons?"

"First, my mistress will never love you."

"How do you know that."

"You have cut her to the heart!"

"I? How on earth can I have offended her, I who ever since I met her have groveled at her feet like a slave! Speak, I beg you!"

"I will never confess that to any man save him who can read into the very depths of my soul."

Once again D'Artagnan examined Kitty curiously, noting her youthful freshness and beauty for which many a duchess would have given away her coronet.

"Kitty," he told her, "I am the man to read to the depths of your soul, whenever you like. Don't make any mistake about that." And he gave her a kiss at which the poor girl turned red as a cherry.

"No, no!" Kitty objected. "You do not love *me*, you love my mistress. You just said so a moment ago."

"Does that prevent you from telling me your second reason?"

"My second reason?" the soubrette replied, emboldened first by D'Artagnan's kiss and further by the expression in the young man's eyes. "My second reason is: In love, each for himself!"

Then only D'Artagnan recalled Kitty's languishing glances . . . their frequent meetings in the antechamber, in the corridor or on the stairs . . . the way her hand managed to brush against his every time she passed him . . . and the deep sighs she could not quite stifle. . . . Absorbed by his desire to please the great lady, he had disdained the soubrette; he who hunts the eagle has no eye for the sparrow.

But this time our Gascon saw at a glance all the advantages to be derived from the love Kitty had just confessed so innocently or so boldly: he could intercept the letters addressed to the Comte de Vardes, he had a faithful intelligencer on the spot, and he could enter Kitty's room adjacent to Milady's whenever he cared to. Manifestly the perfidious deceiver was already scheming to sacrifice the poor girl in order to obtain Milady willy-nilly.

"Tell me, Kitty dear, would you like me to give you proof of this love you appear to doubt?"

"What love?" asked the young girl.

"The love I am ready to offer you."

"What proof will you give?"

"Tonight . . . the hours I usually spend with your mistress . . . shall I spend them with you instead . . . ?"

"Oh, yes," said Kitty clapping her hands. "Please, please do!"

D'Artagnan settled himself in an easy chair, then turned to the soubrette again.

"Very well then, come here, my dear," he urged, "and I shall tell you that you are the prettiest soubrette I have ever laid eyes on."

Which he proceeded to do so profusely and so eloquently that the poor child, who asked for nothing better than to believe him, did believe him. Yet to D'Artagnan's vast astonishment, the comely Kitty resisted his advances resolutely.

Time passes quickly, especially when it is devoted to offensive and de fensive operations. Suddenly midnight sounded and almost at the same time Milady's bell rang in the adjoining apartment.

"Heavens!" Kitty cried in alarm. "My mistress is calling me! Go, my lover, please go at once!"

D'Artagnan rose and took his hat as if he intended to obey; but instead of opening the door leading to the staircase, he whisked open the door of a great closet and buried himself among Milady's robes and dressing-gowns.

"What are you doing?" Kitty gasped.

D'Artagnan, who had secured the key, locked himself in the closet from the inside without deigning to reply.

"Well," Milady called sharply, "are you asleep? Or will you answer the bell when I ring?"

D'Artagnan heard the door open violently.

"Here I am, Milady, here I am," cried Kitty, rushing forward to meet her mistress.

Together the two women returned to Milady's bedroom; and, as the communicating door remained ajar, D'Artagnan could hear Milady scolding her maid for some time. Presently she calmed down and the conversation turned on him while Kitty was undressing her mistress.

"Well! I have not seen our Gascon tonight," Milady remarked.

"What, Madame, he hasn't come? Can he possibly be fickle before he has been made happy?"

"Oh, no! Doubtless he was detained by Monsieur de Tréville or by Monsieur des Essarts. I know what I am doing, Kitty, and I hold this gallant in the palm of my hand."

"What will you do with him, Madame?"

"Do with him?" Milady repeated emphatically. "Rest easy, Kitty, that man and I have to settle something he does not even dream of. Why, he almost ruined my credit with His Eminence. Oh, but I will be revenged!"

"I thought Madame loved him?"

"*I* love him? I detest him! A ninny who held Lord Winter's life in his hands and did not kill him! I lost an income of three hundred thousand livres by it!"

She went on to explain how her son was his uncle's sole heir and how, until his majority, she would have had the enjoyment of his fortune. D'Artagnan shuddered to the marrow of his bones as he heard this suave creature reproach him—in that sharp, shrill voice that she took such pains to hide—for failing to kill a man, a man whom he had seen showering her with kindnesses.

"What is more," Milady went on, "I should long ago have revenged myself on him. But the Cardinal, I don't know why, requested me to conciliate him."

"But Madame has not conciliated that little woman the Gascon was so fond of."

"You mean the mercer's wife from the Rue des Fossoyeurs. Pooh! he has already forgotten she ever existed. A pretty revenge, that, upon my word!"

A cold sweat broke out over D'Artagnan's brow. Truly the woman was a monster. He resumed his eavesdropping but unfortunately Kitty's ministrations were at an end and Milady was ready for bed.

"That will do," he heard her tell the soubrette. "Go back to your own room and, tomorrow, try again to get me an answer to the letter I gave you."

"The letter for Monsieur de Vardes?"

"To be sure! Monsieur de Vardes!"

"Now there is a man," Kitty observed sententiously, "who appears to me to be the very opposite of poor Monsieur D'Artagnan."

"Go to bed, Mademoiselle," Milady ordered curtly. "I do not relish your comments."

D'Artagnan heard the door close, then the noise of the two bolts by which Milady locked herself up in her room; then, on her side, but as softly as possible, Kitty turned the key in the lock, and at last he opened the closet door.

"Oh, Good Lord!" said Kitty in a low voice. "What is the matter with you? How pale you are!"

"That abominable creature!" murmured D'Artagnan.

"Hush, Monsieur, hush! And please go!" Kitty begged. "There is but a thin wainscot between Milady's room and mine; every word said in one can be heard in the other!"

"That is exactly why I will not go," D'Artagnan explained.

"What!" said Kitty blushing.

"Or at least I will go—later."

He drew Kitty to him. This time she could offer no resistance, for resistance would have made too much noise. Accordingly Kitty yielded.

On D'Artagnan's part, their lovemaking was a movement of vengeance upon Milady, and gratefully he realized how right it is to describe vengeance as the pleasure of the gods. With a little more heart he would have been content with this new conquest; but he could not rise above ambition and pride. Meanwhile, to give him his due, it must be confessed that the first use he made of his influence over Kitty was to try to find out what had become of Madame Bonacieux. But the poor girl swore on the Cross that she knew nothing at all about it: her mistress only disclosed one-half of her secrets. However she believed she could say Madame Bonacieux was not dead.

As for the cause which almost made Milady lose her credit with the Cardinal, Kitty was equally ignorant. But in this instance D'Artagnan was better informed than she. Had he not seen Milady on board a vessel just as he was leaving England? Surely then it was the affair of the diamond studs that had brought disfavor down upon her head.

But the clearest thing of all was that the hatred, the deep and inveterate hatred that Milady felt for him, sprang from the fact that he had not killed her brother-in-law.

Next day D'Artagnan returned to Milady's to find her in a very disagreeable humor; he could not doubt that her irritability was provoked by lack of an answer from the Comte de Vardes. When Kitty came in, Milady treated her very crossly. The glance the soubrette cast at D'Artagnan seemed to say:

"You see what I am going through on your account!"

Toward the close of the evening, however, the beautiful lioness grew milder; Milady listened smilingly to D'Artagnan's honeyed compliments and even gave him her hand to kiss.

D'Artagnan departed, scarcely knowing what to think. But as he was a lad who did not easily lose his head, he had framed a little plan while continuing to pay his court to Milady.

He found Kitty at the door and, as on the preceding evening, accompanied her to her chamber. Kitty had been accused of negligence and roundly scolded. Milady could not possibly understand why the Comte de Vardes persisted in his silence; she had ordered Kitty to come to her at nine o'clock in the morning to take a third letter.

D'Artagnan made Kitty promise to bring him that letter the following morning; the poor girl agreed to all her lover wished, for she was mad with love.

Things passed as they had the previous night: D'Artagnan concealed himself in the closet, Milady called for Kitty, made her preparations to retire, dismissed the soubrette, and closed her door again. Again, as on the previous night, D'Artagnan did not leave for home before five o'clock in the morning.

At eleven o'clock, true to her promise, Kitty called at D'Artagnan's apartment with the letter Milady had given her at nine. This time the poor girl did not even try to argue with D'Artagnan; she let him do as he willed, for she belonged body and soul to her handsome soldier.

D'Artagnan opened the note and read the following:

This is the third time I have written to you to tell you that I love you. Beware that I do not write to you a fourth time to tell you that I detest you.

If you repent for having acted toward me as you have, the young girl who bears this note will tell you how a man of spirit may obtain his pardon.

D'Artagnan flushed and grew pale several times as he read this note.

"Oh! you love her still!" said Kitty, who had not taken her eyes off the young man's face for an instant.

"No, Kitty, you are mistaken, I do not love her now. But I want to avenge myself for her contempt."

"Yes, I know the vengeance you plan; you yourself told me!"

"What do you care, Kitty? You know very well that you are my only love!"

"How can I know that?"

"By the humiliation I shall visit upon her shameless head."

Kitty sighed. D'Artagnan took up a pen and wrote:

Madame,

Until the present moment I could not believe that your two previous letters were addressed to me, so unworthy did I seem myself of such an honor. Besides, I was so seriously indisposed that I could not have replied to them in any case.

But now I am forced to believe in your excessive graciousness, for not only your letter but your servant assures me that I have the good fortune to be favored by your affection.

She has no occasion to teach me the way in which a man of spirit may obtain his pardon. I will come to crave mine at eleven o'clock this evening. To delay it a single day would be tantamount in my eyes to committing a fresh offense.

From one whom you have rendered the happiest of men.

Comte de Vardes

This note was in the first place a forgery; it was likewise an indelicacy; it was even, according to present standards, something of an infamy; but in the seventeenth century people were less meticulous on certain subjects than they are today. Besides D'Artagnan knew from Milady's own confession that she was guilty of treachery in far more important matters. He had therefore scant reason to hold her in esteem. And yet, despite this want of respect, he felt a mad uncontrollable passion for this woman blazing within him. It was a passion thirsting to vent its scorn but, passion or thirst, there it was.

D'Artagnan's plan was very simple. By Kitty's room he could gain access to that of her mistress. He would take advantage of the first moment of surprise, shame and terror to triumph over her. He might perhaps fail, certainly; but something must be left to chance. One week hence the campaign of La Rochelle would open and he would have to leave Paris. There was therefore no time for a prolonged love seige.

"There," said the young man, sealing the letter and handing it to Kitty, "give this to Milady. It is Monsieur de Vardes' reply."

Poor Kitty suspected the contents of the note. She turned deathly pale.

"Listen to me, darling," D'Artagnan told her, "you must see that all this has to end some way or other. Milady may discover that you gave her first note to my valet instead of to the Comte de Vardes' lackey and that I opened the other two instead of the Comte. If that happens, she will turn you out into the street and hound you to death. You know she is not the sort of woman to limit her vengeance."

"Alas! for whom have I run such terrible risks?"

"For me, I know it, my sweet girl. I appreciate it and I swear I am deeply grateful to you, dear."

"At least tell me what your note says?"

"Milady will tell you."

"Ah! you do not love me!" Kitty wailed. "I am so unhappy!"

To a reproach of this sort, there is always one answer which will delude any woman. D'Artagnan answered to such effect that Kitty remained completely and thoroughly deluded. Although she wept a great deal before making up her mind to deliver the letter, she finally consented to do D'Artagnan's bidding, which was all D'Artagnan wished.

Besides, he promised that he would leave Milady's early that evening and repair immediately to Kitty's room. This promise completed poor Kitty's consolation.

XXXIV

Concerning the Respective Outfits of Aramis and Porthos

Since the four friends had begun to search each for his own outfit, there had been no fixed meetings between them. They dined apart from one another wherever they chanced to be or rather wherever they could. Duty also consumed a portion of that precious time which was passing so swiftly. However they had agreed to report once a week at about one o'-clock, with Athos for host, since, true to his vow, he would not pass the threshold of his door.

Their first meeting was on the same day that Kitty had visited D'Artagnan. She was no sooner gone than D'Artagnan hastened to the Rue Férou, where he found Athos and Aramis plunged in a philosophical discussion. Aramis felt inclined to resume the cassock; Athos, as usual, neither encouraged nor dissuaded him. Athos believed that every man should be left to his own free will, he never volunteered advice, but when asked to give it, he did so only at the second request.

"People in general ask for advice only in order not to follow it," he used to say, "or if they do follow it, it is to have someone to blame for having given it."

Porthos arrived a minute after D'Artagnan and so the four were reunited—but not for long! These four countenances expressed four very dissimilar frames of mind: Porthos looked tranquil, D'Artagnan hopeful, Aramis uneasy, and Athos careless.

After a moment's conversation, while Porthos was hinting that a lady of lofty rank had condescended to relieve him from his embarrassment, suddenly his valet Mousqueton entered. He begged his master to return to his lodgings where, he said piteously, his presence was urgently required.

"Is it my equipment?"

"Yes and no," Mousqueton replied. "Please come, Monsieur."

Porthos rose, bowed to his friends and followed Mousqueton.

An instant after, Bazin appeared at the door.

"What do you want, my friend?" Aramis inquired with that comity of language he affected whenever his ideas were directed toward the Church.

"A man is waiting to see Monsieur at home," Bazin replied.

"A man? What man?"

"A beggar."

"Give him alms, Bazin, and bid him pray for a poor sinner."

"This beggar insists on speaking to you; he claims that you will be very pleased to see him."

"Did he give you any particular message?"

"Yes. He said: 'If Monsieur Aramis hesitates to come, tell him I am from Tours!'"

"From Tours!" cried Aramis. "A thousand pardons, gentlemen, but no doubt this man brings me some news I was expecting." And, rising in his turn, he too set off hurriedly.

"I wager these fellows have managed their business and are fully equipped," said Athos. "What do you think, D'Artagnan?"

"I know that Porthos is in a fair way to succeeding," D'Artagnan replied. "As to Aramis, truth to tell, I have never been seriously worried about him. But you, my dear Athos—you who so generously distributed the Englishman's pistoles which were your own legitimate property—what do you mean to do?"

"I am quite content with having killed that fellow. Is it not blessèd bread to kill an Englishman? But I had pocketed his pistoles, I would now be eating my heart out with remorse!"

"Bah, my dear Athos, you really have the most extraordinary ideas!"

"Ah well, let it pass! . . . To change the subject: Monsieur de Tréville did me the honor of calling on me yesterday. He told me you were frequenting those suspect English protégés of the Cardinal. What about it?"

"Well, it is true I visit an Englishwoman, the one I told you about."

"Ah, yes, the blonde woman about whom I vouchsafed advice, which you of course took care not to follow."

"I gave you my reasons."

"Yes, I think you said you were looking to that quarter for your equipment."

"Not at all. I have acquired certain knowledge that she is concerned in the abduction of Madame Bonacieux."

"Yes, I understand now: to find one woman, you are courting another. It is the longest way around but undoubtedly the most amusing."

D'Artagnan was on the point of telling Athos the whole story but one point restrained him. Athos was a gentleman, punctilious in points of honor, and the plan D'Artagnan had adopted included certain actions which would not obtain the assent of this Puritan. He therefore said nothing and, as Athos was the least inquisitive man on earth, D'Artagnan's confidence stopped there. We will therefore leave the two friends conversing over unimportant trifles and follow Aramis.

We have seen with what alacrity Aramis followed Bazin when he heard that the visitor came from Tours. Actually he followed him only a few steps, for, having quickly overtaken him, he ran without stopping from the Rue Férou to the Rue de Vaugirard. Entering his apartment, he found a rather short man with intelligent eyes, clad in rags.

"You asked for me?" he inquired.

"I should like to speak to Monsieur Aramis. Is that your name, Monsieur?"

"Yes. You have brought me something?"

"Yes, if you will show me a certain embroidered handkerchief."

Aramis took a small key from his breast pocket, opened a small ebony box inlaid with mother-of-pearl, drew out the handkerchief, and held it out for the other's inspection.

"Here it is: look!"

"That is right," said the beggar, "dismiss your lackey."

Bazin was indeed there, all ears. Curious to find out what the mendicant could want with his master, he had kept pace with him as well as he could, reaching home at almost the same time. But his speed had not profited him. At the beggar's suggestion, Aramis motioned Bazin to retire, which he was reluctantly compelled to do.

Bazin gone, the beggar looked quickly around him to make sure that no one could either see or hear him. Then, opening his ragged vest, perilously held together by a leather belt, he began to rip the upper part of his doublet, from which he drew a letter.

Aramis uttered a cry of joy at the sight of the seal, kissed the writing with almost religious respect, and opened the letter to read the following:

My dear Friend:
It is the will of fate that we should remain separated for some time longer, but the delightful days of youth are not lost beyond return. Perform your duty in the camp, I will do mine elsewhere.

Accept what the bearer brings you. Fight in the campaign like the brave, handsome and true gentleman you are, and think of me who herewith kiss your black eyes ever so tenderly.

Adieu or rather au revoir. . . .

The beggar continued to rip his garments and from amid his filthy rags drew one hundred and fifty Spanish double pistoles which he laid down in shining rows on the table. Then he opened the door, bowed and disappeared before the young man, stupefied, had ventured to say a word to him.

Aramis then reread the letter and this time perceived a postscript:

P.S. You may behave politely to the bearer, who is a Count and a Grandee of Spain.

"Golden dreams!" cried Aramis. "Oh, beautiful life! Yes, we are young; yes, we shall know happy days! My love, my blood, my life, all, all are yours, my beauteous and adorable mistress."

And he kissed the letter passionately without even vouchsafing a glance at the gold which sparkled on the table.

Bazin scratched at the door and, as Aramis had no longer any reason to exclude him, he bade him enter. The servant was so astounded at the sight of the gold that he forgot he had come to announce D'Artagnan who, curious to know who the beggar could be, had come straight to Aramis on leaving Athos. As D'Artagnan did not stand on ceremony with his friend, seeing that Bazin failed to announce him, he announced himself.

"The devil, my dear Aramis!" he cried. "If these are the prunes they send you from Tours, please pay my compliments to the gardener who gathers them."

"You are mistaken, my friend," Aramis replied with his usual tact. "This is from my publisher. It represents my fee for that poem in one-syllable verse which I began when I was in Touraine."

"Indeed! Well, my dear Aramis, your publisher is very generous, that's all I can say!"

"What, Monsieur!" Bazin put in. "A poem sells for that much money. Would you believe it? Oh Monsieur, you always succeed in everything; why, you may become the peer of Monsieur de Voiture and Monsieur de Benserade. I like that idea! A poet is almost as good as an abbé. Ah, Monsieur Aramis, please become a poet for my sake, I beg of you."

"Bazin, my friend, I believe you are interfering in our conversation."

Aware that he was at fault, Bazin bowed contritely and withdrew.

"Well," said D'Artagnan with a smile, "the productions you sell are worth their weight in gold. You are very lucky, my friend. But take care or you will lose that letter which is popping out of your doublet. You would not want to lose a letter from your publisher."

Aramis blushed to the roots of his hair, stuffed the letter deep in his pocket, and buttoned up his doublet.

"My dear D'Artagnan, we will now join our friends, if you please," he suggested. "As I am rich, we will resume our dinners in common until the rest of you are rich in turn."

"By my faith, with great pleasure, Aramis. It is a long time since we ate a decent dinner and I, for my part, have a somewhat hazardous expedition for this evening. I confess, I shall not be sorry to fortify myself with a few bottles of old vintage Burgundy."

"Agreed as to the old Burgundy," said Aramis, his ideas of religious retreat dispelled as by magic by the sight of the letter and the gold. "I myself am not averse to old Burgundy, I may add."

Having pocketed three or four double pistoles for current needs, he placed the others in the ebony box inlaid with mother-of-pearl, over the famous handkerchief which served him as a talisman.

The two friends repaired first to Athos who, still faithful to his vow of remaining closeted at home, undertook to have the dinner served there. As he was brilliantly conversant with all the details of gastronomy, neither D'Artagnan nor Aramis offered the slightest objection to entrusting him with this all-important task.

As they went off in search of Porthos, they met that worthy's valet Mousqueton at the corner of the Rue du Bac, looking most shamefaced and piteous as he drove a mule and a horse before him. D'Artagnan uttered a cry of surprise which was not without a certain note of joy.

"Ah, my yellow horse!" he said. "Aramis, look at that horse!"

"Oh, what a frightful brute!"

"Well, my friend, it was that very horse I rode into Paris!"

"What?" said Mousqueton. "Monsieur knows this horse?"

"It is of a most original color," Aramis opined. "I never saw another one with such a hide in all my life."

"I can well believe it," said D'Artagnan, "that is why I got three crowns for him. It must certainly have been for his hide; that carcass of his wouldn't fetch eighteen livres. But how on earth did you get that nag, Mousqueton?"

"Ah, Monsieur," Mousqueton answered ruefully, "pray do not speak to me about it! It is a frightful trick played on us by the husband of our duchess."

"How is that, Mousqueton?"

"Yes, Monsieur, we are looked upon with a very favorable eye by a lady of quality, the Duchess de—but your pardon, gentlemen, my master has commanded me to be discreet so I dare not mention her name! She had forced us to accept a little keepsake, a magnificent Spanish jennet and an Andalusian mule, which were beautiful to look upon. The husband heard of the affair, confiscated our two splendid beasts on the way, and substituted these horrible animals."

"Which you are returning to him?" D'Artagnan asked.

"Exactly, Monsieur. You may well believe that we cannot accept such freaks in exchange for the thoroughbreds we were promised."

"Lord! I should think not! Still, I should like to have seen Porthos on my yellow horse; it would have given me an idea of what I must have looked like when I arrived in Paris!" D'Artagnan laughed. "But don't let us detain you, Mousqueton, go do your master's bidding. Is he at home?"

"Ay, Monsieur," Mousqueton replied, "but in a very bad humor. Giddy-up, there, get on, get on. . . ."

The wretched valet pursued his way toward the Quai des Grands-Augustins while the two friends went to ring at the bell of the unfortunate Porthos. But their friend, having seen them crossing the yard, took good care not to answer, and they rang in vain.

Meanwhile Mousqueton plodded on, arousing popular curiosity at every step, crossed the Pont Neuf, the two sorry beasts in the van, and reached the Rue aux Ours. Arrived there, following his master's orders, he tied both horse and mule to the knocker of the attorney's door. Then, without worrying about their future, he returned to Porthos to announce that his mission was completed.

In a little while, the two luckless beasts, who had eaten nothing since early morning, created such an uproar by raising the knocker and letting it fall again that the attorney ordered his errand-boy to inquire in the neighborhood to whom this horse and mule belonged.

Madame Coquenard, who of course recognized her gift, could not at first understand the reason for this restitution; but a visit from Porthos speedily enlightened her. The anger that blazed in the musketeer's eyes despite his efforts at self-control terrified his sensitive inamorata. In fact Mousqueton had not concealed from his master that he had met D'Artagnan and Aramis and that in the yellow horse D'Artagnan had recognized the Béarn pony which had brought him to Paris and which he had sold for three crowns.

Porthos left after making an appointment to meet the attorney's wife in the cloister of Saint-Magloire. Seeing Porthos leave the house, the attorney invited him to dinner, an invitation which the musketeer refused with a majestic air.

Madame Coquenard sped trembling toward Saint-Magloire, for she guessed what reproaches awaited her there, but she was also fascinated by her suitor's lordly airs.

All the imprecations and reproaches that a man wounded in his pride and vanity can possibly heap upon a woman's head, Porthos let fall in profusion on the bowed head of Madame Coquenard.

"Alas!" she apologized. "I did it all for the best! One of our clients is a horse-dealer ... he owes money to the office ... he is far behind in his payments ... we cannot collect anything from him ... so I took this mule and this horse for what he owed us ... he swore to me they were fine, thoroughbred steeds...."

"Madame," Porthos said with icy dignity, "if he owed you more than five crowns, your horse-dealer is a thief."

"There is no harm in trying to buy things cheap, Monsieur Porthos," the lady countered, trying to excuse herself.

"No, Madame. But people who are always on the look-out for bargains should permit others to seek more generous friends."

And Porthos, turning on one heel, took one step away from her.

"Monsieur Porthos! Monsieur Porthos!" she cried. "I was wrong, I see it now, I shouldn't have driven a bargain when it came to equiping a cavalier like yourself!"

Without deigning to reply, Porthos took a second step. In her imagination, Madame Attorney saw him in the center of a dazzling cloud, wholly surrounded by duchesses and marchionesses, all of whom cast bags of money at his feet.

"Stop in the name of Heaven, Monsieur Porthos!" she implored. "Stop and let us talk."

"Talking with you brings me misfortune!"

"But tell me, what do you ask of me?"

"Nothing—for that amounts to the same as if I asked you for something."

Madame Coquenard hung on to the musketeer's arm and, in an agony of grief, pleaded:

"Monsieur Porthos, I am ignorant of all such matters. How should I know what a horse is? How do I know about saddles and harness and the rest?"

"You should have left it to me, Madame, because I know very well what they are. But you wished to save your money and consequently to lend at usury."

"It was wrong of me, Monsieur Porthos, I know. But I will repair that wrong, on my word of honor."

"How so?"

"Listen, Monsieur Porthos. This evening Monsieur Coquenard is to visit the Duc de Chaulnes, who has sent for him. It is for a consultation which will last three hours at least. Come, please come. We shall be alone and we can make up our accounts."

"Bravo! Now you are making sense, my dear."

"You have forgiven me?"

"We shall see," said Porthos majestically, and the pair separated saying: "This evening, then?" and "Yes, this evening!"

"A devilish good job!" Porthos mused as he walked away. "Apparently I am getting closer to Maître Coquenard's strong box at last!"

XXXV

AT NIGHT ALL CATS ARE GRAY

That evening, so impatiently anticipated by Porthos and D'Artagnan, at last arrived. As usual D'Artagnan called on Milady at about nine. He found her in a delightful mood; never had he been so well received. A single glanced sufficed to inform him that his note had been delivered and that it had had its effect.

Kitty entered, bringing two glasses of sherbet on a handsome salver. Her mistress smiled on her most graciously but alas! the poor girl was too depressed even to notice Milady's condescension.

As D'Artagnan looked from one woman to the other, he was forced to acknowledge to himself that Nature had blundered when fashioning them: to the great lady she had given a base and venal soul and to the maid, the heart of a duchess.

By ten o'clock Milady seemed restless and fidgety for reasons that D'Artagnan understood perfectly well. She kept eying the clock, rising to her feet, and quickly sitting down again. And she smiled at D'Artagnan as if to say: "You are most *amiable*, to be sure, but you would be *enchanting* if only you would go home!"

D'Artagnan rose and took his hat, Milady offered him her hand to kiss; as he did so he realized that the pressure of her fingers was inspired not by coquetry but by gratitude at his departure. How desperately she must love de Vardes, he thought.

This time Kitty was not waiting for him either in the antechamber or in the corridor or by the main door; D'Artagnan had to make his way alone to the staircase and to Kitty's little room. Opening the door, he found her sitting on her bed, her hands over her face, obviously weeping. Though she heard D'Artagnan enter, she did not look up; when he went up to her and took her hands, she burst into sobs.

D'Artagnan had guessed correctly: Milady received the letter, and in a delirium of joy, told her servant everything. Then, to reward Kitty for executing the commission favorably this time, she gave her a purseful of money. Returning to her own room, Kitty had flung the purse in a corner; it now lay on the floor agape, having disgorged a few gold pieces on the carpet. As D'Artagnan caressed her, the unhappy girl looked up at him. He was alarmed at the change in her countenance as she faced him, clasping her hands in a gesture of supplication, without venturing to speak a word.

However selfish D'Artagnan might be, he was touched by this mute sorrow; but he held too tenaciously to his plans and especially to this particular one to change the programme he had mapped out for himself. He therefore gave Kitty no grounds to hope that she could soften him but represented his action as one of pure vengeance.

The realization of this vengeance now seemed considerably simplified by the fact that Milady, doubtless to conceal her blushes from her lover, had ordered Kitty to extinguish all the lights in the apartment and even in her own room. Just before daybreak Monsieur de Vardes was to make his departure through the darkness.

Presently they heard Milady retire to her room. D'Artagnan slipped into the wardrobe and had hardly crouched down in it when Milady's little silver bell rang. Kitty went to her mistress, closing the door after her, but the partition was so thin that almost everything the two women said was clearly audible.

Milady, who seemed drunk with joy, made Kitty repeat the smallest details of her supposed interview with de Vardes: how had he received the letter, how had he responded, what was the expression on his face, had he appeared to be truly amorous, and the rest. To all these questions poor Kitty, forced to put on a pleasant countenance, replied in a choked voice. But so selfish is happiness that her mistress did not even notice Kitty's doleful accents.

Finally, as the hour of her meeting with de Vardes approached, Milady had all the lights about her extinguished, ordered Kitty back to her own room, and instructed her to introduce de Vardes as soon as he arrived.

Kitty did not have long to wait. The moment D'Artagnan perceived through the keyhole of his wardrobe that the whole apartment was in obscurity, he slipped out from his hiding place just as Kitty was closing the communicating door.

"What is that noise?" Milady demanded.

"It is I," said D'Artagnan, in a low voice. "I, the Comte de Vardes."

"Oh, my God, my God!" Kitty murmured, "he couldn't even bear to wait for the hour he himself had named."

"Well," Milady's voice trembled with desire, "why don't you come in?" Then: "Come in, Comte," she repeated, "you know I await you."

At this appeal, D'Artagnan drew Kitty gently to one side and stole into Milady's chamber.

Rage and sorrow can torture the soul in many ways but the worst way, surely, is when a lover receives under a name which is not his own the declarations of love meant for his fortunate rival. D'Artagnan found himself in a painful situation which he had not foreseen. Jealousy gnawed at his heart; and he suffered almost as much as poor Kitty who at that very moment was weeping bitterly in the adjoining room.

"Oh, Comte, Comte," Milady said in her softest, warmest tone as she pressed his hand in her own, "how happy I am in the love which your glances and words have expressed whenever we have met. I too love you! Tomorrow, yes, tomorrow I must have some token from you which will prove that you are thinking of me. For my part, lest you be tempted to forget me, pray take this, pledge of my abiding love."

With which she slipped a ring from her finger on to D'Artagnan's. D'Artagnan knew this ring well, for he had often seen it on Milady's hand; it was a magnificent sapphire encircled with brilliants. His first reaction was to return it, but Milady refused.

"No, no, keep this ring for love of me. Besides," she added in a voice tremulous with emotion, "by accepting it, you do me a favor greater than you could possibly imagine."

("This woman is replete with mystery," D'Artagnan thought. For a moment he was tempted to reveal everything. He even opened his mouth, prepared to tell Milady who he was and with what a revengeful purpose he had come to her bed.)

"Poor angel!" she continued. "That Gascon monster all but slew you, didn't he?" ("I, a monster?" D'Artagnan wondered.) "Are your wounds still painful?" she concluded.

At loss for an effective answer, D'Artagnan assured her that he was in considerable physical distress.

"Set your mind at rest," Milady murmured, "I myself will avenge you—and cruelly!"

"A pox on it!" D'Artagnan thought. "The moment for confidences has not yet come."

It took D'Artagnan some time to recover from the effects of this brief dialogue, but nevertheless all his plans of immediate vengeance had completely vanished. This woman exerted an unaccountable power over him; he hated her with all the bitterness of offended pride and he loved her with all the fervor of desire unsatisfied. He had never imagined that such conflicting emotions could dwell at once in the same heart and, blending, kindle so strange and so diabolical a lust.

At length the clock struck one, and it was time for him to go. His only feeling as he left Milady was one of sharp regret. Amid the passionate farewells they exchanged, another meeting was appointed for the following week. The luckless Kitty, who had hoped to speak a few words to D'Artagnan when he passed through her chamber, was doomed to disappointment. Milady herself guided him through the darkness and did not leave his side until they reached the staircase.

Next morning D'Artagnan hastened to visit Athos, for, involved in so singular an adventure, he wanted his advice. He therefore told him all. Athos listened without interrupting him but frowned several times in the course of the Gascon's narration.

"Your Milady," he said, "seems to me to be an infamous creature. All the same, you were wrong to deceive her. No matter how you look at it, you have a dangerous enemy on your hands."

As he spoke, Athos looked steadily at the sapphire D'Artagnan wore in place of the Queen's ring, now carefully stored away in a casket.

"I see you are looking at my ring," said the Gascon, proud to show off such an expensive gift.

"Yes. It reminds me of a family heirloom."

"It is beautiful, isn't it?"

"Magnificent! I did not think two sapphires of such water existed. Did you trade your diamond for it?"

"No, it is a gift from my beautiful English mistress—or rather from my beautiful French mistress—for I am convinced she was born in France, though of course I didn't ask her."

"Milady gave you that ring?" Athos gasped.

"Certainly. She gave it to me last night."

"Let me have a look at it."

"With great pleasure," D'Artagnan answered, slipping it off his finger.

Athos examined it carefully and, growing very pale, tried it on the third finger of his left hand; it fitted as though made to order. A shadow of vengeful wrath clouded his usually serene brow.

"It couldn't possibly be the same ring!" Athos murmured. "How could it come into Lady Clark's hands? And how in the world could two jewels look so much alike?"

"You know this ring?"

"I thought I did but I was probably mistaken," Athos replied, handing it back to D'Artagnan but continuing to stare at it. Then after a moment of silence: "Will you please do me a favor?" he asked dully.

D'Artagnan nodded.

"Please take that ring off, D'Artagnan, for my sake. Or else turn the stone around!"

D'Artagnan looked askance.

"You see, it recalls such cruel memories," Athos explained, "that I can scarcely pull myself together to converse with you. Yet you come to ask my advice; you hoped I might tell you what to do." He sighed. "But stop! let me look at that sapphire again. The one I mentioned should have a scratch on one of its faces . . . the result of an accident, I recall . . ."

D'Artagnan again took the ring off his finger and gave it to Athos. Athos started.

"Look," he said sharply, pointing to the scratch he had remembered. "What a coincidence!"

Mystified, D'Artagnan inquired how his friend had ever been in possession of Milady's ring.

"I inherited it from my mother," Athos told him, "and Mother inherited from *her* mother. I told you it was an heirloom, destined never to go out of the hands of our family."

"And you—hm!—you s-s-s-sold it?" D'Artagnan stammered.

"No," said Athos with an enigmatic smile, "I gave it away in a night of love, exactly as it was given to you—in a night of love!"

D'Artagnan in turn lapsed into a pensive silence, speculating what secrets lay deep in the dark mysterious abyss of Milady's heart. Mechanically he took the ring back and slipped it into his pocket. Athos grasped his hand:

"D'Artagnan," he said earnestly, "you know how much you mean to me. Had I a son, I could not cherish him more fervently than I do you. I implore you to follow my advice. For God's sake, give up this woman. To be sure, I do not know her. But a sort of intuition tells me that she is a lost soul and that there is something fatal about her."

"You are right, I will have done with her! Honestly, Athos, she terrifies me!"

"Will you have the courage to break away?"

"Of course I shall. And instantly!"

"Bravo, lad, you will be doing the right thing." Athos pressed the young Gascon's hand with almost paternal affection. "This woman came into your life but yesterday; God grant she leave no terrible traces in it." And Athos nodded dismissal as who would make clear that he wished to be left alone with his thoughts.

When he arrived home, D'Artagnan found Kitty waiting for him. A month of fever could not have ravaged the poor child's countenance more direly than her night of sleeplessness and sorrow. She declared falteringly that her mistress, mad with love and overwhelmed with passion, had dispatched her once again to the Comte de Vardes to ask when this superlative lover would meet her for a second night. Poor Kitty, pale and trembling, awaited D'Artagnan's reply. Thinking it all over—the advice

Athos had given him, the confidence he had in Athos, his pride redeemed, his vengeance satisfied, and finally, the cries of his heart, D'Artagnan was determined to be quit of Milady. Accordingly he penned the following brief missive:

> Do not count upon me to meet you again, Madame. Since my convalescence, I have so many affairs of this sort to settle that I am obliged to regulate them somewhat. When your turn comes again, I shall have the honor to apprize you. Meanwhile, I kiss your hand and remain,
>
> Your Ladyship's most faithful servant,
> de Vardes

Of the sapphire, not one word. Did the Gascon expect to use it as a weapon to be held over her head? Or bluntly, did he keep it to use as a last resource to provide his equipment for the forthcoming campaign?

D'Artagnan showed Kitty what he had written. At first she could not understand; then, after a second reading, his purport dawned upon her. A wild joy coursed through her veins, a tingling happiness she could scarcely bring herself to believe. At her earnest request, D'Artagnan had *viva voce* to renew his written assurances. Despite the danger Kitty ran—given Milady's violent character—she sped blithely back to the Place Royale, fast as her legs could carry her. (Verily, the heart of the kindliest of women is pitiless toward the misery of a rival!)

Milady opened the letter with an expectancy as lively as Kitty's in delivering it; but at the first word she read, she turned livid. Then, furiously, she crushed the paper and, her eyes blazing, demanded:

"What is this?"

"The answer to Milady's letter," Kitty replied, shaking like a leaf.

"Impossible," cried Milady. "Impossible. No gentleman would write such a letter to a woman." Then starting, she cried, "O God!" she cried out. "Can he possibly know—" And she stopped, aghast.

Gnashing her teeth, her face ashen, she tottered toward the window for air. But her strength failed her; she could do no more than stretch out her arms, her legs crumpled, and she collapsed into an armchair. Kitty, fearing she was ill, hastened to her aid. Bending over her mistress, she was about to loose her bodice, when Milady rose fiercely.

"What are you trying to do?" she demanded. "How dare you touch me!"

"I thought Madame was ill," the maid answered, terrified at Milady's savagery. "Forgive me, Madame, I was only trying to help you. I thought you had fainted."

"I, faint? I, ill? Do you take me for a half-woman or a simpering school-girl? When I am insulted, I do not faint and I do not turn ill. No, I seek revenge, do you hear?"

And she motioned to Kitty to leave the room.

XXXVI
DREAMS OF VENGEANCE

That evening—it was a Monday—Milady gave orders that when Monsieur D'Artagnan came as usual, he was to be admitted immediately. But he did not come. Next morning Kitty called again on the young man to report all that had happened the day before. D'Artagnan smiled, for Milady's jealous anger was his revenge.

Tuesday evening Milady was even more impatient than on Monday; she renewed her orders concerning the Gascon, but once again she waited for him in vain.

Wednesday morning, when Kitty stopped in at D'Artagnan's, she was no longer lively and joyous as on the two preceding days, but on the contrary sad as death. D'Artagnan asked the poor girl what was the matter. For all answer she drew a letter from her pocket and handed it to him. It was of course in Milady's handwriting, only this time it was addressed to D'Artagnan not to de Vardes. Opening it, he read:

Dear Monsieur d'Artagnan—
It is wrong of you thus to neglect your friends particularly at the moment when you are about to leave them for so long a time.

My brother-in-law and I expected you yesterday and the day before but in vain.

Will it be the same this evening?

Your very grateful
Lady Clark

"How very simple!" D'Artagnan commented. "Yes, Kitty, I was expecting that letter. My credit rises as that of the Comte de Vardes falls."

"Will you go?" Kitty asked.

"Listen to me, my dear girl," said the Gascon seeking to justify himself in his own eyes for breaking his promise to Athos, "you can understand how impolite it would be not to accept so positive an invitation. If I did not go back, Milady would not understand why I had interrupted my visits. She might suspect something. And who shall say how far a woman of her stamp would go to be revenged?"

"Ah, dear God!" cried Kitty. "You know how to present things in such a way that you are always in the right. You are going to pay court to her again and if you succeed this time in your own name and with your own face, it will be much worse than before."

Instinctively the unhappy girl guessed one part of what was about to happen. D'Artagnan reassured her as best he could, promising her that he would remain adamant before Milady's seductions. He bade her tell her mistress that he was supremely grateful for her kindnesses and that he would be obedient to her orders. (He did not dare write for fear of being unable to disguise his handwriting sufficiently to such experienced eyes as Milady's.)

As nine o'clock struck, D'Artagnan was at the Place Royale. The servants waiting in the antechamber had obviously been warned, for as soon as he appeared, before even he had asked if Milady could receive him, one of them ran to announce him.

"Show the Chevalier in," said Milady in a tone quick and shrill enough for D'Artagnan to hear it in the antechamber. As he was ushered in: "I am at home to nobody," Milady told the lackey. "You understand? To nobody."

The lackey bowed and retired. D'Artagnan cast a quizzical glance at his hostess. She was pale and looked weary; her eyes especially were worn, either from tears or lack of sleep. The number of lights had been purposely diminished but the young woman could not conceal traces of the fever which had wracked her for two days. D'Artagnan advanced with his usual gallantry, at which she made an extraordinary effort to receive him. But never did a more distraught countenance give the lie to a more amiable smile. To D'Artagnan's questions concerning her health:

"I feel poorly," she replied, "very poorly."

"Then I am surely intruding," he said. "No doubt you are in need of rest and I will excuse myself."

"No, no!" she protested. "On the contrary, Monsieur d'Artagnan, do stay. Your agreeable company will divert me."

Observing that she had never been so gracious, D'Artagnan determined to be very much on guard. Indeed Milady assumed her most winning air possible and conversed with utmost brilliancy. At the same time, the fever which had for a moment abated, now returned to give lustre to her eyes, color to her cheeks, and a vermilion glow to her lips. Here once again was the Circe who had woven the spell of her enchantments about D'Artagnan's heart. He had believed that his love for her was dead; it was only dormant and now it awoke within him to sway him with all its passionate ardor. Milady smiled and D'Artagnan was prepared to demand himself for that smile. For a moment he experienced a sort of remorse.

Gradually, Milady became more communicative. She asked D'Artagnan if he had a mistress.

"Alas!" he sighed with the most sentimental air he could summon. "How can you be so cruel as to put such a question to me—to me who from the moment I saw you have breathed and have sighed solely through you and for you?"

"Then you love me?"

"Need I tell you so? Have you not noticed it?"

"Perhaps, who shall tell? But as you know, the prouder a woman's heart is, the more difficult it is to capture."

"Pooh! I am not one to fear difficulties!" D'Artagnan affirmed. "Nothing frightens me save impossibilities."

"Nothing is impossible to true love!" Milady answered.

"Nothing, Madame?"

"Nothing!"

("The Devil!" thought D'Artagnan. "She has changed her tune! Is this fickle and wayward beauty about to fall in love with me, by any chance? Will she be disposed to give the real me another sapphire like the one I got for playing de Vardes?")

Impulsively he drew his chair closer to Milady's.

"Tell me now," she coaxed, "what would you do to prove this love you boast of?"

"Everything that could be required of me. Command me, I am at your service."

"Everything?"

"Everything!" D'Artagnan promised blithely, for he knew he had little to risk in making such a pledge.

"Well then, let us talk it over," she suggested as in her turn she drew her armchair closer to D'Artagnan's chair.

"I am all attention, Madame."

For a moment Milady seemed pensive and undecided; then, as if abruptly coming to a decision:

"I have an enemy," she began.

"You, Madame?" cried D'Artagnan, feigning surprise. "How in Heaven's name is that possible? An enemy—you, good and beautiful as you are?"

"A mortal enemy."

"I cannot believe it."

"An enemy who has insulted me so cruelly that it is war to the death between us. May I reckon upon you as an ally and an auxiliary?"

D'Artagnan immediately understood on what ground the vindictive creature wished to base the argument.

"You may indeed, Madame," he said grandiloquently. "My arm and my life belong to you, as does my love, forever!"

"Ah, since you are as generous as you are loving—"

She stopped.

"Well?"

"Well," Milady continued after a moment of silence, "pray cease from this moment on to talk about impossibilities."

"Oh, do not overwhelm me with happiness," cried D'Artagnan, throwing himself on his knees and showering kisses upon the hands she surrendered to him.

("Avenge me upon that infamous de Vardes," Milady muttered between her teeth, "and I shall easily get rid of you, too, you preposterous moon calf, you animated swordblade!")

("O hypocritical and dangerous woman, throw yourself willingly into my arms after having abused me so brazenly," mused D'Artagnan, "and, when it is over, I shall laugh at you with the man you wish me to kill!")

D'Artagnan raised his head:

"I am ready!" he declared.

"So you have understood me, my good Monsieur D'Artagnan."

"I could read your thought in a single one of your glances."

"And that arm of yours which has already won so much renown—you would employ it on my behalf."

"Instantly, if you command."

"But on part, Monsieur, how am I to repay such a service?" she asked. "I know what lovers are. They never do something for nothing."

"Madame, you know the only reply I crave, the only one worthy of you and me!"

As he drew nearer to her, she scarcely resisted.

"You look to your own advantage," she said, smiling.

D'Artagnan, now really swept away by the passion this woman could so easily arouse within him, gazed ardently at her.

"Ah," he said fervently, "that is because my happiness seems so impossible to me! I yearn to make a reality of it because I fear so much that it may vanish like a dream!"

"All you need do is to merit this pretended happiness."

"I am at your orders, Madame."

"Are you quite certain?" Milady asked with a lingering doubt.

"Name the scoundrel who has brought tears to your beautiful eyes and I—"

"Who told you I had been weeping?"

"It seemed to me, Madame—"

"Such women as I never weep."

"So much the better!" said D'Artagnan. "But come, tell me the villain's name."

"Remember, his name is *my* secret."

"Yet I must know it, Madame."

"Ay, you must know it. See what confidence I have in you."

"You overwhelm me with joy. What is his name?"

"You know him."

"Indeed?"

"Yes."

"Surely it is not one of my friends?" D'Artagnan asked, affecting hesitation in order to confirm her belief in his ignorance.

"Would you hesitate if it were?" Milady demanded, with a threatening gleam in her eye.

"Not if it were my own brother!" D'Artagnan vowed, as though carried away by enthusiasm. Our Gascon assuredly promised this without risk, for he knew exactly what was involved.

"I love your devotedness," Milady told him.

"Alas, is that all? Do you love nothing else in me?"

"Yes, *you*." She took his hand. "I love *you*, too, for *yourself*!"

The burning pressure of her hand made him tremble; her mere touch set him afire, as if that fever which consumed Milady had attacked him and was now blazing through his veins.

"So you love me!" he cried hoarsely. "*You* love *me*! Oh, if that were really so, I would go mad!"

He clasped her in his arms. She made no effort to turn her lips away from his kisses but she did not respond to them. Her lips were cold. It was as if he had embraced a statue. But he was none the less drunk with joy and wild with desire. He almost believed in Milady's tenderness, he almost credited de Vardes with the crime he knew de Vardes had not committed. If at that moment the Comte de Vardes had stood before him, D'Artagnan would have killed him then and there. Milady seized the occasion:

"His—name—is—"

"De Vardes, I know it!"

Milady grasped both his hands, stepped back, and looked deep into his eyes, as though to read into the very depths of his heart. Her gaze brought him back to his senses. He realized that by allowing himself to be carried away, he had blundered.

"Tell me, tell me, I say, *how* do you know it!"

"How do I know it?"

"Yes."

"I know it because yesterday in a salon where I happened to be visiting, Monsieur de Vardes displayed a ring which he said he had received from you."

"The wretch!"

This epithet, quite understandably, re-echoed in D'Artagnan's inmost heart.

"And so—?" Milady challenged.

"And so I will avenge you of this wretch," D'Artagnan boasted, with all the airs of Don Japhet of Armenia.

"Oh, thanks, my brave friend," Milady cried. "I cannot thank you enough. And when shall I be avenged?"

"Tomorrow ... immediately ... when you please...."

About to cry out "Immediately!" Milady checked herself, reflecting that such precipitation was scarcely flattering to D'Artagnan. Besides she had a thousand precautions to take and a thousand counsels to give her champion for he must avoid any argument with de Vardes in the presence of witnesses. Her anxiety was dispelled by D'Artagnan's promise:

"Tomorrow you will be avenged or I shall be dead."

"No, you will avenge me and you will not die because he is a coward."

"A coward with women, perhaps, but not with men; remember, I know something of him."

"And yet in your bout with him, it seems to me fortune smiled on you."

"Fortune is a harlot; favorable to a man yesterday, she may turn her back on him tomorrow."

"Which means that you are beginning to waver?"

"God forbid! But would it be just to send me to a possible death without granting me something more tangible than merely hope?"

Milady answered with a glance which he interpreted as a belittling of the favor and an encouragement to speak out. Then she capped her glance with four tender words of explanation:

"That is only equitable!"

"Oh, you are an angel!" he cried triumphantly.

"Then all is agreed?"

"All save what I ask of you, sweet love."

"But I have assured you that you can rely upon my tenderness."

"I cannot wait until tomorrow."

"Hush, I hear my brother. There is no point in his finding you here."

She rang the bell and Kitty appeared.

"Go out this way," she ordered, opening a small secret door, "and come back at eleven. We will then conclude our conversation. Kitty will show you to my apartment."

The unhappy soubrette almost fainted at these words.

"Well, Mademoiselle, what are you doing, standing there like a statue? Come, show the Chevalier out at once. And this evening at eleven—you heard what I said."

("Apparently all her appointments are set at eleven o'clock," D'Artagnan thought. "It is a settled custom, a sort of tradition!")

Milady held out her hand. Bowing, he kissed it tenderly.

("Now D'Artagnan," he told himself as he retreated with utmost speed from Kitty's reproaches, "you must not play the fool. This woman is undoubtedly an unparalleled criminal. You must take the utmost care!")

XXXVII
Milady's Secret

Despite Kitty's entreaties, instead of going up at once to her chamber, he left the mansion. He did so for two reasons: first, he could thus avoid her reproof, recriminations and prayers; secondly, he was not sorry to read his own thoughts and, if possible, to fathom the thoughts of this woman.

That D'Artagnan loved Milady to the point of madness and that she loved him not at all was crystal clear. It required but an instant's reflection to realize what he had best do. He should go home and write Milady a long letter confessing that he and de Vardes were, up to the present moment, one and the same person, and consequently that he could not undertake to kill de Vardes, short of suicide. On the other hand, a fierce lust for revenge spurred him on; he wished to possess this woman in his own name. The notion of such a vengeance appealed to him as too sweet to forgo.

He paced round the Place Royale five or six times, turning at every ten steps to look at the light shining through the blinds of Milady's apartment. This time, he mused, she was not so anxious to return to her bedroom as she had been after their first tryst.

At length the light went out and with it the last irresolution in D'Artagnan's heart disappeared. Recalling all the details of the first night with a pounding heart and a brain on fire, he returned to the mansion and rushed up to Kitty's chamber.

The poor girl, pale as a ghost and trembling in all her limbs, sought to stop her lover. But Milady, listening for every sound, had heard D'Artagnan enter. She opened her door to him.

"Come in!" she said.

She was so incredibly brazen and so monstrously ruttish that D'Artagnan could scarcely believe his sight or his hearing. It was as if he were being drawn in some fantastic situation as occurs only in the world of dreams. Yet this did not prevent him from rushing up to Milady, drawn to her as inevitably as iron is drawn to a loadstone.

As the door closed behind them, Kitty darted toward it. Jealousy, rage, offended pride, in a word all the passions which dispute the heart of a woman in love, drove her to reveal the hoax. But she realized that she would be utterly lost if she admitted having assisted in such a scheme and, worse, that D'Artagnan would be lost to her forever. This last thought of love counseled her to make one last bitter sacrifice.

As for D'Artagnan, he had attained the sum of all his hopes; it was no longer for his rival's sake that Milady showed him favor; she now seemed to prize him on his own account. Faintly, deep in his heart, a secret voice warned him that she was using him as the tool of her vengeance, to be caressed only until he had dealt the death she craved. But pride, self-conceit and folly silenced the feeble murmur of the voice of reason. Then, our Gascon, with the abundant self-confidence characteristic of him, began to compare himself with de Vardes and to wonder why after all he should not be loved for himself.

The sensations of the moment absorbed him entirely. Milady ceased to be the woman whose fatal intent had for an instant terrified him; now she was an ardent, passionate mistress, abandoning herself utterly to a conjunction in which she herself experienced raptures of delight.

When, two hours later, the transports of the two lovers were somewhat calmed, Milady, who had not the same motives for forgetfulness as D'Artagnan, was the first to come back to reality. Had he already planned exactly how he would bring about a duel with de Vardes on the morrow, she asked.

But D'Artagnan, whose thoughts were following quite another course, foolishly forgot himself and replied gallantly that it was too late at night to consider duels and sword-thrusts.

His cold reception of the only interests which occupied her mind frightened Milady and she began to question him more pressingly. D'Artagnan, who had never given this impossible duel a serious thought, attempted to change the conversation. But this proved impossible; Milady held him fast within the limits determined by her irresistible spirit and her iron will.

D'Artagnan fancied himself very canny in suggesting to Milady she forgive de Vardes and forgo her impetuous plans. But at the first word, the young woman gave a start and moved away from him.

"Are you afraid, perhaps, my dear D'Artagnan?" she asked in a shrill scornful voice which rasped strangely across the darkness.

"You surely cannot think so, dear love. But suppose this poor Comte de Vardes were less guilty than you imagine?"

"At all events, he has deceived me," Milady insisted. "Having deceived me, he deserves death."

"He shall die then, since you condemn him!" D'Artagnan vowed with a firmness that convinced Milady of his unwavering devotion. And she at once returned gratefully to nestle against him.

It would be difficult to say how long the night seemed to Milady, but D'Artagnan would have sworn that it was barely two hours before daylight peeped through the shutters, then darted its pallid, intrusive rays into the chamber. Milady, knowing that D'Artagnan was about to leave her, recalled his promise to avenge her on de Vardes.

"I am quite ready," he assured her. "But first I should like to be certain of one thing."

"Certain of what?"

"Certain that you really love me."

"Have I not given you sufficient proof?"

"Ay, you have, and I am yours, body and soul."

"Thank you, my brave and gallant lover! But as I have just proven my love for you, so you in turn must now prove your love for me. Will you do that?"

"Of course I will. But if you love me as much as you say, why do you entertain no fear for what might happen to me?"

"What could possibly happen to you?"

"Well, I might be dangerously wounded or even killed!"

"Impossible," Milady demurred. "Are you not a valiant man and an expert swordsman?"

D'Artagnan then suggested that she might prefer some means of revenge which, while proving as effective, would not necessitate a duel. Milady gazed at her lover in silence. The wan rays of the early morning light lent her eyes a strange, deadly expression.

"So!" she said disparagingly, "I suppose Monsieur is wavering now?"

"No, I'm not wavering. But honestly, I *do* feel sorry for poor de Vardes since you have ceased to love him. I would say that to lose your love was the supreme punishment and that no other punishment could hurt him more grievously."

"How do you know that I ever loved him?" she asked sharply.

In a warm, caressing tone, D'Artagnan told her that now, without being too fatuous, he felt justified in assuming Milady loved some other, happier cavalier than de Vardes. Nevertheless, he went on, he could not help repeating his concern for the Comte.

"You?"

"Yes, I."

"And why are *you* concerned with de Vardes?"

"Because I alone know—"

"What?"

"—that he is far from being, or rather from having been, as guilty as you think."

"Indeed!" Milady seemed somewhat uneasy. "Pray make yourself clear; I really do not know what you mean." And, locked in D'Artagnan's embrace, she stared up at him, her gaze growing brighter apace. Determined to come to an end:

"Well, *I* am a man of honor," D'Artagnan declared. "Since your love is now mine, and I am sure of it—for I can be sure of it, can I not?"

"Of course, my love is wholly yours. Go on."

"To be honest, I am swept off my feet, and—" he paused, "a confession weighs on my mind."

"A confession!"

"If I felt the slightest doubt of your love, I would not be making this confession. But you love me, my beautiful mistress, do you not?"

"I do!"

"Then if my excessive love for you has made me guilty of offending you, you will forgive me?"

"Perhaps!"

As D'Artagnan, summoning his tenderest and most convincing smile, sought to draw her lips to his, Milady evaded him. Turning very pale, she ordered him to confess at once.

"You invited de Vardes to visit you in this very room last Thursday, I believe."

"No, no, that is not true," Milady dissented with such assurance in her voice and such steadfastness in her expression that D'Artagnan, under different circumstances, would inevitably have believed her.

"Do not lie to me, my beautiful angel!" He smiled. "That would be useless!"

"What do you mean? Speak, speak! You will be the death of me if you do not confess!"

"Pray remain calm, my love, you are not guilty toward me. I have already forgiven you."

"What next, what next?"

"De Vardes cannot boast of anything."

"Why? You yourself told me that the ring—"

"That ring, my love, I have it. The Comte de Vardes of last Thursday night and the D'Artagnan of last night are one and the same person."

The rash young man expected Milady to display a certain surprise, mingled with shame, creating a minor tempest which would resolve itself into a flood of tears. But he was completely mistaken, nor did he have long to wait before he realized his error.

Pale and trembling, Milady sat bolt upright, repulsed of D'Artagnan's attempted embrace with a violent push, and sprang out of bed. It was almost broad daylight. D'Artagnan held her back by her fine India-linen nightdress, imploring her pardon; but with a powerful jerk, she strove to shake herself free. This movement tore the cambric at the neck of her gown, exposing her beautiful, white, exquisitely rounded shoulders. On one of these shoulders D'Artagnan was inexpressibly shocked to see the fleur-de-lis, that indelible flower branded upon criminals by the degrading iron of the royal executioner.

"O God!" D'Artagnan gasped, loosing his hold of her nightgown and falling back on the bed, mute, motionless and frozen. In the look of terror that swept over his face, Milady read her own denunciation. He had seen the worst, he now possessed her secret, that terrible secret she had concealed from all save him. She turned upon him, no longer a furious woman now, but a wounded panther in all its savage lust.

"Ah, wretch, you have betrayed me! You know my secret! You shall die for it." Darting across the room to an inlaid casket on her dressing table, she flung it open with feverish, trembling hand, seized a small dagger with a golden handle and sharp, thin blade, and wheeling round again, threw herself with one bound upon the half-naked D'Artagnan.

Now D'Artagnan was a brave man, as his deeds proved. But he was aghast at her distorted features, her horribly dilated pupils, her livid cheeks and her bleeding red lips. He recoiled toward the space between bed and wall as he would have done before the onset of a serpent crawling toward him. As he moved back, his sword came into contact with his cold, clammy hand; nervously, almost unconsciously, he drew it. Milady, undaunted by the naked blade, tried to climb on to the bed in order to get near enough to stab him; nor did she cease her efforts until she felt the sharp point of his sword at her throat. Then she attempted to seize the blade with her hands, but D'Artagnan kept it free from her grasp, now holding it leveled at her eyes, now at her breast. This manoeuvre enabled him to glide behind the bed, whence he hoped to retreat through the door leading to Kitty's apartment.

Meanwhile Milady continued to rush at him, striking with relentless fury and shrieking like a madwoman. All this was not unlike a duel, so presently D'Artagnan came to his senses and step by step, assumed command of the situation.

"Well, well, beautiful lady!" he taunted her. "For Heaven's sake calm yourself or I shall have to engrave a second fleur-de-lis on one of your lovely cheeks!"

"You wretch! You beast!"

Very gradually D'Artagnan worked his way toward the door ever on the defensive. At the uproar they made, Milady overturning the furniture in her efforts to reach him, D'Artagnan moving it to barricade himself against her, Kitty opened the door. By now D'Artagnan had edged his way to within three feet of it. With one spring, he was in Kitty's room and quick as lightning, he had slammed the door upon Milady. As he leaned against it with all his weight, Kitty promptly shot the bolts and locked it.

With a strength and violence far beyond those of a normal woman, Milady attempted to tear down the doorcase but, finding this impossible, she kept stabbing frenetically at the door as, time after time, the thin blade of her dagger pierced through the woodwork. With every blow, she uttered the most terrible imprecations.

"Quick, Kitty quick!" D'Artagnan whispered behind the locked door. "Help me get out of here! Unless we look sharp, she will have me killed by the servants."

"But you can't go out like that," Kitty objected. "You are stark naked."

"Why, so I am," D'Artagnan exclaimed, realizing for the first time how he was dressed—or rather undressed. "Get me some clothes, any clothes, but hurry, my dear girl, it is a matter of life and death."

Kitty understood this only too well. In a turn of the hand she muffled him up in a flowered robe, a big hood and a cloak and she gave him some slippers to cover his bare feet. Then she ushered him downstairs. It was in the nick of time; Milady had already awakened the whole mansion. The porter had not finished drawing the cord to open the street door when Milady, half-naked too, screamed from her window:

"Porter! Don't let anyone out!"

The young man fled down the street as Milady threatened him with an impotent gesture. When he rounded the corner and vanished, Milady fell back, fainting, into her room.

XXXVIII

HOW ATHOS WITHOUT LIFTING A FINGER
PROCURED HIS EQUIPMENT FOR THE CAMPAIGN

D'Artagnan rushed on, too bewildered to worry about what would happen to Kitty; he dashed across half Paris, and stopped only when he reached the sanctuary he hoped Athos might provide for him in the Rue Férou. His extreme mental confusion, the terror that spurred him, the cries of some patrolmen who started in pursuit of him, and the hooting of passersby, off to work despite the early hour, all combined to make him run the faster.

Crossing the court, he leaped up the two flights to his friend's apartment and at long last came to a halt. Before even catching his breath, he pounded at the door as if to wake the dead. As Grimaud appeared, rubbing his eyes still swollen with sleep, D'Artagnan sprang so violently into the room that he almost overturned the astonished lackey. In spite of Grimaud's disciplined taciturnity, this time the poor lad found his tongue:

"Ho, there, what do you want? What are you doing here, you strumpet?"

D'Artagnan threw off his hood and freed his hands from the folds of the cloak. At the sight of his mustache and naked sword, Grimaud realized that he had to deal with a man and concluded it must be an assassin.

"Help! murder! help!" he shouted.

"Hold your tongue, you idiot!" the young man warned him, "I am D'Artagnan, can't you recognize me? Where is your master?"

"You, Monsieur d'Artagnan? Impossible!"

Athos emerged from his room, clad in a dressing gown.

"Grimaud, did I hear you permitting yourself to speak?"

"But, Monsieur, I—"

"Silence!"

Grimaud contented himself with pointing his finger at D'Artagnan, then gazing askance at his master. Athos recognized D'Artagnan and, phlegmatic though he was, burst into laughter. Certainly he had ample cause to as he contemplated D'Artagnan's amazing masquerade: the hood askew over one shoulder, the petticoat and skirt falling in waves over the slippers, the sleeves tucked up awry, and the mustache bristling with agitation.

"For God's sake, don't laugh, my friend!" D'Artagnan besought him. "Don't laugh, for upon my soul this is no laughing matter."

He uttered the words with such a solemn air and with such genuine terror that Athos at once seized his hand, crying:

"Are you wounded, my friend? How pale you are!"

"No, but something frightful has just happened to me. Are you alone, Athos!"

"Ye Gods, who would you expect to find here at this hour?"

"Good! Good!" And D'Artagnan rushed into the musketeer's bedroom.

After closing the door and bolting it so that they would not be disturbed, Athos turned to the Gascon.

"Come, speak. Is the King dead? Have you killed Monsieur le Cardinal? You seem terribly upset. Come, come, tell me, what happened. I am really very much worried."

Shedding his female garments and emerging in his shirt:

"Athos," D'Artagnan said solemnly, "brace yourself up to hear an unheard-of, an incredible story."

"Slip on this dressing-gown first," Athos suggested. "Then go ahead."

D'Artagnan donned the robe so hastily and was still so agitated that he mistook one sleeve for the other.

"Well?" Athos said inquiringly.

"Well," D'Artagnan replied, bending close to the other's ear and speaking in a whisper, "Milady is branded. She bears a fleur-de-lis upon her shoulder."

"Ah!" groaned the musketeer as though he had been shot through the heart.

"Tell me, Athos," D'Artagnan went on, "are you sure *the other woman* is dead?"

"*The other woman?*" Athos mumbled so low that D'Artagnan barely heard him.

"Yes, the woman you told me about one day at Amiens."

Athos groaned again and buried his head in his hands.

"This woman is twenty-six or twenty-eight," D'Artagnan volunteered. "Blonde, is she not?"

"Yes."

"Light blue eyes of a strange brilliancy with very black eyelids and eyebrows."

"Yes."

"Tall? Slender? Shapely? She has lost a tooth, next to the eyetooth on the left?"

"Exactly!"

"The fleur-de-lis is small, russet in color, somewhat faded by the application of poultices?"

"The brand is faint, yes, Athos."

"But you said she was English."

"They call her Milady, but she might well be French. After all, Lord Winter is only her brother-in-law."

"I must see her, D'Artagnan."

"Beware, Athos, beware; you do not really know her. Remember, you tried to kill her. She is the sort of woman to return the compliment and to succeed where you failed."

Athos objected that one word from Milady would suffice to condemn her, to which D'Artagnan replied that Athos had never seen Milady in a fury ... that Milady was a maniac, a tigress, a panther ... that he had witnessed her rages ... that he had incontrovertible evidence of her cold-blooded threats and plans for murder....

"I am very much afraid," he concluded, "that I have invited a terrible vengeance upon both of us!"

"Right you are," said Athos, "with her after me, my life wouldn't be worth a counterfeit soul. Luckily we leave Paris the day after tomorrow, probably for La Rochelle, and once gone—"

"If she recognizes you," D'Artagnan said darkly, "that woman will follow you to the ends of the earth. Let her vent her vengeance on me alone!"

"What matter if she should kill me, my friend? Do you imagine I set much store by life?"

"Athos, there is something horribly mysterious under all this. She is one of the Cardinal's spies, I am certain."

Athos advised his friend to take great care if such were the case. It was possible that the Cardinal might admire D'Artagnan for his brilliant conduct in the London affair even though that affair balked His Eminence's plans. If not, then surely the Cardinal must detest D'Artagnan with all his being. However, all in all, the Cardinal could not accuse D'Artagnan openly. Yet as hatred must find expression, particularly a Cardinal's hatred, D'Artagnan would do well to be extremely vigilant. If he went out, he should never go out alone: when he ate, he should use every precaution against poison. In short he must mistrust everything, even his own shadow.

"As you said, Athos, fortunately all this will be necessary for only thirty-six hours or so," D'Artagnan commented. "Once with the army, I hope we will have only men to fear."

"Meanwhile I shall renounce my vow of seclusion," Athos declared. "I shall go with you wherever you go. You must now return to the Rue des Fossoyeurs; I shall accompany you."

"I live quite near here, I know, Athos!" D'Artagnan surveyed himself in the mirror. "But I can't very well go like this."

"True!"

Athos rang, unbolted the door, and admitted Grimaud. In sign language he ordered him to go to D'Artagnan's to fetch some clothes: Grimaud, having replied in the same medium that he understood perfectly, departed in silence.

"All this is not helping you gather your campaign outfit," Athos remarked. "Unless I err, you have left your clothes at Milady's. I doubt very much that she will be courteous enough to return them to you. Fortunately you have the sapphire."

"The sapphire is yours, Athos. You told me it was a family heirloom."

"Yes, my grandfather gave two thousand crowns for it, he once told me. It was among his wedding presents to his bride. A fine piece, don't you think? In turn, my mother left it to me and I, fool that I am, instead of preserving it as a holy relic, gave it to that fiend!"

"You must take it back, Athos. I can see what it means to you."

"*I—I* take back that ring after it has passed through the hands of that strumpet! Never. That ring has been defiled."

"Sell it then," D'Artagnan suggested.

"Sell a jewel my mother bequeathed me! How could I bring myself to commit such desecration!"

"Pawn it! You can probably borrow over a thousand crowns on it. That sum should solve your immediate problem. Then, when you are in funds again, you can redeem it. Surely it will have been cleansed of its ancient stains after it has passed through the hands of usurers."

"What a delightful companion you are!" Athos smiled. "Your eternal cheerfulness is manna to those poor souls who walk in the ways of affliction. I agree, let us pawn the ring, but only on one condition."

"What?"

"Five hundred crowns for you, five hundred for me."

"Absurd, Athos! I don't need a quarter of the sum. I'm in the guards; I have but to sell my saddle and I am equipped. What do I need? A horse for Planchet, that's all. Besides, you forget I, too, have a ring."

"A ring to which you apparently attach more value than I do to mine," Athos replied.

"True, for in some crisis it might not only save us from considerable trouble but actually rescue us from grave danger. It is not only a valuable diamond, it is an enchanted talisman."

"I don't understand but I'll take your word for it," Athos remarked indifferently. "But to come back to my ring—or rather yours. If you refuse to accept half the proceeds, I swear I will throw it into the Seine, and, since I am no Polycrates, I doubt whether any obliging fish will bring it back to us!"

"In that case, Athos, I accept."

At that moment, Grimaud returned, flanked by Planchet; the latter, worried about his master and curious to know what had happened to him, had insisted in delivering the clothing personally. D'Artagnan dressed; Athos did the same. When they were ready to go out, Athos struck the attitude of a man taking aim; Grimaud nodded and immediately took down his musketoon from its rack and prepared to follow his master.

They reached the Rue des Fossoyeurs safely but found Bonacieux posted on the doorstep. The haberdasher stared at D'Artagnan and with mock affability:

"Make haste, my dear lodger," he cried, "there's a very pretty girl waiting for you upstairs and you know women don't like to be kept waiting."

It could be only Kitty. D'Artagnan darted down the alley, took the stairs three at a time, and, reaching the landing, found her crouching against his door, trembling hysterically. Before he could say a word:

"You swore to protect me," she sobbed. "You swore to save me from her anger, Monsieur le Chevalier. Remember it was you who ruined me."

"Yes, Kitty dear, I know. But don't worry!" He took her hand in his and stroked it. "What happened after I left?"

"How do I know?" Kitty raised her hands to Heaven. "Milady

screamed . . . the lackeys rushed up . . . she was foaming at the mouth . . . she called you names I have never heard. . . . Then I thought she might remember you had gone through my room into hers and that she would think *I* arranged it. So I took my best clothes and what little money I had and here I am."

"I'm so sorry, Kitty dear. But what shall I do? We leave the day after tomorrow."

"Do what you please, Monsieur le Chevalier. But at least help me to get out of Paris! Help me to get out of France!"

"But I can't take you to the Siege of La Rochelle!"

"No, but you can place me somewhere in the provinces with some lady of your acquaintance. Can't you send me to your home, for instance?"

"Alas, my love, the ladies in my part of the world do without chambermaids. But stop! I think I have a solution! Planchet, go fetch Monsieur Aramis at once; tell him it is a matter of utmost importance."

"I see what you are driving at," Athos declared. "But why not Porthos? His marquise—"

"His marquise is chambermaided by her husband's law clerks," D'Artagnan said laughing. "Besides Kitty doesn't want to live in the Rue aux Ours, do you, Kitty?"

"I don't care where I live, Monsieur, so long as I live in hiding."

"Meanwhile, Kitty, we are about to separate. You're not jealous of me any more, are you?"

"Near or far, Monsieur le Chevalier, I shall always love you."

"Where in God's name will virtue perch next?" Athos muttered cynically.

"I shall always love *you*, Kitty," D'Artagnan assured her. "But before we part, I must ask you something." He paused. "Something very important," he went on. "Tell me, have you ever heard about a young woman who was carried off one night?"

"Let me see . . . oh, yes! . . . Ah God! Monsieur le Chevalier, do you still love that woman . . . ?"

"No, no, no! I don't love her. My friend Monsieur Athos loves her."

"I?" Athos cried like a man who suddenly perceives that he is about to tread on an adder.

"Who else but you?" D'Artagnan insisted with a nudge to make his insistence felt. "You know how much we are all interested in poor little Madame Bonacieux. Besides, Kitty won't give us away, will you, Kitty?"

He looked down at her appealingly. "You see, my child, Madame Bonacieux is the wife of that unspeakable baboon you saw on the doorstep."

"Oh, my God, you remind me of the terror I have been through! Pray
Heaven he didn't recognize me!"

"Recognize you? Have you ever seen him before?"

"Certainly. He came to Milady's twice."

"When?"

"About a fortnight ago, I think."

"And—?"

"And he came again yesterday evening."

"Yesterday evening?"

"Yes, just before you came."

"My dear Athos, we are caught in a network of spies," said D'Artagnan.
Then, turning to Kitty: "Do you believe he recognized you, dear?"

"I pulled down my hood when I saw him, but perhaps it was too late."

"Go down, Athos (he mistrusts you less than he does me) and see if he
is still at the door."

Athos went down and returned at once.

"He is gone," he reported, "and the front door is closed."

"He has gone to report that all the birds are hugging the dovecote."

"Very well then, let us all fly," Athos proposed. "We can leave Planchet
here to bring us news."

"Hold on there! What about Aramis? We sent for him."

"Ah, yes," Athos decided, "we shall have to wait for Aramis."

He had no sooner spoken than Aramis entered. The problem was explained to him in full and he was given to understand he had been elected
to find Kitty a position because of all his high connections. Aramis
reflected a moment, blushed and asked D'Artagnan if it would really be
doing him a favor.

"I shall be grateful to you all my life!" the Gascon vowed.

"Well, then," Aramis went on, "as a matter of fact, Madame de Bois-
Tracy asked the other day if I happened to know of a trusty maid. It was
for a friend of hers who lives in the provinces. So if D'Artagnan can answer for Mademoiselle—"

"Oh, Monsieur, please believe that I shall be absolutely loyal and devoted to the lady who enables me to leave Paris."

"Everything is for the best, then," Aramis concluded as he sat down at the table. He proceeded to write a brief note, to seal it with a ring, and to hand it to Kitty.

"And now, Kitty dear," D'Artagnan said, "you know it is not healthy for any of us to be found here. We must separate. We shall meet again in better days."

"Whenever we meet again and wherever it may be," Kitty answered solemnly, "you will find me loving you as deeply as I do today."

"Dicers' oaths, promises like piecrusts!" Athos muttered as D'Artagnan conducted Kitty downstairs. A moment later the three young men separated, agreeing to meet again at four o'clock under the hospitable roof of Athos. Planchet was left to guard the house. Aramis returned home while Athos and D'Artagnan undertook to pawn the sapphire.

As the Gascon had foreseen, they easily raised three hundred pistoles on the ring. Better still, the pawnbroker begged them to sell it to him, since it would make a magnificent pendant for earrings. Were they willing, he promised them five hundred pistoles.

Active as soldiers are and shrewd as connoisseurs, Athos and D'Artagnan assembled the musketeer's full equipment in barely three hours. Besides, Athos was very easy in his ways and lordly to the tips of his fingers; whenever a thing suited him he paid the price sought, without dreaming of asking for a reduction. In vain D'Artagnan remonstrated; Athos merely put his hand on his shoulder and smiled, at which D'Artagnan understood that a little Gascon squirelet like himself might drive a bargain but not a man so princely in his behavior as Athos. The musketeer found a superb Andalusian horse—about six years old—with jet-black coat, slender and beautifully modeled legs and nostrils of fire. He examined the horse carefully; it was sound and flawless. The asking price was one thousand livres, perhaps Athos might have acquired his mount for less. But while D'Artagnan was bargaining with the dealer, Athos was counting out the money on the table.

For Grimaud, Athos purchased a stout, short, powerful cob from Picardy; it cost three hundred livres. But when the saddle and arms for Grimaud were purchased, Athos had not one sou left out of his hundred and fifty pistoles. D'Artagnan offered his friend a part of his own share of the proceeds; Athos could repay it at leisure. But Athos merely shrugged his shoulders.

"What did the pawnbroker say he would give us if we sold the sapphire?"

"Five hundred pistoles."

"In other words, two hundred pistoles more; a hundred for you, a hundred for me. Why, it's a fortune, my friend! Back to the usurer we go!"

"What? You intend to—"

"That ring would only remind me of very bitter things I prefer to forget," Athos explained, "and anyhow we will never be able to raise three hundred pistoles to redeem it. Thus if we do not sell it, we stand to lose two hundred pistoles!"

"Please think it over carefully, Athos."

"Ready money is at a premium these days," Athos replied sententiously, "and we must all learn to make sacrifices. Go D'Artagnan, go see the pawnbroker and sell the ring; Mousqueton will accompany you with his musketoon."

D'Artagnan returned safe and sound a half-hour later with the two thousand livres.

Thus Athos, by staying at home, discovered resources which he would have sought vainly abroad.

XXXIX

A Vision

At four o'clock the four friends were once more together, Athos playing the host. Their anxiety over their equipment had vanished; the face of each of them now preserved only its own secret worry, for behind all present happiness lurks a vague fear of the future.

Suddenly Planchet entered, bringing two letters addressed to D'Artagnan. The first was a small paper, neatly folded, once only, lengthwise. Obviously a private communication, it was prettily sealed by a blob of green wax, with a dove, olive branch and all, stamped upon it. The other was a large square sheet, resplendent with the fearsome arms of His Eminence Duke and Cardinal. At the sight of the little letter, D'Artagnan's heart beat the faster, for he recognized a handwriting which he had seen only once before but which was indelibly stamped upon his memory. So he took it up first and opening it eagerly read the following:

If you happen to stroll along the road to Chaillot next Thursday evening at seven o'clock, be sure to look carefully into the carriages as they pass.

But if you value your life and the lives of those who love you, do not utter a word or make the slightest gesture indicating that you have recognized the woman who is risking everything in order to see you for but an instant.

There was no signature.

"It is obviously a hoax!" said Athos. "Don't go, D'Artagnan."

"And yet the handwriting looks familiar."

"That note could well be a forgery," Athos countered. "At seven in the evening the Route de Chaillot is utterly deserted. You might just as well go for a canter through the forest of Bondy!"

"What if we *all* went?" D'Artagnan suggested. "Surely they cannot gobble up three musketeers, one guardsman, four lackeys, four horses, weapons, harness and the rest?"

"It will give us a chance to parade our equipment," Porthos offered in support of D'Artagnan's suggestion. Aramis, disagreeing, pointed out that if a woman had actually written the note, and if that woman wished to remain unseen, the presence of the three musketeers would compromise her.

"And that, my dear D'Artagnan," he concluded, "is not the part of a gentleman!"

"We can lag in the background," Porthos argued, "and D'Artagnan can go forward alone."

"A pistol shot is easily fired from a carriage traveling at full speed," Aramis declared sententiously.

"Pooh, they'll probably miss me," D'Artagnan scoffed. "Then we'll overtake the carriage and exterminate its occupants! A good job and good riddance! So many enemies the fewer!"

"Right!" Porthos chimed in. "Let us go into action. Here is a splendid chance to try out our battle arms."

"I am with you," Aramis said in his usual silken and nonchalant manner.

"As you please," was all Athos said.

"It is now half-past four, gentlemen," D'Artagnan announced. "We have scarcely time to be on the road to Chaillot by six."

"Besides," Porthos observed, "if we do not set out immediately, no one will see us. That would be a pity, don't you think? Come, gentlemen, let us be off."

Athos reminded D'Artagnan of the second letter.

"What about *that?*" he challenged. "The seal it bears seems to me to warrant some attention. Or am I wrong? For my part, D'Artagnan, I dare say you might find it worthwhile to open it. I fancy that it is more significant than the note you have just slipped so cunningly over your heart."

D'Artagnan, blushing, said:

"Come, lads, let us see what His Eminence wants of me!"

And he opened the second letter. It read:

Monsieur d'Artagnan, of the Royal Guards, Des Essarts, Company Commander, is expected at the Palais-Cardinal this evening at eight o'clock.

La Houdinière
Captain of Guards

"By God," said Athos, "this appointment is far more serious than the other!"

"I shall attend to these appointments in turn," D'Artagnan answered, "the first at seven, the second at eight; there is plenty of time for both."

"Were I you, I should not go at all," Aramis admonished. "A gallant knight should never decline a rendezvous with a lady. But a prudent gentleman can excuse himself from waiting upon His Eminence, especially when he has reason to believe that he is not invited merely to pay his compliments."

"I agree with Aramis," Porthos declared.

"But gentlemen," D'Artagnan remonstrated. "Once before I received such an invitation, through Monsieur de Cavois, I neglected it and next day I suffered a serious misfortune: Constance disappeared! Whatever may come of it, I shall call on the Cardinal!"

"If your mind is made up," Athos advised, "go ahead!"

"And the Bastille?" Aramis queried.

"Bah! if they lock me up, you will get me out," D'Artagnan said confidently.

"Of course we will," said Aramis, and "Certainly!" cried Porthos with such admirable assurance that to rescue a captive from the Bastille seemed like child's play. Naturally they would get him out of prison, but meanwhile, since they were all to set out for the front two days later, D'Artagnan would be wiser not to risk lodgings in a dungeon.

"I have a better plan," Athos proposed. "Let us stick close to D'Artagnan throughout the evening. Each of us can wait at a gate of the palace with three musketeers behind him; if anyone sees a suspiciously darkened carriage drive out, we and our nine fellow-musketeers can fall upon it. It is a long time since we musketeers have had a skirmish with the Cardinal's guards; Monsieur de Tréville must think us dead of inertia."

"Bravo, Athos!" Aramis applauded. "You were born to be a General of the Army! What about the plan Athos has outlined, gentlemen?"

His listeners registered unanimous approval.

"Good!" Porthos added. "I'm off to the Hôtel de Tréville to warn our friends to stand by at eight o'clock. We will meet at the Place du Palais-Cardinal. Meantime, you can arrange to have our lackeys saddle our horses."

"I have no horse," D'Artagnan observed, "but I shall ask for one at the Hôtel de Tréville."

"Don't bother," said Aramis, "take one of mine."

"One of yours! How many have you then?"

"Three," Aramis confessed, smiling.

"Well, my friend," said Athos, "you are most certainly the best mounted poet throughout the length and breadth of France—not to mention Navarre. Recently acquired! Three horses!" Athos said wonderingly. "What can you possibly do with them? I cannot understand what induced you to buy three horses!"

"I only bought two," Aramis replied.

"And the third?" Athos insisted.

Suavely Aramis told how the third horse had turned up at his lodgings that morning. A groom, out of livery and refusing to divulge his master's name, delivered the animal as ordered.

"Ordered by his master," D'Artagnan insinuated, "or by his mistress?"

"What matter?" said Aramis, blushing. "At all events, the fellow informed me that his mistress had ordered him to place this horse in my stable without telling me whence it came."

"That could happen to none but a poet!" Athos commented sententiously.

"I have an idea!" D'Artagnan proclaimed. "Tell me, Aramis, which of the two horses will you ride: the one you bought or the one that was given to you?"

"The one that was given to me, of course. You understand, D'Artagnan, that I cannot offend—"

"The anonymous donor!" D'Artagnan broke in.

"And who might the mysterious lady be?" Athos asked casually.

"Is the horse you bought useless to you now that you have another from an anonymous donor who may be a mysterious lady?"

"Practically useless," Aramis replied.

"And you yourself chose it?"

"With the greatest care. As you know the safety of a horseman almost always depends upon his horse."

"Splendid!" said D'Artagnan. "Can you let me have him for the price he cost you?"

"My dear D'Artagnan, I was about to suggest you take the horse and settle the bagatelle involved at your convenience."

"How much did you pay?"

"Eight hundred livres."

"Here are forty double pistoles, my friend," said D'Artagnan, producing the requisite sum. "You are paid in coin of the sort for your poems, I trust."

"Then you are really affluent?" Aramis asked, incredulous.

"My dear fellow, I belch gold like Croesus," D'Artagnan answered, jingling the coins in his pocket.

"Send your saddle to the Hôtel de Tréville, D'Artagnan, and they will bring your horse here with ours."

"Good! But it is almost five o'clock. Let us make haste!"

Within fifteen minutes, Porthos, superb in his proud joy, loomed at the end of the Rue Ferou mounted upon a most impressive jennet, Mousqueton in his wake, astride a small but handsome horse bred in Auvergne.

Simultaneously, Aramis appeared at the other end of the street, riding a spanking English charger, Bazin at his heels, on a serviceable roan, with the stout Mecklemburg cob that was to be D'Artagnan's.

The two met at the door; from the window Athos and D'Artagnan observed their meeting.

"A fine mount you have there, Porthos," said Aramis admiringly.

"Ay, it is the one they should have sent to me at first. The husband tried to play a feeble joke on me by substituting that other sorry nag you saw. But he has been punished for it and I have obtained complete satisfaction."

Planchet and Grimaud appeared in turn, leading their masters' steeds. D'Artagnan and Athos left the vantage point of the window, went down into the street, and vaulted into their saddles. Side by side the four companions started off, Athos on the horse he owed to his wife, Aramis on the horse he owed to his mistress, Porthos on the horse he owed to the attorney's lady and D'Artagnan on the horse he owed to his good fortune—the best mistress of all!

The lackeys drew up the rear.

As Porthos expected the cavalcade cut quite a swath; indeed, had Madame Coquenard seen Porthos ride by majestically on his imposing Spanish jennet, she would not have regretted the bleeding she had inflicted upon her husband's strongbox.

Near the Louvre the four friends met Monsieur de Tréville who was returning from Saint-Germain. He stopped them to compliment them on their equipment, whereupon a crowd of idlers and gapers collected about them in an instant. D'Artagnan profited by the circumstance to tell Monsieur de Tréville about the letter with the great red seal and the Cardinal's signet. Needless to say he breathed no word about the other letter. Monsieur de Tréville approved of D'Artagnan's decision, adding that if D'Artagnan failed to appear on the morrow, he himself would undertake to find him, no matter where he might be.

At this moment the clock of La Samaritaine struck six and the four friends, pleading an engagement, took their leave of the Captain of Musketeers.

A lively canter brought them to the Route de Chaillot by twilight. The traffic moved by, to and fro, as D'Artagnan, his friends watching over him from some distance, peered into every carriage as it passed him. But he failed to recognize a single face. At length, after they had waited a quarter of an hour, just as night was falling, a carriage appeared, speeding down the Sévres road. A presentiment told D'Artagnan instantly that this carriage bore the person who had arranged the rendezvous; he himself was astonished to feel his heart beating so violently against his ribs. Suddenly a woman's face appeared at the window, two fingers on her mouth as though to enjoin silence or to blow him a kiss. D'Artagnan uttered a cry of joy. The carriage had passed by, swift as a vision, but the apparition was a woman and the woman was Madame Bonacieux.

Involuntarily and despite the warning given, D'Artagnan spurred his horse into a gallop, overtaking the carriage in a few strides. But he found the window hermetically closed and the vision had vanished.

Then he recalled the injunction: "If you value your life and the lives of those who love you do not utter a word or make the slightest gesture. . . ." He stopped therefore trembling not on his own account but for the poor woman who had obviously exposed herself to danger by arranging for this rendezvous.

The carriage pursued its way at the same swift pace, entered Paris and disappeared. D'Artagnan, dumbfounded, stood rooted to the spot. What was he to think? If it was Madame Bonacieux and if she was returning to Paris, why this fugitive meeting, why this simple exchange of glances, why this lost kiss? If, on the other hand, it was not Madame Bonacieux—a perfectly plausible conjecture, since his eyes might well have mistaken him in the near-darkness—was this not a plot in which his enemies were using for decoy the woman he was known to love?

His three friends joined him. All had clearly distinguished a woman's face at the carriage window, but only Athos knew Madame Bonacieux. According to him, it was certainly she; but as Athos was less intent upon that pretty face, he had, he fancied, seen a man beside her in the carriage.

"In that case," D'Artagnan said, "they are undoubtedly transferring her from one prison to another. But what can they intend to do to the poor girl? And how shall I ever meet her again?"

"My friend," Athos told him gravely, "remember this: it is only the dead whom we are not likely to meet again on earth. You know something about this just as I myself. Well, if your mistress is not dead and if it is she we have just seen, you will meet her again one of these days. And perhaps," he added in a characteristically misanthropic tone, "perhaps sooner than you wish."

They heard the half-hour strike from a belfry nearby; it was seven thirty. His friends reminded D'Artagnan that he had a visit to pay, adding significantly that he still had time to change his mind. But at once headstrong and curious, D'Artagnan was determined to go to the Cardinal's palace. He must at all cost find out what His Eminence had to say to him. Nothing could possibly dissuade him from following his plans.

Soon they were in the Rue Saint-Honoré and presently in the Place du Palais-Cardinal. They found the nine comrades they had summoned to support them. These gentlemen had reported punctually to a man without knowing what was expected of them.

Apprised of the situation, they were delighted to stand by, for D'Artagnan was popular among the Honorable Company of Royal Musketeers. Most of them, knowing he would one day take his place among them, already looked upon him as a comrade. Accordingly the nine supporters assumed their duties, the more cheerfully because they foresaw the probability of doing the Cardinal and his henchmen an ill turn. Expeditions of that sort were always highly welcome.

Athos divided them into three groups, took command of one and assigned the other two respectively to Porthos and Aramis. Each group took its stand in the darkness close to one of the side entrances to the palace. D'Artagnan, for his part, boldly entered through the main gate.

Though he felt himself ably supported, the young Gascon was not wholly at ease as he ascended the great staircase, step by step. His behavior toward Milady had been pretty close to treachery and he strongly suspected the political relations which existed between her and His Eminence. Worse still, de Vardes, whom he had treated so ill, was a henchman of the Cardinal's, and D'Artagnan knew that Richelieu was as passionately attached to his friends as he was implacable toward his enemies.

"If de Vardes has told the Cardinal about our differences, which seems certain, and if he recognized me, which is probable, then I must consider myself practically doomed," D'Artagnan thought. He shook his head ruefully. "But why has he waited till now?" he wondered. Then: "It is all crystal clear, Milady must have complained about me with all the hypocritical grief that makes her so interesting, and this, my latest crime, has made the pot boil over!"

Yet there was some consolation. "Luckily my loyal friends are down yonder," he mused. "They would never allow me to be taken away without a battle royal!" But his confidence was short-lived as he reflected that Monsieur de Tréville's musketeers could not wage a private war against the Cardinal who commanded the armed forces of all France, reduced the Queen to impotence, and crippled the King's will.

"D'Artagnan, my friend, you are brave and you have excellent qualities," he soliloquized, "but women will ruin you in the end!"

Having reached this melancholy conclusion, he entered the antechamber, presented his letter to the usher on duty, was shown into a vestibule and then passed into the interior of the palace. In the vestibule he saw five or six of the Cardinal's guardsmen who recognized him as the man who had wounded Jussac. It seemed to D'Artagnan that they smiled significantly as he went by.

This augured poorly, he thought. But he was not one to be easily intimidated. Or rather, with the colossal pride of a native Gascon, he refused to betray his thoughts when those thoughts were close akin to fear. Smiling, too, he stood smartly up to the Cardinal's guardsmen, his hand on his hip, every inch a gentleman, a soldier and a man.

Returning, the usher motioned to D'Artagnan to follow him. As D'Artagnan did so he thought he heard the Cardinal's guardsmen whispering among themselves. The usher led him down a corridor, across a vast salon and into a library where he found a man seated at a desk, writing. He heard the usher announce him, then bow his way out silently. D'Artagnan stood on the threshold, waiting.

At first he thought he was up against some magistrate who was looking over the record, prior to questioning him. On closer examination, he saw that the man seated at the desk was writing or rather correcting a text with lines of unequal length and counting syllables on his fingers. Here then was a poet!

Suddenly the poet snapped his manuscript within a portfolio whose covers bore the legend:

MIRAME

A Tragedy in Five Acts

It was the Cardinal.

XL

Wherein D'Artagnan Meets His Eminence and Milady Speeds Him Off to War

The Cardinal's elbow rested on his manuscript, his chin rested in the palm of his hand. He looked very intently at the young man. D'Artagnan, marveling at the intensity of this scrutiny, was hard put to it to hide his nervousness. His Eminence's glance was piercing as a drill.

But the Gascon kept a good countenance and stood, hat in hand, awaiting the Cardinal's pleasure without too much assurance or too much humility.

"You are a certain D'Artagnan from Béarn," the Cardinal observed.

"Ay, Monseigneur."

"There are several branches of that family at Tarbes and thereabouts. To which branch do you belong?"

"Monseigneur, I am the son of the D'Artagnan who served in the Wars of Religion under our great King Henry IV of blessed memory."

"Good!" said the Cardinal. "Good!"

There was a silence. Then Richelieu continued:

"You set out from Gascony some seven or eight months ago to try your fortune in the capital?"

"Ay, Monseigneur."

"You passed through Meung where something untoward occurred. I do not know what but there was some sort of trouble—"

"Monseigneur, this is what happened. I—"

"Never mind, young man." The Cardinal smiled as though to show that he could tell the whole story quite as accurately as D'Artagnan if not more accurately. "You were recommended to Monsieur de Tréville, were you not?"

"Yes, Monseigneur, but in the trouble at Meung—"

"Yes, yes, I know, you lost your letter of recommendation. However Monsieur de Tréville being a skilled physiognomist judged you at a glance and arranged for you to join the Royal Guards—"

"Ay, Monseigneur."

"—your commanding officer being Monsieur des Essarts, brother-in-law of Monsieur de Tréville—"

"Yes."

"And you were led to hope that some day or other you might join the Royal Musketeers."

"Monseigneur is perfectly informed," said D'Artagnan, bowing.

"Since then your life has, I believe, been eventful. One day you happened to stroll by the Convent of the Carmes-Deschaux when it would have been healthier for you to be elsewhere. Another day you and your friends journeyed to Forges, doubtless to take the waters; but they stopped en route, whereas you continued. It is all quite simple: you had business in England."

"Monseigneur, I was going—"

"You were going hunting at Windsor, I dare say, or elsewhere. At all events, that is your own business. However, it is my business to know what is going on. I may add that on your return you were received by an august personage. I am happy to see that you wear the keepsake that lady gave you."

Too late D'Artagnan twirled his ring inward to conceal the jewel.

"The following day," His Eminence continued, "you received a visit from Monsieur de Cavois. He invited you to report here but you saw fit to ignore his request."

"Monseigneur—"

"You were wrong; you should have obeyed his summons."

"I feared I had incurred Your Eminence's displeasure."

"Pray why, Monsieur? Could you incur my displeasure for carrying out orders from your superiors with more courage and intelligence than most men would have done? I punish those who fail in obedience, not those who like yourself carry out their orders—all too well! For proof of it I ask you to recall the exact date on which I invited you to call on me. I also ask you to search your memory in order to recall what happened that very evening."

That was the very evening that Madame Bonacieux was abducted. D'Artagnan shuddered, remembering how just half an hour ago the poor woman had passed close to him, doubtless carried off by the same power that had caused her disappearance.

"In fine," the Cardinal continued, "having heard nothing of you for some time, I wished to know what you were doing. Besides you *do* owe me some thanks. You must yourself have noticed how considerately you were treated in all these circumstances."

D'Artagnan bowed respectfully.

"This was done not only in a spirit of sheer equity, but also because of a place which I had in mind for you in the future."

D'Artagnan looked more and more astonished. "I wanted to disclose this plan to you the day you received my first invitation, but you did not come. Fortunately, nothing is lost through this delay and you shall hear my plan now. Sit down there in front of me, Monsieur d'Artagnan; you are too well-born to stand listening to me like a lackey."

The Cardinal pointed to a chair, but the young man was so amazed that he waited for a second sign from the Cardinal before obeying.

"You are a brave man, Monsieur d'Artagnan, but you are also a cautious man, which is even better. I like men of heart—I mean courage, and men of head—I mean tact. But I must warn you that here, on the threshold of your career, you have powerful enemies. Be very careful, Monsieur, or they will destroy you!"

"Alas, Monseigneur, they can readily do so, for they are strong and well supported, whilst I stand alone!"

"True. But however lonely you may be, you have already accomplished a great deal and you will accomplish even more, I am sure. Still I feel you need guidance in the adventurous career you have undertaken, for if I am not mistaken you came to Paris with the lofty ambition of making your fortune?"

"I am young, Monseigneur, my age is that of extravagant optimism."

"Extravagant optimism is pabulum for fools, Monsieur, and you are a man of intelligence. Tell me, what would you say to a commission as ensign in my guards and to a lieutenancy after the campaign?"

"Ah, Monseigneur—"

"You accept, do you not?"

D'Artagnan, deeply embarrassed, could but repeat:

"Ah, Monseigneur!"

"You refuse, then?"

"I serve in His Majesty's Guards, Monseigneur, and I have no reason to be dissatisfied."

"But it seems to me that my guards are also His Majesty's Guards. Any one serving in a French corps serves the King."

"Your Eminence misunderstood me."

"You want an excuse to transfer, is that it? Well, here it is. I offer you promotion; the campaign is about to open; opportunity knocks at your door. So much for the outside world! For yourself personally, you are assured protection in high places." The Cardinal cleared his throat. "You must realize, Monsieur d'Artagnan, that I have received serious complaints against you. It would seem that you do not devote your days and nights exclusively to His Majesty's service."

D'Artagnan blushed.

"Moreover—" the Cardinal placed his hand on a sheaf of papers, "I have here a complete file concerning you. But before reading it I wished to talk to you. I know you to be a man of character and determination. Under guidance your services might lead to the greatest advantages instead of precipitating your ruin. Think it over, young man, and make up your mind."

"Your kindness overwhelms me, Monseigneur; Your Eminence's magnanimity makes me seem mean as an earthworm. But since you permit me to speak frankly—"

D'Artagnan stopped short.

"Certainly; speak out—"

"Then I would presume to say that all my friends serve in either the Royal Musketeers or in the King's Guards ... that all my enemies, by an inconceivable quirk of fortune, are in the service of Your Eminence. ... So that if I accepted your flattering offer, I would be ill regarded among the King's forces and ill received among Your Eminence's."

The Cardinal smiled disdainfully.

"Are you so conceited as to believe my offer does not match your merits?" he asked.

"Monseigneur, you are a hundred times too kind to me. On the contrary, I do not think that I have so far done anything to be worthy of your favors. The siege of La Rochelle is about to open, Monseigneur. I shall be serving under the eyes of Your Eminence. If I am fortunate enough to perform some brilliant action there, I shall feel I have earned the protection with which Your Eminence honors me. All in its good time, Monseigneur. Hereafter perhaps I shall win the right of *giving* myself; today I would seem to be *selling* myself."

The Cardinal glanced shrewdly at D'Artagnan with an expression of annoyance, tempered by a certain reluctant esteem.

"In other words you refuse to serve me, Monsieur."

"Monseigneur—"

"Well, well, keep your freedom then, preserve your sympathies, cherish your hatreds—"

"Monseigneur—"

"I wish you no ill, Monsieur. Remember, though, that we are sufficiently hard put to it to defend and reward our friends; we owe nothing to our enemies. Let me give you a final word of advice: watch your behavior, Monsieur d'Artagnan! The moment I withdraw my protecting hand, I would not give a straw for your life—"

"I shall do my best," the Gascon promised with noble assurance.

Richelieu looked meaningfully at him and stressing his words:

"In the future," he said, "if some mischance should happen to befall you, remember that it was *I* who sought *you* out and that I did what I could to forestall a catastrophe."

"Whatever may happen," D'Artagnan placed his hand to his heart and bowed, "I shall entertain an everlasting gratitude to Your Eminence for what you now do for me."

"Well, then, so be it, Monsieur; we shall meet again after the campaign. Anyhow, I shall keep an eye on you for I shall be at the siege—" he pointed to a magnificent suit of armor which he was to wear, "and on our return, well—we shall take stock of the situation."

"I beg Your Eminence to spare me the burden of your disfavor," D'Artagnan ventured. "Pray remain neutral, Monseigneur, if you find that I act as becomes a true and gallant gentleman."

"Young man, if I can some day repeat what I have said to you today, I promise you I shall do so."

These final words, conveying the grim doubt they did, dismayed D'Artagnan more than any threat could have done. They constituted a warning. The Cardinal was seeking to preserve him from some misfortune which menaced him. D'Artagnan opened his mouth to reply, but with a haughty gesture the Cardinal dismissed him.

D'Artagnan took his leave. At the door his heart almost failed him and he was on the point of returning, but the grave, stern countenance of Athos rose before his eyes. If D'Artagnan made the pact which the Cardinal proposed, Athos would repudiate him, he could never again shake hands with him. The influence of a truly great character being powerful, it was the mere thought of Athos that kept D'Artagnan from retracing his steps.

Taking the stairway by which he had come, D'Artagnan found Athos and his three supporters awaiting his return with considerable apprehension. D'Artagnan reassured them with a word and Planchet ran to inform the other sentinels that it was useless to stand by any longer because his master had emerged from the palace safe and sound.

When the friends were assembled in the Rue Férou, Aramis and Porthos pressed D'Artagnan to explain this curious interview. He contented himself with telling them that Monsieur le Cardinal had sent for him to propose he enter the Cardinal's Guards with the rank of ensign. He hastened to add that he had refused this honor.

"You did well!" said Porthos.

"Bravo!" Aramis commented.

Athos, falling into a brown study, said nothing. But when he was alone with D'Artagnan:

"You did what you should have done, D'Artagnan," he declared. "But perhaps you were wrong, at that!"

D'Artagnan sighed ruefully, for this reasoning corresponded to that of a secret voice within him which told him that great misfortunes lay in store for him.

380 · *Alexandre Dumas*

All next day was spent in preparations for departure. D'Artagnan paid Monsieur de Tréville a farewell call. At the time, the separation of the musketeers and the guards was supposed to be but a temporary measure, since the King was holding his Parliament that very day and proposing to leave on the morrow. Monsieur de Tréville therefore merely asked D'Artagnan whether he could be of any use to him, to which D'Artagnan replied proudly that he was supplied with all he needed.

That night all the comrades of Monsieur des Essarts' guards and of Monsieur de Tréville's musketeers convened to affirm their long-standing friendship. They were parting to meet again if or when it pleased God. As may be imagined, the night proved a boisterous and riotous one. At such times, extreme preoccupation yields to a gay insouciance.

At the first peals of reveille, the friends parted company, the musketeers hastening to the Hôtel de Tréville, the guards to the Hôtel des Essarts. Each Captain then led his company to the Louvre where the King was to hold his review.

His Majesty looked out of sorts and ill, which detracted considerably from his usual proud bearing. Indeed, the day before a fever seized him in the midst of the parliamentary session; but he determined nevertheless to leave that very evening. Despite all remonstrances offered, he also insisted on reviewing his troops; by vigorously defying it, he hoped to master his illness.

The review over, the guards set forward alone, the musketeers standing by to escort the King. This enabled Porthos to pass down the Rue aux Ours in his magnificent equipment.

Madame Attorney, who saw him go by in his new uniform and on his fine steed, loved him far too dearly to allow him to part thus. She motioned him to dismount and to come to her. Porthos was magnificent: his spurs jangled, his breastplate gleamed, his sword clanked proudly against his massive leg. This time the law clerks felt no temptation to laugh: Porthos looked too much like an authentic clipper of ears and ripper of gullets.

The musketeer was ushered into Monsieur Coquenard's presence; the attorney's little gray eyes sparkled with anger as he saw his cousin so handsomely turned out. But there was one consolation: rumor had it that the campaign would be a hard one. He therefore breathed a silent prayer that Porthos might be killed on the field of honor.

Porthos paid his compliments to the attorney and bade him farewell;

the attorney, in return, wished the musketeer all manner of good fortune. As for Madame Coquenard, she could not check her tears. But no one placed a dubious construction on her sorrow; she was known to be much attached to her relatives and she had always quarreled bitterly with her husband on their behalf. The real farewells, however, took place in Madame Coquenard's room and they were heartrending.

As long as Madame Attorney could follow her lover down the street with her eyes, she stood at the window, leaning out so far that she looked for all the world as if she intended to leap out of it. Porthos received all these attentions like a man accustomed to such demonstrations; but on rounding the corner he lifted his hat jauntily and waved it to her in a gesture of farewell.

For his part, Aramis spent his last moments in Paris writing a long letter. To whom? Nobody knew. Kitty, who was to leave next day for Tours, was waiting in the next room.

As for Athos, he found time to sip his last bottle of Spanish wine to the lees.

Meanwhile D'Artagnan was marching off to the front with his company. At the Faubourg Saint-Antoine he turned round to gaze at the Bastille, half in relief, half in amusement. So absorbed was he in surveying it that he failed to notice a blonde blue-eyed lady mounted on a light chestnut horse. At her side stood two evil-looking men. As she pointed to D'Artagnan, they drew up close to the ranks in order to get a good view of him. They stared up at her questioningly; she nodded affirmatively. Then, certain that there could be no misunderstanding about the execution of her orders, Milady set spurs to her horse and disappeared amid the crowd.

The two men then followed Monsieur des Essart's company and, as it debouched from the Faubourg Saint-Antoine, they mounted two horses, fully equipped, which a lackey out of livery held in readiness.

XLI
THE SIEGE OF LA ROCHELLE

The siege of La Rochelle proved to be one of the great political events of the reign of Louis XIII and one of the Cardinal's great military enterprises. It therefore warrants some comment, both for its own sake and because its vicissitudes were intimately connected with the history we have undertaken to relate.

The general political views of the Cardinal when he undertook this siege were far-reaching. There were also specific private views which were probably quite as important to him.

Of the large cities given up by Henry IV to the Huguenots as places of safety there remained only La Rochelle. It became necessary therefore to reduce this last bulwark of Calvinism, a dangerous leaven constantly impregnated by ferments of civil revolt or foreign war. Spaniards, Englishmen, Italians, malcontents and adventurers from every nation, and soldiers of fortune of every sect, flocked under the standard of the Protestants at the first call and were organized in a vast association whose branches spread at will over Europe.

La Rochelle, having gained new importance as a result of the ruin of the other Calvinist cities, was now the focus of dissensions and ambitions of every sort. More, its port was the last port in the kingdom of France still open to the English; by closing it against England, our hereditary enemy, the Cardinal was completing the work of Joan of Arc and of the Duc de Guise.

So intricate and involved were the issues that François de Bassom-pierre, a Protestant by conviction, a Catholic as Commander of the Order of the Holy Ghost, a German by birth and a Frenchman at heart, a virtually autonomous commander at the siege of La Rochelle, could observe to several noblemen, Protestants like himself, as they charged the Huguenot lines:

"Mark my words, gentlemen, we shall be fools enough to capture La Rochelle."

Bassompierre was right. The bombardment of the Ile de Ré foretold the dragonnades that were to crush the Protestants in the Cévennes during the next reign and the capture of La Rochelle prefaced the revocation of the Edict of Nantes.

But against these simplifying and leveling views of a Minister which belong to history, the honest chronicler is in duty bound to recognize the petty aims of an unrequited lover and jealous rival. Richelieu, as everyone knows, had been in love with the Queen. Was his love a mere political expedient? Or was it the natural consequence of some deep passion such as Anne of Austria inspired in many persons with whom she came into contact? The evidence points either way. At all events, the present chronicle has already recorded how Buckingham triumphed over Richelieu and how he did so on two or three occasions—particularly in the affair of the diamond studs—thanks to the devotion of three musketeers and the valor of a Royal Guardsman named D'Artagnan. Ay, Buckingham had fooled the Cardinal cruelly.

Accordingly, Richelieu meant not only to rid France of a public enemy but to avenge himself upon a private rival. This vengeance, moreover, was to be a signal and striking one, worthy in all ways of a man who wields the forces of an entire kingdom much as an expert duelist wields his sword.

Richelieu knew that in fighting England he was fighting Buckingham . . . in triumphing over England he was triumphing over Buckingham . . . and finally in humiliating England in the eyes of Europe he was humiliating Buckingham in the eyes of the Queen. . . .

For his part Buckingham, pretending to maintain the honor of England, was prompted by interest as personal as the Cardinal's but diametrically opposed. Buckingham, too, pursued a private vengeance; unable to return to France as ambassador under any pretext whatever, he determined to return as conqueror. In a word, then, the true stake of this game, which two of the most powerful kingdoms played for the good pleasure of two hapless lovers, was merely a friendly glance from Anne of Austria.

The Duke of Buckingham won the first advantage. Arriving unexpectedly off the Ile de Ré with ninety vessels and some twenty thousand men, he surprised the Comte de Toirac, Royal Governor of the island and, after a bloody struggle, effected a landing. (Incidentally, in the course of this engagement, a certain Baron de Chantal fell on the field of honor, leaving a daughter eighteen months old who was destined to achieve immortality as Madame de Sévigné, the greatest letter-writer of all ages!) The Comte de Toirac withdrew to the citadel of Saint Martin with his garrison and threw a hundred men into a tiny stronghold called the Fort de la Prée.

This event hastened the Cardinal's resolve. It was determined that the King and the Cardinal were to assume personal command. But until this could be done, the Duc d'Orléans, the King's brother, was dispatched to direct preliminary operations and to organize all available troops at the theatre of war. D'Artagnan figured among the earliest units to proceed to the front.

His Majesty was to follow so soon as the parliamentary session was over. On June 23, despite his high fever, the King insisted upon setting forth but his condition grew worse and he was forced to halt at Villeroi.

Wherever the King halted, so did the musketeers. Thus D'Artagnan, a mere guardsman, was separated from his friends; it occasioned him a certain annoyance which would have been an extreme anxiety had he suspected what unknown dangers surrounded him. Nevertheless he reached the camp before La Rochelle on September 10, 1627, to find things at a stalemate. The Duke of Buckingham and his Englishmen were still masters of the Ile de Ré; they were vainly pursuing the siege of the citadel of Saint Martin and of the Fort de la Prée. Hostilities with La Rochelle had started two or three days before, over a fortress newly set up close to the city walls by the Duc d'Angoulême. His Majesty's Guards, under the command of Monsieur des Essarts, took up quarters at the Convent of the Minim Friars. D'Artagnan, intent on transferring to the musketeers, formed few friendships with his own comrades; he was lonely, a prey to his own thoughts.

These thoughts were far from pleasurable. Since his descent upon Paris—now long ago or was it yesterday?—he had been embroiled in public affairs. But his private affairs showed scant progress, whether in his amours or in making of his fortune. As to love, the only woman he craved was Madame Bonacieux and Madame Bonacieux had vanished into thin air.

As for making his fortune, humble though he was, he had made a sworn enemy of the Cardinal before whom even the King trembled. The Cardinal could so easily crush him; and the marvel was that he had not yet done so. In the forbearance of the prelate, D'Artagnan saw a ray of light beckoning toward a more promising future.

There was another enemy, too, less to be feared, perhaps, but not to be dismissed blithely: Milady.

Against this, D'Artagnan had acquired the protection and the friendship of the Queen. But Her Majesty's protection was one more cause for immediate persecution. Of what avail had the Queen's benevolence been for Monsieur de Chalais and, more recently, for Madame Bonacieux?

His clearest gain in all this was the diamond, worth five or six thousand livres, which he sported on his finger. Yet of what use was it at the moment? Suppose he kept it and, in better days, presented it to the Queen as a reminder of the circumstances in which she had given it? Today it was worth no more than the stones he trod underfoot.

The stones he trod underfoot? Ay, for as he meditated D'Artagnan was walking alone down an attractive lane which led from the camp to the village of Angoutin. His musings took him farther afield than he realized; the last feeble rays of the setting sun showed him that he was far beyond the camp limits. Suddenly he started in surprise as he detected what looked like the glitter of a musket barrel behind a hedge to his right. Quick of eye and ready of understanding, he realized that this musket was not planted there of its own volition and that whoever shouldered it was no friend. He therefore decided to take to the open when on his left, behind a rock, he glimpsed the muzzle of another musket.

"I am between the devil and the deep blue sea!" he mused. "An ambush, God help me!"

Looking swiftly at the first musket, he noticed somewhat anxiously that it was being slowly leveled in his direction; then, the moment he saw the muzzle come to a standstill, he threw himself flat on the ground. A shot whizzed by just over his head.

Aware he had no time to lose, D'Artagnan sprang up just in time to miss a bullet from the left, which scattered the gravel on which he had lain a moment before.

Now D'Artagnan was no foolhardy hero who seeks a ridiculous death in order to be acclaimed for refusing to withdraw an inch. Besides, sheer courage was out of the question here; he was trapped and had no means of facing his enemies.

"A third shot and I am done for!" he thought as he took to his heels, darting back to camp at the double, with all the celerity of a Gascon— and Gascons are noted for their nimbleness and wind. Fast though our Gascon sped, the first bandit had reloaded his musket and fired again, this time so accurately that the bullet pierced D'Artagnan's hat and sent it flying ten feet before him. Since D'Artagnan possessed no other headgear, he picked it up on the run, and reached his quarters very pale, out of breath and unnerved. Exhausted, he sat down and began to reflect.

What was this all about, he wondered.

The first and most natural explanation was that the men of La Rochelle had laid an ambush for him. They would not be displeased to kill one of His Majesty's Guards because this would make one enemy the less and because the victim might have a well-lined purse in pocket. (He picked up his hat, examined the bullet hole and shook his head. The bullet came from no musket but from an harquebus. The accuracy of marksmanship proved that the weapon used was no campaign firearm but a special and costly precision weapon. Here was no military ambush, the more so since the bullet was not of regular military caliber.)

A second explanation occurred: perhaps the Cardinal had taken this occasion to remind D'Artagnan of his lively concern for him. D'Artagnan recalled that just as he had sighted the first barrel in the dying rays of the sun, he had been meditating upon the Cardinal's forbearance. (But no, this was no work of the Cardinal's. Why should His Eminence resort to such elaborate means when he had merely to stretch out his hand in order to destroy D'Artagnan?)

There was a third possibility and the likeliest: Milady! (But D'Artagnan sought vainly to recall the features or dress of the murderers; he had escaped so rapidly that he had seen only the two gleaming barrels.)

"Athos, Porthos, Aramis, where are you now, my dear friends?" he murmured. "How sorely I miss you!"

He spent a very bad night, awaking with a start several times; nightmares possessed him and twice at least he imagined he saw a man approaching his bed, dagger in hand. At long last day brought him the comfort of light, but he felt certain that his troubles had been merely postponed. So he spent the whole day in his quarters, persuading himself that he did so only because of the wretched weather.

Two days later at nine o'clock, the drums beat to arms; the Duc d'Orléans was making a surprise inspection. He passed along the front of the line; one by one, the commanding officers approached him to pay their compliments, Monsieur des Essarts among them. Presently D'Artagnan fancied that Monsieur des Essarts was motioning him to step forward, but diffidently he awaited a fresh sign from his superior. As the Captain motioned again, D'Artagnan stepped out of rank and advanced to receive orders.

"The Duc d'Orléans, our Commander-in-Chief, is about to call on volunteers for a special mission," Monsieur des Essarts explained. "It is a dangerous mission but it will bring honor to those who undertake it. I thought you might be interested, Monsieur."

"My deepest thanks, *mon capitaine!*" D'Artagnan bowed. What a stroke of luck! Here was a possibility of distinguishing himself under the eye of the Lieutenant-General.

The Duc d'Orléans explained that the men of La Rochelle had sallied during the night and recaptured a bastion which the Royal Army had taken two days earlier. The point was to ascertain by a desperate reconnaissance how heavily this bastion was manned. Raising his voice, he said:

"I shall need four or five volunteers, Captain, and a dependable man in charge."

"This is the man we need," Monsieur des Essarts answered, pointing to D'Artagnan. "As for the volunteers, Monsieur d'Artagnan has but to make his wishes known and the men will not be wanting."

D'Artagnan turned about face, saluted the ranks, and cried:

"Four men wanted, front and center, to risk being killed with me!"

Two fellow guardsmen sprang forward; two common soldiers joined them, and D'Artagnan accepted the four as escort.

"First come, first served," he told the others who had offered their services.

Whether the sallying forces from La Rochelle, having seized the bastion, evacuated or manned it was not known. D'Artagnan's mission was to draw close enough to the place to report on this score. He set out along the trench with his four companions, the two guards abreast of him, the privates at their heels. Screened by the parapet, they were within sixty yards of the bastion when D'Artagnan, turning around suddenly, noticed that the privates had disappeared.

"We are minus two," he told his fellow-guardsmen. "I suppose they funked it. No matter, gentlemen, let us proceed!"

As they rounded the counterscarp, they were within twenty yards of the bastion. There was no one in sight; the bastion appeared to be deserted.

"A sleeveless errand!" said Guardsman Number One.

"A forlorn hope!" said Guardsman Number Two.

Then, as they were deliberating whether to advance or retreat, suddenly a circle of smoke emerged from the bastion and a dozen bullets whizzed past D'Artagnan and his two comrades.

"We know what's what, eh?" D'Artagnan commented. "That bastion is substantially garrisoned. To stay here any longer is useless. Let us go back!"

And they beat a hasty retreat that might well be termed a flight.

As they reached the corner of the trench which was to serve them as a rampart, one of the guardsmen fell, shot through the chest. The other, unhurt, scampered back to camp. D'Artagnan, unwilling to abandon his wounded comrade, bent over him and sought to raise him to his feet. As he did so, two shots whistled past him, one shattering the head of the wounded guardsman, the other flattening itself against the rock within two inches of D'Artagnan.

The Gascon whirled round. Those shots, he knew, could not have come from the bastion, for the parapet protected him on that side. Was it the two soldiers who had abandoned him? Two soldiers—and two assassins with barrels gleaming through the hedge, right and left, in the last rays of the sun, two days ago? This time D'Artagnan resolved to face the issue and discover whom he was dealing with. He fell over his comrade's corpse as though he too had been shot. Presently he saw two heads rise above an abandoned earthwork some thirty feet away. Obviously they belonged to the two privates who had hung back, then followed him only to try to kill him, trusting that his death might be ascribed to an enemy bullet.

For their part, thinking D'Artagnan might have been only wounded and could therefore return to camp and denounce them, they advanced to make sure and, if necessary, to dispatch him. Fortunately for D'Artagnan, when they saw him topple over, they neglected to reload their guns. When they were within ten paces, he sprang forward, sword in hand. The ruffians understood that they must either dispatch their man and return to camp or go over to the enemy. One of them seized his gun by the barrel and, wielding it as a club, aimed a smart blow at D'Artagnan. D'Artagnan dodged it by leaping aside, but in doing so, left the way clear for the other bandit to make for the bastion. The men of La Rochelle, knowing nothing of the rascal's intentions, opened fire upon him and he fell, his shoulder broken.

Meanwhile D'Artagnan, sword in hand, soon mastered the second soldier, who had only his unloaded harquebus for weapon. D'Artagnan's blade grazed the barrel of the useless firearm and pierced the ruffian's thigh; D'Artagnan then pressed the point of his sword against his throat.

"Spare me, spare me, I beg you!" the ruffian cried. "I promise to tell you all."

"Is your secret worth your life?"

"Ay, Monsieur, if life means anything to as pretty a gentleman as yourself at twenty years of age and handsome and brave into the bargain."

"Speak quickly, swine! Who employed you to murder me?"

"A woman, Monsieur ... I don't know who ... they call her Milady...."

"If you don't know her, how do you know her name?"

"My comrade knew her . . . he called her Milady . . . she made the bargain with him not with me . . . he even has a letter from her in his pocket . . . a letter you would give your eye-teeth to read, so he says. . . ."

"How did you let yourself in for this dirty job?"

"My friend made me an offer and I accepted."

"On what terms?"

"A hundred louis, Monsieur."

D'Artagnan laughed.

"A hundred louis, eh? I see Milady considers me valuable property. A hundred louis! I can see how that sum would tempt a pair of rascals like you." D'Artagnan paused significantly. "Well, I understand how you came to accept such a dirty job and I shall spare your life—but on one condition."

"What, Monsieur?" the man asked anxiously. D'Artagnan's swordpoint, tickling his Adam's apple, convinced him that all was not over.

"You must go fetch me the letter your comrade has in his pocket."

"But that means certain death, Monsieur, death as certain as your sword at my throat! How can I go fetch that letter under fire from the bastion?"

"Take your choice, man. Either you fetch it or you die by my hands."

"Ah, Monsieur, be generous, be merciful. In the name of that young lady you love . . . in the name of the lady you may believe to be dead but who is alive—" He edged away from D'Artagnan's blade, propped himself on one knee in a gesture of supplication, leaning forward, head bowed, weak for loss of blood.

"How do you know there is a young woman I love? How do you know I believed her dead?"

"The letter, Monsieur! The letter my pal has in his pocket."

"I must have that letter!" D'Artagnan insisted. "Come now, no more nonsense. However reluctant I am to soil my sword in the blood of a swine like yourself, I swear by my word as a gentleman—"

With which D'Artagnan made so fierce a gesture that the wounded man arose.

"Mercy, Monsieur, stop, stop!" Terror revived his courage. "I will go, I swear I will, so but you spare me!"

D'Artagnan took the man's harquebus from him and drove him forward, prodding his back with the point of his sword. Slowly the fellow crept on, step by step, leaving a trail of blood behind him, inching his way toward his accomplice at a crawl, lest he be observed from the bastion. D'Artagnan, taking pity on him, said contemptuously:

"By God, man, I will show you the difference between a man of courage and a coward like yourself. Stay where you are; I shall fetch that letter."

And with nimble step, his eye alert for every movement of the enemy, his progress using every accident of the terrain to advantage, the Gascon eventually reached his objective. Here he was faced with two ways of attaining his end. He could either search the corpse on the spot or carry it back, using it as a shield to protect himself and search it in the trench. Deciding in favor of the latter course, he had barely lifted the corpse to his shoulders when the enemy opened fire. A slight shock, the dull thud of three bullets penetrating into human flesh, a final gasp and a shudder of agony proved to D'Artagnan that his would-be assassin had just saved his life. D'Artagnan reached the trench safely and laid the corpse beside the wounded man. Then he went through his pockets. A leather wallet, a purse in which there was evidently a part of the sum he had received, a dice box and a pair of dice—such were the bandit's heirlooms. D'Artagnan left box and dice where they had fallen, tossed the purse to the bandit's confederate and wrenched open the wallet. Among various papers of no importance he came upon the following:

> I regret to hear that you have lost all trace of the woman. She is now safe in a convent which you should never have allowed her to reach.
>
> Try at least to get the man.
>
> If you fail, remember that my hand stretches very far and that you shall pay dearly for the hundred louis I advanced.

There was no signature but the letter was obviously from Milady. Retaining it as evidence and sheltered in his trench, D'Artagnan questioned the wounded man.

"My friend and I, Monsieur," the ruffian admitted, "we undertook a job to carry off a young woman who was meant to leave Paris by the Porte de La Vilette. But we stopped off to drink at a tavern so we missed the carriage by ten minutes and two drinks—"

"What were you told to do with this woman?" D'Artagnan asked, trembling with anguish.

"We were to take her to a mansion in the Place Royale, Monsieur—"

"Yes, yes, to Milady's!" D'Artagnan murmured as the whole pattern became clear to him.

First there was Milady with a lust for vengeance that impelled her to destroy not only him, but all those who loved him. How well informed she was about matters at Court! How easily she had discovered everything! But how could she have done so except through the Cardinal?

But there was also cause for joy. The Queen, having finally discovered the prison in which poor Madame Bonacieux was expiating her loyalty, had set her free from that prison. The mysteries of Madame Bonacieux's letter to D'Artagnan and of her passage along the Chaillot road—a passage more like an apparition—were now crystal clear. As Athos had predicted, there was hope of finding Madame Bonacieux. No convent was impregnable; he had but to discover to what convent the Queen had committed her.

Immensely cheered, D'Artagnan turned to the wounded man who was observing him anxiously. Holding out his arm:

"Come, lad," D'Artagnan urged, "I'll not leave you like this. Take my arm or lean on my shoulder. I'll trundle you back to camp."

"Ay, Monsieur, thank you kindly." The ruffian found it difficult to credit such magnanimity. "Back to camp to have me hanged, eh?"

"No, I give you my word. For the second time, I prefer to save your life."

The other fell to his knees, seeking to kiss the feet of his savior, but D'Artagnan cut short these tokens of gratitude. There was no point in remaining so close to the enemy bastion even in a trench surmounted by a healthy parapet.

As D'Artagnan and the ruffian hobbled into camp they were received with surprise and delight, for the guardsman who had returned safely reported his four comrades as dead.

D'Artagnan explained the ruffian's swordthrust by a sortie, the details of which he improvised with gusto; the other soldier's death he explained quite as glibly. His recital occasioned a veritable triumph for him. For a day the whole army spoke of nothing else and the Duc d'Orléans sent D'Artagnan his personal congratulations.

Any brave exploit bears its own private reward. D'Artagnan's restored to him the peace of mind he had lost. Of the two ruffians sent to murder him, one was dead and the other was now devoted to his interests. D'Artagnan had ample cause to congratulate himself upon his tranquillity—a tranquillity which proved one thing, namely, that he did not yet know Milady.

XLII

Of Anjou Wine and Its Salubrious Virtues

After the most disheartening news of the King's health, reports of his convalescence reached the camp. As His Majesty was very eager to participate personally in the siege it was announced that he would set forth as soon as he could mount a horse. Meanwhile the Duc d'Orléans did very little. He knew he might be removed from his command any day and replaced by either the Duc d'Angoulême or by Bassompierre or Schomberg, rivals for his post. So he wasted day after day wavering and attempting to feel out the enemy. He dared attempt no large scale enterprise to drive the English from the Ile de Ré where they were still laying siege to the citadel of Saint Martin and to the Fort de La Prée just as the French were besieging La Rochelle.

(Speculation ran rife as to the three candidates for the supreme command. There was Charles de Valois, Duc d'Angoulême, the bastard son of King Charles IX of France and Marie Touchet, whom that monarch celebrated in verse. The Duc d'Angoulême was now fifty-two years old. At sixteen he had been named Grand Prior of France; shortly after he had inherited large estates left by Catherine de' Medici and at the age of eighteen he was dispensed from his vows of the order of Malta and was allowed to marry. A Colonel of Horse under Henry IV, he had plotted against the King to force him to abjure the Queen and marry his mistress, the Marquise de Verneuil. Thirty years ago, he had plotted with Spain, been condemned to death, then to perpetual imprisonment in the Bastille where he had spent eleven years. Released in 1616, he had served the crown in various military and diplomatic capacities. Ten years later he was to serve as General of the French Army in Lorraine during the Thirty Years' War.

There was Bassompierre, who was now forty-eight. Twenty years before he had shared in the dissipations of court life under Henry IV; he had also fought in the Savoy campaign and in 1603 in Hungary against the Turks. Six years ago he had supported Louis XIII against the rebel Huguenots on this same field of La Rochelle. In 1630 he was to be a plotter against Richelieu in the famous conspiracy of the Day of Dupes and, like d'Angoulême, he was to spend twelve long years in the Bastille. He was to die at the age of eighty-seven.

The third candidate for the supreme command was Henri de Schomberg, Marshal of France and son of a Marshal of France. He was connected with a German family, several of whose members had fought in the French cause. One indeed had been killed in the service of Henry IV at Ivry.)

D'Artagnan meanwhile had become somewhat more easy, as always happens after a danger has passed and seems to have completely vanished. His only anxiety was at hearing no tidings from his friends. But one morning early in November everything was explained by the following letter, dated from Villeroi:

Monsieur d'Artagnan:
Messieurs Athos, Porthos and Aramis, having dined well at my establishment and being in very high spirits, created such a disturbance that the provost of the château, a very strict man, ordered them confined to quarters for several days. But, carrying out their orders, I am sending you a dozen bottles of my Anjou wine, of which they thought most highly. They hope you will drink to their healths in their favorite wine.

In obeying them, Monsieur, I commend myself to you most respectfully,

Your most humble and obedient servant.
Godeau
Purveyor and Steward to the Musketeers.

"Bravo!" D'Artagnan cried. "They remember me in their pleasures as I remember them in my troubles. I shall most assuredly drink to their healths with all my heart. But I will not drink alone."

And he hastened off to invite two guardsmen, to whom he was closer than the others, to share the light toothsome Anjou wine he had just received. As one of his comrades was engaged that evening and the other one the next day, the meeting was fixed for two days later.

D'Artagnan therefore sent the twelve bottles to the guard's canteen with orders that they be carefully stored. Then on the festive day, as the dinner was to take place at noon, he dispatched Planchet to the canteen at nine o'clock to prepare everything for the entertainment.

Planchet, very proud at being promoted to the dignity of maître d'hôtel, determined to make all necessary arrangements in the most intelligent manner. With this purpose he enlisted the services of the lackey of one of the guests, a lad named Fourreau, and of the cowardly soldier who had attempted to kill D'Artagnan. The convalescent, whose name was Brisemont, belonged to no troop; he therefore entered the service of D'Artagnan or rather of Planchet, serving in fact as a servant's servant.

The hour of the feast arrived. The two guests took their places; the viands were laid out upon the table. Planchet, a napkin folded over his arm, was to serve the guests. Fourreau was uncorking the bottles and Brisemont was decanting the wine which seemed to have acquired a good deal of sediment as a result of the shaking of the journey. The first bottle looked somewhat cloudy at the bottom; Brisemont poured the dregs into a glass which D'Artagnan permitted him to drink, for the poor devil was still very shaky because of his wound.

The guests, having partaken of soup, were about to lift the first glass to their lips when suddenly the cannon of Fort Louis and Fort Neuf fired full blast. The guardsmen, thinking it meant a surprise attack either from the English or from the Huguenots, sprang to their swords. Host and guests sped to their posts. They had barely left the canteen when they discovered the cause of the firing. Cries of "Long live the King!" and "Long live the Cardinal!" rang out from all sides and the drums throughout the camp beat out a salute. The King in his impatience to reach La Rochelle had proceeded by forced marches, arriving at that very moment with his entire household and a reinforcement of ten thousand men, his musketeers preceding and following him. D'Artagnan, lining the route with his company, greeted his friends with a gesture; their eyes soon met his, especially since it was Monsieur de Tréville who first picked him out of the crowd. Then, the parade over, the four friends were reunited.

"God bless us," cried D'Artagnan, "you fellows could not have arrived more opportunely. The food on the table must still be piping hot—" he turned to appeal to the guardsmen, "don't you think so, gentlemen?" Then he presented them to his friends.

"So we are banqueting, eh?" Porthos asked.

"I hope there are no women at your dinner," Aramis observed.

"Is there any drinkable wine in your shanty?" Athos inquired.

"Of course, my dear friends, there is your wine."

"Our wine?" Athos asked in astonishment.

"Yes, the wine you sent me."

"We sent you wine?"

"Yes ... you know ... that little wine from the slopes of Anjou. ..."

"I know the wine you mean," Athos conceded.

"It is the wine you prefer," D'Artagnan insisted.

"Ay, if there is no Champagne or no Chambertin."

"Well, for want of Champagne or Chambertin you will have to put up with it."

"So you sent for Anjou wine!" Porthos approved. "Hats off to the connoisseur!"

"No, this is the wine *you* sent *me*."

"What!" exclaimed Athos. "I sent you no wine. Did you, Aramis—"

"No, Athos!"

"Or you, Porthos?"

"Certainly not."

"Well, anyhow, gentlemen, your steward sent me some wine."

"Our steward?"

"Yes, your steward, Godeau, purveyor to the musketeers."

"Never mind where it comes from," Porthos urged. "Let us taste it; if it is any good, let us drink it."

"No," Athos warned. "Let us drink no wine that comes to us from an unknown source."

"Right, Athos!" D'Artagnan agreed. "But did none of you instruct Godeau to send me wine?"

"Certainly not. Yet you say he sent you some as a present from us?"

"Here is the letter," said D'Artagnan.

"That's not Godeau's handwriting!" Athos declared. "I know his writing because I settled regimental mess accounts before we left."

"An obvious forgery!" Porthos scoffed. "We were never confined to quarters."

Aramis eyed D'Artagnan reproachfully.

"How could you think we created a disturbance?"

D'Artagnan grew pale and shivered.

"*Tu m'effrayes,*" said Athos, using the familiar *tu* of which he was ever sparing. "You frighten me! What on earth is all this about?"

A horrible suspicion crossed D'Artagnan's mind.

"Come, friends," he begged. "Let us go back to the canteen at once and find out whether this is another vengeance on the part of that woman?"

It was now Athos who turned pale as the six comrades made for the canteen. There, the first thing D'Artagnan sighted was Brisemont stretched out on the floor, writhing in horrible convulsions. Planchet and Fourreau, completely at a loss, were ministering to him. But it was quite plain that Brisemont was beyond mortal aid. His features contorted in agony:

"Ha!" he cried, "shame upon you! You pretend to pardon me and now you poison me!"

"What? What's that, you wretch? *I* poison you?"

"*You* gave me the wine . . . *you* told me to drink it . . . you are revenged upon me and I say it is a dastardly act. . . ."

"No, no, Brisemont, do not believe it! I vow, I swear . . ."

"God is above, Monsieur, and He will punish you! May God make you suffer some day just what I am now suffering."

"I swear by the Bible that I had nothing to do with this!" D'Artagnan kneeled over the dying man. "I never suspected the wine was poisoned; I was about to drink it myself, just as you did."

"I don't believe you," the soldier gasped as he expired, writhing.

Athos shook his head ruefully. Porthos busied himself breaking the bottles and spilling the wine, while Aramis gave somewhat belated orders to fetch a confessor.

"Once again you have saved my life, friends—not only my life but the lives of these two gentlemen!" D'Artagnan motioned toward the guardsmen. "Gentlemen," he said, "may I ask you to maintain the deepest silence regarding this whole affair? It may well be that lofty personages have had a hand in the distressing scene you have just witnessed. Were it to be made public, we might all get into considerable trouble."

"Monsieur!" Planchet breathed, more dead than alive, "Monsieur, what a narrow escape I had!"

"What, you rascal! You were going to drink my wine?"

"To the King's health, Monsieur. I was just about to take a token drink when Fourreau told me somebody was calling for me."

"Alas!" Fourreau confessed, his teeth chattering, "I wanted him out of the way so I could drink by myself."

"Gentlemen," D'Artagnan told his fellow guardsmen, "you may readily understand that we cannot continue this banquet. Pray accept my excuses; we will put it off for another day."

The guardsmen bowed and, realizing that the four friends wished to be left alone, withdrew. The door closed upon their guests. Our friends looked at one another gravely, the full impact of the situation suddenly striking them.

"First let us leave this room," Athos suggested. "The dead are not pleasant company particularly when they have died a violent death."

"Planchet," D'Artagnan ordered, "I commit the corpse of this poor wretch to your care. Let him be buried in holy ground. He was a criminal, to be sure, but he repented."

With which the four comrades went out, leaving to Planchet and Four-reau the duty of rendering mortuary honors to Brisemont.

The steward gave them another room, where he served them some boiled eggs; they drank water which Athos in person drew from the well. In a few words, Porthos and Aramis were supplied with full information about what had led up to the present situation.

D'Artagnan turned to Athos.

"As you see, my dear friend, this is war to the death."

Athos nodded.

"I see that quite plainly," Athos agreed. "But do you think it is—er—it is *that* woman!"

"I am certain of it."

"I still have my doubts."

"But that fleur-de-lis on her shoulder?"

"She could easily be an Englishwoman who committed some crime in France and was branded for it."

"No, Athos, it is your wife! Don't you recall how our descriptions tallied?"

"Yes!" Athos stroked his chin. "Still, I should have thought that the other one was dead. I certainly strung her up systematically to that tree!"

It was D'Artagnan's turn to shake his head.

"What are we to do?" he asked.

"Gentlemen, we cannot go on with a sword eternally dangling over our heads," Athos replied. "We must solve this problem."

"But how?"

"Well, D'Artagnan, try to meet her again; discuss things with her; tell her this is a question of peace or war! Give her your word as a gentleman never to say or do anything about her in return for her solemn oath to remain neutral with regard to yourself. Tell her that otherwise you will apply to the Chancellor, to the King, to the public hangman. Tell her you will move the courts against her and denounce her as branded. Tell her that you will have her tried and that if she were miraculously acquitted, you yourself will strike her down as you would a mad dog."

"The idea appeals to me," D'Artagnan confessed. "But how shall I meet her again?"

"By the grace of time, my friend!" Athos explained. "Time is the father of opportunity; opportunity is the martingale of man. The more we have at stake, the more we stand to gain by waiting."

"Yes—but to wait surrounded by assassins and poisoners—?"

"Pooh!" said Athos, "God has preserved us so far, He will preserve us further."

"And, what's more, we are men. After all, to risk ou[...] lot." D'Artagnan paused. "But what of *her*?"

"Her?" Athos looked puzzled. "You mean—"

"Constance, Constance Bonacieux—"

"Madame Bonacieux, of course," Athos sighed. "[...] friend, I had forgotten you were in love."

"Cheer up," Aramis put in. "The letter you fou[...] proves that Madame Bonacieux is alive and in a co[...] tions in our convents are quite comfortable. As so[...] Rochelle is over, I promise you, on my part—"

"Excellent, my dear Aramis!" Athos observed coolly. "We all know your views incline strongly to religion."

"I am only a musketeer ad interim," Aramis said humbly.

"Apparently he has had no word from his mistress for some time," Athos whispered to D'Artagnan. "But never mind that! We know all about it."

"I see no great difficulty," Porthos ventured.

"How do you mean?"

"The lady is in a convent, you say?"

"Yes, Porthos."

"Well, the siege over, we shall take her out of the convent."

"But we still have to know in what convent she is now."

"True!" sighed Porthos.

"I think I have a clue," Athos announced. "Didn't you tell us the Queen chose her convent, D'Artagnan?"

"I think so."

"In that case Porthos can help us," Athos suggested.

"How so, if you please?"

"We can appeal to your marquise, your duchess, your princess. She must have a long arm, Porthos?"

"Hush, man!" Porthos placed a chubby finger on his lips. "I fear she is a cardinalist. She must know nothing of the matter."

"In that case," Aramis spoke up, "I will make myself responsible to find out exactly where Madame Bonacieux is at the present time."

"*You*, Aramis?" D'Artagnan asked.

"What can *you* do?" Athos inquired.

"You!" Porthos echoed.

Aramis blushed.

"I happen to know the Queen's almoner," he explained.

On this assurance, their modest meal finished, the quartet separated, promising to meet again in the evening. D'Artagnan returned to his chores; the three musketeers repaired to Royal Headquarters to prepare their lodging.

XLIII
AT THE SIGN OF THE RED DOVECOTE

Meanwhile the King, who shared the Cardinal's hatred of Buckingham, but with greater cause, was impatient to meet the enemy. He had no sooner reached the front than he wished to begin operations. He therefore ordered all necessary preparations to be made in order first to drive the English from the Isle of Ré and next to press the siege of La Rochelle. But despite all his efforts, he was delayed by dissensions which broke out between Bassompierre and Schomberg on one hand and the Duc d'Angoulême on the other.

Bassompierre and Schomberg, as Marshals of France, claimed their right to command the army under the orders of the King. But the Cardinal, knowing Bassompierre to be a Huguenot at heart, feared that he might not exert himself sufficiently against the English and the men of La Rochelle, his brothers in religion. The Cardinal therefore supported the Duc d'Angoulême whom the King at his instigation had named Lieutenant General. As a result, in order to prevent Bassompierre and Schomberg from deserting the army, a separate command had to be given to each. Bassompierre took up his quarters to the north of the city, between La Leu and Dompierre; the Duc d'Angoulême to the east, from Dompierre to Périgny; and Schomberg to the south, from Périgny to Angoutin.

The quarters of the Duc d'Orléans were at Dompierre; the King's quarters were sometimes at Etré, sometimes at La Jarrie; the Cardinal's quarters were on the dunes, by the bridge of La Pierre, in a simple house without intrenchment of any sort. Thus the Duc d'Orléans could keep an eye on Bassompierre, the King on the Duc d'Angoulême, and the Cardinal on Schomberg. As soon as this organization was established, they all set about driving the English out of the island.

The conjuncture was favorable. The English, who require good fare above all else to fight well, subsisted on salted meat and wretched biscuits. Many of them fell sick. Worse, the sea, very rough at this time of year all along the sea-coast, destroyed some little vessel or other day-in day-out. At every tide the shore from the point of Aiguillon to the trenches was literally strewn with the wrecks of pinnaces, *roberges* and feluccas. Thus even if the French remained quietly intrenched in their camp, it was evident that Buckingham, who was hanging on in the Ile de Ré through sheer obstinacy, must perforce raise the siege soon.

Yet Monsieur de Toirac reported that preparations for a fresh assault were being made in the enemy camp; so King Louis, judging it best to put an end to the whole business, gave the necessary orders for a decisive action.

It is not our intention to give an account of the siege but merely to describe events connected with the tale that we are relating. We need but state that the expedition succeeded, to the vast astonishment of the King and to the greater glory of Monsieur le Cardinal. The English, repulsed foot by foot, beaten in all encounters and crushed in the passage of the Ile de Loix, were forced to sail away, leaving numerous casualties on the field, including five colonels, three lieutenant-colonels, two hundred and fifty captains and twenty gentlemen of rank. Four pieces of cannon fell into the hands of the French; sixty flags, likewise captured, were taken to Paris by Claude de Saint-Simon and suspended amid great pomp under the arches of Nôtre-Dame. Te Deums were chanted in camp and the news spread throughout France.

The Cardinal was now free to carry on the siege without having anything to fear, for the present at least, from the English. But this security proved short-lived indeed.

An envoy of the Duke of Buckingham, Lord Montagu, having been captured, proof was obtained of a league between the Empire, Spain, England and Lorraine. This league was of course directed against France. Further proof was found in Buckingham's quarters which he had been forced to abandon more hurriedly than he expected; these papers confirmed the existence of this league; and, as the Cardinal later asserted in his *Memoirs,* they strongly compromised Madame de Chevreuse and consequently the Queen.

The whole responsibility for meeting this problem fell squarely on the Cardinal's shoulders, for no man can be a despotic minister without incurring vast liabilities. All the resources of his mighty genius were employed night and day in learning and analyzing the vaguest rumors afoot in the great kingdoms of Europe.

The Cardinal was acquainted with Buckingham's activity and more particularly with the hatred Buckingham bore him. If the league which threatened France were to triumph, Richelieu's influence would be at an end; Spanish policy and Austrian policy would have representatives in the Louvre cabinet, where as yet they had only partisans, and he, Richelieu, the French minister, the national minister par excellence, would be ruined. Though the King obeyed him like a child, he detested him too, as a child detests his master. Louis XIII would surely abandon him to the personal vengeance of the Duc d'Orléans and the Queen; Richelieu would then be lost and France perhaps with him. It was imperative that he prepare now against any such eventuality.

And so, in the little house by the bridge of La Pierre that served as Richelieu's headquarters, night and day in rapid succession and in ever-increasing numbers, the couriers arrived, paused and departed on their mysterious errands. There were monks who wore the frock with such an ill grace that obviously they belonged to the church militant... there were women somewhat inconvenienced by their costume as pages and not wholly able to conceal their rounded forms despite the wide trousers they wore... and there were peasants with blackened hands but of noble form who smacked of the man of quality a league off.... There were also other less agreeable visitors, for it was reported that the Cardinal had narrowly escaped assassination two or three times.

Truth to tell, certain enemies of His Eminence accused him of having himself set these bungling assassins to work in order to create justification for reprisals if these became necessary. But statements made by ministers or by their enemies are not always to be credited.

These attempts did not prevent the Cardinal, to whom his most inveterate detractors have never denied personal bravery, from making nocturnal excursions, sometimes to communicate important orders to the Duc d'Angoulême, sometimes to confer with the King, sometimes to interview a messenger he was unwilling to meet at home.

Meanwhile the musketeers, having little to do, were not under strict orders. They led a carefree, joyous life, our three companions in particular. As friends of Monsieur de Tréville, they easily obtained special leave to be absent from camp.

One evening when D'Artagnan, on duty in the trenches, could not accompany them, Athos, Porthos and Aramis, mounted on their steeds and buried in their cloaks, their hands on their pistol-butts, were returning from a tavern called the *Sign of the Red Dovecote*. Athos had discovered it two days before on the La Jarrie road. They were riding home to camp, very much on their guard for fear of an ambuscade, when at about a quarter of a league from the village of Boisnau, they heard the sound of horses approaching. Immediately all three halted, closed in tightly and waited in the middle of the road. A moment later, as the moon broke from behind a cloud, they saw two horsemen at a bend in the road. Perceiving the musketeers, the two strangers stopped in their turn, apparently to deliberate whether they should continue on their way or retreat. This hesitation aroused the suspicion of the musketeers. So Athos, advancing a few paces in front of the others, cried in a firm voice:

"Who goes there?"

"Who goes there, yourselves?" one of the horsemen replied.

"That is no answer," Athos called back. "Who goes there? Answer or we charge."

"Beware of what you are about, gentlemen!" said a clear voice in tones accustomed to command.

"It is some higher officer making his night-rounds," said Athos. "What do you wish, gentlemen?"

"Who are you?" said the same voice in the same commanding tone. "Answer in your turn or you may well repent of your disobedience."

"Royal Musketeers," said Athos, ever more convinced that their questioner had full authority to challenge them.

"What company?"

"Monsieur de Tréville's."

"Advance and give an account of what you are doing here at this hour."

The three companions advanced rather shamefacedly, for all were now certain they had to deal with someone more powerful than themselves. As usual, by tacit agreement, Athos filled the rôle of spokesman.

The horseman who had spoken so authoritatively sat erect and still in his saddle, some ten paces in front of his companion. Athos signaled to Porthos and Aramis to remain in the rear and rode his horse forward at a walk.

"Your pardon, Sir," he said, "but we did not know whom we were speaking to. As you saw we were keeping close watch."

"Your name?" asked the officer, drawing up his cloak to cover his face.

"But yourself, Monsieur," Athos protested, now somewhat annoyed at this inquisition. "I beg you to give me some proof of your right to question me."

"Your name?" the horseman repeated sharply as he drew his cloak down, leaving his face uncovered.

"Monsieur le Cardinal!"

"Your name?" His Eminence cried for the third time.

"Athos."

The Cardinal motioned to his attendant to draw near.

"These three musketeers shall follow us," he said in an undertone. "I do not care to have it known that I left camp. If they follow us, we shall be certain they will tell nobody."

"We are gentlemen, Monseigneur," Athos objected. "Ask us but to give you our word, you need worry no further. Thank God we can keep a secret."

The Cardinal fixed his piercing eyes on his courageous interlocutor.

"You have a sharp ear, Monsieur Athos," he said. "But now listen to this. It is not from mistrust I request you to follow me but for reasons of my personal security. Doubtless the gentlemen accompanying you are Messieurs Porthos and Aramis?"

"Ay, Your Eminence," Athos nodded as his two friends rode forward slowly, hat in hand.

"I know you, gentlemen, I know you!" the Cardinal said. "I am aware that you are not exactly my friends and I am sorry for it. But I am also aware that you are brave, loyal, trustworthy gentlemen. I shall therefore ask you, Monsieur Athos, and your two friends, to do me the honor to accompany me. You will thus be providing me with an escort fit to excite envy in even His Majesty should we chance to meet him."

The three musketeers bowed so low that their chins grazed the necks of their horses.

"Upon my honor," Athos exclaimed, "Your Eminence is right in taking us with you. We saw several ruffian faces on the road and we even had a quarrel at the *Sign of the Red Dovecote* with four of those faces."

"A quarrel? For what reason, gentlemen? You know I do not like quarrels."

"That is exactly why I have the honor to inform Your Eminence of what happened. Otherwise you might learn about it from others, and, on the strength of false witness, believe us to be at fault."

"And how was this quarrel settled?" the Cardinal demanded, knitting his brow.

"My friend Aramis, here, was pinked in the arm. But, as Your Eminence can see, his wound is not serious enough to prevent him from going into action tomorrow, if Your Eminence orders an escalade."

"But surely, gentlemen, you are not the kind of men who blithely allow themselves to be wounded," the Cardinal observed. "Come, be frank with me; I am sure you have settled accounts with somebody. Confess! You know I have the right to give absolution."

"As for me, Monseigneur," Athos explained, "I did not even draw my sword. I took the fellow who offended me round the waist and tossed him out of the window. It appears that in falling," Athos continued with some hesitation, "he broke his thigh."

"Well, well! And you, Monsieur Porthos?"

"Monseigneur, I know that dueling is prohibited. I therefore seized a bench and brought it down on one of the brigands so hard that I fancy his shoulder is broken."

"So!" said the Cardinal in a dulcet ironic tone. "And Monsieur Aramis?"

"For my part, Monseigneur, I am of a very mild disposition. Besides— perhaps Your Eminence is not aware of it—I am about to enter Holy Orders. I endeavored to appease my comrades when one of those rascals dealt me a treacherous swordblow across the left arm. I must admit I lost my patience then, drew my sword and, as he attacked me again, I had the impression that in charging violently he must have run into my sword. I *do* know that he fell and I rather imagine he was conveyed from the scene with his two companions."

"The devil, gentlemen!" grumbled the Cardinal. "Three soldiers placed *hors de combat* in a tavern brawl! I must say you don't do your work by halves! Pray what was the cause of the quarrel?"

"These wretches were drunk," Athos elucidated. "Knowing that a lady had arrived at the inn this evening, they sought to force their way into her room."

"To force their way into her room? For what purpose?"

"Doubtless to have their will of her, Monseigneur," Athos specified. "I have had the honor of informing Your Eminence that these men were drunk."

"What of the lady?" the Cardinal inquired with a certain anxiety. "Was she young and comely?"

"We did not see her, Monseigneur."

"You did not see her? Ah, well! You acted rightly in defending a woman's honor, gentlemen. As I am now myself going to the *Red Dovecote*, I shall find out if you have told me the truth."

"Monseigneur, we are gentlemen," Athos retorted haughtily. "We would not tell a lie even if our heads hung in the balance."

"I do not doubt it for a minute, Monsieur Athos," the Cardinal agreed. Then, changing the conversation:

"Was this lady alone?" he added.

"There was a cavalier closeted with her. Strangely enough, despite the uproar, this cavalier did not show his face. Obviously a coward, Monseigneur!"

" 'Judge not according to the appearance' says the Gospel."

Athos bowed.

"And now, gentlemen, everything is in order," the Cardinal continued, "I know what I wished to know. Follow me."

The three musketeers fell in behind His Eminence who again buried his face in his cloak and started his horse off at a walk, keeping some ten paces ahead of his companions.

Soon they reached the silent, solitary inn. The landlord, doubtless aware of how illustrious the visitor he expected, had got rid of all intruders. Ten paces from the door, the Cardinal signaled to his esquire and the musketeers to halt. A saddled horse stood by the wall, his bridle fastened to the shutter of the window. The Cardinal rapped against the shutter three times, in a peculiar staccato manner.

Immediately a man wrapped deep in a cloak emerged, exchanged a

few rapid words with the Cardinal, climbed into the saddle again and galloped off toward Surgères, along the road that led on to Paris.

"Advance, gentlemen," the Cardinal ordered. Then, turning to the
musketeers: "You have told me the truth, gentlemen, and it will not be my
fault if our encounter this evening does not prove of advantage to you.
Meanwhile, follow me."

The Cardinal dismounted, the musketeers followed suit; the Cardinal
tossed the bridle of his horse to his esquire and the musketeers fastened
their horses to the shutter.

The landlord stood at the door, indicating in no way that the Cardinal
was more than an ordinary officer coming to visit a lady.

"Have you a room on the ground floor where these gentlemen can wait
around a good fire?" the Cardinal asked.

The landlord opened the door of a large room in which an old stove
had recently been replaced by a large and excellent chimney.

"I have this room, Monsieur," he said.

"That will do very well," the Cardinal said. "Come in, gentlemen, and
kindly wait for me here. I shall not be more than half an hour."

As the three musketeers filed in, His Eminence, without more ado, ascended the staircase like a man who did not need to be shown the way.

XLIV

Of the Utility of Stovepipes

It was evident that our three friends, moved only by their chivalrous and
adventurous character, had just rendered a service to somebody whom the
Cardinal honored with his special protection.

But who was this somebody? They puzzled over that question at
length; then, realizing that none of their conjectures was satisfactory,
Porthos called the host and asked for dice.

As Porthos and Aramis sat down at a table and began to play, Athos
paced the room, deep in thought. Moving back and forth, he kept passing
by the broken stovepipe which obviously communicated with the room
above; each time he did so, he could hear a murmur of voices which
finally succeeded in attracting his attention. Drawing closer to the pipe,
Athos distinguished a few words which appeared to him so interesting

that he motioned to his companions to be silent. Then he bent down, his ear glued to the lower end of the pipe.

"I beg you to listen, Milady," the Cardinal was saying, "this matter is highly important. Pray sit down and let us talk."

"Milady!" Athos murmured and winced as he heard a woman's voice replying:

"I am listening to Your Eminence most attentively."

"A small vessel with an English crew, whose captain is at my orders, awaits you at the mouth of the Charente, at the fort of La Pointe. It will sail tomorrow morning."

"I must go there tonight?"

"Instantly—that is, of course, after you have received my instructions. As you leave this house, you will find two men at the door; they will serve as your escorts. You will allow me to leave first; then, half an hour later, you yourself will go."

"I understand, Monseigneur. Now let us come back to the mission you are willing to entrust to me. Since I desire to continue to merit the confidence Your Eminence places in me, I beg you to give me clear and precise instructions. I would not wish to make the slightest mistake."

A moment of deep silence ensued. Clearly the Cardinal was weighing the terms in which he was about to speak; Milady, meanwhile, was steeling all her intellectual faculties in order thoroughly to grasp his orders and to impress them upon her memory.

Profiting by this moment of silence, Athos signaled to his companions to close the door and to join him at his listening-post. Loving their ease as they did, Porthos and Aramis drew up three chairs and the trio sat down; then, their heads close together and their ears cocked, they listened avidly.

"You are to go to London," the Cardinal continued. "Once there, you are to see Buckingham."

"I must remind Your Eminence that the Duke of Buckingham has always suspected me of responsibility in the affair of the diamond studs. His Grace of Buckingham distrusts me."

"This time you need not trouble to gain his confidence. You have but to present yourself frankly and loyally as a negotiator."

"Frankly and loyally?" Milady repeated with an indescribable expression of duplicity.

"Frankly and loyally," the Cardinal echoed evenly: "The present negotiation is to be carried on quite openly."

"I shall follow Monseigneur's instructions to the letter. I await Your Eminence's pleasure; pray tell me what I am to do."

"You will go to Buckingham on my behalf. You will tell him I know of all the preparations that he is making. You will add that I am not uneasy because, at the first move he makes, I shall ruin the Queen."

"Will he believe that Your Eminence is in a position to carry out this threat?"

"Certainly. I have the necessary proofs in hand."

"But I must be able to present these proofs."

"Undoubtedly. Simply tell him that I can publish the reports submitted by Bois-Robert and by the Marquis de Beautru on the Duke's meeting with the Queen at the house of Madame la Connêtable on the evening of Madame le Connêtable's masquerade. To convince him, you will tell him that he attended the fête disguised as the Great Mogul in a costume supposed to be worn by the Chevalier de Guise, purchased from the Chevalier for the sum of three thousand pistoles."

"Very well, Monseigneur."

"You will tell him that I know every detail of his movements the night he entered the palace disguised as an Italian fortune-teller." The Cardinal paused, probably to make sure Milady seized each detail she was to communicate to Buckingham. Apparently satisfied, he went on briskly. "To substantiate this, you will remind him that under his cloak he wore a white robe embroidered with black tears, death's heads and cross-bones."

(By this disguise Buckingham had hoped, in case of surprise, to pass for the ghost of the White Lady who, according to legend, returns to the Louvre whenever some great event is impending.)

"Is that all, Monseigneur?"

"Tell him that I know every detail of the adventure at Amiens. Tell him that I shall have some writer make a charming little novel out of it, wittily turned, illustrated with a map of the garden and portraits of the principal characters in that nocturnal romance."

"I will, Monsieur le Cardinal."

Richelieu further instructed Milady to inform Buckingham that Montagu, the English envoy, was being held in the Bastille . . . that no letters were found upon his person but that torture might easily make him tell what he knew or even what he did not know . . . that Buckingham, in his flight from the Ile de Ré, had neglected to take along a certain letter from Madame de Chevreuse . . . and that this letter thoroughly compromised the Queen, because Her Majesty, beyond loving the King's enemies, had actually plotted with the enemies of France. . . .

"You recollect all I have said," the Cardinal concluded.

"Your Eminence will judge of that," Milady answered. "One, the ball given by Madame la Connêtable; two, the night at the Louvre; three, the evening at Amiens; four, the arrest of Montagu; five, the letter from Madame de Chevreuse."

"That is correct," said the Cardinal, "you have an excellent memory, Milady."

Milady nodded respectfully at the Cardinal's flattery. But, she inquired, what if in spite of all these reasons, the Duke refused to give in and continued to threaten France?

"The Duke is in love with all the ardor of a madman," His Eminence countered with great bitterness, "or rather with all the ardor of a fool! Like the paladins of old, he undertook this war solely to win one glance from the woman he worships. If ever he can be made to realize that this war may cost the lady of his thoughts, as he calls her, her honor and perhaps her liberty, I assure you he will think twice."

"But if he persists?" Milady returned to the charge with a vigor that proved her will to see clearly the end of her mission. "What if he persists?"

"If he persists," the Cardinal paused, then: "That is not likely!" he concluded.

"Yet it is possible, Monseigneur."

"Well then, if he persists—" His Eminence paused again. "Well, in that case, I shall hope for one of those events which change the destinies of nations."

Milady begged His Eminence to quote some such historical event: it might bring her to share his confidence in the future.

"There are plenty of such incidents," the Cardinal replied, "nor have we to look too far back to find them. In 1610, for instance, our own King Henry IV of glorious memory was about to invade both Flanders and Italy in order to attack Austria on both flanks. He was inspired to do so for a cause similar to that which now inspires Buckingham. And what happened?" Milady made no answer. "What saved Austria? One of those historical events!" Still Milady said nothing. "Why should not the present

King of France profit as much today by a lucky accident as the Emperor profited in 1610?"

"Your Eminence refers to the stabbing in the Rue de la Ferronnerie?"

"Exactly."

"But Ravaillac was tortured and mutilated for killing King Henry IV," Milady argued. "His punishment should deter anyone who might dream of following his example."

"In all times and in all countries, particularly in countries torn by religious strife, there are always fanatics who ask nothing better than to become martyrs. Just as Ravaillac killed Henry IV, so Jacques Clément, twenty years before, killed Henry III. Surely England today offers another case in point. Are not the Puritans furious against the Duke of Buckingham? Do not their preachers describe him as Antichrist?"

"Well?"

"Well!" the Cardinal continued in an indifferent tone, "we need but find some beautiful and clever young woman who has personal reasons to take revenge on the Duke. Such women are legion, for the Duke has had many love affairs. If he has fostered many loves by promises of eternal constancy, he must also have inspired as many hatreds by his eternal infidelities."

"Undoubtedly such a woman could be found," Milady replied coldly.

"Such a woman, placing the knife of Jacques Clément or that of Ravaillac in the hands of a fanatic, would save France!"

"Yes, but she would become the accomplice of an assassin."

"Has anyone ever discovered the accomplices of Ravaillac or of Jacques Clément?"

"No, but perhaps they were so high placed that no one dared look for them. It is not everyone who can get the Palais de Justice burned down, Monseigneur."

As though the question were of no importance:

"So you think the fire at the Palais de Justice was not an accident?" Richelieu asked.

"Monseigneur, I do not think anything. I quote an historical fact, no more. I can only add that were I Mademoiselle de Montpensier or Queen Marie de' Médicis, I could afford to be less cautious than I am. But I am merely Lady Clark."

"True. What do you require, then?"

"I require an order ratifying beforehand whatever act I may consider proper for the greatest good of France."

"Ah, but we must first find some woman who wishes to avenge herself upon the Duke of Buckingham."

"She is found," Milady assured him.

"Next, we must find a miserable fanatic willing to serve as an instrument of the justice of God."

"He will be found."

"When that is done, it will be time to write the order you ask for."

"Your Eminence is right," Milady granted, "and I was wrong in seeing in the mission with which you honor me anything but what it actually is. To sum up my instructions, I am to tell His Grace of Buckingham that you know the various disguises he used in order to approach the Queen at the fête given by Madame la Connétable . . . that you have proofs of the interview at the Louvre granted by the Queen to a certain Italian astrologer who was no other than the Duke of Buckingham . . . that you have ordered a very satirical little romance to be written on the adventures at Amiens, along with a map of the garden where the affair took place, and portraits of the actors who figured in it . . . that Montagu is in the Bastille and that torture may make him tell what he remembers and even what he has already forgotten . . . and finally that you possess a certain letter from Madame de Chevreuse, which not only compromises its sender but also its addressee. . . . Then, if he still persists in the face of all this, my mission will have been accomplished and I have but to pray to God to perform a miracle for the salvation of France. That is correct, is it not, Monseigneur? I have nothing else to do?"

"That is correct," the Cardinal agreed.

Without appearing to notice the Cardinal's change of tone and attitude, Milady asked:

"Now that I have received Your Eminence's instructions concerning his enemies, will Monseigneur permit me to say a few words about mine?"

"You have enemies, Milady?"

"Ay, Monseigneur, enemies against whom you owe me all your support, because I made them while serving you."

"Who are they?"

"In the first place, a meddlesome, intriguing little woman called Bonacieux."

"She is in the prison of Mantes."

"That is to say she *was* there," Milady corrected. "But the Queen obtained an order from the King whereby the Bonacieux woman was transferred to a convent."

"To a convent?"

"Ay, to a convent."

"What convent?"

"That, I do not know. The secret has been well guarded."

"But *I* shall find out."

"And Your Eminence will let me know where the woman is?"

"I do not see why not."

"Good! But I have another enemy much more to be dreaded than this little Madame Bonacieux."

"Who?"

"Her lover."

"What is his name?"

"Oh, Your Eminence knows him well," Milady exclaimed carried away by anger, "he is the evil genius of both of us. It was he who in an encounter with Your Eminence's guards decided the victory in favor of the Royal Musketeers . . . who dealt your emissary de Vardes three serious wounds . . . who caused the affair of the diamond studs to fail . . . and who, knowing that I had caused Madame Bonacieux's abduction, has sworn my death. . . ."

"Ah! I know whom you—"

"I mean that scoundrel D'Artagnan."

"He is a bold fellow."

"That makes him the more dangerous."

"I must have a proof of his connection with Buckingham."

"A proof!" cried Milady. "I will furnish Your Eminence with ten!"

"In that case, nothing could be simpler. Give me that proof and I will send him to the Bastille."

"Capital, Monseigneur!" Milady beamed. "But afterward?"

"Once a man is in the Bastille, there is no afterward," said the Cardinal in a hollow voice. "By my faith, if my enemy were as easy to get rid of as yours are, and if it was against such people that you craved impunity—"

"Monseigneur," Milady rejoined, "bargain for bargain, life for life, man for man: give me one, I will give you the other."

"I do not know what you mean nor do I even care to know. But I do wish to be of service to you and I see no objection to granting you what you ask with regard to so insignificant a creature, especially since you say that this paltry fellow D'Artagnan is a libertine, a duelist and a traitor."

"A scoundrel, Monseigneur, an infamous scoundrel."

"Give me paper, a quill and some ink, then."

"Here they are, Monseigneur."

There was a moment of silence; the Cardinal was perhaps thinking of what terms to use or perhaps actually writing the note. Athos, who had lost no word of the conversation, took his companions by the hand and led them to the far end of the room.

"What do you want?" Porthos asked. "And why do you not let us hear the end of the conversation?"

"Hush!" Athos warned. "We have heard all we need to hear. Besides I am not preventing you from listening to the end. But *I* must be off."

"Off where?" Porthos challenged. "And if the Cardinal asks for you, what are we to tell him?"

"Do not wait until he asks for me. Speak before he does. Tell him I have gone on the lookout because the landlord gave me reason to believe that the road is unsafe. I will tell the Cardinal's esquire the same thing. As for the rest, that is my business. Leave it to me and do not worry."

"Be cautious, Athos!" Aramis counseled.

"You may rest easy on that score. You know I am a cool customer!"

Porthos and Aramis returned to their places by the stovepipe.

Meanwhile Athos went out casually, took his horse, which was tied to the shutter with those of his friends, convinced the esquire in a few words of the necessity of a vanguard for the return journey, pointedly examined the priming of his pistol, drew his sword, and, as though following a forlorn hope, took the road leading to the camp.

XLV

HUSBAND AND WIFE

As Athos had foreseen the Cardinal soon came down. Opening the door, he found Porthos dicing furiously with Aramis. He glanced swiftly around the room and found one of the company missing.

"Where is Monsieur Athos?" he inquired.

Porthos explained that Athos, gathering from the landlord's conversation that the road was not entirely safe, had gone out to reconnoitre.

"And what have you been doing, Monsieur Porthos?"

"I have just won five pistoles from Aramis, Monseigneur."

"Well, will you return with me now?"

"We are at your Eminence's orders."

"To the horse then, gentlemen, for it is getting late."

The Cardinal's esquire stood at the door holding His Eminence's horse by the bridle. A few steps away a group of two men and three horses stood waiting in the shadows; they were to escort Milady to the Fort de La Pointe and see her safely aboard ship. The esquire confirmed what the musketeers had told the Cardinal about Athos; His Eminence nodded in approval and retraced his route with the same precautions he had employed in coming.

As for Athos, he had ridden off at an even clip until he was out of sight; then, turning to the right, he had described a circle and returned within twenty paces of a tall hedge whence he heard the Cardinal and his little troop make off. He actually caught a glimpse of the gold-laced hats of his companions and of the Cardinal's gold-fringed coat. When the horsemen had rounded the corner of the road Athos galloped back to the inn.

The landlord recognized him.

"My Commanding Officer forgot to give the lady an important piece of news," he explained. "I mean the lady on the first floor. He sent me back to—"

"Walk right up, Monsieur, the lady is still here."

Availing himself of the permission, Athos climbed the stairs blithely and from the landing, through the open door, saw Milady putting on her hat. Crossing the threshold, he closed the door behind him and bolted it; at the sound, Milady turned back to face him. He stood before her, wrapped in his cloak, his hat pulled over his eyes. Seeing this figure silent and motionless as a statue, Milady was frightened.

"Who are you," she demanded, "and what do you want?"

"Yes, yes!" said Athos and slipping out of his cloak and removing his hat as he strode toward Milady, "You are certainly the woman I am looking for. Do you recognize me, Madame?"

Milady took one step forward, then drew back as though a snake lay in her path.

"So far so good!" Athos went on. "I see you know who I am."

"The Comte de La Fère!" Milady murmured, turning pale and recoiling step by step to the wall.

"Yes, Milady, the Comte de La Fère in person. He has come expressly from the other world in order to enjoy the pleasure of seeing you again. Let us sit down and talk, as the Cardinal says."

Milady, a prey to indescribable terror, sat down without uttering a word.

"Truly you are a demon sent to plague this earth!" Athos said calmly. "Your power is great I know; but *you* know that with God's help, men have often vanquished the most terrible of demons. Once before, Madame, you crossed my path and I thought I had felled you; but either I was mistaken or Hell has resuscitated you."

Milady bowed her head, groaning.

"Ay, Hell has resuscitated you, Hell has made you rich, Hell has given you another name, Hell has almost lent you another countenance. But it has effaced neither the stains upon your soul nor the brand upon your body."

Milady sprang up as though loosed by a powerful spring. Her eyes flashed lightning. Athos did not turn a hair.

"You thought me dead, did you not, just as *I* thought *you* dead? The name of Athos concealed the Comte de La Fère just as that of Lady Clark concealed that of Anne de Bueil. It was under that name that your honorable brother married us, was it not? Our position is truly a strange one!" Athos laughed wryly. "We have gone on living only because each of us believed the other dead, and because a memory, however torturous, is less oppressive than a living creature."

"Tell me, Monsieur," Milady said in a faint, hollow voice, "what brings you back to me? What do you want?"

"First, I must inform you that while I have remained out of your sight, I have kept an eye on you."

"You know what has happened to me?"

"I can tell you what you have been doing, day by day ever since you entered the service of the Cardinal."

A smile of incredulity fluttered across Milady's pallid lips.

"So you doubt me, eh?" Athos smiled ironically. "Well, listen carefully, Milady. I know it was you who cut off the two diamond studs from the shoulder of the Duke of Buckingham ... it was you who contrived the abduction of Madame Bonacieux ... it was you who, in love with de Vardes and thinking to spend the night with him, opened your door and bed to Monsieur d'Artagnan ... it was you who, believing de Vardes had deceived you, tried to have him killed by his rival ... when this rival discovered your infamous secret, it was you who sought to have him killed by two murderers you sent in pursuit ... when the bullets missed him, it was you who attempted to poison him by means of a case of Anjou wine and a forged letter ... and it was you who a few moments ago sat in this chair I now occupy and promised the Cardinal to murder the Duke of Buckingham in exchange for his permission to let you assassinate D'Artagnan. ...."

Milady turned livid.

"You must be Satan!" she murmured.

"Possibly I am," Athos replied jauntily, "but Satan or not, let me tell you this: you may murder Buckingham or have him murdered, it is all one to me. I do not know His Grace and anyhow he is an Englishman. But if you lay one finger on one hair of D'Artagnan's head, I swear by God and by the memory of my father that it will be your last gesture."

"But, Monsieur—"

"There are no buts."

"But Monsieur d'Artagnan offended me cruelly," Milady objected in low, throaty tones. "Monsieur d'Artagnan shall die."

"Is it really possible to offend you, Madame?" he asked. "So my friend 'offended' you and must pay for it with his life?"

"Exactly. First your friend, then the Bonacieux creature."

Athos felt his head spinning. The sight of this beautiful woman, a monster at heart, filled him with loathing. Memories of her fascination and villainy rose within him. He recalled how in less dangerous times he had once wished to sacrifice her to his honor. Suddenly his desire to destroy her coursed feverishly through him; he rose, drew a pistol from his belt and cocked it carefully. Milady, pale as a corpse, tried to cry out but her swollen tongue failed her. Hoarsely she groaned like a wild beast. Standing immobile, etched against the dark tapestry, her hair disheveled, she looked for all the world like the incarnation of terror. Slowly Athos raised his pistol, stretched out his arm so that the weapon almost touched Milady's forehead and in a voice the more terrible because so calm and so resolute:

"Madame," he said, "you will this instant give me the paper the Cardinal signed or upon my soul I will blow your brains out."

With any other man Milady might have preserved some doubt, attempted to parley or tried to evade the issue. With Athos she knew this was useless. Yet she stood motionless.

"Madame," Athos warned, "you have exactly five seconds in which to make up your mind."

By his frown and the contraction of his features Milady knew that he was in deadly earnest. One second—two—three—and she reached quickly into her bosom, drew out a paper and handed it to Athos.

"Here it is," she snarled, "and be damned to you!"

Athos took the paper, restored the pistol to his belt, drew up the lamp to make sure it was the proper document, and read:

December third, 1627
It is by my order and for the service of the State that the bearer of this note has done what he has done.
 Signed by my hand at the Camp of La Rochelle

             Richelieu

Satisfied, Athos put on his cloak again, crammed his hat on his head and without vouchsafing her a glance:

"Farewell, viper," he said. "I have at last drawn your teeth; bite me if you can."

At the door, he found the two men Richelieu had appointed to escort Milady.

"Gentlemen," he said, "you know the orders His Eminence gave you. You are to convey this woman forthwith to the Fort de La Pointe without leaving her out of your sight until she is safely embarked."

As this agreed perfectly with their previous instructions, the pair bowed. Athos swung into his saddle and galloped down the road but when out of sight turned across country, pausing every now and then to listen. Presently he heard the sound of hoofs on the road and, certain it was the Cardinal and his escort, he wisped his horse down with heather and leaves and suddenly appeared on the highway two hundred yards from the camp.

"Who goes there?" he challenged as the horsemen advanced.

"That must be our gallant musketeer," said the Cardinal.

"Ay, Monseigneur, at your service."

"Monsieur Athos, my thanks for your assuring my security," the Cardinal said. "And thank you, too, gentlemen," he said to the others. "We are home safe and sound. Take the gate on the left, my friends. The password is *Roi et Rè*. Goodnight and thanks again."

His Eminence was no sooner out of earshot than Porthos inquired: "The Cardinal signed her paper, eh?"

And Aramis:

"What happened?"

"I have the paper," Athos told them. His taciturnity prevailed upon them; no word was exchanged save the watchword as the three friends were challenged by sentries. Reaching their quarters, they dispatched Mousqueton with orders to invite D'Artagnan to call on them next day.

Meanwhile, as Athos had foreseen, Milady found her escort and made no difficulty in following. For an instant she had felt inclined to ask to be conducted back to the Cardinal and to report all that had happened. But she quickly realized that any revelation on her part would bring about a revelation on the part of Athos. She might tell how Athos had hanged her but then he would tell that she was branded. It was best to preserve silence, she decided, to set off discreetly, to accomplish her difficult mission with her usual skill and then, when all had been done to the Cardinal's satisfaction, to go back to him and claim her vengeance.

After traveling all night she reached the Port de La Pointe at seven o'-clock; by eight she had embarked, and at nine the vessel (which bore letters of marque from the Cardinal and was supposedly sailing for Bayonne) quietly raised anchor and steered its course toward the English coast.

XLVI

THE BASTION SAINT-GERVAIS

On arriving at the lodgings of his three friends, D'Artagnan found them together in the same room; Athos was meditating, Porthos was curling his mustache and Aramis was reading his prayers out of an attractive little Book of Hours, bound in blue velvet.

"Pardieu, gentlemen!" cried D'Artagnan. "I hope what you have to tell me is worth the telling. Otherwise I warn you I shan't forgive you for summoning me here when I might be getting a little rest after a night spent in capturing and dismantling a bastion. Oh, if only you had been there, gentlemen; I had a hot time of it!"

"We were somewhere else," said Porthos, twirling his mustache with a characteristic flourish. "And the temperature was far from cool."

"Quiet!" Athos admonished, frowning slightly.

"Well, well," D'Artagnan exclaimed, understanding the musketeer's reaction. "Apparently there is something new afoot."

Athos turned to Aramis.

"The day before yesterday, Aramis, you breakfasted at the *Sign of the Heretic*, did you not?"

"Certainly."

"Is it any good?"

"For my part, I fared poorly. It was a day of fasting and they had nothing but meat."

"What?" Athos asked, incredulous. "No fish at a seaport?"

"They say," Aramis explained as he returned to his pious reading, "that the dike the Cardinal is building has driven all the fish out to sea."

"That is not what I asked you," Athos objected. "I want to know if you were left alone and if no one bothered you."

"Come to think of it, there were not too many intruders. Indeed, Athos, for what you have in mind, we would do quite well at the *Sign of the Heretic*."

"Let us go there, then," Athos suggested, "because here the walls are thin as paper."

D'Artagnan was accustomed to his friend's behavior; he could sense immediately by a word, gesture, or sign from him that the situation was very serious. He therefore took the musketeer's arm and they went out together in silence. Porthos followed, chatting with Aramis.

On their way they met Grimaud. Athos beckoned him to follow; Grimaud, according to custom, obeyed in silence. (The poor lad had almost reached the point of forgetting how to speak.)

They arrived at the tavern of the inn at seven o'clock, in early daylight. Having ordered breakfast they repaired to a room, where, according to the innkeeper, they would not be disturbed.

Unfortunately they had chosen a bad hour for a secret conference. Reveille had just sounded; from all parts of the camp the troops, shaking off the drowsiness of night and eager to dispel the humid chill of the morning air, flocked to the inn for an eye-opener. Dragoons, Swiss mercenaries, guardsmen, musketeers and hussars appeared with a rapidity much appreciated by the innkeeper but most unwelcome to our four friends. They replied to the greeting, toasts and jokes of the other patrons with a very sullen air.

"O Lord!" Athos groaned. "I see what is going to happen. We shall get into some gay little brawl or other and that is the last thing we should do at the moment. Come, D'Artagnan, tell us about your experiences last night and we will tell you about ours."

"Yes, yes," said a hussar who had overheard them. Sipping his brandy mincingly, he struck a foppish attitude. "I hear the guardsmen held the line last night. They seem to have been handled rather roughly by the defenders of La Rochelle."

D'Artagnan looked up at Athos inquiringly. Should he answer this intruder?

"Well, D'Artagnan," Athos asked. "Monsieur de Busigny has done you the honor of speaking to you. These gentlemen are eager to know what happened last night. Won't you satisfy their curiosity?"

"Dittent you shtorm a pashtyun?" asked a Swiss mercenary, who was drinking rum out of a beer glass.

"Yes, Monsieur!" D'Artagnan bowed. "We had the honor of storming a bastion. Perhaps you have heard that we also set a barrel of powder under one of the angles. The fireworks, when it blew up, made a sizable breach in the walls. I might add that since that bastion was not built yesterday, the whole structure was considerably unsettled."

"What bastion was that?" asked a dragoon on his way to the fireplace, his sabre spiking a goose he was about to roast.

"The Bastion Saint-Gervais," D'Artagnan answered. "The bastion from behind which the men of La Rochelle were irking our workmen."

"Did you have a hot time of it?"

"Tolerably hot. We lost five men, those of La Rochelle lost eight or ten."

"Balzempleu! Py te ploot of Gott!" cried the Swiss who, despite the admirable collection of oaths afforded by the German language, had acquired a habit of swearing in French.

The hussar shrugged his shoulders: "This morning they will probably send in a squad of pioneers to repair the damage."

"Yes," D'Artagnan agreed. "They probably will."

"Is any gentleman here willing to lay a wager on it?" Athos asked.

"A vacher, ja, a vacher!" said the Swiss.

"What kind?" asked the hussar.

"A wager on what?"

"Just a minute," the dragoon interrupted, setting his sabre like a spit on the huge andirons in the fireplace.

"If you are betting, count me in! Ho, landlord, damn you, fetch me a pan forthwith! I'll not lose a drop of the fat dripping from this estimable fowl."

"Recht he iss," agreed the Switzer. "Ffatt of goosse she is fery goot mit schweetmeats."

"There; I've cooked my goose! Now—what price your wager, Monsieur Athos?" the dragoon challenged. "We are listening!"

"The wager!" cried the hussar, "the wager, Monsieur Athos!"

"Very well, gentlemen, here it is. I bet that my three friends, Porthos, Aramis, D'Artagnan, and myself will breakfast in the Bastion Saint-Gervais and that we will stay there over an hour, watch in hand, no matter what the enemy might do to dislodge us."

Porthos and Aramis exchanged glances; they were beginning to understand what Athos had planned.

"Look here, Athos," D'Artagnan whispered, "you are about to send us out to slaughter!"

"We are far more likely to be slaughtered if we don't go."

"To the wager, gentlemen, to the wager," said Porthos, tipping his chair and twirling his mustache. "May it be a good one!"

"Done!" said Monsieur de Busigny. "What is the stake to be?"

"We are four and there are four of you," Athos replied. "The stake is a dinner for eight convivials, with no limits on the menu."

"Agreed!" said Monsieur de Busigny.

"I concur!" said the dragoon.

"Vell, I vill bett ahlso!" said the Switzer.

The fourth challenger, who had said no word, raised his hand in agreement!

"Breakfast is ready, gentlemen," the innkeeper announced.

"Bring it in then!" said Athos.

When the innkeeper had obeyed, Athos sent for Grimaud, pointed to a large basket which lay in one corner of the room and signaled to Grimaud to wrap up the food in the napkins. Grimaud understanding that Athos planned a luncheon *al fresco* packed food and bottles in the basket and picked it up.

"Where are you going to eat my breakfast?" the innkeeper asked.

"What business of yours, so long as we pay for it?" Athos replied, tossing two pistoles majestically onto the table.

"Do you wish the change, Lieutenant?"

"No, landlord. Just add two bottles of champagne. What is left will pay for the napkins."

The innkeeper, disappointed in the profits he had hoped for, made amends by supplying two bottles of Anjou instead of two bottles of champagne.

"Monsieur de Busigny," said Athos, "will you be so kind as to set your watch with mine, or permit me to set mine with yours?"

"Certainly, Monsieur," the hussar replied, producing a most handsome watch, studded with diamonds. "It is now half-past seven."

"I am five minutes fast," said Athos, "I make it twenty-five minutes to eight. Pray to take note of this, Monsieur."

Bowing to an astounded company, the four young men set out toward the Bastion Saint-Gervais, Grimaud in their wake, the basket under his arm, unaware of where they were off to but passively obedient by wont, never dreaming of questioning his master.

Whilst they crossed the camp, the four friends proceeded in silence, followed by a lot of soldiers who had heard about the wager and were anxious to know what would come of it. But once they had cleared the line of circumvallation and found themselves in the open, D'Artagnan, completely mystified, thought it timely to ask for an explanation.

"Now, my dear Athos," he pleaded, "will you kindly tell me where we are going?"

"To the bastion, of course. Can't you see that?"

"What shall we do there?"

"You know quite well we are going to breakfast there."

"And why did we not breakfast at the *Sign of the Heretic?*"

"Because we have some very important matters to discuss. It was impossible to hear oneself talk in that tavern, what with all those bores coming and going, bowing, scraping and mulling about. There, at least," Athos pointed to the bastion, "no one can disturb us."

"But Athos," D'Artagnan remarked with that prudence which allied itself so naturally with excessive bravery, "it seems to me we could have found some quiet place in the dunes by the seashore."

"No good, D'Artagnan. The four of us would have been seen conferring together and within a quarter of an hour, the Cardinal would have learned from his spies that we were holding a council."

"Athos is right," Aramis announced, "*Animadvertuntur in deserto,* they are seen in the wilderness."

"A wilderness wouldn't have been bad at all," said Porthos, "the point was to find one!"

"There is no desert where a bird cannot fly overhead or a fish jump out of the water or a rabbit dart out of his burrow, and I firmly believe that bird, fish and rabbit are spying for the Cardinal. We had therefore best continue our venture especially since we cannot retreat without dishonor. We have made a wager in circumstances that could not be foreseen and for reasons which I challenge anyone to explain. In order to win this wager, we are about to occupy the bastion for an hour. Either we shall be attacked or we shall not. If we are not, we shall have plenty of time to talk without anyone overhearing us, for the walls of that bastion have no ears, I warrant you. If we are attacked, we shall discuss our business just the same. Moreover, in defending ourselves we shall cover ourselves with glory. Thus, as you see, everything is to our advantage."

"Yes, yes," said D'Artagnan, "and we shall undoubtedly serve as targets for some pretty marksmanship!"

"Alas, my friend," Athos replied, "you know quite well that the firing we have most to fear will not come from the enemy."

"But on such an expedition surely we should have brought our muskets along?"

"Don't be so foolish, friend Porthos. Why load ourselves with a useless burden?"

"I do not consider a good musket, twelve cartridges, and a powder flask very useless when you are facing the enemy."

"But, Porthos, surely you recall what D'Artagnan told us?" Athos asked.

"What did he say?"

"D'Artagnan told us that in last night's attack, eight or ten Frenchmen and about as many men from La Rochelle were killed."

"What then?"

"The bodies were not plundered, were they? Apparently the victors had something more urgent to do."

"Well?"

"Well, we shall collect their muskets, powder flasks and cartridges. Instead of four musketoons and twelve bullets, we shall have fifteen matchlocks and about a hundred charges to fire."

"Oh, Athos! Truly you are a great man," said Aramis admiringly; Porthos nodded in agreement; D'Artagnan alone did not seem convinced.

Grimaud evidently shared the young man's misgivings, for as the party continued walking toward the bastion—a possibility he had until then doubted—he tugged at his master's coat and, by gestures more effective than words could be, inquired whither they were bound. Athos pointed to the bastion. Grimaud, in the same mute idiom, remonstrated that they would all be killed there.

Athos raised an index finger and both eyes toward the firmament. Grimaud put his basket on the ground, sat down on it and shook his head disparagingly. Whereupon Athos took a pistol from his belt, made sure it was properly primed, cocked it, and pressed the muzzle persuasively close to Grimaud's ear. Reacting like some mechanism released automatically, Grimaud leaped to his feet; Athos motioned him to pick up his basket and to lead the way. Grimaud obeyed; all that he had gained by this brief pantomime was to be promoted from the rear of the procession to the vanguard.

Reaching the bastion, the four friends turned round. More than three hundred soldiers of all kinds were clustered around the camp gate; a small, separate group, formed by Monsieur de Busigny, the dragoon, the Switzer and the fourth bettor stood out clearly to one side.

Removing his hat, Athos placed it on the end of his sword and waved it in the air. As one, all the spectators returned his salute, accompanying this courtesy with loud cheers of encouragement.

Then the quartet followed Grimaud into the bastion.

XLVII

The Council of the Musketeers

As Athos had foreseen, the bastion was occupied by but a dozen dead bodies, some French and some of La Rochelle.

"Friends," said Athos who had assumed command of the expedition, "while Grimaud is laying out our breakfast, let us start collecting the guns and cartridges. We can talk while accomplishing this task; these gentlemen," he pointed to the dead, "cannot overhear us."

"But still we could throw them into the ditch," Porthos suggested, "of course after making sure there is nothing in their pockets."

"Yes, that is Grimaud's job," Athos observed.

"Then let Grimaud search them and throw them over the walls immediately."

"By no manner of means," Athos replied, "for they may still be of use to us."

"These bodies of use to us?" Porthos scoffed. "Look here, Athos, are you going mad?"

"Judge not rashly, say the Gospel and the Cardinal," Athos replied. "How many guns, gentlemen?"

"Twelve."

"How many cartridges?"

"About a hundred."

"That is all we need, let us load the guns."

The four musketeers set to work and just as they were loading the last musket Grimaud signaled that breakfast was ready. Athos replied by gestures that it was well and, pointing to a kind of turret shaped like a pepperbox, indicated that Grimaud was to stand guard there. To lighten the boredom of this duty, Athos permitted him to take along a loaf of bread, two cutlets and a bottle of wine.

"And now to table!" said Athos briskly.

The four friends sat on the ground, their legs crossed like Turks or tailors.

"Now that there is no danger of being overheard," D'Artagnan suggested, "I trust you will tell us your mysterious secret."

"My friends, I hope to procure you both amusement and glory," Athos began. "I have taken you out for a very jolly walk; here is a most toothsome breakfast; and yonder, as you may see through the loopholes, stand five hundred persons who take us for madmen or heroes, two species of idiots which are not unlike."

"But the secret, Athos, the secret."

"The secret is that I saw Milady yesterday."

D'Artagnan was raising his wine to his lips. At the name of Milady his hand shook so violently that he had to put the glass on the ground again for fear of spilling its contents.

"You saw your wi—"

"Hush!" Athos interrupted in a quick whisper. "You forget, my friend, that these gentlemen are not initiated into my family secrets." Then, aloud: "I saw Milady," he concluded.

"Where?"

"About two miles from here, at the *Sign of the Red Dovecote.*"

"In that case I am a lost man!" D'Artagnan groaned.

"No, not quite yet, for she must certainly have left the shores of France by now."

D'Artagnan breathed again.

"Come, now, after all, who is this Milady?" Porthos inquired.

"A charming woman," Athos explained, sipping a glass of sparkling wine. "Damnation! that scoundrelly innkeeper gave us Anjou instead of champagne and he thinks we can't tell the difference! . . . Yes, as I was saying, Milady is a charming woman who bestowed her favors upon D'Artagnan. Our friend played her some nasty trick or other. Seeking revenge, she tried to have him shot a month ago, to poison him last week and yesterday to demand his head of the Cardinal."

"What! she demanded my head of the Cardinal?" cried D'Artagnan, pale with terror.

"That is Gospel truth," Porthos testified. "I heard it with my own ears."

"So did I," Aramis confirmed.

"In that case, all further struggle is useless!" D'Artagnan let his arm fall to his side in discouragement. "I may as well blow my brains out and end it all."

"That is the ultimate folly to commit," Athos commented, "seeing that it is the only one for which we have no remedy."

"But with such enemies," D'Artagnan objected, "how can I ever escape? First, the stranger of Meung . . . then the Comte de Vardes whom I wounded thrice . . . then Milady whose secret I discovered . . . and now the Cardinal whose revenge I foiled. . . ."

"Well, that only makes four, and there are four of us, so we are evenly matched," Athos said easily. Then: "By God, look at Grimaud! From the signs he is making I judge we are about to face a far larger number of people than that! What is it, Grimaud?" he called. "In view of the seriousness of the situation I permit you to speak, my friend. But pray be laconic. What do you see?"

"A troop."

"How many?"

"Twenty."

"What sort of men?"

"Sixteen sappers, four soldiers."

"How far off?"

"Five hundred paces."

"Good; we still have time to finish this fowl and to drink one glass to your health, D'Artagnan!"

"Your health," Porthos and Aramis repeated.

"Well, then, to my health, though I scarcely believe your good wishes will be of much use to me."

"Nonsense," said Athos. "God is great, as the Mohammedans say, and the future lies in the hollow of his palm."

Then, draining his glass, which he set down beside him, Athos rose nonchalantly to his feet, picked up the first musket at hand and took his stand near one of the loopholes. Porthos, Aramis and D'Artagnan followed suit; Grimaud was told to stand behind the four friends in order to reload their weapons.

After a moment or two the troop appeared. It advanced along a communication trench which linked the city to the bastion.

"God help us!" Athos scoffed. "It was certainly not worth while to disturb ourselves for a score of oafs armed with pickaxes, mattocks and shovels! Grimaud need but have waved to them to go away and I am sure they would have left us in peace."

"I doubt it; they are advancing very resolutely. Besides, they are not all pioneers. There are four soldiers and a corporal armed with muskets."

"Pooh!" Athos shrugged his shoulders. "They probably haven't seen us."

"I must confess I feel it most distasteful to fire on these poor devils of civilians."

"It is a bad priest who takes pity on heretics," said Porthos sententiously.

"Aramis is right," Athos contradicted. "Let me go warn them."

"What the devil do you mean?" cried D'Artagnan. "You will be shot down like a pheasant."

Paying no heed to D'Artagnan's remonstrance, Athos mounted the breach, his musket in one hand, his hat in the other and saluting courteously, shouted:

"Gentlemen, your attention, please!"

Amazed, the troop halted some fifty paces from the bastion.

"Gentlemen," Athos continued, "a few friends and myself are breakfasting together in this bastion. Now you know nothing can be so annoying as to be disturbed at mealtime. We therefore beg you, if you have absolutely imperative business here, either to wait until we finish our meal or to come back later. Unless, of course, you are so well advised as to quit the side of the rebels and come here to join us in drinking to the health of the King of France."

"Look out, Athos!" D'Artagnan warned him. "Can't you see they are taking aim?"

"Certainly, but they are only civilians, very indifferent marksmen who will surely miss me."

At the same instant four shots rang out and the bullets flattened themselves out against the wall around Athos without a single one touching him. Four shots answered them almost immediately but, much better aimed than those of the aggressors, they hit their mark. Three soldiers fell dead and one pioneer was wounded.

"Grimaud, another musket!" Athos called, still atop the breach.

Grimaud promptly obeyed. His three friends had reloaded and a second discharge followed. The corporal and two sappers fell dead; the rest of the troop took to their heels.

"Now gentlemen, a sally!" Athos ordered.

The four friends rushed out of the fort, reached the scene of battle, picked up the soldiers' muskets and the corporal's short pike, and, certain that the fugitives would not stop until safely within the city again, they calmly returned to the bastion bearing the trophies of their victory.

"Reload the weapons, Grimaud," Athos commanded. "As for us, gentlemen, let us return to our breakfast and resume our conversation. Where were we?"

"We were discussing Milady," D'Artagnan said. "You told us she had left the shores of France," he added, for he was greatly concerned over her itinerary.

"She is going to England," Athos vouchsafed.

"For what purpose?"

"For the purpose of assassinating the Duke of Buckingham or, at any rate, having someone assassinate him."

D'Artagnan uttered an exclamation of surprise and indignation.

"But that is infamous!" he cried.

"Bah, I beg you to believe that to me this matter is but of little moment!" Turning toward his servant: "Now that you have finished, Grimaud," he called, "take the corporal's pike, tie a napkin to it and plant it on top of our bastion so that the rebels of La Rochelle may see they are dealing with brave and loyal soldiers of the King."

Grimaud obeyed without replying. An instant after, the white flag was floating over the heads of the four friends. Across the plain a thunder of applause greeted its appearance; half the camp stood at the barriers.

"Why do you worry so little whether Milady murders Buckingham or not?" D'Artagnan inquired. "The Duke is our friend."

"The Duke is an Englishman, the Duke is fighting against us, let her do what she likes with the Duke." Athos picked up a bottle and poured its contents into his glass to the very last drop. "The Duke? I care no more for him than I do for an empty bottle." And he sent the bottle hurtling through the air a distance of twenty paces.

"Hold on," D'Artagnan argued, "I don't intend to abandon Buckingham so blithely. He gave us some very handsome horses, didn't he?"

"And some very handsome saddles, too," chimed in Porthos who at the moment was wearing the gold lace from his on his coat.

"Besides," Aramis said gravely, "God wishes the conversion of a sinner, not his death."

"Amen," said Athos, "and we shall return to the subject presently if you so desire. But my chief and immediate concern was much more urgent and I am sure D'Artagnan will appreciate this. I was determined to confiscate from that woman a kind of blanket order which she had extorted from the Cardinal and which she meant to use to get rid of you, D'Artagnan, and perhaps of all of us, with impunity."

"But this creature is a demon!" Porthos remarked, holding out his plate to Aramis who was carving the fowl.

"What of this blanket order?" D'Artagnan asked. "Has she still got it?"

"No, I have. But I would be lying if I told you I got it without trouble."

"My dear Athos, I shall give up counting the number of times I owe my life to you."

"So you left us to go to her?" asked Aramis.

"Exactly."

"And you have that letter of the Cardinal's?" D'Artagnan queried.

"Here it is," said Athos, drawing the precious paper from the pocket of his uniform. D'Artagnan unfolded it with a hand whose trembling he did not even attempt to conceal, and read:

> December third, 1627
> It is by my order and for the service of the State that the bearer of this note has done what he has done.
>   Signed by my hand at the Camp of La Rochelle
>   Richelieu

"Indeed, this is an absolution in every sense," Aramis declared, "and in all due form."

"We must destroy this paper," D'Artagnan urged, for in it he fancied he read his own death sentence.

"On the contrary, we must keep it preciously," said Athos. "I would not surrender it for as many gold pieces as would cover it."

"Now you have the paper," D'Artagnan ventured uneasily, "what is she going to do?"

"Oh, she will probably write to the Cardinal," Athos replied with utmost indifference. "I suppose she will tell him that a damned musketeer named Athos forcibly robbed her of her safe-conduct. By the same token, she will probably advise His Eminence to get rid of this musketeer's two friends Porthos and Aramis at the same time. The Cardinal will recall that these are the same men who have crossed his path so often. So one fine morning he will have D'Artagnan arrested and to save his prisoner the pangs of loneliness he will send us three to keep D'Artagnan company in the Bastille."

"Look here, my dear fellow," Porthos grumbled, "you seem to be making a very dull joke of it in very poor taste."

"I am not joking," Athos insisted.

"By God!" Porthos exploded. "To wring that damned Milady's neck would be much less of a sin than to do so to those poor Huguenot devils who have committed no crimes other than singing in French the psalms we sing in Latin."

"What does the Abbé have to say to that?"

"I, Athos? I say I thoroughly agree with Porthos."

"And so do I!" D'Artagnan said warmly.

"Fortunately she is far away!" Porthos spoke consolingly. "I must confess her presence here would make me very uncomfortable."

"Her presence in England makes me just as uncomfortable as her presence in France," said Athos.

"Her presence anywhere makes me terribly nervous," D'Artagnan confessed.

"But Athos, when you had her in your power," Porthos said reproachfully, "why didn't you drown her or strangle her or hang her? The dead alone do not come back to harm you."

"Do you believe that, Porthos?" Athos asked, his lips twisted in a wry smile which only D'Artagnan understood.

"I have an idea," D'Artagnan said suddenly.

"Well?"

But before D'Artagnan could speak:

"To arms, gentlemen!" Grimaud shouted. The young men sprang up and seized their muskets.

A small troop was advancing toward the bastion. There were about twenty-five men; but this time they were not sappers. Their uniform and gait indicated clearly that they were garrison soldiers.

"Hadn't we better make for camp?" Porthos suggested. "The odds against us are pretty grim."

"That is impossible on three counts," Athos answered. "First, we have not finished breakfasting... second, we still have important matters to discuss... and third, we have been here only fifty minutes...."

"All right," Aramis agreed, "but we must draw up a definite plan of action."

"Very simple!" Athos told him. "As soon as the enemy come within range, we fire; if they continue to advance, we fire again; and we keep firing so long as our ammunition holds out. If the enemy survivors then try to storm the bastion, we let them advance as far as the ditch and then we push this strip of wall down on their heads. Look at it, lads, it seems to be standing only by a miracle of balance."

"Bravo, Athos!" Porthos applauded. "You were born to be a general. The Cardinal fancies himself a great captain but compared to you he is very small beer indeed."

"Gentlemen, let us have no duplication," Athos called out crisply. "Let each of us pick his own man."

"I have mine covered," said D'Artagnan.

"Mine is as good as dead!" Porthos boasted.

"Mine is marked!" said Aramis.

"Fire!" Athos commanded.

The four shots rang as one, four men fell. The drum immediately beat and the little troop advanced at the double. From then on, the volleys followed irregularly but with the same telling effect; but the men of La Rochelle, as if aware of the defenders' numerical weakness, pressed on. On every three shots from the bastion, at least two men fell but the advance of those unscathed was by no means slackened.

When the assailants reached the foot of the bastion, they still numbered a dozen or more. A final salvo greeted them but it did not halt their progress as they jumped into the ditch and prepared to scale the breach.

"Now, lads, let us finish them off. To the wall, to the wall, and one good push—"

The quartet, seconded by Grimaud, pushed with the barrels of their muskets against an enormous fragment of masonry. It bent, as if rocked by the wind. Then, loosened from its base, it fell with a deafening crash into the ditch. A horrible clamor arose, a cloud of dust spread toward the heavens—and all was over.

"Do you think we have crushed every last one of them?" Athos asked.

"It certainly looks like it," D'Artagnan assured him.

"No," Porthos corrected, "there go a few, hobbling away."

In point of fact, three or four of these unfortunates caked with mud and blood were retreating painfully along the communication trench toward the city. These were all that remained of the little troop. Athos looked at his watch:

"Gentlemen," he announced, "we have stayed here for an hour and thus won our wager. But let us be good sportsmen and stay on a while. Besides, D'Artagnan has not had a chance to tell us about his idea."

And with his usual calm, Athos sat down again before the remnants of the meal.

"My idea?"

"Ay, you were saying you had an idea when we were suddenly interrupted."

"Now I remember. My idea is for me to go to England a second time and find Lord Buckingham."

"You shall do nothing of the sort!" Athos countered sternly.

"Why not? I did it before!"

"True, but at that time we were not at war. At that time, Lord Buckingham was an ally, not an enemy. What you propose to do has none too pleasant a name. It is known as treason."

D'Artagnan, realizing the strength of the argument, relapsed into an awkward silence.

"Ho!" Porthos proclaimed joyfully. "*I* have an idea now, I think."

"Silence, gentlemen!" Aramis admonished. "Monsieur Porthos has an idea!"

"My idea is for me to ask Monsieur de Tréville for leave on any excuse you care to invent, for I confess I'm not very inventive myself. Milady doesn't know me from Adam. I can approach her without arousing her suspicions. Then, when I catch my beauty, I simply strangle her."

"Not a bad idea!" Athos conceded.

"Come now, you can't kill a woman! Shame on you! I—but wait, listen to me, *I* have the *right* idea!"

"Let's hear it, Aramis!" Athos replied eagerly, for he entertained a high regard for the young man's intelligence.

"We must warn the Queen."

"Right you are!" Porthos exclaimed, and "By Heaven," D'Artagnan added, "I really think we are getting somewhere."

"Warn the Queen? How? Have we connections at Court? Could we dispatch anyone to Paris without the whole camp knowing about it? One hundred and forty leagues separate us from Paris; our letter could not even reach Angers before we were clapped in jail."

Aramis, blushing, suggested timidly: "If it is a question of getting a letter safely into Her Majesty's hands, I know a very clever person in Tours," and stopped as he saw Athos smile.

"Well, Athos, what about it?" D'Artagnan challenged.

"I do not altogether reject the idea," Athos replied. "But I do wish to point out that Aramis cannot leave camp . . . that none save ourselves is to be trusted . . . that, two hours after the messenger left, every capuchin, every policeman and every bailiff of the Cardinal's would know your letter by heart . . . and that you and your very clever person would be safe behind bars. . . ."

"Not to mention the fact," Porthos concurred, "that the Queen would save Lord Buckingham but would certainly not bother about us."

"What Porthos says makes excellent sense," D'Artagnan agreed.

"Look, gentlemen!" Athos pointed toward La Rochelle. "What can be going on in the city?"

"It's a general alarm!"

The four friends, listening, could distinguish the drums calling out the garrison for assembly.

"You watch," said Athos. "They will send a whole regiment against us."

"You don't propose holding out against an entire regiment, do you?" Porthos asked.

"Why not?" Athos answered. "I feel in fine fettle and if we had only been intelligent enough to bring a dozen more bottles along, I could face a whole army."

"The drums seem to be drawing near," D'Artagnan said.

"Let them come with their drummers!" Athos flicked the dust off his sleeve. "It takes a quarter of an hour to go from here to town; *ergo* it takes a quarter of an hour to come from town out here. This allows us ample time to establish a plan of battle. If we leave this place we shall never find another one as suitable; besides, I'm getting rather attached to our bastion. What is more important, gentlemen, the right idea has suddenly occurred to *me!*"

"Let's have it, Athos."

"First, let us give Grimaud some indispensable instructions."

Athos motioned his lackey to approach.

"Grimaud!" He pointed to the dead lying under the wall of the bastion. "Pick up these gentlemen, prop them against the wall, put their hats on their heads and their muskets in their hands."

"Oh, Athos, what a genius you are!" D'Artagnan enthused. "Now I understand what you are planning."

"You understand?" Porthos asked incredulously.

"Do *you* understand, Grimaud?" Aramis inquired. The lackey nodded affirmatively.

"So long as Grimaud understands, that is all we need," Athos declared. "Now, back to my idea."

"I still should like to know what you are driving at," said Porthos.

"Never mind, Porthos, you will, in good time."

"Come, Athos, your idea!" cried D'Artagnan, and "We are listening," said Aramis.

"Here it is. This Milady, this woman, this creature, this demon has a brother-in-law, you said, eh, D'Artagnan?"

"Yes, I know him fairly well. I also know there is very little love lost between them."

"Capital! The more he hates her, the better for us."

"You can be sure he hates her, Athos."

"I should still like to know what Grimaud is up to," Porthos interrupted.

"Quiet, Porthos!" Aramis enjoined.

"What is her brother-in-law's name?"

"Lord Winter."

"Where is he now?"

"He went back to London at the first rumor of war."

"He is just the man we want," Athos said. "It is he we must warn. We will let him know that his sister-in-law is planning to assassinate someone and we will ask him to keep his eye on her. Surely they have some institution for wayward women in London like our Madelonnettes or Filles Repenties—in a word some sort of reformatory. He can have his sister-in-law put away in such a place and we will all breathe more easily."

"Ay, until she breaks loose!"

"Confound it, D'Artagnan, you require too much. I have given you all I had; I assure you I have come to the end of my tether."

"Athos has a good idea, I think," said Aramis. "We must warn both the Queen and Lord Winter."

"Yes, but who will take our messages to Tours and to London?"

"I can vouch for Bazin," said Aramis.

"And I for Planchet," said D'Artagnan.

"Of course," said Porthos. "We cannot leave camp, but certainly our lackeys can."

"Splendid!" Aramis said blithely. "This very day we shall write the letters, give our lackeys money and send them off."

"Money!" Athos broke in. "So you are in funds, Aramis?"

The four friends looked at one another. A cloud passed over their brows which, for a moment, had been so serene.

"To arms, friends!" cried D'Artagnan, "I see some black and red specks moving across the plain, yonder. Did you say a regiment, Athos? This is a veritable army!"

"Well, well, here they come!" Athos said coolly. "But what sneaks they are to creep up without a beating of drums or a flourish of trumpets! Ho there, Grimaud, have you finished?"

Grimaud nodded affirmatively, pointing to a dozen corpses which he had placed in the most picturesque and lifelike attitudes: some were port-ing arms, others seemed to be taking aim, still others stood as though ready, sword in hand.

"Bravo, Grimaud, this does honor to your imagination."

"I still should like to know what it all means," Porthos complained.

"Let us beat a retreat first," cried D'Artagnan. "You'll understand later."

"One moment, gentlemen, one moment: give Grimaud a chance to clear away our dishes."

"These black specks and red specks are growing larger and larger," Aramis observed. "I agree with D'Artagnan; we have no time to lose if we want to get back to camp."

"Bless my soul, I have no objection now to an orderly retreat. We wagered would stay here an hour and we have been here an hour and a half!" Athos seemed highly pleased. "That's all there is to it, gentlemen. Let us away!"

Grimaud had already started off, basket in hand, bearing the dishes and remnants of food back to camp. The four friends followed him out. But they had gone only a dozen yards when Athos exclaimed:

"What the devil are we up to, gentlemen?" he asked, turning back to look anxiously at the bastion.

"Have you forgotten something?" Aramis asked.

"The flag, *morbleu*! We cannot leave a flag in enemy hands even though that flag is but a napkin."

Whereupon Athos rushed back into the bastion, mounted the platform and seized the flag. Just then, the enemy, having come within range, opened a murderous fire upon him. Far from being perturbed, Athos seemed to delight in exposing himself to danger. He seemed to bear a charmed life; the bullets whizzed all around him but not one of them so much as grazed him. Athos waved his flag proudly, turned his back on the enemy and calmly saluted the men in the camp. Cries of anger rose from the rebel ranks, cries of enthusiasm from the French.

A second volley followed the first and three bullets piercing the napkin made of it a real battle-stand. From all parts of the camp shouts rose: "Come down, man!"—"For God's sake—"—"Don't stay there, idiot!"— and the like. Athos complied in leisurely fashion and rejoined his friends in his own good time. Their anxiety turned to joy as he reached them.

"Come, Athos, hurry up!" D'Artagnan begged him. "Now we have settled every problem except the money problem, it would be foolish to get ourselves killed."

But Athos continued to walk at a slow, stately pace despite all urgings of his comrades, who seeing their pleas were vain, adjusted their step to his. Grimaud and his basket, far ahead, were both already out of range. Suddenly a furious fusillade thundered across the air.

"What in God's name is that? What are they firing at now?" Porthos asked. "No one is in the bastion."

"They are firing on our dear departed enemies," said Athos.

"But corpses cannot return fire."

"Perhaps. But the rebels will imagine an ambush, they will pause to take counsel, they will send someone forward to parley and by the time they have found out how we duped them, we shall be well out of range. That is why it is useless to catch cold by running—an exercise I have always considered to be highly diaphoretic."

"Now I understand!" Porthos gasped, marveling.

"It's about time!" said Athos with a shrug.

Cries of relief and cheers of approval kept rising from the camp as the French observed the four friends returning at a walk. For a moment all was silence, then a fresh volley of bullets spattered among the stones about our friends and whistled past their ears. The rebels had at last occupied the bastion.

"Bunglers, those rebels!" Athos remarked. "How many did we shoot down?"

"Fifteen!"

"And how many did we crush?"

"Eight or ten."

"And not a scratch in return. But no! Look at D'Artagnan's hand. You're bleeding, lad."

"I'm all right!"

"A spent bullet?"

"Not even that."

"What is it, then?" Athos loved the young Gascon like a child. Gloomy and imperturbable though he was, at times Athos felt all the anxiety and solicitude of a father for his son.

"A mere scratch!" D'Artagnan smiled. "I caught my fingers between two stones—one from the wall, one on my ring—and it tore the skin."

"That is what you get for wearing diamonds, my master," Athos observed contemptuously.

"I have an idea!" cried Porthos triumphantly.

"Silence, all," said Aramis. "Porthos has an idea."

"Let us hear it!"

"Well," said Porthos deliberately, "we have a diamond, haven't we? And, having a diamond, why the devil are we complaining about a lack of funds?"

"Quite so!" said Aramis.

"Good man, Porthos!" Athos approved. "That really *is* a fine idea!"

"We have a diamond," Porthos repeated, preening himself on the compliment Athos had paid him. "Therefore, let us sell it!"

"But it is the Queen's—"

"All the more reason to sell it, D'Artagnan," Athos interrupted. "Her Majesty is saving the life of her lover, Lord Buckingham, which is as it should be. But by the same reasoning, Her Majesty is morally bound to save us, her friends. Sell the diamond, I say. Porthos has already expressed himself cogently on the subject; what says Monsieur l'Abbé?"

Aramis blushed.

"My own feeling," he said slowly and deliberately, "is that since the ring is not the gift of a mistress, and hence not a talisman of love, D'Artagnan would be justified in selling it!"

"My friend, you speak like theology incarnate. So your advice is—"

"—to sell the diamond."

"Sell it we shall," cried D'Artagnan gaily, "and let us drop the matter."

The rebels continued to fire from the bastion but our friends were out of reach; the shooting was but a token gesture by disappointed marksmen seeking to ease their consciences.

"God's truth, it was high time Porthos conceived this idea," Athos concluded, "for here we are at camp again. Accordingly, gentlemen, not one word of this matter to anyone. Remember, we are being observed. Here come our friends to meet us. They will probably bear us back in triumph shoulder-high."

And so it was. The entire camp was agog; more than two thousand spectators had been watching every move in this exploit as avidly as though it were a rousing drama produced for their entertainment. How indeed could they suspect that this bravado offered the only means whereby our friends could hold a council of war which turned into a battle royal? Cheers of *"Vivent les Mousquetaires!"* and huzzahs of *"Vivent les Gardes!"* rose on every side.

Monsieur de Busigny was the first to reach Athos and wring his hand. Jubilantly he admitted he had lost the wager. Close on his heels, the dragoon and the Swiss guardsman offered their awed congratulations, followed by a host of soldiery who did likewise, amid embraces, handclasps, felicitations, benedictions and endless laughter at the expense of the men of La Rochelle. So great was the uproar that the Cardinal, imagining a mutiny was afoot, dispatched La Houdinière, Captain of his Guards, to ascertain what was happening. Soldiers crowded about the Cardinal's orderly officer to explain their various versions of the heroic exploit.

"Well?" asked the Cardinal as La Houdinière reappeared.

"A curious story, Monseigneur," the captain replied. "It seems that the three musketeers and one Royal Guardsman wagered with Monsieur de Busigny that they would go to breakfast at the Bastion Saint-Gervais. While breakfasting they held out for two hours against the rebels, killing an untold number of them."

"Did you inquire who the three musketeers were?"

"Yes, Monseigneur."

"Their names?"

"Athos, Porthos and Aramis."

"Always the same three heroes—" the Cardinal murmured. "And the guardsman?"

"Monsieur d'Artagnan."

"—always flanked by the same young scapegrace! I must positively enlist these four men in my service."

The same evening His Eminence spoke to Monsieur de Tréville of the day's exploit which was still the sole topic of conversation throughout the camp. Tréville, who had received an account of it from the mouths of the actors themselves, repeated it in full to His Eminence, not omitting the episode of the napkin.

"Splendid, Monsieur de Tréville. Pray have that napkin sent me. I will have three lilies embroidered upon it in gold and I will give it to your company as a standard."

"Monseigneur, I fear that would be doing the Royal Guards an injustice. Monsieur d'Artagnan is not one of my men, he serves under Monsieur des Essarts."

"Well then, take him!" said the Cardinal. "When four brave men are so attached to one another, they should not serve in different companies."

That evening Monsieur de Tréville bore the good news to the three musketeers and to D'Artagnan, inviting all four to lunch with him on the morrow. They were overjoyed.

"God bless us, Athos, that was a triumphant idea of yours. As you promised, we have acquired glory and we were enabled to carry on a most important conversation."

"A conversation we can now continue without fear of suspicion, for, God help us, we shall henceforth be considered cardinalists."

That evening D'Artagnan called to pay his respects to Monsieur des Essarts and to inform him of the promotion he had just received. The Captain, who was very fond of D'Artagnan, offered him his good offices, for this change of corps would involve heavy additional expenses for equipment. D'Artagnan declined gratefully but, using the opportunity to advantage, asked Monsieur des Essarts to have the diamond valued, appraised and sold.

Next morning at eight o'clock Monsieur des Essarts' valet called on D'Artagnan and handed him a bag containing seven thousand gold livres, the price of the Queen's diamond.

XLVIII

A FAMILY AFFAIR

It was Athos who first used the term "family affair." A family affair was not subject to investigation by the Cardinal; it concerned nobody; anyone might conduct a family affair in broad daylight while all the world looked on.

Athos thus discovered the phrase (family affair); Aramis discovered the idea (the lackeys); Porthos discovered the means (the diamond); D'Artagnan alone discovered nothing at all. This was surprising, for he was usually the most inventive of the quartet; alas! in the present juncture the mere name of Milady paralyzed him. But no! he did discover something, after all; he discovered a purchaser for his diamond.

The luncheon at Monsieur de Tréville's was very gay and enjoyable. D'Artagnan already wore his uniform, thanks to Aramis. Having been so handsomely paid by the bookseller who purchased his poem Aramis had bought double of everything. As D'Artagnan and he were of the same size, Aramis cheerfully yielded his friend a complete outfit. D'Artagnan would have been overjoyed had he not constantly seen Milady, hovering like a dark cloud on the horizon.

After luncheon Athos and his friends agreed to meet at his billet that night to complete their deliberations. Only three things remained to be decided upon: first, what they should write to Milady's brother . . . next, what they should write to the adroit person in Tours . . . and finally which two valets were to carry the letters. . . .

Each musketeer offered his own. Athos praised the discreet Grimaud who never spoke a word save when his master unlocked his mouth. Porthos boasted of the powerful Mousqueton, able single-handed to thrash four men of ordinary size. Aramis, confident in Bazin, launched into a pompous eulogy of his infinite resourcefulness. And D'Artagnan, championing Planchet's bravery, reminded them how he had behaved in the ticklish affair at Boulogne. For a long time the virtues of discretion, strength, ingenuity and valor disputed the prize, inspiring magnificent speeches somewhat too long to reproduce here. Athos summed up the situation:

"The trouble is that the man we send must possess in himself alone all four of these qualities."

"But where is such a lackey to be found?"

"Nowhere. He does not exist, I know. Therefore, choose Grimaud."

"Choose Mousqueton."

"Choose Bazin."

"Choose Planchet. He is both brave and shrewd; thus he fulfills two of the four requisites."

"Gentlemen," Aramis intervened, "the point is not to decide which of our lackeys is the most discreet, the strongest, the cleverest or the bravest but which one of them is fondest of money."

"What Aramis says is compact and of sound judgment," Athos agreed. "We must speculate upon the faults of people and not upon their virtues. Monsieur l'Abbé, you are a great moralist."

"I dare say," Aramis nodded. "We require excellent service in order to succeed, granted; but there is more to it than that. We also require excellent service in order not to fail, for if ever we fail the matter involves not the heads of our lackeys but our own."

"Speak lower," Athos warned.

"What I have said holds good not for the lackey in question but for the master, or even for the *masters*," Aramis observed significantly. "I ask you this: are our lackeys sufficiently devoted to us to risk their lives for us? No!"

"Upon my word, I would almost vouch for Planchet," D'Artagnan said.

"Well, then, my friend, double your voucher. To his natural loyalty add a good round sum of money. Thus instead of answering for him once, answer for him twice."

"To be disappointed just the same," Athos grumbled, ever an optimist where things were concerned and a pessimist when it came to men. "They will promise you anything for the sake of money, but once on the road fear will prevent them from acting. Once caught, they will be pressed; once pressed, they will confess everything. Devil take it, we are not children. To reach England—" Athos lowered his voice, "—our messenger must cross most of France which is honeycombed with cardinalist spies. He needs a passport to embark. And he must know English in order to ask his way to London (if ever he lands in England!). Really the whole thing is very difficult!"

But D'Artagnan, determined that the mission be accomplished, contradicted him:

"Not at all! For my part I think it quite easy! Of course if we send Lord Winter extravagant tirades about the horrors the Cardinal perpetrates—"

"Don't shout!" Athos warned.

"—about intrigues and secrets of state," D'Artagnan continued, lowering his tone, "then we will all undoubtedly be broken on the wheel. But for God's sake, don't forget this, which you yourself mentioned, Athos: we are writing to him about family affairs, no more. Our sole purpose in communicating with him is to beg him to meet Milady the moment she reaches London and to make it impossible for her to injure us. I shall write to him more or less like this—"

"Well, let's hear you!" Aramis broke in quietly, assuming a critical look.

D'Artagnan began phrasing his message before putting pen to paper:

"Monsieur et Cher Ami—"

Athos immediately stopped him:

"Ah, yes, D'Artagnan, you call an Englishman 'dear friend.' Bravo, a capital beginning! For that alone you would be quartered instead of broken on the wheel."

"Well, then, I shall say just: Monsieur."

"You may even say My Lord," Athos suggested, invariably a stickler for form.

"Milord, do you recall the little goat pasture of the Luxembourg—?"

"Good God! The Luxembourg, now! Anyone reading that would be certain to see a reference to the Queen Mother. You're a subtle fellow, D'Artagnan."

"All right, let us put it this way: Milord, do you recall a certain little enclosure where your life was spared—"

"My dear D'Artagnan, you will never be anything but a very poor letter-writer. 'Where your life was spared!' Bah, that is ignoble. No one reminds a gentleman of such favors received. A benefit reproached is an offense committed."

"You're unbearable, my dear Athos. If this letter is to be written under your censure, I beg to resign."

"You will be doing rightly, my friend. Handle musket or sword and you will always come off splendidly; but leave the pen to Monsieur l'Abbé, for literature is *his* province."

"Ay," Porthos concurred. "Hand the pen to Aramis. He writes these in Latin."

"So be it. You draw up the note for us, Aramis. But by our Holy Father the Pope, be concise or I shall pare you and prune you to the bone, I warn you."

"I don't at all mind helping you," Aramis declared with the ingenuous confidence inherent in every poet. "But let me first hear something more definite about the subject matter. One way or another I gather the sister-in-law is a vile woman; I judged as much when I listened to her conversation with the Cardinal."

"God's death, man, speak lower!" Athos growled.

"What I need is more facts," Aramis elaborated. "The details escape me."

"I'd like to know more about all this, too," said Porthos.

D'Artagnan and Athos exchanged a long glance. Presently Athos, rousing himself from his meditation, nodded assent to D'Artagnan's unspoken query. He was even paler than usual. D'Artagnan, feeling free to talk, said:

"You must write something of this sort, Aramis: Milord, your sister-in-law is a villainous woman who has sought to kill you in order to inherit your wealth. But she has never been really married to your brother because she still has a husband in France and because she—"

D'Artagnan paused, searching for appropriate terms. He looked askance at Athos who suggested:

"Because her husband drove her out of his house?"

"He drove her out of his house," D'Artagnan repeated, "because she had been branded!"

"Branded?" Porthos exclaimed. "Impossible."

"It is God's truth!"

"And she sought to kill her brother-in-law!"

"Ay," Athos admitted dully.

"So she was previously married in France?" Aramis asked. "That would make her a bigamist, would it not?"

"Ay," Athos repeated hoarsely.

"And her husband discovered a fleur-de-lis branded on her shoulder," Porthos supplied.

"Ay," Athos said for the third time in a voice now the grimmer for being under perfect control.

"And who actually saw this brand?" Aramis inquired.

"D'Artagnan and I." Athos coughed. "Or to observe chronological sequence, I and D'Artagnan."

"And the woman's first husband is still alive?"

"Very much so."

"Are you sure?"

"Absolutely certain," said Athos. "I happen to be the husband." A leaden silence fell upon them. Then, to ease the situation: "D'Artagnan has stated the argument of our letter quite clearly," he went on; "let Aramis write it."

"Heaven help me, Athos, this message is devilishly hard to convey. The Lord Chancellor himself would find it hard to know what to say, yet he can certainly turn a pretty phrase! No matter, hold your tongues and I shall do my best."

Aramis took up the quill, meditated for a few moments and wrote some ten lines in a neat somewhat feminine hand. Then, speaking softly and deliberately as if each word had been scrupulously weighed, he read:

My Lord:
The person who writes these lines had the honor of crossing swords with you in the little inclosure off Rue d'Enfer. Since then, you have several times declared your feelings of friendship toward the writer.

Accordingly he considers it his duty to repay you in kind by sending you some urgent advice.

Twice already you have almost fallen a victim to a close relative of yours whom you believe to be your heir because you do not know that before contracting a marriage in England she had not dissolved a previous marriage in France.

She will make a third attempt upon your life very shortly. She sailed from La Rochelle last night, bound for England.

Pray be on the alert for her, she has vast and terrible plans. If you would be convinced of her wickedness, you have but to read her past history upon her left shoulder.

"Bravo, Aramis, you have the pen of a Secretary of State," Athos approved. "Should your letter reach Lord Winter, he will be on his guard; should even His Eminence intercept it, we shall not be compromised. However, the lackey we send might easily stop at Châtellerault and pretend he has been to London and back. I suggest we give him only one-half the sum promised, agreeing to pay the other half in exchange for the answer. Have you your diamond, D'Artagnan?"

"I have something more useful," D'Artagnan replied. "I have its value in cash."

He tossed a bag on the table. Hearing the gold pieces jingle, Aramis raised his eyes, Porthos started, but Athos remained impassive.

"How much is there in that little bag?"

"Seven thousand livres in louis, each worth twelve francs apiece."

"Seven thousand livres!" Porthos gasped. "That poor little diamond was worth—"

"Apparently, for here is the money," Athos replied. "I doubt very much whether our friend D'Artagnan has added any money of his own to the amount."

"But gentlemen," D'Artagnan urged briskly, "in all this we are not thinking of the Queen. Let us take some heed of the welfare of her beloved Buckingham. That is the least we owe her."

"Very true!" Athos agreed. "But that matter concerns Aramis."

"Well, what do you want me to do?" asked Aramis, blushing.

"It's quite simple. Just write a second letter to that very clever person in Tours."

Aramis picked up his pen, reflected a moment and wrote the following lines, which he immediately submitted to the approval of his friends.

"My dear Cousin—" he began.

"Ah! So you are related to this clever person?"

"We are first cousins."

"Go on then, leave it 'My dear Cousin!' "

My dear Cousin:

His Eminence the Cardinal whom God preserve for the happiness of France and the confusion of her enemies is on the point of putting an end to the heretical rebellion of La Rochelle. Probably the succor of the English fleet will never even arrive within sight of the city. I will even venture to say that I am certain Lord Buckingham will be prevented by some great event from even setting out.

As you know His Eminence is the most illustrious and determined statesman of times past, of times present and probably of times to come. He could extinguish the sun if the sun stood in his way.

Pray give these happy tidings to your sister, my dear cousin. I dreamed that this accursed Englishman was dead. I cannot remember now whether it was by steel or poison but I can well remember I dreamed of his death. As you know, my dreams never deceive me. How many have failed to come true in the past?

You may be sure, then, of seeing me return soon.

"Excellent!" Athos approved. "You are the king of poets, my dear Aramis; you speak like the Apocalypse and you are as authentic as the Gospel. All you need now is to address the letter."

"That is soon done!" Aramis folded the letter neatly and elegantly, took up his pen and wrote:

> *To Mademoiselle Michon*
> *Seamstress*
> *Tours*

The three friends glanced at one another and laughed at the ease with which Aramis had foiled their curiosity.

"Now you will understand, gentlemen, that Bazin alone can carry this letter to Tours," Aramis announced. "My cousin knows nobody and trusts nobody except Bazin; any other person would therefore fail. Besides Bazin is ambitious and learned; Bazin has read history, gentlemen, and he knows that Sixtus the fifth became Pope after having been a swineherd.

Well, as he means to enter the Church at the same time as I do, he does not despair of becoming Pope, in his turn, or at least Cardinal. You can understand that a man with such aims will never allow himself to be captured or, if captured, will suffer martyrdom rather than speak."

"I heartily agree and I vote for Bazin," D'Artagnan spoke up, "but grant me Planchet. Milady had him thrown out of her house one day amid a thumping and thwacking of cudgels. Now Planchet has a good memory and I guarantee that if he can invent some possible vengeance, he will allow himself to be flayed alive before he abandons it. If the affairs of Tours concern you, Aramis, those of London are mine. I request then that Planchet be chosen, especially as he has already been to London with me and can say very correctly: 'London, sir, if you please,' and 'My master, Lord d'Artagnan!' With that equipment you may rest satisfied; he will make his way handily, both going and returning."

"In that case Planchet must receive seven hundred livres for going and seven hundred for coming back," Athos advised, "and Bazin three hundred for going and three hundred for returning. That will reduce our general assets to five thousand livres. We will each take one thousand livres to be employed as each sees fit and we will leave a fund of one thousand livres under the guardianship of Monsieur l'Abbé, here, for extraordinary occasions or for common necessities. Will that do?"

"My dear Athos, you speak like Nestor," Aramis declared, "and Nestor, as all men know, was the wisest among the Greeks."

"Good, that's settled!" Athos said with some satisfaction. "Planchet and Bazin shall be our messengers. All in all, I am not sorry to retain Grimaud. He is accustomed to my ways and I am very particular. Yesterday's affair must have shaken him a little and this journey would utterly unnerve him."

Planchet was summoned and given his instructions; D'Artagnan had already broached the matter to him, pointing out first how much money, next how much glory and third how much danger were involved.

"I will slip the letter in the lining of my coat," the lackey said, "and if I am caught, I will swallow it."

"But how will you fulfill your mission then?" D'Artagnan objected.

"Monsieur need but give me a copy this evening and I shall learn the text by heart overnight."

D'Artagnan looked quizzically at his comrades as though to invite them to confirm his faith in Planchet and to congratulate him on his lackey's resourcefulness. Then, turning to Planchet:

"You have sixteen days in all: eight days to get to Lord Winter and eight days to return here. If you are not here at exactly eight o'clock in the evening on the sixteenth day—I mean eight and not even five minutes past—then you will receive no money whatever for the return journey."

"Well, then, Monsieur must buy me a watch."

"Take this watch," Athos interrupted with his usual careless generosity, sliding his own watch across the table, "take it and be a good lad. Remember that if you gossip or babble or lag on the way you are risking the head of a master who believed so roundly in your loyalty that he answered for you and persuaded us to choose you for this mission. But remember this too: if through your fault anything untoward befalls Monsieur d'Artagnan, I swear I shall find you wherever you may be and I shall make a point of ripping up your belly!"

Planchet flushed, at once humiliated by the suspicion and terrified at the musketeer's icy calm.

"Monsieur may trust me—" he said meekly.

"And remember," Porthos put in, "remember I will skin you alive!"

"Oh, Monsieur—"

"As for me," Aramis added in his soft melodious voice, "remember I will roast you before a slow fire like a savage."

"Oh, Monsieur—"

And Planchet began to weep, perhaps from terror at these threats or perhaps from tenderness at seeing these four friends so closely united. D'Artagnan clasped the lackey's hand and embraced him:

"Cheer up, Planchet," he said comfortingly, "these gentlemen are saying all this out of love for me. At bottom they have a great respect for you."

"Monsieur, I shall succeed or I shall be cut in quarters, and if they cut me in quarters, not a morsel of me will speak!"

It was resolved that Planchet should set out next morning at eight in order to have ample time to memorize the letter and to rest before leaving. He gained just twelve hours by this arrangement since he was scheduled to return on the sixteenth day by eight in the evening.

In the morning D'Artagnan, who deep in his heart felt a certain partiality for Buckingham, drew Planchet aside just as the lackey was about to mount his horse.

"Listen carefully," he enjoined. "After you have given Lord Winter the letter and he has read it, tell him: 'Watch over Lord Buckingham for they wish to assassinate him.' Do you understand?"

"Ay, Monsieur: 'Watch over Lord Buckingham for they wish to assassinate him.' "

"Planchet, this is so serious and so important that I did not tell even my friends I meant to entrust this secret to you. And I would not put it in writing, no! not even for a Captain's commission!"

"Do not worry, Monsieur, you shall see how reliable I am."

With which Planchet, mounted on an excellent horse he was to leave sixty miles further when he took the post, galloped off, somewhat hurt by the triple threat the musketeers had made but otherwise as cheerful as could be.

On the morrow Bazin set out for Tours, being allowed eight days for his mission.

During the absence of their messengers our friends eyed the watch around the dial, thrust their noses to the wind and kept their ears peeled. Day by long day they collected and sifted any rumors they might overhear, they observed the Cardinal's actions minutely and they spied upon every courier that set foot in camp. More than once when called out on special duty, they were seized with uncontrollable misgivings. Also they had constantly to look to their own safety, for Milady was the type of phantom which, once arisen, did not allow its victims to sleep very soundly thereafter.

The morning of the eighth day Bazin, fresh and deliberate and smiling as ever, entered the Parpaillot tavern as the musketeers were sitting down to breakfast and, as had been agreed upon, announced:

"Monsieur Aramis, here is the answer from your cousin."

The quartet exchanged joyous glances, relieved to know that half the work was done. To be sure it was the shortest and easiest part but it augured well for the other. Aramis, blushing in spite of himself, took the letter which was couched in a large coarse hand.

"God help us," he laughed, "I quite despair of my poor Michon. She will never write like Monsieur de Voiture."

"Vot doss you mean, dot poor Mischon," asked the Swiss who was sitting with our friends.

"I mean nothing serious," Aramis assured him. "This is a note from a charming little seamstress whom I love very dearly. I asked her to write me just for remembrance."

"Teffil you say, if she pe so pig a lady as her hantwritink, ten you are a lucky tamn fellow, my frient."

Aramis read the letter and passed it to Athos telling him to examine it. Athos glanced over it and to scatter any suspicions that might have arisen, read aloud:

My dear Cousin:
My sister and I are skilful at interpreting dreams and we are terrified by them anyhow.

In the case of yours, I hope we will be able to say that dreams are but lies and illusions.

Farewell. Take care of yourself. And act in such a way that we may from time to time hear of your prowesses.

Aglae Michon

The dragoon, who had drawn up to the table as Athos was reading, asked what the dream in question might be.

"Ja," the Swiss concurred. "Vot is tiss tream?"

"Oh, just a dream," Aramis said airily. "I had a dream and I told her about it."

"Yess, py Gott, it iss siimple to tell off a tream. Pot I neffer tream mineself."

"You are very fortunate," Athos said, rising. "Would I could say as much myself."

"I neffer neffer tream," the Swiss insisted, charmed that a man like Athos could envy him anything. "Neffer in mine life!"

D'Artagnan, seeing Athos rise, followed suit, took his arm and accompanied him out while Porthos and Aramis remained to bandy jests with the dragoon and the Switzer. As for Bazin, he found himself a truss of straw and lay down upon it. He soon fell asleep and, more imaginative than the Swiss, dreamed that Aramis, become Pope, had adorned his head with a cardinal's hat.

So far so good; Bazin's auspicious return had somewhat eased the anxiety that weighed upon our friends. But Planchet remained to be accounted for. Periods of expectation always seem to draw out interminably, and D'Artagnan would have sworn that the days were forty-eight hours long. He forgot the necessary slowness of navigation and he overstressed the power of Milady. Likening this woman to a demon, he endowed her with auxiliaries as supernatural as herself. No noise however slight but he imagined he was about to be arrested and forced with his friends to confront a Planchet in irons. Day by day, hour by hour, his confidence in the worthy Picard lackey waned. Worse, his attack of nerves assumed a sort of panic fear as it spread to Porthos and Aramis. Athos alone remained unshakable, as if, running no danger, he could afford to relax as usual.

On the sixteenth day in particular, the three uneasy friends could not contain themselves; singly or in pairs they wandered like lost souls along the road by which Planchet was expected. Athos, cool as a cucumber, lectured them in his usual dégagé fashion:

"Upon my word, you are behaving like children; surely no woman could so terrify three men? All in all, what is there to fear? Prison, ay; but if we go there, we will get out, just as Madame Bonacieux got out. Execution, ay; but day-in day-out here in the trenches we go cheerfully to expose ourselves to worse than that. Remember that a surgeon would give us more pain by amputating a leg than an execution by chopping off our heads. Wait, be patient, rest easy. In two or four or six hours at most, Planchet will be here; he promised and I trust him implicitly because he seems to be a very good lad indeed."

"What if he doesn't come?"

"Well, D'Artagnan, if he doesn't come, it will be because of some delay. He may have tumbled off his horse or fallen on some slippery deck or ridden so fast against the wind that he is ill with a fever. Let us allow for the unforeseen, gentlemen, since all is a gamble and life a chaplet of minor miseries which, bead by bead, your philosopher tells with a smile. Be philosophers as I am, friends; sit down here and let us drink. Nothing on earth makes the future so rosy as to look at it through a glass of Chambertin."

"That's all very well," D'Artagnan grumbled, "but I am tired of it all! Every time I open up a fresh bottle I tremble lest the wine comes from Milady's cellar."

"How fastidious you are, D'Artagnan! Such a beautiful woman!"

"A woman of mark!" Porthos observed, guffawing.

Athos shuddered, mopped his brow and rose to his feet with a kind of irritable movement he could not check.

The day crawled on; evening came slowly but at long last fell. The taverns were filled with drinkers. Athos, who had pocketed his share of the diamond, seldom left the Parpaillot. In Monsieur de Busigny, who incidentally had treated the musketeers to a magnificent dinner, he found a partner worthy of his attention. They were gambling together as usual when seven o'clock sounded; Athos could hear the patrols passing to double the posts. At half-past seven, the drums sounded retreat.

"The game is up, eh?" Athos repeated loudly, drawing four pistoles from his pocket and tossing them on the table. "Come, gentlemen, the tattoo has sounded; let us to bed!"

Very calmly he rose and moved out, D'Artagnan at his heels, Porthos and Aramis arm in arm bringing up the rear. Aramis was mumbling poetry to himself; from time to time Porthos pulled a hair or two from his mustaches to mark his despair.

Suddenly a shadow rose against the darkness . . . a shadow that D'Artagnan knew . . . a shadow that loomed large as life and dearer, even . . . and a familiar voice said very simply:

"Monsieur, I brought you your cloak. It is chilly this evening."

"Planchet!" D'Artagnan cried, overwhelmed with joy and, "Planchet! Planchet!" Porthos and Aramis echoed.

"Of course it's Planchet," Athos said calmly. "What is so strange about that? He promised to be back by eight o'clock and eight is striking. Good evening, Planchet, and congratulations! You are a man of your word. If ever you leave your master, I promise to take you on in my service."

"Thank you, Monsieur, but I will never leave Monsieur d'Artagnan." And, as he spoke, he slipped a note into his master's hand.

D'Artagnan felt strongly prompted to embrace Planchet as he had embraced him on his departure. But he feared lest this mark of affection, bestowed upon a lackey in the open street, appear extraordinary to passers-by and he restrained himself.

"I have the answer," he whispered to his friends.

"Good! Let us go home and read it."

The note burned in his hand; he tried to quicken their steps but Athos took his arm and forced him to walk slowly. At last they reached the tent, lit a lamp and, as Planchet stood guard at the entrance, D'Artagnan broke the seal and, with trembling hand, opened the long-awaited letter. It contained a half-line traced in eminently British handwriting and utterly Spartan in its laconism:

Thank you, be easy.

D'Artagnan's meagre stock of English sufficed to enable him to translate this. Athos then took the letter from D'Artagnan, set it over the lamp and did not relinquish it until it was reduced to ashes.

"Now, my lad," Athos said, "you may claim your seven hundred livres. But you certainly ran no great risks with a note like that."

"I am not to blame, Monsieur, for having tried every which way to make it short."

"Well, tell us all about it," D'Artagnan cried.

"Good Lord, Monsieur, it's a long story."

"You are right, Planchet," Athos declared. "Besides the tattoo has sounded and we must not keep this light on."

"So be it," D'Artagnan conceded. "Go to bed, Planchet, and sleep well."

"God's truth, Monsieur, it will be my first sound sleep in sixteen days."

"And mine!" said D'Artagnan.

"Mine too!" said Porthos.

"Same here!" said Aramis.

"And, truth to tell, mine too!" said Athos.

XLIX

FATALITY

Meanwhile Milady, drunk with passion and roaring on deck like a captive lioness, was sorely tempted to dive overboard and swim ashore. She could not rid her mind of the idea that she had been insulted by D'Artagnan, that she had been threatened by Athos and that she was leaving France without being revenged on them. Soon this thought became a veritable obsession and so intolerable that she implored the Captain to put her ashore no matter how terrible the risks to herself. But the Captain was eager to escape from his difficult position—he was hemmed in between French and English cruisers like a bat of the fable between the rats and the birds. It was imperative that he hasten to reach England; he therefore refused obstinately to heed what he considered to be a woman's whim. But since his fair passenger had been particularly recommended by the Cardinal, he promised to land her, the sea and the French permitting, at some port in Brittany, say Lorient or Brest. Unfortunately the wind continued contrary and the sea rough, so they tacked, beating to windward. Nine days after leaving the Charente, Milady, pale from disappointment and vexation, saw only the blue coast of Finistère heave into sight.

She calculated that she would require at least three days to cross this corner of France and to return to the Cardinal; an additional day for landing would make it four, four days. Add these four days to the nine past and it would mean thirteen days lost—days during which so many important events might occur in London. She also reflected that the Cardinal, furious at her return, would be more likely to listen to complaints against her than to her complaints against others. Abandoning all efforts to influence the Captain, she allowed the vessel to pass Lorient and Brest without a word; he, for his part, was careful not to remind her of her request. Milady therefore continued her voyage and on the very day Planchet embarked at Portsmouth for France the fair messenger of His Eminence entered that harbor triumphantly.

The whole town was in a state of extraordinary excitement. Four large vessels, recently built, had just been launched. At the end of the jetty, his clothes lavishly braided with gold, glittering as usual with diamonds and precious stones, his hat adorned with a white plume that swooped over his shoulder, Buckingham stood with a staff of officers almost as brilliant as himself.

It was one of those rare, beautiful winter days when England remembers that there is a sun over the island. The star of day, pale yet splendent, was sinking on the horizon, turning sea and firmament roseate with bands of fire and casting upon the towers and old houses of the city one last golden ray which made the windows sparkle like the reflection of a conflagration; Milady, breathing the sea-breeze, found it much more invigorating and softer as they approached land. Avidly she contemplated all these preparations which she was commissioned to destroy, all the might of this army which she, a woman, was to combat alone with the help of a few bags of gold. Looking out across the water, she compared herself mentally to Judith, the terrible Jewess, when she penetrated the camp of the Assyrians and beheld the enormous mass of chariots, horses, men and arms which a gesture of her hand was to scatter like a cloud of smoke.

They entered the roadstead but as they were about to cast anchor a formidably armed little cutter, apparently on coast guard duty, approached the merchantman. A few moments later the cutter put out a rowboat manned by a naval officer, a mate and eight oarsmen; as it reached the ladder of the merchantman, only the officer came on board, where he was received with all the deference due his uniform.

The officer conversed for a few moments with the skipper, showed him several papers he was carrying and then, at the skipper's order, both crew and passengers were summoned on deck.

When this had been done the officer inquired aloud about the brig's port of departure, its route and its landings; the skipper answered all these questions without hesitation or difficulty. Next the officer began to examine all the persons on deck, one after the other, and stopping when he came to Milady, he surveyed her intently but without uttering a word.

Then returning to the skipper, he spoke to him again very briefly and, as if from that moment the vessel was under his command, he ordered a manoeuvre which the crew executed immediately. The brig resumed its course, still escorted by the little cutter which sailed alongside, menacing it with the mouths of its six cannon. The rowboat followed in the wake of the brig, a mere speck beside this enormous mass.

While the officer had been scrutinizing Milady, she for her part was scrutinizing him quite as thoroughly. Yet despite the extraordinary power this woman with eyes of flame commanded when it came to reading the hearts of those whose secrets she wished to divine, on this occasion she met with a countenance so impassive that her investigation proved fruitless. The officer who had stopped in front of her and studied her silently with so much care, was about twenty-five years old. He was of pale complexion, with clear blue eyes, rather deeply set . . . his fine well-chiseled mouth remained cast in its natural lines . . . his strong, bold chin denoted that will power which, in the ordinary British type, indicates mere obstinacy . . . his brow, slightly receding as is proper for poets, enthusiasts and soldiers, was scantily shaded by short, thin hair . . . the beard covering the lower part of his face, was, like his hair, of a beautiful deep chestnut color. . . .

When they entered the harbor, night had already fallen. The fog increased the darkness and, falling on the ship's lights and lanterns of the jetties, formed a circle like that on the moon when rain threatens. The atmosphere was dank, cold and dismal. Milady, courageous though she was, shivered in spite of herself.

The officer pointed to Milady's baggage, had it placed in the rowboat, and invited her to descend by offering her his hand. She looked at him hesitantly.

"Who are you, Sir," she asked, "and why are you so kind as to trouble yourself so particularly on my account?"

"You must see by my uniform, Madame, that I am an officer in the Royal Navy."

"But is it usual for officers in the Royal Navy to place themselves at the service of their women compatriots when they land at an English port, and to carry their gallantry so far as to conduct them ashore?"

"Yes, Madame, it is usual, not through gallantry but for security reasons. In time of war, foreigners are conducted to particular hostelries in order that they may remain under government surveillance until complete information be obtained about them."

Though the officer spoke with a most scrupulous politeness and the most perfect calm, his words failed to convince Milady.

"But I am not a foreigner, Sir," she protested in the purest English accent ever heard between Portsmouth and Manchester. "My name is Lady Clark and this measure—"

"This measure is general, Madame, and you will seek in vain to evade it."

"Very well, Sir, I will follow you."

Accepting the officer's hand, she started down the ladder, at the foot of which the rowboat waited. The officer followed her. A large cloak had been spread in the stern of the rowboat; the officer bade her be seated on it and then himself sat down beside her.

"Row!" he told the sailors.

Eight oars fell at once into the sea making but a single sound and moving in but a single stroke as the boat seemed to fly over the face of the waters. Within five minutes they reached land; the officer leaped to the pier and offered his hand to Milady. A carriage awaited them on the quay.

"Is this carriage for us?" Milady asked.

"Yes, Madame."

"Then the hostelry is quite far?"

"At the other end of town."

"Very well, let us go," said Milady, entering the carriage resolutely.

The officer saw that the baggage was securely fastened behind the carriage, then sat down beside Milady and shut the door. Immediately, without any order or any indication of his destination, the coachman set off at a gallop through the streets.

So strange a reception naturally gave Milady ample food for thought.

Seeing that the young officer was not at all disposed for conversation, she leaned back in her corner of the carriage and reviewed all the surmises which passed successively through her mind.

They drove on for a quarter of an hour. Surprised at the length of the journey, Milady leaned forward to try to ascertain where they were going. There were no houses in sight now; only great trees appeared in the darkness like gaunt phantoms chasing one another across the night. Milady shuddered.

"But we are no longer in the city, sir," she protested.

The young officer remained silent.

"I warn you, sir, I shall go no farther unless you tell me where you are taking me."

Her threat elicited no information.

"Oh, this is too much!" she cried. "Help! help!"

But no voice replied as the carriage bowled forward. The officer at her right sat motionless as a statue. Milady cast him one of her characteristically frightening and usually very effective glances; anger made her eyes flash in the darkness. But the young man preserved his immobility. Milady next tried to open the door and jump out.

"Take care, Madame," the young man said coolly, "you will kill yourself if you jump."

She sat down again fuming with rage. The officer leaned forward, looking at her in his turn; he appeared surprised that a face so beautiful a few moments before could suddenly become so distorted and almost hideous in its impotent rage. Milady, who was nothing if not artful, at once realized that she was injuring herself by thus betraying her true nature. Collecting herself, she composed her features, asked in a quavering voice:

"In the name of Heaven, sir, pray tell me if it is to you, to your government or to an enemy that I must attribute the violence done me?"

"No one is doing you violence, Madame. What is happening to you is the result of a very simple measure, which we are forced to adopt with all who land in England."

"Then you do not know me, sir?"

"This is the first time I have had the honor of seeing you."

"And on your honor you have no reason to hate me?"

"None at all, I swear."

There was so much serenity, coolness and gentleness, even, in the young man's voice that Milady felt reassured.

At length, after about an hour's journey, the carriage stopped before an iron gate at the entrance to a narrow road which led to a castle, severe in form, massive and isolated. As the wheels rolled over a fine gravel, Milady heard a vast roaring which she immediately recognized as the surge of surf breaking over a rocky coast.

The carriage passed under two arched gateways and at last drew up in a square, gloomy court. Almost immediately the door of the carriage swung open, the young man sprang lightly out and offered his hand to Milady, who leaned upon it and in turn alighted with tolerable calm.

"So I am a prisoner!" she commented, glancing about her and then back at the young officer with a gracious smile. "But surely it will not be for long. My conscience and your politeness are guarantees of that."

Flattering though the compliment was, the officer made no reply. From his belt he drew a small silver whistle such as boatswains use on battleships and he whistled three times in three different keys. Immediately several men appeared, unharnessed the steaming horses and pushed the carriage into a coach house.

The officer, still with the same calm politeness, invited his fair prisoner to enter the house. With the same gracious smile, Milady took his arm and together they passed under a low arched door which, by a vaulted passageway lighted only at the farther end, led to a stone staircase, winding around a heavy stone pillar. They then came to a massive door; the young man produced a key from his pocket, turned the lock and the door swung heavily upon its hinges, revealing the chamber Milady was to occupy.

With one glance the prisoner took in the apartment in its minutest details. The furniture was appropriate for either a prisoner or a free man; but the bars at the windows and the outside bolts on the door smacked of the prison rather than the guest room.

For an instant all this woman's strength of mind, though drawn from the most vigorous sources, seemed to abandon her. She sank into a large easy-chair, arms crossed, head bowed, expecting every moment to see a judge enter to interrogate her. But no one entered except some marines who brought in her trunks and bags, set them down in one corner and retired without speaking.

The officer presided over all these details with the same tranquillity as before; he too spoke no word but enforced his orders by a gesture of his hand or a note of his whistle. It was as if spoken language did not exist or had become useless between this man and his inferiors. Unable to hold out any longer, Milady broke the silence:

"In the name of Heaven, sir, what does all this mean? Pray put an end to my doubts: I have courage enough for any peril I can foresee or any misfortune I can grasp. Where am I and why am I here? If I am free, why all these bars and bolts? If I am a prisoner, what crime have I committed?"

"You are here in the apartment that has been prepared for you, Madame. I received orders to meet you on shipboard and to conduct you to this castle. I believe I have fulfilled these orders with the firmness of a soldier, but also with the courtesy of a gentleman. Thus for the present, so far as you are concerned, my mission is at an end. The rest concerns another person."

"And who is that other person?" Milady asked impatiently. "Can you not tell me his name?"

As she spoke a loud jingling of spurs echoed through the corridor, voices passed by and died out in the distance, then the sound of a single footstep approached the door.

"That person is here, Madame," the officer said stepping aside to leave the entrance clear and assuming an attitude of great respect.

The door opened, a man appeared on the threshold. He was hatless, he wore his sword by his side and his fingers toyed with a handkerchief.

Milady thought she recognized this shadow in the gloom, with one hand she leaned heavily on the armchair and craned her neck forward as if to face a certainty.

The stranger advanced slowly and as he came into the circle of light projected by the lamp, Milady involuntarily recoiled. Then, when there was no longer any possible doubt, she cried in amazement:

"What, brother, is it you?" Overwhelmed with surprise: "You?"

"Yes, fair lady!" Lord Winter made a bow that was half courteous and half ironical. "Yes, it is I myself, in the flesh!"

"Then this castle—?"

"Is mine."

"This room—?"

"Is yours."

"Then I am your prisoner?"

"Virtually."

"But this is a frightful abuse of power!"

"No hifalutin words, Madame! Come, let us sit down and chat quietly as brother and sister ought to do."

Then, turning toward the door and noticing that the young officer stood waiting for further orders:

"All is well, I thank you. Now please leave us, Mr. Felton."

L

OF AN INTIMATE CONVERSATION BETWEEN BROTHER AND SISTER

Lord Winter closed the door, fastened a loose shutter and drew up a chair close to his sister-in-law.

Milady seemed lost in thought. Staring into space, she searched the limits of possibility without imagining what had befallen her and what would come of it. Her brother-in-law was, as she knew, a gentleman, a loyal and decent man, a great huntsman, an inveterate gambler, a wooer of women, but no plotter or intriguer. Could he possibly have discovered the hour of her arrival and had her seized and abducted? If so, why was he holding her?

There was Athos, of course, who had insinuated that her conversation with the Cardinal had not been unheard. But surely Athos could not have acted so promptly?

Perhaps her previous activities in England had come to light. Buckingham might well have discovered that it was she who had stolen the two diamond studs. He might well wish vengeance. Yet Buckingham was temperamentally incapable of persecuting a woman, particularly if that woman was probably moved by jealousy.

Was her past catching up with her or was her future in jeopardy: there lay the whole problem and she inclined toward the former solution. All in all she congratulated herself on falling into the hands of her brother-in-law. A stranger would have been more direct, intelligent and vigorous. Her immediate problem was to find out from Lord Winter what to do in the immediate future. He might not know what this operation signified or he might be hedging. Accordingly she smiled on him and waited for him to react to her charm. She did not have long to wait.

"So you decided to return to England?" he said very evenly. "Against every oath you swore to in Paris, here you are in Britain, eh?"

Question to question, Milady thought, and using enemy tactics:

"May I ask how you were able to know so intimately of my movements? May I ask since when you kept so close a watch upon me? Port of landing, day and hour, even?"

Lord Winter countered in kind:

"What brings you to England, sister?"

"The desire to see you."

"To see me?"

"Why not? Is that strange?"

"So you have crossed the Channel just to see me."

"Yes, My Lord and brother!"

"How dearly you must love me, My Lady."

"You are my only kinsman," Milady sighed ingenuously.

"Your only kinsman, ay. That makes you my only heir, Madame!"

Milady started. Obtuse as Lord Winter was, he could not fail to observe her dismay. The thrust was direct and deep. Had Kitty betrayed her, Milady wondered. Had Kitty told Lord Winter of certain indiscreet remarks, of certain expressions of dislike, confessed by mistress to servant and inspired wholly by greed of gain? Why had Milady been so indifferent and callous on the evening when Lord Winter introduced D'Artagnan to her as the man who had saved her life? And there was Kitty's disappearance, too.

"My dear brother—" she stalled. "I do not follow you." She must at all cost let him declare himself. "What on earth do you mean? What mystery lurks behind your words?"

"No mystery at all, my dear sister," he replied. (Was his joviality spontaneous or assumed?) "So you came to England to see me, eh? Knowing this, I spared you all sorts of annoyance: I sent you an officer to land you easily, I had a carriage at your disposal, you arrive here under my roof, you find a very comfortable room at your disposal, and we shall meet daily. What could be more natural? Certainly, what I tell you is as natural as what you tell me."

"But how did you know I was coming, brother?"

"Quite simple, Milady. The skipper of your vessel asked for permission to enter this port. He forwarded his logbook and his register. I am Governor of the Port; I consulted these records and I recognized your name. My heart told me what your lips have just confirmed. A choppy sea . . . a great many formalities ... your yearning to see me again—all these considerations inspired me to send my cutter to meet you. You know the rest. . . ."

"Tell me, My Lord and brother—" Milady, terrified, paused for a moment. "Didn't I see His Grace of Buckingham on the jetty?"

"Very likely. He is often at Admiralty Headquarters. Coming from France as you do, I suppose the sight of him impressed you. In France, I hear, there is much talk of British armament and preparations for invasion. Apparently this disturbs your friend the Cardinal."

"My friend the Cardinal!"

"Do you not acknowledge the friendship of His Eminence? Strange, I thought you both hand in glove. But we can discuss Richelieu and Buckingham at some other time. Meanwhile you came, I think you said, in order to visit me?"

"Exactly."

"As I remarked, you shall have your wish. We shall see each other daily."

"Then I am to stay—?"

"You will be comfortably lodged, sister. If there is anything you lack, you have but to ask for it."

"But I have no maid or lackeys."

"You shall not want for service, Madame: I would not venture to guess upon what footing your first husband established your household but, brother-in-law as I am, I shall match it."

"My first husband!"

"I mean your *French* husband, not my brother, who was perhaps your *second* husband. Or have you forgotten? At all events, you have a French husband still living. I am quite willing to write to him."

"You are joking, brother," Milady said airily. But a cold sweat broke over her brow.

"Do I look like a jester?"

"No. You look like someone who is trying to insult me!"

"Insult you! Is it humanly possible to insult *you?*"

"God help us, My Lord and brother, you are either in your cups or out of your senses. I beg you to withdraw and send me a maidservant."

"Women are discreet, eh, sister? Shall I play the maid to you? Family secrets—"

"Coward!" Milady looked angrily at him, then sprang across the room. "Coward!" she repeated.

"Well, well, well," Lord Winter replied, his arms crossed but his right hand on the pommel of his sword. "Murder is murder and you are skilled in the art. But I warn you I can defend myself even against you."

"Yes, you are cowardly enough to draw your sword against a woman."

"It would not be the first time a man raised his hand against you in punishment," he said, pointing to her left shoulder. "Snarl all you wish, tigress sister," he went on, "but do not bite, for it will not profit you. Here are no lawyers to settle an estate in advance ... and no knights errant to quarrel with me for the sake of the female I hold incommunicado ... here are only judges and righteous judges. ... They will make short shrift of a bigamist, however charming; and I warn you they will hand you over to a hangman who will make your two shoulders as like as a brace of cherries on one stem."

Milady's eyes flashed and, though armed, Lord Winter cowered. The chill of fear stole over him but with rising anger.

"Yes, I know your game," he continued, "you inherited my brother's fortune, now you plan to inherit mine. But, kill me or not, I am forewarned. Not one penny of mine can possibly go to you. Are you not rich enough? God knows you 'inherited' almost a million. But it was not enough; you had perforce to pursue your wicked career. Tell me—" he glanced speculatively at her, "was it greed of gain that possessed you or love of evil for evil's sake?"

"My Lord—"

"At all events I can tell you this. Were my brother's memory not sacred to me, you would now be rotting in a state dungeon or providing a spectacle to entertain the curiosity of sailors at Tyburn. For my part I shall not unmask you: by the same token, I advise you to take your imprisonment calmly. Within two or three weeks I go to La Rochelle with the army. The day before I sail, a vessel will come for you and I shall see you off to our colonies in the south. You may be assured of a bodyguard who will blow your brains out at the first effort you make to return to England or to the Continent."

Milady, her fiery eyes dilated, listened with extreme concentration.

"Thus for the present you are to remain here in this castle," Lord Winter went on. "Its walls are thick, its doors are strong, its bars are stout. Besides, your window juts out over the deep blue sea. My men, who are devoted to me body and soul, stand watch around this apartment; they guard every passage leading to the courtyard; even if you managed by some miracle to reach the courtyard, you would still have to pass through three iron gates. My orders are positive: one step, one move, one word suggesting escape and you will be shot down. Should you be killed, English justice will, I trust, be beholden to me for having spared it some work."

Milady stared at him coldly as though he was speaking in some foreign language.

"Ha, I see!" he said. "You are calm again, your features placid and your countenance serene as ever. 'Two weeks,' you say, 'three weeks, pshaw! I have an inventive mind. Between now and then I shall contrive something. My soul was fashioned in hell, I shall soon find a victim to spirit me out of here!' Well, Madame, my only answer is: Try it!"

Milady, her innermost thoughts betrayed, dug her nails into her flesh to restrain any expression other then one of painful apprehension. Lord Winter continued:

"The officer in command here during my absence you already know, for he brought you here from Portsmouth. You observed how implicitly he obeys orders, for I am sure you could not have traveled together all that way without your attempting to sound him out. Tell me, was marble statue ever more impassive and more mute? Ah, you have tried your powers of seduction on many men and unfortunately you have always succeeded. Now try them upon this one; by God, if you get the better of him, I shall certify you to be Satan himself."

Walking across to the door, he flung it open:

"Send for Mr. Felton," he ordered. Then turning to Milady: "In a few moments I shall recommend you to his care."

A strange silence ensued between the two. Presently slow regular footsteps could be heard approaching; soon a human form loomed in the shadows of the corridor and Felton stood at attention, awaiting his master's orders.

"Come in, my dear John," said Lord Winter, "come in and close the door." As the young officer obeyed: "Now, John, look carefully at this woman. She is young, she possesses all earthly seductions and charms but she is a fiend incarnate. At twenty-five this monster stands guilty of as many crimes as you could read of in a year in the archives of our courts-at-law. Her voice is prepossessing, her beauty serves as a lure for her victims; and her body pays what she promises—that, at least, I must grant her. She will attempt to seduce you, she may even attempt to kill you."

Lord Winter coughed, looked frankly at Felton, paused for another moment, and in simple sincere tones pursued:

"I rescued you from a life of wretchedness, John; I obtained your Lieutenant's commission for you and I once saved your life, you recall on what occasion. I am not only your protector but your friend; I am not only your benefactor but almost your father. This woman here came to England in order to plot against my life; I now hold the snake in my hands. So I have sent for you to tell you: 'Friend Felton, my dear lad, beware of this woman for my sake but especially for yours. Swear to me by your hope of salvation that you will preserve her for the punishment she has so richly deserved. John Felton, I trust in your pledged word; Lieutenant Felton, I trust in your loyalty.' "

The young man's mild calm expression changed; he flushed with all the hatred he could find in his heart:

"My Lord," he said solemnly, "your orders will be carried out."

Her eyes on his face, Milady received Felton's harsh glance with the air of a gentle victim, innocence and submission written large upon her exquisite features. Even Lord Winter found it difficult to believe that here was the tigress he had been ready to strike down a few moments ago.

"This woman is never to leave this room under any circumstances whatever, do you understand, John? She is to communicate with no one by writing, and orally with you alone. Whether or not you do her the honor of replying is your own affair."

"I understand, My Lord. I have given you my word of honor."

Lord Winter nodded. Then to Milady:

"Now that Man has passed judgment upon you, Madame," he advised, "try to make your peace with God."

Milady bowed her head as if crushed by the overwhelming justice of this sentence; Lord Winter beckoned to Felton to follow and the door closed upon them. A moment later the steady tread of a sentry echoed up and down the corridor with the occasional clank of a musket against wall or floor.

Suspecting that somebody might be spying up on her through the keyhole, Milady sat stock-still for some minutes. Then raising her head she stared into space, her features contracted in defiance and menace. Presently she edged toward the door to listen; then she crossed to the window to look down on the sea; and at last she sank back into her armchair, lost in thought.

LI

OF AN OFFICER OUT ON A STROLL

Meanwhile the Cardinal was anxiously awaiting news from England; but none came save of the most unpleasant and threatening nature.

La Rochelle was thoroughly invested; every precaution had been taken and the dike, which prevented the entrance of even a skiff into the beleagured city, augured certain success. Yet the blockade might last quite a while, which would prove a great affront to the King's arms and a great inconvenience for the Cardinal. True, Richelieu need no longer embroil the King with Anne of Austria; he had already accomplished this. But he had still to accommodate matters between Monsieur de Bassompierre and the Duc d'Angoulême who were on very bad terms. As for the Duc d'Orléans, brother to the King, having begun the siege, he left the task of finishing it to the Cardinal.

Notwithstanding the incredible perseverance of their Mayor, the citizens of La Rochelle had attempted a mutiny of sorts to force him to surrender. The Mayor hanged the ringleaders. This show of force quieted the unruly who resolved to die of hunger, a slower and less drastic death than strangulation.

The besiegers, for their part, occasionally intercepted couriers sent by the men of La Rochelle to Buckingham or spies sent by Buckingham to the men of La Rochelle. Justice in either case was swiftly rendered. The Cardinal merely uttered the word "Hanging!" and a man hung. His Majesty was invariably invited to witness the execution. The King arrived languidly, occupied a favored place whence he could observe each detail of the operation, was invariably somewhat entertained and felt the siege to be less of a chore. But he was very bored indeed and spoke constantly of returning to Paris. Thus had there been a lack of La Rochelle messengers and English spies, His Eminence, despite his imagination and resource, would have found himself in an awkward position.

Time passed on and still the city showed no sign of surrendering. The most recent spy captured was the bearer of a letter informing Buckingham that the city was desperate. But instead of saying: "If your succor is not forthcoming within a fortnight we shall surrender," it read: "If your succor does not arrive within a fortnight we shall all be dead of hunger when it does arrive."

Buckingham, then, was the sole hope of the citizenry of La Rochelle; he was their Messiah. Obviously if once they learned for certain that they could no longer count on him their courage would collapse with their hopes.

Accordingly His Eminence waited avidly for tidings from England to the effect that Buckingham would not come.

The question of storming the city was frequently debated in the Royal Council and invariably rejected. In the first place, its battlements seemed impregnable. Further whatever His Eminence might have said he realized that he could not set Frenchmen against Frenchmen. The horrors of a bloody civil war would have marked current policy as a retrogression to the savagery of sixty years before. His Eminence was what we of the nineteenth century call a man of progress. Indeed, in 1628, the sack of La Rochelle and the slaughter of three or four thousand Huguenots who would have borne too much resemblance to the Massacres of Saint Bartholemew in 1572. The King, staunch Catholic though he was, would not have objected in the least to such categoric and sanguinary measures. But he always bowed before the argument of the besieging generals; La Rochelle, they all agreed, was impregnable save by famine.

Often the Cardinal thought uncomfortably and with a certain fear of Milady. Her strange dual character . . . the mixture of beauty and horror in her . . . the dove, the lion, the snake. . . . Had she betrayed him? Was she dead? Friend or foe, acting for or against him, he knew that nothing save the greatest obstacles could immobilize a woman of her energy. But who could have set these obstacles in her path?

Fundamentally he felt he could rely on her and with reason. There must be something so ghastly in this woman's past that only his red mantle could cover it. This woman was his own, his creature, for only in him could she find support stronger than the dangers which threatened her.

The stake he had in her being so tenuous, the Cardinal decided to wage war single-handed; any success from abroad would be a stroke of chance. He would continue to raise the famous dike which was to starve La Rochelle and, as it rose higher, day by day, he stared across at the unhappy city. What profound wretchedness and what heroic virtues it contained! The Cardinal thought of King Louis XI his political predecessor—as akin to himself as his successor Robespierre was to be—and he remembered the words of the King's minister and toady, Tristan L'Hermite: "Divide in order to rule."

Henry IV when besieging Paris had ordered his soldiers to toss bread and provisions over the walls to the enemy. His Eminence arranged for short notes to be tossed over the walls of La Rochelle in which he pointed out to its inhabitants how unjust, selfish and barbarous was the conduct of their leaders. These leaders, said the text, possessed wheat in abundance yet they would not share it with the population. Their slogan—for they had their slogans too—was that women, children and oldsters should die so long as those who manned the walls remained well-fed, healthy and strong.

Thanks to the loyalty of the citizens or to their inability to resist, this principle had not been universally adopted but it was partially observed; it had passed from theory to practice. Richelieu's propaganda injured it considerably. It reminded the men that the luckless folk they allowed to die were their own wives, children and parents. The evident conclusion was that if all the inhabitants were reduced to a common misery such equal conditions must inevitably result in unanimity of decision.

These broadcasts met with all the effect their writer anticipated, for they determined a large number of inhabitants to open private negotiations with the Royal Army.

The Cardinal had cause to congratulate himself; his methods were bearing fruit and the future looked rosy. But at precisely this juncture a citizen of La Rochelle tossed a figurative bombshell into His Eminence's real expectations. Despite the vigilance of Bassompierre, of Schomberg and of the Duc d'Angoulême, themselves under the Cardinal's unflagging surveillance, a man of La Rochelle had regained the city from England with word that he had himself seen a splendid fleet in Portsmouth harbor ready to sail within a week. Lord Buckingham, he added, wished the Mayor of La Rochelle to tell his fellow-citizens that the Great League was about to declare itself and that France was soon to be invaded simultaneously by English, Imperial and Spanish armies. This letter was read publicly in every square of the city, copies were posted on all street corners and even those who had begun negotiations with the Royal Army now desisted, pending the succor so nobly and handsomely promised.

This unexpected circumstance revived Richelieu's early anxiety and forced him reluctantly to cast his eyes once more across the Channel.

Such high concerns did not affect the Royal Army. Exempt from the worries of its sole and true chief, it led a carefree, joyous life. Provisions and money were plentiful; the various units vied in gaiety and daring. For the citizenry of La Rochelle, a prey to famine and apprehension, the days were interminable; for the Cardinal who had bottled up the city, they were long enough; for the troops, they were a prolonged holiday. To catch a spy and hang him they invented the wildest expeditions and carried them out over the dike or at sea with consummate phlegm.

At times His Eminence, in no wise distinguishable from the humblest trooper in his army, would ride the dunes. As he gazed over the harbor works which kept pace with his wishes so slowly, he marveled that engineers recruited all over France had been so laggard. Whenever he met any musketeers of Monsieur de Tréville's company, he found himself wondering why none was Athos, Porthos, Aramis or D'Artagnan. Then, shaking his head, he would stare out to sea again, his thoughts on more vital matters. One day, oppressed by intolerable ennui, in despair of negotiating with the city and utterly without news from England, His Eminence set out for a stroll along the beach with no purpose other than to take the air: Cabusac and La Houdinière alone followed him. Pacing his horse at a slow walk, His Eminence stared out across the slate-gray sea. Presently his horse brought him to the top of a dune whence he sighted a hedge. From this height His Eminence espied, over the hedge, a group of men reclining in a valley of sand. A last faint light of premature dusk, rare in that season, enabled him to distinguish seven men reclining amid a circle of empty bottles.

(Need I say that the seven were four musketeers, poised to hear one of them read a letter he had just received. Need I add that the letter was so vital that they had tossed their cards and dice onto the drumhead? Must I explain how the other three, evidently lackeys, were engaged in opening a demijohn of Colliure wine?)

His Eminence was in extremely low spirits and when depressed he could not bear to see others happy. Psychologically, too, he fancied somewhat strangely that his melancholy created gaiety in others. Motioning to Cabusac and La Houdinière to halt, His Eminence dismounted and advanced on tiptoe toward these suspect merrymakers. The sand would deaden his footsteps, the hedge conceal his approach; he could doubtless overhear them without fear of detection. He had not taken ten steps before he recognized a rollicking Gascon accent; he knew the men were musketeers; undoubtedly here were the youth he had wondered about and the inseparable Athos, Porthos and Aramis.

He was therefore all the more eager to hear what they were saying. His eyes took on a strange air of expectancy and, catlike, His Eminence crept toward the hedge. Crouching behind it he caught only a few meaningless syllables when suddenly a loud cry made him start. The musketeers looked up.

"Attention gentlemen!" Grimaud bawled.

"You spoke, scoundrel?" Athos cried incredulously. He raised himself on one elbow, brushed the sand off his shoulder with his free hand and stared at Grimaud, his eyes flashing. "You dared speak!"

Awed, Grimaud said no more. But he pointed toward the hedge. In a trice the musketeers rose to their feet, stood at attention and saluted with impeccable smartness. His Eminence seemed disgruntled.

"Well, gentlemen," he observed sourly, "I notice the musketeers post sentinels about them. Can the English be planning to land or do the musketeers consider themselves to be Field Officers?"

Amid the general consternation Athos alone preserved his calm. Cool as a cucumber, self-possessed as ever, he faced the Cardinal as a nobleman, equal to equal.

"Monseigneur," he said evenly, "when off duty, His Majesty's musketeers drink and dice. They are not commissioned, but to their lackeys they are the equals of the highest Field Officers."

"Lackeys, you say," the Cardinal grumbled, "lackeys ordered to alert their masters when someone passes by are sentries, not lackeys."

"Yet Your Eminence must see that we have posted no sentries. We were taken by surprise. Indeed we might well have let Your Eminence pass without paying our respects and offering our thanks for past favors." Athos paused a moment, drew himself up and: "D'Artagnan," he said, "you have been waiting for a chance to express your gratitude to the Cardinal. Well, here is your chance."

Athos spoke with all the assurance and imperturbability that distinguished him in times of crisis. Ever calm, he was kingly when danger threatened. D'Artagnan stumbled forward, mumbled a few words of thanks, and relapsed into silence under the Cardinal's disapproving stare.

Richelieu, apparently in no wise diverted from his original purpose by the incident Athos had created, looked stonily ahead of him and said:

"All this is beyond the point, gentlemen. Because private soldiers happen to be privileged to serve in a crack regiment, they are not to play the part of great noblemen. I do not like it. Discipline is the same for one and all."

Athos bowed.

"Monseigneur," he said firmly, "we have not violated military discipline. We are now off duty and being off duty we fancied we could spend our time as we pleased. If Your Eminence sees fit to order us to perform some task in the line of duty we would be much honored." Athos frowned, for the Cardinal's specious interrogation was beginning to try his patience. "As Your Eminence may observe, we did not venture forth unarmed."

Athos looked significantly at the four muskets stacked beside the drum on which lay an assortment of cards and dice.

Recovering his senses, D'Artagnan suggested that the musketeers would not have failed to go to meet His Eminence had they imagined he was coming into their midst so poorly attended. The Cardinal pursed his lips.

"Do you know what you look like? Always together, always armed, always guarded by your lackeys? Why, you look like four conspirators."

"True, Monseigneur, we *do* conspire. But as Your Eminence observed the other day, we conspire against the men of La Rochelle."

"Well, gentlemen politicos—" the Cardinal frowned in his turn, "I dare say many mysteries might be solved if one could read your minds as blithely as you were reading that letter when I drew up. I may add that I was as quick to see you hide it as you were to do so."

Athos, flushing, stepped forward.

"Judging by this inquisition, it would seem as though Your Eminence really suspected us of conspiracy. If so, we trust Monseigneur will deign to explain so that we may at least know where we stand."

"Inquisition or no, Monsieur Athos, others have submitted to it and answered in all honesty."

"We are prepared to answer in all honesty to any question Your Eminence may be pleased to ask."

"I see." There was a long silence. Then, turning on Aramis, the Cardinal barked: "What was in the letter you were reading, Monsieur, and why did you hide it when I appeared?"

"A letter from a lady, Monsieur."

"Ah, yes, that sort of letter commands discretion!" The Cardinal coughed. "Still, it may well be shown to a confessor; as you know I have been admitted to Holy Orders."

With a calmness the more terrifying because he knew he might well pay for it with his head, Athos admitted the letter was from a lady but was signed neither by Marion de Lorme nor by Madame d'Aiguillon.

The Cardinal turned very pale, his eyes darted lightning, and he turned as if to give an order to Cahusac and La Houdinière. Athos, seeing the movement, stepped toward the stacked muskets. His companions eyed their weapons like men ill disposed to submit meekly to arrest. The Cardinal's party numbered three, His Eminence included; the musketeers with their lackeys numbered seven. His Eminence judged very wisely that if Athos and his friends were really plotting, the contest would prove all the more uneven. With one of those sudden reversals by which he so often profited, all his anger faded into a smile.

"Enough!" he said affably, "I know you to be brave young men, proud in the daylight and loyal in the dark. There is no harm in posting men to watch over yourselves when you watch so well over others. I have not forgotten the night when you escorted me to and from the *Red Dovecote*, gentlemen. Were there any danger on the road I am about to take, I would beg you to accompany me. But since I am quite safe, pray stay where you are and finish your bottles, your gambling and your love letters. Gentlemen, I bid you adieu."

Cahusac led up the Cardinal's horse. His Eminence sprang into the saddle, waved his hand in farewell and rode off. The four young men watched him disappear and looked at one another in dismay. To be sure his leave-taking had been friendly but each knew that the Cardinal was in a towering rage. Only Athos smiled, an authoritative and disdainful smile. The Cardinal out of sight, Porthos, venting his ill humor on the nearest butt at hand, growled:

"That fellow Grimaud warned us too late!"

The lackey was about to apologize; but Athos raised his hand, enjoining silence.

"Would you have handed over your letter?" D'Artagnan asked Aramis.

"I?" Aramis asked back in his most melodious voice. The others looked at him curiously. "Yes," he said. "My mind was made up. I would have given him the letter with one hand and, with the other, plunged my sword through his body."

"So I thought," said Athos. "That is why I stepped forward between you and His Eminence. I must say that cleric is rash to speak to any self-respecting men as he did to us. You might suppose he had dealt all his life with women and children."

"Heaven knows I admire you, Athos," D'Artagnan said. "But after all you were in the wrong."

"I, in the wrong? God help us, whose is this air we breathe, whose this ocean we survey, whose this sand we rest on, whose the letter from your mistress, D'Artagnan? Do any of these belong to the Cardinal? I swear I think that man imagines that he owns the entire world. And there you stood before that man, flustered, stammering, stultified. Anyone might have supposed the Bastille gaped to receive you or the gigantic Medusa had turned you to stone. You are in love; does that make you a conspirator? You are in love with a woman His Eminence clapped into jail and you want to get her back for yourself. There you stand, gambling against His Eminence; the letter is the ace in your hand, why expose it to your opponent? No one ever does that. Let him guess, well and good; we can guess what trumps *he* holds."

D'Artagnan conceded that what Athos said was eminently sensible.

"In that case, let us forget this unpleasant interlude. Come, Aramis, read us the letter from your cousin. I must say I have forgotten how it ran, what with all these interruptions."

Aramis pulled the letter from his pocket, his friends drew together around him, the three lackeys took their stand around the demijohn as though the Cardinal had never appeared.

"You had only read a line or two," said D'Artagnan. "Start again from the beginning."

"With pleasure," said Aramis. "Here you are:

My dear Cousin:

I think I shall decide to leave for Stenay where my sister has entered our little maid in the Carmelite convent. The poor child is quite resigned to this as she knows she cannot live elsewhere without endangering her hopes of sanctity and salvation.

If our family affairs permit, as we hope, I believe she will ultimately return to those she longs for, even though she run the risk of being damned for it. I say this because I know how she realizes that they think of her constantly.

Meanwhile she is not too unhappy. What she most craves is a letter from her swain. Such communications are difficult to pass through convent gratings but, if I can go, I will undertake the task. As you know I have not proved unskilful in the past. So much for that.

As for my sister, she thanks you for your loyal and enduring remembrance. For a while she experienced considerable distress but now she is somewhat reassured, for, to forestall any untoward circumstances, she has dispatched her secretary to the place you know.

Adieu, fair cousin. Let us hear from you as often as you can—I mean as often as you can safely.

I embrace you
Marie Michon"

"How much I owe you, Aramis!" D'Artagnan sighed. "Thanks to you I have news of my beloved Constance after all these weeks. She is alive; she is safe in a convent; she is at Stenay. Where is Stenay, Athos?"

"Stenay is in Lorraine, a few leagues from the Alsatian border," Athos replied. "The siege done, we can take a turn in that direction."

"It won't be long now, let us hope," Porthos put in. "This very morning they hanged a spy who had confessed that the men of La Rochelle were down to shoe leather. The leather eaten, suppose they eat up the soles, I can't see what they can do after that but eat one another."

Athos drained a glass of excellent Bordeaux, a wine which, without enjoying the reputation it does today, deserved it nevertheless: "Poor fools!" he said. "As though the Roman Catholic faith were not the most profitable and agreeable of religions!"

Smacking his tongue against his palate in appreciation of the wine: "No matter, they are gallant men!" he went on. Then, turning on Aramis: "What the devil are you about?" he asked. "Why are you cramming that letter into your pocket?"

"Well, I—"

"Athos is right," D'Artagnan broke in. "We must burn that letter. And even if we do we must pray that His Eminence does not collect the ashes and read them by some process of his own."

"I am certain he has some such process," Athos agreed.

"Grimaud, front and centre!" Athos commanded. And, as the lackey stepped forward: "My friend, contrary to all orders, you spoke without permission. For punishment, you shall please eat this paper. And in reward for the great service you did us, you shall wash it down with a glass of wine. Here is the paper; chew it up carefully!" Grimaud smiled. His eyes fixed on the glass Athos held up, he ground the paper between his teeth, rolled it up in his mouth, and, moistening it with all the saliva he could muster, swallowed it effortlessly.

"Bravo, Grimaud, here you are! Bottoms up and don't bother to thank me."

Grimaud sipped the glass silently but throughout this occupation his eyes, raised heavenward, spoke a language the more expressive for being mute.

"And now," said Athos, "unless Monsieur le Cardinal should be inspired to dissect Grimaud, I think we may feel pretty safe about the letter."

Meanwhile His Eminence was pursuing his dull, melancholy ride back to camp, murmuring between his mustaches:

"Come what may, I must win those four men over to my cause."

LII
Captivity: The First Day

While all this was going on in France, Milady, across the Channel was still a prey to complete dispair. Plunged in an abyss of dismal meditation, a dark hell at whose gate she had almost abandoned all hope, for the first time in her life she experienced doubt and fear.

Twice before, luck had deserted her; twice before, she had been exposed and betrayed and twice before, she had fallen the victim to the same fatal genius whom God must have appointed to be her undoing. D'Artagnan had conquered her despite her apparently invincible force for evil.

He had deceived her in love, humbled her in her pride, thwarted her of her ambition; now he was ruining her fortunes, depriving her of liberty and threatening her very life. Worse still, he had partly raised her mask; he had thrust aside the shield which was at once her protection and her strength.

D'Artagnan had diverted from Buckingham (whom she hated as she hated all those she had loved) the threat Richelieu held over his head in the person of the Queen. D'Artagnan had impersonated de Vardes for whom she entertained the tigerish fancy such women are apt to feel. D'Artagnan had confiscated the blanket order which she had obtained from Richelieu as an instrument of her vengeance upon her enemy.

D'Artagnan, having caused her arrest, was about to banish her to some shameful Tyburn in the old world or to some horrible Botany Bay in the Indian Ocean!

For all this D'Artagnan was solely responsible. Who but he could have heaped so much shame upon her head? Who but he could have told Lord Winter all the terrible secrets which he had so providently discovered one after another? He knew Lord Winter, he must undoubtedly have written to him.

What a witch's brew of hatred she distilled as she sat there in her lonely room, motionless, her eyes burning and fixed. How well the tumult of her hoarse deep-fetched moans of fury and exasperation blended with the surge of the surf as it rose, growled, roared and spent itself, as though in eternal and powerless despair, against the rocks topped by this dark and lofty castle! In the lightning flashes of her tempestuous rage, what magnificent vengeance she plotted against Madame Bonacieux, against Buckingham and especially against D'Artagnan in the future, immediate or remote!

True, but to revenge herself she must be free and to go free a prisoner must pierce a wall, unfasten bars cut through a floor—all of which tasks can be accomplished by a strong patient man but before which the feverish irritations of a woman must give way. Besides, to do all this, time was necessary—months, even years—and Lord Winter, her fraternal and terrifying jailer had warned her that she had but ten or twelve days. Were she a man, she would try to escape, however heavily the odds were stacked against her, and who knows: she might even succeed! But Heaven had committed the hideous error of misplacing a manlike soul in her frail and delicate body.

These, the first few moments of her imprisonment, were a veritable agony as she paid her debt of feminine weakness to nature amid paroxysms of rage that swept her headlong. Presently, little by little, she overcame the outbursts of her insensate rage. The nervous tremblings which wracked her body subsided and she recoiled within herself like an exhausted serpent in repose.

"Ah, God! I must have been mad to lose my self-control!" she mused, gazing into the mirror which reflected her own burning, questioning glance. "Enough of violence; violence is a proof of weakness; what is more, I have never succeeded by that means. Perhaps if I employed my strength against women I might find them weaker than I am and consequently vanquish them. But I am struggling against men to whom I am but a woman. Let me fight like a woman, my whole strength lies in my frailty."

As if to prove to herself what changes she could impose upon her expressive and mobile countenance, she assumed all manner of varied expressions from that of a passionate anger which convulsed her features to that of the gentlest, most affectionate and seductive serenity. Then under her skilful hands her hair successively took on all the forms which she believed might best flatter her face. At last satisfied, she murmured:

"Ah well, nothing is lost! I am still beautiful!"

It was then nearly eight o'clock in the evening. Milady decided that a rest of several hours would refresh not only her head and her ideas but also her complexion. But a still better idea occurred to her before she retired. She had overheard some talk about supper and she had already been in this chamber an hour; they would surely be bringing her some food before long. Determined not to lose a moment of precious time, she planned this very evening to reconnoitre the terrain by carefully studying the characters of the men to whose guardianship she was committed.

Presently a light under the door announced the return of her jailers. Milady rose hastily from her bed, flung herself into the armchair, tilted her head back, let her beautiful hair fall disheveled over her shoulders, half-bared her bosom under her crumpled lace, and placed one hand on her heart, dangling the other helplessly at her side. The bolts were drawn, the door grated on its hinges, the sound of approaching footsteps reechoed in her room.

"Put the table there," said a voice which she recognized as Felton's. "Bring lights in and relieve the sentinel."

This double order given to the same men convinced Milady that her servants were her guards too, in other words soldiers. Felton's orders were executed with a silent rapidity that spoke worlds for the discipline he maintained. At last Felton, who had not yet looked at Milady, turned toward her, "Ah!" he said, "she is asleep. When she wakes up she can sup!" And he took several steps toward the door.

"No, Lieutenant," said a soldier who, less stoical than his chief, had approached Milady, "this woman is not asleep."

"What, not asleep? What is she doing, then?"

"She has fainted. She is deathly pale. I listened closely but I cannot hear her breathe."

"You're right," said Felton, after examining Milady without moving from the spot where he stood. "Go tell Lord Winter that his prisoner has fainted. Personally I do not know what to do. We had not foreseen this."

As the soldier moved away to carry out Felton's orders, Felton sat down on an armchair close to the door and waited, wordless and motionless.

Milady possessed one great art which women cultivate assiduously, that of looking through her long eyelashes without appearing to open her eyelids. She watched Felton, who sat with his back to her, steadily for almost ten minutes. During all this time, he never once turned around.

She realized that Lord Winter would be coming in shortly and that his presence would strengthen Felton's indifference. Her first attempt had failed. Acting like a woman who exploits all her resources, she raised her head, opened her eyes and uttered a helpless sigh. Felton wheeled around:

"Ah, you are awake, Madame," he said, "then I have nothing more to do here. If you want anything, you can ring!"

"Ah God, my God, how I have suffered!" Milady moaned in that melodious voice which like those of the enchantress of old, charmed all whom they wished to destroy. And, sitting up in her armchair, she assumed a still more graceful and abandoned position than when she had reclined. Felton rose to his feet.

"You will be served three times a day, Madame: breakfast at nine, dinner at one, supper at eight. If that does not suit you you may tell us what hours you prefer and we will comply with your wishes."

"But am I to remain always alone in this huge dismal room?"

"A woman of the neighborhood has been sent for. She will come to the castle tomorrow and will return whenever you desire her presence."

"I thank you, sir," replied the prisoner humbly.

Felton made a slight bow and started toward the door. As he was about to clear the threshold, Lord Winter appeared in the corridor, followed by the soldier sent to apprise him of Milady's swoon. He held a vial of smelling salts in his hand.

"Well, what is this? What on earth is going on here?" he jeered, as he saw his prisoner sitting up and Felton about to leave the room. "Has this corpse come to life already? Tut, tut, Felton my lad, can't you see that she takes you for a greenhorn? This is but Act One of a comedy which we shall doubtless have the pleasure of applauding as the plot unfolds!"

"I thought so, My Lord, but after all the prisoner is a lady. I wished to pay her all the attention that a gentleman owes a lady, if not on her account, at least on my own."

Milady shuddered from head to toe as Felton's matter-of-fact words passed like ice through her veins.

Lord Winter laughed.

"Behold the beautiful hair so artfully disheveled, that white skin and that languishing glance! So they have not seduced you yet, O heart of stone!"

"No, My Lord," the phlegmatic youth answered. "Believe me, it requires more than the tricks and coquetry of a woman to corrupt me."

"In that case my gallant lieutenant, let us leave Milady to invent something else and let us adjourn to supper. Rest assured she possesses a fruitful imagination and Act Two of the comedy will be forthcoming soon!"

With which Lord Winter passed his arm through Felton's and led him out, still laughing at his joke.

"I will be a match for you yet!" Milady vowed through clenched teeth. "Of that you may be certain, you poor sanctimonious would-be monk, you wretched little mock-soldier with your uniform cut out of God knows what flyblown canonicals!"

"By the way," Lord Winter added, looking back across the doorway, "pray do not suffer this check to take away your appetite. Taste that fowl and that fish; on my honor, they are not poisoned. I have an excellent cook and, as he is not my heir, I trust him completely and utterly. Do just as I do! Adieu then, dear sister, until your next swoon!"

It was all Milady could endure. Her hands grasped her armchair, she ground her teeth furiously, her eyes followed the door as it closed behind Felton and Lord Winter. The moment she was alone, a fresh fit of despair seized her. Glancing at the table, she saw a knife glittering up at her, darted toward it and took it up. But her disappointment was cruel indeed: the blade was round and of flexible silver.

A burst of laughter sounded on the other side of the door, which had not been properly closed and which now swung open again.

"Ha, ha, ha!" Lord Winter mocked. "Ha, ha, ha! You see, my dear Felton, you see what I told you? That knife was for you, my lad; she would have killed you. You see, one of her peculiarities is to rid herself in one way or another of anybody who stands in her way. If I had listened to you, that knife would have been pointed and of steel. That would have meant good-bye, Felton; she would have cut your throat and after that turned on the rest of us! See, John, see how well she handles a knife!"

Milady stood there, still holding the harmless weapon in her clenched fist; but at these last words, at this supreme insult, her hands, her strength and even her will faltered. The knife fell clattering down on the floor.

"You were right, My Lord," Felton admitted in a tone of such profound disgust that Milady's heart sank within her. "Ay, you were right and I was wrong."

Once again they walked away. This time Milady listened more carefully until she could no longer hear their footsteps.

"I am lost!" Milady murmured. "Now I am in the power of men on whom I have no more influence than on statues of bronze or granite! They know me by heart and are steeled against all my artifices. But no! it shall not be! It is impossible that this should end as they have decreed."

Fear and weakness could not dwell long in her wilful and passionate spirit; instinctively she clutched at hope. Sitting down at the table, she ate from several dishes, drank a little Spanish wine and felt all her resolution returning.

Before going to bed she pondered and analyzed the words, the steps, gestures and even the silences of her interlocutors. From this deep, skilful and meticulous study she concluded that Felton was the more vulnerable of her two persecutors. One expression especially recurred to her mind: "If I had listened to you," Lord Winter had said to Felton. Felton must have spoken in her favor since Lord Winter had been unwilling to listen to him.

"Weak or strong," Milady repeated, "that man has at least a spark of pity in his soul. I shall fan that spark into a flame that shall devour him. As for the other, he knows me, he fears me and he realizes what to expect if ever I escape from his hands. It is futile to attempt anything with him, but Felton—he is something else again! He is a young, ingenuous and pure young man; he appears to be virtuous. Him there are means of destroying!"

Milady sighed, went to bed and fell asleep with a smile on her lips. Anyone who had seen her thus would have said that here was a young girl dreaming of the crown of flowers she was to wear on her brow on the Feast Day.

LIII

CAPTIVITY: THE SECOND DAY

Milady dreamed that she at long last held D'Artagnan in her power. She was witnessing his execution; his blood was streaming under the axe of the executioner. This welcome fancy lent her features a great calm and her lips an innocent red smile. She slept the sleep of a captive who is confident of speedy release.

On the morrow when the orderly entered she was still abed. Felton stood in the doorway and ushered in the woman who was to wait on Milady.

"May I help Your Ladyship?" the crone asked, approaching the bed.

"No, I am feverish. I have not slept all night. I am in terrible pain. Pray be kinder than the others were yesterday and leave me to myself."

"Shall I fetch a physician, Ma'am?"

Felton, speechless, watched and listened. He noted that Milady, naturally fair of complexion, was now paler than wax. For her part Milady realized that the more people she had about her the more people she would have to cope with. Besides Lord Winter would increase his vigilance. And the physician might well declare her illness feigned. Having lost the first round in this bout, Milady was determined to win the second.

"Fetch a physician?" said she. "What good would that do? Yesterday these gentlemen declared that my illness was a comedy; today it would be the same. It is somewhat late to be sending for a doctor!"

"Will you kindly tell us yourself, Madame, what treatment you would wish to follow?" Felton interrupted with some impatience.

"Ah, God, how do *I* know! *I* know that I am suffering, that is all. Give me what you will, I do not care."

"Send for Lord Winter," said Felton, wearied by these everlasting complaints.

"Oh, no, no! please do not call him, I beseech you. I am well, I want nothing!"

Milady uttered this plea with such vehemence and such burning eloquence that Felton, attracted despite himself, took a few steps into the room.

He has come in, Milady thought.

"Madame, if you really are in pain, I shall have a doctor sent for. If you

are deceiving us, so much the worse for you. Thus we shall have no reason to reproach ourselves."

For her only reply Milady buried her beautiful head in the pillow and
sobbed bitterly. Felton gazed at her for a moment with his usual impassivity. Then, seeing that the crisis threatened to be a long one, he went out,
the servant following him. Lord Winter did not appear.

"I fancy I am beginning to see my way," Milady mused with savage joy,
drawing the bedclothes over her face to conceal her satisfaction from anyone who might be spying on her.

Two hours later she decided it was time for her illness to cease. She
would get up and contrive somehow to gain an advantage of some sort.
She had only ten days in all; two were already gone. Earlier the orderly
had brought her breakfast; surely someone would be coming shortly to remove the table. And surely Felton would appear too.

She was not mistaken. Felton returned, and without noticing whether
Milady had touched the food or not, motioned to the orderly to carry
away the table. He stood by the doorway, alone, still silent, a book in his
hand.

Milady, deep in a chair beside the fireplace, a picture of beauty, pallor
and resignation, looked for all the world like a saintly virgin awaiting martyrdom. Felton approached her and said:

"Lord Winter, a Roman Catholic like yourself, believes that you might
suffer at being deprived of the rites and ceremonies of *your* faith. He sends
you this book so you may read the ordinary of *your* mass every day. Here
it is!"

At the manner in which Felton placed the book on the little table near
which Milady sat, at the tone in which he said *your* faith and *your* mass, and
at the disdainful smile which accompanied them, Milady concentrated
her attention on him. Then, noting the plain, severe arrangement of his
hair, the exaggerated simplicity of his dress and the marmorean polish,
hardness and impassivity of his brow, she recognized him for one of those
somber Puritans whom she had so often met both at the Court of King
James and at that of the King of France, where despite memories of the
massacre of Saint Bartholomew's Day, they sometimes sought refuge.

A sudden inspiration swept through her mind, the sort of guiding impulse which occurs only to people of signal genius and only in times of
great crisis which are to decide their fortunes or their very lives. Felton's
mere emphasis of the pronoun *your* as he referred to faith and mass, and

a cursory glance at him, sufficed to dictate Milady's future strategy and to reveal to her all its importance.

With the quick intelligence that characterized her, she protested:

"*I* a papist?" The contempt in her voice matched his. "*I,* say a Romish mass? Heavens, sir, Lord Winter, that corrupt Catholic, knows very well that I am not of his superstition. This is a trap he is setting for me!"

"And to what faith do you belong, Madame?" Felton asked with an astonishment he could not wholly conceal.

With feigned exaltation:

"I shall tell you," Milady cried, "when I have accomplished the full suffering I must undergo for the sake of my beliefs."

Felton's look disclosed to Milady the extent of the progress she had made thanks to these few words. Nevertheless the young officer stood silent and motionless; only his glance had betrayed him.

"I am in the hands of mine enemies!" she continued with all the fervor she knew that Puritans affected. "So, let my God preserve me or let me perish for His sake! I beg you to convey this to Lord Winter." She pointed toward the missal but forbore to touch it, as if to do so must inevitably contaminate her. "Take *this* back," she commanded, "and make use of it yourself, for I am sure you are doubly the tool of Lord Winter—an accomplice in his persecutions and an accomplice in his heresies."

Still silent, Felton picked up the book with the same repugnance he had shown in delivering it, and retired, wrapped in thought.

At about five o'clock that evening, Lord Winter appeared. Milady had found time aplenty to trace her plan of action; she received him with the air of a woman who has already recovered all her advantages. His Lordship sat down in an armchair facing hers and, stretching his legs nonchalantly on the hearth:

"Apparently we have decided to go in for a bit of apostasy?" he jeered.

"I do not know what Your Lordship means."

"I mean since we last met you have changed your religion. Have you by any chance married again—this time a Protestant!"

"I beg you to explain," the prisoner countered regally. "I vow I can hear what you say but it all makes no sense."

"It amounts to this, Madame: you have no religion whatever. It is best so."

"Atheism would seem more in keeping with *your* principles."

"I confess it is all one to me what you believe in."

"Why bother to profess your godlessness, My Lord? Your debauchery and crimes speak for themselves."

"What! you dare speak of debauchery, *you*, Messalina, *you*, Lady Macbeth! Either I misunderstand you or else you are confoundedly impudent!"

"You talk so because we are being overheard, sir," Milady replied frigidly; "you seek to prejudice your jailers and your hangmen against me."

"My jailers, my hangmen! Ha, Madame, you speak very poetically. Yesterday's comedy is turning to tragedy, eh? Ah, well, within a week you will be where you belong and good riddance, too. My task will then be over."

"A task of infamy," Milady retorted with the exaltation of a victim provoking a judge. "An impious horror!"

"God save us, I vow the hussy is going quite mad! Come, come, be calm, Madame Puritan or I shall consign you to a cell. By Heaven, it must be my Spanish wine that has gone to your head. Never mind, that type of drunkenness is innocuous and without consequence."

With which Lord Winter withdrew, swearing as lustily as ever gentleman swore in that age of profanity and invective. And Felton, stationed behind the door, just as Milady had supposed, missed no word of the scene.

"Yes, go, go," Milady adjured her brother. "But remember: the consequences of your iniquity are upon you, while you, weak fool, will wake up to them too late!"

Silence fell once again over her prison. Two hours passed by. When the orderly brought in Milady's supper, she was lost in her devotions. Prayers she had heard from the lips of an austere Puritan, an old servant of her second husband, rose melodic and eloquent out of her ecstasy. She paid not the slightest attention to what was going on. Felton motioned to the orderly not to disturb her and, when all was arranged, he went out quietly with the soldiers.

Knowing she might be watched, Milady continued her prayers to the end. It seemed to her, as clearly as she could judge under the circumstances, that the sentry halted occasionally to listen to her. For the time being nothing could have pleased her better. She rose, stepped toward the table, ate but scantily and drank only water. An hour later the orderly came to remove the table. This time, Milady noted, Felton did not accompany him.

Immensely excited, she realized it was because he feared to see her too often. She turned toward the wall to smile triumphantly, conscious that her mere expression would have betrayed her hypocrisy.

She allowed a half-hour to pass. Then, when all was silence in the old castle save for the eternal murmur of the waves as the vast sea broke against the rocks, she began to sing. In a pure, harmonious and vibrant voice, she chanted a psalm she knew to be in greatest favor with the Puritans at the time:

> Lord Thou hast now forsaken us
> To try our faith and strength,
> Yet merciful and generous
> Thou shalt forbear at length.

These verses were anything but poetic but the Puritans cared little for artistic ornament.

As she sang, Milady listened. The sentry on guard stopped; there was no more pacing outside her door. Congratulating herself upon the effect of her psalmody, she continued to sing with inexpressible feeling and fervor; the notes seemed to her to spread far down the corridor and to echo progressively, from vault to vault, bearing some magic charm to soften the hearts of her jailers. However the sentry, doubtless a zealous Roman Catholic, was presumably able to shake off the spell. For, through the door:

"Hold your tongue, Madame," he enjoined. "Your song is as dismal as a *De Profundis*. It's bad enough to be on duty here, but if we have to listen to such doldrum lamentation, it's more than mortal man can bear."

A stern voice broke in. Milady instantly recognized it as Felton's:

"Hush, man! What business is this of yours, you rascal? Have you had orders to stop this woman singing? No: you were told to guard her and to fire on her if she attempted to escape. Very well, do as you were told and don't let me catch you going beyond your orders."

An expression of unspeakable joy illumined Milady's countenance, but it was as fleeting as the reflection of a flash of lightning. Without appearing to have heard the dialogue, she continued to sing, summoning all the charm, power and seduction Satan had bestowed upon her voice:

> Despite my tears, despite my cares,
> My exile and my chains
> I have my youth, my loving prayers
> And God who knows my pains.

To the rude, unpolished poetry of this psalm, Milady's voice lent a grace and an effect which the most impassioned Puritans, finding them seldom present in the songs of their brethren, had perforce to conjure up with all the resources of imagination. Felton would have vowed he was hearing that angel who brought consolation to the three Hebrews in the burning, fiery furnace. Milady continued:

> Oh God, most powerful and just,
> The day of our release must come,
> We shall reach Heaven if so we must,
> Or die in martyrdom.

This verse, into which this accomplished enchantress put all her passion, struck home. The young officer, thoroughly bewildered, flung open the door and stood there, pale as ever but with eyes aflame:

"Why are you singing?" he mumbled. "That voice . . . that voice of yours . . ."

"I crave your pardon, sir!" Milady was all humility, "I forgot that my songs are out of place in this house. Perhaps I offended you in your beliefs. But it was not purposely, I vow. Forgive me, then, for a wrong which may seem serious but which was certainly not intended."

Milady was so beautiful at this moment and her religious ecstasy cast so luminous an expression upon her features that Felton, dazzled, fancied he was beholding that angel whom had only heard.

"Ay, Madame," he mumbled, "you are troubling and exciting the people who are meant to watch over you."

Nor did the witless young man gauge the incoherence of his words as Milady's lynx eyes read into the depths of his heart.

"I shall not worship," Milady said, her eyes downcast, her voice mellow, her attitude resigned. "I shall pray inwardly."

"No, Madame, I beg you," Felton said uncertainly, "But at night especially, pray do not sing so loud."

And, feeling he could no longer maintain his severity toward such a prisoner, he took to his heels. As he walked down the corridor:

"You are right, Lieutenant," the sentry said. "Such songs upset a body. And yet, heigh-ho! we get used to them, sir. The lady prisoner has a lovely voice!"

LIV
CAPTIVITY: THE THIRD DAY

Felton had come to see her, certainly, but there was still another step to take: Milady must detain him and they must remain together quite alone. At present she only sensed obscurely how to achieve this result.

There was even more to do: he must be made to speak in order to be spoken to. Milady knew very well that her greatest charm lay in her voice which, in its richness and variety ran the gamut of tones, from the speech of humans to the melopoeia of angels.

Yet despite her powers of seduction, Milady might well fail, for Felton was forewarned against the slightest hazard. From that moment on, she watched over her every gesture and her every word, from the simplest glance and the merest reflex down to her very breath, for a breath might well be interpreted as a sigh. In short, she studied every reaction of hers, much as a clever actor who has just been assigned a new rôle in a type of acting to which he is unaccustomed.

In so far as Lord Winter was concerned, her plan of conduct was easier; she had already determined upon it the night before. She would remain silent and dignified in his presence; now and again, she would irritate him by affected disdain or by a contemptuous word; she would provoke him to outbursts and threats that offered a contrast to her own resignation. Felton would see this; he might perhaps say nothing, but he would have seen everything.

Next morning Felton came as usual, but Milady allowed him to preside over all the preparations for breakfast without addressing a word to him. As he was about to withdraw, a ray of hope cheered her, for she fancied he was about to speak. But his lips moved without uttering a sound. With a powerful effort to control himself, he recommitted to his heart the words about to escape his lips and he left hastily.

Toward noon, Lord Winter entered. It was a rather fine winter's day; a few rays of that pale English sunshine, which sparkles but does not warm, filtered through the prison bars. Milady, gazing out of the window, pretended not to hear the door as it opened.

"Well, well!" said Lord Winter, "after playing comedy and then tragedy I see we are now playing melancholy."

The prisoner vouchsafed no reply.

"I understand," Lord Winter went on. "Quite! How happy you would be to have the freedom of that shore! How happy to be on a fine ship cleaving the waves of that emerald-green sea! How happy, whether on land or water, to catch me in one of those nice little ambushes you are so adept at laying. Patience, patience! Only four days more and you shall feel the shore beneath your feet, the sea will be open to you—more open perhaps than you would wish—and England will at long last be rid of you!"

Milady clasped her hands and raising her beautiful eyes to heaven:

"O Lord, O Lord my God!" she said with an angelic meekness of gesture and tone. "Forgive this man as I myself forgive him."

"Pray on, damned soul that you are!" Lord Winter sneered. "Your prayers are the more generous since you are in the power of a man who will never forgive you, I swear it!"

With which he left her. But as he went out, she sensed a piercing glance fixed upon her through the half-opened door, and as she looked up, she glimpsed Felton moving aside hastily to prevent her seeing him. Encouraged, she fell to her knees and began to pray:

"O my God, my God," she cried, "Thou knowest in what holy cause I endure tribulation. Give me then strength, I pray, to bear my trial with fortitude and charity!"

The door opened gently; the beautiful supplicant, pretending to hear nothing, continued in a tearful voice:

"O God of vengeance, O God of grace, wilt Thou suffer the abominable plots of this man to be carried out!"

Then only she feigned to hear the sound of Felton's footsteps. Rising, quick as thought, she blushed as if ashamed of being surprised on her knees.

"I would not wish to disturb anyone who is praying, My Lady," said Felton gravely. "Pray continue your devotions, I would not wish you to interrupt them on my account."

"How do you know that I was praying, sir?" she asked in a voice broken by sobs. "You are mistaken I assure you; I was *not* praying."

In the same serious voice but in a gentler tone, Felton went on:

"Surely you do not think I assume the right to prevent a fellow creature from bowing down before the Creator? God forbid! Besides, My Lady, repentance becomes the guilty. Whatever crime they may have committed, I hold the guilty to be sacred when they do obeisance at the feet of God."

"Guilty?" Milady protested. "I, guilty?" Her smile would have disarmed the angel on the Day of Judgment: "Guilty! Ah God, Thou knowest whether I am innocent or guilty! Say that I have been sentenced, sir, if you will; but as you know, that God Who loves martyrs sometimes allows the innocent to be condemned."

"Your condemnation itself is reason enough for prayer," Felton replied. "But if you are innocent, the stronger the reason, and I shall add my own prayers on your behalf."

"Oh! how just, how righteous a man you are!" cried Milady throwing herself at his feet. "I cannot hold out any longer; I am desperately afraid of weakening when I shall be called upon to face the ordeal and confess my faith. I implore you, sir, to listen to the plea of a woman in despair. You have been deceived about me but that is not the question. I only ask one favor, no more; if you grant it, I shall bless you both in this world and in the next."

"You must speak to my master, Madame," Felton replied. "I am not so fortunately placed as to mete out pardon or punishment. God has placed this responsibility in the hands of one who is of loftier station than I."

"No, I shall speak to you, to you alone! I beg you to listen to me instead of contributing to my shame and ruin."

"If you deserved this shame and invited this ruin, you must submit to it as an offering to God."

"What? What are you saying, man? Oh, why can't you understand? When I speak of shame, you think I speak of some sort of punishment—prison, say, or the gallows? Would to Heaven these might be my lot! What do *I* care about prison or death?"

"Now I, in turn, do not understand."

"Or rather you pretend not to understand me, sir," the prisoner replied, smiling incredulously.

"Nay, on my honor as a soldier and my faith as a Christian, I swear that is not true."

"Do you mean to tell me you are ignorant of Lord Winter's designs upon my person?"

"I assure you I am quite ignorant of them."

"Impossible. You are his confidant!"

"I beg you to observe that I am not in the habit of lying, My Lady."

"But Lord Winter makes no mystery of his purpose. How can you help but guess it?"

"I have no wish to guess anything," Felton explained. "I wait until someone confides in me. Except for what Lord Winter has told me in your presence, he has confided nothing to me."

"So you are not his accomplice!" Milady cried with a feigned sincerity that was utterly convincing. "Then you did not even suspect that he intends to bring down upon my head a disgrace that all the punishments of all the earth cannot match in their horror?"

"You are mistaken, My Lady," Felton protested, blushing. "Lord Winter is incapable of any such crime."

"Perfect!" Milady said to herself. "He knows nothing about all this, yet he calls it a crime! I am making good headway!" Then aloud: "The son of Satan will stop at nothing."

"And who is the son of Satan?"

"Are there two men in England who may be so described?"

"You mean George Villiers?" Felton asked, his eyes blazing.

"I mean George Villiers whom the godless and the libertines call Duke of Buckingham. I never dreamed there was a single Englishman in all England who requires such lengthy explanations to make him know who I meant."

"The hand of the Lord hangs heavy over his head," Felton intoned sententiously, "nor shall he escape the punishment which he has earned."

With regard to the Duke, Felton was merely voicing the execration all Englishmen entertained toward a man whom the Roman Catholics themselves called the extortioner, the peculator and the profligate, and whom the Puritans referred to simply as Satan, Abaddon, Apollyon or Belial.

"Ah, God! ah, God!" Milady wrung her hands. "When I crave that Thou visit upon this miscreant the chastisement which he so richly merits, Thou knowest well that I seek not mine own vengeance but rather the deliverance of a whole nation which is in helpless bondage!"

"You know the Duke of Buckingham?" Felton inquired.

Gratified that Felton should at last question her and happy that she had achieved this so readily and profitably:

"Know him?" Milady repeated. "Know him? Alas, I know him to my great sorrow and my eternal grief." And she wrung her hands as if in a paroxysm of agony.

Felton, for his part, felt his strength failing; he stumbled toward the door. But the prisoner, watching his every step, sprang forward to intercept him.

"Be generous, be merciful and listen to my prayer," she pleaded. "I had a knife as you know; Lord Winter's fatal prudence deprived me of it because he well knows to what use I would put it. Oh, please do not leave me; please hear me to the end! Give me back that knife for one minute only in the name of pity and charity. I am at your knees, a woman groveling in front of you. Look at me before you close the door upon me; tell me you know I do not seek to harm you." She paused dramatically, flung her arms about his knees. "To harm *you!*" she went on. "You, the only just, good and compassionate being I have ever met; you, who may well be my savior. Give me that knife for an instant, I beseech you, for an instant only, and I shall return it to you by the grating. One infinitesimal moment, Mr. Felton, and you will have saved my honor!"

"You mean to kill yourself!" Felton asked, forgetting in his terror to withdraw his hands from her grasp. "You mean to kill yourself?"

With consummate artistry, Milady fell back as in a swoon.

"God have mercy upon me!" she murmured as she sank to the floor, "I have given myself away. He knows my secret and I am lost!"

Felton hovered over her, motionless and nonplussed. Milady, recognizing that he was still somewhat dubious, blamed herself for underacting her part. Suddenly footsteps in the corridor brought them both to their senses; both recognized Lord Winter's tread. Felton edged toward the door, Milady sprang toward him.

"Do not breathe a word of this, I beg you," she urged in a tense, sultry voice. "Not one word to that man or I am lost and you, you, you will be—"

Then as the steps drew nearer, fearing that she might be overheard, she pressed her beautiful hand on Felton's lips with a gesture of extreme terror. Felton gently repulsed her and tottering across the room she sank into a chaise-longue.

Lord Winter passed by the door without stopping; the echo of his footsteps grew fainter in the distance.

Felton, pale as death, stood there straining his ears. When all was silence in the corridor, he sighed deeply, like a man suddenly awaking from a dream. Suddenly he darted out of the room. Milady in turn listened to departing footsteps as Felton moved off in the opposite direction from that Lord Winter had taken.

"Ah!" Milady breathed triumphantly. "At last you are mine!" Then her countenance darkening: "But if he speaks to Lord Winter I am irremediably lost," she thought. "Winter knows quite well that I will never kill myself; he himself will hand me a knife in Felton's presence and Felton will soon see that my great despair was but a farce." She walked to her mirror and gazing into it congratulated herself that she had never before looked more beautiful. She smiled. "True, true," she concluded confidently. "But Felton will *not* speak to him."

That evening Lord Winter entered with the servant who brought Milady's dinner tray.

"My Lord," she protested, "is your presence a necessary accessory to my imprisonment? Could you not spare me the increase of torment your visits cause me?"

"What, my dear sister?" Winter replied in mock surprise. "Didn't you yourself inform me, with those same pretty lips that are so cruel today, that you had come to England for the sole purpose of seeing me quite freely! To be deprived of that joy was so grievous, you told me, that you risked everything: seasickness, tempests, even captivity! Very well, here I am; you should be grateful. What is more, this time my visit has a definite purpose."

Convinced that Felton had spoken to him, Milady shuddered. Certainly in the course of her life this extraordinary woman had experienced the most powerful and conflicting emotions; but never before had she felt her heart beat so violently.

She remained seated; Lord Winter drew up an armchair and sat down beside her. Then he took a slip of paper from his pocket and unfolded it slowly.

"Pray examine this," he urged, looking up at her. "I want you to see the kind of passport I myself drew up for you. Henceforth it will serve to identify you in the life I am willing to allow you to live."

Turning away from Milady to scan the paper again, he read:

Order of Duty on His Majesty's Service

You are hereby commanded to conduct to————the female person named Charlotte Backson, duly and lawfully condemned to branding, for crimes committed, by order of the courts of justice of the Kingdom of France, and released after fulfillment of sentence.

Said Charlotte Backson shall reside permanently in the aforementioned place, whence she shall be forbidden to adventure more than a distance of three leagues (nine miles). In the event of attempted escape, the penalty of death shall be imposed forthwith without benefit of trial. Said Charlotte Backson shall be allowed five shillings per day for board and lodging.

Lord Winter cleared his throat, folded the paper and went on:
"You will note that your place of destination has been left blank. If you have any preference, you will inform me; provided it be at least three thousand miles from London, your wish will be granted."

"That order does not concern *me*," Milady said coldly. "It bears another's name."

"A name? Have you a name, pray?"

"I bear your brother's name."

"No you do not!"

"I—"

"My brother is only your second husband; your first husband is still alive! Tell me his name and I will substitute it for Backson."

Milady did not move.

"So, you will not tell me his name? Very well then you shall be entered on the prisoners' docket under the name of Charlotte Backson."

Milady said nothing but this time her silence was not a piece of strategy. She was mortally afraid. The order, she judged, was ready for execution; Lord Winter, hastening her departure, had probably condemned her to leave that very evening. For a moment her mind went blank, everything fell away from her, she was stunned. Suddenly she noticed that the order bore no signature and her joy at this discovery was beyond control. Lord Winter, his eyes fastened upon her, read her thoughts as he might read an open book.

"Yes, yes," he said quickly. "You are looking for the signature and seal. All is not lost, you think, for the order is not signed; he is showing it to me only to terrify me, you say. But you are sorely mistaken! Tomorrow this order will go to My Lord of Buckingham; next day he will return it signed and sealed; and within four-and-twenty hours I shall myself be responsible for its execution. This is all I had to say to you, Madame: I therefore bid you good-bye!"

"And I tell you, sir, that this abuse of power, which exiles me under a fictitious name, is infamous."

"Would you prefer to be hanged under your own name, My Lady? As you know, here in England our law is inexorable on the chapter of marriage. Speak out and tell me what you want. Though my name, or rather my brother's name, were to suffer for it I am determined to hazard the scandal of a public trial in order to be certain that I shall be rid of you once and for all."

Milady, pale as a corpse, made no answer. There was a silence.

"Well, well," Lord Winter went on, "I must conclude you prefer to prolong your peregrinations. So much the better, Madame. You know the old saw: 'A-travel I would go....' Upon my word you are not wrong; life is very sweet. That is why I do not intend to forfeit mine at your hands."

Milady stared at him but said nothing.

"The only thing that remains to be settled is your allowance of five shillings. You consider me somewhat parsimonious, do you not? The reason is that I do not care to furnish you with the means of corrupting your jailers. Anyhow, you will always have your charms left with which to seduce them. Employ them then if your failure with Felton has not disgusted you at attempts of the sort."

"Felton has not told him," Milady mused. "Nothing is lost, then."

"And now, My Lady, au revoir until we meet again tomorrow when I shall call on you to announce the departure of my messenger."

Lord Winter rose, bowed ironically to her and left.

Milady breathed again: she still had four days before her and four days would suffice to complete the seduction of Felton. But suddenly a terrifying thought flashed through her mind. Suppose Lord Winter were to send Felton himself to get the order signed by the Duke of Buckingham? In that case Felton would escape her, since the accomplishment of her plan depended on the magic of a continuous fascination. Still there was one reassuring aspect to her plight: Felton had not spoken.

Determined not to appear unnerved by Lord Winter's threats, she sat down at the table and ate her dinner. Then she fell to her knees as she had done the evening before and said her prayers aloud. Once again the soldier stopped pacing up and down the corridor to listen to her. Presently she heard footsteps lighter than those of the sentinel; someone was coming toward her cell. As the steps stopped before her door:

"It is Felton, it is he!" she said and began singing the hymn which had excited Felton so violently the previous evening. But though her voice— a sweet, full sonorous voice—rang quite as melodically and pathetically as ever, the door remained shut. To be sure, in one of the furtive glances she darted from time to time at the grating of the door, she thought she detected the ardent eyes of the young man through the serried wires.

Whether this was true or whether she imagined it, this time at least Felton mustered sufficient self-control not to enter. And yet a few moments later Milady fancied she heard a deep sigh. Then the same steps she had heard approach now withdrew slowly and as though regretfully.

LV
Captivity: The Fourth Day

Next day when Felton entered Milady's apartment he found her standing on a chair, holding in her hands a kind of rope. Apparently she had made it by tearing some cambric handkerchiefs into strips, twining the strips one with another and tying them end to end. At the noise Felton made in entering, Milady jumped lightly to the ground from her armchair, sat down in it and tried to conceal this improvised cord by dropping it behind her.

The young man was even paler than usual and his eyes, reddened by want of sleep, proved that he had spent a feverish night. His expression was more austere and stern than ever. He advanced slowly and taking one end of the suicidal rope, which by mistake or design she had allowed to appear:

"What is this, Madame?" he inquired coldly.

"That?" Milady smiled with that expression of appealing melancholy which she assumed so skilfully. "Boredom is the mortal enemy of prisoners. I was listless so I amused myself twining this rope."

Felton glanced at the wall toward which he had found Milady reaching when he entered; over her head he noticed a gilt-headed peg fixed in the wall and used for hanging up clothes and weapons. He gave a start which the prisoner observed through her lashes.

"What were you doing standing on that chair?"

"What can that matter to you?"

"I wish to know."

"Do not question me, sir, you know that we true Christians are forbidden to utter falsehoods."

"Well, then, I shall tell you what you were doing or rather what you were about to do. You meant to complete the fatal plan you cherish. Remember, Madame, if God forbids us to lie, He forbids us much more sternly to commit suicide."

"When God sees one of His creatures persecuted unjustly and placed between suicide and dishonor," Milady answered with ringing conviction, "God pardons suicide because such suicide is martyrdom."

"You say either too much or too little. Speak, My Lady. In Heaven's name, make yourself clear."

"Ay, you wish me to tell you my misfortunes so you may treat them as fables; you wish to know my plans so you may denounce them to my persecutor. No, I could never bear that! Besides, why should *you* care about the life or death of an unhappy woman, unjustly condemned? You are answerable for my body alone, are you not? Provided you produce a corpse that can be recognized as mine, no one will ask aught else of you. Indeed, you may perhaps earn a double reward."

"I, Madame," Felton protested indignantly. "Can you dream I would accept a reward for your life? Oh, you cannot possibly believe what you are saying."

"Let me act as I please," Milady cried with increasing excitement. "Every soldier should be ambitious, eh? You are now a lieutenant, are you not? Well, when you follow me to the grave you will be a captain."

"What have I done to you," Felton asked, "that you should burden me with such a responsibility before God and man?" He seemed considerably shaken. "In a few days you will have left here, My Lady. Your life will no longer be under my care and—" he sighed, "you can do what you will with it, because—"

As though unable to resist giving vent to a holy indignation, Milady interrupted:

"So you, a pious man, you who are called righteous and just, you ask for but one thing? And what is that thing, alas? Merely that you may not be involved in my death or held to account for it."

"I am in duty bound to watch over your life, My Lady, and I shall do so."

"But do you understand the mission you are charged with? A cruel enough mission if I am guilty. But what name can you give to it and what name will the Lord give to it if I am innocent?"

"I am a soldier, Madame, and I obey orders."

"Do you actually believe that on the Day of Judgment, God will separate the blind executioner from the iniquitous judge? You refuse to let me kill my body yet you are the agent of the man who has determined to kill my soul."

"But I repeat: no danger threatens you. I will answer for Lord Winter as I would for myself."

"Poor deluded soul, what madness to dare answer for another when the wisest and most Godfearing dare not answer for themselves? You are ranged on the side of the strongest and most fortunate of men, even if it means crushing the helpless and most unhappy of women."

"Impossible, Madame!" Deep in his heart Felton knew that the argument he was about to give her was a just one. "A prisoner, you shall not recover your freedom through me; living, you shall not lose your life through me."

"True, but I shall lose something dearer than life, Felton, I shall lose my honor. And it is you I shall hold accountable before God and men for my shame and my infamy."

Impassive as Felton was or appeared to be, this time he could not resist the secret influence which had begun to possess him. To see this woman, beautiful and splendent as a vision, to repel at once the ascendancy of grief and comeliness proved too much for him. It was beyond the power of a visionary, beyond the power of a brain undermined by the ardent dreams of an ecstatic faith, beyond the power of a heart corroded by the love of Heaven that burns and the hatred of men that devours.

Milady perceived his disquiet. Intuitively she felt the flame of the opposing passions which set the young zealot's blood afire. Like a skilful strategist who, seeing his enemy about to fly, marches toward him with a cry of victory, she rose, superb as an ancient priestess, inspired as a Christian virgin, her arms raised, her throat uncovered, her hair disheveled. With one hand she held her gown modestly drawn over her high, firm breasts, and, her look blazing with the fervor which had already raised such havoc in the young man's heart, she stepped forward and raised her usually low, melodious voice to a pitch of prophetic frenzy, singing:

> To Baal doom the innocent,
> To beasts their martyr prey,
> Our God shall force thee to repent
> Who saveth His alway.

Felton stood listening to this strange invocation, like one petrified. Then, trembling:

"Who are you?" he asked, clasping his hands. "Are you a messenger from God or a minister from Hell? Are you angel or demon? Are you Eloah or Astarte?"

"Don't you know me, Felton? I am neither angel nor demon, I am a daughter of earth, I am your sister in the true faith, that is all."

"Yes, I doubted, but now I believe!"

"You believe, yet you suffer me to languish in the hands of that child of Belial whom men call Lord Winter? You believe, yet you deliver me to that villain who fills and defiles the world with his heresies and debaucheries, to that infamous Sardanapalus whom the blind call Duke of Buckingham but whom true believers call Antichrist!"

"*I* deliver you up to Buckingham? What can you possibly mean?"

"Having eyes, see ye not?" Milady quoted. "Having ears, hear ye not?"

"Yes, it is true," Felton exclaimed, passing his hand over his perspiring brow as if to remove his last doubt. "Yes, I recognize the voice which speaks to me in my dreams . . . I recognize the features of the angel that appears to me every night . . . I recognize that spirit which says to my sleepless soul: 'Arise, strike! Save England and save thyself else thou shalt die without having satisfied thy God. . . .' " Felton drew a deep breath and: "Speak, speak," he begged Milady, "I understand you now."

A flash of unholy joy, swifter than thought, gleamed in Milady's eyes. Fleeting though it was, Felton saw it and started back, aghast, as though its light had illuminated the dark abysses of this woman's heart. Suddenly he recalled Lord Winter's warnings, the seductions of Milady and her first attempts on her arrival. He stepped back, hanging his head, but still looking at her as if, fascinated by this strange creature, he could not remove his eyes from hers.

Milady was not a woman to misunderstand this hesitation. Under her apparent emotions, her icy coolness never abandoned her. Before Felton had a chance to reply and before she should be forced to resume a conversation so difficult to sustain in the same exalted tones, she let her hands fall helplessly to her side. It was as if the weakness of the woman could not live up to the enthusiasm of the inspired fanatic:

"But no! I am not strong enough to be the Judith to deliver Bethulia from this Holofernes. The sword of the Eternal is too heavy for my arm. Let me die, then, to avoid dishonor; let me take refuge in martyrdom. I do not ask you for liberty as a guilty woman would nor for vengeance as a pagan would. Let me die, that is all I beg and implore you on bended knee; let me die, and my last sign shall be a blessing upon you for saving my soul!"

Hearing that voice (so gentle and suppliant!) and seeing that look (so timid and downcast!) Felton reproached himself for his hesitation. Step by step, the enchantress had resumed that magic adornment which she donned or doffed at will, that adornment of beauty, meekness and tears, and that irresistible attraction of mystical voluptuousness, the most devouring of all.

"Alas, there is but one thing I can do, namely, to pity you if you prove to me you are a victim. Lord Winter has brought up cruel charges against you. You are a Christian and my sister in the true faith; I feel drawn toward you, I who have loved no one but my benefactor and who have met none but traitors and impious men all the days of my life. But you, Madame, so beautiful in reality and so pure in appearance, you must have committed great crimes for Lord Winter to pursue you thus."

"Having eyes, see ye not?" Milady repeated with an accent of indescribable grief. "Having ears, hear ye not?"

"Well then, speak, speak—"

"You wish me to confide my shame to *you*?" A blush of modesty suffused her cheeks. "Ay, it *is* my shame, for often the crime of one becomes the shame of another."

"I do not understand—"

"I cannot confide my shame to *you*, a man!" Covering her lovely eyes virtuously with her hand: "Never, never! I *could* not do it!"

"But—am I not your brother?"

Milady looked at him for some time with an expression which the young officer mistook for doubt but which was partly scrutiny and chiefly the will to fascinate. Felton, supplicant in his turn, clasped his hands.

"Well, then," Milady conceded, "I trust my brother and I will dare to—"

At this moment Lord Winter's footsteps echoed down the corridor. This time Milady's relentless brother-in-law was not content to stop before the door and move on as he had the days before. Instead he exchanged a few words with the sentinel, then the door swung open and he stood on the threshold. Felton, hearing his voice, had stepped back. When Lord Winter entered the young officer was several paces away from the prisoner. Lord Winter walked in slowly, his inquisitorial glance first leveled at Milady then turning on Felton.

"You've been here a long time, John," he said. "Has this woman been telling you about her crimes? If so, I can understand your long stay."

Felton winced. Milady realized that if she did not come to the help of her disconcerted Puritan all was lost.

"So you fear your prisoner may escape?" She turned scornfully toward her brother-in-law. "Well, just ask your worthy jailer what favor I was even now soliciting of him."

"You were soliciting a favor?" Lord Winter inquired suspiciously.

"Ay, she was, my Lord," Felton confessed with some embarrassment.

"Come, what favor?"

"She asked me for a knife which she promised to return to me through the grating a moment after she had received it."

"There must be someone concealed here whose throat this amiable lady would wish delicately to slit!" Lord Winter observed in an ironical, contemptuous tone.

"There is myself," Milady replied very evenly.

"I have given you your choice of America or Tyburn! Choose Tyburn, My Lady. Believe me, the cord is more certain than the knife."

Felton turned pale and made a step forward, remembering that at the moment he entered Milady had a rope in her hand.

"Quite so, My Lord, I have often thought of it." Then, lowering her voice: "And I will think of it again."

Felton shuddered and Lord Winter advised:

"Be on your guard, John. I have placed my trust in you. Beware, friend; I have warned you." He cleared his throat. "Cheer-up, lad, we shall be delivered of this creature within three days. And where I shall send her she can harm nobody."

"Hear him, oh, hear him!" Milady cried with such vehemence that Lord Winter might believe she was addressing Heaven and Felton might understand that she was addressing him.

Felton bowed his head, apparently deep in thought. His master took the young officer by the arm and led him out, keeping his eye on his sister-in-law all the while.

"Alas!" mused Milady, "I fear I am not so far advanced as I expected. Lord Winter has exchanged his natural stupidity for a prudence hitherto quite alien to him. Truly the desire for vengeance is a wonderful thing and how it moulds a man's character! As for Felton, he is hesitant. Ah, he is not a man like that accursed D'Artagnan. A Puritan adores only virgins and expresses his adoration by clasping his hands. A musketeer loves women and expresses his love by clasping his hands about them."

Meanwhile Milady waited with much impatience, fearing the day might pass without her seeing Felton again. But within one hour she heard someone speaking in a low voice at the door; soon after it opened and, to her surprise, there he stood. Felton advanced quickly into the room, leaving the door open behind him. He signaled to Milady to be silent. He seemed very much agitated.

"What do you want of me?" she demanded.

"Listen," Felton said in a low voice, "I have just sent away the sentinel so I could stay here without anyone knowing about it. I came to speak to you without being overheard. Lord Winter has just told me a most horrible story."

Milady, reassuming the smile of a resigned victim, shook her head.

"Either you are a demon," Felton went on, "or Lord Winter, my benefactor, my father, is a monster. I have known you just four days, I have loved him for years; I therefore may hesitate between you. Do not be afraid at what I say, I want to be convinced. I shall come to see you tonight, shortly after twelve; I shall hear your story and you will convince me."

"No, Felton, no, my brother, your sacrifice is too great and I know what it costs you. No, I am ruined; do not let me encompass you in my ruin. My death will speak for me much more eloquently than my life; the silence of the corpse will convince you more surely than the words of the prisoner."

"Hush My Lady, do not speak thus! I came to implore you to promise upon your honor and to swear by all you hold most sacred that you will not make an attempt upon your life."

"I will not promise, Felton, for no one has more respect for a promise or an oath than I have. If I make a promise, I must keep it."

"Very well. But promise me you will do nothing until we have met again. After we have talked, if you still persist, then you shall be free and I myself will give you the weapon you desire."

"For your sake, I will wait."

"Swear it!"

"I swear I will, by our God, the true God. Are you satisfied?"

"I am. Till tonight, then!"

Whereupon he darted out of the room, closed the door, and waited in the corridor, the sentry's short pike in his hand, as if he had mounted guard in his place. When the soldier returned, Felton gave him back his weapon. Milady, peeping through the grating, saw the young officer cross himself with delirious fervor. From his expression, she was convinced he was beyond himself with joy.

For her part she returned to a chair. A smile of savage contempt curled her lips. And, blaspheming, she repeated the awesome name of that God by whom she had sworn without ever having learned to know Him.

"O God, what an insane fanatic!" she sneered. "Did I say God? I am my own God, vengeance is mine, I will repay. And that young Puritan fool will help me do so!"

LVI
CAPTIVITY: THE FIFTH DAY

The half-triumph she had achieved heartened Milady and doubled her strength. Hitherto she had found no difficulty in conquering men who allowed themselves to be seduced and whose education in gallantry at Court made them an easy prey. She was beautiful enough not to encounter much resistance on the part of the flesh and clever enough to overcome all the obstacles of the spirit.

This time, however, she had to contend with a rude, concentrated nature, whose austerity foiled even the most skilful appeal to the senses. Religion and penitence had made of Felton a man inaccessible to ordinary seductions. Such vast, grandiose and tumultuous plans stormed his fanatical brain that no place remained for any love, whether capricious or material, because love feeds upon leisure and grows by dint of corruption.

Thanks to her sham virtue, Milady had made a breach in the opinion of a man horribly prejudiced against her; by her beauty she had made inroads upon the heart of a heart hitherto chaste and pure. Her successful experiment taught her the full efficacy of her charms. Had she not just reduced to her will the most refractory subject that nature and religion could possibly have offered?

Yet throughout the evening she had often doubted of fate and despaired of herself. She called upon God solely for purposes of humbug and these purposes had been fruitful. Her true faith rested in the genius of evil, whose boundless sovereignty reigns over every detail of human life. As the Arab proverb says, a single pomegranate seed suffices to reconstruct a ruined world.

Confident of her sway over Felton, Milady had ample leisure to draw up her plan of campaign for the morrow. She had but two days left until the order for her deportation was submitted to Buckingham. Obviously Buckingham would sign the more readily, since the name on the document was a false one and he could not know it was Milady he was getting rid of. She would be put aboard immediately by Lord Winter. Ruefully she reflected that women sent to the colonies are less influential for purposes of seduction than your so-called virtuous lady, whose beauty is illumined by the brilliance of society, whose charm is lauded by the world of fashion, and whose allure is enhanced by a halo of aristocracy. Sentenced to a wretched and infamous punishment, a woman may still remain beautiful, but, beauty or no, she loses her power.

Like all persons of true genius, Milady knew how, where and when she could best utilize her advantages and profit thereby. Poverty was abhorrent to her, degradation would rob her of virtually all her greatness. Milady, one queen among many queens, required the joy of pride fulfilled in order to establish her domination. To give orders to inferiors was for her more humiliating than pleasurable.

She did not doubt a moment that she would return from exile. But how long would this exile last? Days unprofitable to private ambition were so many days lost to a person like Milady. What then of days not neutral and uneventful only but retrogressive and ruinous? To waste one year or two or three spelled an eternity to her. Was she to return to witness a triumphant D'Artagnan and his jubilant comrades receive the laurels he had so richly earned in the service of the Queen? The mere thought was odious. She raged inwardly. Had her bodily means matched her mental purpose, she would have wrenched asunder the bolts and bars of her prison with a mere fillip.

There was an even more painful rub. What of the Cardinal? What must that mistrustful, restless and suspicious soul be thinking of? His Eminence was not only her sole prop and support but the very instrument of her career and of her vengeance. She knew him of old and she knew him well. If she returned after a sleeveless errand, she could invoke the sorrows of her imprisonment and enlarge upon the sufferings she had undergone. His Eminence, caustic as usual, would shrug his shoulders with all the mockery of a skeptical and forceful genius, and say:

"You should not have allowed yourself to be trapped, Madame."

Milady concentrated all her energies. There was only one man who could help her, Felton. Over and again she repeated his name as though breathing a prayer. Felton, Felton, the only dim light in her darkling inferno. Just as a snake coils and recoils to ascertain his strength ring by ring, so Milady, brooding, wrapped Felton about in the myriad toils of her fertile imagination.

Time passed. The hours, one by one, seemed to awaken the bells. Each stroke of the clapper resounded deep in Milady's heart. At nine o'clock Lord Winter made his usual visit. He examined the window and bars, he sounded the flooring and the walls, he inspected the fireplace and the doors. During his lengthy and minute investigation no word passed between the lord of the manor and his captive. Both realized that it was idle to bandy words in order merely to vent their anger. As Lord Winter retired he bowed, and:

"Well, My Lady," he assured his prisoner, "you will not escape tonight, I imagine."

At ten o'clock Milady recognized Felton's familiar footstep; she was now as familiar with it as is a mistress with every move made by the lover of her heart. Yet she hated and despised him for a weak fanatic.

But this was not the appointed hour; Felton walked past and she had to wait two hours more until, at twelve o'clock, the guard was changed. Impatiently she listened to the sentry march off and his relief start his pacing up and down. Two minutes later Felton paused before her door. Straining her ears, she heard him say to the sentry:

"Look here, my lad, you must not leave this door for any reason whatsoever. As you know His Lordship punished a soldier last night because he quitted his post for a minute, even though I myself replaced the fellow while he was absent."

"Ay, Lieutenant, I heard about it."

"Very well, then: be sure to keep the strictest watch. I for my part am going to inspect this woman's room once again. I am convinced she plans to do away with herself and I have orders to keep her under observation."

Milady thrilled as she overheard the austere Puritan telling a falsehood on her behalf. As for the soldier, he merely laughed, and:

"The deuce, Lieutenant," he said, "you are a lucky man to have that detail, especially if His Lordship authorized you to look into her bed, too!"

Felton blushed. Under any other circumstances he would have reprimanded the soldier for taking such liberties. But his conscience was irking him too much; he opened his lips but could make no sound. He coughed. At length:

"If I call you," he ordered briefly, "be sure to come in. And if anyone comes down the passage, call me at once."

"Ay, Lieutenant."

Felton then entered Milady's room. She rose to her feet.

"So you have come?"

"I promised to; I have kept my promise."

"You promised me something else, too."

"What else?" the young man groaned. Despite his self-control, he felt his knees tremble. A cold sweat broke over him. "What else did I promise you?"

"You promised to bring me a knife and to leave it with me after we had talked."

"Do not dream of that, Madame. . . . There can be no plight, however dreadful, which permits one of God's creatures to take his own life. I have thought it over carefully. I can never be guilty of such a sin."

"So you have thought it over, eh?" Milady sat down in her armchair and smiled contemptuously. "I have been thinking things over too."

"What, for instance?"

"For one thing that I have nothing to say to a man who breaks his word."

"Ah, God!—"

"You may withdraw, sir, I have nothing further to say."

"Here you are, Madame!" Felton said, drawing the knife meekly from his pocket. He had been unwilling to produce it, but all his objections vanished before her scorn.

"Let me see it!"

"Why—?"

"I vow on my honor I will return it to you in a moment. Lay it down on this table and you can stand guard over it."

Felton handed the weapon to Milady who carefully felt its blade and tested its point on the tip of her finger. Then, returning it to the young officer: "This is good, fine steel," she commented. "Thank you, Felton, you are a loyal friend."

Felton took back the weapon and laid it on the table behind him as he had agreed with the prisoner. Milady followed him with her eyes and made a gesture of satisfaction.

"Now," she said, "listen to me."

Her injunction was quite unnecessary; the young officer stood upright before her, curiosity writ large upon his features.

Very solemnly and in tragic tones Milady asked Felton to suppose it was his own sister, his father's daughter, who was speaking. What would he do if she were to say to him:

"While still young and still beautiful enough for my own undoing, I was tricked and snared; I resisted! Every type of pitfall and violence was made use of; I resisted! The creed I profess and the God I adore were blasphemed because I invoked their aid in my affliction; I resisted! No outrage but was heaped upon me; I resisted. Then, as my enemy could not destroy my soul, he tried to defile my body forever. Finally—"

Milady paused. A bitter, sad little smile hovered over her lips.

"Go on, My Lady, what then?"

"Finally one evening my enemy resolved to paralyze the resistance he had been unable to overcome; one evening someone slipped a drug, a powerful narcotic, into my water. I had scarcely finished my meal than I felt myself gradually sinking into a strange torpor. I did not suspect what had happened yet a vague fear seized me. Stubbornly I sought to fight off my drowsiness. I rose, attempted to reach the window and cry for help. But my legs refused to carry me. It was as though the ceiling was sinking upon my head and crushing me under its weight. I stretched out my arms, I tried to speak but I could only utter inarticulate sounds. An irresistible numbness overwhelmed me. I clutched at a chair feeling that I was about to fall, but this support soon proved unavailing because my arms were too weak. I fell on one knee, then on both; I strove to pray but my tongue was frozen. God doubtless neither saw nor heard me. I sank on the floor, a prey to a slumber that was like death.

"How long I slept or what happened while I did, I cannot know. I remember that I awoke in a circular chamber, sumptuously furnished. Light penetrated only through an opening in the ceiling. Stranger still, no door gave entrance to the room which might be well described as a magnificent prison.

"It took me a long time to establish what kind of place I was in and to make out the details I have just described to you. My mind struggled vainly to shake off the heavy pall of the sleep that had possessed me. Blurred intimations of something that must have happened to me seeped eerily through my dulled senses: the rumbling of a coach . . . a long long drive . . . a terrible dream in which my strength was exhausted. . . . But these perceptions were so shadowy and so indistinct in my mind that they seemed to have happened to some other woman in some other existence, yet were somehow linked with me and my life by some fantastic duality.

"For a long time, I assured myself, I must be dreaming. I arose tottering. My clothes were near me on a chair, yet I could not remember having undressed or gone to bed. Then, very slowly, the truth began to dawn upon me with all the horror it held to a chaste girl. I was no longer at home . . . in so far as I could judge by the sunlight, the day was already two-thirds spent . . . it was the evening before that I fell asleep . . . my slumber must have lasted twenty-four hours. . . . But what had occurred during this long coma?

"I dressed as quickly as I could, each slow and benumbed movement of mine proving to me that the effect of the narcotic had not yet worn off. I realized grimly that the room I occupied had obviously been furnished to receive a woman; the most finished coquette could not have asked for anything that was not ready at hand. Certainly I was not the first woman to be held captive in this splendid prison; but you can understand, Felton, the handsomer the prison, the greater my terror.

"Luxurious though the chamber was, it was a prison nevertheless. I essayed in vain to get out. I sounded all the walls, seeking to discover a door; everywhere only a dull, flat thud replied to my beating fists. I made the rounds of the room a score of times at least, hoping against hope to find some exit. As last, baffled, I fell into a chair, crushed by fright and fatigue.

"Meanwhile night was fast falling and, with night, my terrors increased. What was I to do? Should I sit still where I was? What else *could* I do? I sensed I was beset with all manner of unknown dangers; any step I took might cast me into them. Though I had eaten nothing since the day before, my fears prevented me from feeling hungry.

"No noise reached me from the outside or I might have measured the passage of time. I could only guess that it was probably now seven or eight o'clock in the evening, for it was in October all this happened and everything was quite dark.

"Suddenly the creaking of a door turning on its hinges made me start. A globe of fire appeared above the glazed opening in the ceiling. By the brilliant light it cast into my chamber, I perceived with dismay that a man loomed up within a few steps of me. A table set for two, bearing a supper ready to serve, stood as if by magic in the middle of the apartment.

"Alas it was the man who had pursued me for a whole year . . . who had sworn my dishonor . . . and who, by the first words he uttered, gave me to understand that he had accomplished it the previous night. . . ."

"The scoundrel!" Felton shuddered. "Oh, what infamy!" The officer frowned, his eyes seemed to hang on her lips. Milady, her eyes downcast, nevertheless noted the interest her Puritan took in this bizarre recital.

"What baser infamy can you imagine, Felton?" she asked helplessly. "This man believed that by triumphing over me in my sleep, he had settled everything satisfactorily . . . he came, trusting that I would accept my disgrace . . . he was prepared to offer his fortune in exchange for my love. . . .

"All the contempt and scorn that can rise in the heart of a virtuous woman I poured upon that man. I dare say he was accustomed to reproaches of the sort. He listened to me calmly, smiling, his arms crossed; then, thinking I had had my say, he stepped forward. I sprang toward the table, seized a knife and placed its point against my breast."

"And then, Madame?" Felton asked impatiently.

And then, Milady explained, she told her seducer that if he took one step more he would have her death on his conscience as well as her dishonor. Apparently something in her looks, her voice and her whole attitude must have reflected that sincerity of gesture, of pose and of accent which carries conviction to even the most perverse souls. The man did not move. But he did speak, banteringly, his lips curled. Her death, he told her, was not what he wished. She was far too desirable a mistress for him to lose her thus after the joys of possessing her only one night. Bowing, he bade his "lovely beauty" farewell and promised to visit her again when she was in a better humor. Having spoken, he blew on a silver whistle. The globe of fire which lighted the room reascended and disappeared and she was again plunged into the dark. Again she heard the noise of a door opening and closing; again the flaming globe descended and again Milady was left completely alone. It was a desperate moment for her. Any doubts she might have entertained about her misfortune had now been scattered by an overwhelming reality. She was in the clutches of a man she not only hated but despised; her captor had already gone to fatal lengths to betray his corruption, but had he reached the limits of his wickedness?

"Who was the man?" Felton interrupted.

"I spent the night sitting bolt upright on a chair," Milady went on, ignoring his question. "At about midnight, the lamp went out and I was in darkness once more. Vague sounds reached my ears; I started up at the merest echo. Fortunately night passed without any further attempt on the part of my persecutor. Day broke: the table had disappeared and I sat there, knife in hand. In that knife lay my only hope!

"I was worn out with fatigue, my eyes burned from lack of sleep, I had not dared relax for an instant. The light of day reassured me; I flung myself on my bed, fully clothed, and hid the knife under my pillow.

"When I awoke I found a table in the middle of the room, freshly set and covered with viands. Despite my suspicions and my worries, I felt ravenous, for I had touched no food in forty-eight hours. So I ate some bread and fruit; then, remembering the drugged water that had brought about my downfall, I was careful not to pour any water from the carafe that stood on the table. Instead I filled my glass at a marble fountain fastened into the wall over my dressing-table.

"Cautious though I had been, I remained anxious. This time, however, my fears were groundless. I passed the day without experiencing anything of the symptoms I dreaded.

"I had taken care to empty out half the carafe so that my suspicions might escape notice. Evening came on and with it the darkness to which my eyes were gradually becoming accustomed. Amid the shadows, I discerned the table sinking through the floor. A quarter of an hour later, it reappeared with my supper, and a moment thereafter the same lamp appeared, lighting up my room. I was determined to eat only such foods as could not be mixed with a soporific. My meal consisted of two eggs and some fruit; I drew some water from my blessed fountain and began to drink. But the first few mouthfuls convinced me that this water did not taste like the water I had drunk that morning. Instinctively I stopped, but I had already drunk about half a glassful. I threw away the rest with revulsion and I sat there, waiting, as a heavy sweat broke over my brow. I could not but doubt that some invisible spy had observed me that morning and taken advantage of my guilelessness in order the better to make sure of my ruin, so coolly plotted and so cruelly pursued.

"Half an hour later the same symptoms reappeared. Luckily I had only taken half a glass this time. I resisted longer. Instead of falling sound asleep, I relapsed into a state of somnolence which felt me aware of what was happening around me, though I was too weak either to defend myself or to seek flight. I dragged myself toward the bed to seize the only defense left to me—the knife which was to save me. But I could not reach the pillow. I swayed, slipped to the ground and clasped my arms about one of the bedposts. Then I knew I was indeed lost!"

Felton, hearing, gave a shudder. His hands twitched convulsively. Milady continued in tones as dramatic as though she were even now a victim of that anguish she had experienced in the moment she was describing so vividly.

"Worst of all," she whimpered, "this time I was conscious of the danger that threatened me." She regained control of herself. "My body, drugged, was half-asleep but my mind registered everything I saw and heard. True, all this passed through veils of dreams but it was none the less ghastly.

"I saw the lamp ascend, leaving me in the darkness. I heard the awful creaking of the door, distinguished but twice before, yet how familiar! I felt intuitively that someone was approaching. Felton, they say that natives, lost in the jungles of America, can sense the approach of a cobra; that is exactly what I sensed that night.

"Desperately I made an effort, I strained every nerve in order to cry out; at incredible pains, I even managed to rise to my feet. But I sank down immediately and fell into the arms of my persecutor."

"When will you tell me who this man was?" the young man pleaded.

One glance satisfied Milady of the pain and revulsion she had inspired in Felton by dwelling upon every detail of her story. But she wished to spare him no pang. The more deeply she could harrow his heart, the more certainly he would avenge her. The name of her seducer she reserved for the climax of her recital. Until then, she nursed every possible effect. On this latest visit, she told Felton, the villain was not contending with an inert acquiescent body, bereft of all feeling. Though Milady was unable to regain the complete exercise of her faculties, nevertheless she was possessed of a sense of immediate danger. Accordingly she struggled with all her might and, weak though she was, she must have put up a determined resistance, for presently she heard him damn "these wretched Puritan swine," and amid much profanity declare that he knew they tired out their executioners but thought them to be less recalcitrant toward their lovers.

"Alas, my fiercest exertions could not last forever. I felt my strength waning and this time the coward took advantage not of my sleep but of my swooning!"

Felton made almost no sound, save for his harsh, throaty breathing. But sweat streamed over his marble brow and his hand, under his coat, tore nervously at his breast.

"On coming to," Milady resumed, "my first impulse was to feel under my pillow for the knife I had been unable to reach. It had not availed to defend me, it might still serve in expiation. But as I picked up this knife, Felton, a terrible idea occurred to me. I have sworn to tell you everything and I shall tell you everything; I have promised you the truth and you shall hear it, were it to mean my ruin!"

"I can guess," said Felton. "You wanted to avenge yourself on this man, did you not?"

"Ay, and how passionately! Here was no Christian feeling, I know. Doubtless that eternal enemy of our souls, that lion that rages ever about us, inspired me with his fury." Meek, a frail woman accusing herself of a monstrous piece of wickedness, Milady whispered: "The idea *did* occur to me and probably, for all my prayers, it has remained deep within me. Probably, too, I am now bearing the punishment of my homicidal lust."

"Go on, Madame," Felton urged. "You see how carefully I listen and how eager I am to learn what happened."

"I was resolved to commit the crime as soon as possible; I had no doubt my seducer would return the following night. During the day I had nothing to fear.

"Accordingly, when the hour for breakfast came, I did not hesitate to eat and drink, but I was only going to pretend to eat supper. Thus I had to fortify myself with my morning nourishment against my evening fast. But I did hide a glass of water, part of my breakfast, because thirst had been my chief suffering during my forty-eight hours without food or drink.

The day passed without any effect on me other than to strengthen me in the resolve I had taken. But I was careful lest my face betray the thoughts in my heart. I was positive I was being watched. At times I felt a smile on my lips but I quickly covered it with my hand. Ah, Felton, I dare not tell you what made me smile; you would be horrified—"

"Madame, tell me what happened next?"

"Evening came, the routine events took place. As before, my supper appeared under cover of the darkness, the lamp was lighted and I sat down at table. I ate only some fruit. I pretended to pour some water from the carafe but I drank only that which I had kept in my glass. I made the substitution skilfully enough to elude the suspicion of the spies, if spies there were.

"After supper I feigned the same signs of numbness as before; but this time, as if succumbing to fatigue or over-familiar with danger, I dragged myself to my bed, undressed and went to bed. I had no trouble in finding my knife under the pillow and all the while I pretended to be falling asleep I grasped its handle firmly. Two hours or so must have passed; nothing happened. Who could have imagined the night before that this could be? I began to fear he would not come!

"But at length I saw the lamp slowly rise and disappear into the depths of the ceiling; my room was plunged in darkness but I strained my eyes, hoping to distinguish the form of my persecutor. Some ten minutes elapsed. I could hear no sound above the beating of my heart. I implored Heaven that the villain might come. Evidently my prayer was being answered, for I heard the door open and close and, though the carpet was very thick, I distinguished a footstep which made the floor creak and across the obscurity I discerned a shadow advancing toward my bed."

"Go on, My Lady, make haste," Felton begged her. "Can't you see that every word you say burns me like molten lead?"

"I gathered all my strength, Felton, and I remembered that the hour for vengence—or rather for justice—had struck at last. I felt I was another Judith, I poised myself, knife in hand, and when I saw him near me, his arms outstretched to grasp his victim, I uttered a supreme cry of agony and despair as I struck him full in the chest. But oh! the coward had foreseen every eventuality. His chest was covered with a coat of mail; the knife slanted off."

Her seducer had then seized her arm and wrenched the weapon from her grasp.

"So you have designs on my life, my lovely Puritan?" he mocked. "Lud! this is more than aversion, it is plain ingratitude! Come, come, calm yourself, my pretty pet. I thought you had grown more tender but I see I was wrong. Heigh-ho, I am not the sort of despot who detains a woman by force. You do not love me! With my usual fatuousness, I doubted it; but now I am convinced. Tomorrow you shall go free."

Desiring nothing from him save death at his hands:

"Have a care," she told him, "my liberty spells your dishonor."

"Explain, fair Sibyl."

"No sooner do I leave this place than I shall tell everything: I shall make known the violence which you employed against me, I shall recount my captivity and I shall denounce this palace of abominations. You are highly exalted, My Lord, and you sit in the seat of the mighty. But, above you, thrones the King, and above the King thrones the Lord God."

Her persecutor was by nature a master of callousness and self-control, yet he could not wholly disguise his anger. Milady could not see the expression on his face but her hand was on his arm and she felt he was trembling. Curtly he announced that if such were the case he would not allow her to leave.

"As you will," she countered, "my torture chamber will be my grave. I shall die here, granted. But you will see whether a phantom accusing is not a more terrible thing than a human being who but threatens."

"You shall be left no weapon—"

"I need none save that which despair supplies to any creature brave enough to use it. I shall starve myself to death."

He had then assured her that peace was much better than so uneven a war. Why did she not accept her freedom at once and he would proclaim her virtue, naming her the Lucretia of England? To which she replied that she would name him the Sextus of England, prosecuting him before men as she had prosecuted him before God. And if, like Lucretia, she must sign his accusation in her blood, she would so sign it.

"Tut, tut," he jeered, "that is quite another matter. Meanwhile, after all, you are comfortable here, you shall want for nothing and if you care to starve to death, that is your own concern."

"With these words, he retired, Felton," Milady continued. "I listened to the door as it opened and closed. Oh, Felton, I was not so much wracked by my sorrow, I confess, as by my shame at failing to avenge myself.

"My seducer kept his word. All that day and the following night he left me unmolested; but I too kept my word and night and day I neither ate nor drank. I had warned him I was resolved to starve; so I passed all those long hours in fervent prayer, trusting that God would forgive me for taking my own life.

"The second night the door opened; I was lying on the floor, my strength ebbing fast. At the sound I raised myself on one hand and I heard that hateful voice challenging me:

" 'Well, now, are we a whit meeker? And will we not pay for our liberty with a promise of silence? Come, my dear, I am a cheerful fair-minded sort of fellow. Though I frankly dislike men of the Puritan faith I do them justice exactly as I do justice to Puritan women when they are pretty. Come now, a very short oath upon the Cross, that is all I ask of you.' "

Felton craned his neck forward, his eyes bulging:

"He asked you to swear upon the Cross, My Lady?"

"Yes, Felton, this idolater and adulterer did exactly that! Suddenly all my strength returned. I rose to my feet. I said:

" 'I swear upon the Cross that never promise nor threat nor torture will seal my lips. I swear upon the Cross that I shall expose you everywhere as a murderer, a despoiler of honor and a dastard. I swear upon the Cross that if ever I escape from here I shall beseech all mankind to visit upon you the vengeance you deserve!'

" 'Have a care!' He spoke more threateningly than I had ever heard him speak. 'I still have a supreme means of making you hold your tongue. I do not wish to employ it save as a last resort. It is a dire one. It may not seal your lips completely but it will prevent anyone from believing a word you utter.'

"I rallied all my spent strength to laugh defiantly. He understood that thenceforth it was war to the death between us.

" 'Listen carefully,' he told me. 'I will give you the rest of this night and all day tomorrow to reflect. Think carefully, pledge silence and riches, consideration and honors are yours; breathe but a word of this, and I will condemn you to infamy.'

" 'You? To *infamy*?'

" 'Ay, to irremediable and everlasting infamy.' "

Milady concluded:

"I told him that unless he withdrew from my presence, I would bash my brains out against the wall of the room. He repeated I had until the next evening to make up my mind. As he left I fell to the floor and gnawed the carpet for very ignominy and pain! I—I—"

And she sobbed softly, her head on her shoulder. But this position did not prevent her from noticing that Felton was leaning for support on a stool near by. Triumphant in her knowledge that her recital had struck home, she smiled demoniacally.

LVII

How Milady Employed the Technique of Classical Tragedy to Prepare a Modern One

There was a moment of silence which Milady employed in observing her young listener. Then she continued her recital.

It was more than three days, she related, since she had touched food or drink . . . she was suffering atrocious tortures . . . at times clouds passed over her, dimming her eyes and pressing heavily down on her forehead as through a haze she realized this was delirium. . . . When evening came she was so weak that she kept fainting at every moment and each time she fainted she thanked God because she believed she was about to die. Suddenly, in the midst of one of these fainting spells, she heard the door open. Terror brought her back to consciousness.

"And then," Milady told her rapt listener, "he came in. He was masked but I recognized his step, I knew his voice and that proud, impressive air which hell bestowed upon his person for the ruin of humanity."

He was followed, she added, by a companion, also masked. Her persecutor spoke up:

"Well!" he asked, "have you made up your mind to swear the oath I asked of you?"

To which Milady replied that her torturer had himself admitted that Puritans have but one word . . . that he had heard hers . . . and that she meant to pursue him on earth before the tribunals of men until she could do so before the Court of God in Heaven.

"So you persist?"

"I swear it before the God Who now hears me. I will call all earth to bear witness to your crime—that is, until I shall have found an avenger!"

"You are a whore," he thundered, "and you shall submit to the punishment of common whores. Branded in the eyes of the world you hope to appeal to, how will you prove that you are neither guilty nor insane?"

Then, turning to his companion;

"Executioner," he said, "do your duty."

"His name, his name," Felton pleaded. "Please tell me his name."

"Then in spite of my cries, in spite of my resistance—for I realized I was facing something worse than death—the executioner seized me, threw me to the floor and pinned me down. I was choking with sobs, almost unconscious, calling for help from a God who did not heed me. Suddenly I shrieked for pain and humiliation. A burning fire, a red-hot iron, and the executioner had branded his mark upon my shoulder."

Felton groaned.

"Look for yourself," Milady said, rising with the majesty of a queen, "here, Felton, behold the new martyrdom invented for a pure young girl, the victim of a scoundrel's brutality. Learn to know the hearts of men and henceforth do not offer yourself so readily to serve as the instrument of their iniquitous vengeance."

With a swift gesture, Milady opened her dress, tore aside the cambric which covered her breast and, blushing with feigned anger and simulated shame, bared the ineffaceable imprint which marred her beautiful shoulder.

"But that is a fleur-de-lis!" Felton cried.

"That is the most shameful part of it all," Milady answered. "Had the brand been the brand of England, it would have been necessary to prove what court had sentenced me; I could have made a public appeal to every court in the kingdom. But the brand of France! Ah, here was truly the brand of infamy!"

This was too much for Felton. Pale, stock-still, aghast at the horror of this revelation and dazzled by the beauty of this woman who bared herself before him with an immodesty which he found sublime, he finally fell on his knees before her. With just such fervor, the early Christians were wont to fall on their knees before the Virgin martyrs whom the emperors delivered in the circus to the bloodthirsty lubricity of the populace. The brand disappeared, beauty alone remained.

"Forgive me, forgive me," Felton cried.

"Love me, love me!" Milady read in his glance as:

"Forgive you for what?" she asked.

"Forgive me for having joined with your persecutors."

Milady held out her hand.

"So young! so beautiful!" Felton whispered, covering her hand with kisses. Milady, sure of herself, flashed on him the sort of look that makes a slave of a king. Felton, born and bred a Puritan, relinquished her hand and bowed down to kiss her feet. He no longer loved her now, he adored her.

The crisis past, Milady seemed to have recovered a self-possession which she had never lost; and Felton saw the veil of chastity once again cover those treasures of love so well hidden from him that they but made him desire them the more.

"Ah, now," he pleaded, "I have only one more thing to ask you: the name of the real executioner. There can be but one; the other was merely the instrument of his wickedness."

"Oh, my friend, my brother, need I name the villain? Can't you guess—"

"So it's he—he again—always he, the great criminal!"

"Ay, the arch criminal, the plague of England, the persecutor of true believers, the fiend who has ravished the honor of so many women. It is he who to satisfy a whim of his corrupt heart is about to plunge England into bloodshed. It is he who protects the Protestants today and will betray them tomorrow—"

"Buckingham!" Felton cried, exasperated. "So it was Buckingham!"

Milady hid her face in her hands, as though unable to bear the burden of shame this name recalled.

"Buckingham, the torturer of this angelic creature!" Felton moaned. "And Thou didst not destroy him with Thy thunder, O God? Instead Thou hast left him noble, honored and powerful to the greater ruin of us all?"

"God abandons those who abandon themselves, Felton."

"But Buckingham will draw upon his head the punishment reserved for the damned!" Felton cried with growing excitement. "Buckingham invites human justice to forestall that of Heaven?"

"Men fear him and spare him."

"Not I," Felton protested. "I do not fear him and shall not spare him!"

An unholy joy swept over Milady. Surely her victim and her victim's victim now lay in the hollow of her hand. Yet Felton, won over completely, nevertheless was inquiring:

"But how could Lord Winter, my protector, be mixed up in all this?"

"Ah, my friend, often the most cowardly and despicable of men dwell side by side with great and generous creatures. I was engaged to such a man whom I loved and who loved me. He had a heart like yours, Felton; he was a man like yourself. I went to him and told him all; he knew me, that man did, and he never for a moment doubted me. He was a great nobleman, a peer of Buckingham's in every way. He said nothing; he merely reached for his sword, threw his cloak over his shoulder and made straight for Buckingham's mansion."

"Ah, yes, I see what he meant to do," Felton commented. "But with men like Buckingham, you do not use a sword, it were too noble. You use a dagger!"

"Buckingham had left England the day before on a mission as Ambassador to Spain where he was to solicit the hand of the Infanta for King Charles the first, who was then but Prince of Wales. My fiancé returned, sad at heart.

" 'Darling,' he told me, 'this scoundrel has gone and so he has escaped my vengeance for the time being. Meanwhile let us marry as we had planned. Then, leave it to Lord Clark to uphold his honor and that of his wife.' "

"Lord Clark!" cried Felton. "Why, that was the——"

"The brother of Lord Winter. Now you must certainly understand everything? Buckingham stayed abroad almost a year! One week before his return, Lord Clark died, leaving me his sole heir. How did he come to die and whence came the blow? God, Who knows all, can answer. For my part I accuse nobody, yet——"

"What an abyss of infamy!"

"Lord Clark died without revealing anything to his brother. My terrible secret was to be scrupulously concealed until it burst, like a thunderbolt, over the head of the guilty. Your protector disapproved of this marriage between his elder brother and a girl without dowry or means; I felt I could not expect support from a man disappointed in his hopes of an inheritance. I therefore moved to France, resolved to spend the rest of my life there. But my entire fortune is in England. The war interrupted all communication between the two countries and I was in want of everything. Forced to return, I landed at Portsmouth six days ago."

"And then——?"

"Then Buckingham must somehow or other have learned of my return. He spoke of me to Lord Winter who was already prejudiced against me, describing me as a prostitute and a branded woman. The pure, noble voice of my husband was not there to defend me. Lord Winter believed everything Buckingham told him, the more readily since it was to his interest to do so. He caused me to be arrested, conveyed me here and put me under your guard. The rest you know: the day after tomorrow, he is having me banished and deported, the day after tomorrow he is relegating me to the criminal classes. Ah, the web of treachery is shrewdly spun, I tell you! the plot is skilful! How can my honor avail against it? No, Felton, I must die; there is no other solution! Give me that knife!"

With these words, as though all her strength were exhausted, Milady sank back, weak and languishing, into the arms of the young officer. Mad with love, trembling with anger and swayed by strange new sensations, sensual and voluptuous, Felton pressed her against his heart, shuddering as he felt the breath from her red passionate mouth fanning his cheek and distracted by the contact of her firm throbbing breasts against his chest.

"No, no," he vowed, "you shall live honored and pure, to triumph over your enemies."

Milady put him away from her slowly with her hand, drawing him nearer the while with her glance. Felton, in turn, advanced to embrace her, his arms clasped close about her, imploring her as he might a goddess.

"O death, death!" she whispered, lowering her voice, her eyes half-closed. "Death rather than shame. Felton, my friend, my brother, have mercy upon me!"

"No, you shall live and you shall live avenged!"

"Alas, Felton, I bring disaster to all who come near me! Leave me, abandon me to my fate, let me die—"

"Well, then, we shall die together!" he cried, pressing his lips to hers.

There was a knocking at the door; this time Milady pushed him away in earnest.

"Listen! We are caught! People are coming. All is over; this is the end!"

Felton assured her that it was only the sentinel warning him that they were about to change guard.

"Then run to the door and open it yourself."

Felton obeyed like a child, for her merest orders were now his every thought, his entire soul. In the doorway stood a soldier and, a few paces away, a sergeant commanding a watch patrol.

"Well, what is it, man?" the young lieutenant asked.

"You told me to open the door if I heard anyone cry out, sir," the soldier replied. "But you forgot to leave me the key. I heard you cry out but I could not make out what you were saying. I tried to open the door but it was locked on the inside. So I called for the sergeant of the guard."

"And here I am, Lieutenant," the sergeant spoke up.

Felton, bewildered, almost crazed, stood quite speechless. Milady perceived instantly it was for her to cope with the situation. Running to the table, she seized the knife Felton had laid down.

"By what right will you prevent me from dying?" she cried theatrically.

"Great God!" Felton gasped as he saw the knife glittering in her hand.

An ironical burst of laughter resounded through the corridor. Lord Winter, attracted by the noise, stood in the doorway, clad in a dressing-gown:

"Well, well, well," he said, "so this is the last act of the tragedy, eh? You see, Felton, the drama has followed all the phases I cited. But do not worry, no blood will flow."

Milady knew that all was lost if she did not give Felton an immediate and terrible proof of her courage.

"You are mistaken, My Lord," she said evenly. "Blood *will* flow and may it fall back on those who cause bloodshed."

With a cry, Felton rushed toward her, but he was too late; Milady had already stabbed herself.

As luck—or better, as Milady's skilled hand—would have it, the blade struck the iron busk of Milady's corset, glanced down, ripped her gown and penetrated obliquely between her flesh and ribs. Her robe was nevertheless immediately stained with blood. She fell backwards as though in a faint. Felton snatched the knife from her limp hand.

"See, My Lord," he said in a gloomy voice, "this woman was under my guard and she has killed herself!"

"Rest easy, Felton, she is not dead," Lord Winter told him. "No demon dies so easily! Calm yourself and go wait for me in my room."

"But, My Lord—"

"Go, sir, I command you."

At this injunction from his superior, Felton obeyed; but as he went out he slipped the knife under his shirt. As for Lord Winter, he contented himself with summoning the woman who waited upon Milady. When she was come, he commended the still unconscious prisoner to her care and left the two women together. But since, all things considered, the wound might be serious, he sent a man off on horseback to fetch a physician.

LVIII

Escape

As Lord Winter had thought, Milady's wound was not dangerous. As soon as she found herself alone with the woman, she suffered herself to be undressed, then she opened her eyes.

But she must still feign weakness and pain which was no difficult task for a consummate actress like Milady. Accordingly, the poor chambermaid was so completely duped by the prisoner that despite Milady's entreaties, she insisted on sitting up with her all night. Her presence did not prevent Milady from thinking over her plight from every point of view.

There could be no doubt that she had convinced Felton: he was now wholly hers! Had an angel from Heaven appeared to the young man to denounce Milady, in his present frame of mind Felton would certainly have taken the apparition for a fiend sent by the Evil One. Milady smiled at this thought, for Felton was now her only hope, her only means of safety.

There was also an unfavorable possibility: perhaps Lord Winter might suspect him and Felton might even now be under surveillance himself.

Toward four o'clock in the morning the doctor arrived, but in the interval since Milady had stabbed herself the wound had already healed. The doctor could therefore judge neither its direction nor its depth. He contented himself with taking the patient's pulse; it proved that the case was not serious.

Later in the morning Milady, pretending that she had not slept all night and that she needed rest, dismissed the woman who had watched by her bedside. She had one hope, namely, that Felton would come at breakfast time. But he did not appear.

Were her fears realized? Would Felton, suspected by Lord Winter, fail at the decisive moment? She had only one day left: Lord Winter had given her notice that she was to embark on the twenty-third and today was the twenty-second. Nevertheless she still waited quite patiently until the dinner hour.

Though she had eaten nothing for breakfast, dinner was brought at the usual time. Milady was horrified to notice that the uniforms of the soldiers who guarded her had changed. When she ventured to ask what had become of Felton she was told he had left on horseback an hour ago. She inquired whether Lord Winter was still at the castle; the soldier replied that he was and that he had given orders to be informed if the prisoner wished to speak to him. Milady answered that she was too weak at present and that her only desire was to be left alone. The soldier went out, leaving the dinner served.

So Felton had been sent away, the marine guard had been relieved; therefore Felton was obviously under suspicion. This was the last cruel blow Lord Winter had reserved for her.

Left alone, she arose. The bed which she had hugged through prudence in order that they might believe her seriously wounded burned like a bed of fire. Glancing at the door, she noted that Lord Winter had had a plank nailed over the grating. Doubtless he feared that this opening might furnish her with some diabolical means to corrupt her guards. Milady smiled with joy. She was free now to give way to her transports without being observed. She paced the room with all the frenzy of a maniac, with all the fury of a tigress caged. Certainly if she had still possessed the knife, she would not have dreamed of killing herself; she would have plunged it into Lord Winter's heart.

At six o'clock Lord Winter entered, armed to the teeth. This man, who hitherto had always seemed to her but a plain somewhat witless gentleman, had become an admirable jailer. Apparently he could foresee, divine and anticipate everything. One glance at Milady told him what was on her mind.

"I see," he said, "I see! But you shall not kill me today. You have no weapon now and besides I am on my guard. You had begun to pervert my poor Felton. He was yielding to your infernal influence. But I will save him. He will never see you again. All is over. Get your belongings together and pack them up. Tomorrow you go! I had arranged for you to sail on the twenty-fourth but I have decided that the sooner you go the better and safer for all concerned. Tomorrow, by twelve o'clock, I shall have the order for your exile, signed, *Buckingham*. If you utter one word to anyone before boarding the vessel my sergeant will blow your brains out. He has received orders to do so. If, once aboard, you utter one word to anyone before the captain permits you, he will have you tossed into the sea. This has all been agreed upon.

"*Au revoir*, then! That is all I have to say today. Tomorrow I will see you again to take my leave of you and bid you farewell."

Milady had listened to the whole menacing tirade with a smile of disdain on her lips but with rage in her heart. Now she saw him bow and leave the room. Supper was served. Milady ate heartily, for she felt that she stood in need of all her strength. Anything—a miracle or a catastrophe—might well happen during this night which was approaching so menacingly. Great clouds rolled across the sky; distant flashes heralded a fierce storm.

The storm burst at about ten o'clock. Milady derived a consolation of sorts as she saw Nature partaking in the disorders of her heart. The thunder growled in the air like the anger and fury in her mind. It was as if the blast, whirring across the earth to bow the branches of the trees and to strip them of their leaves, were lashing her and disheveling the very hairs on her head. She too howled like the hurricane as her voice was lost in the great voice of Nature which seemed to Milady to be wailing for despair, like herself.

Suddenly she heard a tap at her window and, as the lightning flashed, discerned a man's face behind the bars. She ran to the window and opened it.

"Felton!" she cried. "I am saved!"

"Yes," said Felton, "but hush, hush! I must have time to saw the bars. *You* make sure that they do not see you through the grating."

"They cannot, Felton, and there is another proof that the Lord is on our side! They have boarded up the grating."

"Capital! God in His Wisdom has made them witless!"

"But what must I do?"

"Nothing, My Lady, nothing. Just shut the window. Go to bed or at least get into bed with all your clothes on. When I have finished, I shall rap at the window. But will you be able to follow me?"

"Oh, yes!"

"Your wound?"

"It troubles me. But I can walk!"

"Then stand by for the first signal."

Milady shut the window, blew out the lamp and, obeying Felton's injunctions, curled up in bed. Amid the roars and moans of the storm, she could distinguish the steady grinding of the file upon the bars and by the light of every flash she perceived Felton's shadow across the panes. She spent a whole hour breathless, panting, a cold sweat pearling her brow, her heart wrung by excruciating anguish each time she heard a move in the corridor. Time crawled by. There are moments which last a lifetime.

An hour later, Felton rapped again. Milady sprang out of bed and opened the window. The removal of two small bars formed an opening through which a man could pass comfortably.

"Are you ready?"

"Yes. Shall I take anything with me?"

"Money, if you have some!"

"Yes! Thank God, they left me the money I had."

"So much the better. I have spent all mine in chartering a vessel."

"Take this," Milady urged, placing a bag full of louis in Felton's hands. Felton took the bag and dropped it to the foot of the wall.

"Now," he said, "will you come?"

"I am ready."

Milady mounted on a chair and passed the upper part of her body through the window. She saw the young officer suspended above the abyss on a rope-ladder. For the first time a feeling of terror reminded her that she was a woman. The yawning emptiness frightened her.

"I expected this," Felton said grimly.

"No, never mind, it's nothing at all," Milady assured him. "I will go down with my eyes shut."

"Do you trust me?" asked Felton.

"What a question!"

"Put your two hands together. Cross them. That's right."

Felton bound her wrists together with his handkerchief, then knotted a cord around the handkerchief.

"What are you doing?"

"Put your arms around my neck and fear nothing!"

"But I shall make you lose your balance and we will both be dashed to pieces."

"Don't be afraid. I am a sailor."

There was not a second to lose. Milady clasped her arms around Felton and slipped out of the window.

Felton began to descend the ladder slowly, rung by rung. Despite the weight of their bodies, the blast of the hurricane swung them in the air. Suddenly Felton stopped.

"What's wrong?"

"Quiet!" Felton warned. "I hear footsteps."

"We are lost!"

For several seconds all was silent.

"No," said Felton, "it is nothing."

"But what is that noise?"

"The patrol making its rounds."

"Which way does it pass?"

"Directly below us."

"They will surely discover us!"

"Not if there is no lightning."

"They will run into the bottom of the ladder."

"Luckily it is six feet too short."

"There they are! Oh, my God!"

"Hush!"

Both remained suspended, motionless and breathless within fifty feet of the ground while the soldiers passed below, laughing and talking. It was a horrible moment for the fugitives.

The patrol passed. The noise of retreating footsteps growing fainter, the murmur of voices died gradually away.

"Now," said Felton, "we are safe!"

Milady heaved a sigh of relief and fainted.

Felton continued to descend. Near the bottom of the ladder when he felt there was no support left for his feet, he clung on with his hands, his legs dangling in the void. Presently he reached the last rung. Hanging on by the strength of his wrists, he touched ground. Stooping down, he picked up the bag of gold and placed it between his teeth. Then he took Milady in his arms and set off briskly in the direction opposite to that which the patrol had taken. He soon left the path under patrol, climbed down across the rocks, and reaching the sea, emitted a swift, shrill whistle.

A similar signal replied. Five minutes later a boat appeared, rowed by four men. The boat approached as close as it could to the shore but the water was not deep enough for it to touch land. Felton walked into the water up to his waist, unwilling to entrust his precious burden to anyone.

Fortunately the storm began to subside though the sea was still choppy. The little boat bounded over the waves like a nutshell.

"To the sloop!" Felton ordered, "and row smartly!"

The four men bent their oars but the sea was too high for them to make much headway. However, inch by inch, they were leaving the castle behind; that was the main thing. It was almost pitch dark. Already they could barely see the shore from the boat; it seemed even less likely that those ashore could possibly distinguish them.

A black dot was floating on the sea. It was the sloop. While the boat was advancing with all the strength its four rowers could muster, Felton unknotted the cord and untied the handkerchief which bound Milady's hands together. When her hands were free he cupped up some sea-water and sprinkled it over her face. Milady heaved a sigh, opened her eyes, and:

"Where am I?" she asked.

"You are safe!" the young officer told her.

"Oh, safe! safe!" she exclaimed. "Yes, there is the sky, here is the sea! This air I breathe is the air of liberty. Oh, thank you, Felton, thank you and God bless you!"

The young man pressed her close against his heart.

"But what is the matter with my hands?" cried Milady. "It feels as if my wrists had been crushed in a vise."

And she raised her arms to survey her bruised wrists.

"Alas," exclaimed Felton, looking at her beautiful hands and shaking his head sorrowfully.

"Oh, it's nothing, nothing!" Milady protested. "Now I remember all that happened." Then she looked around her as if in search of something.

"Here it is!" Felton reassured her, touching the moneybag with his foot.

They drew near the sloop. A sailor on watch hailed the boat, the boat replied.

"What vessel is that?" Milady asked.

"The vessel I hired for you."

"Where will it take me?"

"Wherever you wish, provided you first put me ashore at Portsmouth."

"What are you going to do in Portsmouth?"

"I shall carry out Lord Winter's orders," Felton replied with a gloomy smile.

"What orders?"

"Then you don't understand?"

"No, please explain, I beg you."

"As he mistrusted me, he determined to guard you himself. So he sent me in his place to get Buckingham to sign the order for your deportation."

"But if he mistrusted you, how did he come to trust you with such an order?"

"How could I be expected to know what papers I was bearing?"

"That is true. And so you are going to Portsmouth?"

"I have no time to lose. Tomorrow is the twenty-third and Buckingham sets sail tomorrow with his fleet."

"He sets sail tomorrow? Where for?"

"For La Rochelle."

"He need not necessarily set sail!" Milady cried, her usual presence of mind abandoning her.

"Rest easy: he will not sail."

Milady started with joy. She could read into the very depths of this young man's heart and there she saw Buckingham's death sentence written in all its particulars.

"Felton, you are as great as Judas Maccabaeus!" she thrilled. "If you die, I will die with you. That is all I can say to you."

"Hush! We must go aboard!"

Indeed the boat was now alongside the sloop. Felton mounted the ladder first and gave his hand to Milady, while the sailors supported her because the sea was still choppy. A moment later they were on the deck.

"Captain," said Felton, "this is the lady I mentioned. You are to convey her safe and sound to France."

"On payment of one thousand pistoles," the captain agreed.

"I have paid you five hundred on account."

"That's correct."

"Here are the other five hundred, Captain," Milady broke in, reaching for her bag of gold.

"No, Ma'am," the Captain replied. "I make but one bargain and I have agreed with this young man that the remainder is to be paid me only on arrival in Boulogne."

"Shall we land there?"

"Safe and sound, Ma'am, as true as my name's Jack Butler."

"Well, if you keep your word, instead of five hundred pistoles I will give you a thousand."

"Hurrah for you then, beautiful lady!" the Captain cried. "May God often send me such passengers as Your Ladyship."

"Meanwhile," said Felton, "take us to the little bay of————. As you recall it was agreed you should put in there."

For sole answer the skipper ordered the necessary manoeuvres and toward seven in the morning the little vessel cast anchor as desired.

During the passage, Felton related everything to Milady: how, instead of going to London, he had chartered the little vessel ... how he had returned ... how he had scaled the wall by fastening cramps in the interstices of the stones as he ascended in order to give him foothold ... finally, how, when he had reached the bars he had made the ladder fast.... As for the rest, he concluded modestly, Milady had herself witnessed it.

Milady, for her part, strove to encourage Felton in his project; but at the first words she uttered, she plainly saw that the young fanatic needed rather to be restrained than to be urged on.

It was agreed that Milady would wait for Felton until ten o'clock; if he did not return by then she was to set sail for France. If for some reason he could not join her aboard but was at liberty, he would catch a later ship and rejoin her in France, at the Convent of the Carmelites at Béthune.

LIX
Of What Occurred at Portsmouth on August 23, 1628

Kissing her hand casually, Felton took leave of Milady as a brother might do of his sister, bound for a casual excursion. His whole attitude was calm as usual. But an unwonted brilliance in his glance betrayed an inward fever; he looked paler; his teeth were clenched; his crisp, clipped speech showed how nervous he was.

So long as he sat in the rowboat bearing him to land, he kept his eyes on Milady. She too, standing on deck, gazed steadfastly at him. Each knew there was no immediate danger of pursuit.

Felton jumped ashore, climbed the little slope that led to the clifftop, waved to Milady for the last time, and made for the city. A thousand yards further he could barely distinguish the mast of the sloop bobbing up and down on the distant waters. Portsmouth stood about two miles ahead of him; across the haze of early morning, he could make out its houses and towers. He sped on. Beyond Portsmouth lay the sea, dotted with vessels whose masts, like a forest of poplars in winter, bent with each gust of wind.

Felton looked back over his life, his underprivileged youth, his years among the Puritans, and all the accusations these Puritans leveled at Buckingham, the favorite of two kings, James I and Charles I.

Comparing the crimes with which public opinion charged this minister—glaring, national and even European crimes, so to speak—with the humbler, private and unknown crimes that Milady invoked, Felton was convinced that, in Buckingham's dual conduct, the latter were the more reprehensible. In love for the first time in his life, swayed by a novel and strange and ardent urge, he viewed the infamous and imaginary accusations of Milady as through a magnifying glass. In his eyes, her grievances assumed an infinitely exaggerated stature. Thus a scientist, looking through a lens at a molecule invisible to the naked eye when placed beside an ant, sees it as a monster of titanic proportions.

As Felton raced on, his ardor grew apace. His temples throbbed as the blood rose to his head. Was he to leave the woman he loved or, better, the saint he adored, at the mercy of the most dastardly vengeance? The variety of emotions he had experienced, his present fatigue, and his rising excitement contributed to exalt his mind above all rational, human considerations.

Reaching Portsmouth at eight, he found the whole population astir. Drums were beating in the streets and in the port; the troops about to embark were marching toward the docks. Covered with dust and streaming with perspiration, his face purple with heat and excitement, Felton sought to enter the Admiralty Building. The sentry refused him access; Felton called for the Orderly Officer.

"I am Lieutenant Felton, sir, of the Royal Navy," he said, coming to attention and saluting smartly. "I bear urgent dispatches from Lord Winter."

And he produced the letter his protector had addressed to Buckingham.

As Lord Winter was known to be an intimate of the Duke's, the officer motioned to him to pass and Felton darted into the palace. Just as he passed into the vestibule another man entered, dusty and breathless as Felton. (So great was his haste that he had left his posthorse at the gate without flinging the reins to a groom. The horse had fallen on its foreknees, exhausted.) Shoulder to shoulder, the two men raced up the steps; they addressed Patrick, the Duke of Buckingham's confidential valet, simultaneously. But Felton named Lord Winter, whereas the stranger declined to identify himself to anyone save His Grace in person. Each sought to gain access to Buckingham before the other.

Patrick knew that Lord Winter belonged to the service and that he was a personal friend of his master's. Quite naturally, therefore, he gave preference to Felton. The stranger, who had perforce to wait, could not conceal his displeasure.

Patrick led Felton across a large hall where the deputies of La Rochelle, headed by the Prince de Soubise, who three years before had seized Oléron from the Royalists and had fought doggedly for the Huguenots for some years. Hard on Patrick's heels, Felton proceeded down a corridor to a dressing room where Buckingham, just out of the bathtub, was putting on his clothes, a matter upon which he always bestowed the most meticulous attention.

"Lieutenant Felton with dispatches from Lord Winter," Patrick announced.

"From Lord Winter, eh? Well, send the Lieutenant in."

Felton entered into the presence of a minister who, having tossed a richly gold-embroidered dressing gown over an armchair, was trying on a sky blue velvet doublet, studded with pearls.

"Why did not My Lord come himself?" Buckingham demanded. "I expected him this morning."

"Lord Winter requested me to present his compliments and to inform Your Grace that he was unavoidably detained because of the prisoner at the castle."

"Yes, yes, I know—I know he has a prisoner—"

"It is about that prisoner that I beg to speak to Your Grace."

"Well, speak up, then."

"What I have to tell Your Grace is extremely confidential."

"You may go, Patrick," Buckingham told his valet. "But keep within reach; I shall be ringing for you presently." Patrick gone, Buckingham looked at Felton. "Now we are alone, sir, tell me what all this means."

"If Your Grace recalls, Lord Winter wrote recently requesting you to sign an embarkation order for a young woman named Charlotte Backson."

"Certainly; I asked him to send me the order and I promised to sign it."

"Here is the order, My Lord."

Taking the paper from Felton, Buckingham glanced casually at it and, realizing it was the one mentioned, he put it on the table, took up a quill and prepared to sign it.

"Begging Your Grace's pardon," Felton said stepping forward, "Your Grace knows that Charlotte Backson is not the real name of this young woman."

"Certainly, sir, I know that," the Duke replied as he dipped his quill in the inkhorn.

"Then Your Grace knows her real name?" Felton asked sharply.

"Yes, I know that too," Buckingham acknowledged as he put pen to paper.

"And knowing that—" Felton's voice trembled, "Your Grace will sign this order all the same?"

"Certainly. With the greatest pleasure, twice or thrice over!"

Felton's voice grew sharper and though low-pitched assumed a certain shrillness. His words came increasingly staccato:

"Does Your Grace realize that the deportee is Lady Clark?" he asked.

"Of course I do. But how do you know?"

"I know, My Lord, by this means or that. But I cannot understand how Your Grace dare venture in all conscience to sign this order for deportation—"

Buckingham stared haughtily at him.

"Look here, sir, your questions sound very strange and I am very foolish to answer."

"Your Grace *must* answer. The circumstances are even more serious than Your Grace imagines."

Knowing that the youth came from Lord Winter, Buckingham supposed that he spoke in his master's name. Somewhat less sternly:

"I shall sign this order without a qualm," he told Felton. "Lord Winter knows as well as I that the person concerned is a criminal. She is very lucky to get off with deportation—" he concluded, about to set pen to paper. Felton took two steps forward.

"You will not sign that order, My Lord!" he said.

"I will not sign that order? And why not, pray?"

"Because Your Grace will look into your heart and will do this lady justice."

"I would do her justice by sending her to Tyburn. This lady is infamous."

"Your Grace, Lady Clark is an angel, as you well know, and I demand that you set her free."

"You demand—look here, man, are you mad, to talk thus to me?"

"Forgive me, My Lord, I am speaking as best I can. And I am restraining myself, at that. I implore you to think of what you are about to do. Let Your Grace beware of going too far!"

"What's that you say? Damme, I believe the fellow is threatening me."

"No, My Lord, I am still pleading. And I say to you: one drop of water suffices to make the full vessel overflow. Just one slight mistake—" Felton stared meaningfully at Buckingham, "one slight mistake can bring down punishment upon the mightiest head, spared hitherto despite so many crimes."

"Mr. Felton," said Buckingham, "you will withdraw and place yourself under arrest forthwith."

"You shall hear me out, My Lord. You seduced this young woman, you outraged and defiled her. Now you have a chance to repair your crime. Let her go free and I shall require nothing else from you."

"You will require—?" Buckingham stared at Felton in astonishment, pronouncing the three words with great emphasis.

"My Lord—" Felton grew more and more excited as he spoke. "Beware! All England is weary of your iniquities. Your Lordship has abused, nay, almost usurped the royal power, and you stand an object of horror to God and man. God will punish you hereafter, but I will punish you here and now!"

"This is too much!" cried Buckingham, making for the door. But Felton blocked his passage.

"I ask Your Lordship most humbly to sign the order for this lady's liberation," he pleaded with a return of calm. "Remember she is a woman whom you have dishonored."

"Withdraw forthwith, sir, or I shall call my attendant and have you put in irons."

"You shall *not* call!" Felton cried, thrusting himself between the Duke and the bell which stood on a small silver-encrusted table. "Beware, My Lord!" his eyes blazed. "You are in the hands of God!"

"In the hands of the Devil, you mean," Buckingham cried, raising his voice so as to be heard by his servants without actually calling for them.

"I insist Your Lordship sign," Felton insisted threateningly as he held a paper before the Duke. "Sign the liberation of Lady Clark."

"*I* sign by force! You are joking. Ho, Patrick!"

"Sign, My Lord!"

"Certainly not!"

"You *must* sign!"

"Never!"

Buckingham sprang for his sword, reached it but could not draw it; Felton was upon him. From under his shirt, Felton drew the knife Milady had given him. Buckingham cried for help. Suddenly Patrick appeared.

"A letter from France, My Lord."

Buckingham looked up . . . Patrick advanced, letter in hand . . . Felton lunged. . . .

"Thus die all traitors, villains and fornicators," said Felton solemnly.

Buckingham gasped.

"Ah, you have killed me!" he cried.

Patrick rushed to his support. Felton, seeing the door free, took to his heels. . . .

Felton entered the antechamber where the deputies of La Rochelle awaited His Grace's pleasure, crossed it rapidly and was about to rush down the staircase when on the top step he ran into Lord Winter. Seeing how pale and confused Felton was, staring into space, his face and hands spattered with blood, the nobleman seized him, crying:

"God have mercy on me, I knew it. And I have come just one minute too late! Fool and wretch that I am!"

Felton offering no resistance, Lord Winter placed him in the hands of the guards who, pending further orders, led him to a small terrace overlooking the sea. Then Lord Winter hastened to Buckingham's apartment.

Meanwhile, close upon the Duke's cry: "Ah, you have killed me!" and Patrick's appeal for help, the gentleman with news from France entered Buckingham's dressing room. He found the Duke stretched out on a sofa, pressing his clenched hands over his wound.

"La Porte," the Duke whispered, "La Porte, do you come from her?"

"Ay, Milord and perhaps too late," the Queen's loyal secretary replied with tears in his eyes.

"Hush, La Porte, not so loud," Buckingham spoke effortfully. "We might be overheard." He coughed. "Patrick, let no one enter. Ah, God, I am dying and I shall never know what message she sent!" And the Duke fainted.

Just then Lord Winter, the deputies from La Rochelle and the leaders of the expedition all made their way into His Grace's presence. Exclamations of surprise, horror and despair filled the little room. Those within explained what had happened to their friends in the corridor, the news spread like wildfire throughout the palace and presently throughout the city.

A moment later the report of heavy cannon announced that something new and unexpected had taken place. Lord Winter tore his hair in an agony of self-reproach.

"Too late," he groaned, "too late by one minute! My God, my God, what a tragedy!"

(At seven o'clock that morning he had been informed that a rope ladder was dangling from one of the windows of the castle . . . rushing to Milady's room he had found it empty, the window open and the bars sawed through . . . suddenly he had recalled the verbal caution D'Artagnan's messenger had transmitted . . . in panic, fear of what might befall, the Duke had darted to the stables . . . without waiting to have his own horse saddled he had leaped on the first one at hand . . . he had galloped off to the Admiralty . . . he had climbed the stairs three at a time . . . and at the top of the staircase he had met Felton. . . .)

The Duke was not dead—not yet, thought Winter. Buckingham recovered a little and opened his eyes again. Hope sprang anew in the hearts of his friends.

"Gentlemen," the Duke said faintly, "I beg you to leave me alone with Patrick and La Porte." Then, noticing his friend: "Ah, you Winter!" he said. "You sent me a curious lunatic this morning; look at what he did to me!"

"My Lord, God help me, I shall never forgive myself!"

"That would be quite wrong, my dear Winter," said Buckingham stretching out his hand to him, "what man on earth deserves to leave another inconsolable? But pray leave us, I entreat you."

Lord Winter withdrew, sobbing with grief, the door closed upon him, and the wounded Duke, La Porte and Patrick remained closeted in the dressing room. A doctor was being sought but so far without success.

Kneeling beside the Duke's sofa, Anne of Austria's faithful servant said tremulously:

"Your Grace will live, I know it. Your Grace will live."

"What has she written to me, La Porte?" Buckingham inquired feebly, covered with blood and overcoming the most atrocious pain in order to speak of the woman he loved. "What has she written? Read me her letter."

"Oh, Milord!"

"Do as I say, La Porte. Don't you see I have no time to lose?"

La Porte broke the seal and placed the parchment before the Duke's eyes.

"Read, I say, read. *I* cannot see clearly; soon, perhaps, I shall not be able to hear. Read, man, so I may know what she wrote me before I die."

La Porte made no further protest and read:

My Lord:

By what I have suffered through you and for you since I have known you, I conjure you, if you have any regard for my well-being, to interrupt those great armaments you are preparing against France. I beseech you by the same token to cease this war which is generally said to be due to religious causes but privately whispered to spring from the love you bear me.

This war may not only visit great catastrophes upon England and France but great misfortunes upon your own head, My Lord, which would leave me inconsolable.

Pray watch carefully over your life which is threatened and which will be dear to me from the moment I no longer have cause to regard you as an enemy.

Your affectionate
Anne

Buckingham collected all his remaining strength to listen attentively; when the reading was done he sank back disconsolate, as he had never expected to find this letter so bitterly disappointing.

"Have you nothing further to tell me, La Porte? No oral message."

"Yes, Milord. Her Majesty charged me to beg you to be very careful. She had learned recently that a plot was afoot to murder Your Grace."

"Is that all, La Porte? Is that all?"

"Her Majesty charged me also to tell Your Grace—" La Porte lowered his voice, "to tell Your Grace that she still loved you."

"God be praised, I can die in peace! To her, my death will not be the death of a stranger!"

La Porte burst into tears.

"Patrick," the Duke ordered, "bring me the casket in which the diamond studs were kept."

As Patrick obeyed, La Porte recognized the casket as having once belonged to the Queen.

"Now the white satin sachet, on which her cipher is embroidered in pearls."

Patrick again obeyed.

"Here, La Porte, here are the only tokens I ever received from her: a silver casket and these two letters! You will return them to Her Majesty. And as a last remembrance—" Buckingham looked around him for some valuable object, "you will also give her—"

He still searched about him, but his eyes, dimmed by approaching death, fell upon nothing save the knife that had fallen from Felton's hands. Following his gaze, La Porte noted that the blade was still red with Buckingham's blood.

"—you will also give her this knife!" Buckingham gasped, pressing La Porte's hand.

He found just strength enough to place the sachet at the bottom of the silver casket and drop the knife in. Next he motioned to La Porte that he was no longer able to speak. Then, in a final convulsion he could not master, he slid from the sofa to the floor. Patrick uttered a loud cry. Buckingham attempted to smile a last time but Death arrested his thought, which remained impressed upon his brow like a last kiss of love.

At this moment the Duke's physician arrived, much distraught. They had not been able to reach him before because he had already boarded the flagship. He approached the Duke, took his hand, held it for an instant in his and letting it fall:

"All is useless," he whispered, "His Grace is dead."

"Dead!" Patrick screamed. "His Grace dead!"

At this cry the crowd returned to Buckingham's apartment to mourn the passing of their master. Lord Winter, assured that Buckingham had expired, ran to the terrace where Felton was still under guard. By now the young man had regained his natural coolness and self-possession.

"You traitor, you wretch, what have you done?" the nobleman said.

"I have avenged myself!"

"Avenged yourself?" Lord Winter stared, incredulous. Then mastering his fury: "Say rather that you have served as the tool of that accursed woman. But remember, I swear by all that is holy, this crime shall be her last!"

Felton looked him in the eye with perfect composure.

"I do not know what you mean, My Lord!" He bowed his head. "I do not know of whom you speak. I killed the Duke of Buckingham because he twice refused you my commission as Captain. I punished him for his injustice, that is all."

Lord Winter, nonplussed, watched the men bind Felton: he could make nothing, absolutely nothing of such callousness in one so young and recently so close to his heart. One thing alone, he thought, could cast a shadow over the youth's pallid brow. And, observing Felton, Lord Winter guessed that at every sound he heard, the naïve Puritan fancied he recognized the step and voice of Milady, coming to throw herself in his arms, to accuse herself and to share his death.

Suddenly Felton started. His glance, ranging over the harbor, had become fixed on a tiny speck out at sea. With the eagle eye of a sailor he had identified what the average man would have mistaken for a gull poised on the waves. It was the white sail of a sloop heading for France.

Felton turned ashen, placed his hand upon his heart which was breaking and suddenly understood the full extent of all her treachery.

"One last favor, My Lord!" he begged.

"Well?"

"What o'clock is it?"

The nobleman drew out his watch.

"It lacks ten minutes to nine."

Milady had sailed more than an hour before the time stipulated. Hearing the cannon boom, she had immediately given orders to weigh anchor. Now the sloop was bobbing under a bright blue sky far and safe from shore.

With the inherent fatalism and resignation of the fanatic:

"God has willed it so, God's will be done!" Felton sighed. But he could not tear his glance away from that ship and from the vision he glimpsed of the white phantom for whom he had sacrificed his life.

"You shall be punished in your own person, poor wretch," Lord Winter declared. "But on the head of my brother whom I loved so dearly, I vow that your accomplice will suffer a worse fate!"

Felton bowed his head without uttering a syllable. Lord Winter swung on his heel, ran down the stairs and made straight for the port.

On hearing of Buckingham's death, Charles I, King of England, was desperately afraid lest the news discourage his allies of La Rochelle. As Richelieu was to write later in his memoirs, the British monarch attempted to keep this news a secret as long as he could. He closed all the ports in his kingdom and saw to it that no vessel left the island until the forces that Buckingham had mustered were on their way to France. Buckingham gone, His Majesty himself undertook to direct preparations for the campaign. He actually went so far as to detain in England the Danish ambassadors, who had taken their leave, and the Ambassador Ordinary of Holland, who was to return to the port of Flushing the India merchant vessels which Charles had decided to restore to the United Provinces.

But King Charles did not think of giving these orders until five hours after the murder of Buckingham. It was then two o'clock in the afternoon and two vessels had already made off. One of these bore Milady to France. Suspecting what had happened, she was confirmed in her belief as she sailed past the flagship of the fleet and saw a black ensign flying at the mast head. Of the second ship, more anon.

Meanwhile at the French camp outside La Rochelle things were at a standstill. King Louis XIII, bored as usual but perhaps even more so in camp than elsewhere, decided to go to Saint-Germain to celebrate the feast day of his patron saint. He therefore requested of the Cardinal an escort of musketeers—only twenty, since His Majesty was to travel incognito. His Eminence, often infected by the monarch's tedium, granted his royal lieutenant this leave of absence with the utmost pleasure. The King promised to return about the fifteenth of September.

His Eminence notified Monsieur de Tréville who had his baggage immediately prepared. The Captain of musketeers was aware that our four friends, impelled by urgent reasons which he did not know, were most anxious to return to Paris. He therefore detailed them at once as part of the royal escort. Indeed they learned the great news only a quarter of an hour after Monsieur de Tréville himself, for they were the first to whom he imparted it. It was then that D'Artagnan appreciated to its full extent the favor the Cardinal had conferred on him by allowing him at long last to transfer to the musketeers. Otherwise he would have been forced to remain in camp whilst his companions sped joyfully back to Paris.

This impatience to return to the capital was of course dictated by thoughts of the danger Madame Bonacieux would run in meeting Milady, her mortal enemy, at the Convent of Béthune. Plans to avert this danger had long since been made and partially carried out. First Aramis had written to Madame Michon, the beautiful seamstress of Tours who had acquaintances in such high circles. Aramis asked that she obtain from the Queen authority for Madame Bonacieux to leave the convent and to retire either to Lorraine or to Belgium. The reply was very prompt; within ten days, Aramis received the following letter:

My dear Cousin:
Herewith is the authorization from my sister enabling our little servant to withdraw from the Convent of Béthune. I am sorry the air there, as you wrote, is so bad for her. My sister takes great pleasure in sending you this authorization, for she is very fond of the girl, whom she expects further to befriend hereafter.

My fondest love to you.
Marie Michon

The paper enclosed read as follows:

The Mother Superior of the Convent of Béthune is instructed to deliver into the hands of the bearer of this note, the novice who entered the convent on my recommendation and under my patronage.

Done by my hand at the Palace of the Louvre this tenth day of August in the year of Our Lord one thousand six hundred and twenty-eight.

Anne

Naturally the family ties between Aramis and a seamstress who called the Queen her sister amused the young men no end and aroused their barbed, their sharpest witticisms. But Aramis, having blushed several times to the roots of his hair at the ribald jests of Porthos, begged his friends to drop the subject. If he heard another word of this, he threatened, he would never again implore his cousin to intervene in an affair of this sort.

Marie Michon therefore ceased to be a theme of conversation between them. They had obtained what they wanted, namely, the order to remove Madame Bonacieux from the Carmelite Convent of Béthune. This order was of no great use to them so long as they were in camp near La Rochelle, with half of France between them and Madame Bonacieux. D'Artagnan was on the point of taking Monsieur de Tréville fully into his confidence, stressing the urgency of the affair and requesting a leave of absence, when suddenly they learned from the Captain of musketeers that they were among the twenty musketeers detailed to accompany the King to Paris. Their joy at these tidings knew no bounds; the lackeys were sent on beforehand with the baggage and the expedition set out on the morning of September sixteenth. The Cardinal accompanied His Majesty from Surgères to Mauzé, where they parted with great demonstrations of friendship.

The King traveled as fast as possible, for he was determined to reach Paris by September twenty-third. But on the road, now and then, the expedition would stop to fly the King's falcons and hawks at magpies, larks and quails. Falconry was a favorite sport of the King's; years ago, when Louis was still Dauphin, the Duc de Luynes had initiated him in the technique of this form of hunting and he had always retained a great predilection for it. Whenever the expedition paused for this hunting, sixteen of the twenty musketeers were jubilant, our friends alone cursing the delay roundly. D'Artagnan in particular felt a perpetual buzzing in his ears, a phenomenon Porthos readily diagnosed.

"A very great lady once told me," he explained, "that when you experience a ringing in the auditory center, it is caused by the fact that somebody somewhere is talking about you!"

The escort finally crossed Paris on the night of the twenty-third; His Majesty thanked Monsieur de Tréville and permitted him to grant a four-day furlough to his men on condition that none thus favored should appear in a public place under penalty of immediate incarceration in the Bastille.

As may readily be imagined, the first four leaves granted went to our friends. Even better, Athos obtained six days instead of four, adding two nights as well, by prevailing upon Monsieur de Tréville to let them leave on the twenty-fourth at five o'clock in the evening and in his kindness, to postdate their orders to the morning of the twenty-fifth.

D'Artagnan, sanguine as only a Gascon and confidently making molehills of mountains, grumbled to his friends.

"I think we are making a great to do about something very simple," he observed. "I can reach Béthune in forty-eight hours by riding three horses to the death, but that matters little for I have plenty of money. At Béthune, I merely hand the Queen's letter to the Mother Superior and I convey my beloved Constance not to Lorraine nor to Belgium but back here to Paris. Don't you agree that she can hide much more safely here, particularly so long as the Cardinal remains in La Rochelle? Then, when we return from the campaign, partly through the protection of her cousin, partly through what we have personally done for her, we can obtain what we wish from the Queen. I therefore suggest that you stay here, my friends, and take things easy. There is no point in tiring yourselves out needlessly. An errand as simple as this calls for only myself and Planchet to bestir ourselves."

To which Athos countered very evenly:

"We too have plenty of money left. I have not yet drunk up all my share of the diamond; and Porthos and Aramis have not taken out all theirs in gourmandizing and gluttony. Thus we can each afford to wear out three horses apiece just as easily as you can." His face clouded, and he resumed in a voice so gloomy that D'Artagnan shuddered: "Remember that Béthune is the town where the Cardinal has made an appointment with a woman who brings misery in her wake wherever she sets foot. If you had but to overcome four men, D'Artagnan, I would cheerfully allow you to go alone. But you have to face that woman. So the four of us shall go together and, with our four lackeys, pray God we shall prove numerous enough."

"You terrify me, Athos. What in God's name do you fear?"

"I fear the worst," Athos replied. "To horse, then, gentlemen!"

As they rode out silently, D'Artagnan glanced at his comrades frequently; like Athos, the two others betrayed signs of deep anxiety. All pressed forward at top speed in complete silence.

On the evening of September twenty-fifth, they entered Arras. D'Artagnan had just alighted before the inn called the *Herse d'Or, At the Sign of the Golden Harrow,* and was slaking his thirst, when a horseman, emerging from the posting yard where he had just changed horses, galloped off toward Paris. As he was passing through the gateway into the street, a gust of wind blew open the cloak in which he was muffled and unsettled his hat. Hastily the stranger caught it and crammed it down over his eyes. D'Artagnan, who had recognized him, turned deathly pale and let his glass clatter to the pavement.

"What is the matter, Monsieur?" Planchet inquired. "Help, gentlemen," he called to the others. "Please come here, my master is ill!"

The three friends rushed to D'artagnan's assistance, but far from being ill he waved them away and sprang for his horse. They stood fast and held him at the door.

"What the devil are you up to now?" Athos demanded.

"Where on earth are you going?" Aramis asked.

"The fellow is mad!" Porthos commented.

Trembling with anger, white as a sheet, a cold sweat pouring in beads over his forehead:

"That's the man!" D'Artagnan cried, "my enemy! Let me catch up with him!"

"What man?" Athos inquired; and Aramis: "Please explain what all this is about?"

"That man who just rode by—"

"What about him?"

"He is my evil genius, the curse upon my life, the bane of my existence. Always I have met him when threatened with some terrible misfortune. He was with that horrible woman when I met her for the first time . . . I was after him when I offended Athos . . . I saw him the very morning of the day when Madame Bonacieux was carried off . . . and now I see him again. . . . I recognized him clearly when the wind blew his cloak open."

"Devil take it," Athos murmured, lost in thought.

"To horse, gentlemen, to horse; let us pursue and overtake him."

Aramis offered sager advice.

"My dear fellow," he remarked, "remember that he is going in an opposite direction from ours . . . that he has a fresh horse and ours are tired . . . that we would only disable ours to no effect . . . and that you should let the man go and save the woman. . . ."

Suddenly a stable boy came running out of the posting yard in search of the stranger.

"Ho, Monsieur, ho!" he called, "here is a paper that fell out of your hat!" And he looked vainly about him.

"My friend," said D'Artagnan, "a half-pistole for that paper."

"With pleasure, Monsieur, here it is."

Enchanted with his financial coup, the stable boy returned to the yard, bowing.

"Well?"—"What is it?"—"Read it?" asked the friends.

"Nothing. Just one word!"

"Yes, but that word is the name of some town or village," Aramis pointed out.

"Armentières," Porthos read, "Armentières! I never heard of it."

"The name of that town or village is in *her* handwriting," Athos reported.

"Come, let us preserve this piece of paper carefully," D'Artagnan suggested. "Perhaps I have not wasted my last pistole. To horse, my friends, to horse!"

And they galloped off toward Béthune.

LXI

Of What Occurred at the Convent of the Carmelite Nuns in Bethune

Great criminals bear a kind of predestination which enables them to overcome all obstacles and to escape all perils until a wearied Providence sets up a pitfall to mark the end of their impious fortunes.

So it was with Milady. She had the good luck to sail blithely through the fleets of two enemy nations without mishap until Fate was presently to catch up with her.

Landing at Portsmouth, Milady was an Englishwoman driven from La Rochelle by the persecutions of the French; landing at Boulogne after a two days' crossing, she was a Frenchwoman driven from Portsmouth by the persecution of the English.

Milady also possessed the most efficient of passports: her beauty, her noble manner and the generosity with which she distributed her pistoles. Freed from the usual formalities by the affable smile and gallant manners of the aged Governor of the Port, who kissed her hand and conducted her unexamined through the police and customs offices, she stayed in Boulogne only long enough to dash off the following note:

To His Eminence Monseigneur Cardinal de Richelieu at his camp before La Rochelle:

Monseigneur:

Your Eminence need have no cause for alarm. His Grace the Duke of Buckingham cannot possibly set out for France. Boulogne, the evening of the 25th.

Lady Clark

P.S. In accordance with the wishes of Your Eminence, I am leaving for the Convent of the Carmelites at Béthune where I await further orders.

Traveling rapidly that day, Milady spent one night at an inn on the road, and after a journey of three hours next morning, reached Béthune at eight o'clock. At the Carmelite convent, she was received by the Mother Superior, produced her order from the Cardinal, was immediately assigned to a chamber and given a hearty breakfast. As she partook of it cheerfully, every detail of her past faded into oblivion; the roseate perspective of the future beckoned as she basked in the aura of favors to come from the Cardinal she had served so well. Best of all, the name of Richelieu had not been mentioned in the whole murderous affair. Surely then her discretion merited the highest recompense in His Eminence's gift? In her body and her heart, passion succeeded passion, consuming her ever anew; her life took on the color and movement of clouds that float across the firmament, tinged now with azure, now with fire, and now with the blackness of a tempest which leaves in its wake no trace of aught but devastation and death.

After breakfast the Mother Superior paid Milady a visit. In general there are few distractions in a convent and a new arrival, particularly one as attractive as Milady, provides considerable entertainment. The good nun sought her out with anticipatory relish. Milady, on her part, used all her wiles in order to please the Mother Superior; this was not difficult, what with the grace of her person and the variety and ease of her conversation.

The Mother Superior was of noble birth ... she welcomed all manner of Court gossip which so rarely travels to the confines of the realm ... she was awed by the type of tidings which infrequently scale the walls of convents ... and she was dazzled by these secular rumors which burst upon the godly silence of her little world. ...

Milady, on the contrary, was thoroughly conversant with all the aristocratic intrigues amid which she had constantly lived for the past few years. She therefore made it her business to amuse the worthy nun with an abundance of anecdotes about the French Court. Discreetly she unfolded the mundane practices of the great lords and ladies whom the Mother Superior knew perfectly well by name . . . skilfully she retailed the exaggerated devoutness and eccentric devotions of the King . . . lightly she exposed the scandals of this or that amour between this or that noble . . . airily she told of the love affair between Her Majesty and Buckingham. . . . In brief she spoke a great deal with assumed candor in order to move her auditor to speak ever so little.

But the Mother Superior simply sat back listening avidly, vouchsafing no word and smiling encouragement. Milady, aware that this type of conversation pleased the nun, developed various themes of Court chatter, endeavoring slowly and warily, to bring the Cardinal into the discussion.

Her problem was a thorny one, for she did not know whether the Mother Superior was a royalist or a cardinalist. Accordingly she steered a safe middle-course. Meanwhile the nun maintained an even more cautious reserve, nodding her head gravely whenever Milady chanced to mention the Cardinal by name.

As the conversation continued, Milady, beginning to feel that conventual life promised to prove extremely tedious, resolved to take a risk in order to ascertain how matters stood. To test the discretion of the nun, she related an ugly rumor about the Cardinal, circumspectly at first, then thoroughly circumstantiated. It concerned Monseigneur's reputed liaison with Madame d'Aiguillon, his niece, which afforded the fillip of incest to her tale . . . of Monseigneur's reputed liaison with Marion de Lorme, the versatile courtesan whom des Barreaux, the rake and poet, initiated into the ways of carnality and who bedded with Saint Evremond, the wit and littérateur and with the great Condé among others . . . and finally of Monseigneur's reputed liaison with a good many other ladies of light virtue. . . .

Out of the corner of her eye, Milady noticed gratefully that the Mother Superior appeared to listen more attentively, to grow more animated and here and there even to smile. Encouraged, Milady mused:

"Good, the woman is interested in what I am telling her. If she is a cardinalist, at least she is no fanatic!"

And she went on to describe the persecution His Eminence exercised upon his enemies, while, at each instance cited, the Mother Superior made a sign of the cross, registering neither approval nor disapproval. The nun's attitude confirmed Milady's suspicion that she was dealing with a royalist. Presently the Mother Superior ventured:

"I am little acquainted in all such matters. We are far removed from Court life, as you know. Yet remote as we are from the world and its turmoil, occasionally we find tragic examples of what you tell me."

Milady glanced questioningly at the nun. "Yes," the nun went on, "we happen to have a young woman staying here at this very moment who has had much to suffer from the vengeance and persecution of the Cardinal."

"A guest of yours, here in this convent, Reverend Mother!" Milady exclaimed. "Poor woman, how I pity her!"

"You have good reason to do so, my daughter. She has suffered imprisonment, menaces, abuse, ill-treatment, in a word, everything. But after all," the nun sighed, "perhaps the Cardinal has sound reasons for acting thus. Though this young woman looks like an angel, who can tell? Appearances are so often deceptive."

Milady, suspecting she was in luck and might discover something of interest, assumed an expression of utmost candor.

"Alas!" she sighed. "I know! Some say that we are wrong to trust in appearances and that the most beautiful face may conceal the most evil of hearts. But how else should we judge? Surely the human countenance is the most beautiful work Our Lord created? I may well be mistaken all my life long, but I vow I shall always have faith in anyone whose looks please me."

"You think this young woman innocent, then?"

"The Cardinal does not pursue criminals exclusively," Milady said. "He has been known to harass the most virtuous of women—"

"Your pardon, Madame, I do not follow you—"

"What do you mean, Reverend Mother?" Milady countered with extreme ingenuousness.

"I mean I do not understand your language—"

Milady smiled.

"What is so strange about my language?"

"Well, Madame, you are a friend of the Cardinal's. It was he sent you here. And yet—"

"And yet I speak ill of him?"

"You say no good of him, my daughter."

"That is because I am his victim," said Milady, heaving a sigh, "his victim, Reverend Mother, and not his friend."

"What of your letter of recommendation? It is signed by the Cardinal."

"It is merely an order for my temporary confinement, Reverend Mother. I expect some satellite of His Eminence's to arrive here at any moment and to spirit me away."

"Why did you not run away?" the nun asked pertinently.

"Where to, Madame? Could I flee to any place on earth the Cardinal cannot reach? Were I a man, I might stand a chance; but what can a poor helpless woman do?" Milady paused dramatically. "What of your guest, Madame? Has *she* attempted to run away?"

"Her case is different, my child. I suspect she is staying in France because of some love affair."

"Ah, if she is in love, then, she cannot be so utterly miserable!"

And as Milady sighed the nun looked at her with new interest.

"So you too are a hapless victim of persecution?" she asked.

"Alas, yes!"

The Mother Superior scrutinized Milady as though to solve a fresh problem:

"You are n-n-n-ot an en-n-nemy of our H-h-h-oly F-f-f-faith?"

"I, a Protestant!" Milady cried. "Reverend Mother, I call upon God Who hears us to witness that I am a devout, fervent and practicing Catholic."

The nun smiled.

"In that case, Madame," she said, "you may set your mind at ease. This house will not be a harsh prison; we will do all in our power to make you enjoy your captivity. And you will find pleasant companionship. The young woman I mentioned is, like yourself, a victim of Court intrigues. That is a bond in common; and she too is both attractive and mannerly."

"Who is she, Reverend Mother?"

"She was sent to me by a person of the highest rank. I know her only under the name of Kitty. I have not attempted to discover her real name."

"Kitty! Kitty! Are you sure, Madame?"

"That is the name she goes under," the nun answered. "But why do you ask? Do you know her?"

Milady shrugged her shoulders and smiled. Could this attractive victim of the Cardinal's persecution be her erstwhile soubrette? Recalling

Kitty's unexplainable disappearance, a surge of anger swept over her, hatred and lust for vengeance distorted her features. Then, mastering herself, she reassumed that placid, benevolent expression which was but one of her many disguises.

"When may I see this poor young woman?" she asked with errant innocence. "I feel sure I shall like her ever so much!"

"You may see her this evening. But you have been traveling these four days, as you yourself told me. You arose this morning at five o'clock, you must rest, my dear. Lie down and go to sleep; we will call you in time for dinner."

Excited as Milady was by the prospect of a new panel in her gallery of intrigues she could have done without sleep, despite the ardors and endurances of her journey. Nevertheless she obeyed the Mother Superior. A fortnight of various and harrowing experiences could not exhaust her physically, but mentally she must have rest.

She therefore excused herself, curtsied to the Mother Superior and went to bed, lulled to a quiet sleep amid notions of vengeance suggested by the mere name of Kitty. She recalled the virtually complete authority the Cardinal had promised so but she succeed in her mission. She had succeeded; D'Artagnan was in her power.

There was, however, a considerable fly in her generous ointment. The thought of it prickled her. Uncomfortably she remembered a certain Comte de La Fère, whom she had once married and whom she had thought dead or at least expatriated. But he was neither dead nor expatriated; he was resurrected in the person of Athos, D'Artagnan's bosom friend. As such he must certainly have aided D'Artagnan in all the manoeuvres whereby the Queen had foiled the Cardinal's plans; as such he was undoubtedly the enemy of His Eminence; as such she could probably include him in the plans of vengeance she had elaborated against the young Gascon. Lulled by such pleasant thoughts, Milady enjoyed golden slumbers.

Milady was awakened by a gentle voice. Starting up, she saw the Mother Superior and a young woman at the foot of her bed. The young woman was blonde, demure and of delicate complexion; she was eying Milady with a kindly curiosity.

Milady had never seen the novice before. The two looked at each other with scrupulous attention as they exchanged the usual courtesies, both beautiful but how different in their beauty! Milady smiled triumphantly as she realized her own advantage as to grand manners and aristocratic bearing; her rival did not indicate that the robe of a novice was not calculated to favor her in a duel of this kind. The Mother Superior presented the two young women to each other; this formality accomplished, she explained that her duties called her to chapel, and left them alone.

The novice, seeing that Milady remained in bed, made to follow the Mother Superior, but Milady checked her.

"Come, Madame, we have barely met and you seek to deprive me of your company. I must confess I had looked forward to chatting with you and making friends—"

"I beg your pardon, Madame. I thought I had come at the wrong time. You were sleeping; you must be very tired."

"What pleasanter, my dear, than to be roused from sleep to find you at my bedside?" Milady said affably. "My awakening was a happy one; do let me enjoy it at leisure." Rising in bed, she grasped the novice's hand and drew her to a chair close to her bed. "Tell me about yourself," she urged.

The novice sat down and:

"Dear Heaven!" she said, "how unhappy I am! I have been here for six long months without the slightest amusement or distraction. Now you come, we meet, I am sure we will be friends—and I may have to leave here at any moment."

"What? You are leaving?"

"I hope so, Madame," said the novice beaming. "I *do* hope so!" she insisted, with no effort to conceal her joy.

"I hear you have suffered at the hands of the Cardinal, my dear. That strengthens the bonds of sympathy between us."

"So what our good Mother told me is true, Madame. You too are the victim of that wicked priest?"

"Hush, my dear, we must not speak of him thus, even here. All my misfortunes come from my saying more or less what you just said. A woman I believed to be my friend overheard me. She betrayed me." Milady sank back against the pillows. "I dare say you too are the victim of a friend's betrayal."

"No, Madame, I am the victim of my loyalty to a woman I loved, for whom I would have given my life and for whom I would give my life today."

"And she has abandoned you, poor child?"

"I was unjust enough to believe so. But in the last few days I have obtained proof to the contrary, God be praised, for I would have been deeply hurt had she forgotten me." The novice sighed. "But you, Madame," she continued, "you seem to be free. If you wish to escape there is nothing to prevent you."

"And where am I to go?" Milady asked ruefully. "I have no friends and no money, I know nothing of this part of the country, for I have never been here before—"

"Oh, *you* would find friends wherever you went. You are so kind and so beautiful!"

"That," Milady replied, softening her smile and assuming an angelic expression, "does not save me from solitude and persecution."

"Believe me, Madame, "the novice urged, "we must have faith in Heaven. There always comes a moment when the good you have done pleads your cause before God. Who knows, perhaps it is lucky for you to have met me, humble and powerless though I be. For if I leave here— well, I shall have a few powerful friends who after working on my behalf will work on yours."

Milady was quick to judge that by talking of herself, she could probably get the novice to reply in kind.

"When I said I was alone," she said, "I did not mean to say that I had not powerful friends in high places. But these friends themselves tremble before the Cardinal. Even the Queen does not dare to oppose the fearsome minister; I have proof that Her Majesty, generous though she be, has more than once been forced to abandon to the Cardinal's anger people who had served her loyally and well."

"Believe me, Madame, the Queen may seem to have abandoned these persons but you must not judge by appearances: the more direly her servants are persecuted, the more the Queen thinks of them. Very often, just when these unhappy victims least expect it, they are given proofs of Her Majesty's charitable remembrance."

"Alas, yes! I suppose this is true! The Queen is so good."

"So you know her, Madame? You know our noble, beautiful and gracious Queen?"

"I have never had the honor of being presented to Her Majesty in person," Milady explained, "but I know a great many of her most intimate friends: I know Monsieur de Putange ... Monsieur Dujart in England ... and Monsieur de Tréville. ..."

"Monsieur de Tréville!" cried the novice, "you know Monsieur de Tréville?"

"Yes, indeed. As a matter of fact, I know him intimately."

"The Captain of the Royal Musketeers?"

"The Captain of the Royal Musketeers."

"See, Madame, how closely that brings us together. It makes us excellently acquainted, we are almost friends. If you know Monsieur de Tréville so well, you must have visited him."

"Often, my child," said Milady, congratulating herself on the successful falsehood.

"You must have met some of his musketeers, then?"

"I have met all those he usually receives," Milady replied, glowing with pleasure at the turn the conversation was taking.

"Will you name some of them, Madame? I wonder if any of them are also friends of mine."

"Well," Milady said slowly, concealing her embarrassment, "I know Monsieur de Souvigny . . . Monsieur de Courtivron . . . Monsieur de Férussac . . ."

The novice watched her expectantly, then, seeing her stop, she asked:

"Do you happen to know a gentleman named Athos?" she inquired.

Milady turned white as the sheets in which she was lying. Mistress of her movements though she was, she could not help uttering a cry, seizing the young woman's hand and staring deep into her eyes.

"What is the matter, Madame?" The novice was aghast. "Have I said anything to offend you?"

"No, child, but that name struck me! I know that gentleman and it seemed so strange to find someone else who knows him well."

"Ay, Madame, I know him very well and I know his friends too: Monsieur Porthos and Monsieur Aramis."

"I also know them," Milady blurted, chilled to the marrow of her bones.

"Well, then, you must be aware what true and loyal men they are. Why not appeal to them if you need help?"

"To be quite accurate," Milady stammered, "they are not really close friends. I know them chiefly through stories I have heard from one of their comrades, Monsieur d'Artagnan."

"So you know Monsieur d'Artagnan!" the novice gasped as she, in turn, seized Milady's hand and stared deep into her eyes. Then observing the extraordinary expression on Milady's face:

"Forgive me for asking you, dear Madame, but what is D'Artagnan to you?"

"A friend ... just a casual friend ... yes, a friend. ..."

"You are deceiving me, Madame, you have been his mistress."

"It is *you* who have been his mistress," Milady retorted.

"I, Madame—" the novice faltered.

"Yes, *you*. I know who you are now. You are Madame Bonacieux." The young woman started back in surprise and terror. "Yes, you are Constance Bonacieux! Do you deny it?"

"No, Madame; I see you know who I am. But are we rivals?"

So savage and malign a joy blazed over Milady's features that in any other circumstances, Madame Bonacieux would have fled in terror. But in this moment the poor young woman was consumed with jealousy. Summoning a vehemence of which she would have seemed incapable, she pleaded: "Tell me the truth, Madame, I can face it. Were you ever his mistress? Are you his mistress now?"

"Of course not!" Milady's accents admitted of no doubt. "Of course not!"

"I believe you, Madame, but pray tell me why you were so upset when I—?"

Already Milady had overcome her agitation and with complete calm:

"Don't you understand?" she demanded.

"Understand what, Madame? Pray tell me what you mean?"

"Don't you understand that Monsieur d'Artagnan is my friend and that he has told me everything—"

"Everything?"

"Yes, child, I know all about how you were carried off from the cottage at Saint Cloud ... how D'Artagnan was plunged in despair ... how he marshaled his friends and how they searched for you in vain ... how at this very moment they are worrying about you.... Monsieur d'Artagnan and I have spoken so often of you, he told me all the adoration he had for you and he made me love you long before I ever laid eyes on you. And so, now we meet! At last, my dear Constance, at long last we meet!"

With which, Milady stretched out her arms to Madame Bonacieux, who, convinced by her words, saw in Milady not the rival she had believed but a sincere, cordial and devoted friend.

"Forgive me, Madame, forgive me!" Constance, locked in Milady's embrace, was weeping over her shoulder. "I was jealous. But I *do* love him so!"

For a moment the two women remained silent, their arms about each other as Madame Bonacieux wept softly. Had Milady's strength equalled her hatred, she would have strangled her. Instead she smiled.

"What a poor, pretty, devoted creature you are!" she said unctuously. "And how happy I am to see you!" Unclasping her arms, she raised Madame Bonacieux to her feet and surveyed her as a beast of prey surveys its timid victim. "Ay, it is Constance Bonacieux. Everything D'Artagnan told me was true; I recognize you perfectly."

Madame Bonacieux saw in the other's eyes only pity and sympathy. Indeed it would have called for much experience to read in the brilliance of Milady's glance and in the purity of her expression the hatred and ferocity that possessed her.

"You know what I have suffered," the novice said, "and you know how unhappy he has been! But to suffer for his sake is to be happy beyond all telling."

"Quite so!" Milady replied mechanically, her thoughts elsewhere.

"But my troubles are over," Madame Bonacieux continued, "my torment is at an end. Tomorrow—or perhaps this very evening—I shall see him again and the past will be no more than a bad dream."

"Tomorrow? This evening?" The words roused Milady from her reverie as she repeated them. "What do you mean, child? Do you expect news of him?"

"I expect *him* . . . himself . . . in person. . . ."

"You expect D'Artagnan?"

"Yes, Madame."

"Impossible, child. D'Artagnan is at the siege of La Rochelle with the Cardinal. He cannot leave until the city has fallen."

"You may think so, Madame. But the truth is that a noble and loyal gentleman like my D'Artagnan can accomplish miracles."

"Perhaps. But how can he leave the front?"

"Read this, Madame," the young woman cried in excess of pride and joy as she handed Milady a letter.

Milady recognized the handwriting of Madame de Chevreuse.

"I always suspected some secret intelligence in that quarter," she mused. Then avidly she read the following:

My dear child:

Hold yourself in readiness. Our friend (and of course you know whom I mean) will be seeing you soon. His sole purpose in coming is to release you from the imprisonment to which you had to be committed for your own security. So make ready to leave the convent and never despair of us.

Our charming Gascon has just proved himself to be as brave and faithful as ever. Tell him that certain parties are very grateful to him for the warning he has given them.

"Well, the letter is clear enough," Milady commented. "Do you happen to know what D'Artagnan's warning referred to?"

"No, Madame, but I can guess. I suppose he warned the Queen against some fresh machination of the Cardinal's."

"Yes, that must be it!" Milady returned the letter to Madame Bonacieux. "Yes, certainly." She bowed her head pensively over her bosom. Suddenly the echo of a horse's hoofs sent Madame Bonacieux darting to the window.

"It is probably D'Artagnan!" she cried, wild with joy.

For once Milady was at a loss. So many things were happening to her with such startling suddenness that she could but lie back in bed, wide-eyed.

"You mean D'Artagnan . . . ? D'Artagnan is coming here . . . ? Now . . . ?"

"Alas, no!" Madame Bonacieux peered through the window. "It is not D'Artagnan!" She sighed. "The horseman is stopping at the gate." A pause. "Now he is ringing."

Milady sprang out of bed.

"You are quite sure it is not D'Artagnan?" she asked.

"I am certain—"

"Are you sure you can really see—?"

"I could recognize my D'Artagnan by the plume in his hat, the tip of his cloak and the sword under it—"

Milady began to dress.

"Where is this man now?" she asked.

"He is coming in here."

"He has come either for you or for me."

"Oh, Madame, how nervous you are. Do take things calmly."

"Yes, I am nervous, I admit. I have not your confidence. And I am desperately afraid of the Cardinal."

"Hush, Madame, someone is coming!"

The door swung open and the Mother Superior appeared on the doorsill.

"Did you come from Boulogne?" she asked Milady.

"Yes, I did, Reverend Mother." Milady sought to regain her calm. "Who wants me?"

"A gentleman who refuses to give his name. He told me to say he comes from the Cardinal."

"He wants to speak to *me?*"

"He wants to speak to a lady who arrived from Boulogne."

"Then let him come in, if you please, Madame."

"Ah, God, can it be bad news?" Madame Bonacieux groaned. "Perhaps—"

"I fear it is *very* bad news."

"I will leave you with this stranger, Madame. But the moment he goes, I will return, if you permit."

"If I *permit?* I *beseech* you to do so."

The Superior and Madame Bonacieux retired; Milady, alone, drew herself up and stared at the door. An instant later the jangling of spurs resounding on the staircase . . . the sound of footsteps drew near . . . the door opened . . . a man stood on the threshold. . . .

Milady uttered a cry of joy. It was the Comte de Rochefort, the *âme damnée,* the demoniacal tool of His Eminence the Cardinal.

LXII

Of Two Varieties of Demons

"*You,* Chevalier!" Milady cried in surprise.

"*You,* Milady!" Rochefort cried with like incredulity.

"You come from where, Chevalier?"

"From La Rochelle, Milady. And you?"

"From England!"

"What of Buckingham?"

"Buckingham is either dead or desperately wounded. Just as I left without having been able to obtain anything from him, I heard that some fanatic had stabbed him."

"What a piece of luck!" Rochefort smiled. "His Eminence will be delighted. Did you inform him of it?"

"I wrote him from Boulogne. But what brings *you* here?"

"His Eminence was worried and sent me in search of you."

"I arrived only yesterday."

"And what have you been doing since yesterday?"

"I have not wasted my time."

"Oh, I am sure of that!"

"Do you know whom I met here?"

"No."

"Guess?"

"How can I—?"

"The young woman the Queen freed from prison."

"The mistress of young D'Artagnan?"

"Yes ... Madame Bonacieux ... even the Cardinal did not know where she was hidden. ..."

"Upon my word, this piece of luck matches your news of Buckingham. His Eminence is indeed a fortunate man, Milady."

"I leave you to imagine how amazed I was to find myself face to face with the woman."

"Does she know you?"

"No, she does not!"

"She looks upon you as a stranger, then?"

Milady smiled enigmatically and: "I am her best friend!" she explained coolly.

"Upon my honor, only yourself, dear Milady, can perform such miracles!"

"Little good it does me, Chevalier."

"Pray why?"

"You don't know what is happening?"

"No, Madame."

"Tomorrow or the day after, this woman is being withdrawn from the convent on orders from the Queen."

"How and by whom?"

"By D'Artagnan and his friends."

"Honestly, those fellows will go so far one of these days that we shall have no choice but to clap them into the Bastille."

"What are you waiting for?"

"The Cardinal seems to entertain a certain weakness or laxity in regard to these four men. I scarcely know why."

"Well, tell him this, Rochefort, from *me*. Listen carefully. Those same four men overheard the conversation His Eminence and I held at the *Sign of the Red Dovecote* . . . after the Cardinal's departure, one of them broke into my room . . . the fellow abused me and seized the safe-conduct His Eminence had given me . . . the four of them warned Lord Winter of my journey to England . . . once again, they almost foiled my mission, just as they had in the affair of the diamond studs. . . ."

Rochefort asked: "But how——?"

"Tell His Eminence that of the four, two only are dangerous: D'Artagnan and Athos . . . that the third, Aramis by name, happens to be the lover of Madame de Chevreuse and therefore, since we know his secret he should be spared, for he may well come in useful . . . and the fourth, a fellow called Porthos, is a fool, an oaf, a fathead and a blusterer beneath the notice of anyone. . . ."

"But these four men must surely be at the siege of La Rochelle?"

"That is what I thought, too. Meanwhile Madame Bonacieux was rash enough to show me a letter from Madame la Connétable. The text leads me to believe that all four are on their way here to remove her from this convent."

"Devil take it! What are we to do?"

"What did the Cardinal say about me?"

"He ordered me to ask you to communicate to me any orders you have—written or verbal—and to return post-haste. As soon as he learns what you have done, he will consider what you are to do hereafter."

"So I am to stay here?"

"Here or in the neighborhood."

"Can you not take me with you?"

"No, Milady, my orders are imperative. Near the camp you might well be recognized and your presence, you must realize, might compromise His Eminence."

"Well, I suppose I shall have to wait here or somewhere near by."

"I am afraid so, Milady. But be sure to tell me where you settle, so that the Cardinal's orders can reach you promptly."

Milady explained that she would probably be unable to stay at the convent because her enemies would be arriving at any moment.

"So this little woman is to slip through the Cardinal's fingers?" Rochefort asked.

Again Milady smiled an enigmatic smile all her own.

"You forget I told you I was her best friend," she answered.

"True, Milady. I can therefore tell the Cardinal that in so far as this little woman is concerned—"

"He may rest easy."

"That is your only message?"

"His Eminence will know what I mean."

"At least he will make a shrewd guess. Now, let us see: what had I better do?"

"You must go back at once. Surely the news I have given you deserves to be immediately communicated to the Cardinal?"

"My chaise broke down as we drove into Lilliers."

"Excellent! Nothing could be better!"

"What do you mean?"

"I mean I can use your chaise."

"And how am I to travel?"

"Full speed on horseback."

"Easy enough to say. But I have almost six hundred miles to cover."

"That is soon done. A horseman like you—"

"Granted. But what then—?"

"As you pass through Lilliers, send your servant in your chaise with instructions to obey all my orders implicitly."

"What then, Milady?"

"You must have some sort of credentials from the Cardinal, my dear Rochefort."

"Indeed I have. I am granted full powers—"

"Show your orders to the Mother Superior . . . tell her someone or other will come to fetch me today or tomorrow . . . say that I am to follow the bearer of your note. . . ."

"Good."

"When you speak to the Mother Superior, don't forget to speak ill of me."

"Why, Milady?"

"Because I am passing as a victim of the Cardinal. I *must* have some means of inspiring confidence in poor little Madame Bonacieux."

"True enough. Now will you give me a detailed report of all that has happened?"

"I have told you everything," Milady insisted. "You have an excellent memory; just repeat what I have told you. To put all that in writing is useless. Papers are easily lost."

"Yes, but I must know where you are going. I cannot roam the neighborhood looking for you to bring you the Cardinal's orders. Do you want a map?"

"No, no, I know this part of the country quite well."

"Really!"

"Yes, I was brought up here," Milady told him. "It does come in useful to have been brought up somewhere, don't you think?"

"I shall send my chaise to you," Rochefort decided. "But where will I find you later?"

"Let me think? Ah, I have it, Chevalier: I will stay at Armentières!"

"Where and what is Armentières?"

"A small town on the River Lys. I need but cross the river and I am on foreign soil."

"Agreed. But you will cross the river only in case of the gravest danger—?"

"Certainly."

"But if you cross, how shall I find you?"

"Your lackey ... you don't need him ... can he be trusted ... ?"

"I don't need him and he is thoroughly trustworthy."

"Let me have him," Milady suggested. "Nobody here knows him. I can leave him at the place I leave the chaise and he can wait for you there."

"At Armentières, then, Milady."

"At Armentières."

"Do write that name on a piece of paper, Milady, lest I forget it. The name of a town can compromise nobody."

"*Anything* can compromise *anybody*," Milady replied, "but never mind." Tearing a sheet in half, she wrote the word "Armentières." "I don't mind compromising myself to that extent," she added.

Rochefort took the paper, folded it and placed it in the lining of his hat.

"Don't worry," he assured her, "I shall do as children do: for fear of losing the paper, I shall repeat the name all along the road. Is there anything else?"

"Plenty," Milady answered with a certain asperity.

"Let me see: Buckingham dead or at death's door ... your conversation with the Cardinal overheard by the four musketeers ... Lord Winter informed of your arrival at Portsmouth ... D'Artagnan and Athos to be committed to the Bastille ... Aramis, lover of Madame de Chevreuse ... Porthos a lout and an oaf ... Madame Bonacieux whom you discovered in hiding here ... the chaise to come for you here as soon as possible ... my valet at your disposal ... you, a victim of the Cardinal's, in order to dispel any suspicions the Mother Superior may entertain ... and Armentières on the banks of the Lys our next meeting-place. . . . Am I right?"

"Ay, Chevalier, your memory is flawless. But there is still something."

"What, Milady?"

"There is a very pretty wood close to the convent garden. Tell the Mother Superior to allow me to stroll there. Who can tell? I may need a back door to assure my escape."

"You think of absolutely everything, Milady."

"And you, Chevalier, forget—"

"I forget what—?"

"You forget to ask me whether I need money?"

"Do you? How much, Milady?"

"All the gold you have on your person."

"I have about five hundred pistoles."

"I have the same amount," Milady said. "With a thousand pistoles we can face all emergencies. Turn out your pockets."

"Here you are then."

"Splendid! When do you leave?"

"Within an hour ... just enough time to snatch a bite to eat ... and while I sup, I shall send somebody to fetch me a horse ..."

"All is settled, then. Farewell, Monsieur."

"Good-bye, Milady."

"Pray commend me to the Cardinal."

"Pray commend me to Satan, Madame."

Milady and Rochefort smiled beautifully upon each other and parted. Within an hour Rochefort was galloping along the road and within five he had passed through Arras, where, as may be recalled, D'Artagnan recognized him, and was with difficulty prevented by his comrades from pursuing him, and accordingly made for his goal with greater enthusiasm and celerity. . . .

LXIII

OF WINE AND WATER

Rochefort had scarcely departed when Madame Bonacieux returned to face Milady who was wreathed in smiles.

"Well, what you dreaded has happened, Madame. The Cardinal is sending somebody to take you away this evening or tomorrow."

"Who told you, child?"

"The messenger himself."

"Come sit by me," Milady said.

"Here I am, Madame."

"Sit close to me. Now wait—we must make sure no one is listening."

"Why all these precautions, Madame?"

"I shall explain in good time."

Milady rose, opened the door, looked into the corridor, closed the door again and returned to her place.

"Well, the lad has made a good job of it!" she sighed.

"Who, Madame?"

"The man who impersonated the Cardinal's envoy."

"So he was playing a part?"

"Yes, child."

"Then the man I spoke to—?"

"The man you spoke to," Milady lowered her voice confidentially, "is my brother."

"Your brother, Madame?"

"You alone know this secret, my dear. If you reveal it to anyone in the world, I shall be lost and you too perhaps."

"Ah, God! Madame—"

"Listen carefully. This is exactly what happened. My brother was coming to my rescue to take me away from here by force if necessary. On the way he met the Cardinal's emissary, followed him and at a lonely stretch of the road compelled the Cardinal's man to hand over his credentials. The fellow put up a fight, so my brother killed him in self-defense!"

"How dreadful, Madame!" the novice said shuddering.

"What else could he do?" Milady insisted.

Madame Bonacieux shrugged her shoulders helplessly. Milady went on:

"My brother decided to substitute cunning for violence. Making the papers, he presented himself as the Cardinal's messenger and within an hour or two a carriage will come to fetch me away in the Cardinal's name."

"Your brother is sending the carriage, Madame?"

"Exactly. But that is not all. That letter you received—that letter you think comes from Madame de Chevreuse—"

"Well?"

"—is a clumsy forgery!"

"How can that be, Madame?"

"A clumsy forgery intended to prevent your resisting when they come for you."

"But D'Artagnan himself is coming."

"No, child, D'Artagnan and his friends are detained at the siege of La Rochelle."

"How do you know that, Madame?"

"My brother met some of the Cardinal's men disguised in the uniform of musketeers. The plan was to have you summoned to the gate and, as you advanced to meet people you believed were friends, to seize you and carry you off to Paris."

"Ah, God, what evil! I vow my senses fail me amid this chaos of iniquities! If this continues, I shall go mad!"

"One moment! Wait!"

"What is it?"

"I hear a horse's hoofs; that must be my brother setting off again. I shall wave him farewell. Come to the window."

Motioning to the novice to join her, she threw open the window and leaned out, the novice joining her. Below, Rochefort galloped by.

"Good-bye, brother," Milady called.

The Chevalier looked up, perceived the two young women and without stopping raised his hand in friendly salute.

"Bless his heart!" Milady said closing the window, her expression at once melancholy and affectionate. And she returned to her chair as if she were plunged in purely personal reflections.

"Forgive me for interrupting you, dear Madame," the novice ventured.

"But I implore you to tell me what you advise me to do. You have so much more experience than I. Speak and I shall obey you."

"To begin with, I may be wrong," Milady said confidently, "and it is barely possible that D'Artagnan and his friends are really coming to your rescue."

"That would be too wonderful!" the novice exclaimed. "Surely so much happiness is not in store for me!"

"Well, if your friends *are* coming, the whole thing boils itself down to a question of time, a kind of race. Who will reach there first? If your friends are the speedier, you are saved; if the Cardinal's henchmen outride them, you are lost."

"Yes, hopelessly lost! But what shall I do, Madame, what shall I do?"

"There is one quite simple, quite natural way—"

"What way, Madame?"

"You might wait in hiding somewhere in the neighborhood until you made sure exactly who was coming to fetch you."

"But where can I wait?"

"*That* is easy! I myself am going to hide a few leagues from here until my brother can join me. Suppose I take you with me and we wait in hiding together."

"But I will not be allowed to leave, Madame," the novice objected. "I am virtually a prisoner here."

"As they think I am leaving on orders from the Cardinal no one will dream that you wish to follow me."

"What then, Madame?"

"My carriage is at the gate . . . you are bidding me adieu . . . you mount the step to embrace me for the last time . . . suddenly my brother's lackey signals to the postillion and we drive off. . . ."

"But D'Artagnan, Madame? What of D'Artagnan, if he comes?"

"We shall know if he comes, my dear."

"How, Madame?"

"We can trust my brother's lackey . . . we will send him back to Béthune . . . he can assume a disguise and take lodgings opposite the convent . . . if the Cardinal's emissaries turn up first, he makes no move . . . if it is Monsieur D'Artagnan and his friends, he brings them to us. . . ."

"The lackey knows Monsieur d'Artagnan?"

"Certainly. Has he not seen him often at my house?"

"Yes, yes, Madame, I had forgotten. All is for the best, I am sure. But let us not go too far away from here."

"Eight leagues at most, child. We shall settle close to the border. At the first sign of danger, we can leave France."

"But what in the meantime?"

"We must wait patiently. It will not be long."

"But what if D'Artagnan and his friends arrive?"

"My brother's carriage will be here first."

"What if I should be away when the carriage calls for you?" the novice asked. "I might be in the refectory at dinner or supper for instance."

"Why not ask our good Mother Superior to allow you to share my meal?"

"Will she permit it?"

"Why should she object?"

"Yes, that is a splendid idea, Madame. We need not be separated for an instant."

"Quite so, my dear. Now run down to make your request. I feel dizzy; my head is spinning; I think I shall go for a stroll in the garden."

"Where shall I meet you, Madame?"

"Right here in an hour."

"Very well, Madame; right here in an hour from now. Oh, how kindly and gracious you are and how thankful I am to you!"

"Why should I not be interested in you? You are beautiful and you are charming. And one of my best friends is in love with you."

"How grateful D'Artagnan will be, Madame!"

"I hope so indeed." Milady smiled. "Come, now that all is arranged, let us go downstairs."

"You are going to the garden, Madame?"

"Yes, my dear. How do I get there?"

"Just follow this corridor until you reach a small staircase on the right and walk down one flight."

"Thank you so much!" Milady beamed.

Milady had told the truth: she felt dizzy and her head was spinning because her ill-ordered plans clashed chaotically. She must have time to sort out her thoughts. Vaguely she foresaw the future, but she required quiet and silence to shape it up properly. The principal and most urgent matter was to carry Madame Bonacieux off to some safe place where she could hold her as a hostage, if necessary. She recognized her danger and frankly admitted to herself that her enemies were no less dogged than she. And, as a sailor senses a squall, she sensed that the contest was clear-cut, desperate and close at hand.

"The Bonacieux woman, that is the answer," she thought. "I must keep her in my power . . . she means more to D'Artagnan than his very life . . . if I hold her, I have him at my beck and call. . . ."

Madame Bonacieux would undoubtedly follow Milady without misgivings; once they were in hiding at Armentières, Milady could easily persuade her that D'Artagnan had never come to Béthune. Within a fortnight at most, Rochefort would return; meanwhile Milady could plot how best to wreak vengeance upon her four enemies. No moment would be lost, praise God! as she enjoyed to the full the perfection, step by step, of her retaliation. Dreaming of each successive and gratifying blow she hoped to inflict upon her enemies, Milady looked about her, taking in the topography of the garden. A woman, and a beautiful one at that, she remained as realistic and as masculine as a general who, balancing possibilities of victory and defeat, allows for a lightning advance or a precipitous retreat. Presently she heard Madame Bonacieux calling her. The Mother Superior had agreed; novice and guest were to sup together.

As Milady and her companion crossed the courtyard they heard the rumble of a carriage drawing up at the gate.

"Listen!"

"Ay, it is a carriage, Madame."

"It is my brother's carriage."

"Ah, God!"

"Come, child, courage!"

The bell of the convent gate rang. Milady had timed her manoeuvre perfectly.

"Run to your room," she told Madame Bonacieux. "You must have some jewels you want to take along."

"I have D'Artagnan's letters!"

"Go fetch them, dear, then join me in my room. We will sup together in haste. We may have to travel part of the night; we must take nourishment to keep up our strength."

The novice clutched her throat.

"I am stifling," she moaned. "I cannot move! I cannot breathe!"

"Courage, my dear, just one effort! Remember that in a quarter of an hour you will be safe. Remember that what you are about to do is for *his* sake!"

"Yes, yes, everything for him! You have restored my courage with a single word. Go, Madame, I shall join you at once."

Milady ran quickly up to her room, found Rochefort's lackey waiting and gave him her instructions. He was to stand by the gate. If by chance the musketeers appeared, the carriage was to start off at top speed, drive around the convent walls and await Milady in a hamlet at the edge of the woods behind the convent. In this case, Milady would cross the garden, pass through the wood and reach the hamlet on foot. She congratulated herself on her knowledge of the countryside.

If, on the contrary, the musketeers did not appear, things were to follow the original plan: Madame Bonacieux was to jump onto the carriage step as if to bid Milady farewell and they were to drive off.

Madame Bonacieux joined her and, to dispel any suspicions the novice might have, Milady made a point of repeating in her presence the latter part of her instructions, as the lackey stood by, listening intently. She also asked several questions about the carriage; the lackey replied that it was a chaise drawn by three horses and driven by a postillion. The lackey himself would ride ahead as courier.

Milady's fears as to any suspicion on her victim's part were groundless. Poor Constance Bonacieux was too innocent to imagine such treachery on the part of any woman. Besides the name of the Comtesse de Clark, which she had heard from the Mother Superior, was quite unknown to her. How could she be expected to see in this beautiful, brilliant and resourceful fellow-sufferer, the creature who was responsible for so many fatal misfortunes that had befallen her.

The lackey gone, Milady turned to Madame Bonacieux and with a sigh of satisfaction: "You see, dear, everything is ready . . . the Mother Superior thinks I am being taken away on orders from the Cardinal . . . this man is off to give his last orders . . . and in a quarter of an hour. . . ."

Madame Bonacieux swayed.

"Here, drink a finger of wine, it will comfort you. Then let us be off!"

"Ay, let us be off!" Madame Bonacieux echoed mechanically.

Milady motioned her to sit down opposite her, poured out a small glass of Spanish wine and served her a breast of chicken.

"Really, everything favors us!" she said gaily. "The night is almost fallen and by daybreak we shall be in our retreat. Who on earth can guess where it is? Courage, child, eat a few morsels and drink a drop or two."

Still dazed, Madame Bonacieux automatically swallowed four or five mouthfuls and barely touched the glass with her lips.

"Come, child, do as I," Milady urged, raising her glass with a gesture that suggested she was about to drain it. But it remained suspended in mid-air for she had just heard a rumble from the road which sounded like the echo of horses' hoofs galloping up from afar. Then, as the sounds grew clearer, she fancied she could distinguish the neighing of horses. This rumor scattered her joy much as a clap of thunder dispels the most golden of dreams. She grew very pale and ran to the window; Madame Bonacieux, rising all atremble, leaned on her chair for support. It was impossible to see anything yet; but the approaching noise was undoubtedly that of horses at a gallop.

"Ah God! what can that be?" Madame Bonacieux whimpered.

"Our friends or our enemies," Milady declared with frightening calm. "Stay where you are, I shall let you know in a moment."

Madame Bonacieux stood speechless, rigid and pale as a statue.

The noise grew louder, the horses could not be more than a hundred and fifty paces distant; only a crook in the road made them invisible. A second later the echo was distinct enough for Milady to count them by the syncopated rattle of their hoofs. Straining her eyes, she stared across the dusk; there was just light enough for her to recognize the approaching horsemen.

Suddenly at the bend in the road she saw the glitter of gold-laced hats and flowing plumes . . . she counted first two, then five, then eight horsemen . . . and she noticed that one was several lengths ahead of his comrades. . . . Milady uttered a stifled moan: in the horseman in the lead she had recognized D'Artagnan.

"Ah God, Madame, what is it?" Madame Bonacieux whimpered.

"It is the Cardinal's Guards, I can tell by their uniforms. We have not a moment to lose. Let us fly."

"Yes, Madame, let us fly—" the novice repeated. But she stood there, rooted in terror to the spot, unable to move an inch. Meanwhile the horsemen could be heard clattering by under the window.

"Come along, for God's sake, come along." Milady attempted to drag the young woman by the arm. "We can still escape through the garden, I have the key. But do hurry! In five minutes it will be too late."

Madame Bonacieux tried to walk, took two paces and fell to her knees. Milady tried to lift her and carry her on but could not manage it. At that moment she heard the rumbling of a carriage setting out at a gallop. Then came an exchange of shots.

"For the last time, will you come?" Milady insisted.

"I can't. Oh, my God, don't you see my strength fails me. I cannot walk. You must flee alone!"

"And leave you here, child. Never!"

Milady suddenly paused, looming over the other; a livid flame flashed from her eyes. Then, running back to the table, she twirled open the bezel of her ring with extraordinary speed, and emptied its contents into Madame Bonacieux's glass. The ring contained a tiny reddish pill which dissolved immediately. Then grasping the glass firmly:

"Drink," she said, "this wine will give you strength. Drink!"

And she pressed the glass to the lips of the young woman who gulped obediently.

"That was not the revenge I planned!" Milady mused, smiling and replacing the glass on the table. "Ah, well, we do our best!" And she rushed out of the room.

Madame Bonacieux watched her disappear without being able to follow her; she was like the victim of a nightmare in which she was being pursued but was pinned down helpless to her bed. Several minutes passed but she did not move. Then there was a great tumult at the convent gate and she expected Milady to reappear at any moment but in vain. In her terror and dismay, she felt an icy sweat break over her burning forehead.

At length she heard the grating of hinges as the gates swung open with a crash. There was a trampling of boots, a rattling of spurs and a hubbub of voices on the stairs. And then she heard or dreamed she was hearing someone call her by name.

Suddenly she uttered a great cry of joy and darted toward the door for she had recognized the voice of D'Artagnan.

"D'Artagnan, D'Artagnan! Is it you?" she cried. "This way, this way!"

"Constance, where are you?"

The door of the cell sprang open. As several men rushed in, Madame Bonacieux sank back into an armchair unable to move. D'Artagnan tossed a pistol, still smoking, to the floor and fell on his knees before his mistress. Athos replaced his pistol in his belt. Porthos and Aramis, who had entered sword in hand, returned the weapons to their scabbards.

"Oh, D'Artagnan, my beloved D'Artagnan! Here you are at last! You kept your word! It is you, is it not? Tell me it is *you* I see!"

"Ay, Constance, we are together again!"

"*She* told me you were not coming. I knew you were, but *she* seemed so sure. I hoped in silence. I did not want to flee with her. How right I was, darling, and how happy I am!"

At the word *she,* Athos, who had sat down quietly, started up.

"*She?*" D'Artagnan asked. "Who do you mean?"

"Why, my companion and friend . . . the lady who tried to get me away from my persecutors . . . the lady who mistook you for Cardinalist Guards and has just fled. . . ."

D'Artagnan turned paler than the white veil of his mistress.

"Your companion, dear Constance?" he asked, utterly baffled. "What companion do you mean?"

"The lady whose carriage was at the door! She told me she was a friend of yours, D'Artagnan. She said you had told her everything."

"Her name, her name! Can't you recall her name?"

"Yes, I think so. The Mother Superior told me but I forget. It is a strange name. Oh, God, my head swims—I cannot see—"

"Help, help, my friends, her hands are icy cold," said D'Artagnan. "She is ill. Dear God! She is losing consciousness!"

While Porthos bellowed for help, Aramis moved toward the table for a glass of water. But he stopped suddenly at the sight of Athos. A terrible change had come over Athos as he stood before the table, his hair bristling, his eyes frozen in a stupor. Staring into one of the glasses, Athos appeared to be a prey to the most horrible doubt.

"No, no, it is impossible," he muttered. "God would not permit such a crime."

"Water," cried D'Artagnan, "bring some water!"

"Poor woman!" Athos murmured brokenly.

Madame Bonacieux opened her eyes under the kisses of D'Artagnan.

"She is coming to!" cried our Gascon. "Thank God!"

"Madame," Athos asked, "in the name of Heaven, whose is that empty glass?"

"It is mine, Monsieur," the young woman answered in a dying voice.

"But who poured you the wine that was in it?"

"*She* did—"

"But who is she?"

"Oh, I remember now ... *she* is the Comtesse de Clark ..." She gasped for breath, then, having spoken, she turned livid, a sharp spasm passed over her frame and she would have fallen but for Porthos and Aramis who held out their arms to support her. D'Artagnan seized the hand of Athos with indescribable anguish.

"Do you think—?" he paused, choking. "Do you think—?" and his voice was drowned in a sob.

"I think the very worst!" Athos answered, biting his lips.

"D'Artagnan, D'Artagnan!" Madame Bonacieux moaned. "Don't leave me, my lover. Where are you? You see I am dying."

Releasing Athos, whose hand he had held clenched in his hands, D'Artagnan hastened to her side. Her beautiful face was distorted in agony, her bright eyes were now fixed in a glassy stare, her lovely body trembled convulsively, the sweat rolled off her brow.

"For God's sake, get some help, Porthos, Aramis. What are you waiting for?"

"It is quite useless," Athos said bitterly. "For the poison *she* pours, there is no antidote."

"Help me, my dear friends," Madame Bonacieux pleaded. "I am in such pain!"

Then, gathering all her strength, she took the young man's head between her two hands, looked at him for a moment as though to concentrate her entire soul in this gaze of farewell, and with a sobbing cry, pressed her lips on his.

"Constance, Constance!"

A sigh escaped her, D'Artagnan felt her breath grazing his lips and slowly she sank back. How good, how chaste, how loving she had been, he thought, and now it was a dead woman he held in his embrace. With a cry, he fell beside her, pale and icy as herself.

Porthos was weeping unashamedly, Athos shook his fist toward Heaven, Aramis made the sign of the Cross.

Suddenly a man appeared in the doorway, panting and almost as upset as those in the room. Looking around him he noticed Madame Bonacieux dead and D'Artagnan in a faint. At a glance he realized that he was witnessing the moment of general stupor which follows upon great catastrophes.

"I was not mistaken," he said, "this is Monsieur d'Artagnan, and you three are his friends, Messieurs Athos, Porthos and Aramis."

The musketeers looked up in surprise at hearing their names. Each sought to recall the stranger who seemed not unfamiliar yet they could not quite place him.

"Like yourselves, gentlemen, I am in search of a woman—" he gave a bitter smile, "—a woman who must have passed this way, for I see a corpse here."

The friends remained silent. Surely they had met this man, but where? His voice as well as his face recalled someone they had encountered, but in what circumstances?

"Gentlemen," the stranger continued, "since you do not recognize a man whose life you have saved twice, I must need introduce myself. I am Lord Winter, brother-in-law of *that* woman."

The three friends cried out in surprise. Athos rose and held out his hand:

"Be welcome, Milord," he said courteously. "You are one of us."

"I left Portsmouth five hours after she did," Lord Winter explained. "I reached Boulogne three hours after her. I missed her by twenty minutes at Saint-Omer. Finally at Lilliers I lost all trace of her. I was on her trail, searching haphazard and inquiring of everybody who passed. Suddenly I saw you gallop past and I recognized Monsieur d'Artagnan. I shouted to you but you did not reply. I tried to overtake you but my horse could not keep up with yours. So in spite of all your diligence you arrived too late."

"As you see," Athos said, pointing to Madame Bonacieux, while Porthos and Aramis attempted to revive the Gascon.

"Are they both dead?" Lord Winter inquired sternly.

"No," Athos assured him. "Fortunately Monsieur d'Artagnan has only fainted." And at that moment, as though to reassure the stranger, D'Artagnan opened his eyes, tore himself away from Porthos and Aramis and flung himself like a madman on the body of his mistress. Athos rose, walked over to his friend with slow and solemn step, tenderly embraced him and, as D'Artagnan broke into sobs, he said in his mellow, persuasive voice:

"Friend, be a man! Women weep for the dead; men avenge them!"

"Ay, we must avenge her. Lead the way, Athos, I am ready to follow you!"

Athos profited by this moment of strength inspired in his friend by hope of vengeance to motion Porthos and Aramis to fetch the Mother Superior. They found her in the corridor, dismayed and distraught at the strange events that had broken in on her religious quietude. She summoned several nuns, who against all monastic custom were ushered into the presence of five men.

"Madame," said Athos, passing his arm under D'Artagnan's, "we abandon to your pious care the precious remains of this unfortunate woman. She was an angel on earth before becoming an angel in Heaven. Pray treat her as one of your own sisters. We will return some day to pray over her grave."

D'Artagnan hid his face against the shoulder Athos offered and burst into sobs.

"Ay, weep, lad!" he whispered. "Weep, heart full of love, alive with youth, and pulsing with life! Would I too could weep!"

And he helped his friend out of the room, handling him with all the affection of a father, the charity of a priest and the sympathy of a man who has suffered much.

All five, followed by five lackeys leading their horses by the bridle, walked into the town of Béthune and stopped at the first inn they found.

"What!" D'Artagnan protested vehemently. "Are we not going in pursuit of *that woman?*"

"Later," Athos said soothingly. "I have certain measures to take."

"She will slip through our fingers, Athos, and you will be to blame."

"No, D'Artagnan, I guarantee we will find her."

Athos spoke with such quiet conviction and D'Artagnan trusted him so implicitly that he bowed his head in consent and entered the inn without replying. Porthos and Aramis looked at each other in puzzlement, wondering how Athos was so confident. Lord Winter suggested to them in a whisper that Athos had spoken so in order to soothe D'Artagnan's sorrow.

Having ascertained that there were five vacant rooms in the inn, Athos proposed that each retire.

"D'Artagnan needs to be alone to mourn, to find calm and to go to sleep. I promise to take charge of everything; I promise you I know what I am doing."

Lord Winter seemed somewhat taken aback.

"If there are certain measures to be taken against Lady Clark, it concerns me too, Monsieur. She is my sister-in-law—"

"I have a prior and more valid claim," Athos said coldly. "She is my wife!"

D'Artagnan smiled. He understood that to reveal so horrible a secret, Athos must be certain of his prey. Porthos and Aramis exchanged another of those quizzical glances that enigmatic statements from Athos invariably aroused. As for Lord Winter, he was convinced Athos was completely mad.

"Pray retire then, gentlemen, and let me act. You must perceive that, I being the lady's husband, the affair is wholly my concern. But look here, D'Artagnan: if you have not lost it, give me the paper that dropped from that man's hat—you recall, it bore the name of a village—the village of—"

"Ah! that name—in her handwriting . . ."

"Ay, D'Artagnan, that village." Athos bowed to his companion. "As you see, D'Artagnan, God is in His Heaven!"

LXIV

The Man in the Red Cloak

When Athos first looked down upon Madame Bonacieux writhing in agony, he was seized with a despair which he concealed by speaking with the utmost phlegm. Then the implications of what had occurred concentrated his grief and heightened the lucidity of his thought. One thing alone moved him now. He had made a promise and assumed a heavy responsibility. That alone mattered.

He was therefore careful to retire only after he had made sure his companions were safe in their rooms. Next, he begged the landlord to bring him a map of the province and studying every line traced upon it, he ascertained that four different roads connected Béthune with Armentières. Then he sent for the lackeys.

Planchet, Grimaud, Mousqueton and Bazin appeared successively and received clear, positive and ironclad instructions. They were to set out at daybreak and to proceed to Armentières, each by a different road. Planchet, the most intelligent of the four, was to take the road followed by the carriage upon which their masters had fired that evening.

A thorough strategist, Athos put the lackeys into the field first because he had had occasion to appreciate their individual talents and to size up each of them. Besides on the highway, when a lackey asks a stranger for directions or information, he is more likely to find help than his master would be. In the third place, Milady knew the four friends but she knew none of the lackeys who, for their part, knew her perfectly.

The lackeys, each proceeding according to directions, were to meet again at eleven o'clock on the morrow. If by then they had discovered Milady's hiding place, three would mount guard and the fourth report back to Béthune.

The lackeys having been thoroughly briefed, Athos rose from his chair, clasped on his sword, wrapped himself in his cloak, and left the inn. It was ten o'clock. In the provinces, as we all know, the streets are little frequented at that hour, yet Athos combed them, apparently looking for someone to question. Finally, encountering a belated passer-by, he accosted him and whispered a few words. The man, drawing back in terror, replied with a gesture of the hand. Athos offered him half a pistole to accompany him, but he shook his head.

Athos then started down the street which the man had pointed out but, reaching a square where four roads crossed, was visibly embarrassed. However, since the crossroads offered him the best chance of meeting somebody, he walked. Indeed within a few moments a night watchman passed. Athos repeated the same question he had asked the first man. The patrolman evinced the same terror, refused in his turn to accompany Athos, and merely pointed his finger toward the road Athos was to take.

Following the direction indicated, Athos reached the outskirts of the city diametrically opposite to those where he and his companions lodged. Then once again, anxious and at a loss, he stopped for the third time. Fortunately a beggar passed and, accosting him, implored alms. Athos offered him a crown on condition he accompany him to his destination. The mendicant hesitated at first but the sight of the silver coin shining through the half-darkness was too much for him. Bracing himself up, he nodded consent and set out ahead of Athos.

Reaching a street corner, he pointed to a small house in the distance, isolated, lonely and dismal. Athos approached it while the beggar, having received his reward, ran off as fast as his legs could carry him.

Athos walked around the house before he could distinguish the door from amid the reddish paint with which its walls were daubed. No light glimmered through the cracks of the shutters, no sound gave reason to suppose the house was inhabited. All was dark and silent as the tomb.

Athos knocked twice without receiving an answer. At his third knock he heard footsteps within. Presently the door swung ajar and a tall, very pale man with black hair and a black beard, thrust his neck forward.

Athos and the man exchanged a few whispered words, then the man motioned Athos to enter. Athos immediately complied and the door closed behind him.

The man Athos had come so far to seek and had found with such difficulty ushered him into his laboratory where he was engaged in lashing the rattling bones of a skeleton with wire to make them fast. The torso was already reconstituted but the skull lay wobbling on a table.

The rest of the furnishings indicated that the occupant of the house was interested in the natural sciences. There were jars filled with snakes, labeled according to their species; dried lizards, set in large frames of black wood, shone like cut emeralds; and bunches of wild odoriferous herbs Athos had never seen hung down from the ceiling. Athos found no signs of a family or a servant; undoubtedly the tall man lived quite alone.

Athos surveyed the laboratory with a cold indifferent glance and, at the other's invitation, sat down. The tall man remained standing. Athos then explained the reason for his visit and the favor he requested; but he had barely finished when the stranger recoiled with terror, shaking his head in refusal. Athos then drew from his pocket a small piece of paper containing two lines accompanied by a signature and a seal, and handed it to the man who had given such premature signs of repugnance. The tall man read the two lines, noticed the signature and recognized the seal; then he bowed to indicate that he had no longer any objection to make and that he was ready to obey.

Athos required no more. He rose, bowed, left the house, returned as he had come, and went up to his room. At dawn D'Artagnan entered, asking what they were to do.

"We have but to wait," Athos replied mechanically.

Two hours later Aramis came back from the convent where he had called on the Mother Superior. The burial, he said, was to take place at noon. Of the poisoner, there were no tidings. She must have escaped by way of the garden, for her footprints were evident on the damp gravel; the garden gate was locked; the key had disappeared.

At the appointed hour, Lord Winter and the four friends repaired to the convent. The bells were tolling; the chapel was open. At the chapel door D'Artagnan felt his courage fail anew and turned to look for Athos. But Athos had disappeared. Within, the grating of the choir was closed. In the middle of the choir, the body of the victim, clothed in her novitiate dress, made a white blur against the dark woodwork. The entire community of the Carmelite nuns was assembled on either side of the choir, behind the gratings opening out onto the convent; the sisters followed the divine service from there, without seeing the profane and unseen by them but mingling their chant with the chant of the priests.

Faithful to the avenging mission he had undertaken, Athos had slipped away and requested to be taken to the garden. There over the damp gravel, he followed the light tracks of the woman who left a trail of horror wherever she passed. Reaching the gate which led to the wood he had it opened and plunged into the thicket.

All his suspicions then found confirmation. The road by which the carriage had disappeared circled the forest. Athos followed this road for a time, his eyes fastened on the ground; slight bloodstains coming from a wound inflicted either on the courier or on one of the horses, speckled the road. About a mile further on some hundred odd yards from the hamlet of Festubert, he distinguished a much larger patch, marking what had been a pool of blood. Here the earth bore traces of the tramping of horses. A little beyond the wood and a few feet short of the churned earth, Athos detected the same footprints he had followed through the garden. Obviously Milady had emerged from the wood and entered the carriage here.

Satisfied with this discovery which confirmed all his suspicions, Athos returned to the inn, where he found Planchet awaiting him impatiently.

Everything had taken place as Athos had foreseen. Planchet, having followed the road as Athos had just done, noticed the bloodstains and noted the spot where the horses had stopped. But he pushed on farther than Athos had. Stopping at a tavern in the village of Festubert, he did not even have to ask of news; his fellow-drinkers volunteered the information that the evening before at half past eight, a wounded man and a lady had driven up to the inn. Apparently the man could go no further. The accident was attributed to robbers who had held up the chaise in the forest. The man remained in the village, the woman had hired a relay of horses and continued her journey.

Planchet sought out the postillion who had driven the chaise and found him. He had taken the lady as far as Fromelles; from Fromelles she had set out for Armentières. Planchet took the crossroad and by seven in the morning he was at Armentières.

There was only one inn at Armentières, the Hôtel de la Coste. Planchet presented himself there as a lackey out of work. He had not spoken ten minutes with the people at the inn before ascertaining that a woman had arrived at eleven o'clock the previous evening, had sent for the innkeeper and told him she intended to stay in the neighborhood for some time.

This was all Planchet needed to learn. Speeding to the appointed meeting place, he found his three colleagues at their posts, placed them as sentries at each exit of the inn and sped back to Béthune. Just as Planchet finished his report, the others returned from the convent. They were a sad, gloomy group; even the gentle countenance of Aramis looked down and almost harsh.

"What now?" D'Artagnan asked curtly.

"We must wait."

Without protest or comment each of them withdrew to his room. At eight o'clock that evening, Athos ordered the horses to be saddled and sent word to Lord Winter and to his friends that they would be leaving soon. The party was ready in a few moments. Each of them examined his arms and put them in order. Athos, the last to come downstairs, found D'Artagnan already mounted and chafing at the delay.

"Patience, my friend," he said coolly. "One of our party is still missing."

His companions looked about in surprise, wondering who this other person might be. Just then Planchet brought out Athos' horse and the musketeer leaped lightly into the saddle.

"Wait for me," he said. "I will be back in a moment!" and he galloped off.

Within a quarter of an hour he returned, accompanied by a tall man who wore a mask over his eyes and was swathed in a vast red cloak. Lord Winter and the musketeers exchanged questioning glances. None could enlighten the others; none had the faintest notion who the stranger might be. But they trusted Athos and, since Athos had so arranged, they would not question or demur. At nine o'clock, guided by Planchet, the little cavalcade started off along the road the carriage had taken.

These six men presented a melancholy sight as they rode forward in silence, each deep in his own thoughts, dark as despair and gloomy as retribution.

LXV

DAY OF JUDGMENT

It was a dark, tempestuous night. Vast tenebrous clouds raced across the heavens, obscuring the light of the stars. The moon would not be rising until about midnight. Now and then, thanks to a flash of lightning on the horizon, the cavalcade could see the road stretching out before them, white and solitary. Then, the flash spent, the riders were plunged into murky darkness.

Time and again Athos had to call D'Artagnan back to his place in the cavalcade; obsessed by one thought, to speed forward fast as he could, the Gascon kept pushing on too far in advance of his comrades.

They passed in silence through the hamlet of Festubert, where the wounded courier lay; they skirted the forest of Richebourg, and at Herlier, Planchet who led the column, turned to the left. Lord Winter or Porthos or Aramis tried several times to engage in conversation with the red-cloaked stranger. At each effort they made he merely bowed, without replying. Realizing from his attitude that he must have some mysterious but compelling reason for his silence, they abandoned all thoughts of sociability.

The storm increased in intensity, flash succeeded ever more rapidly on flash, the thunder growled ominously and the wind, forerunner of a hurricane, whistled through the feathers of the horsemen's hats and through their hair.

They broke into a fast trot.

A little beyond Fromelles the storm burst in great fury and the horsemen put on their greatcoats. They still had some ten miles to cover, which they did under torrents of rain. D'Artagnan, who alone had not put on his greatcoat, now took off his hat; he enjoyed letting the cold rain beat down on his burning brow and trickle refreshingly over his feverish body.

Just as the little troop cleared the village of Goskal and drew close to the Post House where relays were stationed, a man sheltered by a tree and rendered invisible by its trunk, stepped out onto the road and held up one arm high over his head. As they halted, he brought one finger to his lips. Athos recognized Grimaud.

"What is it?" cried D'Artagnan, "Has she left Armentières?"

Grimaud nodded affirmatively; D'Artagnan gnashed his teeth, and cried: "But look here—"

"Hush, D'Artagnan!" Athos ordered. "*I* am in charge of this operation and *I* shall question Grimaud." Turning back to Grimaud: "Where is she?" he asked.

Grimaud pointed toward the River Lys.

"How far from here?"

Grimaud merely crooked his finger.

"Is she alone?"

Grimaud nodded.

"Gentlemen," Athos said, "she is alone, she is half a league from here, somewhere by the river."

"Bravo, my good Grimaud, take us there at once," D'Artagnan ordered.

Grimaud then led them across some fields toward a brook, some five hundred yards distant, which they forded. Thanks to a flash of lightning they perceived the hamlet of Enguinghem.

"Is that the place, Grimaud?"

Grimaud shook his head negatively and the avengers continued on their way. Presently another flash of lightning wreathed its serpentine way across the heavens. Grimaud raised his arm and they perceived a small lonely house on the banks of the river, three hundred feet from the ferry.

"This is the place," Athos announced. Just then a man who had been lying in a ditch arose; it was Mousqueton. He pointed to the lighted window.

"She is in there, gentlemen!" he said.

"And Bazin?"

"I have been watching the window," Mousqueton replied. "He is watching the door."

"Good," said Athos, "my compliments. You are excellent servants."

With which he sprang from his horse, tossed the bridle to Grimaud and approached the window, motioning to the others to make for the door.

The little house was surrounded by a low quickset hedge which Athos hurdled; then he moved toward the window. There were no shutters, but the half-curtains were carefully drawn. Athos stepped on to the outer window-sill in order to peer over the curtains.

By the light of a lamp within, he distinguished a woman wrapped in a dark colored mantle, seated on a stool close to a dying fire; her elbows rested on a mean table and she held her head in between her hands, white as ivory. He could not make out her face, but a sinister smile flickered across his lips. There could be no mistake; here was the woman they sought.

Suddenly one of their horses neighed. Milady looked up toward the window to see the drawn pallid face of Athos, glued to the window pane.

Realizing that she had recognized him, Athos pushed the pane in with hand and knee; the glass yielded and fell clattering to the floor. Athos, the very specter of vengeance, leaped into the room.

Milady rushed to the door and opened it; at the threshold, even paler and more threatening than Athos, stood D'Artagnan.

Milady recoiled with a cry. D'Artagnan, thinking she had some means of escape, drew a pistol from his belt. But Athos raised his hand in warning.

"Put back that weapon," he ordered. "We must judge this woman, not murder her. Be patient for a few moments and you shall find satisfaction."

And he invited the others to enter.

There was something so impersonal, so solemn and so commanding in the attitude of Athos that D'Artagnan could not but obey, meekly as a child. It was as if out of a worldly musketeer some force had suddenly created a justiciar, sent from heaven, to preside with complete equity over an all-too-human lawsuit. Porthos, Aramis, Lord Winter and the man in the red cloak entered the house; the lackeys stood guard at door and window.

Milady fell back into a chair, her hands outstretched as though to conjure away this terrible apparition. Recognizing her brother-in-law, she uttered a cry of surprise and terror.

"What do you want?" she screamed.

"We want Charlotte Backson," Athos replied impersonally, "who was first called the Comtesse de la Fère and subsequently Lady Clark, Baroness of Sheffield."

"Well, here I am!" Milady murmured in a paroxysm of terror. "What do you want of me?"

"We want to judge you according to your crimes," Athos replied. "You shall be free to defend yourself and to justify yourself if you can. Monsieur D'Artagnan, it is for you to accuse her first."

D'Artagnan stepped forward.

"Before God and before man," he said, "I accuse this woman of having poisoned Constance Bonacieux, who perished yesterday evening."

He looked up at Porthos and at Aramis.

"I bear witness to the truth of it!" said Aramis and Porthos: "I swear this is the truth."

D'Artagnan continued:

"Before God and before man, I accuse this woman of having tried to poison me, too, with wine she sent to me together with a forged letter explaining that it came from my friends. God in His mercy saved my life but a man died in my stead. The victim's name was Brisemont."

"I saw him die!" said Aramis, and Porthos: "Upon oath, I declare this to be the truth."

"Before God and before man, I accuse this woman of having sought to make me kill the Comte de Vardes. Since no one else can certify to this fact, I beg that my solemn word of honor be accepted." He paused a moment. "I have finished," he concluded and crossed the room to join Porthos and Aramis.

"It is your turn now, Milord," said Athos, and the Englishman stepped forward.

"Before God and before man," said Lord Winter slowly, "I accuse this woman of having caused the murder of George Villiers, Duke of Buckingham."

"Buckingham!" D'Artagnan gasped.

"Buckingham dead?" said Porthos and "What in the world—?" cried Aramis. Alone Athos and the masked man in the red cloak betrayed no change of expression and made no comment.

"His Grace the Duke of Buckingham has just been assassinated," the Englishman went on evenly. "On the strength of the letter I received from you gentlemen, I had this woman arrested. I placed her in the hands of a true and loyal servant. She corrupted this man, set a dagger in his hand and sent him forth to kill the Duke. At this very moment, the assassin is probably paying with his life for the crime committed by this fury."

Amazed at the import of the Englishman's news and baffled by the extent of Milady's powers of evil, they stood by, silent and lost in wonder.

"There is more," Lord Winter pursued. "My brother bequeathed his all to this woman. Within three hours after he had signed his will, he died of a mysterious illness which left long livid streaks over his body. Tell me, my dear sister, how did your husband die?"

"Horrible!" said Porthos. Aramis stood motionless. D'Artagnan looked critically at Milady as he recalled his amorous passages with her.

"For the murder of Buckingham, for the murder of Felton and for the murder of my brother, I demand that justice be done. If this woman is not punished for her crimes, then I vow to punish her by my own hand."

And Lord Winter joined the group across the room, leaving his corner free for other plaintiffs. Milady buried her face in her hands, striving desperately to collect her thoughts as her head whirled dizzily.

"It is now my turn," Athos declared impassively, but he was shaking a little, and D'Artagnan, his eyes fastened on his friend, could think only of a lion, trembling ever so merely at the sight of a serpent. "It is now my turn," Athos repeated with utmost calm. He walked over to the corner whence the preceding accusers had testified and said:

"I married this woman when she was a young girl, against the wishes of my whole family. I gave her my name and my wealth. One day I discovered that she was branded; there was a fleur-de-lis stamped upon her left shoulder."

Milady rose indignantly to her feet:

"I defy you," she said fiercely, "to find any tribunal which passed this infamous sentence upon me. I was innocent. No court in France could have branded me. Tell me then how it came about?"

"Silence, woman, it is my turn to speak."

From the depths of the room, the man in red cloak rose to full height, dominating the others:

"My turn at last," he added in ominous tones.

"Who are *you*?" cried Milady, choking.

Her spell of coughing done, her disheveled hair streaming above the hands that held her head, she ventured a glance at the speaker. She was aghast, thought Porthos, with something akin to pity in his heart. Aramis, watching her, thought that her hair had come alive and was writhing like that of the Medusae. All eyes were turned toward the stranger, for none save Athos had the faintest idea who he could be. Yet Athos appeared to lose his composure and to be gazing at the man in the red cloak with as vast an astonishment as his friends. The stranger did not make for the corner the previous plaintiffs had occupied but instead approached Milady with a long, slow, firm step, advancing so near that only the narrow table separated them.

With increasing fright, Milady stared up at him. Then, noting his haggard face framed by sable-black hair and beard, she shuddered. The stranger maintained an icy impassiveness.

"No, no, no!" Milady sobbed. Rising she shrank back to the wall. "You are a figment of my imagination, an apparition from Hell! Help, help!" she screamed, tearing at the wall as though to pull it down with her hands.

"But how do you know this woman?" Aramis asked discreetly.

"This woman will tell you," the stranger replied. "As you see, she appears to have recognized me."

"The executioner of Lille!" Milady moaned, clutching at the wall to avoid falling. The whole company stepped back; now the man in the red cloak stood alone in the middle of the room.

"Forgive me!" Milady sobbed, falling to her knees and mumbling incoherently.

The stranger waited for silence, then continued very evenly:

"As I said, this woman recognized me. I am the executioner of Lille."

His audience looked raptly at him, eager for the solution of the enigma. Staring straight before him the man in the red cloak stated in a monotonous voice that the accused was once as beautiful a girl as she was now a beautiful woman, that she had been a nun in the Benedictine Convent at Templemar, and that in this convent she had seduced a candid sincere young priest.

"He was all innocence and all duty but she gained her ends. She would have seduced a saint."

The vows of both priest and nun were sacred and irrevocable; their love affair could not last long without bringing them both to ruin. The woman therefore persuaded her lover to leave that part of the country and to go with her where no one knew them. But for this, money was necessary and neither of them had a sou. So the young priest stole the sacred vessels and sold them. But as the pair were preparing to abscond, they were apprehended.

A week later, the woman seduced the jailer's son and thus escaped; the young priest was condemned to serve ten years in irons and to be branded.

"I was the executioner of Lille," the speaker insisted. "I was forced to brand the guilty man, and the guilty man, gentlemen, was my own brother!

"I did my duty. This woman had ruined my brother; she was more than a party to the crime, she had instigated it. Then and there, I swore that she should not go unpunished. I found out where she was hiding, I caught up with her and I marked upon her shoulder the same brand my brother bore. That, gentlemen, is why there are no records of this sentence; it was unofficially executed by the official executioner of the City of Lille."

Returning to Lille next day, the executioner discovered that his brother, too, had broken out of jail. He was therefore held in prison in his brother's place until the other gave himself up.

"My poor brother knew nothing of this," the plaintiff said. "He had joined this woman. They had fled southward to the province of Berry, where he found a small living. This woman passed herself off as his sister.

"The lord of the estate where they settled met the young priest's alleged sister and fell madly in love with her. They married and she forsook the man she had ruined for him she was about to ruin. As Comtesse de La Fère—"

All eyes turned toward Athos who simply nodded assent.

The young priest, out of his senses and desperate, resolved to put an end to an existence of which this woman had robbed honor, happiness and all else.

"My poor brother returned to Lille," the man in the red cloak said, "and learning of the judgment which had condemned me in his stead, he gave himself up. He took my place. That evening he hanged himself on the vent of his cell. To give them their due, the men who had sentenced me kept their word. I was at once set free." Milady cowered at his glance. "I have stated why I punished this woman before and why I seek to punish her again."

When he had moved aside, Athos turned to D'Artagnan:

"Monsieur d'Artagnan, what sentence should be passed upon this woman?"

"I request the penalty of death."

"Lord Winter, what judgment is to be inflicted upon the accused?"

"On three counts, the sentence of death."

Athos looked at Porthos and Aramis. "You two gentlemen are judges," he stated. "What punishment do you please to impose upon this woman?"

"Death!" they answered in one voice.

Their stern, hollow tones rang through the room. Milady uttered a shriek, fell to her knees and crept, inch by inch, toward her accusers.

"Charlotte Backson, Comtesse de La Fère and Lady Clark—" Athos paused significantly, "your presence has too long importuned men on earth and offended God in his Heaven. Should you happen to know a Christian prayer, now is the time to say it. You are hereby sentenced to death for your crimes. May God have mercy upon your unfortunate soul."

Aware that these words left her without hope of appeal, Milady rose to her feet and sought to speak. But her strength failed her. It was as though an implacable hand had seized her by the hair and must drag her as irrevocably to her doom as the hand of fate drags men whither it would have them go. Beyond all resistance, she merely bowed her head and left the cottage.

One by one, Lord Winter, D'Artagnan, Athos, Porthos and Aramis followed her out. The lackeys fell in behind their masters. The room was left empty, its window broken, its door wide open, and its smoky lamp burning dimly on the table.

LXVI
OF HOW JUDGMENT WAS ACCOMPLISHED

It was now almost midnight. The waning sickle-shaped moon rose ruddy and as though emblooded by the last vestiges of the storm. It soared slowly over the village of Armentières, its wan light etching the dark line of the houses and the silhouette of its tall belfry against a darkling background. The Lys rolled by like a river of molten lead. Beyond it, a black mass of trees standing out against an angry sky heavy with fat coppery clouds, re-created a sort of twilight amid the fulness of the night. To the left, from an old deserted mill, an owl hooted, strident, monotonous and at unfailing intervals. Here and there across the plain to the right and left of the road, a few squat and stunted trees stood like so many dwarfs (rising from what sinister cave?) to spy upon these men abroad at so unwonted an hour.

From time to time a broad, powerful sheet of lightning illumed the entire horizon, darting over the black leaves of the trees, slashing sky and stream asunder. No wisp of wind now freshened the oppressive atmosphere. A deathlike silence reigned over all nature. The ground was sodden and slippery with the recent rain. There was a cool redolence of grass.

Grimaud and Mousqueton led Milady forward, their hands pinned under her arms. The executioner followed hard by. Then respectively came Lord Winter, D'Artagnan, Athos, Porthos and Aramis. Planchet and Bazin brought up the rear.

Painfully Milady moved, or better, was moved toward the river. She did not say a word, but her eyes, extraordinarily brilliant, seemed to be pleading as she gazed in turn on each of her escort. As she and the valets gained some ground, she whispered:

"A thousand pistoles for each of you if you help me escape. But if you give me up to your master, I have friends who will make you pay dearly for my death."

Grimaud hesitated; Mousqueton trembled. Athos, hearing Milady's voice, ran up. "Planchet!" he called. "Bazin! Front and center!" And in an undertone to Lord Winter: "She has spoken to these two; they are no longer trustworthy." Planchet and Bazin came up, Grimaud and Mousqueton fell behind.

When they reached the river bank, the executioner advanced to tie a cord about Milady's hands and feet. She screamed:

"Cowards! You are all miserable cowards! Ten murderers against a defenseless woman! Shame upon you! If I am not saved, I shall be avenged."

"You are no woman," said Athos. "You do not belong to the human species, you are a demon from Hell and back to Hell you shall go."

"Ha, gallant and virtuous gentlemen that you are, pray remember that whoever touches one hair of my head becomes a murderer too!"

"The public executioner, Madame, can destroy life without being guilty of murder," said the man in the red cloak, clapping his hand against the scabbard of his broadsword. "He is the final judge and no more: *Nachrichter*, our German neighbors call him."

As he bound her, Milady uttered piercing cries that echoed and were lost, dismally, in the depths of the wood.

"Suppose I *am* guilty," Milady protested when she had come to her senses, "take me to court. Who appointed *you* judges of my so-called crimes?"

"I offered you Tyburn and you refused," said Lord Winter.

"I do not want to die," Milady answered, writhing in her bonds. "I am too young to die."

"So too was the woman you poisoned at Béthune," D'Artagnan put in. "She was younger than you, yet she is dead!"

"I swear to enter a convent ... I will become a nun ..."

"You were cloistered and you were a nun," the executioner replied. "You left the convent to bring ruin upon my brother."

Milady uttered a cry of horror and fell on her knees. The hangman, picking her up under the arms, sought to take her toward the boat moored near by.

"Ah, God, do you mean to drown me?" she whimpered.

There was something so pathetic and so appealing in her voice that even D'Artagnan, from the first her most dogged pursuer, slumped down on a tree trunk and, bowing his head, stopped up his ears with his fingers. Nevertheless he could not drown out her shrieks and threats. The youngest of them all, D'Artagnan felt his courage fail him.

"I cannot bear to see this sight!" he moaned. "I cannot stand by and let a woman die like this."

Hearing him, Milady clutched at a shadow of hope.

"D'Artagnan," she cried, "remember that I loved you!"

The Gascon rose dully and took a few steps toward her, but Athos, looming between them, his sword drawn, barred the way.

"One more step, D'Artagnan, and we fight, for all our friendship," he threatened.

D'Artagnan sank to his knees and prayed.

"Come," Athos commanded, "do your duty, executioner."

"Willingly, Monsieur," the man of Lille replied. "As a good Catholic, I swear I am but performing the duties of my office in destroying this woman."

Athos took one step forward and facing Milady:

"I forgive you the evil you have done me," he said. "I pardon you for my future blasted, my honor lost, my love defiled and salvation forever warped by the despair you visited upon me. God rest you, may you die in peace!"

Lord Winter advanced.

"I forgive you for poisoning my brother, for murdering His Grace the Duke of Buckingham, for causing the death of young Felton and for your attempts upon my own life. May you die in peace!"

"For my part," said D'Artagnan, "*I* beg *your* forgiveness. By trickery unworthy of a gentleman, I provoked your anger and moved you to vengeance. In return for such forgiveness, I forgive you that cruel vengeance and the death of my poor mistress. God grant you die in peace!"

"I am lost!" Milady cried in English. "I must die," and immediately after, in French: "*Je suis perdue, je dois mourir!*"

Then, unaided, she rose, stood erect and glanced about her, her eyes shining in the night like a flame. But she saw nothing; and, pausing to listen, she heard no sound.

"Where am I to die?" she asked.

"Across the river," said the man of Lille, helping her into the boat. When both were settled, Athos handed the executioner a sum of money.

"Here is your fee for the execution," he said. "It must be made quite plain that we are acting only as judges."

"I thank you, Monsieur," the man in the red cloak replied, tossing the money into the river. "This woman must know that I am not accomplishing my public duties as professional executioner but my private duties as a God-fearing man."

The boat glided toward the left bank of the Lys as the company fell to their knees. Slowly the boat followed the ferry rope under the shadow of a pallid cloud that descended very gradually over the waters. Our friends, following the boat's progress, watched it reach the bank opposite; the figures of executioner and condemned were clearly discernible, outlined in black against the faintly reddish horizon.

Milady, during the crossing, had contrived to shake free from the rope binding her feet. Reaching shore, she jumped lightly from the boat and took to her heels. But the ground was wet. Having scaled the bank, she slipped and fell to her knees.

What passed through her mind at that instant? Perhaps she realized fatalistically that all was at an end. Perhaps, even she, adamant by nature, was at long last beaten. Perhaps she felt, superstitiously, that Heaven itself had vowed her destruction. At all events, she stayed very still there, kneeling on the top of the embankment.

The executioner raised his arms very slowly . . . a ray of moonlight illumined the blade of his broadsword . . . his arms fell down again smartly . . . the whir of his weapon cut across the silent air (or did the spectators imagine it?) . . . and, after one terrified shriek, his victim fell, severed under the blow. . . .

The man from Lille then took off his red cloak, spread it out on the turf, placed the body upon it and tossed the head on it after the body. Then he gathered it up and, his grisly burden over his shoulder, returned to his boat.

Midstream, he swung his boat round. Raising his red cloak and its contents over the water:

"God's justice and will and mercy be done!" he cried in a loud voice.

Then he dropped the cloak overboard and the waters closed up about it.

Three days later, the musketeers returned to Paris. They had not overstayed their leave of absence and, on the evening of their arrival, they paid their customary call on Monsieur de Tréville.

"Well, gentlemen," the good Captain inquired, "did you enjoy yourselves on your excursion?"

"Prodigiously!" Athos replied, speaking for one and all.

LXVII

Of the Cardinal, His Agent and a Lieutenant's Commission

On the sixth day of the following month the King, true to the promise he had made to My Lord Cardinal, left his capital, still stunned by the news—which was spreading like wildfire—of Buckingham's assassination.

The Queen of course had frequently been warned that the man she loved so passionately was in great danger, but when she heard of his death she refused to believe it. Rashly she exclaimed:

"It cannot be true, he has just written to me!"

On the morrow, however, she was forced to credit the fatal tidings, for La Porte arrived from London to confirm them. Like everyone else, he had been detained by order of King Charles I; now he came back bearing the Duke's dying gift to the Queen.

King Louis, overcome with joy, did not even trouble to dissemble; indeed he paraded his delight before the Queen with immense affection. Like all weak-spirited men, Louis XIII was wanting in generosity.

Soon, however, he relapsed into boredom and ill-health, for he was the least cheerful and sanguine of men. He knew that, returning to the Army, he would be returning to slavery. Nevertheless that is exactly what he did. The Cardinal was for him the fascinating serpent, himself was the fascinated bird which hops from branch to branch without power to escape.

Thus the journey to La Rochelle was full of melancholy. Our four friends, in particular, amazed their comrades by their unwonted dejection, as they advanced, side by side as usual but with heads bowed and eyes averted. Athos alone looked up from time to time, his eyes flashing and his lips curled in a wry smile. Then, like his comrades, he sank back again into deep meditation.

Arriving at a city, as soon as the escort had conducted the King to his quarters, the four friends either retired directly to their bullets or sought out some secluded tavern where they neither gambled nor drank but merely conversed in hushed tones, looking carefully about them to make sure no one was listening.

One day the King stopped off for some shooting, the magpies being particularly tempting. Our four friends as usual preferred a quiet tavern on the main road to a few hours of sport.

As they sat talking, a man came galloping up from La Rochelle, stopped at the door to order a glass of wine and as he did so stared into the room where the four friends were seated.

"Ho, there, Monsieur," he cried. "You are Monsieur d'Artagnan, are you not?"

Glancing up, D'Artagnan uttered a cry of joy. Here was the man he called his phantom, the stranger he had encountered first at Meung, next in the Rue des Fossoyeurs in Paris, then in Arras, and now, at long last, on the road to La Rochelle.

D'Artagnan drew his sword and sprang toward the door. But this time, instead of taking to his heels, the stranger leaped from his horse and strode forward.

"So, Monsieur, we meet at last," said the Gascon. "But *this* time you shall not escape me!"

"I have no intention of doing so, Monsieur," the stranger replied. "*This* time, *I* am after *you*! In the name of His Majesty the King, I have the honor to put you under arrest. I order you to yield your sword, Monsieur, without resistance. I also warn you that your head is at stake."

"And who may you be, Monsieur?" D'Artagnan inquired, lowering his sword but still holding it firmly in his grasp.

"I am the Chevalier de Rochefort, the equerry of Monseigneur le Cardinal de Richelieu. I have orders to conduct you to His Eminence forthwith."

Suddenly Athos stepped forward, and:

"We are on our way to the Cardinal's," he explained. "You will please take Monsieur d'Artagnan's word for it that he will proceed immediately to La Rochelle."

"I am in duty bound to hand him over to the guards. They will take him into camp."

"I pledge our word as gentlemen that we will be his guards," Athos countered. "But, by the same token—our gentleman's word—we and Monsieur d'Artagnan shall not part company."

The Chevalier de Rochefort, turning, saw that Porthos and Aramis had moved up behind him and cut off his retreat. He understood that he was completely at the mercy of the four comrades.

"Very well, gentlemen," he conceded. "If Monsieur d'Artagnan will surrender his sword and add his word of honor to yours, I shall be satisfied with your promise to convey Monsieur d'Artagnan to the quarters of Monseigneur the Cardinal."

"I give you my word, Monsieur," said D'Artagnan. "Here is my sword!"

"So much the better," Rochefort exclaimed, "because I must continue my journey."

"If you propose to join Milady, yours is a sleeveless errand," said Athos, coolly. "You will not find her."

"What has become of her?" Rochefort asked eagerly.

"Come back to camp with us and you will find out."

Rochefort made no immediate reply. Obviously he was turning the matter over in his mind. As Surgières, where the Cardinal awaited His Majesty, was only a day's journey distant, Rochefort decided to accept the advice Athos proffered. Besides, to return with our friends gave him the advantage of keeping an eye on his prisoner. So the five took to the road again.

They reached Surgières next day at three o'clock in the afternoon. The Cardinal had made elaborate preparations to greet his sovereign; their meeting was most cordial. They embraced each other, they exchanged numerous compliments, salutes, blandishments, and congratulations on the lucky accident which had rid the realm of France of an inveterate enemy who had roused all Europe against her. Whereupon the Cardinal, aware that D'Artagnan was under arrest and anxious to see him, took ceremonious leave of the King. As they parted, it was decided that His Majesty would inspect and dedicate the dyke, the works of which were now completed.

Returning in the evening to his headquarters close to the bridge of La Pierre, the Cardinal found D'Artagnan standing swordless in front of the house, the three musketeers, fully armed, beside him. This time, well attended by a bodyguard, His Eminence stared sternly at them and, with eye and hand, beckoned D'Artagnan to follow him. As the young Gascon obeyed:

"We shall wait for you, D'Artagnan," Athos said loudly enough for the Cardinal to hear him.

Richelieu frowned, stopped for a moment, then went on his way. D'Artagnan followed and as he disappeared four guards took their stand by the door. Richelieu entered the room that served him for a study, walked over to the mantelpiece, and, leaning against it, motioned to

Rochefort to usher D'Artagnan in. Our Gascon appeared, bowed courteously and faced the great Cardinal for his second interview, which, years
later, D'Artagnan was to confess he was sure was to be his last. Richelieu,
without moving, declared:

"You have been arrested by my orders, Monsieur."

"So I have been told, Monseigneur."

"Do you know why?"

"No, Monseigneur, I do not. Certainly there are grounds for my arrest,
but Your Eminence has not yet learned them."

Richelieu looked steadily at the young man.

"What, Monsieur?" he asked. "What do you mean?"

"If Monseigneur will be kind enough to tell me in the first place what
crimes I am charged with, I shall then inform him of what I have already
done."

"You are charged with crimes which have brought down far loftier
heads than yours, Monsieur."

"What crimes, Monseigneur?" D'Artagnan asked with a calmness that
amazed the Cardinal.

"You are indicted for correspondence and intelligence with the enemies of the Kingdom, for violation of secrets of State, and for attempting
to thwart the plans of your Commanding General."

"But by whom were these charges preferred, Monseigneur?" D'Artagnan asked, knowing that it was certainly Milady.

And before the Cardinal could speak, he was answering his own question:

"By a woman whom the justice of our country has branded: by a
woman who espoused one man in France and another in England; by a
woman who poisoned her second husband and who attempted both to
poison and to slay me."

"What in the world are you saying, Monsieur? What woman are you
talking about?"

"I am talking about Lady Clark. Since you have honored me with your
confidence, Monseigneur, I have no doubt you are ignorant of Milady's
crimes."

"If Lady Clark has committed these crimes, Monsieur, you may be
sure she will be duly punished."

"Monseigneur, she has already been punished."

"By whom, pray?"

"By my three friends and myself."

"She is in prison?"

"She is dead."

"Dead!" the Cardinal exclaimed incredulously. "Dead! You say she is dead?"

"Thrice she attempted to kill me and I pardoned her," D'Artagnan said. "But when she murdered the woman I loved, my friends and I seized, tried and sentenced her."

D'Artagnan then related how Madame Bonacieux was poisoned in the Carmelite convent at Béthune, how the trial was held in the lonely house and how Milady was executed on the banks of the Lys.

The Cardinal, a man renowned for his phlegm, shuddered at the recital. Then, perhaps reacting to some secret thought, he seemed to change completely. His gloomy expression gradually cleared and, perfectly serene:

"So you and your friends dared to sit as judges!" he declared in a tone that contrasted strangely with the severity of his words. "Do you realize that those who punish without license to punish are guilty of murder?"

"I swear to you, Monseigneur, that it never for a moment occurs to me to defend my life against you," D'Artagnan answered. "I shall willingly submit to any punishment Your Eminence may please to order. I have never held life so precious as to be afraid of death."

"Monsieur, I know you to be a brave man," the Cardinal said almost affectionately. "I can therefore tell you immediately that you will be tried and probably convicted."

"Another might assure Your Eminence that he had his pardon in his pocket. For my part, I am content to say: 'Command as you see fit, Monseigneur, I shall obey.' "

"Your pardon in your pocket?" said Richelieu, surprised.

"Ay, Monseigneur!"

"A pardon signed by whom?" Richelieu asked, adding with a singular tone of contempt: "By the King?"

"No, by Your Eminence."

"By *me*? You are insane, Monsieur."

"Surely Monseigneur will recognize his own handwriting?" D'Artagnan said. And he handed over the precious note which Athos had seized from Milady and had given him to serve for a safeguard. His Eminence accepted the paper, scanned it carefully, and read the text slowly, syllable by syllable:

> December third, 1627
> It is by my order and for the service of the State that the bearer of this note has done what he has done.
>
> Signed by my hand at the Camp of La Rochelle
Richelieu

Having read this document, the Cardinal sank into a profound reverie, paper in hand. D'Artagnan felt sure that His Eminence was meditating by what sort of punishment he should kill him.

"Well," mused the young musketeer, who was excellently disposed to meet his end heroically, "he shall see how a gentleman goes to his death."

Richelieu remained plunged in thought, rolling and unrolling the paper in his hands. At length he raised his head, fastened his eagle glance upon the other's loyal, open, intelligent countenance, and on that countenance, furrowed by tears, read all the sufferings D'Artagnan had endured for the last month. For the third or fourth time the Cardinal reflected what a brilliant future lay before this youth of twenty-one and what resources his activity, courage and shrewdness might offer to a good master. Recalling too how the crimes, power and infernal genius of Milady had more than once terrified him, he felt a kind of secret joy at being relieved forever of so dangerous an accomplice. Slowly, the Cardinal tore up the paper which D'Artagnan had generously relinquished.

"This is the end!" D'Artagnan thought. And he bowed deeply to the Cardinal, as who might say: "Lord, Thy will be done!"

His Eminence moved over to his desk and without sitting down wrote a few lines on a parchment two-thirds of which were already filled and affixed his seal to it.

"This is the order for my execution," D'Artagnan thought. "Monseigneur is sparing me the tedium of the Bastille or the protracted formalities of a trial. That is very gracious of him."

"Here, Monsieur," the Cardinal told him, "I have taken a *carte blanche* document from you, so I shall give you another. The name is wanting on this commission; you can write it in yourself."

D'Artagnan took the paper hesitantly and looked it over; it was a Lieutenant's commission in the Musketeers. He fell to one knee before His Eminence.

"Monseigneur, my life is yours," he declared, "do with it henceforth what you will. But I do not deserve the favor you have bestowed upon me. I have three friends all of whom are worthier and more deserving—"

"You are a gallant lad, D'Artagnan," the Cardinal interrupted, tapping him on the shoulder and savoring the pleasure of having at last overcome this rebellious nature. "Do with the commission what you will. But remember, though the bearer's name is blank, it is to you I give it."

"I shall never forget it, Your Eminence may be certain of that!"

The Cardinal turned and called in a loud voice: "Rochefort!" The Chevalier, who was doubtless close to the door, entered immediately.

"Rochefort," said His Eminence, "here you see Monsieur d'Artagnan. I number him among my friends. Pray greet each other and behave yourselves if you hope to keep a head on your shoulders!"

Rochefort and D'Artagnan embraced each other somewhat coldly as the Cardinal stood over them, his vigilant eye observing all that occurred. But when they had left the room together:

"We shall meet again, Monsieur, shall we not?" Rochefort demanded.

"Whenever you please."

"The opportunity will surely arise," Rochefort asserted.

"Eh, what's that?" asked the Cardinal, pushing the door ajar.

The two exchanged smiles, shook hands and saluted His Eminence. D'Artagnan sped down the stairs and rushed up to his friends.

"We were growing rather impatient," Athos remarked.

"Well, here I am, friends, not only free as air but in high favor, too!"

"Tell us about it."

"I will this evening," D'Artagnan replied. "But for the moment let us separate."

Accordingly that evening D'Artagnan sought out Athos whom he found well on the way to emptying a bottle of Spanish wine, an occupation which he accomplished religiously every night. D'Artagnan related what had passed between the Cardinal and himself and, drawing the commission from his pocket, said:

"Here, my dear Athos, this naturally belongs to you!"

Athos smiled—a proud, gracious smile—answering:

"My friend, for Athos this is too much; for the Comte de La Fère, it is too little. Keep the commission, it is yours. God knows you have bought it all too dearly."

Taking his leave of Athos, the young Gascon called upon Porthos. He found this worthy clothed in a magnificent costume, covered with splendent embroidery. Porthos was busy gazing at his reflection in the mirror.

"Ah, so it's you, is it?" Porthos exclaimed. "Tell me, my friend, do these garments fit me?"

"They fit you to perfection," D'Artagnan assured him. "But I have come to offer you a costume that will suit you even better."

"What costume?"

"The uniform of a Lieutenant of Musketeers," D'Artagnan said proudly. Then, having given Porthos a summary of his interview with the Cardinal, he drew the commission from his pocket and:

"Here, my friend," he urged. "Write your name on this and please be a good chief to me!"

Porthos glanced over the parchment and to D'Artagnan's immense surprise handed it back to him.

"Thank you," Porthos said. "This is very flattering, of course. But I would not have time enough to enjoy this distinction. During our expedition to Béthune, the husband of my duchess passed away. The coffers of the dear departed beckon me with open arms—or rather doors! I shall marry the widow. As you see, I was trying on my wedding clothes when you came in. So keep the lieutenancy, my friend, keep it for yourself."

D'Artagnan then hastened to offer the commission to Aramis. He found him kneeling before a *prie-Dieu,* his head bowed over an open prayer book. For the third time, D'Artagnan gave an account of his interview with the Cardinal and, drawing his commission from his pocket for the third time, said:

"Aramis, you are our friend, our guiding light, our invisible protector; pray accept this commission. By your wisdom and by your advice which has invariably led to the happiest results, you have proved yourself the best qualified to do so."

"I am sorry, my friend," Aramis said, "I must decline. Our recent adventures have disgusted me with both secular and military life. This time my mind is irrevocably set. The siege ended, I shall join the Lazarists. Keep the commission, D'Artagnan; the profession of arms suits you admirably, you will make a brave and resourceful captain."

D'Artagnan went back to visit Athos again. His eyes were moist with gratitude but he was beaming with joy. He found Athos still at table, contemplating his last glass of Malaga admiringly by the light of his lamp.

"Well," D'Artagnan announced, "the others refused too."

"That is because no one deserves it more than you," said Athos. Then, taking up a quill, he wrote boldly into the blank in the commission:

D'ARTAGNAN

and returned it to him.

"I have lost my friends," D'Artagnan said ruefully, burying his head in his hands. "I have nothing left but the bitterest of recollections. . . ."

Two large tears rolled down his cheeks.

"You are young," Athos answered. "Your bitter recollections have the time requisite to change into the happiest of memories."

LXVIII

EPILOGUE

After a year's siege, La Rochelle, deprived of the assistance of the British fleet and of the diversion promised by Buckingham, surrendered. The capitulation was signed on October 28, 1628.

The King returned to Paris on December twenty-third of the same year, receiving as triumphant a welcome as if he came from conquering an enemy rather than his fellow-Frenchmen. He entered the city by the Faubourg Saint-Jacques under arches of greenery.

D'Artagnan assumed his lieutenancy. (Eventually Planchet obtained a sergeancy in the Piedmont Regiment.)

Porthos, having left the service, married Madame Coquenard in the course of the following year. The coffers so avidly coveted yielded eight hundred thousand livres. (Mousqueton, clad in a magnificent livery, enjoyed the satisfaction of his supreme ambition: to ride behind a gilded carriage.)

Aramis, after a journey into Lorraine, suddenly vanished without a word to his friends. Later they learned through Madame de Chevreuse, who told it to a few intimates, that he had retired to a monastery—no one knew where. (Bazin became a lay brother.)

Athos remained a musketeer under D'Artagnan's command until 1633 when, after a journey to Touraine, he too quitted the service, under the pretext that he had inherited a small property in Roussillon. (Grimaud followed him.)

D'Artagnan fought with Rochefort thrice and thrice he wounded him.

"I shall probably kill you the fourth time," he declared, as he helped Rochefort to his feet.

"We had therefore best stop where we are," the wounded man answered. "God's truth, I am a better friend than you imagine. After our first encounter, by saying one word to the Cardinal, I could have had your throat slit from ear to ear."

This time they embraced heartily, all malice spent; indeed, it was Rochefort who found Planchet his sergeancy.

As for Monsieur Bonacieux, he lived on very quietly, wholly ignorant of what had become of his wife and caring very little about it. One day he was rash enough to recall himself to the Cardinal's memory. His Eminence replied that he would provide for the haberdasher so thoroughly that he would never want for anything in the future. In fact, Monsieur Bonacieux, having left his house at seven o'clock in the evening to go to the Louvre, never set foot again in the Rue des Fossoyeurs. In the opinion of those who seemed best informed, he is lodged and fed in some royal stronghold at the expense of His Generous Eminence.

COMMENTARY

MARGARET OLIPHANT

BRANDER MATTHEWS

G. K. CHESTERTON

MARGARET OLIPHANT

[We] owe more innocent amusement [to Alexandre Dumas] than to almost any other writer of his generation.

We would not, however, have it supposed that in saying this we are setting up Alexandre Dumas as a model writer, or recommending his works as a moral regimen for the young. Nothing could be further from our intention. All that we venture to assert is, that he is purity itself and good taste itself in comparison with the more recent and much more pretentious school of fiction which has openly dedicated itself to the study and elucidation of vice, and which is generally meant when the contemptuous phrase "French novel" drops from British lips.

It is not from the modern inspiration of fiction, but from [the] wild source of boundless adventure and incident, that [Dumas] draws his power. He appeals not to the deeper principles of nature in his hearers, nor to their sympathy with the struggles of heart and soul, the complications of will and passion, which are the true subjects of poetry; but to that which is most universal in us, the intellectual quality (if it can be justly called intellectual at all) which most entirely pervades humanity, which is common to the child and the sage, the simplest and the most educated—that primitive Curiosity and thirst for story without which man would scarcely be man.

His was not the art of reflection, of careful balance, and elaborate completeness. He produced his effects *sur-le-champ*, by chance, by the inspiration of the moment, without pausing to consider, or making any conscious selection of circumstances. He began—but there never appeared to him any necessity to close. The story which he told was one long-continued tale, such as children and simple natures love—a story without an end. With a wild and gay and careless exuberance of strength and of material such as none of his contemporaries could equal, he rushed on from incident to incident, each new adventure leading to another, like the endless peaks of a mountain-range. From one day to another, from one year to another, what matter how far the story led him, he carried his audience on with unflagging interest and frequent excitement.... The charm of dramatic suspense, of uncertainty, and eager curiosity—those universal stimulants of the common mind—attended him wherever he moved.

[In our opinion, Dumas's greatest work] was the "Trois Mousquetaires." ... It is the most spontaneous and dazzling, the most joyous, effortless, and endless of romances.... What gay vitality overflows in it, what bustling scenes open around its heroes!—scenes which are so real, so crowded, so full of incident, that we never dream of inquiring into their historical accuracy, nor of bringing them to that dull standard of fact which is alien to romance. Such scenes indeed do not belong to one historical period or another, nor can the bold and brilliant narrative be bound down to formal limits of costume, or the still harder bondage of actual events. They belong rather to that vague period "once upon a time," familiar to all primitive audiences, in which the action of all fairy tales is laid, and which is the age proper to the primary poet, vague in chronology but dauntless in invention, who is always the earliest chronicler.

[The] unbounded vivacity of the narrative, its endless variety, the delightful prodigality of movement and frolic-wealth, is to the *blasé* reader of more reasonable and profitable literature like a dip into some sunshiny sea with flashing waves and currents, with wild puffs of wind and dashes of spray, after the calm navigation of stately rivers. Athos, Porthos, and Aramis are as delightfully real as they are impossible. Does any one ask whether we believe in them? we laugh at the question, and at all the gravity and conformance to ordinary rule which it implies. Believe in them! we know that our four paladins are impossible—as impossible as the seven champions of Christendom, but equally delightful and true to the instincts which, once in a way, ask something more from imagination than sketches of recognisable men and comprehensible circumstances. They are possible as Puck and Ariel are possible, though they are not at all ethereal, but most vigorous and solid human beings, with swords of prodigious temper, and arms of iron, giving blows which no man would willingly encounter. Their combination of ancient knight-errantry with the rude and careless habits of a modern soldier of fortune, their delicate honour and indifferent morals, their mutual praise and honest adulation, combined with the perfect frankness of the author as to their faults, give a reality to these martial figures which no chronological deficiency can detract from, and which even their wonderful and unheard-of successes do not abate.

[The] author never forgets the characteristic differences of his adventurers. The calm and somewhat sad indifferentism of Athos, the sentimentalism of Aramis, the sturdy conviviality of Porthos, are kept up throughout with unfailing consistency; and nothing can be more individual than the character of d'Artagnan, who is more distinctly the soldier of fortune than any of his friends, and who, . . . in the very heat of adventure keeps always a corner of his eye upon his own advantage, or rather the advantage of the brotherhood, which to each of the four is as his own. The perpetual contrast and variety thus kept up adds immensely to our interest in the Mousquetaires. It supplies the charm of character which is sometimes wanting to the rapid strain of the improvisatore, and adds what is in its way a distinct intellectual enjoyment to that pleasure which can scarcely be called intellectual—the delight of simple story, a primitive and savage joy.

The tragic thread which runs through this record of warlike exploits, and which brings in certain chapters which we would gladly get rid of, has on the whole but little to do with the adventures of our Mousquetaires. The portentous creation of Milady, the depraved and dishonoured woman whom we divine at once to have been the wife of the proud Athos and cause of his misfortunes, has little attraction to the wholesome imagination, though she has been the origin of a whole school of wicked heroines. . . . [We] cannot take upon us to say that any of the women who figure now and then in the story do any credit to Dumas. The best that can be said for him is, that he brings them in only when he cannot help it, and has himself no predilection for scenes of passion, or any intrigues except those which are political. Embarrassing situations and the "delicate" suggestions of vice in which some other French writers delight, are entirely out of the way of the honest *raconteur.*

From "Alexandre Dumas," published in *Blackwood's Edinburgh Magazine,* July 1873

BRANDER MATTHEWS

Ben Jonson, we are told, once dreamed that he saw the Romans and Carthaginians fighting on his big toe. No doubt Dumas had not dissimilar dreams; for his vanity was at least as stalwart and as frank as Ben Jonson's. To defend himself against all charges of plagiarism, the French dramatist echoed the magniloquent phrase of the English dramatist, and declared that he did not steal, he conquered [see excerpt dated 1833]. It is but justice to say that there was no mean and petty pilfering about Dumas. He annexed as openly as a statesman, and made no attempt at disguise. In his memoirs he is very frank about his sources of inspiration, and tells us at length where he found a certain situation, and what it suggested to him, and how he combined it with another effect which had struck him somewhere else. When one goes to the places thus pointed out, one finds something very different from what it became after it had passed through Dumas's hands, and, more often than not, far inferior to it. It can scarcely be said that Dumas touched nothing he did not adorn; for he once laid sacrilegious hands on Shakspeare, and brought out a "Hamlet" with a very French and epigrammatic last act. But whatever he took from other authors he made over into something very different, something truly his own, something that had *Dumas fecit* in the corner, even though the canvas and the colors were not his own. . . . In a word, all his plagiarisms, and they were not a few, are the veriest trifles when compared with his indisputable and extraordinary powers.

Besides plagiarism, Dumas has been accused of "devilling," as the English term it; that is to say, of putting his name to plays written either wholly or in part by others. There is no doubt that the accusation can be sustained, although many of the separate specifications are groundless. The habit of collaboration obtains widely in France; and collaboration runs easily into "devilling." When two men write a play together, and one of them is famous and the other unknown, there is a strong temptation to get the full benefit of celebrity, and to say nothing at all about the author whose name has no market-value. That Dumas yielded to it now and then is not to be wondered at. There was something imperious in his character, as there was something imperial in his power. He had dominion over so many departments of literature, that he had accustomed himself to be monarch of all he surveyed; and if a follower came with the germ of a plot, or a suggestion for a strong situation, Dumas took it as tribute due to his superior ability. In his hands the hint was worked out, and made to render all it had of effect. Even when he had avowed collaborators, as in *Richard Darlington,* he alone wrote the whole play. His partners got their share of the pecuniary profits, benefiting by his skill and his renown; and most of them did not care whether he who had done the best of the work should get all the glory or not.

That Dumas plagiarized freely in his earliest plays, and had the aid of "devils" in the second stage of his career, is not to be denied, and neither proceeding is praiseworthy; but, although he is not blameless, it irks one to see him pilloried as a mere vulgar appropriator of the labors of other men. The exact fact is, that he had no strict regard for mine and thine. He took as freely as he gave. In literature, as in life, he was a spendthrift; and a prodigal is not always as scrupulous as he might be in replenishing his purse. Dumas's ethics deteriorated as he advanced. One may safely say, that there is none of the plays bearing his name which does not prove itself his by its workmanship. When, however, he began to write serial stories, and to publish a score of volumes a year, then he trafficked in his reputation, and signed his name to books which he had not even read. An effort has been made to show that even *Monte Cristo* and the *Three Musketeers* series were the work of M. Auguste Maquet, and that Dumas contributed to them only his name on the title page.... I must confess that I do not see how any one with any pretence to the critical faculty can doubt that *Monte Cristo* and the *Three Musketeers* are Dumas's own work. That M. Maquet made historical researches, accumulated notes, invented scenes even, is probable; but the mighty impress of Dumas's hand is too plainly visible in every important passage for us to believe that either series owes more to M. Maquet than the service a pupil might fairly render to a master. That these services were considerable is sufficiently obvious from the printing of M. Maquet's name by the side of Dumas's on the title pages of the dramatizations from the stories. That it was Dumas's share of the work which was inconsiderable is as absurd as it is to scoff at his creative faculty because he was wont to borrow. Señor Castelar has said that all Dumas's collaborators together do not weigh half as much in the literary balance as Dumas alone; and this is true. I have no wish to reflect on the talents of Dinaux, the author of *Thirty Years, or a Gambler's Life,* and of *Louise de Lignerrolles,* or on the talents of M. Maquet himself, whose own novels and plays have succeeded, and who is so highly esteemed by his fellow-dramatists as to have been elected and re-elected the president of the Society of Dramatic Authors; yet I must say that the plays which either Dinaux or M. Maquet has written by himself do not show the possession of the secret which charmed us in the work in which they helped Dumas. It is to be said, too, that the later plays taken from his own novels, in which Dumas was assisted by M. Maquet, are very inferior to his earlier plays, written wholly by himself. They are mere dramatizations of romances, and not in a true sense dramas at all. The earlier plays, however extravagant they might be in individual details, had a distinct and essential unity not to be detected in the dramatizations, which were little more than sequences of scenes snipped with the scissors from the interminable series of tales of adventure. . . . Full as these pieces are of life and bustle and gayety, they are poor substitutes for plays, which depend for success on themselves, and not on the vague desire to see in action figures which the reader has learned to like in endless stories. These dramatizations were unduly long-drawn, naturally prolix, not to say garrulous. When his tales were paid for by the word, when he was "writing on space," as they say in a newspaper office, Dumas let the vice of saying all there was to be said grow on him. On the stage, the half is more than the whole.

From "Alexandre Dumas," *French Dramatists of the 19th Century,* 1901

G. K. CHESTERTON

Dumas's fame is wrapped in similar clouds to those which wrap the fame of about half of the great Elizabethans. Nobody is quite certain that any idea which Dumas presented was invented by him. Nobody is quite certain that any line which Dumas published was written by him. But for all that, we know that Dumas was, and must have been, a great man. There are some people who think this kind of doubt clinging to every specific detail does really invalidate the intellectual certainty of the whole. They think that when we are in the presence of a mass that is confessedly solid and inimitable, we must refrain from admiring that mass until we have decided what parts of it are authentic; where the fictitious begins and where the genuine leaves off. Thus, they say that because the books of the New Testament may have been tampered with, we know not to what extent, we must, therefore, surrender altogether a series of utterances which every rational person has admitted to strike the deepest note of the human spirit. They might as well say that because Vesuvius is surrounded by sloping meadows, and because no one can say exactly where the plain leaves off and the mountain begins, therefore there is no mountain of Vesuvius at all, but a beautiful, uninterrupted plain on the spot where it is popularly supposed to stand. Most reasonable people agree that it is possible to see, through whatever mists of misrepresentations, that an intellectual marvel has occurred. Most people agree that, whatever may be the interpolations, an intellectual marvel occurred which produced the Gospels. To descend to smaller things, most people agree that whatever lending and stealing confused the Elizabethan Age, an intellectual marvel occurred which produced the Elizabethan drama. And to descend to things yet smaller again, most people agree that whatever have been the sins, the evasions, the thefts, the plagiarism, the hackwork, the brazen idleness of the author, an intellectual miracle occurred which produced the novels of Dumas.

In novels of this kind, novels produced in such immeasurable quantities, of such prodigious length, and marked throughout with its haste of production and dubiety of authorship, it is, indeed, impossible that we should find that particular order of literary merit which marks so much of the work that is now produced and is so much demanded by modern critics; the merit of exact verbal finish and the precision of the *mot juste*. Stevenson would have lain awake at night wondering whether, in describing the death of a marquis in a duel he should describe a sword as glittering or gleaming, or speak of the stricken man staggering back or reeling back. Dumas could not, in the nature of things, have troubled his head about such points as that, so long as somebody killed the marquis for him at a moderate figure. All technical gusto, the whole of that abstract lust for words which separates the literary man from the mere thinker, were certain, through the facts of the case, to fade more or less out of Dumas. The supreme element of greatness in him . . . [may be described as] the power of massing a building. He was a great architect, and stands among his hired scribblers like Sir Christopher Wren among the masons at work upon St. Paul's. The idea that he did actually publish books written in detail by others is very much borne out by the fact that nothing is more noticeable in his work than that its talent is chiefly shown in the planning of an incident or a series of incidents. Without going into any of the actual examples, we can ourselves imagine the class of eventualities which are the glory of Dumas's romances; and we can imagine Dumas planning them out as a general plans a campaign. We can imagine him telling a secretary, as he went out for the day, that the two cavaliers were to go to six inns, one after another, and find in each a huge banquet prepared for them by an unknown benefactor, or a man in a mask seeking to fix a quarrel upon them. We can imagine him scribbling on a loose piece of paper a list of six Royal Princes, each of whom in succession was to be summoned by the King to assist him against an assassin, and each of whom in turn was to turn his sword against the King. It was in this dramatic sequence that Dumas was greatest and most readable; he excelled in a kind of systematic disaster and a kind of orderly crime. He was, after all, a Frenchman in more ways than one, and with all his violence, worldliness and appetite there remains in his work something fundamentally logical. The man who made the finest scenes in his romantic writings turn on tangles of relationship, like the triple due! which opens *The Three Musketeers,* had almost the mind of a mathematician.

This structural, systematic, almost numerical method of Dumas's is really important as throwing some light on the conditions which produce romance so popular and so great as his. There is a very general notion in existence that romance depends upon the unexpected. This is altogether an error: romance depends upon the expected. Unless the elements already existing in the story point to and hint at more or less darkly, but more or less inevitably, the thing that is to follow, the mere brute occurrence of that thing, without rhyme or reason, does not either excite or entertain us. . . . Anybody could make a mad bull enter the drawing-room in the middle of one of Miss Fowler's epigrammatic conversations, or make one of Mr. W. W. Jacobs's stories end abruptly with the blowing of the trump of the Resurrection. Nothing could be more unexpected than these things would be; but they would not excite us; they would bore us like the conversational rambling of an idiot in a cell. Romance depends, if not absolutely upon the expected, at least upon something that may be called the half-expected. The true romantic ending is something that has been prophesied by our subconsciousness. We feel the spirit of romance when Ulysses springs upon the table, his rags falling from him, and shoots Antinous in the throat. It would be much more unexpected, if that were all, if he turned three somersaults in the air and announced that he was only Ulysses's ship's carpenter playing a practical joke. Similarly, we feel the spirit of romance when D'Artagnan joins his three adversaries in turning their swords against the musketeers of the Cardinal. It is not unexpected that the four should thus get into a fight together. The most unexpected thing one can imagine in Dumas would be that they should not get into one.

[Dumas's large scheme of orderly and successive adventures] is his great merit as an artist. He had the power of making us feel that his heroes were moving parts of a great scheme of adventures, a scheme as wide, as politic, as universal and sagacious as one of the plots of his own Cardinal Richelieu. And it is in this that almost all his imitators fail; they imagine that his triumph consisted in the swaggering inconsequence of his events, in innumerable drawn swords; in ceaseless torrents of blood; in the mere multiplication of cloaks, and feathers, and halberds, and rope ladders. These things are not romance: here, as everywhere, materials and materialism mislead us. Dumas was a great romanticist, because he had the sense of something solid and eternal in old valour, in old manners, in old friends. But a mere drawn sword is no more poetical than a pocket-knife. A mere dead man is not in any sense so dramatic as a living one. Men who find no romance in life will certainly find none in death.

From "Alexandre Dumas," in *The Bookman,* July 1902

Reading Group Guide

1. Discuss Dumas's use of historical events in the novel. Do you think a knowledge of history is necessary or unnecessary in order to enjoy the novel? Discuss the ways in which Dumas alters or takes liberties with real events in order to suit the story. Is his view of history sanitized in any way?

2. Dumas is thought of as the chief popularizer of French Romantic drama. In considering *The Three Musketeers*, do you think this reputation is an accurate one? How does Dumas use dramatic effect in the novel?

3. Contemporary critics were offended by the scenes depicting vice and violence in the novel. Do you find these scenes arbitrary or not?

4. Many critics have described the musketeers as well-developed stereotypes, but are there ways in which the musketeers transcend these stereotypes? Are there other, perhaps more complex ways of interpreting the four protagonists?

5. Discuss Dumas's female characters, in particular Milady. What is her role in the novel, and what does this reveal about Dumas's views of women, if anything? Does Dumas depict a war between the sexes?

6. How do the chapter endings contribute to Dumas's masterly maintenance of pace? How does this kind of device recall a play, and how does this speak to Dumas's strengths stylistically?

7. In what ways is *The Three Musketeers* a bildungsroman? Would you characterize the work as a youthful novel?

A Note on the Type

The principal text of this Modern Library edition
was set in a digitized version of Janson,
a typeface that dates from about 1690 and was cut by Nicholas Kis,
a Hungarian working in Amsterdam. The original matrices
have survived and are held by the Stempel foundry in Germany.
Hermann Zapf redesigned some of the weights and sizes for Stempel,
basing his revisions on the original design.

MODERN LIBRARY IS ONLINE AT
WWW.MODERNLIBRARY.COM

MODERN LIBRARY ONLINE IS YOUR GUIDE
TO CLASSIC LITERATURE ON THE WEB

THE MODERN LIBRARY E-NEWSLETTER

Our free e-mail newsletter is sent to subscribers, and features sample chapters, interviews with and essays by our authors, upcoming books, special promotions, announcements, and news.

To subscribe to the Modern Library e-newsletter, send a blank e-mail to: sub_modernlibrary@info.randomhouse.com or visit www.modernlibrary.com

THE MODERN LIBRARY WEBSITE

Check out the Modern Library website at
www.modernlibrary.com for:

- The Modern Library e-newsletter
- A list of our current and upcoming titles and series
- Reading Group Guides and exclusive author spotlights
- Special features with information on the classics and other paperback series
- Excerpts from new releases and other titles
- A list of our e-books and information on where to buy them
- The Modern Library Editorial Board's 100 Best Novels and 100 Best Nonfiction Books of the Twentieth Century written in the English language
- News and announcements

Questions? E-mail us at modernlibrary@randomhouse.com.
For questions about examination or desk copies, please visit
the Random House Academic Resources site at
www.randomhouse.com/academic